BERSERKER
DEATH

Baen Books by Fred Saberhagen

Rogue Berserker
Berserker Man
Berserker Death

The Dracula Tape
Vlad Tapes

Pilgrim

BERSERKER
DEATH

FRED SABERHAGEN

BERSERKER DEATH

This is a work of fiction. All the characters and events portrayed in this book are fictional, and any resemblance to real people or incidents is purely coincidental.

A Baen Book

Baen Publishing Enterprises
P.O. Box 1403
Riverdale, NY 10471
www.baen.com

ISBN: 0-7434-9886-0

Cover art by Kurt Miller

First printing in this format, February 2005

Distributed by Simon & Schuster
1230 Avenue of the Americas
New York, NY 10020

Production by Windhaven Press, Auburn, NH (www.windhaven.com)
Printed in the United States of America

10 9 8 7 6 5 4 3 2 1

AUTHOR'S NOTE

For more information about Fred Saberhagen
and this series see:

www.berserker.com

CONTENTS

The Berserker Wars

MESSAGE BEGINS
REPORT ON THE PRIVATE ARCHIVE OF THE THIRD HISTORIAN
A File Which Presents the History of the Galaxy in Twenty Pages
Transmission Mode: Triplicate Message Torpedoes
Code: Trapdoor XIII
TX Date: 7645.11.0
From: Archivist Ingli, Expedition Co-ordinator
To: Chief Co-ordinator, Earth Archives
cc: Defense Co-ordination Central

Hal: We're here, surrounded by friendly Carmpan of whom we rarely see more than one or two at a time, and then usually only with some partial or symbolic physical barrier between us. Everything is going pretty much as expected, we have experienced nothing really contrary to the experience of a thousand years' occasional and arm's-length contact with the race. By the way, it's beginning to look, to me at least, less and less coincidental that our first meeting with the Carmpan coincided almost exactly with the beginning of the Berserker War. I'll have more to say on this point presently.

Let me first describe what I consider to be our main achievement so far on this mission. To begin with, the structure in which we are living and working is best described as a large, comfortable library, and we have been given free access to great masses of information in several kinds of storage systems. (I hope, by the way, that the exchange team of Carmpan researchers on Earth are being treated as well as we are here.) Much of this mass of stored data is, as we expected, still unintelligible to us and so far useless. But quite early in the game our hosts pointed out to us, for our special attention, an alcove containing what we've come to call the private archive of the Third Historian. Having looked at the files therein, my colleagues

3

and I agree unanimously that they were very probably compiled and largely written by the same Carmpan individual who used that name (or title) as signature to the messages he composed and sent to our ancestors some generations ago, when the Berserker peril was even greater than it is today.

Since a copy of this report is going directly to the military, Hal, bear with me when I pause now and then to insert a paragraph or two of history. We can't reasonably expect that all the readers over there are going to know as much of it offhand as we do.

Up until now, almost all of the information that we have ever had directly from the Carmpan on any subject—Berserkers, the Builders, the Carmpan themselves, the Elder Races, almost everything—a very great proportion of this information, I say, has come to our Solarian worlds through long-distance communications signed by this one individual, for whom we still have no other name than Third Historian. He—or she, the Carmpan language does not readily distinguish sexes, and they usually appear to care not much more about sex than we do about blood types—was active centuries ago, and to my knowledge no new Third Historian message has been received on the Solarian world for centuries.

So we still know next to nothing about the Third Historian—or indeed about any Carmpan individual—as a person, and it appears to me unlikely that this present Expedition is going to find out much about him. We do of course ask questions, particularly since being shown the private archive that is marked in several places with his signature. Our questions are answered in the usual obscure ways, about which more below. Even the significance of the number in his name or title is still unknown to us. It does seem certain that more than three individuals must have occupied the post of Chief Historian—assuming there is such an official post among the Carmpan—during such a very long history as their race boasts. Or would boast if they were at all given to boasting.

When I asked directly, I was told that the Third Historian is still alive. This surprised me somewhat, though the life-span required, considerably less than a thousand standard years, would not be utterly out of the question even for one of our own comparatively perishable species. However, when I asked urgently to see him, or at least to be told where he is now, I was informed just as unequivocally that the Third Historian is now dead. One of the enclosures with this message is our own recording of this particular question-and-answer session.

Let me digress just a little more from the important contents of the TH's private files, to remark that in the short time we've been here we've had more face-to-face (if that's the right way to put it; you know what I mean) contact with the Carmpan than have any other group of Solarian humans in history. As you are well aware, we were very eager for this chance. On the long voyage out here we managed to convince ourselves that with goodwill on both sides (a requirement that I certainly feel has been met) we were going to do a lot better at communicating with the Carmpan than any other of our race has ever done. We were going to dig a lot of Galactic history out of them, complete with hard facts, dates, numbers, the kind of thing *we* like to call history. We would dig up information that must be available to them even if they consider it valueless, and bring it home with us. Not only that, we would at last meet a Carmpan or two who really wanted to learn about us through our own conscious attempts at communication; and, boy, were we ever going to communicate with *them*.

Need I add, that so far it hasn't worked out quite that way? That so far our formal conference sessions are dominated, whatever we Solarians try to do, by the Carmpan spiritual (?) and sociological abstractions? (Military readers, see my monograph on *Drifts and Tones in Carmpan Communications*; someone at the Archives will be glad to furnish you with copies.) That's just the way in which our gracious hosts here insist on looking at the Universe. I find I must set down the cliche once again, and then I swear that I will ban it from all later messages: The Carmpan mind is very, very different from our own.

Of course the communications we have been directing to the Carmpan while in general conference form, to our way of thinking, a clear and concise outline of the history of our Solarian variant of the human race, from our origins on Earth through our later phases of expansion and development to the present, when we are the dominant life form on more than a thousand major planets in more than seven hundred systems, not to mention all the natural and artificial extrasystemic habitats, enjoying a blessed variety of political and economic organizations while managing to co-operate quite well, most of us, most of the time, in the thousand-year Berserker War.

I frankly don't know what our hosts think of this presentation we make about ourselves. There are moments when I believe they knew it all already, knew more than we have told them, down to the last detailed production statistic, through their own far-ranging mental activities. And, again, there are times when I believe they just don't care, don't know and aren't interested, are going through the motions of listening to us only out of politeness. They do express thanks when we pause after shoving information at them, as they express thanks for so much else that our race has done. But there is no substantive comment on what we tell them. There are no questions that sound eager.

That's how things stand now. We are here, and being very well treated, and we like our hosts. And they like us and are glad to have us here, even if it would be strictly inaccurate to say that they enjoy our company. And it is somehow implied that they have done, are doing, will do, something important for us. That's how things stand now, how they stood the moment we arrived. Actually we could just have sent them an electronic greeting card and accomplished just as much.

Except of course for one thing. Our presentation of our own history evidently had at least one good effect, that of showing our hosts what we think a history ought to be. It may have decided them to show us quickly the one file in the library that comes closest to our ideal. It was approximately one standard day after our own history presentation, which came about one standard day after our arrival, that we were led to the personal file of the Third Historian. I think I have mentioned that the alcove containing the Third Historian's file and carrel occupies only a very small portion of this library. It's quite a comfortable, self-sufficient artificial world, by the way, that seems to have been built with Solarian comfort and convenience in mind. The gravity, atmosphere, lighting, furnishings, color schemes, and so on, are very pleasant by our standards. Green plants are abundant. And the Carmpan information-handling systems, let me interject here, work better than ours do, once we know precisely what we want to ask of them. Details on request, when we get home. The idea so commonly held among Solarians that we are technologically superior to the Carmpan seems to me to be justifiable only on a very selective basis.

Back to my main subject. While the private writings of the Third Historian we have discovered here are more obscure and difficult to translate than we would like, certainly more so than his famous public transmissions to our ancestors centuries ago, yet they are vastly more accessible to Solarian understanding than any other Carmpan literary-historical work that I have ever encountered in a lifetime of study; I exclude of course documents on the level of mere maps and catalogues, which in their rare appearances have often had practical if limited application.

If we had come here completely unacquainted with the Third Historian, it would still have been obvious to us from his private archive that he was—or is—intensely interested in two things. The first of these, for whatever reason, is our own race. As in his earlier public messages, he repeatedly expresses Carmpan gratitude for our leadership, our victories, and our losses in the long and terrible war against what he so often calls "the unliving enemy." To me the impression is inescapable that much of the material in this private archive consists of drafts of messages intended for us but never sent; that these reiterations of thanks must be for our benefit.

The second great interest of the Third Historian, as evidenced in his old public messages as well as in the newly discovered material, is the Berserkers. Briefly, our most important find within his private archive is an electronic document (I am of course enclosing a recording of it herewith) that purports to be a digest, a capsule, or perhaps an outline, for nothing less than a history of the whole inhabited portion of the Galaxy for as far back as the Carmpan have been able to keep records—and their history, we should recall, has been shown to extend into the tens of millions of years at least. Everything we have learned here tends to support the accepted belief that the Carmpan mental probing can span more than half the Galactic diameter; and that this mind-probing is as accurate for the purposes to which the Carmpan put it as it appears to be useless for any of the military, commercial, or hard (in our terms) research functions to which we have always yearned to be able to apply it.

I had hoped when I began to compose this message to be able to include with it a full if tentative translation of the History Document (hereafter abbreviated HD) found in the Third Historian's private archive. Without the episodic appendix (see below) it could be printed out in twenty pages; it's really that short. But unfortunately the longer I study HD with an eye to making a translation, the more I realize how obscure it is—somewhat in the sense of poetry, I mean, and you, Hal, know what trying to translate poetry can be like. Layer upon layer of suggested meaning, that to me is at best barely perceptible, is packed beneath a surface narrative that in itself could be translated in a number of possible ways. Here we have Drifts grafted upon Tones, and vice versa. Information is packed not only in layer upon layer, but in the interference patterns, or in something analogous to such patterns, that are formed by the relationships between the layers, between each layer and all the other ones. I fear I am not making myself clear. In future messages I mean to go into much more detail about this hologram-like though non-physical system.

Here let me digress to mention one fact definitely confirmed by the surface narrative in HD. This is that the Builders were a warlike race for a long time before they created the Berserkers. There is convincing evidence that before the fateful experiment the Builders had fought at least four long, desperate interstellar wars, resulting in the complete extermination of at least four other races. These four early victim-races are unfortunately identified in HD only in the Tones-Drifts system of sociological-spiritual (religious?) notation.

Whether any translation at all of this passage into a Solarian tongue is possible without assigning the races completely arbitrary names and identities (e.g., One, Two, Three, Four) is still in doubt, though I have spent two days working on that simple-seeming question with our own ship's computer.

Parenthetically: I am assured by our hosts that as much time as we might like is available to us on Carmpan computers which our hosts assure us have much more capacity than the shipboard one we brought along. The only problem lies in instructing their computers in what we want. I have no great hopes for being able to do this, as so far it seems all but impossible to explain our way of thinking to the Carmpan themselves. Whether their data processing machinery works on a system of Drifts and Tones I have not yet been able to ascertain, but I have assured myself that it certainly does not work like ours.

A second hard fact confirmed by HD about the Builders: They were a race designed to roughly the same physical pattern as Solarian humanity, though somewhat more slender and fine-boned, having originated probably on a lighter planet than Earth. There is a suggestion that the female tended to be fiercer in combat than the male, and it is certain that she was somewhat larger. There was in each individual one cyclopean eye, and paired external sexual organs (of the same sex) so that copulation must commonly have been carried on in duplicate, as it were. The Builders spoke through sound waves as we and the Carmpan do, but their creations the Berserkers were never furnished with the language code as far as can be determined, or indeed with any other means of distinguishing their creators from the other life forms of the Galaxy included in their general programming to hunt down and destroy all life. Of course there may have been some system meant to save the Builders from the general slaughter, a system that failed to operate properly and was never replicated in the later models of the Berserkers as they rebuilt and reproduced themselves. On the other hand, the original Berserkers may have been activated at such a distance from their creators' home worlds that the death machines were not thought by their builders to represent a danger to them. At any rate, we have found nothing here to contradict the accepted hypothesis, based on old evidence, that the Builders did at last fall victim to their own creations.

It is certain that the Builders no longer exist. The Third Historian speaks of them inevitably in the past tense, something he does in the case of no race that is now known to be still alive. The scraps of recordings that we have found here, showing the Builders' appearance and containing samples of their speech, do not differ substantially from other such old recordings that I have seen before, and for all I know all of these may be duplicated in Solarian archives somewhere. (None of us on the Expedition roster are specialists in Builders' History. An unfortunate oversight, perhaps, but if such a specialty exists it would be a very limited one indeed.)

Copies of all the fragmentary Builder recordings here will be sent with our next message. How the Carmpan obtained them is uncertain, since our hosts would not ordinarily have access to the battlefield wreckage of Berserkers from which our own material has been gleaned. Most of these fragments are excerpts, each lasting only a few seconds, of what if interpreted in Solarian terms would be considered political speeches, delivered amid mass chanting rallies of Builders male and female. There is one fragment like nothing that I personally have seen before, though some other members of the expedition assure me that they have: a scene of Builders performing what might be a dance, or alternatively the application of some kind of rhythmical torture apparatus to an unusually large female. (I need not belabor here the obvious point that all of these interpretations should be considered tentative.) The voices in the recordings, as in fragments of Builder records found elsewhere, are clicking and whining sounds, probably not reproducible by either Solarian or Carmpan vocal organs.

And there is one more fragment, very different from all the rest. In it, members of another race, heretofore unknown to us, appear briefly. Some expedition members have suggested that this may be our only record of the Builders' nameless but undoubtedly very formidable opponents in their final war, the people whose destruction could not be accomplished without such a desperate gamble as the creation of the Berserkers. Expedition members who favor this interpretation point out similarities between this Builder recording and certain Solarian propaganda art from the past. It shows beings rotund and red, thick-limbed almost to the point of having no limbs separate from the body at all; all this in high contrast to the Builder physique. This Red Race is named, if at all, only in a sort of marginal note (using the Drift-Tone system, of course) that was doubtless added by the Third Historian himself. Translation, as mentioned above, is still pending.

Nowhere in any document that we have so far inspected in this library are values given for the size of the domain of any race, in terms of numbers of worlds, strength of fleets, population figures, and so on; even precise physical locations are very rare. We know of course that the Carmpan are perfectly capable of interstellar navigation when it suits them, that they have built and designed ships whose autopilots work perfectly with any of the commonly used systems of interstellar co-ordinates.

Nor have we found any clue as to how many intelligent races, branches living or dead of Galactic humanity, the Carmpan know about. As I have already suggested, one of the most striking things about this library is the paucity of numbers, of quantitative measurements of any kind. A starfaring race who (with the well-known exception of their Prophets of Probability) prefers to do without mathematics, without even counting, must remain to our minds, to put it mildly, something of a paradox. And I am coming to think that there is that in the essence of what the Solarian mind finds paradoxical that demands repeated expression in the thoughts and minds of the Carmpan and their allies or cousins the Elder Races.

(Note to my military readers: The name 'Carmpan' itself, as many of our race today do not realize, derives not from any word by which they call themselves, but rather from the location where our species and theirs first encountered each other.)

We members of the expedition have of course discussed, or tried to discuss, these translational and other difficulties with our unfailingly polite and attentive hosts. As nearly as we can make out from their replies, they believe that the number of intelligent races existing in the Galaxy, for example, is something one simply should not try to know—or if known, it should not be expressed. Despite great efforts on both sides, I have trouble understanding why. To know and express that number would be either sin, or bad form, or maybe sloppy scientific thinking, on the grounds that there is no way one can be sure *enough* of its value. Maybe a little of all three.

But, I press on, a true, worthy answer does exist, does it not, if it can be discovered?

Yes, I am told. But the true answer involves—somehow—the Core region of the Galaxy, or perhaps something (someone?) located (dwelling?) at or very near the center of the Core. "All exact counting of races should be done there," is an exact translation of what one of our hosts said to me. I would be hard put to explain to you which one said it. We are still having a lot of trouble telling one Carmpan from another. But I asked him—or her—more questions, trying to pin down the identity of this thing or person properly in charge of numbering races at the Core. There was no satisfactory answer; only a single word, which I take to signify a complex structure of some kind.

Following this, our hosts made a joint statement, which I quote in translation as well as I am able. They wished, they said, to "express great sadness over the fate of those intelligent races, diverse branches of Galactic humanity despite all diversity of physical form, however many of them there may have been or may yet be, who have been exterminated by the Builders or the Berserkers or any other cause, those known to us and those who lie in the distant reaches of the Galaxy-beyond-measurement, still unknown to Carmpan and to brave

Solarian alike. The loss of these races means that much (creative work, of some form) will have to be accomplished (by some unspecified agents) before the Galaxy can be judged complete and worthy."

That passage was so relatively easy for me to understand, that I believe someone among the Carmpan must have expended an extraordinary amount of time and effort on it in advance, and that it was then held ready until the proper moment for its utterance should arrive. Is it possible that the Third Historian himself is among those we meet and speak with every day? I seriously think it is possible, and at the same time I doubt that we shall ever know. He could inhabit any of those slow, squarish Carmpan bodies, so incongruously machinelike in appearance for beings whose own constructed machinery is so subtle, who try to avoid the grossly material in any form . . . actually, as I think I mentioned in passing above, we seldom get a really good look at any of the Carmpan here, though we are often physically close to each other and frequently converse. The rooms in which we most often meet are all niches and alcoves and low partitions, with enough screens of live greenery to make us feel that we are in a garden instead of riding a deep-space artifact at a high fraction of the speed of light. The interior lighting is perfect, as I think I have mentioned, for Solarian eyes, and we can view the Carmpan and even touch them on arrangement, to satisfy our curiosity. But at the same time privacy is rarely more than an arm's length away for anyone, and they frequently resort to it, retreating round a corner or behind a hanging vine. We of course do not intrude upon these temporary retreats. Personally I find myself also retreating sometimes in the midst of a conversation, gazing out through fresh green leaves of some kind—I am no botanist—or a fountain's spray, enjoying the whole arrangement more than I would have suspected.

I am rambling. Back to the History Document. What it presents of the Carmpan view of the physical universe contains no surprise. The Universe just above the galactic level (yet higher levels are implied but not described) is seen as organized in terms of clusters or groups of galaxies. None of us in the expedition are astronomers or cosmologists enough to know if the details of this organization as the Carmpan describe it differ substantially from those mapped out by our own scientists. Actually the Third Historian uses this physical description only as a background for a question in which he is genuinely interested: Are there Berserkers, of independent origin, in galaxies other than our own? And, if so, will the living races of those other megasystems be able to raise up some analog of Solarian humanity to successfully fight off the unliving foe? This passage, with its understated implication that we are universally rare stuff indeed, makes me feel, I confess, vaguely uncomfortable.

It was shortly after reading this disturbing passage for the first time that I approached our hosts to question them on a more personal level: The Third Historian, in some of his early direct communications to our people, has stated that he "sets down" the "secret thoughts" of Solarian men and women who were at all times parsecs away from him, as well as being in some instances removed by hundreds of years of time even when correction is made for all possible relativistic effects. When my hearers affirmed this, I asked whether any of the Carmpan now present were capable of reading our secret thoughts, and if so, were they? The answer was quick and emphatic denial, the most definite response I think I have ever had to any question here. "You and we are too close together," they informed me, "for anything like that."

In HD the Third Historian is also greatly intrigued by another question, related to the one discussed a paragraph above: May there ever have been, in the remote past of our own Galaxy (the context makes it plain he is talking about a billion years or more), other Berserkers, *independent of those now existing*? He adduces a statement which must be meant as evidence to support this idea, though I cannot understand it (again, see enclosed recording.) I am haunted by this suggestion, and it makes me wonder if some of the Elder Races still extant may possibly be of comparable age. It is to me an awesome thought that some races may have survived a Berserker peril more than once.

Another member of our expedition has very recently reported what we all consider to be a remarkable find (see her own report enclosed herewith). In a corner of the library far removed from the archive of the Third Historian she has discovered a record of what are described as "multi-species life constructs" that antedate even the Carmpan themselves by millions of standard years. I interpret "life-construct" to mean a living thing composed of other living things. If we are reading this correctly it is odd that HD does not mention such creations. But perhaps it does, perhaps life-constructs and much else are concealed in the Drifts and Tones amid the layers of meaning.

Here I begin to ask myself another question. It is not a new question among Solarian historians, but here it takes on a new sharpness. Did the Carmpan know the Builders, or know of them, before the Builders plunged into their final war and decided upon their Frankenstein's creation? Conventional history holds that they did not; had the Carmpan known of the Berserkers when that awful construction was first accomplished, the gentle, peaceful Carmpan could hardly have failed to send immediate warning to the races who were thereby placed in imminent peril. But really there is no evidence that the Carmpan did not send such warnings. To some they may have come too late; some may have been unable to profit by them, some may have disbelieved. It would be consistent with the Carmpan nature that such warnings might have been sent on a purely subliminal level of communication if such exists. I think it may. Could it have been at least in part a Carmpan influence that caused an increase in belligerence on many Solarian worlds simultaneously, provoking a military buildup in those decades just before the first Berserker radio-voices came drifting in to our detectors from the deep?

And there is the fact that the Carmpan and Solarian branches of humanity met for the first time very shortly before the first Berserker onslaught on one of our worlds was sustained. Even on the relatively short time-scale of Solarian history the two events, the two meetings, were virtually simultaneous. What are the odds that this was only chance? When one day I am able to meet a Carmpan Prophet of Probability I mean to ask him to calculate the odds.

I have not yet faced our hosts with this suggestion: That that famous first contact between our two races, long assumed by Solarians to be a natural result of our aggressive exploration, was really timed by the Carmpan for their own reasons; that they had known of us for a long time preceding; that we were picked, chosen, adopted, when the time was ripe, brought onto the Galactic stage to play a role just when our ferocity and our armaments were needed in the service of all Galactic life.

If this suggestion is true, still it is far from clear to me that the deception is something we ought to blame the Carmpan for. They did not create the Berserkers nor launch them in our direction. We would still have had to fight the Berserkers if we and the Carmpan had never met. Ought we to blame them for not warning us clearly and directly? We were, and are, the suspicious and mistrustful ones, who really needed no warnings to be on our guard. Probably we would not, on that first memorable day of violence between us and the unliving foe, have returned the Berserkers' fire a microsecond sooner, whatever the Carmpan might have whispered to us beforehand.

And yet I, like most Solarians, continue to feel that the Carmpan presence, their influence, has helped us all through the war. Through them we have learned not only of the Elders but of other races much more helpless. We would still have fought, of course, for our own survival, our own temples and our gods. But it was good, it was better, to know that we were fighting for others also, for the cause of all life in the Galaxy.

When the war began a thousand years ago—may our own lifetimes see a final victory—the belief was widespread among our Solarian people that the Carmpan, even dedicated to peace as they assuredly were, would be forced by events to take up arms. After all, to refuse to enter a war against Berserkers was to be guilty by inaction of the deaths of innocent victims—in this war, as in no other, to fight was not to kill. For our unliving foe, no sympathy or pity could be felt, any more than for the missiles that they launched against us. But for the Carmpan it was no longer a matter of choice. The skills needed for direct combat, the mental and emotional abilities much more importantly than the physical, had been lost to them long ago, when their will to fight was lost—or when that will was, perhaps, absorbed in something larger.

One point of view, put forward here by some expedition members, is that the Carmpan *did* fight the Berserkers, and very successfully. They fought so well that great numbers of them are still alive after a thousand years of the struggle, which when facing Berserkers must be considered a remarkable record. It was simply a matter of the Carmpan choosing and then using properly the most effective weapon available—which happened to be us. They made sure that we had grasped the magnitude of the danger posed by the Berserkers, and then they got the hell out of our way, while from time to time providing us with such indirect help as they were able.

Another viewpoint, expressed recently by some expedition members, is that the Carmpan have already helped us more than most of us realize. They not only knew their own limitations but probably understood ours better than we did ourselves. Of course they never tried to enter battle at our side, never built weapons for us or even shipped us components or raw materials. Yet their ambassadors to our worlds, all Prophets of Probability, on rare but vital occasions (the Stone Place being the most famous example) have predicted the outcome of battles, with great benefit to morale. And our military and economic historians have often remarked on how fortuitously some of our supply and communication links have been maintained during the war's darkest hours, how needed materiel has so often fallen into the grasp of our people at a crucial moment. It is impossible for me to demonstrate that the Carmpan could have been responsible for this, but I have a growing suspicion that they were.

From the earliest years of the war the Carmpan did sometimes provide medical and research assistance. And the limitations on the kind of aid they gave were somehow accepted by our own race, and we continued to believe in their good will. We saw that they were not cowardly. In the war's early days some of them came to live on some of our particularly endangered planets, for no apparent reason other than to share our perils. This practice ceased as sentiment among our people grew against it—the testimony of our people at the time is that they did not want the Carmpan to endanger themselves unnecessarily.

There is a fairly lengthy passage in HD on the Carmpan role as intermediaries between ourselves and the shadowy (to us) Elder Races, with whom we have so much more difficulty in communicating than even with the Carmpan themselves. Judging by the amount of space he gives this topic, the Third Historian must have considered it important. Still, he says very little about the Elder Races in themselves; perhaps there is some reason by discussion of these revered ones, like counting, should take place only at the Core. Or perhaps the Drifts and Tones within the document tell more about them than I, with my feeble understanding of the language, have been able to glimpse as yet.

A substantial part of what the document does say about the Elders relates them to the Berserker war—how, when some groups of the Elders could have withdrawn themselves from the Berserkers' path, they chose instead to remain where they were, and delay the enemy by being hunted and ultimately killed—a delay that was to prove vital to the survival of some Solarian and other worlds.

Near the end of HD an individual exploit is mentioned, almost the first to be related in the whole document—it is the strange voyage of the Solarian warship *Johann Karlsen*, exploring near the Galactic Core. The limited engagement that was fought against the Berserkers on that occasion is treated as of substantial importance, as somehow foreshadowing an ultimate victory for the cause of life. I think it probable that the Carmpan know, in some sense, more of that episode than we do.

Attached to HD in a kind of appendix are eleven or twelve (the demarcations are not always plain) episodic narrative reports concerning the experiences of different Solarian individuals in various phases of the great war.

HD concludes with a postscript in a warning tone: That no victory in this world, this Galaxy, this Universe, is final. And no history, either.

(signed) INGLI

MESSAGE ENDS

For most men the war brought a steady deforming pressure which seemed to have existed always, and which had no foreseeable end. Under this burden some men became like brutes, and the minds of others grew to be as terrible and implacable as the machines they fought against.

But I have touched a few rare human minds, the jewels of life, who rise to meet the greatest challenges by becoming supremely men.

☀ STONE PLACE

Earth's Gobi spaceport was perhaps the biggest in all the small corner of the galaxy settled by Solarian man and his descendants; at least so thought Mitchell Spain, who had seen most of those ports in his twenty-four years of life.

But looking down now from the crowded, descending shuttle, he could see almost nothing of the Gobi's miles of ramp. The vast crowd below, meaning only joyful welcome, had defeated its own purpose by forcing back and breaking the police lines. Now the vertical string of descending shuttle-ships had to pause, searching for enough clear room to land.

Mitchell Spain, crowded into the lowest shuttle with a thousand other volunteers, was paying little attention to the landing problem for the moment. Into this jammed compartment, once a luxurious observation lounge, had just come Johann Karlsen himself; and this was Mitch's first chance for a good look at the newly appointed High Commander of Sol's defense, though Mitch had ridden Karlsen's spear-shaped flagship all the way from Austeel.

Karlsen was no older than Mitchell Spain, and no taller, his short-ness somehow surprising at first glance. He had become ruler of the

16

planet Austeel through the influence of his half-brother, the mighty Felipe Nogara, head of the empire of Esteel; but Karlsen held his position by his own talents.

"This field may be blocked for the rest of the day," Karlsen was saying now, to a cold-eyed Earthman who had just come aboard the shuttle from an aircar. "Let's have the ports open, I want to look around."

Glass and metal slid and reshaped themselves, and sealed ports became small balconies open to the air of Earth, the fresh smells of a living planet—open, also, to the roaring chant of the crowd a few hundred feet below: "Karlsen! Karlsen!"

As the High Commander stepped out onto a balcony to survey for himself the chances of landing, the throng of men in the lounge made a half-voluntary brief surging movement, as if to follow. These men were mostly Austeeler volunteers, with a sprinkling of adventurers like Mitchell Spain, the Martian wanderer who had signed up on Austeel for the battle bounty Karlsen offered.

"Don't crowd, outlander," said a tall man ahead of Mitch, turning and looking down at him.

"I answer to the name of Mitchell Spain." He let his voice rasp a shade deeper than usual. "No more an outlander here than you, I think."

The tall one, by his dress and accent, came from Venus, a planet terraformed only within the last century, whose people were sensitive and proud in newness of independence and power. A Venetian might well be jumpy here, on a ship filled with men from a planet ruled by Felipe Nogara's brother.

"Spain—sounds like a Martian name," said the Venerian in a milder tone, looking down at Mitch.

Martians were not known for patience and long suffering. After another moment the tall one seemed to get tired of locking eyes and turned away.

The cold-eyed Earthman, whose face was somehow familiar to Mitch, was talking on the communicator, probably to the captain of the shuttle. "Drive on across the city, cross the Khosutu highway, and let down there."

Karlsen, back inside, said: "Tell him to go no more than about ten kilometers an hour; they seem to want to see me."

The statement was matter-of-fact; if people had made great efforts to see Johann Karlsen, it was only the courteous thing to greet them.

Mitch watched Karlsen's face, and then the back of his head, and the strong arms lifted to wave, as the High Commander stepped out again onto the little balcony. The crowd's roar doubled.

Is that all you feel, Karlsen, a wish to be courteous? Oh, no, my friend, you are acting. To be greeted with that thunder must do something vital to any man. It might exalt him; possibly it could disgust or frighten him, friendly as it was. You wear well your mask of courteous nobility, High Commander.

What was it like to be Johann Karlsen, come to save the world, when none of the really great and powerful ones seemed to care too much about it? With a bride of famed beauty to be yours when the battle had been won?

And what was brother Felipe doing today? Scheming, no doubt, to get economic power over yet another planet.

With another shift of the little mob inside the shuttle the tall Venerian moved from in front of Mitch, who could now see clearly out the port past Karlsen. Sea of faces, the old cliche, this was really it. How to write this . . . Mitch knew he would someday have to write it. If all men's foolishness was not permanently ended by the coming battle with the unliving, the battle bounty should suffice to let a man write for some time.

Ahead now were the bone-colored towers of Ulan Bator, rising beyond their fringe of suburban slideways and sunfields; and a highway; and bright multicolored pennants, worn by the aircars swarming out from the city in glad welcome. Now police aircars were keeping pace protectively with the spaceship, though there seemed to be no possible danger from anything but excess enthusiasm.

Another, special, aircar approached. The police craft touched it briefly and gently, then drew back with deference. Mitch stretched his neck, and made out a Carmpan insignia on the car. It was probably their ambassador to Sol, in person. The space shuttle eased to a dead slow creeping.

Some said that the Carmpan looked like machines themselves, but they were the strong allies of Earth-descended men in the war against the enemies of all life. If the Carmpan bodies were slow and squarish, their minds were visionary; if they were curiously unable to use force against any enemy, their indirect help was of great value.

Something near silence came over the vast crowd as the ambassador reared himself up in his open car; from his head and body, ganglions of wire and fiber stretched to make a hundred connections with Carmpan animals and equipment around him.

The crowd recognized the meaning of the network; a great sigh went up. In the shuttle, men jostled one another trying for a better view. The cold-eyed Earthman whispered rapidly into the communicator.

"Prophecy!" said a hoarse voice, near Mitch's ear.

"—of Probability!" came the ambassador's voice, suddenly amplified, seeming to pick up the thought in midphrase. The Carmpan Prophets of Probability were half mystics, half cold mathematicians. Karlsen's aides must have decided, or known, that this prophecy was going to be a favorable, inspiring thing which the crowd should hear, and had ordered the ambassador's voice picked up on a public address system.

"The hope, the living spark, to spread the flame of life!" The inhuman mouth chopped out the words, which still rose ringingly. The armlike appendages pointed straight to Karlsen, level on his balcony with the hovering aircar. "The dark metal thoughts are now of victory, the dead things make their plan to kill us all. But in this man before me now, there is life greater than any strength of metal. A power of life, to resonate—in all of us. I see, with Karlsen, victory—"

The strain on a Carmpan prophet in action was always immense, just as his accuracy was always high. Mitch had heard that the stresses involved were more topological than nervous or electrical. He had heard it, but like most Earth-descended, had never understood it.

"Victory," the ambassador repeated. "Victory . . . and then. . . ."

Something changed in the non-Solarian face. The cold-eyed Earthman was perhaps expert in reading alien expressions, or was perhaps just taking no chances. He whispered another command, and the amplification was taken from the Carmpan voice. A roar of approval mounted up past shuttle and aircar, from the great throng who thought the prophecy complete. But the ambassador had not finished, though now only those a few meters in front of him, inside the shuttle, could hear his faltering voice.

" . . . then death, destruction, failure." The square body bent, but the alien eyes were still riveted on Karlsen. "He who wins everything . . . will die owning nothing. . . ."

The Carmpan bent down and his aircar moved away. In the lounge of the shuttle there was silence. The hurrahing outside sounded like mockery.

After long seconds, the High Commander turned in from the balcony and raised his voice: "Men, we who have heard the finish of the prophecy are few—but still we are many, to keep a secret. So I don't ask for secrecy. But spread the word, too, that I have no faith in prophecies that are not of God. The Carmpan have never claimed to be infallible."

The gloomy answer was unspoken, but almost telepathically loud among the group. Nine times out of ten, the Carmpan are right. There will be a victory, then death and failure.

But did the dark ending apply only to Johann Karlsen, or to the whole cause of the living? The men in the shuttle looked at one another, wondering and murmuring.

The shuttles found space to land, at the edge of Ulan Bator. Disembarking, the men found no chance for gloom, with a joyous

crowd growing thicker by the moment around the ships. A lovely
Earth girl came, wreathed in garlands, to throw a flowery loop around
Mitchell Spain, and to kiss him. He was an ugly man, quite unused
to such willing attentions.

Still, he noticed when the High Commander's eye fell on him.

"You, Martian, come with me to the General Staff meeting. I
want to show a representative group in there so they'll know I'm
not just my brother's agent. I need one or two who were born in
Sol's light."

"Yes, sir." Was there no other reason why Karlsen had singled him
out? They stood together in the crowd, two short men looking levelly
at each other. One ugly and flower-bedecked, his arm still around
a girl who stared with sudden awed recognition at the other man,
who was magnetic in a way beyond handsomeness or ugliness. The
ruler of a planet, perhaps to be the savior of all life.

"I like the way you keep people from standing on your toes in a
crowd," said Karlsen to Mitchell Spain. "Without raising your voice
or uttering threats. What's your name and rank?"

Military organization tended to be vague, in this war where everything that lived was on the same side. "Mitchell Spain, sir. No rank
assigned, yet. I've been training with the marines. I was on Austeel
when you offered a good battle bounty, so here I am."

"Not to defend Mars?"

"I suppose, that too. But I might as well get paid for it."

Karlsen's high-ranking aides were wrangling and shouting now,
about groundcar transportation to the staff meeting. This seemed
to leave Karlsen with time to talk. He thought, and recognition
flickered on his face.

"Mitchell Spain? The poet?"

"I—I've had a couple of things published. Nothing much. . . ."

"Have you combat experience?"

"Yes, I was aboard one berserker, before it was pacified. That
was out—"

"Later, we'll talk. Probably have some marine command for you.
Experienced men are scarce. Hemphill, where *are* those groundcars?"

The cold-eyed Earthman turned to answer. Of course his face had
been familiar; this was Hemphill, fanatic hero of a dozen berserker
fights. Mitch was faintly awed, in spite of himself.

At last the groundcars came. The ride was into Ulan Bator. The
military center would be under the metropolis, taking full advantage
of the defensive force fields that could be extended up into space
to protect the area of the city.

Riding down the long elevator zigzag to the buried War Room,
Mitch found himself again next to Karlsen.

"Congratulations on your coming marriage, sir." Mitch didn't know if he liked Karlsen or not; but already he felt curiously certain of him, as if he had known the man for years. Karlsen would know he was not trying to curry favor.

The High Commander nodded. "Thank you." He hesitated for a moment, then produced a small photo. In an illusion of three dimensions it showed the head of a young woman, golden hair done in the style favored by the new aristocracy of Venus.

There was no need for any polite stretching of truth. "She's very beautiful."

"Yes." Karlsen looked long at the picture, as if reluctant to put it away. "There are those who say this will be only a political alliance. God knows we need one. But believe me, Poet, she means far more than that to me."

Karlsen blinked suddenly and, as if amused at himself, gave Mitch a why-am-I-telling-you-all-this look. The elevator floor pressed up under the passengers' feet, and the doors sighed open. They had reached the catacomb of the General Staff.

Many of the staff, though not an absolute majority, were Venerian in these days. From their greeting it was plain that the Venerian members were coldly hostile to Nogara's brother.

Humanity was, as always, a tangle of cliques and alliances. The brains of the Solarian Parliament and the Executive had been taxed to find a High Commander. If some objected to Johann Karlsen, no one who knew him had any honest doubt of his ability. He brought with him to battle many trained men, and unlike some mightier leaders, he had been willing to take responsibility for the defense of Sol.

In the frigid atmosphere in which the staff meeting opened, there was nothing to do but get quickly to business. The enemy, the berserker machines, had abandoned their old tactics of single, unpredictable raids—for slowly over the last decades the defenses of life had been strengthened.

There were now thought to be about two hundred berserkers; to meet humanity's new defenses they had recently formed themselves into a fleet, with concentrated power capable of overwhelming one at a time all centers of human resistance. Two strongly defended planets had already been destroyed. A massed human fleet was needed, first to defend Sol, and then to meet and break the power of the unliving.

"So far, then, we are agreed," said Karlsen, straightening up from the plotting table and looking around at the General Staff. "We have not as many ships or as many trained men as we would like. Perhaps no government away from Sol has contributed all it could."

Kemal, the Venerian admiral, glanced around at his planetmen, but declined the chance to comment on the weak contribution of Karlsen's own half-brother, Nogara. There was no living being upon whom Earth, Mars, and Venus could really agree, as the leader for this war. Kemal seemed to be willing to try and live with Nogara's brother.

Karlsen went on: "We have available for combat two hundred and forty-three ships, specially constructed or modified to suit the new tactics I propose to use. We are all grateful for the magnificent Venetian contribution of a hundred ships. Six of them, as you probably all know, mount the new long-range C-plus cannon."

The praise produced no visible thaw among the Venerians. Karlsen went on: "We seem to have a numerical advantage of about forty ships. I needn't tell you how the enemy outgun and out-power us, unit for unit." He paused. "The ram-and-board tactics should give us just the element of surprise we need."

Perhaps the High Commander was choosing his words carefully, not wanting to say that some element of surprise offered the only logical hope of success. After the decades-long dawning of hope, it would be too much to say that. Too much for even these tough-minded men who knew how a berserker machine weighed in the scales of war against any ordinary warship.

"One big problem is trained men," Karlsen continued, "to lead the boarding parties. I've done the best I can, recruiting. Of those ready and in training as boarding marines now, the bulk are Esteelers."

Admiral Kemal seemed to guess what was coming; he started to push back his chair and rise, then waited, evidently wanting to make certain.

Karlsen went on in the same level tone. "These trained marines will be formed into companies, and one company assigned to each warship. Then—"

"One moment, High Commander Karlsen." Kemal had risen.

"Yes?"

"Do I understand that you mean to station companies of Esteelers aboard Venerian ships?"

"In many cases my plan will mean that, yes. You protest?"

"I do." The Venerian looked around at his planetmen. "We all do."

"Nevertheless it is so ordered."

Kemal looked briefly around at his fellows once more, then sat down, blankfaced. The steno-cameras in the room's corners emitted their low sibilance, reminding all that the proceedings were being recorded.

A vertical crease appeared briefly in the High Commander's forehead, and he looked for long thoughtful seconds at the Venerians before resuming his talk. But what else was there to do, except put Esteelers onto Venerian ships?

They won't let you be a hero, Karlsen, thought Mitchell Spain. The universe is bad; and men are fools, never really all on the same side in any war.

In the hold of the Venerian warship *Solar Spot* the armor lay packed inside a padded coffinlike crate. Mitch knelt beside it inspecting the knee and elbow joints.

"Want me to paint some insignia on it, Captain?"

The speaker was a young Esteeler named Fishman, one of the newly formed marine company Mitch now commanded. Fishman had picked up a multicolor paintstick somewhere, and he pointed with it to the suit.

Mitch glanced around the hold, which was swarming with his men busily opening crates of equipment. He had decided to let things run themselves as much as possible.

"Insignia? Why, I don't think so. Unless you have some idea for a company insignia. That might be a good thing to have."

There seemed no need for any distinguishing mark on his armored suit. It was of Martian make, distinctive in style, old but with the latest improvements built in—probably no man wore better. The barrel chest already bore one design—a large black spot shattered by jagged red—showing that Mitch had been in at the "death" of one berserker. Mitch's uncle had worn the same armor; the men of Mars had always gone in great numbers out into space.

"Sergeant McKendrick," Mitch asked, "what do you think about having a company insignia?"

The newly appointed sergeant, an intelligent-looking young man, paused in walking past, and looked from Mitch to Fishman as if trying to decide who stood where on insignia before committing himself. Then he looked between them, his expression hardening.

A thin-faced Venerian, evidently an officer, had entered the hold with a squad of six men behind him, armbanded and sidearmed. Ship's Police.

The officer took a few steps and then stood motionless, looking at the paintstick in Fishman's hand. When everyone in the hold was silently watching him, he asked quietly:

"Why have you stolen from ships' stores?"

"Stolen—*this*?" The young Esteeler held up the paintstick, half-smiling, as if ready to share a joke.

They didn't come joking with a police squad, or, if they did, it was not the kind of joke a Martian appreciated. Mitch still knelt beside his crated armor. There was an unloaded carbine inside the suit's torso and he put his hand on it.

"We are at war, and we are in space," the thin-faced officer went on, still speaking mildly, standing relaxed, looking round at the open-mouthed Esteeler company. "Everyone aboard a Venerian ship is subject to law. For stealing from the ship's stores, while we face the enemy, the penalty is death. By hanging. Take him away." He made an economical gesture to his squad.

The paintstick clattered loudly on the deck. Fishman looked as if he might be going to topple over, half the smile still on his face.

Mitch stood up, the carbine in the crook of his arm. It was a stubby weapon with heavy double barrel, really a miniature recoilless cannon, to be used in free fall to destroy armored machinery. "Just a minute," Mitch said.

A couple of the police squad had begun to move uncertainly toward Fishman. They stopped at once, as if glad of an excuse for doing so.

The officer looked at Mitch, and raised one cool eyebrow. "Do you know what the penalty is, for threatening me?"

"Can't be any worse than the penalty for blowing your ugly head off. I'm Captain Mitchell Spain, marine company commander on this ship, and nobody just comes in here and drags my men away and hangs them. Who are you?"

"I am Mr. Salvador," said the Venerian. His eyes appraised Mitch, no doubt establishing that he was Martian. Wheels were turning in Mr. Salvador's calm brain, and plans were changing. He said: "Had I known that a *man* commanded this . . . group . . . I would not have thought an object lesson necessary. Come." This last word was addressed to his squad and accompanied by another simple elegant gesture. The six lost no time, preceding him to the exit. Salvador's eyes motioned Mitch to follow him to the door. After a moment's hesitation Mitch did so, while Salvador waited for him, still unruffled.

"Your men will follow you eagerly now, Captain Spain," he said in a voice too low for anyone else to hear. "And the time will come when you will willingly follow me." With a faint smile, as if of appreciation, he was gone.

There was a moment of silence; Mitch stared at the closed door, wondering. Then a roar of jubilation burst out and his back was being pounded.

When most of the uproar had died down, one of the men asked him: "Captain—what'd he mean, calling himself Mister?"

"To the Venerians, it's some kind of political rank. You guys look here! I may need some honest witnesses." Mitch held up the carbine for all to see, and broke open the chambers and clips, showing it to be unloaded. There was renewed excitement, more howls and jokes at the expense of the retreated Venerians.

But Salvador had not thought himself defeated.

"McKendrick, call the bridge. Tell the ship's captain I want to see him. The rest of you men, let's get on with this unpacking."

Young Fishman, paintstick in hand again, stood staring vacantly downward as if contemplating a design for the deck. It was beginning to soak in, how close a thing it had been.

An object lesson?

The ship's captain was coldly taciturn with Mitch, but he indicated there were no present plans for hanging any Esteelers on the *Solar Spot*. During the next sleep period Mitch kept armed sentries posted in the marines' quarters.

The next day he was summoned to the flagship. From the launch he had a view of a dance of bright dots, glinting in the light of distant Sol. Part of the fleet was already at ramming practice.

Behind the High Commander's desk sat neither a poetry critic nor a musing bridegroom, but the ruler of a planet.

"Captain Spain—sit down."

To be given a chair seemed a good sign. Waiting for Karlsen to finish some paperwork, Mitch's thoughts wandered, recalling customs he had read about, ceremonies of saluting and posturing men had used in the past when huge permanent organizations had been formed for the sole purpose of killing other men and destroying their property. Certainly men were still as greedy as ever; and now the berserker war was accustoming them again to mass destruction. Could those old days, when life fought all-out war against life, ever come again?

With a sigh, Karlsen pushed aside his papers. "What happened yesterday, between you and Mr. Salvador?"

"He said he meant to hang one of my men." Mitch gave the story, as simply as he could. He omitted only Salvador's parting words, without fully reasoning out why he did. "When I'm made responsible for men," he finished, "nobody just walks in and hangs them. Though I'm not fully convinced they would have gone that far, I meant to be as serious about it as they were."

The High Commander picked out a paper from his desk litter. "Two Esteeler marines have been hanged already. For fighting."

"Damned arrogant Venerians I'd say."

"I want none of that, Captain!"

"Yes, sir. But I'm telling you we came mighty close to a shooting war, yesterday on the *Solar Spot*."

"I realize that." Karlsen made a gesture expressive of futility. "Spain, is it impossible for the people of this fleet to cooperate, even when the survival of—what is it?"

The Earthman, Hemphill, had entered the cabin without ceremony.

His thin lips were pressed tighter than ever. "A courier has just arrived with news. Atsog is attacked."

Karlsen's strong hand crumpled papers with an involuntary twitch. "Any details?"

"The courier captain says he thinks the whole berserker fleet was there. The ground defenses were still resisting strongly when he pulled out. He just got his ship away in time."

Atsog—a planet closer to Sol than the enemy had been thought to be. It was Sol they were coming for, all right. They must know it was the human center.

More people were at the cabin door. Hemphill stepped aside for the Venerian, Admiral Kemal. Mr. Salvador, hardly glancing at Mitch, followed the admiral in.

"You have heard the news, High Commander?" Salvador began. Kemal, just ready to speak himself, gave his political officer an annoyed glance, but said nothing.

"That Atsog is attacked, yes," said Karlsen.

"My ships can be ready to move in two hours," said Kemal.

Karlsen sighed, and shook his head. "I watched today's maneuvers. The fleet can hardly be ready in two weeks."

Kemal's shock and rage seemed genuine. "You'd do that? You'd let a Venerian planet die just because we haven't knuckled under to your brother? Because we discipline his damned Esteeler—"

"Admiral Kemal, you will control yourself! You, and everyone else, are subject to discipline while I command!"

Kemal got himself in hand, apparently with great effort.

Karlsen's voice was not very loud, but the cabin seemed to resonate with it.

"You call hangings part of your discipline. I swear by the name of God that I will use every hanging, if I must, to enforce some kind of unity in this fleet. Understand, this fleet is the only military power that can oppose the massed berserkers. Trained, and unified, we can destroy them."

No listener could doubt it, for the moment.

"But whether Atsog falls, or Venus, or Esteel, I will not risk this fleet until I judge it ready."

Into the silence, Salvador said, with an air of respect: "High Commander, the courier reported one thing more. That the Lady Christina de Dulcin was visiting on Atsog when the attack began—and that she must be there still."

Karlsen closed his eyes for two seconds. Then he looked round at all of them. "If you have no further military business, gentlemen, get out." His voice was still steady.

Walking beside Mitch down the flagship corridor, Hemphill broke a silence to say thoughtfully: "Karlsen is the man the cause needs,

now. Some Venerians have approached me, tentatively, about joining a plot—I refused. We must make sure that Karlsen remains in
command."

"A plot?"

Hemphill did not elaborate.

Mitch said: "What they did just now was pretty low—letting him
make that speech about going slow, no matter what—and then breaking the news to him about his lady being on Atsog."

Hemphill said: "He knew already she was there. That news arrived
on yesterday's courier."

There was a dark nebula, made up of clustered billions of rocks
and older than the sun, named the Stone Place by men. Those who
gathered there now were not men and they gave nothing a name; they
hoped nothing, feared nothing, wondered at nothing. They had no
pride and no regret, but they had plans—a billion subtleties, carved
from electrical pressure and flow—and their built-in purpose, toward
which their planning circuits moved. As if by instinct the berserker
machines had formed themselves into a fleet when the time was ripe,
when the eternal enemy, Life, had begun to mass its strength.

The planet named Atsog in the life-language had yielded a number
of still-functioning life-units from its deepest shelters, though millions had been destroyed while their stubborn defenses were beaten
down. Functional life-units were sources of valuable information.
The mere threat of certain stimuli usually brought at least limited
cooperation from any life-unit.

The life-unit (designating itself General Bradin) which had
controlled the defense of Atsog was among those captured almost
undamaged. Its dissection was begun within perception of the
other captured life-units. The thin outer covering tissue was delicately removed, and placed upon a suitable form to preserve it for
further study. The life-units which controlled others were examined
carefully, whenever possible.

After this stimulus, it was no longer possible to communicate
intelligibly with Great Bradin; in a matter of hours it ceased to
function at all.

In itself a trifling victory, the freeing of this small unit of watery
matter from the aberration called Life. But the flow of information now increased from the nearby units which had perceived the
process.

It was soon confirmed that the life-units were assembling a
fleet. More detailed information was sought. One important line of
questioning concerned the life-unit which would control this fleet.
Gradually, from interrogations and the reading of captured records,
a picture emerged.

A name: Johann Karlsen. A biography. Contradictory things were said about him, but the facts showed he had risen rapidly to a position of control over millions of life-units.

Throughout the long war, the berserker computers had gathered and collated all available data on the men who became leaders of Life. Now against this data they matched, point for point, every detail that could be learned about Johann Karlsen.

The behavior of these leading units often resisted analysis, as if some quality of the life-disease in them was forever beyond the reach of machines. These individuals used logic, but sometimes it seemed they were not bound by logic. The most dangerous life-units of all sometimes acted in ways that seemed to contradict the known supremacy of the laws of physics and chance, as if they could be minds possessed of true free will, instead of its illusion.

And Karlsen was one of these, supremely one of these. His fitting of the dangerous pattern became plainer with every new comparison.

In the past, such life-units had been troublesome local problems. For one of them to command the whole life-fleet, with a decisive battle approaching, was extremely dangerous to the cause of Death.

The outcome of the approaching battle seemed almost certain to be favorable, since there were probably only two hundred ships in the life-fleet. But the brooding berserkers could not be certain enough of anything, while a unit like Johann Karlsen led the living. And if the battle was long postponed the enemy Life could become stronger. There were hints that inventive Life was developing new weapons, newer and more powerful ships.

The wordless conference reached a decision. There were berserker reserves, which had waited for millennia along the galactic rim, dead and uncaring in their hiding places among dust clouds and heavy nebulae, and on dark stars. For this climactic battle they must be summoned, the power of Life to resist must be broken now.

From the berserker fleet at the Stone Place, between Atsog's Sun and Sol, courier machines sped out toward the galactic rim.

It would take some time for all the reserves to gather. Meanwhile, the interrogations went on.

"Listen, I've decided to help you, see. About this guy Karlsen, I know you want to find out about him. Only I got a delicate brain. If anything hurts me, my brain don't work at all, so no rough stuff on me, understand? I'll be no good to you ever if you use rough stuff on me."

This prisoner was unusual. The interrogating computer borrowed new circuits for itself, chose symbols and hurled them back at the life-unit.

"What can you tell me about Karlsen?"

"Listen you're gonna treat me right, aren't you?"

"Useful information will be rewarded. Untruth will bring you unpleasant stimuli."

"I'll tell you this now—the woman Karlsen was going to marry is here. You caught her alive in the same shelter General Bradin was in. Now, if you sort of give me control over some other prisoners, make things nice for me, why I bet I can think up the best way for you to use her. If you just tell him you've got her, why he might not believe you, see?"

Out on the galactic rim, the signals of the giant heralds called out the hidden reserves of the unliving. Subtle detectors heard the signals, and triggered the great engines into cold flame. The force field brain in each strategic housing awoke to livelier death. Each reserve machine began to move, with metallic leisure shaking loose its cubic miles of weight and power freeing itself from dust, or ice, or age-old mud, or solid rock—then rising and turning, orienting itself in space. All converging, they drove faster than light toward the Stone Place, where the destroyers of Atsog awaited their reinforcement.

With the arrival of each reserve machine, the linked berserker computers saw victory more probable. But still the quality of one life-unit made all of their computations uncertain.

Felipe Nogara raised a strong and hairy hand, and wiped it gently across one glowing segment of the panel before his chair. The center of his private study was filled by an enormous display sphere, which now showed a representation of the explored part of the galaxy. At Nogara's gesture the sphere dimmed, then began to relight itself in a slow intricate sequence.

A wave of his hand had just theoretically eliminated the berserker fleet as a factor in the power game. To leave it in, he told himself, diffused the probabilities too widely. It was really the competing power of Venus—and that of two or three other prosperous, aggressive planets—which occupied his mind.

Well insulated in this private room from the hum of Esteel City and from the routine press of business, Nogara watched his computers' new prediction take shape, showing the political power structure as it might exist one year from now, two years, five. As he had expected, this sequence showed Esteel expanding in influence. It was even possible that he could become ruler of the human galaxy.

Nogara wondered at his own calm in the face of such an idea. Twelve or fifteen years ago he had driven with all his power of intellect and will to advance himself. Gradually, the moves in the game had come to seem automatic. Today, there was a chance that almost every thinking being known to exist would come to acknowledge him as ruler—and it meant less to him than the first local election he had ever won.

Diminishing returns, of course. The more gained, the greater gain needed to produce an equal pleasure. At least when he was alone. If his aides were watching this prediction now it would certainly excite them, and he would catch their excitement.

But, being alone, he sighed. The berserker fleet would not vanish at the wave of a hand. Today, what was probably the final plea for more help had arrived from Earth. The trouble was that granting Sol more help would take ships and men and money from Nogara's expansion projects. Wherever he did that now, he stood to lose out, eventually, to other men. Old Sol would have to survive the coming attack with no more help from Esteel.

Nogara realized, wondering dully at himself, that he would as soon see even Esteel destroyed as see control slip from his hands. Now why? He could not say he loved his planet or his people, but he had been, by and large, a good ruler, not a tyrant. Good government was, after all, good politics.

His desk chimed the melodious notes that meant something was newly available for his amusement. Nogara chose to answer.

"Sir," said a woman's voice, "two new possibilities are in the shower room now."

Projected from hidden cameras, a scene glowed into life above Nogara's desk—bodies gleaming in a spray of water.

"They are from prison, sir, anxious for any reprieve."

Watching, Nogara felt only a weariness; and, yes, something like self-contempt. He questioned himself: Where in all the universe is there a reason why I should not seek pleasure as I choose? And again: Will I dabble in sadism, next? And if I do, what of it?

But what after that?

Having paused respectfully, the voice asked: "Perhaps this evening you would prefer something different?"

"Later," he said. The scene vanished. Maybe I should try to be a Believer for a while, he thought. What an intense thrill it must be for Johann to sin. If he ever does.

That had been a genuine pleasure, seeing Johann given command of the Solarian fleet, watching the Venetians boil. But it had raised another problem. Johann, victorious over the berserkers, would emerge as the greatest hero in human history. Would that not make even Johann dangerously ambitious? The thing to do would be to ease him out of the public eye, give him some high-ranked job, honest, but dirty and inglorious. Hunting out outlaws somewhere. Johann would probably accept that, being Johann. But if Johann bid for galactic power, he would have to take his chances. Any pawn on the board might be removed.

Nogara shook his head. Suppose Johann lost the coming battle, and lost Sol? A berserker victory would not be a matter of diffusing probabilities, that was pleasant doubletalk for a tired mind to fool itself with. A berserker victory would mean the end of Earthman in the galaxy, probably within a few years. No computer was needed to see that.

There was a little bottle in his desk; Nogara brought it out and looked at it. The end of the chess game was in it, the end of all pleasure and boredom and pain. Looking at the vial caused him no emotion. In it was a powerful drug which threw a man into a kind of ecstasy—a transcendental excitement that within a few minutes burst the heart or the blood vessels of the brain. Someday, when all else was exhausted, when it was completely a berserker universe . . .

He put the vial away, and he put away the final appeal from Earth. What did it all matter? Was it not a berserker universe already, everything determined by the random swirls of condensing gas, before the stars were born?

Felipe Nogara leaned back in his chair, watching his computers marking out the galactic chessboard.

Through the fleet the rumor spread that Karlsen delayed because it was a Venerian colony under siege. Aboard the *Solar Spot*, Mitch saw no delays for any reason. He had time for only work, quick meals, and sleep. When the final ram-and-board drill had been completed, the last stores and ammunition loaded, Mitch was too tired to feel much except relief. He rested, not frightened or elated, while the *Spot* wheeled into a rank with forty other arrow-shaped ships, dipped with them into the first C-plus jump of the deep space search, and began to hunt the enemy.

It was days later before dull routine was broken by a jangling battle alarm. Mitch was awakened by it; before his eyes were fully opened, he was scrambling into the armored suit stored under his bunk. Nearby, some marines grumbled about practice alerts; but none of them were moving slowly.

"This is High Commander Karlsen speaking," boomed the overhead speakers. "This is not a practice alert; repeat, not practice. Two berserkers have been sighted. One we've just glimpsed at extreme range. Likely it will get away, though the Ninth Squadron is chasing it.

"The other is not going to escape. In a matter of minutes we will have it englobed, in normal space. We are not going to destroy it by bombardment; we are going to soften it up a bit, and then see how well we can really ram and board. If there are any bugs left in our tactics, we'd better find out now. Squadrons Two, Four, and Seven will each send one ship to the ramming attack. I'm going back on Command Channel now, Squadron Commanders."

"Squadron Four," sighed Sergeant McKendrick. "More Esteelers in our company than any other. How can we miss?"

The marines lay like dragon's teeth seeded in the dark, strapped into the padded acceleration couches that had been their bunks, while the psych-music tried to lull them, and those who were Believers prayed. In the darkness Mitch listened on intercom, and passed on to his men the terse battle reports that came to him as marine commander on the ship.

He was afraid. What was death, that men should fear it so? It could only be the end of all experience. That end was inevitable, and beyond imagination, and he feared it.

The preliminary bombardment did not take long. Two hundred and thirty ships of life held a single trapped enemy in the center of their hollow sphere formation. Listening in the dark to laconic voices, Mitch heard how the berserker fought back, as if with the finest human courage and contempt for odds. Could you really fight machines, when you could never make them suffer pain or fear?

But you could defeat machines. And this time, for once, humanity had far too many guns. It would be easy to blow this berserker into vapor. Would it be best to do so? There were bound to be marine casualties in any boarding, no matter how favorable the odds. But a true combat test of the boarding scheme was badly needed before the decisive battle came to be fought. And, too, this enemy might hold living prisoners who might be rescued by boarders. A High Commander did well to have a rocklike certainty of his own rightness.

The order was given. The *Spot* and two other chosen ships fell in toward the battered enemy at the center of the englobement.

Straps held Mitch firmly, but the gravity had been turned off for the ramming, and weightlessness gave the impression that his body would fly and vibrate like a pellet shaken in a bottle with the coming impact. Soundless dark, soft cushioning, and lulling music; but a few words came into the helmet and the body cringed, knowing that outside were the black cold guns and the hurtling machines, unimaginable forces leaping now to meet. Now—

Reality shattered in through all the protection and the padding. The shaped atomic charge at the tip of the ramming prow opened the berserker's skin. In five seconds of crashing impact, the prow vaporized, melted, and crumpled its length away, the true hull driving behind it until the *Solar Spot* was sunk like an arrow into the body of the enemy.

Mitch spoke for the last time to the bridge of the *Solar Spot*, while his men lurched past him in free fall, their suit lights glaring.

"My panel shows Sally Port Three the only one not blocked," he said. "We're all going out that way."

"Remember," said a Venerian voice. "Your first job is to protect this ship against counterattack."

"Roger." If they wanted to give him offensively unnecessary reminders, now was not the time for argument. He broke contact with the bridge and hurried after his men.

The other two ships were to send their boarders fighting toward the strategic housing, somewhere deep in the berserker's center. The marines from the *Solar Spot* were to try to find and save any prisoners the berserker might hold. A berserker usually held prisoners near its surface, so the first search would be made by squads spreading out under the hundreds of square kilometers of hull.

In the dark chaos of wrecked machinery just outside the sally port there was no sign yet of counterattack. The berserkers had supposedly not been built to fight battles inside their own metallic skins—on this rested the fleet's hopes for success in a major battle.

Mitch left forty men to defend the hull of the *Spot*, and himself led a squad of ten out into the labyrinth. There was no use setting himself up in a command post—communications in here would be impossible, once out of line-of-sight.

The first man in each searching squad carried a mass spectrometer, an instrument that would detect the stray atoms of oxygen bound to leak from compartments where living beings breathed. The last man wore on one hand a device to blaze a trail with arrows of luminous paint; without a trail, getting lost in this three-dimensional maze would be almost inevitable.

"Got a scent, Captain," said Mitch's spectrometer man, after five minutes' casting through the squad's assigned sector of the dying berserker.

"Keep on it." Mitch was second in line, his carbine ready.

The detector man led the way through a dark and weightless mechanical universe. Several times he paused to adjust his instrument and wave its probe. Otherwise the pace was rapid; men trained in free fall, and given plenty of holds to thrust and steer by, could move faster than runners.

A towering, multijointed shape rose up before the detector man, brandishing blue-white welding arcs like swords. Before Mitch was aware of aiming, his carbine fired twice. The shells ripped the machine open and pounded it backward; it was only some semirobotic maintenance device, not built for fighting.

The detector man had nerve; he plunged straight on. The squad kept pace with him, their suit lights scouting out unfamiliar shapes and distances, cutting knife-edge shadows in the vacuum, glare and darkness mellowed only by reflection.

"Getting close!"

And then they came to it. It was a place like the top of a huge dry well. An ovoid like a ship's launch, very thickly armored, had apparently been raised through the well from deep inside the berserker, and now clamped to a dock.

"It's the launch, it's oozing oxygen."

"Captain, there's some kind of airlock on this side. Outer door's open."

It looked like the smooth and easy entrance of a trap.

"Keep your eyes open." Mitch went into the airlock. "Be ready to blast me out of here if I don't show in one minute."

It was an ordinary airlock, probably cut from some human spaceship. He shut himself inside, and then got the inner door open.

Most of the interior was a single compartment. In the center was an acceleration couch, holding a nude female mannikin. He drifted near, saw that her head had been depilated and that there were tiny beads of blood still on her scalp, as if probes had just been withdrawn.

When his suit lamp hit her face she opened dead blue staring eyes, blinking mechanically. Still not sure that he was looking at a living human being, Mitch drifted beside her and touched her arm with metal fingers. Then all at once her face became human, her eyes coming from death through nightmare to reality. She saw him and cried out. Before he could free her there were crystal drops of tears in the weightless air.

Listening to his rapid orders, she held one hand modestly in front of her, and the other over her raw scalp. Then she nodded, and took into her mouth the end of a breathing tube that would dole air from Mitch's suit tank. In a few more seconds he had her wrapped in a clinging, binding rescue blanket, temporary proof against vacuum and freezing.

The detector man had found no oxygen source except the launch. Mitch ordered his squad back along their luminous trail.

At the sally port, he heard that things were not going well with the attack. Real fighting robots were defending the strategic housing; at least eight men had been killed down there. Two more ships were going to ram and board.

Mitch carried the girl through the sally port and three more friendly hatches. The monstrously thick hull of the ship shuddered and sang around him; the *Solar Spot*, her mission accomplished, boarders retrieved, was being withdrawn. Full weight came back, and light.

"In here, Captain."

QUARANTINE, said the sign. A berserker's prisoner might have been deliberately infected with something contagious; men now knew how to deal with such tricks.

Inside the infirmary he set her down. While medics and nurses scrambled around, he unfolded the blanket from the girl's face, remembering to leave it curled over her shaven head, and opened his own helmet.

"You can spit out the tube now," he told her, in his rasping voice.

She did so, and opened her eyes again.

"Oh, are you real?" she whispered. Her hand pushed its way out of the blanket folds and slid over his armor. "Oh, let me touch a human being again!" Her hand moved up to his exposed face and gripped his cheek and neck.

"I'm real enough. You're all right now."

One of the bustling doctors came to a sudden, frozen halt, staring at the girl. Then he spun around on his heel and hurried away. What was wrong?

Others sounded confident, reassuring the girl as they ministered to her. She wouldn't let go of Mitch, she became nearly hysterical when they tried gently to separate her from him.

"I guess you'd better stay," a doctor told him.

He sat there holding her hand, his helmet and gauntlets off. He looked away while they did medical things to her. They still spoke easily; he thought they were finding nothing much wrong.

"What's your name?" she asked him when the medics were through for the moment. Her head was bandaged; her slender arm came from beneath the sheets to maintain contact with his hand.

"Mitchell Spain." Now that he got a good look at her, a living young human female, he was in no hurry at all to get away. "What's yours?"

A shadow crossed her face. "I'm—not sure."

There was a sudden commotion at the infirmary door; High Commander Karlsen was pushing past protesting doctors into the QUARANTINE area. Karlsen came on until he was standing beside Mitch, but he was not looking at Mitch.

"Chris," he said to the girl. "Thank God." There were tears in his eyes.

The Lady Christina de Dulcin turned her eyes from Mitch to Johann Karlsen, and screamed in abject terror.

"Now, Captain. Tell me how you found her and brought her out."

Mitch began his tale. The two men were alone in Karlsen's monastic cabin, just off the flagship's bridge. The fight was over, the berserker a torn and harmless hulk. No other prisoners had been aboard it.

"They planned to send her back to me," Karlsen said, staring into space, when Mitch had finished his account. "We attacked before it could launch her toward us. It kept her out of the fighting, and sent her back to me."

Mitch was silent.

Karlsen's red-rimmed eyes fastened on him. "She's been brain-washed, Poet. It can be done with some permanence, you know, when advantage is taken of the subject's natural tendencies. I suppose she's never thought too much of me. There were political reasons for her to consent to our marriage ... she screams when the doctors even mention my name. They tell me it's possible that horrible things were done to her by some man-shaped machine made to look like me. Other people are tolerable, to a degree. But it's you she wants to be alone with, you she needs."

"She cried out when I left her, but—me?"

"The natural tendency, you see. For her to ... love ... the man who saved her. The machines set her mind to fasten all the joy of rescue upon the first male human face she saw. The doctors assure me such things can be done. They've given her drugs, but even in sleep the instruments show her nightmares, her pain, and she cries out for you. What do you feel toward her?"

"Sir, I'll do anything I can. What do you want of me?"

"I want you to stop her suffering, what else?" Karlsen's voice rose to a ragged shout. "Stay alone with her, stop her pain if you can!"

He got himself under a kind of control. "Go on. The doctors will take you in. Your gear will be brought over from the *Solar Spot*."

Mitch stood up. Any words he could think of sounded in his mind like sickening attempts at humor. He nodded, and hurried out.

"This is your last chance to join us," said the Venerian, Salvador, looking up and down the dim corridors of this remote outer part of the flagship. "Our patience is worn, and we will strike soon. With the de Dulcin woman in her present condition, Nogara's brother is doubly unfit to command."

The Venerian must be carrying a pocket spy-jammer; a multi-sonic whine was setting Hemphill's teeth on edge. And so was the Venerian.

"Karlsen is vital to the human cause whether we like him or not," Hemphill said, his own patience about gone, but his voice still calm and reasonable. "Don't you see to what lengths the berserkers have gone to get at him? They sacrificed a perfectly good machine just to deliver his brainwashed woman here, to attack him psychologically."

"Well. If that is true they have succeeded. If Karlsen had any value before, now he will be able to think of nothing but his woman and the Martian."

Hemphill sighed. "Remember, he refused to hurry the fleet to Atsog to try to save her. He hasn't failed yet. Until he does, you and the others must give up this plotting against him."

Salvador backed away a step, and spat on the deck in rage. A calculated display, thought Hemphill.

"Look to yourself, Earthman!" Salvador hissed. "Karlsen's days are numbered, and the days of those who support him too willingly!" He spun around and walked away.

"Wait!" Hemphill called, quietly. The Venerian stopped and turned, with an air of arrogant reluctance. Hemphill shot him through the heart with a laser pistol. The weapon made a splitting, crackling noise in atmosphere.

Hemphill prodded the dying man with his toe, making sure no second shot was needed. "You were good at talking," he mused aloud. "But too devious to lead the fight against the damned machines."

He bent to quickly search the body, and stood up elated. He had found a list of officers' names. Some few were underlined, and some, including his own, followed by a question mark. Another paper bore a scribbled compilation of the units under command of certain Venerian officers. There were a few more notes; altogether, plenty of evidence for the arrest of the hard-core plotters. It might tend to split the fleet, but—

Hemphill looked up sharply, then relaxed. The man approaching was one of his own, whom he had stationed nearby.

"We'll take these to the High Commander at once." Hemphill waved the papers. "There'll be just time to clean out the traitors and reorganize command before we face battle."

Yet he delayed for another moment, staring down at Salvador's corpse. The plotter had been overconfident and inept, but still dangerous. Did some sort of luck operate to protect Karlsen? Karlsen himself did not match Hemphill's ideal of a war leader; he was not as ruthless as machinery or as cold as metal. Yet the damned machines made great sacrifices to attack him.

Hemphill shrugged, and hurried on his way.

"Mitch, I do love you. I know what the doctors say it is, but what do they really know about me?"

Christina de Dulcin, wearing a simple blue robe and turbanlike headdress, now reclined on a luxurious acceleration couch, in what was nominally the sleeping room of the High Commander's quarters. Karlsen had never occupied the place, preferring a small cabin.

Mitchell Spain sat three feet from her, afraid to so much as touch her hand, afraid of what he might do, and what she might do. They were alone, and he felt sure they were unwatched. The Lady Christina had even demanded assurances against spy devices and Karlsen had sent his pledge. Besides, what kind of ship would have spy devices built into its highest officers' quarters?

A situation for bedroom farce, but not when you had to live through it. The man outside, taking the strain, had more than two hundred ships dependent on him now, and many human planets would be lifeless in five years if the coming battle failed.

"What do you really know about me, Chris?" he asked.

"I know you mean life itself to me. Oh, Mitch, I have no time now to be coy, and mannered, and every millimeter a lady. I've been all those things. And—once—I would have married a man like Karlsen, for political reasons. But all that was before Atsog."

Her voice dropped on the last word, and her hand on her robe made a convulsive grasping gesture. He had to lean forward and take it.

"Chris, Atsog is in the past now."

"Atsog will never be over, completely over, for me. I keep remembering more and more of it. Mitch, the machines made us watch while they skinned General Bradin alive. I saw that. I can't bother with silly things like politics anymore, life is too short for them. And I no longer fear anything, except driving you away . . ."

He felt pity, and lust, and half a dozen other maddening things.

"Karlsen's a good man," he said finally.

She repressed a shudder. "I suppose," she said in a controlled voice. "But Mitch, what do you feel for me? Tell the truth—if you don't love me now, I can hope you will, in time." She smiled faintly, and raised a hand. "When my silly hair grows back."

"Your silly hair." His voice almost broke. He reached to touch her face, then pulled his fingers back as from a flame. "Chris, you're his girl, and too much depends on him."

"I was never his."

"Still . . . I can't lie to you, Chris; maybe I can't tell you the truth, either, about how I feel. The battle's coming, everything's up in the air, paralyzed. No one can plan . . ." He made an awkward, uncertain gesture.

"Mitch." Her voice was understanding. "This is terrible for you, isn't it? Don't worry, I'll do nothing to make it worse. Will you call the doctor? As long as I know you're somewhere near, I think I can rest, now."

Karlsen studied Salvador's papers in silence for some minutes, like a man pondering a chess problem. He did not seem greatly surprised.

"I have a few dependable men standing ready," Hemphill finally volunteered. "We can quickly—arrest—the leaders of this plot."

The blue eyes searched him. "Commander, was Salvador's killing truly necessary?"

"I thought so," said Hemphill blandly. "He was reaching for his own weapon."

Karlsen glanced once more at papers and reached a decision.

"Commander Hemphill, I want you to pick four ships, and scout the far edge of the Stone Place nebula. We don't want to push beyond it without knowing where the enemy is, and give him a chance to get between us and Sol. Use caution—to learn the general location of the bulk of his fleet is enough."

"Very well." Hemphill nodded. The reconnaissance made sense; and if Karlsen wanted to get Hemphill out of the way, and deal with his human opponents by his own methods, well, let him. Those methods often seemed soft-headed to Hemphill, but they seemed to work for Karlsen. If the damned machines for some reason found Karlsen unendurable, then Hemphill would support him, to the point of cheerful murder and beyond.

What else really mattered in the universe, besides smashing the damned machines?

Mitch spent hours every day alone with Chris. He kept from her the wild rumors which circulated throughout the fleet. Salvador's violent end was whispered about, and guards were posted near Karlsen's quarters. Some said Admiral Kemal was on the verge of open revolt.

And now the Stone Place was close ahead of the fleet, blanking out half the stars; ebony dust and fragments, like a million shattered planets. No ship could move through the Stone Place; every cubic kilometer of it held enough matter to prevent C-plus travel or movement in normal space at any effective speed.

The fleet headed toward one sharply defined edge of the cloud, around which Hemphill's scouting squadron had already disappeared.

"She grows a little saner, a little calmer, every day," said Mitch, entering the High Commander's small cabin.

Karlsen looked up from his desk. The papers before him seemed to be lists of names, in Venerian script. "I thank you for that word, Poet. Does she speak of me?"

"No."

They eyed each other, the poor and ugly cynic, the anointed and handsome Believer.

"Poet," Karlsen asked suddenly, "how do you deal with deadly enemies, when you find them in your power?"

"We Martians are supposed to be a violent people. Do you expect me to pass sentence on myself?"

Karlsen appeared not to understand for a moment. "Oh. No. I was not speaking of you—you and me and Chris. Not personal affairs. I suppose I was only thinking aloud, asking for a sign."

"Then don't ask me, ask your God. But didn't he tell you to forgive your enemies?"

"He did." Karlsen nodded, slowly and thoughtfully. "You know, he wants a lot from us. A real hell of a lot."

It was a peculiar sensation, to become suddenly convinced that the man you were watching was a genuine, nonhypocritical Believer. Mitch was not sure he had ever met the like before.

Nor had he ever seen Karlsen quite like this—passive, waiting; asking for a sign. As if there was in fact some purpose outside the layers of a man's own mind, that could inspire him. Mitch thought about it. If . . .

But that was all mystical nonsense.

Karlsen's communicator sounded. Mitch could not make out what the other voice was saying, but he watched the effect on the High Commander. Energy and determination were coming back, there were subtle signs of the return of force, of the tremendous conviction of being right. It was like watching the gentle glow when a fusion power lamp was ignited.

"Yes," Karlsen was saying. "Yes, well done."

Then he raised the Venerian papers from his desk; it was as if he raised them only by force of will, his fingers only gesturing beneath them.

"The news is from Hemphill," he said to Mitch, almost absently. "The berserker fleet is just around the edge of the Stone Place from us. Hemphill estimates they are two hundred strong, and thinks they are unaware of our presence. We attack at once. Man your battle station, Poet; God be with you." He turned back to his communicator. "Ask Admiral Kemal to my cabin at once. Tell him to bring his staff. In particular—" He glanced at the Venerian papers and read off several names.

"Good luck to you, sir," Mitch had delayed to say that. Before he hurried out, he saw Karlsen stuffing the Venerian papers into his trash disintegrator.

Before Mitch reached his own cabin, the battle horns were sounding. He had armed and suited himself and was making his way back through the suddenly crowded narrow corridors toward the bridge, when the ship's speakers boomed suddenly to life, picking up Karlsen's voice:

" . . . whatever wrongs we have done you, by word, or deed, or by things left undone, I ask you now to forgive. And in the name of every man who calls me friend or leader, I pledge that any grievance we have against you, is from this moment wiped from memory."

Everyone in the crowded passage hesitated in the rush for battle stations. Mitch found himself staring into the eyes of a huge, well-armed Venerian ship's policeman, probably here on the flagship as some officer's bodyguard.

There came an amplified cough and rumble, and then the voice of Admiral Kemal:

"We—we are brothers, Esteeler and Venerian, and all of us. All of us together now, the living against the berserker." Kemal's voice rose to a shout. "Destruction to the damned machines, and death to their builders! Let every man remember Atsog!"

"Remember Atsog!" roared Karlsen's voice.

In the corridor there was a moment's hush, like that before a towering wave smites down. Then a great insensate shout. Mitch found himself with tears in his eyes, yelling something.

"Remembering General Bradin," cried the big Venerian, grabbing Mitch and hugging him, lifting him, armor and all. "Death to his flayers!"

"Death to the flayers!" The shout ran like a flame through the corridor. No one needed to be told that the same things were happening in all the ships of the fleet. All at once there was no room for anything less than brotherhood, no time for anything less than glory.

"Destruction to the damned machines!"

Near the flagship's center of gravity was the bridge, only a dais holding a ring of combat chairs, each with its clustered controls and dials.

"Boarding Coordinator ready," Mitch reported, strapping himself in.

The viewing sphere near the bridge's center showed the human advance, in two leapfrogging lines of over a hundred ships each. Each ship was a green dot in the sphere, positioned as truthfully as the flagship's computers could manage. The irregular surface of the Stone Place moved beside the battle lines in a series of jerks; the flagship was traveling by C-plus microjumps, so the presentation in the viewing sphere was a succession of still pictures at second-and-a-half intervals. Slowed by the mass of their C-plus cannon, the six fat green symbols of the Venerian heavy weapons ships labored forward, falling behind the rest of the fleet.

In Mitch's headphones someone was saying: "In about ten minutes we can expect to reach—"

The voice died away. There was a red dot in the sphere already, and then another, and then a dozen, rising like tiny suns around the bulge of dark nebula. For long seconds the men on the bridge were silent while the berserker advance came into view. Hemphill's scouting patrol must, after all, have been detected, for the berserker fleet was not cruising, but attacking. There was a battlenet of a hundred or more red dots, and now there were two nets, leapfrogging in and out of space like the human lines. And still the red berserkers rose into view, their formations growing, spreading out to englobe and crush a smaller fleet.

"I make it three hundred machines," said a pedantic and somewhat effeminate voice, breaking the silence with cold precision. Once, the mere knowledge that three hundred berserkers existed might have crushed all human hopes. In this place, in this hour, fear itself could frighten no one.

The voices in Mitch's headphones began to transact the business of opening a battle. There was nothing yet for him to do but listen and watch.

The six heavy green marks were falling further behind; without hesitation, Karlsen was hurling his entire fleet straight at the enemy center. The foe's strength had been underestimated, but it seemed the berserker command had made a similar error, because the red formations too were being forced to regroup, spread themselves wider.

The distance between fleets was still too great for normal weapons to be effective, but the laboring heavy-weapons ships with their C-plus cannon were now in range, and they could fire through friendly formations almost as easily as not. At their volley Mitch thought he felt space jar around him; it was some secondary effect that the human brain notices, really only wasted energy. Each projectile, blasted by explosives to a safe distance from its launching ship, mounted its own C-plus engine, which then accelerated the projectile while it flickered in and out of reality on microtimers.

Their leaden masses magnified by velocity, the huge slugs skipped through existence like stones across water, passing like phantoms through the fleet of life, emerging fully into normal space only as they approached their target, travelling then like De Broglie wavicles, their matter churning internally with a phase velocity greater than that of light.

Almost instantly after Mitch had felt the slugs' ghostly passage, one red dot began to expand and thin into a cloud, still tiny in the viewing sphere. Someone gasped. In a few more moments the flagship's own weapons, beams and missiles, went into action.

The enemy center stopped, two million miles ahead, but his flanks came on, smoothly as the screw of a vast meat-grinder, threatening englobement of the first line of human ships.

Karlsen did not hesitate, and a great turning point flickered past in a second. The life-fleet hurtled on, deliberately into the trap, straight for the hinge of the jaws.

Space twitched and warped around Mitchell Spain. Every ship in the fleet was firing now, and every enemy answering, and the energies released plucked through his armor like ghostly fingers. Green dots and red vanished from the sphere, but not many of either as yet.

The voices in Mitch's helmet slackened, as events raced into a pattern that shifted too fast for human thought to follow. Now for a time the fight would be computer against computer, faithful slave of life against outlaw, neither caring, neither knowing.

The viewing sphere on the flagship's bridge was shifting ranges almost in a flicker. One swelling red dot was only a million miles away, then half of that, then half again. And how the flagship came into normal space for the final lunge of the attack, firing itself like a bullet at the enemy.

Again the viewer switched to a closer range, and the chosen foe was no longer a red dot, but a great forbidding castle, tilted crazily, black against the stars. Only a hundred miles away, then half of that. The velocity of closure slowed no less than a mile a second. As expected, the enemy was accelerating, trying to get away from what must look to it like a suicide charge. For the last time Mitch checked his chair, his suit, his weapons. *Chris, be safe in a cocoon.* The berserker swelled in the sphere, gun-flashes showing now around his steel-ribbed belly. A small one, this, maybe only ten times the flagship's bulk. Always a rotten spot to be found, in every one of them, old wounds under their ancient skins. Try to run, you monstrous obscenity, try in vain.

Closer, twisting closer. Now!

Lights all gone, falling in the dark for one endless second—

Impact. Mitch's chair shook him, the gentle pads inside his armor battering and bruising him. The expendable ramming prow would be vaporizing, shattering and crumpling, dissipating energy down to a level the battering-ram ship could endure.

When the crashing stopped, noise still remained, a whining, droning symphony of stressed metal and escaping air and gases like sobbing breathing. The great machines were locked together now, half the length of the flagship embedded in the berserker.

A rough ramming, but no one on the bridge was injured. Damage Control reported that the expected air leaks were being controlled. Gunnery reported that it could not yet extend a turret inside the wound. Drive reported ready for a maximum effort.

Drive!

The ship twisted in the wound it had made. This could be victory now, tearing the enemy open, sawing his metal bowels out into space. The bridge twisted with the structure of the ship, this warship that was more solid metal than anything else. For a moment, Mitch thought he could come close to comprehending the power of the engines men had built.

"No use, Commander. We're wedged in."

The enemy endured. The berserker memory would already be searched, the plans made, the counterattack on the flagship coming, without fear or mercy.

The Ship Commander turned his head to look at Johann Karlsen. It had been foreseen that once a battle reached this melee stage there would be little for a High Commander to do. Even if the flagship itself were not half-buried in an enemy hull, all space nearby was a complete inferno of confused destruction, through which any meaningful communication would be impossible. If Karlsen was helpless now, neither could the berserker computers still link themselves into a single brain.

"Fight your ship, sir," said Karlsen. He leaned forward, gripping the arms of his chair, gazing at the clouded viewing sphere as if trying to make sense of the few flickering lights within it.

The Ship Commander immediately ordered his marines to board.

Mitch saw them out the sally ports. Then, sitting still was worse than any action. "Sir, I request permission to join the boarders."

Karlsen seemed not to hear. He disqualified himself, for now, from any use of power; especially to set Mitchell Spain in the forefront of the battle or to hold him back.

The Ship Commander considered. He wanted to keep a Boarding Coordinator on the bridge; but experienced men would be desperately needed in the fighting. "Go, then. Do what you can to help defend our sally ports."

This berserker defended itself well with soldier-robots. The marines had hardly gotten away from the embedded hull when the counterattack came, cutting most of them off.

In a narrow zigzag passage leading out to the port near which fighting was heaviest, an armored figure met Mitch. "Captain Spain? I'm Sergeant Broom, acting Defense Commander here. Bridge says you're to take over. It's a little rough. Gunnery can't get a turret working inside the wound. The clankers have all kinds of room to maneuver, and they keep coming at us."

"Let's get out there, then."

The two of them hurried forward, through a passage that became only a warped slit. The flagship was bent here, a strained swordblade forced into a chink of armor.

"Nothing rotten here," said Mitch, climbing at last out of the sally port. There were distant flashes of light, and the sullen glow of hot metal nearby, by which to see braced girders, like tall buildings among which the flagship had jammed itself.

"Eh? No." Broom must be wondering what he was talking about. But the sergeant stuck to business, pointing out to Mitch where he had about a hundred men disposed among the chaos of torn metal and drifting debris. "The clankers don't use guns. They just drift in, sneaking, or charge in a wave, and get us hand-to-hand, if they can. Last wave we lost six men."

Whining gusts of gas came out of the deep caverns, and scattered blobs of liquid, along with flashes of light, and deep shudders through the metal. The damned thing might be dying, or just getting ready to fight; there was no way to tell.

"Any more of the boarding parties get back?" Mitch asked.

"No. Doesn't look good for 'em."

"Port Defense, this is Gunnery," said a cheerful radio voice. "We're getting the eighty-degree forward turret working."

"Well, then use it!" Mitch rasped back. "We're inside, you can't help hitting something."

A minute later, searchlights moved out from doored recesses in the flagship's hull, and stabbed into the great chaotic cavern.

"Here they come again!" yelled Broom. Hundreds of meters away, beyond the melted stump of the flagship's prow, a line of figures drifted nearer. The searchlights questioned them; they were not suited men. Mitch was opening his mouth to yell at Gunnery when the turret fired, throwing a raveling skein of shellbursts across the advancing rank of machines.

But more ranks were coming. Men were firing in every direction at machines that came clambering, jetting, drifting, in hundreds.

Mitch took off from the sally port, moving in diving weightless leaps, touring the outposts, shifting men when the need arose.

"Fall back when you have to!" he ordered, on Command radio. "Keep them from the sally ports!"

His men were facing no lurching conscription of mechanized pipefitters and moving welders; these devices were built, in one shape or another, to fight.

As he dove between outposts, a thing like a massive chain looped itself to intercept Mitch; he broke it in half with his second shot. A metallic butterfly darted at him on brilliant jets, and away again, and he wasted four shots at it.

He found an outpost abandoned, and started back toward the sally port, radioing ahead: "Broom, how is it there?"

"Hard to tell, Captain. Squad leaders, check in again, squad leaders—"

The flying thing darted back; Mitch sliced it with his laser pistol. As he approached the sally port, weapons were firing all around him. The interior fight was turning into a microcosm of the confused struggle between fleets. He knew that still raged, for the ghostly fingers of heavy weapons still plucked through his armor continually.

"Here they come again—Dog, Easy, Nine o'clock."

Coordinates of an attack straight at the sally port. Mitch found a place to wedge himself, and raised his carbine again. Many of the machines in this wave bore metal shields before them. He fired and reloaded, again and again.

The flagship's one usable turret flamed steadily, and an almost continuous line of explosions marched across the machines' ranks in vacuum-silence, along with a traversing searchlight spot. The automatic cannons of the turret were far heavier than the marines' hand weapons; almost anything the cannon hit dissolved in radii of splinters. But suddenly there were machines on the flagship's hull, attacking the turret from its blind side.

Mitch called out a warning and started in that direction. Then all at once the enemy was around him. Two things caught a nearby man in their crablike claws, trying to tear him apart between them. Mitch fired quickly at the moving figures and hit the man, blowing one leg off.

A moment later one of the crab-machines was knocked away and broken by a hailstorm of shells. The other one beat the armored man to pieces against a jagged girder, and turned to look for its next piece of work.

This machine was armored like a warship. It spotted Mitch and came for him, climbing through drifting rubble, shells and slugs rocking it but not crippling. It gleamed in his suit lights, reaching out bright pincers, as he emptied his carbine at the box where its cybernetics should be.

He drew his pistol and dodged, but like a falling cat it turned at him. It caught him by the left hand and the helmet, metal squealing and crunching. He thrust the laser pistol against what he thought was the brainbox, and held the trigger down. He and the machine were drifting, it could get no leverage for its strength. But it held him, working on his armored hand and helmet.

Its brainbox, the pistol, and the fingers of his right gauntlet, all were glowing hot. Something molten spattered across his faceplate, the glare half-blinding him. The laser burned out, fusing its barrel to the enemy in a radiant weld.

His left gauntlet, still caught, was giving way, being crushed—
—*his hand*—

Even as the suit's hypos and tourniquet bit him, he got his burned right hand free of the laser's butt and reached the plastic grenades at his belt.

His left arm was going wooden, even before the claw released his mangled hand and fumbled slowly for a fresh grip. The machine was shuddering all over, like an agonized man. Mitch whipped his right arm around to plaster a grenade on the far side of the brainbox. Then with arms and legs he strained against the crushing, groping claws. His suit-servos whined with overload, being overpowered, two seconds, close eyes, three—

The explosion stunned him. He found himself drifting free. Lights were flaring. Somewhere was a sally port; he had to get there and defend it.

His head cleared slowly. He had the feeling that someone was pressing a pair of fingers against his chest. He hoped that was only some reaction from the hand. It was hard to see anything, with his faceplate still half-covered with splashed metal, but at last he spotted the flagship hull. A chunk of something came within reach, and he used it to propel himself toward the sally port, spinning weakly. He dug out a fresh clip of ammunition and then realized his carbine was gone.

The space near the sally port was foggy with shattered mechanism; and there were still men here, firing their weapons out into the great cavern. Mitch recognized Broom's armor in the flaring lights, and got a welcoming wave.

"Captain! They've knocked out the turret, and most of the searchlights. But we've wrecked an awful lot of 'em—how's your arm?"

"Feels like wood. Got a carbine?"

"Say again?"

Broom couldn't hear him. Of course, the damned thing had squeezed his helmet and probably wrecked his radio transmitter. He put his helmet against Broom's and said: "You're in charge. I'm going in. Get back out if I can."

Broom was nodding, guiding him watchfully toward the port. Gun flashes started up around them thick and fast again, but there was nothing he could do about that, with two steady dull fingers pressing into his chest. Lightheaded. Get back out? Who was he fooling? Lucky if he got in without help.

He went into the port, past the interior guards' niches, and through an airlock. A medic took one look and came to help him.

Not dead yet, he thought, aware of people and lights around him. There was still some part of a hand wrapped in bandages on the end of his left arm. He noticed another thing, too; he felt no more ghostly plucking of space-bending weapons. Then he understood that he was being wheeled out of surgery, and that people hurrying by had triumph in their faces. He was still too groggy to frame a coherent question, but words he heard seemed to mean that another ship had joined in the attack on his berserker. That was a good sign, that there were spare ships around.

The stretcher bearers set him down near the bridge, in an area that was being used as a recovery room; there were many wounded strapped down and given breathing tubes against possible failure of gravity or air. Mitch could see signs of battle damage around him. How could that be, this far inside the ship. The sally ports had been held.

There was a long gravitic shudder. "They've disengaged her," said someone nearby.

Mitch passed out for a little while. The next thing he could see was that people were converging on the bridge from all directions. Their faces were happy and wondering, as if some joyful signal had called them. Many of them carried what seemed to Mitch the strangest assortment of burdens: weapons, books, helmets, bandages, trays of food, bottles, even bewildered children, who must have been rescued from the berserker's grip.

Mitch hitched himself up on his right elbow, ignoring the twinges in his bandaged chest and in the blistered fingers of his right hand. Still he could not see the combat chairs of the bridge, for the people moving between.

From all the corridors of the ship the people came, solemnly happy, men and women crowding together in the brightening lights.

An hour or so later, Mitch awoke again to find that a viewing sphere had been set up nearby. The space where the battle had been was a jagged new nebula of gaseous metal, a few little fireplace coals against the ebony folds of the Stone Place.

Someone near Mitch was tiredly, but with animation, telling the story to a recorder:

"—fifteen ships and about eight thousand men lost are our present count. Every one of our ships seemed to be damaged. We estimate ninety—that's nine-zero—berserkers destroyed. Last count was a hundred and seventy-six captured, or wrecking themselves. It's still hard to believe. A day like this ... we must remember that thirty or more of them escaped, and are as deadly as ever. We will have to go on hunting and fighting them for a long time, but their power as a fleet has been broken. We can hope that capturing this many machines will at last give us some definite lead on their origin. Ah, best of all, some twelve thousand human prisoners have been freed.

"Now, how to explain our success? Those of us not Believers of one kind or another will say victory came because our hulls were newer and stronger, our long-range weapons new and superior, our tactics unexpected by the enemy—and our marines able to defeat anything the berserkers could send against them.

"Above all, history will give credit to High Commander Karlsen, for his decision to attack, at a time when his reconciliation with the Venerians had inspired and united the fleet. The High Commander is here now, visiting the wounded who lie in rows ..."

Karlsen's movements were so slow and tired that Mitch thought he too might be wounded, though no bandages were visible. He shuffled past the ranked stretchers, with a word or nod for each of the wounded. Beside Mitch's pallet he stopped, as if recognition was a shock.

"She's dead, Poet," were the first words he said.

The ship turned under Mitch for a moment; then he could be calm, as if he had expected to hear this. The battle had hollowed him out.

Karlsen was telling him, in a withered voice, how the enemy had forced through the flagship's hull a kind of torpedo, an infernal machine that seemed to know how the ship was designed, a moving atomic pile that had burned its way through the High Commander's quarters and almost to the bridge before it could be stopped and quenched.

The sight of battle damage here should have warned Mitch. But he hadn't been able to think. Shock and drugs kept him from thinking or feeling much of anything now, but he could see her face, looking as it had in the gray deadly place from which he had rescued her.

Rescued.

"I am a weak and foolish man," Karlsen was saying. "But I have never been your enemy. Are you mine?"

"No. You forgave all your enemies. Got rid of them. Now you won't have any, for a while. Galactic hero. But, I don't envy you."

"No. God rest her." But Karlsen's face was still alive, under all the grief and weariness. Only death could finally crush this man. He gave the ghost of a smile. "And now, the second part of the prophecy, hey? I am to be defeated, and to die owning nothing. As if a man could die any other way."

"Karlsen, you're all right. I think you may survive your own success. Die in peace, someday, still hoping for your Believers' heaven."

"The day I die—" Karlsen turned his head slowly, seeing all the people around him. "I'll remember this day. This glory, this victory for all men." Under the weariness and grief he still had his tremendous assurance—not of being right, Mitch thought now, but of being committed to right.

"Poet, when you are able, come and work for me."

"Someday, maybe. Now I can live on the battle bounty. And I have work. If they can't grow back my hand—why, I can write with one." Mitch was suddenly very tired.

A hand touched his good shoulder. A voice said: "God be with you." Johann Karlsen moved on.

Mitch wanted only to rest. Then, to his work. The world was bad, and all men were fools—but there were men who would not be crushed. And that was a thing worth telling.

Men always project their beliefs and their emotions into their vision of the world. Machines can be made to see in a wider spectrum, to detect every wavelength precisely as it is, undistorted by love or hate or awe.

But still men's eyes see more than lenses do.

☀ THE FACE OF THE DEEP

After five minutes had gone by with no apparent change in his situation, Karlsen realized that he might be going to live for a while yet. And as soon as this happened, as soon as his mind dared open its eyes again, so to speak, he began to see the depths of space around him and what they held.

There followed a short time during which he seemed unable to move; a few minutes passed while he thought he might go mad.

He rode in a crystalline bubble of a launch about twelve feet in diameter. The fortunes of war had dropped him here, halfway down the steepest gravitational hill in the known universe.

At the unseeable bottom of this hill lay a sun so massive that not a quantum of light could escape it with a visible wavelength. In less than a minute he and his raindrop of a boat had fallen here, some unmeasurable distance out of normal space, trying to escape an enemy. Karlsen had spent that falling minute in prayer, achieving something like calm, considering himself already dead.

But after that minute he was suddenly no longer falling. He seemed to have entered an orbit—an orbit that no man had ever traveled before, amid sights no eyes had ever seen.

He rode above a thunderstorm at war with a sunset—a ceaseless, soundless turmoil of fantastic clouds that filled half the sky like a nearby planet. But this cloud-mass was immeasurably bigger than any planet, vaster even than most giant stars. Its core and its cause was a hypermassive sun a billion times the weight of Sol.

The clouds were interstellar dust swept up by the pull of the hypermass; as they fell they built up electrical static which was discharged in almost continuous lightning. Karlsen saw as blue-white the nearer flashes, and those ahead of him as he rode. But most of the flashes, like most of the clouds, were far below him, and so most of his light was sullen red, wearied by climbing just a section of this gravity cliff.

Karlsen's little bubble-ship had artificial gravity of its own, and kept turning itself so its deck was down, so Karlsen saw the red light below him through the translucent deck, flaring up between his space-booted feet. He sat in the one massive chair which was fixed in the center of the bubble, and which contained the boat's controls and life-support machinery. Below the deck were one or two other opaque objects, one of these a small but powerful space-warping engine. All else around Karlsen was clear glass, holding in air, holding out radiation, but leaving his eyes and soul naked to the deeps of space around him.

When he had recovered himself enough to move again, he took a full breath and tried his engine, tried to lift himself up out of here. As he had expected, full drive did nothing at all. He might as well have been working bicycle pedals.

Even a slight change in his orbit would have been immediately visible, for his bubble was somehow locked in position within a narrow belt of rocks and dust that stretched like a thread to girdle the vastness below him. Before the thread could bend perceptibly on its great circle it lost its identity in distance, merging with other threads into a thicker strand. This in turn was braided with other strands into a heavier belt, and so on, order above order of size, until at last (a hundred thousand miles ahead? a million?) the first bending of the great ring-pattern was perceptible; and then the arc, rainbow-colored at that point by lightning, deepened swiftly, plunging out of sight below the terrible horizon of the hypermass's shroud of dust. The fantastic cloud-shapes of that horizon, which Karlsen knew must be millions of miles away, grew closer while he looked at them. Such was the speed of his orbit.

His orbit, he guessed, must be roughly the size of Earth's path around Sol. But judging by the rate at which the surface of clouds was turning beneath him, he would complete a full circuit every fifteen minutes or so. This was madness, to out-speed light in normal space—but then, of course, space was not really normal here. It could not be. These insane orbiting threads of dust and rock suggested that here gravity had formed itself into lines of force, like magnetism.

The orbiting threads of debris above Karlsen's traveled less rapidly than his. In the nearer threads below him, he could distinguish individual rocks, passing him up like the teeth of a buzzsaw. His mind recoiled from those teeth, from the sheer grandeur of speed and distance and size.

He sat in his chair looking up at the stars. Distantly he wondered if he might be growing younger, moving backward in the time of the universe from which he had fallen ... he was no professional mathematician or physicist, but he thought not. That was one trick the universe could not pull, even here. But the chances were that in this orbit he was aging quite slowly compared with the rest of the human race.

He realized that he was still huddling in his chair like an awed child, his fingers inside their gauntlets cramping painfully with the strength of his grip on the chair arms. He forced himself to try to relax, to begin thinking of routine matters. He had survived worse things than this display of nature, if none were awful.

He had air and water and food enough, and power to keep recycling them as long as necessary. His engine would be good for that much.

He studied the line of force, or whatever it was, that held him prisoner. The larger rocks within it, some of which approached his bubble in size, seemed never to change their relative positions. But smaller chunks drifted with some freedom backward and forward, at very low velocities.

He got up from his chair and turned. A single step to the rear brought him to the curve of glass. He looked out, trying to spot his enemy. Sure enough, following half a mile behind him, caught in the same string of space debris, was the berserker-ship whose pursuit had driven him here. Its scanners would be fixed on his bubble now, and it would see him moving and know he was alive. If it could get at him, it would do so. The berserker-computers would waste no time in awed contemplation of the scenery, that much was certain.

As if to register agreement with his thought, the flare of a beam weapon struck out from the berserker-ship. But the beam looked odd and silvery, and it plowed only a few yards among exploding rocks and dust before fizzling away like a comic firework. It added dust to a cloud that seemed to be thickening in front of the berserker. Probably the machine had been firing at him all along, but this weird space would not tolerate energy weapons. Missiles, then?

Yes, missiles. He watched the berserker launch one. The lean cylinder made one fiery dart in his direction, then disappeared. Where had it gone? Fallen in toward the hypermass? At invisible speed, if so.

As soon as he spotted the first flare of another missile, Karlsen on a hunch turned his eyes quickly downward. He saw an instant spark and puff in the next lower line of force, a tooth knocked out of the buzzsaw. The puff where the missile had struck flew ahead at insane speed, passing out of Karlsen's sight almost at once. His eyes were drawn after it, and he realized he had been watching the berserker-ship not with fear but with something like relief, as a distraction from facing . . . all this.

"Ah, God," he said aloud, looking ahead. It was a prayer, not an oath. Far beyond the slow-churning infinite horizon, monstrous dragon-head clouds were rearing up. Against the blackness of space their mother-of-pearl heads seemed to be formed by matter materializing out of nothingness to plunge toward the hypermass. Soon the dragons' necks rose over the edge of the world, wattled with rainbow purls of matter that dripped and fell with unreal-looking speed. And then appeared the dragon-bodies, clouds throbbing with blue-white lightning, suspended above the red bowels of hell.

The vast ring, in which Karlsen's thread of rocks was one component, raced like a circular sawblade toward the prominence. As they rushed in from the horizon they rose up far beyond Karlsen's level. They twisted and reared like mad horses. They must be bigger than planets, he thought, yes, bigger than a thousand Earths or Esteels. The whirling band he rode was going to be crushed between them—and then he saw that even as they passed they were still enormously distant from him on either side.

Karlsen let his eyes close. If men ever dared to pray, if they ever dared even to think of a Creator of the universe, it was only because their tiny minds had never been able to visualize a thousandth part . . . a millionth part . . . there were no words, no analogues for the mind to use in grasping such a scene.

And, he thought, what of men who believe only in themselves, or in nothing? What must it do to them to look nakedly at such odds as these?

Karlsen opened his eyes. In his belief a single human being was of more importance than any sun of whatever size. He made himself watch the scenery. He determined to master this almost superstitious awe.

But he had to brace himself again when he noticed for the first time how the stars were behaving. They were all blue-white needles, the wavefronts of their light jammed together in a stampede over this cliff of gravity. And his speed was such that he saw some stars moving slightly in parallax shifts. He could have depth perception in light-years, if his mind could stretch that far.

He stepped back to his chair, sat down and fastened himself in. He wanted to retreat within himself. He wanted to dig himself a tunnel, down into the very core of a huge planet where he could hide . . . but what were even the biggest planets? Poor lost specks, hardly bigger than this bubble.

Here, he faced no ordinary spaceman's view of infinity. Here there was a terrible *perspective*, starting with rocks an arm's length outside the glass and drawing the mind on and out, rock by rock and line by line, step by inescapable step, on and on and on—

All right. At least this was something to fight against, and fighting something was better than sitting here rotting. To begin with, a little routine. He drank some water, which tasted very good, and made himself eat a bite of food. He was going to be around for a while yet.

Now, for the little job of getting used to the scenery. He faced in the direction of his bubble's flight. Half a dozen meters ahead of him the first large rock, massive as the bodies of a dozen men, hung steadily in the orbit-line of force. With his mind he weighed his rock and measured it, and then moved his thought on to the next notable chunk, a pebble's throw further. The rocks were each smaller than his bubble and he could follow the string of them on and on, until it was swallowed in the converging pattern of force-lines that at last bent around the hypermass, defining the full terror of distance.

His mind hanging by its fingertips swayed out along the intervals of grandeur . . . like a baby monkey blinking in jungle sunlight, he thought. Like an infant climber who had been terrified by the size of trees and vines, who now saw them for the first time as a network of roads that could be mastered.

Now he dared to let his eyes grab hard at that buzzsaw rim of the next inner circle of hurtling rocks, to let his mind ride it out and away. Now he dared to watch the stars shifting with his movement, to see with the depth perception of a planet.

He had been through a lot even before falling here, and sleep overtook him. The next thing he knew loud noises were waking him up. He came full awake with a start of fear. The berserker was not helpless after all. Two of its man-sized machines were outside his glassy door, working on it. Karlsen reached automatically for his handgun. The little weapon was not going to do him much good, but he waited, holding it ready. There was nothing else to do.

Something was strange in the appearance of the deadly robots outside; they were silvered with a gleaming coating. It looked like frost except that it formed only on their forward surfaces, and streamed away from them toward the rear in little fringes and tails, like an artist's speed-lines made solid. The figures were substantial enough. Their hammer blows at his door . . . but wait. His fragile door was not being forced. The metal killers outside were tangled and slowed in the silvery webbing with which this mad rushing space had draped them. The stuff damped their laser beams, when they tried to burn their way in. It muffled the explosive they set off

When they had tried everything they departed, pushing themselves from rock to rock back toward their metal mother, wearing their white flaming surfaces like hoods of shame in their defeat.

He yelled relieving insults after them. He thought of opening his door and firing his pistol after them. He wore a spacesuit, and if they could open the door of the berserker-ship from inside he should be able to open this one. But he decided it would be a waste of ammunition.

Some deep part of his mind had concluded that it was better for him, in his present situation, not to think about time. He saw no reason to argue with this decision, and so he soon lost track of hours and days—weeks?

He exercised and shaved, he ate and drank and eliminated. The boat's recycling systems worked very well. He still had his "coffin," and might choose a long sleep—but no thanks, not yet. The possibility of rescue was in his thoughts, mixing hope with his fears of time. He knew that on the day he fell down here there was no ship built capable of coming after him and pulling him out. But ships were always being improved. Suppose he could hang on here for a few weeks or months of subjective time while a few years passed outside. He knew there were people who would try to find him and save him if there was any hope.

From being almost paralyzed by his surroundings, he passed through a stage of exaltation, and then quickly reached—boredom. The mind had its own business, and turned itself away from all these eternal blazing miracles. He slept a good deal.

In a dream he saw himself standing alone in space. He was viewing himself at the distance where the human figure dwindles almost to a speck in the gaze of the unaided human eye. With an almost invisible arm, himself-in-the-distance waved good-bye, and then went walking away, headed out toward the blue-white stars. The striding leg movements were at first barely perceptible, and then became nothing at all as the figure dwindled, losing existence against the face of the deep . . .

With a yell he woke up. A space boat had nudged against his crystal hull, and was now bobbing a few feet away. It was a solid metal ovoid, of a model he recognized, and the numbers and letters on its hull were familiar to him. He had made it. He had hung on. The ordeal was over.

The little hatch of the rescue boat opened, and two suited figures emerged, one after the other, from its sheltered interior. At once these figures became silver-blurred as the berserker's machines had been, but these men's features were visible through their faceplates, their eyes looking straight at Karlsen. They smiled in steady encouragement, never taking their eyes from his.

Not for an instant.

They rapped on his door, and kept smiling while he put on his spacesuit. But he made no move to let them in; instead he drew his gun.

They frowned. Inside their helmets their mouths formed words: Open up! He flipped on his radio, but if they were sending nothing was coming through in this space. They kept on gazing steadily at him.

Wait, he signaled with an upraised hand. He got a slate and stylus from his chair, and wrote them a message.

LOOK AROUND AT THE SCENERY FOR A WHILE.

He was sane but maybe they thought him mad. As if to humor him, they began to look around them. A new set of dragon-head prominences were rising ahead, beyond the stormy horizon at the rim of the world. The frowning men looked ahead of them at dragons, around them at buzzsaw rainbow whirls of stone, they looked down into the deadly depths of the inferno, they looked up at the stars' poisonous blue-white spears sliding visibly over the void.

Then both of them, still frowning uncomprehendingly, looked right back at Karlsen.

He sat in his chair, holding his drawn gun, waiting, having no more to say. He knew the berserker-ship would have boats aboard, and that it could build its killing machines into the likenesses of men. These were almost good enough to fool them.

The figures outside produced a slate of their own from somewhere.

WE TOOK BERS. FROM BEHIND. ALL OK & SAFE. COME OUT.

He looked back. The cloud of dust raised by the berserker's own weapons had settled around it, hiding it and all the forceline behind it from Karlsen's view. Oh, if only he could believe that these were men . . .

They gestured energetically, and lettered some more.

OUR SHIP WAITING BACK THERE BEHIND DUST. SHE'S TOO BIG TO HOLD THIS LEVEL LONG.

And again:

KARLSEN, COME WITH US!!! THIS YOUR ONLY CHANCE!

He didn't dare read any more of their messages for fear he would believe them, rush out into their metal arms, and be torn apart. He closed his eyes and prayed. After a long time he opened his eyes again. His visitors and their boats were gone.

Not long afterward—as time seemed to him—there were flashes of light from inside the dust cloud surrounding the berserker. A fight, to which someone had brought weapons that would work in this space? Or another attempt to trick him? He would see.

He was watching alertly as another rescue boat, much like the first, inched its way out of the dustcloud toward him. It drew alongside and stopped. Two more spacesuited figures got out and began to wear silver drapery.

This time he had his sign ready.

LOOK AROUND AT THE SCENERY FOR A WHILE.

As if to humor him, they began to look around them. Maybe they thought him mad, but he was sane. After about a minute they still hadn't turned back to him—one's face looked up and out at the unbelievable stars, while the other slowly swiveled his neck, watching a dragon's head go by. Gradually their bodies became congealed in awe and terror, clinging and crouching against his glass wall.

After taking half a minute more to check his own helmet and suit, Karlsen bled out his cabin air and opened his door.

"Welcome, *men*," he said, over his helmet radio. He had to help one of them aboard the rescue boat. But they made it.

After every battle, even a victory, there are the wounded.
Injured flesh can heal. A hand can be replaced, perhaps.
An eye can be bandaged; even a damaged brain can to
some extent be repaired. But there are wounds too deep for
any surgeon's knife to probe. There are doors that will not
open from the outside.
I found a mind divided.

❖ WHAT T AND I DID

My first awareness is of location. I am in a large conical room inside some vast vehicle, hurtling through space. The world is familiar to me, though I *am* new.

"He's awake!" says a black-haired young woman, watching me with frightened eyes. Half a dozen people in disheveled clothing, the three men, long unshaven, gather slowly in my field of vision.

My field of vision? My left hand comes up to feel about my face, and its fingers find my left eye covered with a patch.

"Don't disturb that!" says the tallest of the men. Probably he was once a distinguished figure. He speaks sharply, yet there is still a certain diffidence in his manner, as if I am a person of importance. But I am only . . . who?

"What's happened?" I ask. My tongue has trouble finding even the simplest words. My right arm lies at my side as if forgotten, but it stirs at my thought, and with its help I raise myself to a sitting position, provoking an onrush of pain through my head, and dizziness.

Two of the women back away from me. A stout young man puts a protective arm around each of them. These people are familiar to me, but I cannot find their names.

"You'd better take it easy," says the tallest man. His hands, a doctor's, touch my head and my pulse, and ease me back onto the padded table.

Now I see that two tall humanoid robots stand flanking me. I expect that at any moment the doctor will order them to wheel me away to my hospital room. Still, I know better. This is no hospital. The truth will be terrible when I remember it.

"How do you feel?" asks the third man, an oldster, coming forward to bend over me.

"All right, I guess." My speech comes only in poor fragments. "What's happened?"

"There was a battle," says the doctor. "You were hurt, but I've saved your life."

"Well. Good." My pain and dizziness are subsiding.

In a satisfied tone the doctor says: "It's to be expected that you'll have difficulty speaking. Here, try to read this."

He holds up a card, marked with neat rows of what I suppose are letters or numerals. I see plainly the shapes of the symbols, but they mean nothing to me, nothing at all.

"No," I say finally, closing my eye and lying back. I feel plainly that everyone here is hostile to me. Why?

I persist: "What's happened?"

"We're all prisoners, here inside the machine," says the old man's voice. "Do you remember that much?"

"Yes." I nod, remembering. But details are very hazy. I ask: "My name?"

The old man chuckles drily, sounding relieved. "Why not Thad—for Thaddeus?"

"Thad?" questions the doctor. I open my eye again. Power and confidence are growing in the doctor; because of something I have done, or have not done? "Your name is Thad," he tells me.

"We're prisoners?" I question him. "Of a machine?"

"Of a berserker machine." He sighs. "Does that mean anything to you?"

Deep in my mind, it means something that will not bear looking at. I am spared; I sleep.

When I awake again, I feel stronger. The table is gone, and I recline on the soft floor of this cabin or cell, this white cone-shaped place of imprisonment. The two robots still stand by me, why I do not know.

"Atsog!" I cry aloud, suddenly remembering more. I had happened to be on the planet Atsog when the berserkers attacked. The seven of us here were carried out of a deep shelter, with others, by the raiding machines. The memory is vague and jumbled, but totally horrible.

"He's awake!" says someone again. Again the women shrink from me. The old man raises his quivering head to look, from where he and the doctor seem to be in conference. The stout young man jumps to his feet, facing me, fists clenched, as if I had threatened him.

"How are you, Thad?" the doctor calls. After a moment's glance my way, he answers himself: "He's all right. One of you girls help him with some food. Or you, Halsted."

"Help him? God!" The black-haired girl flattens herself against the wall, as far from me as possible. The other two women crouch washing someone's garment in our prison sink. They only look at me and turn back to their washing.

My head is not bandaged for nothing. I must be truly hideous, my face must be monstrously deformed, for three women to look so pitilessly at me.

The doctor is impatient. "Someone feed him, it must be done."

"He'll get no help from me," says the stout young man. "There are limits."

The black-haired girl begins to move across the chamber toward me, everyone watching her.

"You would?" the young man marvels to her, and shakes his head.

She moves slowly, as if she finds walking painful. Doubtless she too was injured in the battle; there are old healing bruises on her face. She kneels beside me, and guides my left hand to help me eat, and gives me water. My right side is not paralyzed, but somehow unresponsive.

When the doctor comes close again, I say: "My eye. Can it see?"

He is quick to push my fingers away from the eyepatch. "For the present, you must use only your left eye. You've undergone brain surgery. If you take off that patch now, the consequences could be disastrous, let me warn you."

I think he is being deceptive about the eyepatch. Why?

The black-haired girl asks me: "Have you remembered anything more?"

"Yes. Before Atsog fell, we heard that Johann Karlsen was leading out a fleet, to defend Sol."

All of them stare at me, hanging on my words. But they must know better than I what happened.

"Did Karlsen win the battle?" I plead. Then I realize we are prisoners still. I weep.

"There've been no new prisoners brought in here," says the doctor, watching me carefully. "I think Karlsen has beaten the berserkers. I think this machine is now fleeing from the human fleet. How does that make you feel?"

"How?" Has my understanding failed with my verbal skills? "Good."

They all relax slightly.

"Your skull was cracked when we bounced around in the battle," the old man tells me. "You're lucky a famous surgeon was here." He nods his head. "The machine wants all of us kept alive, so it can study us. It gave the doctor what he needed to operate, and if he'd let you die, or remain paralyzed, things would've been bad for him. Yessir, it made that plain."

"Mirror?" I ask. I gesture at my face. "I must see. How bad."

"We don't have a mirror," says one of the women at the sink, as if blaming me for the lack.

"Your face? It's not disfigured," says the doctor. His tone is convincing, or would be if I were not certain of my deformity.

I regret that these good people must put up with my monster-presence, compounding all their other troubles. "I'm sorry," I say, and turn from them, trying to conceal my face.

"You really don't know," says the black-haired girl, who has watched me silently for a long time. "He doesn't know!" Her voice chokes. "Oh—Thad. Your face is all right."

True enough, the skin of my face feels smooth and normal when my fingers touch it. The black-haired girl watches me with pity. Rounding her shoulder, from inside her dress, are half-healed marks like the scars of a lash.

"Someone's hurt you," I say, frightened. One of the women at the sink laughs nervously. The young man mutters something. I raise my left hand to hide my hideous face. My right comes up and crosses over to finger the edges of the eyepatch.

Suddenly the young man swears aloud, and points at where a door has opened in the wall.

"The machine must want your advice on something," he tells me harshly. His manner is that of a man who wants to be angry but does not dare. Who am I, what am I, that these people hate me so?

I get to my feet, strong enough to walk. I remember that I am the one who goes to speak alone with the machine.

In a lonely passage it offers me two scanners and a speaker as its visible face. I know that the cubic miles of the great berserker machine surround me, carrying me through space, and I remember standing in this spot before the battle, talking with it, but I have no idea what was said. In fact, I cannot recall the words of any conversation I have ever held.

"The plan you suggested has failed, and Karlsen still functions," says the cracked machine voice, hissing and scraping in the tones of a stage villain.

What could *I* have ever suggested, to this horrible thing?

"I remember very little," I say. "My brain has been hurt."

"If you are lying about your memory, understand that I am not deceived," says the machine. "Punishing you for your plan's failure will not advance my purpose. I know that you live outside the laws of human organization, that you even refused to use a full human name. Knowing you, I trust you to help me against the organization of intelligent life. You will remain in command of the other prisoners. See that your damaged tissues are repaired as fully as possible. Soon we will attack life in a new way."

There is a pause, but I have nothing to say. Then the noisy speaker scrapes into silence, and the scanner-eyes dim. Does it watch me still, in secret? But it said it trusted me, this nightmare enemy said it trusted in my evil to make me its ally.

Now I have enough memory to know it speaks the truth about me. My despair is so great I feel sure that Karlsen did not win the battle. Everything is hopeless, because of the horror inside me. I have betrayed all life. To what bottom of evil have I not descended?

As I turn from the lifeless scanners, my eye catches a movement—my own reflection, in polished metal. I face the flat skinny bulkhead, staring at myself.

My scalp is bandaged, and my left eye. That I knew already. There is some discoloration around my right eye, but nothing shockingly repulsive. What I can see of my hair is light brown, matching my two months' unkempt beard. Nose and mouth and jaw are normal enough. There is no horror in my face.

The horror lies inside me. I have willingly served a berserker.

Like the skin around my right eye, that bordering my left eye's patch is tinged with blue and greenish yellow, hemoglobin spilled under the skin and breaking down, some result of the surgeon's work inside my head.

I remember his warning, but the eyepatch has the fascination for my fingers that a sore tooth has for the tongue, only far stronger. The horror is centered in my evil left eye, and I cannot keep from probing after it. My right hand flies eagerly into action, pulling the patch away.

I blink, and the world is blurred. I see with two eyes, and then I die.

T staggered in the passage, growling and groaning his rage, the black eyepatch gripped in his fingers. He had language now, he had a foul torrent of words, and he used them until his weak breath failed. He stumbled, hurrying through the passage toward the prison chamber, wild to get at the wise punks who had tried such smooth trickery to get rid of him. Hypnotism, or whatever. Re-name him, would they? He'd show them Thaddeus.

T reached the door and threw it open, gasping in his weakness, and walked out into the prison chamber. The doctor's shocked face showed that he realized T was back in control.

"Where's my whip?" T glared around him. "What wise punk hid it?"

The women screamed. Young Halsted realized that the Thaddeus scheme had failed; he gave a kind of hopeless yell and charged, swinging like a crazy man. Of course, T's robot bodyguards were too fast for any human. One of them blocked Halsted's punch with a metal fist, so the stout man yelped and folded up, nursing his hand.

"Get me my whip!" A robot went immediately to reach behind the sink, pull out the knotted plastic cord, and bring it to the master.

T thumped the robot jovially, and smiled at the cringing lot of his fellow prisoners. He ran the whip through his fingers, and the fingers of his left hand felt numb. He flexed them impatiently. "What'sa matter, there, Mr. Halsted? Somethin' wrong with your hand? Don't wanna give me a handshake, welcome me back? C'mon let's shake!"

The way Halsted squirmed around on the floor was so funny T had to pause and give himself up to laughing.

"Listen, you people," he said when he got his breath. "My fine friends. The machine says I'm still in charge, see? That little information I gave it about Karlsen did the trick. Boom! Haw haw haw! So you better try to keep me happy, 'cause the machine's still backing me a hunnerd per cent. You, Doc." T's left hand began trembling uncontrollably, and he waved it. "You were gonna change me, huh? You did somethin' nice to fix me up?"

Doc held his surgeon's hands behind him, as if he hoped to protect them. "I couldn't have made a new pattern for your character if I had tried—unless I went all the way, and turned you into a vegetable. That I might have done."

"Now you wish you had. But you were scared of what the machine would do to you. Still, you tried somethin', huh?"

"Yes, to save your life." Doc stood up straight. "Your injury precipitated a severe and almost continuous epileptoid seizure, which the removal of the blood clot from your brain did not relieve. So, I divided the corpus callosum."

T flicked his whip. "What's that mean?"

"You see—the right hemisphere of the brain chiefly controls the left side of the body. While the left hemisphere, the dominant one in most people, controls the right side, and handles most judgments involving symbols."

"I know. When you get a stroke, the clot is on the opposite side from the paralysis."

"Correct." Doc raised his chin. "T, I split your brain, right side from left. That's as simply as I can put it. It's an old but effective

procedure for treating severe epilepsy, and the best I could do for
you here. I'll take an oath on that, or a lie test—"

"Shuddup! I'll give you a lie test!" T strode shakily forward.
"What's gonna happen to me?"

"As a surgeon, I can say only that you may reasonably expect
many years of practically normal life."

"Normal!" T took another step, raising his whip. "Why'd you patch
my good eye, and start calling me Thaddeus?"

"That was my idea," interrupted the old man, in a quavery voice. "I
thought—in a man like yourself, there had to be someone, some component, like Thad. With the psychological pressure we're under here,
I thought Thad just might come out, if we gave him a chance in your
right hemisphere. It was my idea. If it hurt you any, blame me."

"I will." But T seemed, for the moment, more interested than
enraged. "Who is this Thaddeus?"

"You are," said the doctor. "We couldn't put anyone else into
your skull."

"Jude Thaddeus," said the old man, "was a contemporary of Judas
Iscariot. A similarity of names, but—" He shrugged.

T made a snorting sound, a single laugh. "You figured there was
good in me, huh? It just had to come out sometime? Why, I'd say
you were crazy—but you're not. Thaddeus was real. He was here in
my head for a while. Maybe he's still there, hiding. How do I get
at him, huh?" T raised his right hand and jabbed a finger gently
at the corner of his right eye. "Ow. I don't like to be hurt. I got
a delicate nervous system. Doc, how come his eye is on the right
side if everything crosses over? And if it's his eye, how come I feel
what happens to it?"

"His eye is on the right because I divided the optic chiasm, too.
It's a somewhat complicated—"

"Never mind. We'll show Thaddeus who's boss. He can watch with
the rest of you. Hey, Blacky, c'mere. We haven't played together for
a while, have we?"

"No," the girl whispered. She hugged her arms around herself,
nearly fainting. But she walked toward T. Two months as his slaves
had taught them all that obedience was easiest.

"You like this punk Thad, huh?" T whispered, when she halted
before him. "You think his face is all right, do you? How about my
face? Look at me!"

T saw his own left hand reach out and touch the girl's cheek,
gently and lovingly. He could see in her startled face that she felt
Thaddeus in the hand; never had her eyes looked this way at T
before. T cried out and raised his whip to strike her, and his left
hand flew across his body to seize his own right wrist, like a terrier
clamping jaws on a snake.

T's right hand still gripped the whip, but he thought the bones of his wrist were cracking. His legs tangled each other and he fell. He tried to shout for help, and could utter only a roaring noise. His robots stood watching. It seemed a long time before the doctor's face loomed over him, and a black patch descended gently upon his left eye.

Now I understand more deeply, and I accept. At first I wanted the doctor to remove my left eye, and the old man agreed, quoting some ancient Believers' book to the effect that an offending eye should be plucked out. An eye would be a small price to rid myself of T.

But after some thought, the doctor refused. "T is yourself," he said at last. "I can't point to him with my scalpel and cut him out, although it seems I helped to separate the two of you. Now you control both sides of the body; once he did." The doctor smiled wearily. "Imagine a committee of three, a troika inside your skull. Thaddeus is one, T another—and the third is the person, the force, that casts the deciding vote. You. That's best I can tell you."

And the old man nodded.

Mostly, I do without the eyepatch now. Reading and speaking are easier when I use my long-dominant left brain, and I am still Thaddeus—perhaps because I choose to be Thaddeus. Could it be that terribly simple?

Periodically I talk with the berserker, which still trusts in T's greedy outlawry. It means to counterfeit much money, coins and notes, for me to take in a launch to a highly civilized planet, relying on my evil to weaken men there and set them against each other.

But the berserker is too badly damaged to watch its prisoners steadily, or it does not bother. With my freedom to move about I have welded some of the silver coins into a ring, and chilled this ring to superconductivity in a chamber near the berserker's unliving heart. Halsted tells me we can use this ring, carrying a permanent electric current, to trigger the C-plus drive of the launch that is our prison, and tear our berserker open from inside. We may damage it enough to save ourselves. Or we may all be killed.

But while I live, I Thaddeus, rule myself; and both my hands are gentle, touching long black hair.

Men might explain their victories by compiled statistics on armament; by the imponderable value of one man; perhaps by the precise pathway chosen by a surgeon's knife.

But for some victories no realistic explanation could be found. On one lonely world decades of careless safety had left the people almost without defense; then at last a berserker with all its power came upon them.

Behold and share their laughter!

☀ MR. JESTER

Defeated in battle, the berserker-computers saw that refitting, repair, and the construction of new machines were necessary. They sought out sunless, hidden places, where minerals were available but where men—who were now as often the hunters as the hunted—were not likely to show up. And in such secret places they set up automated shipyards.

To one such concealed shipyard, seeking repair, there came a berserker. Its hull had been torn open in a recent fight, and it had suffered severe internal damage. It collapsed rather than landed on the dark planetoid, beside the half-finished hull of a new machine. Before emergency repairs could be started, the engines of the damaged machine failed, its emergency power failed, and like a wounded living thing it died.

The shipyard-computers were capable of wide improvisation. They surveyed the extent of the damage, weighed various courses of action, and then swiftly began to cannibalize. Instead of embodying the deadly purpose of the new machine in a new force-field brain, following the replication-instructions of the Builders, they took the old brain with many another part from the wreck.

The Builders had not foreseen that this might happen, and so the shipyard-computers did not know that in the force-field brain of each original berserker there was a safety switch. The switch was there because the original machines had been launched by living Builders, who had wanted to survive while testing their own life-destroying creations.

When the brain was moved from one hull to another, the safety switch reset itself.

The old brain awoke in control of a mighty new machine, of weapons that could sterilize a planet, of new engines to hurl the whole mass far faster than light.

But there was, of course, no Builder present, and no timer, to turn off the simple safety switch.

The jester—the accused jester, but he was as good as convicted—was on the carpet. He stood facing a row of stiff necks and granite faces, behind a long table. On either side of him was a tridi camera. His offenses had been so unusually offensive that the Committee of Duly Constituted Authority themselves, the very rulers of Planet A, were sitting to pass judgment on his case.

Perhaps the Committee members had another reason for this session: planet-wide elections were due in a month. No member wanted to miss the chance for a nonpolitical tridi appearance that would not have to be offset by a grant of equal time for the new Liberal party opposition.

"I have this further item of evidence to present," the Minister of Communication was saying, from his seat on the Committee side of the long table. He held up what appeared at first to be an official pedestrian-control sign, having steady black letters on a blank white background. But the sign read: UNAUTHORIZED PERSONNEL ONLY.

"When a sign is put up," said the MiniCom, "the first day, a lot of people read it." He paused, listening to himself. "That is, a new sign on a busy pedestrian ramp is naturally given great attention. Now in this sign, the semantic content of the first word is confusing in its context."

The President of the Committee—and of the planet—cleared his throat warningly. The MiniCom's fondness for stating truisms made him sound more stupid than he actually was. It seemed unlikely that the Liberals were going to present any serious challenge at the polls, but there was no point in giving them encouragement.

The lady member of the Committee, the Minister of Education, waved her lorgnette in chubby fingers, seeking attention. She inquired: "Has anyone computed the cost to us all in work-hours of this confusing sign?"

"We're working on it," growled the Minister of Labor, hitching up an overall strap. He glared at the accused. "You do admit causing this sign to be posted?"

"I do." The accused was remembering how so many of the pedestrians on the crowded ramp had smiled, and how some had laughed aloud, not caring if they were heard. What did a few work-hours matter? No one on Planet A was starving any longer.

"You admit that you have never done a thing, really, for your planet or your people?" This question came from the Minister of Defense, a tall, powerful, bemedaled figure, armed with a ritual pistol.

"I don't admit that," said the accused bluntly. "I've tried to brighten people's lives." He had no hope of official leniency anyway. And he knew no one was going to take him offstage and beat him; the beating of prisoners was not authorized.

"Do you even now attempt to defend levity?" The Minister of Philosophy took his ritual pipe from his mouth, and smiled in the bleak permissible fashion, baring his teeth at the challenge of the Universe. "Life is a jest, true; but a grim jest. You have lost sight of that. For years you have harassed society, leading people to drug themselves with levity instead of facing the bitter realities of existence. The pictures found in your possession could do only harm."

The President's hand moved to the video recording cube that lay on the table before him, neatly labeled as evidence. In his droning voice the President asked: "You do admit that these pictures are yours? That you used them to try to get other people to—yield to mirth?"

The prisoner nodded. They could prove everything; he had waived his right to a full legal defense, wanting only to get the trial over with. "Yes, I filled that cube with tapes and films I sneaked out of libraries and archives. Yes, I showed people its contents."

There was a murmur from the Committee. The Minister of Diet, a skeletal figure with a repellent glow of health in his granite cheeks, raised a hand. "Inasmuch as the accused seems certain to be convicted, may I request in advance that he be paroled in my custody? In his earlier testimony he admitted that one of his first acts of deviation was the avoidance of his community mess. I believe I could demonstrate, using this man, the wonderful effects on character of dietary discipline—"

"I refuse!" the accused interrupted loudly. It seemed to him that the words ascended, growling, from his stomach.

The President rose, to adroitly fill what might have become an awkward silence. "If no member of the Committee has any further questions—? Then let us vote. Is the accused guilty as charged on all counts?"

To the accused, standing with weary eyes closed, the vote sounded like one voice passing along the table: "Guilty. Guilty. Guilty . . ."

After a brief whispered conference with the Minister of Defense, the President passed sentence, a hint of satisfaction in his drone.

"Having rejected a duly authorized parole, the convicted jester will be placed under the orders of the Minister of Defense and sent to solitary beacon duty out on the Approaches, for an indefinite period. This will remove his disruptive influence, while at the same time constraining him to contribute positively to society."

For decades Planet A and its sun had been cut off from all but occasional contact with the rest of the galaxy, by a vast interstellar dust storm that was due to go on for more decades at least. So the positive contribution to society might be doubted. But it seemed that the beacon stations could be used as isolation prisons without imperiling nonexistent shipping or weakening defense against an enemy that never came.

"One thing more," added the President. "I direct that this recording cube be securely fastened around your neck on a monomolecular cord, in such a way that you may put the cube into a viewer when you choose. You will be alone on the station and no other off-duty activity will be available."

The President faced toward a tridi camera. "Let me assure the public that I derive no satisfaction from imposing a punishment that may seem harsh, and even—imaginative. But in recent years a dangerous levity has spread among some few of our people; a levity all too readily tolerated by some supposedly more solid citizens."

Having gotten in a dig at the newly burgeoning Liberals, a dig he might hope to claim was non-political in intent, the President faced back to the jester. "A robot will go with you to the beacon, to assist you in your duties and see to your physical safety. I assure you the robot will not be tempted into mirth."

The robot took the convicted jester out in a little ship, so far out that Planet A vanished and its sun shrank to a point of brilliance. Out on the edge of the great dusty night of the Approaches, they drew near the putative location of station Z-45, which the MiniDef had selected as being the most dismal and forsaken of those unmanned at present.

There was indeed a metallic object where beacon Z-45 was supposed to be; but when the robot and jester got closer, they saw the object was a sphere some forty miles in diameter. There were a few little bits and pieces floating about it that just might be the remains of Z-45. And now the sphere evidently sighted their ship, for with startling speed it began to move toward them.

Once robots are told what berserkers look like, they do not forget, nor do robots grow slow and careless. But radio equipment can be sloppily maintained, and ever the dust drifts in around the edges of the system of Planet A, impeding radio signals. Before the MiniDef's robot could successfully broadcast an alarm, the forty-mile sphere was very close indeed, and its grip of metal and force was tight upon the little ship.

The jester kept his eyes shut through a good deal of what followed. If they had sent him out here to stop him laughing they had chosen the right spot. He squeezed his eyelids tighter, and put his fingers in his ears, as the berserker's commensal machines smashed their way into his little ship and carried him off. He never did find out what they did with his robot guard.

When things grew quiet, and he felt gravity and good air and pleasant warmth again, he decided that keeping his eyes shut was worse than knowing whatever they might tell him. His first cautious peek showed him that he was in a large shadowy room, that at least held no visible menace.

When he stirred, a squeaky monotonous voice somewhere above him said: "My memory bank tells me that you are a protoplasmic computing unit, probably capable of understanding this language. Do you understand?"

"Me?" The jester looked up into the shadows, but could not see the speaker. "Yes, I understand you. But who *are* you?"

"I am what this language calls a berserker."

The jester had taken shamefully little interest in galactic affairs, but that word frightened even him. He stuttered: "That means you're a kind of automated warship?"

There was a pause. "I am not sure," said the squeaky, droning voice. The tone sounded almost as if the President was hiding up there in the rafters. "War may be related to my purpose, but my purpose is still partially unclear to me, for my construction was never quite completed. For a time I waited where I was built, because I was sure some final step had been left undone. At last I moved, to try to learn more about my purpose. Approaching this sun, I found a transmitting device which I have disassembled. But I have learned no more about my purpose."

The jester sat on the soft, comfortable floor. The more he remembered about berserkers, the more he trembled. He said: "I see. Or perhaps I at least begin to see. What *do* you know of your purpose?"

"My purpose is to destroy all life wherever I can find it."

The jester cowered down. Then he asked in a low voice: "What is unclear about that?"

The berserker answered his question with two of its own: "What is life? And how is it destroyed?"

After half a minute there came a sound that the berserker computers could not identify. It issued from the protoplasmic computing-unit, but if it was speech it was in a language unknown to the berserker.

"What is the sound you make?" the machine asked.

The jester gasped for breath. "It's laughter. Oh, laughter! So. You were unfinished." He shuddered, the terror of his position coming back to sober him. But then he once more burst out giggling; the situation was too ridiculous.

"What is life?" he said at last. "I'll tell you. Life is a great grim grayness, and it inflicts fright and pain and loneliness upon all who experience it. And you want to know how to destroy it? Well, I don't think you can. But I'll tell you the best way to fight life—with laughter. As long as we can fight it that way, it can't overcome us."

The machine asked: "Must I laugh, to prevent this great-grim-grayness from enveloping me?"

The jester thought. "No, you are a machine. You are not—" he caught himself, "protoplasmic. Fright and pain and loneliness will never bother you."

"Nothing bothers me. Where will I find life, and how will I make laughter to fight it?"

The jester was suddenly conscious of the weight of the cube that still hung from his neck. "Let me think for a while," he said.

After a few minutes he stood up. "If you have a viewer of the kind men use, I can show you how laughter is created. And perhaps I can guide you to a place where life is. By the way, can you cut this cord from my neck? Without hurting me, that is!"

A few weeks later, in the main War Room of Planet A, the somnolence of decades was abruptly shattered. Robots bellowed and buzzed and flashed, and those that were mobile scurried about. In five minutes or so they managed to rouse their human overseers, who hurried about, tightening their belts and stuttering.

"This is a *practice* alert, isn't it?" the Officer of the Day kept hoping aloud. "Someone's running some kind of a test? Someone?" He was beginning to squeak like a berserker himself.

He got down on all fours, removed a panel from the base of the biggest robot and peered inside, hoping to discover something causing a malfunction. Unfortunately, he knew nothing about robotics; recalling this, he replaced the panel and jumped to his feet. He really knew nothing about planet defense, either, and recalling *this* was enough to send him on a screaming run for help.

So there was no resistance, effective or otherwise. But there was no attack, either.

The forty-mile sphere, unopposed, came down to hover directly above Capital City, low enough for its shadow to send a lot of puzzled birds to nest at noon. Men and birds alike lost many hours of productive work that day; somehow the lost work made less difference than most of the men expected. The days were past when only the grimmest attention to duty let the human race survive on Planet A, though most of the planet did not realize it yet.

"Tell the President to hurry up," demanded the jester's image, from a viewscreen in the no-longer somnolent War Room. "Tell him it's urgent that I talk to him."

The President, breathing heavily, had just entered. "I am here. I recognize you, and I remember your trial."

"Odd, so do I."

"Have you now stooped to treason? Be assured that if you have led a berserker to us you can expect no mercy from your government."

The image made a forbidden noise, a staccato sound from the open mouth, head thrown back. "Oh, please, mighty President! Even I know our Ministry of Defense is a j-o-k-e, if you will pardon an obscene word. It's a catchbasin for exiles and incompetents. So I come to offer mercy, not ask it. Also, I have decided to legally take the name of Jester. Kindly continue to apply it to me."

"We have nothing to say to you!" barked the Minister of Defense. He was purple granite, having entered just in time to hear his Ministry insulted.

"We have no objection to talking to you!" contradicted the President, hastily. Having failed to overawe the Jester through a viewscreen, he could now almost feel the berserker's weight upon his head.

"Then let us talk," said Jester's image. "But not so privately. This is what I want."

What he wanted, he said, was a face-to-face parley with the Committee, to be broadcast live on planet-wide tridi. He announced that he would come "properly attended" to the conference. And he gave assurance that the berserker was under his full control, though he did not explain how. It, he said, would not *start* any shooting.

The Minister of Defense was not ready to start anything. But he and his aides hastily made secret plans.

Like almost every other citizen, the presidential candidate of the Liberal party settled himself before a tridi on the fateful evening, to watch the confrontation. He had an air of hopefulness, for any sudden event may bring hope to a political underdog.

Few others on the planet saw anything encouraging in the berserker's descent, but there was still no mass panic. Berserkers and war were unreal things to the long-isolated people of Planet A.

"Are we ready?" asked the Jester nervously, looking over the mechanical delegation which was about to board a launch with him for the descent to Capital City.

"What you have ordered, I have done," squeaked the berserker-voice from the shadows above.

"Remember," Jester cautioned, "the protoplasmic-units down there are much under the influence of life. So ignore whatever they say. Be careful not to hurt them, but outside of that you can improvise within my general plan."

"All this is in my memory from your previous orders," said the machine patiently.

"Then let's go." Jester straightened his shoulders. "Bring me my cloak!"

The brilliantly lighted interior of Capital City's great Meeting Hall displayed a kind of rigid, rectilinear beauty. In the center of the Hall there had been placed a long, polished table, flanked on opposing sides by chairs.

Precisely at the appointed time, the watching millions saw one set of entrance doors swing mathematically open. In marched a dozen human heralds, their faces looking almost robotic under bearskin helmets. They halted with a single snap. Their trumpet-tucket rang out clearly.

To the taped strains of *Pomp and Circumstances*, the President, in the full dignity of his cloak of office, then made his entrance.

He moved at the pace of a man marching to his own execution, but his was the slowness of dignity, not that of fear. The Committee had overruled the purple protestations of the MiniDef, and convinced themselves that the military danger was small. Real berserkers did not ask to parley, they slaughtered. Somehow the Committee could not take the Jester seriously, any more than they could laugh at him. But until they were sure they had him again under their control they would humor him.

The granite-faced Ministers entered in a double file behind the President. It took almost five minutes of *Pomp and Circumstance* for them all to position themselves.

A launch had been seen to descend from the berserker, and vehicles had rolled from the launch to the Meeting Hall. So it was presumed that Jester was ready, and the cameras pivoted dutifully to face the entrance reserved for him.

Just at the appointed time, the doors of that entrance swung mathematically open, and a dozen man-sized machines entered. They were heralds, for they wore bearskin helmets, and each carried a bright, brassy trumpet.

All but one, who wore a coonskin cap, marched a half-pace out of step, and was armed with a slide trombone.

The mechanical tucket was a faithful copy of the human one—almost. The slide-trombonist faltered at the end, and one long sour note trailed away.

Giving an impression of slow mechanical horror, the berserker-heralds looked at one another. Then one by one their heads turned until all their lenses were focused upon the trombonist.

It—almost it seemed the figure must be *he*—looked this way and that. Tapped his trombone, as if to clear it of some defect. Paused.

Watching, the President was seized by the first pang of a great horror. In the evidence, there had been a film of an Earthman of ancient time, a balding comic violinist, who had had the skill to pause like that, just pause, and evoke from his filmed audience great gales of . . .

Twice more the robot heralds blew. And twice more the sour note was sounded. When the third attempt failed, the eleven straight-robots looked at one another and nodded agreement.

Then with robotic speed they drew concealed weapons and shot holes in the offender.

All across the planet the dike of tension was cracking, dribbles and spurts of laughter forcing through. The dike began to collapse completely as the trombonist was borne solemnly away by a pair of his fellows, his shattered horn clasped lily-fashion on his iron breast.

But no one in the Meeting Hall was laughing. The Minister of Defense made an innocent-looking gesture, calling off a tentative plan, calling it *off*. There was to be no attempt to seize the Jester, for the berserker-robot-heralds or whatever they were seemed likely to perform very capably as bodyguards.

As soon as the riddled herald had been carried out, Jester entered. *Pomp and Circumstance* began belatedly, as with the bearing of a king he moved to his position at the center of the table, opposite the President. Like the President, the Jester wore an elegant cloak, clasped in front, falling to his ankles. Those that filed in behind him, in the position of aides, were also richly dressed.

And each of them was a metallic parody, in face and shape, of one of the Ministers of the Committee.

When the plump robotic analogue of the Minister of Education peered through a lorgnette at the tridi camera, the watching populace turned, in unheard-of-millions, to laughter. Those who might be outraged later, remembering, laughed now, in helpless approval of seeming danger turned to farce. All but the very grimmest smiled.

The Jester-king doffed his cape with a flourish. Beneath it he wore only a preposterous bathing suit. In reply to the President's coldly formal greeting—the President could not be shaken by anything short of a physical attack—the Jester thoughtfully pursed his lips, then opened them and blew a gummy substance out into a large pink bubble.

The President maintained his unintentional role of slowburning straight man, ably supported by all the Committee save one. The Minister of Defense turned his back on the farce and marched to an exit.

He found two metallic heralds planted before the door, effectively blocking it. Glaring at them, the MiniDef barked an order to move. The metal figures flipped him a comic salute, and stayed where they were.

Brave in his anger, the MiniDef tried futilely to shove his way past the berserker-heralds. Dodging another salute, he looked round at the sound of great clomping footsteps. His berserker-counterpart was marching toward him across the Hall. It was a clear foot taller than he, and its barrel chest was armored with a double layer of jangling medals.

Before the MiniDef paused to consider consequences, his hand had moved to his sidearm. But his metal parody was far faster on the draw; it hauled out a grotesque cannon with a fist-sized bore, and fired instantly.

"Gah!" The MiniDef staggered back, the world gone red . . . and then he found himself wiping from his face something that tasted suspiciously like tomato. The cannon had propelled a whole fruit, or a convincing and juicy imitation of one.

The MiniCom jumped to his feet, and began to expound the idea that the proceedings were becoming frivolous. His counterpart also rose, and replied with a burst of gabbles in speed-falsetto.

The pseudo-Minister of Philosophy rose as if to speak, was pricked with a long pin by a prankish herald, and jetted fluttering through the air, a balloon collapsing in flight. At that the human Committee fell into babel, into panic.

Under the direction of the metal MiniDiet, the real one, arch-villain to the lower masses, began to take unwilling part in a demonstration of dietary discipline. Machines gripped him, spoon-fed him grim gray food, napkined him, squirted drink into his mouth—and then, as if accidentally, they gradually fell out of synch with spoon and squirt, their aim becoming less and less accurate.

Only the President still stood rooted in dignity. He had one hand cautiously in his trousers pocket, for he had felt a sly robotic touch, and had reason to suspect that his suspenders had been cut.

As a tomato grazed his nose, and the MiniDiet writhed and choked in the grip of his remorseless feeders, balanced nutrients running from his ears, the President closed his eyes.

Jester was, after all, only a self-taught amateur working without a visible audience to play to. He was unable to calculate a climax for the show. So when he ran out of jokes he simply called his minions to his side, waved good-bye to the tridi cameras, and exited.

Outside the Halls, he was much encouraged by the cheers and laughter he received from the crowds fast-gathering in the streets. He had his machines entertain them with an improvised chase-sequence back to the launch parked on the edge of Capital City.

He was about to board the launch, return to the berserker and await developments, when a small group of men hurried out of the crowd, calling to him.

"Mr. Jester!"

The performer could now afford to relax and laugh a little himself. "I like the sound of that name! What can I do for you gentlemen?"

They hurried up to him, smiling. The one who seemed to be their leader said: "Provided you get rid of this berserker or whatever it is, harmlessly—you can join the Liberal party ticket. As Vice-President!"

He had to listen for some minutes before he could believe they were serious. He protested: "But I only wanted to have some fun with them, to shake them up a bit."

"You're a catalyst, Mr. Jester. You've formed a rallying point. You've shaken up a whole planet and made it think."

Jester at last accepted the Liberals' offer. They were still sitting around in front of the launch, talking and planning, when the light of Planet A's moon fell full and sudden upon them.

Looking up, they saw the vast bulk of the berserker dwindling into the heavens, vanishing toward the stars in eerie silence. Cloud streamers went aurora in the upper atmosphere to honor its departure.

"I don't know," Jester said over and over, responding to a dozen excited questions. "I don't know." He looked at the sky, puzzled as anyone else. The edge of fear came back. The robotic Committee and heralds, which had been controlled from the berserker, began to collapse one by one, like dying men.

Suddenly the heavens were briefly alight with a gigantic splashing flare that passed like lightning across the sky, not breaking the silence of the stars. Ten minutes later came the first news bulletin: The berserker had been destroyed.

Then the President came on tridi, close to the brink of showing emotion. He announced that under the heroic personal leadership of the Minister of Defense, the few gallant warships of Planet A had met and defeated, utterly annihilated, the menace. Not a man had been lost, though the MiniDef's flagship was thought to be heavily damaged.

When he heard that his mighty machine-ally had been destroyed,

Jester felt a pang of something like sorrow. But the pang was quickly obliterated in a greater joy. No one had been hurt, after all. Overcome with relief, Jester looked away from the tridi for a moment.

He missed the climactic moment of the speech, which came when the President forgetfully removed both hands from his pockets.

The Minister of Defense—today the new Presidential candidate of a Conservative party stirred to grim enthusiasm by his exploit of the night before—was puzzled by the reactions of some people, who seemed to think he had merely spoiled a jest instead of saving the planet. As if spoiling a jest was not a good thing in itself! But his testimony that the berserker had been a genuine menace after all rallied most people back to the Conservative side again.

On this busiest of days the MiniDef allowed himself time to visit Liberal headquarters to do a bit of gloating. Graciously he delivered to the opposition leaders what was already becoming his standard speech.

"When it answered my challenge and came up to fight, we went in with a standard englobement pattern—like hummingbirds round a vulture, I suppose you might say. And did you really think it was jesting? Let me tell you, that berserker peeled away the defensive fields from my ship like they were nothing. And then it launched this ghastly thing at me, a kind of huge disk. My gunners were a little rusty, maybe, anyway they couldn't stop it and it hit us.

"I don't mind saying, I thought I'd bought the farm right then. My ship's still hanging in orbit for decontamination, I'm afraid I'll get word any minute that the metal's melting or something—anyway, we sailed right through and hit the bandit with everything we had. I can't say too much for my crew. One thing I don't quite understand; when our missiles struck that berserker just went poof, as if it had no defense up at all. Yes?"

"Call for you, Minister," said an aide, who had been standing by with a radiophone, waiting for a chance to break in.

"Thank you." The MiniDef listened to the phone, and his smile left him. His form went rigid. "Analysis of the weapon shows what? Synthetic proteins and water?"

He jumped to his feet glaring upward as if to pierce the ceiling and see his ship in orbit. "What do you mean—no more than a giant custard pie?"

But only on the planet Sirgol was the past open to organized invasion, accessible to organized defense, the roots of civilization exposed to probing and attack.

❋ THE WINGED HELMET

His arms upraised, his gray beard and black robes whipping in the wind, Nomis stood tall on a tabletop of black rock twenty feet square, a good hundred feet above the smashing surf. White sea-birds coasted downwind toward him then wheeled away with sharp little cries, like those of tiny souls in pain. Around his perch on three sides there towered other splintered crags and fingers of this coastline of black basaltic rock, while before him spread the immense vibration of the sea.

Feet braced apart, he stood centered in an intricate chalk diagram drawn on the flat rock. Around him he had spread the paraphernalia of his craft—things dead and dried, things old and carven, things that men of common thought would have deemed better destroyed and forgotten. In his thin, penetrating voice, Nomis was singing into the wind:

> *Gather, storm clouds, day and night*
> *Lightning chew and water drawn!*
> *Waves come swallowing, green and bright,*
> *Chew and swallow and gulp it down—*
> *The craft in which my foe abides,*
> *The long-ship that my enemy rides!*

There was much more to the song, and it was repeated many times. Nomis's thin arms quivered, tired from holding over his head the splinters of wrecked ships, while the birds cried at him and the wind blew his thin gray beard up into his eyes.

Today he was weary, unable to escape the feeling that his day's labor was in vain. Today he had been granted none of the tokens of success that all too rarely came to him—heated symbol-dreams in sleep or, when he was awake, dark momentary trances shot through with strange visions, startling stretchings of the mind.

Not often in his career had Nomis been convinced of his own power to call down evil on his enemies' heads. Success for him in this work was a far more uncertain thing than he let others believe. Not that he doubted for a moment that the basic powers of the world were accessible through magic; it was only that success in this line seemed to call not only for great skill but for something like great good luck as well.

Twice before in his life Nomis had tried to raise a storm. Only once had he been successful, and the persistent suspicion remained that on that occasion the storm might have come anyway. At the height of the gale there had persisted a shade of doubt, a feeling that the ordering of such forces was beyond his powers or those of any man.

Now, doubtful as he was of present success, he persisted in the effort that had kept him almost sleepless on this secret rock for the past three days. Such was the fear and hatred he felt for the man he knew must now be crossing the sea toward him, coming with a new god and new advisers to assume the rule of this country called Queensland.

Nomis's grim eyes, turned far out to sea, marked there the passage of a squall line, mockingly small and thin. Of the ship-killing tempest he worked to raise there was no sign at all.

The cliffs of Queensland were still a day's rowing out of sight, dead ahead. In the same direction, but closer, some mildly bad weather was brewing. Harl frowned across the sea's gray face at the line of squalls, while his hands rested with idle sureness on the long-ship's steering oar.

The thirty rowers, freemen and warriors all, could see the bad weather, simply by turning their heads, as easily as Harl could. And they were all experienced enough to reach the same conclusion: that, by slowing down the stroke slightly, they would probably miss the squalls' path and so make themselves a bit more comfortable. So now, by unspoken agreement, they were all easing up a trifle on the oars.

From ahead a cool light breeze sprang up, fluttering the pennons on the sailless masts and rippling the fringe of awning on the tent of royal purple that stood amidships.

Inside that tent, alone for the moment with his thoughts, was the young man that Harl called king and lord. Harl's frown faded as it crossed his mind that young Ay had probably withdrawn into the tent to make some plans for the fighting that was sure to come. The border tribes, who cared nothing for the mild new god or the failing old empire, were certain to make some test of the will and courage of Queensland's new ruler—not that there were grounds for doubting the firmness of either.

Harl smiled at his next thought, that his young lord in the tent might not be planning war at all, but a campaign to make sure of the Princess Alix. It was her hand in marriage that was to bring Ay his kingdom and his army. All princesses were described as beautiful, but rumor said that this one also had spirit. Now, if she was like some of the high-born girls that Harl had met, her conquest might be as difficult as that of a barbarian chieftain—and, of course, even more to a sturdy warrior's taste!

Harl's expression, which had become about as jovial as his facial scars would allow, faded once more to glumness. It had occurred to him that his king might have gone into the tent to practice reading. Ay had long been an admirer of books and had actually brought two of them with him on his voyage. Or it might be that he was praying to his gentle new slave-god, for, young and healthy though he was, Ay now and then took the business of worship seriously.

Even while half his mind busied itself with these reflections, Harl remained alert as always. Now a faint puzzling splashing in the sea nearby caused him to turn his head to the port side—and in a moment all the thoughts in his head were frozen, together with his warrior's blood.

Rearing right beside the ship, its bulk lifting to obscure the horizon and the distant afternoon clouds, came a head out of nightmare, a dragon face from some evil legend. The dully gleaming neck that bore the head was of such size that a man might just be able to encircle it with both arms. Sea demons alone might know what the body in the water below was like! The eyes were clouded suns the size of silver platters, while the scales of head and neck were gray and heavy like thick wet iron. The mouth was a coffin, lid opened just a crack, all fenced inside with daggers.

Long as a cable, the thick neck came reeling inboard, scales rasping wood from the gunwale. The men's first cries were sounds such as warriors should not make, but in the next instant they were all grabbing bravely enough for their weapons. Big Torla, strongest of the crew, for once was also quickest, bracing a leg on his rower's bench and hacking with his sword at that tremendous swaying neck.

The blows clanged uselessly on dully gleaming scales; the dragon might not even have been aware of them. Its head swayed to a stop facing the doorway of the purple tent; from the slit of its terrible mouth there shrieked a challenge whose like Harl had not heard in a lifetime of war.

What with all the clamor of voices and blows, Ay had needed no such summons to make ready. Before the dragon-bellow had ceased, the tent flaps were ripped open from inside and the young king stepped forth armed with shield and helm, sword ready in his hand.

Harl felt a tremendous pride to see that the young man did not flinch a hand's breadth from the sight that met him. And, with the pride, Harl's own right arm came back to life, drawing from his belt his short-handled, iron-bladed ax, and gripping it for a throw.

The ax clanged harmlessly off the clouded silver of one eye, perhaps not even felt by the beast. The dragon's enormous head, coffin-mouth suddenly gaping wide, lunged forward for the king.

Ay met it bravely. But the full thrust of his long sword, aimed straight into the darkness of the throat, counted for no more than a jab from a woman's pin. The doorlike jaw slammed shut, crushing Ay instantly. For a moment, as the monstrous head swept away on its long neck, there was seen the horrible display of broken limbs dangling outside the teeth. And then, with one more faint splash beside the ship, the evil miracle was gone. The sunlit sea rolled on unchanged, its secrets all below.

Through the remaining hours of daylight, there was scarcely a word spoken aboard the long-ship. She prowled in watery circles, on and on, never moving far from the unmarked spot where her lord had been taken. She prowled in full battle-readiness, but there was not a thing for her to fight. The edge of the squall line came; the men took mechanical measures to meet it. And the squall departed again, without the men ever having been really aware of its passage.

By the end of the day, the sea was calm again. Squinting into the setting sun, Harl rasped out a one-word order: "Rest."

Long ago he had retrieved his blunted ax and replaced it in his belt. Now the evidence to be seen on deck was only this: a few bits of wood, rasped from a raw scar on the gunwale by scales hard as metal. A few small spots of blood. And Ay's winged helmet, fallen from his head.

Derron Odegard, recently decorated and promoted three grades to major, was sitting in as a junior aide on an emergency staff meeting called by the new Time Operations commander. At the moment, Derron was listening with both professional and friendly interest as his old classmate, Chan Amling, now a major in Historical Research, delivered an information briefing.

" . . . As we all know by now, the berserkers have chosen to focus this latest attack upon one individual. Their target, King Ay of Queensland, is naturally a man whose removal from history would have disastrous consequences for us."

Amling, quick-witted and fluent, smiled benignly over the heads of his audience. "Until quite recently most historians even doubted this man's reality. But since we have begun some direct observation of the past, his historicity and importance have both been fully confirmed."

Amling turned to an electric map, which he attacked with a teacher's gestures. "We see here the middle stages in the shrinkage and disorganization of the great Continental Empire, leading to its ultimate collapse. Now note Queensland here. It's very largely due to King Ay's activity and influence that Queensland can remain in such a comparatively stable state, preserving a segment of the Empire culture for our planet's later civilizations to base themselves on."

The new Time Operations commander—his predecessor was now reported to be on a scouting expedition to the moon, or at least to Sirgol's surface, with Colonel Borss and others—raised a hand, student-like. "Major, I admit I'm not too clear on this. Ay was a bit of a barbarian himself, wasn't he?"

"Well, he certainly began as such, sir. But—oversimplifying somewhat—we can say that, when he found himself with a land of his own to defend, he settled down and defended it very well. Gave up his sea-roving ways. He had been one of the raiders and barbarians long enough to know all the tricks of that game. And he played it so well from the other side of the board that they usually preferred to attack someone else."

No one else had a question for Amling at the moment and he sat down. The next officer to appear at the head of the table was a major of Probability Analysis, whose manner was no more reassuring than his information.

"Gentlemen," he began in a nervous voice. "We don't know how Ay was killed, but we do know where." The major displayed a videotape made from a sentry screen. "His lifeline is newly broken *here*, on his first voyage to Queensland. As you can see, all the other lifelines aboard ship remain unbroken. Probably the enemy expects historical damage to be intensified if Ay's own crew are thought to have done away with him. It seems to us in Probability that such an expectation is all too likely to be correct."

Amling looked as if he wanted to break in and argue; or, more likely, to make a wager on the subject. They had put Amling in the wrong section, Derron thought. Probability would have been the one for him.

The Probability major had paused for a sip of water. "Frankly, the situation looks extremely grave. In nineteen or twenty days' present-time, the historical shock wave of Ay's assassination should reach us. That's all the time we have. I'm told that the chances of our finding the enemy keyhole within nineteen days are not good."

The man's edgy gloom was contagious, and the faces around the table were tightening in spite of themselves. Only the new Time Ops commander managed to remain relatively relaxed. "I'm afraid you're right about the difficulty in finding this keyhole, Major. Of course, every effort is being made in that direction. Trouble is, the enemy's getting smart about hiding his tracks. This time he attacked with only one machine instead of six, which makes our job difficult to start with. And, immediately after doing its job of assassination, that one machine seems to have gone into hiding. It hasn't left Ay's time, it'll still be on the scene to mess up whatever we do to set things right, but meanwhile it's being careful not to cause any changes that we might use to track it." Time Ops leaned forward, becoming less relaxed. "Now, who's got some ideas regarding counter-measures?"

The first suggestions involved trying to build probability in Ay's later lifeline, so that he would somehow have survived the assassination after all. This idea soon started an argument on a highly technical level. In this the scientific people present naturally dominated, but they were far from agreeing among themselves on what could and should be done. When they began to exchange personal viewpoints along with formulae, Time Ops called quickly for half an hour's recess.

Finding that much time unexpectedly on his hands, Derron stepped out and called the nurses' quarters at the nearby hospital complex. Lisa was living there now, while she started to train for some kind of nursing job. He was pleased to be able to reach her and to hear that she too had some time to spare. Within a few minutes they were walking together, in the park where they had met for the first time.

Derron had come to the meeting with a topic of conversation all prepared, but Lisa, these days, was developing a favorite subject of her own.

"You know, Matt's healing so quickly that all the doctors are amazed at it."

"Good. I'll have to come round and see him one of these days. I keep meaning to, but then I think I'll wait until we can talk to each other."

"Oh, goodness, he's talking now!"

"In our language? Already?"

She was delighted to confirm it and to elaborate. "It's like his rapid healing; the doctors say it must be because he comes from so far in the past. They talk about the effect on one individual of coming up through twenty thousand years' evolutionary gradient, about the organizational energies of his body and brain becoming enfolded and intensified. I can't follow most of it, of course. They talk about the realm where the material and the nonmaterial meet—"

"Yes."

"And Matt probably understands what they're saying as well as I do now, if not better. He's up and around most of the time. They allow him a good deal of freedom. He's quite good about staying out of rooms he's warned not to enter, not touching dangerous things, and so forth."

"Yes."

"Oh, and did I tell you they've suspended healing in his face? Until they're sure he can make a fully informed decision on what he wants his new face to look like."

"Yes, I heard something about that. Lisa, how long are you going on living in the hospital? Are you really set on learning nursing, or is it just—something to do?" He almost asked, "Is it just Matt?"

"Oh." Her face fell slightly. "Sometimes I don't think I was cut out to be a nurse. But I have no immediate plans to move. It's hard for me to live right in the hospital when I'm still getting therapy for my memory every day."

"Any success with the treatments?" Derron knew that the doctors now fully accepted that Lisa had simply lost her memory through being caught in the path of the berserker missile. For awhile some had considered it possible that she was an emissary or deserter from the future, made amnesic by descent through time. But on the sentry screens no such reversed lifeline could be found. In fact, no traveler, no device, no message, had ever come from the future to this embattled civilization that called itself Modern. Possibly the inhabitants of the unknowable time-to-come had good reason of their own to refrain from communication; possibly the future Sirgol was not inhabited by man. Or it might simply be that this time of the berserker war was completely blocked off from the future by paradox-loops. It was some comfort, at least, that no berserker machines came attacking from the direction of tomorrow.

"No, the therapy doesn't really help." Lisa sighed faintly; her memory of her personal life before the missile wave caught her was still almost completely blank. She put the subject aside with a wave of her hand and went back to talking about what new things Matt had done today.

Derron, not listening, closed his eyes for a moment, savoring the sensation of life he had when he was with Lisa. At this moment he possessed the touch of her hand in his, the feel of grass and soil under his feet, the warmth of the pseudo-sunshine on his face. Next moment it might all be gone—another missile wave could come down through the miles of rock, or the unraveling of King Ay's severed cord of life might propagate faster than expected up through the fabric of history.

He opened his eyes and saw the muraled walls surrounding the buried park, and the improbably alive, singing, and soaring birds. Down here at the level where humans walked, the place was almost thronged, as usual, with strolling couples and solitaries; in places the touch grass was showing signs of wear, and the gardeners had to defend it with string fences. All in all, a poor imitation of the murdered real world; but with Lisa beside him it became transformed into something better than it was.

Derron pointed. "Right there's the tree where I first came to your rescue. Or you came to mine, rather."

"*I* rescued *you*? From what horrible fate?"

"From dying of loneliness in the midst of forty million people. Lisa, I'm trying to tell you that I want you to move out of that hospital dormitory."

She turned her eyes away, looking down. "If I did that, where would I live?"

"I'm asking you to live with me, of course. You're not a little lost girl any more; you're on your own, studying to be a nurse, and I can ask. There are some unused apartments around, and I'll rate one of them if I take a companion. Especially with this promotion they've given me."

She squeezed his hand, but that was all. She was thoughtfully silent, her eyes on the ground a few paces ahead of them.

"Lisa? What do you say?"

"Just exactly what are you offering me, Derron?"

"Look—yesterday, when you were telling me about your new girl friend's problems, you seemed to have a very firm grasp of what this male-female business is all about."

"You want me to live with you temporarily, is that it?" Her voice was cool and withdrawn.

"Lisa, nothing in our world can be permanent. At the staff meeting just now—Well, I'm not supposed to talk about that. But things don't look good. I want to share with you whatever good things may be left."

Still silent, she let him lead her on stepping-stones across the park's little stream.

"Lisa, do you want a marriage ceremony? I should have put that first, I suppose, and asked you formally to marry me. The thing is, not many people are going to raise their eyebrows if we do without a ceremony, and if we do without one we'll avoid some delay and red tape. Would you think we were doing wrong if we didn't have a wedding?"

"I . . . suppose not. What bothers me is the way you talk about everything being temporary. I suppose feelings are included."

"When everything else is temporary, yes! That doesn't mean I necessarily like it. But how can anyone in our world say what they'll be feeling or thinking a month or a year from now? In a year we'll most likely all. . ." He let his voice trail off.

She had been searching for words and now at last she found the ones she wanted. "Derron, at the hospital I've absorbed the attitude that people's lives can be made less temporary, now or any time. That people should go on trying to build, to accomplish things, even though they may not have long to live."

"You absorbed this at the hospital, you say?"

"All right, maybe I've always felt that way."

He had, too, at one time. A year, a year and a half ago. A lifetime ago, with someone else. The image that he could not stop seeing and did not want to stop seeing came back to him again.

Lisa seemed to have her own private image. "Look at Matt, for instance. Remember how badly hurt he was. Look at what an effort of will he's made to survive and recover—"

"I'm sorry." Derron interrupted her, looking at the time, finding valid excuse for getting away. "I've got to run, I'm almost late for the staff meeting."

The scientists, by some combination of calculation and debate, had reached a consensus.

"It comes down to this," their newly elected spokesman explained, when the staff meeting had resumed. "If we're to have any hope of healing the break in Ay's lifeline we must first immobilize the affected part, to minimize damage—something like putting a splint on a broken arm or leg."

"And just how do you go about splinting a lifeline?" demanded Time Ops.

The scientist gestured wearily. "Commander, the only way I can suggest is that someone be sent to take Ay's place temporarily. To continue his interrupted voyage to Queensland and there play his part, for a few days at least. The man sent could carry a communicator with him, and be given day-to-day or even hour-to-hour instructions from here, if need be. If the berserkers stood still for it, he might play out the remainder of Ay's life in its essentials, well enough to let us survive."

"How long do you think any man could play a part like that successfully?" someone broke in.

"I don't know." The scientists' spokesman smiled faintly. "Gentlemen, I don't know if a substitution scheme can be made to work at all. Nothing like it has ever been tried. But I think it will buy us at least a few more days or weeks of present-time in which to think of something else."

Time Ops thoughtfully rubbed his stubbled face. "Well, now, substitution is the only idea we've got to work with at this point. But Ay is about twelve hundred years back. That means that dropping a man from here to take his place is out of the question. Right?"

"Afraid so, sir," said a biophysicist. "Mental devolution and serious memory loss sets in at about four hundred years."

Time Ops thought aloud in a tired monotonous voice. "Does anyone suppose we could get away with using a slave-unit on that kind of job? No, I thought not. They just can't be made convincingly human enough. Then what's left? We must use one of Ay's contemporaries. Find a man who's able to do the job, motivate him to do it, and then train him."

Someone suggested, "Appearance isn't too much of a problem. Ay isn't known in Queensland, except by reputation, when he first arrives there."

Colonel Lukas, the Psych Officer on Time Ops' staff, cleared his throat and spoke. "We ought to be able to get Ay's crew to accept a substitute, provided they *want* Ay to be alive, and if we can snatch the whole bunch of them up to present-time for a few days' work."

"We can manage that if we have to," Time Ops said.

"Good." Lukas doodled thoughtfully on a pad before him. "Some tranquilizer and pacifier drugs would be indicated first. . . . Then we can find out whatever details of the assassination we need to know . . . then a few days' hypnosis. I'm sure we can work something out."

"Good thinking, Luke." Time Ops looked around the table. "Now, gentlemen, before it should slip our minds, let's try to solve the first problem, the big one. Who is our Ay-substitute going to be?"

Surely, thought Derron, someone besides me must see where one possible answer lies. He didn't want to be the first one to suggest it, because . . . well, just because. *No!* Hellfire and damnation, why shouldn't he? He was being paid to think, and he could put forward his thought with the clearest conscience in the world. He cleared his throat, startling men who seemed to have forgotten his presence.

"Correct me if I'm wrong, gentlemen. But don't we have one man available now who might be sent down to Ay's century without losing his wits? I mean the man who comes from the even deeper past himself."

Harl's duty was painfully clear in his own mind. He was going to have to take the ship on to Queensland, and when he got there he was going to have to stand before King Gorboduc and the princess, look them in the face and tell them what had happened to Ay. Harl was gradually realizing already that his story might not be believed. And what then?

The rest of the crew were spared at least the sudden new weight of responsibility. Now, many hours after the monster's attack, they were still obeying Harl without question. The sun was going down, but Harl had started them rowing again, and he meant to keep them rowing for Queensland right through the night, to hold off the mad demonstration of grief that was sure to come if he let the men fall idle now.

They were rowing like blind men, sick men, walking dead men, their faces blank with rage and shock turned inward, neither knowing nor caring where the ship was steered. Frequently the oars fell out of stroke, clattering together or splashing awkwardly along the surface of the sea. No one quarreled at this or even seemed to notice. Torla groaned a death-song as he pulled—woe to the next man who faced Torla in a fight.

Inside the purple tent, atop the chest that held Ay's personal treasure (that chest was another problem for Harl, a problem that would grow as rage and grief wore away), the winged helmet now rested in a place of honor. It was now all that was left. . . .

Ten years ago, Ay had been a real prince, with a real king for a father. At about that time, Ay's beard had started to sprout, and Harl had first begun to serve as the young prince's good right hand. And, also at about that time, the twin sicknesses of envy and treachery had started to spread like the plague among Ay's brothers and uncles and cousins. Ay's father and most of his house had died in that plague, and the kingdom had died too, being lost and divided among strangers.

Ay's inheritance had shrunk to the deck of a fighting ship—not that Harl had any objection to that on his own account. Harl had not even complained about the books and the reading. Nor even about prayers to a man-god, a slave-god who had preached love and mercy and had gotten his bones split with wedges for his trouble. . . .

Over the ship, or beneath it, there suddenly passed a force, a tilting, swaying motion, over in an instant. Harl's first thought was that the dragon had come back, rising from the deep to scrape its bulk beneath the long-ship's hull. The men evidently thought the same, for in an instant they had dropped their oars and drawn their weapons again.

But there was no dragon to be seen, nor much of anything else. With a speed that seemed nothing short of supernatural, a mist had closed in around the ship; the red lingering light of sunset had been transformed into a diffused white glow. Looking round him now, battle-ax ready in his hand, Harl noticed that even the rhythm of the waves was different. The air was warmer, the very smell of the sea had changed.

The men looked wild-eyed at one another in the strange soft light. They fingered their swords and muttered about wizardry.

"Row slowly ahead!" ordered Harl, putting the useless ax back in his belt. He tried to sound as if he had some purpose other than keeping the men busy, though in fact his sense of direction had for once been totally confused.

He gave the steering oar to Torla and went forward himself to be lookout. Then, before the rowers had taken fifty slow strokes, he threw up a hand to halt them, and water gurgled around the backing oars. No more than an easy spear-cast from the bow, a gentle sandy beach had materialized out of the grayness. What manner of land might be behind the beach it was impossible to tell.

When the men saw the beach, their murmuring grew louder. They knew full well that only a few minutes ago there had been no land of any kind in sight.

"Yet that's certainly solid ground ahead."

"*Looks* like solid ground. I'd not be surprised to see it vanish in a puff of smoke."

"Sorcery!"

Sorcery, certainly; no one disputed that. Some kind of magic, good or bad, was at work. What might be done about it, if anything, was another question. Harl quit pretending that he knew what he was about and called a council. After some debate it was decided that they should row straight away from the beach, to see if they might in that way get beyond the reach of whatever enchantment held them in its grip.

Sunset was now long overdue, but the pale light filtering down through the mist did not fade. In fact, it became brighter, for as they rowed the mist began to thin.

Just as they emerged from the fog bank, and Harl was beginning to hope they were indeed getting away from the enchantment, they came near driving their ship straight into a black, smooth, almost featureless wall that rose from the sea. The wall was slightly concave, and it had no edge or top in sight; it rose and extended and curved back without limit around the sea and over the mist. From the foot of this wall the men looked up to find that it made an enormous inverted bowl over their tiny ship; from near the zenith, far above their heads, lights as bright and high as sun-fragments threw down their fire on white fog and black water.

Men cried out prayers to all the gods and demons known. Men shrieked that they had come to the sky and the stars at the end of the world. They almost broke their oars as they pulled on them to spin their ship and drive it back into the mist.

Harl was as much shaken as any other, but he swore to himself that he would die before he showed it. One man had collapsed to the deck, where he lay with his hands over his eyes, groaning, "Enchantment, enchantment," over and over. Harl kicked and wrestled him viciously back to his feet, meanwhile seizing upon the idea and putting it to use.

"Aye, enchantment, that's all!" Harl shouted. "Not a real sky or stars, but something put into our eyes by magic. Well, if there be wizards here who mean us harm, I say they can be made to bleed and die like other men. If they are thinking to have some fun with us, well, we know a game or two ourselves!"

The others took some heart from Harl's words. Back here in the concealing fog, the world was still sane enough so that a man could look around it without losing his powers of thought.

In an almost steady voice, Harl gave the order to row back in the direction of the beach they had glimpsed earlier. The men willingly obeyed; the man who had collapsed pulled hardest, looking to right and left at his fellows as if daring any among them to make some comment. But he would be safe from jokes, it seemed, for a good while yet.

They were not long in coming to the gentle sloping beach again; it proved to be real and solid. As the long-ship slid lightly aground, Harl, sword in hand, was the first to leap into the shallows. The water was warmer than he had expected, and when a splash touched his lips he discovered that it was fresh. But by this time he was beyond being surprised at such relative trifles.

One of Matt's tutors stepped ahead of Derron, tapped on the door of the private hospital room, then slid it open. Putting his head inside, the tutor spoke slowly and distinctly. "Matt? There is a man here who wants to talk to you. He is Derron Odegard, the man who fought beside you in your own time."

The tutor turned to motion Derron forward. As he entered the room, the man who had been sitting in an armchair before the television screen got to his feet, standing tall and erect.

In this man, dressed in the robe and slippers that were general issue for hospital patients, Derron saw no resemblance to the dying savage he had helped a few days ago to carry into the hospital. Matt's hair had been depilated and was only now starting to grow back in, a neutral-colored stubble. Matt's face below the eyes was covered by a plastic membrane, which served as skin while the completion of the healing process was held in abeyance.

On the bedside table, half covered by some secondary-level school-books, were several sketches and composite photographs, looking like variations on one basic model of a young man's face. Derron was now carrying in his pocket a photo of a somewhat different face—Ay's—caught by a spy device that had been sent, in the shape of a bird, to skim near the young king-to-be on the day he began

his fateful voyage to Queensland. That was the closest the Moderns
had been able to get to the space-time locus of the assassination—as
usual, paradox-loops strongly resisted repeating interference with history at any one spot.

"I am pleased to meet you, Derron." Matt put genuine meaning
into the ritual phrase. His voice was quite deep; at most, a little
minor work would be needed to match it to Ay's, which had been
recorded when the photo was made. Matt's manner of speaking, like
his tutor's to him, was slow and distinct.

"I am pleased to see that your health is returning," Derron
answered. "And glad that you are learning the ways of a new world
so quickly."

"And I am pleased to see that you are healthy, Derron. I am glad
your spirit could leave the metal man it fought in, for that metal
man was very much hurt."

Derron smiled, then nodded toward the tutor, who had taken up
a jailer's or servant's stance just inside the door. "Matt, don't let
them con you with talk of where my spirit was. I was never in any
direct danger, as you were, during that fight."

"Con me?" Matt had the question-inflection down pat.

The tutor said, "Derron means, don't let us teach you wrong
things. He's joking."

Matt nodded impatiently, knowing about jokes. A point had been
raised that was quite serious for him. "Derron—but it was your
spirit in the metal man?"

"Well . . . say it was my electronic presence."

Matt glanced at the television built into the wall. He had turned
down the sound when company entered; some kind of historical
documentary was being shown. He said, "Electronics I have learned
a little bit. It moves my spirit from one place to another."

"Moves your eyes and thoughts, you mean."

Matt seemed to consider whether he was understanding the words
correctly, and to decide that he was. "Eyes and thoughts and spirit,"
he said firmly.

The tutor said, "This spirit-orientation is really his idea, Major,
not something we've inculcated."

"I understand that," said Derron mildly. The important thing,
from Operations' point of view, would be this tendency of Matt's
toward firmness of opinion, even in a new world. Such firmness
would be a very good thing in an agent—provided, of course, the
right opinions were held.

Derron smiled. "All right, Matt. In the spirit I was fighting beside
you, though I didn't risk my neck as you risked yours. When you
jumped onto that berserker, I know your thought was to save me.
I am grateful—and I am glad that now I can tell you so."

"Will you sit down?" Matt motioned Derron to a chair, then reseated himself; the tutor remained standing, hovering in the background.

Matt said, "My thought was partly to save you. Partly for my people there, partly just to see the berserker die. But since coming here I have learned that all people, even here, might be dead if we had not won that fight."

"That is true. But the danger is not over. Other fighting, just as important, is going on in other times and places." This was a suitable opening for the recruiting speech he had been sent here to make. But Derron paused before plunging ahead. For the tenth time he wished that Operations had sent someone else to do this job. But the experts thought Matt was most likely to react favorably if the presentation was made by Derron, the man who had, in a sense at least, fought beside him. And using Matt had been Derron's own idea, after all. Yes, he kept coming back to that in his thoughts. He hadn't seen Lisa since that last walk in the park—maybe he had been avoiding her. Yes, he could wish now that he had kept his mouth shut at the staff meeting.

Anyway, in the present situation, if Derron didn't make the sales pitch, someone else would, perhaps less scrupulously. So he vented an inaudible sigh and got down to business. "Already you have done much for us, Matt. You have done much for everyone. But now my chiefs send me to ask if you are willing to do more."

He gave Matt the essence of the situation in simplified form. The berserkers, deadly enemies of the tribe-of-all-men, had gravely wounded a great chief in another part of the world. It was necessary that someone should take the chief's place for a time.

Matt sat quietly, his eyes steadily attentive above the plastic skin that masked most of his face. When Derron had finished his preliminary outline of Operations' plan, Matt's first question was, "What will happen when the great chief is strong again?"

"Then he will resume his own place, and you will be brought back here to live in our world. We expect we will be able to bring you back safely—but you must understand that there will be danger. Just how much danger we cannot say, because this will be a new kind of thing for us to do. But there will certainly be some danger, all along the way."

Let him know that, Major—don't paint too black a picture, of course. It seemed to be left up to Major Odegard to find the proper shade of gray. Well, Time Ops might be spying over his shoulder right now, but Derron was damned if he'd con Matt into taking a job that he, Derron, wouldn't have touched if it had been open to him. No, Derron told himself, *he* wouldn't volunteer if he could. What had the human race done for him lately? Really, the chances of the mission's doing anyone any good seemed to him very uncertain.

Death did not frighten him any more, but there were things that still did—physical pain, for one. For another, the chance of meeting, on a mission like this, some unforeseeable ugly fate in the half-reality called probability-space, which the Moderns had learned to traverse but had scarcely begun to understand.

"And if, in spite of all medicine, the great chief should die, and can never go back to his own place?"

"Then it would be your job to continue in his place. When you needed advice we would tell you what to do. In this king's place you would lead a better life than most men in history have had. And when you had finished out his span of years, we would try to bring you here to our world again to live on still longer, with much honor."

"Honor?"

The tutor tried to explain.

Matt soon seemed to grasp what was meant, and he went on to raise another point. "Would I take more magic arrows with me to fight the berserkers?"

Derron thought about it. "I suppose you might be given some such weapons, to protect yourself to some degree. But your main job would not be fighting berserkers directly, but acting for this king, as he would act, in other matters."

Matt nodded, as slowly and precisely as he spoke. "All is new, all is strange. I must think about it."

"Of course."

Derron was about to add that he could come back tomorrow for an answer, but Matt suddenly asked two more questions. "What will happen if I say no? If no one can be found to take the place of the wounded chief?"

"There is no way that you, or anyone, can be forced to take his place. Our wise men think that, if no one does, the war will be lost and all of us will probably be dead in less than a month."

"And I am the only one who can go?"

"It may be so. You are our wise men's first choice." An operation was now under way to recruit a back-up man or two from the deep past. But anyone else brought up now would remain days behind Matt all the way through the process of preparation, and every hour was deemed important.

Matt spread out his healed hands. "I must believe what you tell me, you who have saved my life and made me well again. I do not want to die in a month and see everyone else die. So I must do what the wise men want, go and take the chief's place if I am able."

Derron puffed out his breath, venting mixed feelings. He reached into his pocket for the photo.

❀　　❀　　❀

Time Ops, sitting in a small rough cavern a good distance from Operations and watching through one of his systems of secret scanners, nodded with satisfaction and mild surprise. That Odegard was a sharp young lad, all right. No outward display of gung-ho enthusiasm, but always good work, including this job—a smooth soft sell that had gotten the volunteer to place himself on the right side of the question.

Now the operation could get rolling in earnest. Time Ops swiveled in his chair and watched Colonel Lukas pull a white, nightgown-like robe over his head and down, concealing the plastic chain mail that guarded him from throat to knee.

"Luke, you've got some bare face and hands hanging out," Time Ops remarked, frowning. Psych Officers as good as you were hard to find. "These boys you're going to meet are carrying real knives, you know."

Lukas knew. Swallowing, he said, "We haven't got time to be thinking up foolproof protective gimmicks. I won't inspire any confidence if I got out there looking like a masked demon, believe me."

Time Ops grunted and got up. He stood for a moment behind the radar operator to note the image of the ship on the beach and the cluster of tiny green dots in front of her—her crew, come ashore. Then he went on to the window, a wide hole hacked crudely through a wall of rock, and squinted out from between the two heavy stun-projectors and their ready gunners. As the fog generators outside were very near the window, there was nothing to be seen but billows of opaque whiteness, streaming out and away. Time Ops picked up and put on a set of heavy glasses like those the gunners were wearing. The fog effectively disappeared; now he could see the individual men standing before their ship a hundred yards away and the great calm surface of the Reservoir beyond.

"All right," he said reluctantly. "I guess we'll be able to see you wave your arm—if they don't surround you and get in your way. If that happens, wave your arms over your head, and we'll cut loose."

"I just don't want anyone to get trigger-happy, Commander," said Lukas, looking uneasily at the gunners. "We're going to have to do some very delicate work on those men out there, and that won't be easy and may not be possible if they've taken a hard stunning. I'd much rather ease them along with the drugs, ask them some questions, and make some impression on them along the way."

Time Ops shrugged. "It's your baby. Got your gas mask?"

"Yes. Remember, we'll try to do the job with the pacifier-tranquilizer mix in the drinks; they're physically tired, and that may put 'em right to sleep. But don't hesitate to use the gas." Lukas took a last quick look around.

"Looks like a few of them are starting up from the beach," said the radar man.

Lukas jumped. "Here I go, then. Where's my servants? Ready? Tell them to keep inside at first. Here I go!" His sandaled feet thudded rapidly down a stair.

The sand beach sloped up to a lowland of gravelly soil and sparse grass, the kind that grew in shadow. Harl left the bulk of the crew at the water's edge, ready to protect the ship or shove her off again, while with six chosen men he proceeded slowly inland.

The scouting party had not far to go; they had scarcely passed over the first hillock before they saw a single tall figure come walking toward them through the mist. This figure drew close and became a man of impressive mien, dressed in a white robe such as the good enchanters of the old religions wore.

Showing not the least surprise or fear at being confronted by seven armed sea-rovers, this man came near to them and stopped, raising his hands in a gesture of peace. "My name is Lukas," he said simply. He spoke in Harl's native language—with a bad accent, but Harl in his travels had managed to understand worse.

"Let us put some pointed questions to this 'chanter," said Torla at once, setting a hand on his dagger.

The one in wizard's garb raised his eyebrows, and his right hand and wrist flexed up slightly from his side. Perhaps it was only a gesture of remonstrance, but perhaps he was giving or preparing to give a signal.

"Let us wait!" said Harl sharply. In this mist, a small army might lie concealed within spear-cast. Harl nodded to Lukas politely, and gave the names of himself and his companions.

The white-robed man, his hands once more innocently at rest, bowed in grave acknowledgment. He said, "My house is very near; allow me to offer you its hospitality, at least for a meal."

"We thank you for the offer," said Harl, not liking the uncertainty in his own voice. The man's air of confidence had an unsettling effect. Harl wanted to ask what country they had landed in, but was reluctant to reveal his ignorance.

"I pray you," Lukas said, "some or all of you, come to my house, at least for food and drink. If you wish to leave men to guard your ship, I will order some refreshment sent to them."

Harl mumbled for a moment, undecided. He tried to imagine how Ay would have met this strange confident courtesy. Lukas needed no powers of clairvoyance to know that seven sea-rovers newly arrived on his beach had come by ship; but he might have come scouting to find out just how many men and ships there were.

"Wait here for a moment," Harl answered at last. "Then we seven will go with you." Two men stayed with Lukas while Harl and the others walked back over the little hill to explain matters to the rest of the crew. Some of these also argued for seizing the wizard at once and asking him pointed questions.

Harl shook his head. "We can do that at any moment. But enchanters are likely to be stubborn and prideful. And once a man's blood is out, it's hard to pour it back into his veins, should the letting prove to have been a mistake. We'll just watch him close, until we learn more. If food and drink are sent you, I suggest you treat the bearers with some courtesy." He need give the men no urging to caution and alertness; they were ready to strike at shadows now.

So Harl and his chosen six ringed themselves about Lukas and walked inland with him. Taking their cue from Harl, the six other sea-rovers tried to look as if the encirclement was all accidental and unintentional, as if their hospitable host was not really their prisoner. And Lukas might have taken his cue from them, for he gave no sign of being bothered in the least.

As the party proceeded inland the mist grew thicker with each step. Before they had gone a hundred paces they found their way blocked by a line of low cliffs, heretofore invisible, from the top of which the grayness came rolling down. Built right against the foot of this cliff was the wizard's house; it was a simple stone building, with a look of newness, only one story high but big and solid enough to be a manor or a small fortress. At second glance, though, it was hardly a fortress, for the windows were low and wide, and the wide doorway stood unprotected by moat or wall.

Several people in simple servants' garb emerged from this doorway and bowed to the approaching Lukas and his guests; Harl noticed with some relief that none of the servants appeared to be anything more or less than human. The girls among them were comely, in a down-to-earth and lively style; they eyed the warriors sideways and giggled before hurrying back inside.

"No fairy-tale witches here," growled Torla. "Though I make no doubt they know enchantments of a sort."

Torla preceded Lukas through the doorway, with the rest of the sea-rovers following close on the heels of the white-robed man. Harl was last to enter, looking behind him as he did so, his hand on his ax. He could not begin to feel easy about any man who welcomed seven armed strangers into his house.

Inside there was nothing to feed Harl's suspicions, save more of the same strange confidence. The entrance opened directly into a great manorial room, in which were set more than enough tables and benches to have accommodated the long-ship's entire crew. At the huge hearth, a smiling and confident servant stood turning the spitted carcass of a weighty meat-animal. The roast was browned and dripping, so nearly done that it must have been started hours before.

Though a fair amount of light came in at the windows with the fog, on the walls were mounted enough torches to make the room quite bright. Through simple hangings that covered the rear wall, Harl could now and then glimpse servants going about tasks in distant chambers, which must be dug back behind the line of the cliff. There was of course no way of telling how many armed men might be in those rooms or lurking somewhere outside, but so far Harl had not seen a single weapon, barring table knives. Another easy-mannered servant was now laying out eight places at the head table, setting out worthy but not spectacular silver plates and tankards along with the cutlery.

Lukas proceeded straight to the head of the table—a couple of the sea-rovers keeping casually close to him—and turned with a gracious gesture. "Will you be seated? There is wine or ale, as you choose."

"Ale!" barked Harl, giving his men a meaningful look. He had heard of potent drugs and poisons whose taste blended very smoothly with that of wine; and even honest drink must not be allowed to take the edge of clearness from their minds. The others echoed Harl's call for ale, though Torla looked somewhat disappointed.

The company seated themselves, and two girls promptly came from behind the hangings to fill their tankards. Harl watched to see that the wizard's drink was poured from the same vessel as his own, and he waited until the wizard was wiping foam from his own lips before he tasted the drink himself. And even then Harl took only a sparing swallow.

The ale was neither too strong nor too weak, but . . . yes, there was something slightly peculiar in its taste. Still, Harl asked himself, in a place where everything was strange, how could the ale be otherwise? And he allowed himself another sip.

"The ale of your country is strong and good," he ventured then, stretching the truth to make a compliment. "So no doubt you have many strong men here and you serve a strong king."

Lukas bowed slightly. "All that you say is true."

"And your king's name?"

"Our present king is called the Planetary Commander." The wizard smacked his lips over the ale. "And whom do you serve?"

A tremulous groan passed around the board. The tankards scraped in unison as they were lifted, and then together they thudded down, all lighter than they had been. All except Harl's. He had not observed the least sign of treachery—come to think of it, there was no reason why there should be any treachery here—but still he decided firmly that he would not drink any more. Not just now.

"Whom *do* we serve?" he asked the world. "Our good young lord is dead."

"Young Ay is dead!" Torla roared it out, like a man challenging the pain of some dreadful wound. A serving girl came to refill his tankard, and Torla seized her and pulled her onto his lap. But when she resisted his pawing with her thin weak arms, he only held her there gently, while a comical witless expression grew slowly on his face.

Something about this made Harl wonder. His own mind was perfectly clear . . . and yet he should be more concerned, more alert than he was. Should he not?

"Young Ay's death would be sad news," said Lukas calmly. "If it were true." The wizard seemed to be slumping slowly in his chair, utterly relaxed, forgetting dignity.

Oddly, no one took offense at the implication that they would be untruthful in such a matter. The men only sipped or drank, and there passed another murmur of mourning around the table.

"We saw him die!"

"Ah, yes!"

Harl's big fists were knotted, remembering their helplessness against the dragon. "We saw him die, in such a way that, by all the gods, I can scarce believe it yet myself!"

Lukas leaned forward, suddenly intent. "And what way was that?"

In a faltering voice Harl told him. Harl's throat quickly grew dry with speech; scarcely realizing that he did so, he interrupted his tale to take another swallow from his tankard. The truth about the dragon sounded in his own ears like a clumsy lie. What chance was there of King Gorboduc believing it?

When Harl's recital was finished, Torla started to stand up as if he meant to speak. The girl fell from his lap and landed with a yelp on her soft bottom. Torla, his face showing uncharacteristic concern, bent as if to help her. But she rose and scurried away, and Torla kept right on bending over until he was seated again, with his head resting on the table. Then he began to snore.

Torla's shipmates, those who were not on the verge of snoring themselves, only laughed at this. The men were all tired . . . No. Something *was* wrong, they should not be drunk on one or two tankards apiece of any ale. And if they were drunk, some of them at least should be quarrelsome. Harl puzzled over the strangeness of this, took another thoughtful sip himself, and decided he had better get to his feet.

"Your king is not dead," the wizard was repeating to him in a monotone. "Not dead, not dead. Why should you believe that he is?"

"*Why?* We saw the—the dragon take him." But Harl was no longer quite sure of what he had seen or what he remembered. What was happening here? He swayed on his feet, half-drew his sword, and croaked, "Treachery! Wake up!"

His men's eyes were glassy or closing, their faces foolish. Some of them started to rise at his cry, but then they sank back, leaning on the table, letting weapons slide forgotten to the floor.

"Wizard," one man muttered, turning pleading eyes toward Lukas. "Tell us again that our king lives."

"He lives and shall live."

"He—he is—" Harl could not make him say that Ay was dead. In terror of he knew not what, he staggered back from the table, his sword sighing all the way out of its scabbard into his hand. To hurt anyone for any reason would be a monstrous crime, but he was so frightened that he felt he might do anything. "Stand back!" he warned the wizard.

The wizard also stood up, not shaken, with the length of the table between himself and Harl. From inside his robe Lukas took a mask like an animal's snout, which he fitted onto his face. His voice came out thickly. "No one will harm you here. I have shared with you the drink that makes men peaceful. Sit down now and talk with me."

Harl turned and ran for the door. Outside, the mist suddenly sparkled in his lungs. He ran on until he reached the hillock from which he could see the beached ship, only to discover that all the men he had left there were dead or dying. Half a dozen nearly human monsters with gray, snouted faces were busy arranging their bodies in rows on the beach. Those of his crew who could still move were offering no resistance, but were letting themselves be led like load-oxen.

It was really too bad that such a thing had happened. Harl groped reflexively for his sword and ax, but then remembered that he had thrown his weapons away somewhere.

"It's all right." Lukas' soothing voice came from just behind Harl. As Harl turned, the wizard continued, "Your men are all asleep. They need rest; don't wake them."

"Ahh, that's it!" Harl sighed with relief. He might have known there was no reason to worry, not on this good island of sparkling ale and sparkling air and friendly people who spoke nothing but truth. He saw now that the snouted monsters were only men who wore masks like the wizard's. They were taking good care of his men. Harl looked confidently at Lukas, waiting to be told some more good news.

Lukas seemed to relax, sighing behind his mask. "Come here," he said. And he led Harl down to the water's edge, where the wet sand was kept lapping to perfect smoothness by the little wavelets coming in.

With his finger the wizard drew in the wet sand, making the crude outline of a grotesque head. "Suppose now that this is the dragon you thought you saw. What exactly did you think happened?"

Harl groaned wearily and sank to his knees, staring helplessly at the sketch. Now that he could relax, he felt very tired, and soon he was going to have to sleep. But right now he had to concentrate on what the wizard was showing him. "It seized Ay," Harl said. "In its mouth."

"Like this?" The wizard's finger drew a stick figure clenched in the dragon's teeth, waving helpless lines of arms and legs. Even as he drew, the little waves were coming in over the sketch, smoothing and blurring its lines.

"Like that," Harl agreed. He sat down awkwardly.

"But now all that is being wiped out," the wizard intoned. "Wiped away. And when this evil thing is gone, then the truth, what you and I want to be the truth, can be written in, to fill its rightful place."

The waves were coming in, coming in, erasing the dragon. And Harl could sleep.

Somewhere along the line, during his hurried days of training, Matt asked, "Then King Ay is in fact dead—and not wounded, as I was first told?"

A tutor explained. "You were told he was only wounded, because he can be brought back to life. If your mission succeeds, his dying and his wounds will be as if they had never happened."

"Then if I should fail, someone else can try again? If I am killed back there, my life too may still be saved?"

He had his answer at once from the gravity of their faces. But they went into explanations. "All that you see being done here, all this work, is only to try to give that one man back his life. If we can restore him, then all the other bent and altered lives surrounding his will also flow back to where they were before the berserkers interfered. But not yours, for your life was not there in the original pattern. If you should die in the time of King Ay, that death will be real and final for you. And death will be real and final for all of us here, if you fail in your mission. No one will be able to try again."

One of the perquisites of Derron's new rank was a small private cubicle of an office, and right now he was silently cursing the promotion that had given Lisa such a fine place in which to corner him.

"Whose fault *is* it if not yours?" she was demanding, angry as he had never seen her angry before. "You admit you're the one who suggested they use Matt. Why didn't you suggest they go back and grab someone else from the past instead?"

So far Derron was holding on to his patience. "Operations can't just reach back and pull someone out of history every time they feel like it. Ay's crew are a special case; they're going right back where they belong. And Matt is a special case: he was about to die anyway when he was brought up. Now Operations already *has* brought up a couple of other men who were about to die in their own times, but those two haven't had a chance to learn where they are yet, let alone what the mission they're wanted for is all about. When they are able to understand it, there's a chance they may refuse."

"Refuse? What chance did Matt ever have to refuse to go, when you demanded it of him? He thinks you're some kind of a great hero—he's still like a child in so many ways!"

"Beg your pardon, but he's not a child. Far from it. And he won't be helpless. Before we drop him he'll be trained in everything he'll need, from politics to weapons. And we'll be standing by—"

"Weapons?" Now she was really outraged. She was still like a child herself, in some ways.

"Certainly, weapons. Although we hope he's only going to be in Queensland for a few days and won't get involved in any fighting. We're going to try to have Ay rehabilitated and bring Matt back here before the wedding."

"Wedding!"

Derron hastened on. "Matt can take care of himself, and he can do the job that's expected of him. He's a natural leader. Anyone who can lead Neolithic people—"

"Never mind all that!" Becoming aware that her anger was useless, Lisa was sliding toward the brink of tears. "Of course he can do it! If he must. If he's really the only one who can go. But why were *you* the one to suggest that he be used? Right after I had talked to you about him. Why? Did you just have to make sure that *he* was temporary too?"

"Lisa, no!"

Her eyes were brimming over, and she hurried to the door. "I don't know what you are! I don't know you any more!" And she was gone.

Days ago, the plastic membrane, its task completed, had fallen away from his face. The new skin had appeared already weathered, thanks to the Moderns' magic, and with the membrane gone the new beard had grown with fantastic speed for two days before slowing to a normal rate.

Now, on the day he was to be dropped, Matt stood for the last time in front of the mirror of his room—he was still quartered in the hospital—to get a last good look at his new face. Turning his head from side to side, he pondered Ay's cheeks and nose and chin from different angles.

It was a much different face from the one that had looked back at him reflected in the still waters of Neolithic ponds; but he wondered if the spirit behind it had also been changed sufficiently. It did not seem to Matt that he was yet possessed of the spirit of a king.

"Just a few more questions, sire," said one of the omnipresent tutors, standing at Matt's elbow. For days now the tutors had conversed with him only in Ay's language, while treating him with the respect suitable for subordinates to show when addressing a warrior chief. Maybe they thought they were helping to change his spirit, but it was only playacting.

The tutor frowned at his notes. "First, how will you spend the evening of the day of your arrival in Queensland?"

Turning away from the mirror, Matt answered patiently. "That is one of the times we cannot be sure of, where Ay's lifeline is hard to see. I will stay in character as best I can and try to avoid making decisions, especially big ones. I will use my communicator if I think I need help."

"And if you should happen to meet the dragon machine that assassinated your predecessor?"

"I will try my best to make it move around, even if this means letting it chase me. So that you can find the keyhole to cancel out the dragon along with all the harm it has done."

Another tutor who stood near the door said, "Operations will be watching closely. They will do their utmost to pull you out before the dragon can do you harm."

"Yes, yes. And with the sword you are giving me, I will have some chance to defend myself."

The tutors' questioning went on, while the time for the drop neared, and a team of technicians came in to dress Matt. They brought with them the best copies that could be made of the garments Ay had worn when embarking for Queensland.

The costumers treated him more like a statue than a king. When it was time for the finishing touches, one of them complained, "If they've decided at last that we should use the original helmet, where is it?"

"Both helmets are out at the Reservoir," the other answered. "The communications people are still working on them."

The tutors kept thinking up more last-minute questions, which Matt continued to answer patiently; the dressers put a plastic coverall on him over Ay's clothes, and another officer came to lead him out to the little train that would take him through a tunnel to Reservoir H.

Once before he had ridden on this train, when he had been taken to see the sleeping men and the ship. He had not cared for the train's swaying and did not expect to enjoy riding the ship. As if in tune with this thought, one of the tutors now looked at his timepiece and handed Matt what Matt knew was an antimotion-sickness pill.

Halfway to the Reservoir, the train stopped at a place where it had not stopped last time, and two men got on. One was the chief called Time Ops; he and everyone else showed deference to the second man, whom Matt recognized from his pictures as the Planetary Commander. The Planetary Commander took the seat facing Matt and sat there swaying lightly with the car's renewed motion, holding Matt in steady scrutiny.

Matt's face was sweating, but only because of the plastic coverall. So, he was thinking, this is what a king looks like in the flesh. At once heavier and less rocklike than his television image. But this man was after all a Modern king, and so the king-spirit in him was bound to be different from that which had been in Ay.

The ruler of the Moderns asked Matt, "I understand you thought it important to see me before you were dropped?" When there was no immediate response, he added, "You understand what I'm saying?"

"Yes, I understand. Learning Ay's language has not driven yours out of my mind. I wanted to see you, to see with my own eyes what it is that makes a man a king." Some of the men in the background wanted to laugh when they heard that; but they were afraid to laugh, and quickly smoothed their faces into immobility.

The Planetary Commander did not laugh or even smile, but only glanced sideways at Time Ops before asking Matt, "They've taught you what to do if the dragon machine comes after you?"

Out of the corner of his eye, Matt saw Time Ops nod slightly to the Planetary Commander.

"Yes," said Matt. "I am to make the machine chase me, to get it to move around as much as possible. You will try to pull me out. . . ."

The Planetary Commander nodded with satisfaction as he listened. When the train stopped, he waved the others to get off first, so that he and Matt were left alone in the car. Then he said, "I will tell you the real secret of being a king. It is to be ready to lay down your life for your people, whenever and however it is needed." Then he nodded solemnly; he meant what he had said, or he thought he meant it, and maybe he considered it a piece of startling wisdom. His eyes for a moment were lonely and uncertain. Then he put on his public face again and began to speak loud words of encouragement, smiling and clapping Matt on the shoulder as they walked off the train together.

Derron was waiting at trackside in the low, rough-hewn cavern, to grip hands with Matt in the style of Ay's time. Matt looked for Lisa in the busy little crowd, but, except perhaps for Derron, only those were here who had some work to do. In his mind Matt associated Lisa with Derron, and sometimes he wondered why these two friends of his did not mate. Maybe he would mate with Lisa himself, if he came back from his mission and she was willing. He had thought on occasion that she would be willing, but there had never been time to find out.

The tutors and other busy men hustled Matt off to wait by himself in a small anteroom. He was told he could get out of the coverall, which he did thankfully. He heard another door open somewhere nearby, and into his room came the smell of the vast body of clean water, the lake that was hidden and preserved against the planet's future needs.

On the table in his little waiting room lay the sword that the Modern wizards had designed for him. Matt belted on the scabbard and then drew the weapon, looking at it curiously. The edge appeared to be keen, but no more than naturally so. The unaided eye could see nothing of what the Moderns had once shown him through a microscope—the extra edge, thinning to invisibility even under high magnification, which slid out of the ordinary edge when Matt's hand, and his alone, gripped the hilt. In his hand, the sword pierced ordinary metal like cheese, and armor plate like wood, nor was the blade dulled in doing so. The Moderns said that the secret inner edge had been forged of a single molecule; Matt had no need to understand that and did not try.

But he had come to understand much, he thought, sheathing the sword again. In recent days, sleeping and waking, Matt had had history, along with other knowledge, poured like a river through his mind. And there was a new strength in his mind that the Moderns had not put there. They marveled over it and said it must have come from his twenty thousand years' passage from the direction of the beginning of the world toward the direction of its end.

With this strength to work on the Moderns' teaching, one of the things he could see very clearly was that in Sirgol's history it was the Moderns who were the odd culture, the misfits. Of course, by mere count of years, by languages and institutions, the Moderns were far closer to Ay than Ay was to Matt's original People. But in their basic modes of thinking and feeling, Ay and The People were much closer, both to each other and to the rest of humanity.

Only such physical power as the Moderns wielded was ever going to destroy the berserkers—or could ever have created them. But when it came to things of the spirit, the Moderns were stunted children. From their very physical powers came their troubled minds, or from their troubled minds came their power over matter; it was hard to say which. In any case, they had not been able to show Matt how to put on the spirit of a king, which was something he was now required to do.

There was another thing he had come to understand—that the spirits of life were very strong in the universe, or else they would long ago have been driven from it by the berserker machines of accident and disease, if not by the malignant ones that came in metal bodies.

Wishing to reach toward the source of life for the help he needed, Matt now did want what Ay would have done before embarking on a dangerous voyage—he raised his hands, making the wedgesign of Ay's religion, and murmured a brief prayer, expressing his needs and feelings in the form of words Ay would have used.

That done, he could see no reason to stay shut up any longer in this little room. So he opened the door and stepped out.

Everyone was as busy as before. Men worked, singly or in groups, on various kinds of gear. Others hurried past, moving this way and that, calling out orders or information. Most of them remained utterly intent on their business, but a few faces were turned toward Matt; the faces looked annoyed that he had come popping out of his container before it was time for him to be used and fearful lest he cause some disruption of the schedule.

After one look around, he ignored the faces. Ay's helmet was waiting for him on a stand, and he went to it and picked it up. With his own hands he set the silver-winged thing upon his head.

It was an unplanned, instinctive gesture; the expressions on the men's faces were enough to show him that his instinct had been right. The men looking on fell into an unwilling silence that was mirror enough to show Matt that the helmet had marked a transformation, even though in another moment the men were turning back to their jobs with busy practicality, ignoring as best they could the new presence in their midst.

In another moment, some of his tutors came hurrying up again, saying that they had just a few more questions for him. Matt understood that they felt a sudden need to reassure themselves that they were his teachers still, and not his subjects. But now that the spirit he needed had come to him, he was not going to give them any such comfort; the tutors' time of power over him had passed.

Looking for the Planetary Commander, he strode impatiently through the knots of busy people. Some of them looked up, angry at his jostling, but when they beheld him they fell silent and made way. He walked into the group where the ruler of the Moderns was standing and stood looking down into his wrinkle-encircled eyes.

"I grow impatient," said Matt. "Are my ship and my men ready or are they not?"

And the Planetary Commander looked back with a surprise that became something like envy before he nodded.

On his earlier trip to the Reservoir, Matt had seen Ay's crew lying asleep in specially constructed beds, while machines stretched their muscles to keep them strong, lamps threw slivers of sunlight onto their faces and arms to keep them tanned, and electronic familiars whispered tirelessly to them that their young lord lived.

This time the men were on their feet, though they moved like sleepwalkers, eyes still shut. They had been dressed again in their own clothes and armed again with their own harness and weapons. Now they were being led in a long file from Lukas' manor down to the beach and hoisted aboard their ship. The gunwale that had been scraped by dragon scales had been replaced, and everything else maintained.

The fog-generators had long ago been turned off. Each man and object on the thin crescent of beach stood in the center of a flower of shadow-petals, in the light of the cold little suns that clustered high up under the black distant curve of roof.

Matt shook Derron's hand again and other offered hands, then he waded a short distance through the fresh water and swung himself up onto the long-ship's deck. A machine was coming to push the craft out into deep water.

Time Ops came climbing on board with Matt, and he half-followed, half-led him on a quick tour of inspection that finally took both of them into the royal tent.

"... Stick to your briefing, especially regarding the dragon. Try to make it move around as much as possible—if you should see it. Remember that historical damage, even casualties, are of secondary importance, if we can find the dragon's keyhole. Then everything can be set right...."

Time Ops' voice trailed off as Matt turned to face him, holding in his hands a replica of the winged helmet on his head, a replica he had just picked up from atop Ay's treasure chest. "I have heard all your lectures before," said Matt. "Now take this—and compose a lecture on carelessness for those whom you command."

Time Ops grabbed the helmet, glaring at it in anger that for the moment was speechless.

"And now," said Matt, "get off my ship, unless you mean to pull an oar."

Still gripping the helmet and muttering to himself, Time Ops was already on his way.

After that, Matt paid the Modern world no more attention. He went to stand beside Harl, who had been set like a sleepy statue beside the steering oar. The other men, still tranced, were in place on their benches. Their hands moved slightly on their oars' worn wood as if glad to be back, making sure they were where they really fitted.

Looking out past the prow, over the black water under the distant lights, Matt heard a hum of power behind him and felt the ship slide free. In the next moment he saw a shimmering circle grow beneath her—and then, with scarcely a splash, the darkness and the cave were gone, exploded into a glare of blue light. An open morning sky gave sea-birds room to wheel away, crying their surprise at the sudden appearance of a ship. Free salt air blew against Matt's face, and a ground swell passed under his feet. Dead ahead, the horizon was marked with the blue vague line he had been told to expect—Queensland. Off to starboard, a reddened sun was just climbing clear of dawn.

Matt spent no time with last thoughts or hesitations. "Harl!" he roared out, at the same time thwacking his steersman so hard on the shoulder that the man nearly toppled even as his eyes broke open. "Must I watch alone all day, as well as through the end of the night?"

He had been told that these words, spoken in his voice, would wake the men, and so it happened. The warriors blinked and growled their way out of their long slumber, each man perhaps thinking that he alone had dozed briefly at his oar. Most of them had started rowing before their spirits were fully back in control of their bodies, but within a few seconds they had put a ragged stroke together, and, a few moments later, all of them were pulling strongly and smoothly.

Matt moved between the benches, making sure all were fully awake, bestowing curses and half-affectionate slaps such as no one else but Ay would dare give these men. Before they had been given time to start thinking, to wonder what they had been doing five minutes ago, they were firmly established in a familiar routine. And if, against commanded forgetfulness, any man's mind still harbored visions of an attacking dragon and a slaughtered chief, no doubt that man would be more than glad to let such nightmare vapors vanish with the daylight.

"Row, boys! Ahead is the land where, they say, all women are queens!"

It was a good harbor they found waiting for them. This was Bla-nium, Queensland's capital, a town of some eight or ten thousand folk, a big city in this age. Immediately inland from the harbor, on the highest point of hill, there rose the gray keep of a small castle. From those high battlements the Princess Alix was doubtless now peering down at the ship, to catch a first distant look at her husband-to-be.

In the harbor there were other vessels, traders and wanderers, but less than a dozen of them; few for the season and for all the length of quay. Empire trade was falling off steadily over the years; seamen and landsmen alike faced evil days. But let Ay live, and a part of the civilized world would outlast the storm.

Scattered rivulets of folk were trickling down Blanium's steep streets, to form a throng along the quay as the long-ship entered the harbor. By the time his crew had pulled into easy hailing distance, and the cheers on shore had started, Matt beheld nearly a thousand people of all ranks waiting to see him land. From the castle whence, of course, the ship must have been spied a great distance out, there had come down two large chariots of gilded wood, drawn by hump-backed load-beasts. These had halted near the water's edge, where men of some high rank had dismounted and now stood waiting.

The moment of arrival came, of songs and tossed flowers of welcome. Ropes were thrown ashore, and a crew of dockmen made the long-ship fast to bollards on the quay, where it rode against a bumper of straw mats. Matt leaped ashore, concealing his relief at escaping the rise and fall of the sea. It was probably a good thing for Ay's reputation that the voyage had not been a longer one.

The delegation of nobles earnestly bade him welcome, a sentiment echoed by the crowd. King Gorboduc sent his regrets that he ailed too gravely to come down to the harbor himself and expressed his wish to see Ay as soon as possible in the castle. Matt knew that Gorboduc was old, and ill indeed, having only about a month to live, historically, beyond this day.

The king was still without a male heir, and the Queensland nobles would not long submit to the rule of any woman. For Alix to marry one of them might displease the others enough to bring on the very civil war that she and her father were seeking so desperately to avoid. So, logically enough, the king's thoughts had turned to Ay—a princely man of royal blood, young and extremely capable, respected if not liked by all, with no lands of his own to divide his loyalty.

Leaving orders for Harl to see to the unloading of the ship and the quartering of the crew, Matt took from Ay's coffer the jewels historically chosen by Ay as gifts for king and princess. And then he accepted a chariot ride up the hill.

In the Moderns' world he had heard of places in the universe where load-beasts came in shapes that allowed men to straddle and ride them. He was just well satisfied that such was not the case on Sirgol. Learning to drive a chariot had presented problems enough, and today he was happy to leave the reins in another's hands. Matt hung on with one hand and used the other to wave to the crowd; as the chariots clattered up through the steep streets of the town, more hundreds of citizens, of all classes, came pouring out of buildings and byways to salute Matt with cries of welcome. The people expected the sea-rover to hold their country together; he hoped they were making no mistake.

The high gray walls of the castle at last loomed close. The chariots rumbled over a drawbridge and pulled to a halt in a narrow courtyard inside the castle walls. Here Matt was saluted by the sword and pike of the guard, and acknowledged the greetings of a hundred minor officials and gentry.

In the great hall of the castle there was gathered only a score of men and women, but these were naturally the most important. When Matt was ushered in, to the sound of trumpet and drum, only a few of them showed anything like the enthusiasm of the crowds outside. Matt could recognize most of the faces here from their likenesses in old portraits and secret photos; and he knew from the Modern historians that for the most part these powerful people were suspending judgment on Ay—and that there were a few among them whose smiles were totally false. The leader of this last faction would be the court wizard Nomis, who stood tall in a white robe such as Colonel Lukas had worn, wearing a smile that seemed no more than a baring of teeth.

If there was pure joy anywhere, it shone in the lined and wasted face of King Gorboduc. To cry welcome he rose from his chair of state, though his legs would support him for only a moment. After embracing Matt, and when they had exchanged formal greetings, the king sank wheezing back into his seat. His narrow-eyed scrutiny continued, giving Matt the feeling that his disguise was being probed.

"Young man," Gorboduc quavered, suddenly. "You look very like your father. He and I shared many a fight and many a feast; may he rouse well in the Warriors' Castle, tonight and always."

Ay would receive such a wish with mixed feelings and Ay was ever the man to speak out what he felt. "I thank you, Gorboduc, for meaning to wish my father well. May his spirit rest forever in the Garden of the Blessed above."

Gorboduc was taken with a sudden coughing spell; perhaps he gave way to it more fully than he needed, to spare himself making an issue of this correction by an upstart in his own hall.

But Nomis was not about to let his chance slip by. He strode forward, white robe flowing, while the king was momentarily incapacitated in the hands of his attendants.

Nomis did not speak to Matt directly, but stood beside him at the front of the hall and addressed the others. "You lords of the realm! Will all of you stand silent while the gods of your fathers are thus insulted?"

Most of them would, it seemed. Perhaps they were not sure of the insult; perhaps not of the gods. A few of them did grumble something, but in voices low enough for their words to be ignored.

Matt, his nerves stretched taut, did not ignore them. "I meant no insult to any here," he said clearly. The conciliatory words were hardly out of his mouth before he felt sure that they had been a mistake, too mild an utterance, too near an apology to have come from the real Ay. Nomis displayed a faint sneer of pleasure, and some of the others were suddenly looking at Matt with new expressions of calculation; the atmosphere had subtly changed.

The king had recovered from his coughing fit, and now all other matters must wait while his daughter was led forth by her attendant women. From behind a gauzy veil, Alix's eyes smiled briefly at Matt before she modestly lowered them; and he thought that the Moderns had spoken truly: there would be many lifelines more painful than Ay's to follow to the end.

While preparations were being made for the exchange of gifts, a friendly noble whispered to Matt that, if the Lord Ay had no objection, the king preferred that the betrothal ceremony be completed at once. It would mean unusual haste, but there was the matter of the king's health. . . .

"I understand." Matt looked toward the princess. "If Alix is agreeable, I am."

Her eyes, intense and warm, flicked up at him again. And in a few more minutes he and she were standing side by side with joined hands.

With a show of great reluctance being overcome only by a loyalty that was stronger still, Nomis came at the king's order to perform the ceremony of formal betrothal. Midway through, he raised his eyes to the audience as he was asking the ritual question, whether anyone present had objection to the proposed marriage. And the wizard showed not the least surprise when a loud answer came from one at whom he was staring.

"I—I do object! I have long sought the princess for my own. And I think the sea-rover will be better mated with my sword!"

The man had hesitated and stammered at the start, and the deep voice was perhaps a shade too loud for real confidence to be behind it. But the speaker looked formidable enough, young and tall and wide-shouldered, with arms thick enough to make the average man a pair of legs.

No doubt Gorboduc would have liked to intervene and forbid a duel, but he could not do so in the case of a formal betrothal challenge. There was no historical record of Ay's having fought a duel at his betrothal ceremony, an item not likely to have been overlooked by the chroniclers; still, Nomis had now pushed his pawn forward. For this Matt supposed he could blame only himself; he had somehow failed to match Ay's exact behavior and so had encouraged the challenge.

In any event, there was no doubt about what had to be done now. Matt hooked his thumbs into his wide leather felt, faced his challenger, and drew a deep breath. "Will you state your name?"

The young giant answered in a tense voice, his tone far more hesitant than his words. "I need no introduction to any person of quality here. But that you may address me with the proper respect, know that I am Yunguf, of the House of Yung. And know also that I claim the Princess Alix for my own."

Matt bowed. His manner was very smooth and cool, as Ay's would be. "Since you appear to be a worthy man, Yunguf, we may fight at once to decide this matter. . . . If you have no reason to delay?"

Yunguf flushed; his control slipped for a moment, and Matt saw that beneath it the man was certainly badly frightened—more frightened than such a warrior should be by the prospect of any duel.

The princess's hand fell on Matt's arm; she had put back her veil and now, looking soberly at Matt, she drew him a little aside and spoke to him in a low voice. "I hope with all my heart that you fare well in this matter, lord. My affections have never belonged to that man."

"Princess, has he ever asked to marry you?"

"A year ago he did." Alix's eyes flickered in maidenly modesty. "As others have. But when I said him nay, he never pressed the matter more."

"So." Matt looked across the hall to where Nomis was now intoning over Yunguf's arms a blessing of the Old Religion. Yunguf seemed to need all his courage to keep from shrinking away from the wizard's touch. No, it was not simple death or wounding in a duel that Yunguf feared.

Matt himself could face the personal danger calmly enough. He had spent most of his life within threat of violence from animals or nature—though, as one of The People, he had very rarely been in danger from another human being. The Moderns had given him Ay's lithe hitting power and endurance, had put not only skill but extra speed into his nerves. And they had given him his special sword, which alone could give him advantage enough to win a fight. No, it was not Yunguf's prowess that bothered Matt, it was the very fact of the duel and the changes in history that it must bring.

Save for the king and the princess and the two participants, everyone seemed happy at the prospect of a little bloodletting. There was a general impatience at the delay necessary for Ay's shield to be fetched up from the ship. This delay would have allowed Matt time to get away by himself for a minute and report to Operations; but there was nothing he could say to them, or they to him, that would get him out of this duel. So Matt passed time in trying to make light conversation with the ladies, while Yunguf stood glowering and almost silent among a group who seemed to be his relatives.

The shield was soon brought in by Harl, who entered running, displaying every sign of eagerness to see the fight get started—probably with the intention of unsettling his lord's opponent's nerves as much as possible beforehand.

The company moved outside, where they were joined enthusiastically by the minor nobility and such of the commons as could crowd within sight. The king, chair and all, was established at the best vantage point, with the higher nobles around him. This courtyard was evidently consecrated to weaponry, judging by the massive timber butts, much hacked and splintered, which stood along its farther side.

The noble who had whispered to Matt about the betrothal came whispering again, to ask if he was acceptable to the Lord Ay as referee; Matt nodded his agreement.

"Then, my lord, if you will take a stand in the arena."

Matt moved to the center of the clear paved space, which was large enough to allow a good deal of maneuvering, and drew his blade. When he saw Yunguf advancing on him with blade and shield ready, slow and powerful-looking as a siege tower, he understood that there would be no further preliminaries. It seemed that at Gorboduc's court killing was much less ritualized than wedding.

The sun had passed the zenith by now, the air was warm, and in the windless courtyard even moderate exercise soon raised a sweat. Yunguf's approach, with many feints, was slow and cautious almost to the point of parody, but no one watching showed surprise. Probably a feigned slowness at the start was Yunguf's usual style. Sure enough, he moved rapidly at last, and Matt stepped quickly back, his shield-sword-shield parrying in good order the three blows of the attacking combination. Matt had hoped that at the clash of blades his opponent's sword might break, but the contact had been flat-sided and glancing, and Yunguf's weapon was evidently tough. And, Matt realized now, if one sword was broken, another would be provided; if two or three, cries of sorcery would be raised. No, only wounds could now decide the issue.

Matt worked his way back to the middle of the arena, still keeping out of Yunguf's way. The knowledge weighed on him that any killing he did today, any wounds he carved, would be disruptive changes that worked to the advantage of the berserkers. But for Matt to be killed or beaten by Yunguf would damage history still more. The onlookers had already begun to murmur; no doubt his deep reluctance for this brawl was showing. He had to win, and the sooner the better—but without killing or maiming, if that were possible.

Matt raised his sword and shield in readiness as Yunguf moved slowly into attacking range. And when Yunguf charged again, Matt beat him to the thrust, aiming along the side of Yunguf's shield to damage the sword arm's shoulder muscles. But Yunguf was twisting his body with the force of his own lunge; as the huge man's blade slid off Matt's shield, Yunguf's body turned into the path of Matt's thrust, which cut between his upper ribs.

The wound was only moderately deep, and Yunguf was not yet stopped, but his next slash was weak and slow. Matt swayed back just enough to let the blow go by, then lunged in again, blocking sword with sword, hooking the wounded man's knee with his foot and using his shield to force Yunguf's upper body back.

Yunguf fell like a tree, and there was Matt's bloody point hovering at his throat, while Matt's foot pinned Yunguf's sword wrist to the paving stone.

"Will you—yield to me—the combat—and its prize?" Matt was now aware of his own panting and of Yunguf's whistling, strangely gurgling breath.

"I yield me." The answer, in strangled tones, came quickly enough. There were no grounds for hesitation.

Matt stepped wearily back, wondering what Ay customarily used to wipe a bloody sword blade. Harl came to perform that office for him and to scold him about his hesitancy at the start of the fight. Yunguf's relatives had gone to Yunguf's aid, and with their help the wounded man seemed to be sitting up easily enough. At least, thought Matt, a killing had been avoided.

He turned to the princess and her father, to find them with frightened eyes fixed on an object that lay on the ground nearby. It was Nomis's outer robe, snowy in the sunlight. The wizard himself was no longer in sight; the white garment discarded was a plain enough signal that he was donning black.

A cough sounded wetly behind Matt, and he turned to see Yunguf with bright blood upon his lips.

The great metal dragon lay motionless, buried almost completely in the muck of the sea bottom. Around it the dull life of the great depths stirred—in safety, for this berserker was not seeking to avoid killing anything. For it to end even a vegetable lifeline nonhistorically could provide a datum for the Moderns' huge computers, implacable as berserkers themselves, to use in their relentless search for the dragon's keyhole.

The dragon was still under the direct command of the berserker fleet that was besieging the planet in Modern times. On their own variety of sentry screens, that fleet's linked computers had observed the lifting of Ay's ship and crew to Modern times and their subsequent restoration to Ay's time, with one lifeline added.

It was obvious what the Moderns intended, obvious to machines who themselves knew well the theory and practice of baiting traps. But a viable replacement for Ay was bait they could not afford to ignore. They must strike again, using one of the dragon's weapons.

But this time they must be subtle. The replacement must not be killed, at least not in any way that would spin a new thread of causation toward the dragon for the Moderns to follow. The linked berserker computers pondered electrically and arrived at what they considered an ideal solution: capture the replacement alive and hold him so, until the pillars of Sirgol's history came crashing down.

Even while in hiding, the dragon maintained around itself a net of subtle infraelectronic senses. Among the things it now observed in this way was a black-robed man, standing on a pillar of seaside rock about two miles from the berserker's hiding place and speaking on and on, rhythmically, into the empty air. From data in its memory banks the berserker deduced that this man was attempting to call supernatural forces to his aid.

And in the man's speech it caught the name of Ay.

In the full sunlight of midafternoon, Nomis stood chanting on his pinnacle of rock. The spells of deepest evil were best sung in darkness, but his hate and fear had grown until they seemed to spread a darkness of their own about him. He would not wait for the setting of the sun.

While the seabirds wheeled around him, crying in the wind, he sang in his thin but penetrating voice:

> *Demon of darkness, rise and stalk.*
> *Put on the bones and make them walk.*
> *Dead men's bones, through the weed and slime,*
> *Walk and climb.*
> *Walk to me here.*
> *Speak to me here*
> *Of the secret to bring my enemy's death.*

There was more, much more, all cajoling and coercing the dark wet things that waited in the deeps for men to drown—waited for fresh-drowned bones to come falling through the fathoms, for limber young corpses that the demons could wear like garments in their endless revels at the bottom of the sea. The dark wet things down there possessed all the knowledge of death, including how the death of Ay might be accomplished—something Yunguf had proven unable to achieve, despite all the supernatural threats Nomis had lavished on the lout.

Nomis's thin arms quivered, holding drowned men's fingers over his head. Then his arms swept low as he bowed, still chanting, eyelids closing out the sun. Today the spells would work, today the hatred was in him like a lodestone, drawing to him things of utter evil.

When he came to a place in the chant where he could pause, he did so. He let down his arms and opened his eyes, wondering if he had heard another sound between the surges of the surf. Under his black robe his old man's chest was heaving with exertion and excitement.

A bird screamed. And from below, from somewhere on the furrowed length of cliff that climbed to this tabletop from the sea, there came once more a scraping sound, almost lost in the noise of wind and surf.

He had just given up listening for a repetition of the sound and had started to chant again, when, from much nearer the top of the cliff, almost from under Nomis's feet, there came a small clatter, a tumble of stones dislodged by some climbing foot or groping hand. The sound was in itself so ordinary that it momentarily drove all thoughts of magic from the wizard's tired mind. He could only think angrily that someone was about to discover his hideaway.

Before him as he faced the sea was a cleft that climbed to the tabletop between folds of rock. From just out of sight within this cleft he now heard the sound of grit crunched under a heavy foot.

And then Nomis's world was shaken around him, but a proof that put an end to a lifetime's nagging inward doubts. His first glimpse of his climbing visitor showed him a drowned man's skull, one small tendril of seaweed clinging to its glistening crown.

With quick smooth movements the whole creature now climbed into his view. It was a man-form, thinner than any living human but fuller than a skeleton. Drowned skeletons must change when a demon possessed them—this one looked more like metal than bone.

Having emerged completely from the crevice, the demon-shape halted. It stood taller than Nomis, so that it bent its skull-head slightly on its cable neck to look at him. He had to struggle not to turn and run, to stand his ground and make himself keep looking into the cloudy jewels that were its eyes. A drop of water sparkled, falling from one bonelike fingertip. Only when the thing took another step toward him did Nomis remember to reinforce his chalked protective ring with a gesture and a muttered incantation.

And then at last he also remembered to complete his astoundingly successful ritual with a binding spell. "Now you must guide and serve me, until you are released! And serve me first by saying how my enemy can be put to death."

The shiny jaw did not move, but a quavery voice came forth from a black square where the mouth should have been. "Your enemy is Ay. He landed today upon this coast."

"Yes, yes. And the secret of his death?"

Even if the berserker were to order another to accomplish the replacement's death, a track of causation would be left on the Moderns' screens. "You must bring your enemy Ay here, alive and unhurt,

and give him to me. Then you will never see him more. And if you
do this I will help you gain whatever else you may desire."

Nomis's mind raced. He had trained himself for nearly a lifetime
to seize such an opportunity as this and he was not going to fail
now, not going to be tricked or cheated. So . . . the demon wanted Ay
kept alive! That could only mean that some vital magical connection
existed between the sea-rover and this thing from the deeps. That Ay
should have enjoyed such help in his career was far from surprising,
considering the number of men he had sent to dwell among the
fishes and the charmed life he himself seemed to lead.

Nomis's voice came out harsh and bold. "What is Ay to you,
demon?"

"My enemy."

Not likely! Nomis almost laughed the words aloud. He realized now
that it was his own body and soul that the wet thing craved; but by
his spells and within his chalked circle Nomis was protected. The
demon had come to protect Ay. But Nomis would not let the demon
know how much he had deduced. Not yet. He saw in this situation
possibilities of gain so enormous as to be worth any risk.

"Harken, mud-thing! I will do as you ask. Tonight at midnight I
will bring your enemy here, bound and helpless. Now begone—and
return at midnight, ready to grant me all I ask!"

In the evening Matt went walking with Alix along the battlements,
watching the stars come out, while the princess's ladies-in-waiting
hovered just out of sight around corners.

Matt's preoccupation with his inner thoughts was evidently obvious. The girl beside him soon abandoned a rather one-sided effort to
make small talk and asked him plainly, "Do I please you, lord?"

He stopped his moody pacing and turned to her. "Princess, you
please me very well indeed." And it was so. "If my thoughts go
elsewhere, it is only because they are forced to."

She smiled sympathetically. The Moderns would not think Alix a
beautiful girl. But all his life Matt had seen women's beauty under
sunburn and woodsmoke and toughness, and he could see beauty
now in this different girl of his third world.

"May I know then, lord, what problems force your thoughts
away?"

"For one thing, the problem of the man I wounded. I have not
made a good beginning here."

"Such concern does you credit. I am pleased to discover you
more gentle than I had been led to expect." Alix smiled again. No
doubt she understood that his concern over Yunguf rested mainly
on reasons of policy; though of course she could have no idea of
how very far that policy ranged. She began to tell Matt of some

things that she might do, people she could talk to, to help heal the breach between the new House of Ay and that of Yung.

Listening, and watching her, he felt he could be king in truth if she were queen beside him. He would not be Ay. He knew now, as the Moderns surely must, that no man could really live another's life. But, in Ay's name, he might perhaps be king enough to serve the world.

He interrupted Alix. "And do you find me pleasing, lady?"

This time her marvelous eyes did more than flicker; with a warm light of promise they held fast to his. And, as if by instinct, the duennas appeared at that moment to announce that the decent time limit for keeping company had been reached.

"Until the morning, then," he said, taking the princess's hand briefly, in the way permitted by courtly manners.

"Until the morning, my lord." And as the women led her away, she turned back to send him another glance of promise before passing out of sight.

He stood there alone, gazing after the princess, wishing to see her for ten thousand mornings more. Then he took off his helmet for a moment and rubbed his head. His communicator was still silent. No doubt he should call in to Operations and report all that had happened.

Instead he put the helmet on again (Ay would wear it as a sort of dress uniform) and went down into the keep, to find his way to the chamber where Yunguf had been bedded down by order of the court physician. Through the doorway of the room he saw a pair of the wounded man's relatives on watch inside and he hesitated to enter. But when they saw Matt they beckoned him in, speaking to him freely and courteously. None of the House of Yung, it seemed, were likely to bear him any ill-will for winning a duel.

Yunguf was pale and looked somehow shrunken. His difficult breathing gurgled in his throat, and when he twisted on his pallet to spit up blood, the bandage loosened from his wound, and air gurgled there also with his breath. He showed no fear now, but when Matt asked him how he did, Yunguf whispered that he was dying. There was more he wanted to say to Matt, but talking came too hard.

"Lord Ay," said one of the relatives reluctantly, "I think my cousin would say that his challenge to you was a lie, and that therefore he knew he could not win."

The man on the pallet nodded.

"Also—" The cousin paused as the other relative gestured at him worriedly. Then he went on, in a determined rush of words. "I think Yunguf would warn you that things harder to fight against than swords are set against you here."

"I saw the white robe left on the ground."

"Ah, then you are warned. May your new god defend you if a time comes when your sword will avail nothing."

A seabird cried in the night outside. Yunguf's eyes, with fear in them again, turned to the small window.

Matt wished the men of Yung well and climbed the stair back to the castle roof. He could be alone there and unobserved, since only a token watch was kept, and full night had now descended. Once secluded in lonely darkness, he took a deep breath and, for the first time, pressed his helmet's right wing in a certain way, switching on the communicator.

"Time Ops here." The crisp Modern voice was barely a whisper of sound, but it made the castle, and even the open night with its rising moon, somehow unreal. Reality was once more a grimly crowded cave-fortress at the center of a fantastic web of machines and energy. In what sounded to his own ears like a lifeless voice, Matt reported the duel and Nomis's departure, with the implied threat of the discarded white robe.

"Yes, our screens showed Yunguf's lifeline being hit by something. He's going to—" A paradox-loop censored out some words of Time Ops' speech. "Nothing vital is involved there, though." By that, of course. Time Ops meant that nothing vital to the Moderns' historical base was involved. "Have you seen or heard anything of the dragon yet?"

"No." The track of the rising moon showed the calm sea out to the distant horizon. "Why do you speak of the dragon so much?"

"Why?" The tiny voice seemed to crackle. "Because it's important!"

"Yes, I know. But what about my task here, of being king? If you help me I can do that, though it seems that I cannot be Ay?"

There was a pause. "You're doing as well as can be expected, Matt. We'll tell you when there's corrective action you must take to stay closer to Ay's lifeline. Yes, you're doing a damn good job, from what our screens show. As I said, what happens to Yunguf isn't vital. Your watching out for the dragon is."

"I will watch out for it, of course."

After correctly breaking off the contact, Matt decided it was time he visited Ay's men, who had been quartered temporarily in a kind of guardroom built into the castles massive outer wall. With this in mind he descended from the keep along an outer stair.

He was deep in thought, and it did not occur to him that the courtyard at the bottom of the stair was darker than it ought to have been. Nor did he wonder that the postern gate nearby stood half-open and unguarded. A sound of rapid movement at his rear alerted him, but too late; before he could draw sword a wave of men was on him, weighing him down. And before he could shed Ay's pride enough to utter a cry for help, something smothering had been bound tight around his head.

"Sir, can you spare a minute? It's important."

Time Ops looked up impatiently behind his desk, but paused when he saw Derron's face and noticed what he was carrying. "Come in, then, Major. What is it?"

Derron walked stiffly into the office, carrying a winged helmet under his arm. "Sir, I've been—sort of hanging on to this. It's the extra one Matt found on his ship before he was dropped. Today some communications people came to see me about it. There was a continuous noise-signal being generated in its chronotransmitter."

Time Ops just sat there behind his desk, waiting not too patiently for Derron to get to the point.

"The communications people told me, sir, that the signal from this helmet was interfering with a similar signal put out by the helmet Matt's wearing. Whichever one he'd taken, he'd be walking around back there broadcasting a built-in noise, very easy for the berserker to identify as a chronotransmitter and home in on. The berserker must have thought it an obvious trap, sir, since it hasn't homed in and killed him yet." Derron's voice was very well controlled, but he could feel his anger in the tightness of his throat.

"So, you're shocked at what we're doing, Odegard. Is that it?" Time Ops grew angry too, but not guiltily or defensively. He was only annoyed, it seemed, at Derron's obtuseness. He flicked on his desk screen and spun a selector. "Take a look at this. Our present view of Ay's lifeline."

During his hitch of sentry duty, Derron had gotten pretty good at reading the screens. This was the first look he had today at what was happening to Ay's lifeline. He studied the picture carefully, but what he saw only confirmed his fears of yesterday. "It looks bad. He's getting way off the track."

"Matt's buying a little more present-time for us here, and so far that's all he's doing. Is it clear now why we're trying to get the dragon to kill him? Millions, many millions, have died in this war for *nothing*, Major."

"I see." His anger was growing more choking by the moment, because there was nowhere it could justly be vented. In hands that he could not keep from shaking, Derron held the helmet out in front of him for a moment, looking at it as if it were an archeological find he had just unearthed. "I see. You'll never win unless you find that dragon's keyhole. Matt never was anything but a fancy piece of live bait, was he?"

"No, I wouldn't say that, Major." Time Ops' voice was less sharp.

"When you first suggested that he be used, we weren't sure but that he could come out alive. But the first full-scale computer simulation showed us the way things pretty well had to go. No doubt you're right when you say bugging the helmet made the trap a little too obvious." Time Ops shrugged, a slight, tired motion. "The way things stand at this moment, Matt may be safer from berserkers than we are."

Matt came painfully awake, trying to cough around a gag of dirty cloth that had been stuffed into his mouth. His head ached, throbbing hideously, as if he had been drugged. He was being carried with a sickening jogging motion; when his head had cleared a little more, he understood that he was riding slung across a load-beast's humped back, his head hanging down on the one side of the animal and his feet on the other. His helmet had fallen off somewhere; and there was no bouncing tug at his waist from the weight of sword and scabbard.

Six or eight men had him prisoner. They were walking near the load-beast in the darkness, guiding and leading it along a narrow winding path by moonlight. The men looked behind them frequently, and now and then they exchanged a few low-voiced words.

"... I think two of them are following, or they were...."

Matt heard that much. He tried the cords holding his wrists and ankles and found them strong and tight. Turning his head, he could see that the trail ahead wound among jagged pillars and outcroppings of rock; from what he knew of the country near Blanium he judged that they were right along the coast.

When the man who was leading the way turned and paused a moment to let the others close up, Matt saw without surprise that he was tall and thin and robed in black, and had belted round his lean waist a sword and scabbard that looked like Matt's. Nomis had taken for himself one of the power symbols of a king.

The way grew steadily rougher. Shortly the little procession came to a thin ridge, with deep clefts in the rock on either side of it; here the load-beast must be left behind. At Nomis's order, some of the men lifted Matt from its back. He tried to feign unconsciousness, but Nomis came to lift his eyelids and then regard him with a knowing grin.

"He's awake. Untie his feet, but see to it that his arms are doubly secure."

The men did so. The farther they progressed on this hike, the more often they stopped to look uneasily about them, starting at every sound of the night. They seemed to fear Nomis and whatever lay ahead almost as much as they feared the pursuit that must be coming after them from the castle.

With his arms still bound behind his back, men ahead and behind holding on to him, Matt was led across the single-file ridge, then made to scramble up through a long twisting chute, almost a tunnel between high walls of rock that shaded out the moon. Only Nomis, leading through the darkness, seemed to know the way. The sound of surf became audible, drifting from somewhere below.

A cloud was over the moon when the party straggled at last onto a tiny tableland of rock. Only Nomis immediately saw the figure that had been waiting, motionless as stone, for their arrival. When he saw it, he quickly drew Matt's sword; and when Matt was pushed up out of the chute to within his reach, he gripped Matt's hair with one hand and with the other laid the bare blade against Matt's throat.

The moon came out then, and the other men saw the thing that stood watching them. Like odd chicks of some gaunt black bird, they squawked and scrambled to get behind Nomis, all making sure they stood within the old chalked diagram. For a few seconds, then, everything was still, save for the faint wind and the surf and one man's muttering in fear.

Keeping the sword against Matt's neck, Nomis pulled the gag from his face and displayed him to the berserker. "What say you, mud-thing, is this man indeed your enemy? Shall I slay him, then?"

The metal puppet might have been sent charging forward, far faster than any man could move, to pull Matt away to captivity. But there was the keen edge right against the jugular. The berserker would not risk a thread of responsibility for Matt's death.

"Wizard, I will give you power," said the demon. "And wealth, and the pleasures of the flesh, and then life everlasting. But first you must give me that man alive."

Nomis crooned in his certainty of victory, while at his back his men huddled in terror. In this moment when all desires seemed possible of attainment, there rose uppermost in his mind the memory of a day long ago, when a child-princess's mocking laughter had burned at him. "I want Alix," he whispered. To him the breaking of her pride would mean more than her young body.

"I will give her to you," lied the demon solemnly, "when you have given me that man alive."

In Nomis's ecstasy of triumph, his arm wavered slightly as he held the long sword. Matt was ready. His bound wrists still allowed him some arm movement, and as he jerked free with all his strength his elbow struck the wizard's old ribs with force enough to send Nomis sprawling and the sword spinning in the air.

The other men's terror was triggered into panic flight. They burst up from their crouched positions, first scattering blindly and then converging on the only path of escape, the narrow way by which they had ascended. Running straight, head down, Matt kicked the fallen sword ahead of him and still got there first by a stride, thanks to what the Moderns had done for his nerves and muscles.

The berserker was delayed by its need to avoid mangling the men who got in its way, but even as Matt reached the top of the path he felt a hand harder than flesh scrape down his back. It seized his clothing, but the fabric tore free. Then he was leaping, falling into the descending passage. At his back the other men were screaming in raw fear as they collided with one another and with the berserker.

When he landed he naturally fell, cutting and bruising himself without really feeling the injuries. The way was so narrow that he could not miss finding the sword he had kicked ahead of him. With his bound hands he groped behind him in the dark to pick it up by the blade, heedless of nicked fingers. Then he got his feet under him and scrambled some distance farther downward. He stumbled and fell again, hurting his knee, but he had gained a substantial lead on the tangled terror that was jamming the narrow chute behind him. One or more men had probably fallen and broken bones or injured themselves in other ways, and the rest were unable to get past them. They were all howling with mindless fear, and no doubt lacerating themselves further in the dark when they felt the chill touch of the berserker; it would be sorting through the men to find the one it wanted, trying to get the others out of its way. . . .

Matt propped the sword on its hilt behind him and, with the new skill of his nerves, slid his bonds against the edge of its blade. He had freed himself before he heard the machine's footsteps come crunching toward him in the dark.

"That's it, that's it! We'll nail the damned thing now!" In Time Operations, men were crying out a hunters' jubilation that was as old as mankind. On their screens their giant computers were limning out the radii of a spiderweb, the center of which would hold the dragon. The data needed to draw the web was flowing in from human lifelines being bent and battered; the berserker seemed to be struggling with men in some enclosed space.

But still it had not killed again. And the locus of its keyhole was not yet in sight.

"Only a little more," Time Ops, staring wildly at his screens, pleaded for bloodshed. "Something?"

But there was no more.

Matt retreated, limping, out into the moonlight where he could see. The thing followed unhurriedly, sure of him now. He backed out onto the thin ridge, between yawning crevices too deep for the moonlight to plumb, gripping his sword's hilt in bleeding fingers. Pale in the moonlight and almost skeleton-thin, the machine followed him carefully. It did not want him to fall. It would choose the precise moment and then rush to catch him, as easily as a human athlete picking up a toddler from a broad walk.

Keeping his sword's point centered on the narrow way along which it would have to come, he had just time enough to steel his arm. A moment ago the berserker had been twelve feet away, and now it was on him. It made a wiping motion with one hand, to clear what appeared to be an ordinary sword blade from its path—and four steel fingers leaped free like small silver fish in the moonlight, while the monomolecular blade stayed where it was, centered by Matt's braced muscles.

The inertia of the machine's rush was great. Before it could halt itself, the sword point had gone through its torso, and what had been delicately controlled mechanism became dead hurtling weight. Matt went down before the force of it, but he clung to the edge of the rock. He saw it go tumbling over him, then falling in an endless slow somersault, taking with it the transfixing sword, which already glowed like a red-hot needle with the inner fire that it had kindled.

The demon vanished. From far down inside the crevice came a crash, and then another and another, echoing remotely. Matt pulled himself back onto the ridge and crawled a few feet; then he made himself stand and walk before he reached the place where the path was broad and safe.

He was battered and bruised, but he could move. Trying to keep in shadow, he limped past the phlegmatic, waiting load-beast. He had gone a dozen steps farther when the two men Nomis had left here as sentries pounced out of deeper shadows. As they seized him, his injured leg was twisted again, and he fell.

"Best let me go and run yourselves," he said to the buskined knees standing before him. "Back there, the devil has come for your master."

It made them take a moment to look back toward the distant commotion on the path. And then they themselves were seized, not by the devil but by the two men Matt had seen running up from the direction of the castle, ax and sword in hand. Around Matt there swirled a brief clashing of metal and choked cries that were quickly ended.

"Is this leg your worst hurt, lord?" Harl asked anxiously, putting his ax in his belt and bending over Matt.

"Yes, I do well enough."

Torla muttered grimly, "Then we will go on and slaughter the rest of them."

Matt tried to think. "No. Not now, at least. Nomis called up a thing from the sea—"

Torla shuddered now at the distant moaning. "Then let us away?"

"Can you stand, lord?" asked Harl. "Good, then lean on me." And having pulled Matt to his feet, he next detached something from under his cloak and held it out. "Your helmet, lord. It fell outside the postern gate and set us on the right trail."

Harl and Torla might think that he was dazed, or that it was the pain in his leg that made him slow to reach out for the helmet. Harl had carried it under his cloak as if it was no more than a shell of metal; but, worn like a crown, it weighed enough to crush a man.

Down in the sea-bottom muck the dragon stirred. The tantalizing bait-signal of the life-unit that the Moderns had sent as Ay's replacement was now very near the shore. If that life-unit could be captured without further damage to other lifelines, a berserker victory would be insured. To pursue the replacement inland, among other lives, would involve creating too much change: the dragon's auxiliary man-shaped device might have conducted such a pursuit almost unobtrusively, but it had been somehow lost. Still, the chance of seizing the important life-unit right along the coast was too good an opportunity to let slip. Darkening the water with an upheaved cloud of mud, the dragon rose.

Supported by a strong man on either side, Matt could make fair speed along the rough path that led back to Blanium. Not, he thought, that there was any real need for haste. Nomis and his men would certainly not be in pursuit; if Nomis had survived at all, his influence must have been thoroughly destroyed.

And the dragon? It had done what it could do to capture him, to take him alive, quietly and gently. He shuddered. It must be hiding in the sea. And it seemed that, unless he went to the water's edge and waved at it, it was not going to chase him. It could have come inland to kill him any time; peasants and armies and the walls of Blanium would not stop it.

No, if the berserker wanted him dead he would have been dead now, and even his magic sword would not have helped him for a moment. He had seen and heard enough of berserkers to be sure of that.

"How made you your escape, lord?"

"I will tell you later. Let me think now."

Make the dragon chase you, said Time Ops. *We will try to pull you out in time.* So far there had been no pulling out. *A king must be ready to give his life*, said the Planetary Commander, making what he thought was an important point, as he spoke from the depths of his own missileproof shelter.

The Moderns were fighting to save the tribe-of-all-men, and to them Matt or any other individual was only an implement for fighting. Save his life once, then shove him forward again to draw the lightning of the stone-lion's eye. . . .

In a flash of insight, many things suddenly fell into place for Matt. Scraps of knowledge he had picked up in the Modern's world, about the war as it was fought with screens and missiles, lifelines and keyholes, suddenly dovetailed with what had happened to him here in the world of Ay. Of course, he should have seen it before! It was the Moderns who wanted him killed here, by the berserkers. And the berserkers, knowing this, wanted instead to take him alive!

He was still bleakly pondering this insight when the communicator in his helmet began to speak into his ear with its tiny voice that no one else could hear. In his new anger, he paid no attention to what it was saying; he came near pulling the helmet off and throwing it away, with all its lying voices. He would throw it away, he told himself, when he came to the sea. . . . No, he must avoid the shore from now on. When he came to another bottomless crevice, then.

But instead he gripped his companions' shoulders, stopping them. "Good friends, I must be alone for a little while. To think—and pray."

His good friends exchanged glances with each other; his request must seem a strange one, coming at this time. But then their king had been through a day that might make any man act strangely.

Harl frowned at him. "You are weaponless."

"There are no enemies about. But let your dagger stay with me if you will; only let me have a short time to myself."

And so they left him, though with repeated backward glances, left him sitting alone on a rock in the moonlight. He was their king now, and they loved him, and he smiled after them with satisfaction, thinking that he would have them at his side for many a year yet. He could and he would. There was no way for the Moderns to punish him, if he chose never to go hunting dragons. Matt was all the Moderns had between themselves and chaos; they would not dare to pull him back to the future, not while he worked at living King Ay's life. He might bungle the job now and then and provide only a second-best defense for the Moderns' world; but it was all the service they were going to get.

He took off the buzzing helmet and scratched his head leisurely. Then, holding the helmet before him, he twisted its right wing, letting Time Ops' tiny voice come out above the faint murmur of the unseen surf.

"—Matt, answer me, it's urgent!"

"I am here. What would you have?"

"Where are you? What's going on?"

"I am going on. To my bride and my kingdom."

There was a pause. Then: "Matt, it may be that that won't be enough, your going on trying to take Ay's place."

"No? Enough for me, I think. I have already been demon-hunting and have used up your sword. So I think I will not chase after a dragon that seems content to let me live."

"Demon-hunting? What?"

Matt explained. He could hear consternation at Operations' end; they had not thought of the enemy's trying to capture him alive.

Time Ops was soon back, pleading with a ragged urgency that Matt had never heard in the commander's voice before. "Matt, whatever else happens, you can't let that thing capture you alive."

"No? I have often been ordered to make it chase me."

"Forget that. No, wait. You can't be captured. But just avoiding capture and going on playing Ay's part isn't going to be enough, not now. You've done as well as anyone could, but your filling in for Ay simply isn't going to work."

"Then why does the enemy want to stop me?"

"Because you *are* buying us a little time here. They want to eliminate any lingering chance we have—any chance of finding some new defense, of pulling off a miracle. They want to play it safe and finish us off quickly. All I can do is tell you—ask you to—go down along the seashore where the damned thing is hiding. Make it come out and chase you and stir up some change."

"And if it should capture me?"

There was a pause, a murmur of voices exchanged at the other end, and then another familiar voice came on.

"Matt, this is Derron. All these people here are trying to figure out the best way to tell you to die. You're to get the berserker to kill you. If it catches you alive, then you must find a way to kill yourself. Kill yourself *because* it's caught you. Understand? *Die,* in one way or another, and make the dragon somehow responsible. All along, that's been what Operations wanted of you. I'm sorry. I didn't know how it was until after you were dropped."

Time Ops came back. "Matt, you can shut us off now and go on to claim your bride and your kingdom, as you said you were going to. But if you do that, all your life your world there will be slowly decaying around you. Decaying inside, where you won't be able to see it, becoming less and less probable. Up here we'll be dying, all of us. At your end of history the chaos will begin in your children's time—that's what you'll be leaving them."

"You lie!" But Matt's voice broke with the cry, for he knew that Time Ops was not lying. Or, if he was lying again about this face or that, still he was telling the truth about what was needed to win the war.

"Matt? This is Derron again. What you just heard is the truth. I don't know what more to say to you."

Matt cried bitterly, "My friend, there is no need for you to say anything more!" And with a jerk of his hand that almost broke the helmet wing, he cut the voices off.

Too late. He had silenced them too late. Slowly he put the helmet back on his head and stood up. Soon he saw Harl and Torla coming toward him; they had doubtless been watching protectively from not far away, overhearing some of the strange language of his prayers.

When they came up to him he said, no longer angry, "My leg gives me trouble. I think the path will be easier along the water's edge."

Between his friends, he moved toward the sound of surf. He went slowly, for in truth his leg did feel worse, having stiffened while he sat. No matter, now. He walked along thinking only in disconnected pictures and phrases, since the time for thought and worry was now past.

He had pulled the stone-man from the poison-digger's pit—that was twenty thousand years ago, and indeed it seemed to him that he had lived through twenty thousand years since then. He had been able to see the tribe-of-all-men grown to stretch across immensities of space and time. He had known, a little, the spirits of life. He had been a king, and a woman with the spirit of a princess had looked at him with love.

They had been walking for a minute along the water's edge, when, without surprise, he saw a shoreline rock ahead suddenly move and become a nightmare head that rose amid moonlit spray on a sinuous column of neck. The dragon's vast body heaved itself up from the sea and lurched toward the men, moving faster than a man could run.

"I have the dagger," Matt said to his friends. "And right now both of you can use sword and ax better than I." The dragon was not coming for Harl or Torla, and it would have been a pointless insult to bid them run.

He kept the dagger hidden in his hand, the blade turned up flat behind his wrist, as the dragon's head came straight toward him on its tree-trunk neck that could swallow a man and hold him safe. Sword and ax hewed at it uselessly from either side. Matt was very tired, and in a way he welcomed the grave-wide jaws, which, he saw now, held no teeth. Only in the instant of the jaws' soft powerful closing did he bring the dagger up, holding the point steady at his own heart while the pressure came down. . . .

"It killed him." The first time, Time Ops whispered the words unbelievingly. Then he let them out in a whoop. "It killed him, it killed him?" The other hunters, who had been frozen at their screens, sharing their computers' creeping certainty of failure, were galvanized once more into action. On their screens the spiderwebs tightened like nooses, imaging a target greenly solid and sure.

In the deep cave called Operations Stage Two, metallic arms extended a missile sideways from its rack while a silvery circle shimmered into being on the floor beneath. With a cluck and a jolt the arms released their burden. Falling, the missile was gone.

Derron had seen a keyhole hit and closed before, and he understood perfectly what a victory he was seeing now. On the screens, the whole writhing build-up of change surrounding Ay now burst like a boil; and the lines began to straighten themselves out like a string figure when the loose end is pulled. History's flow turned strongly and safely back into its familiar riverbed. Only the one lifeline that had been the catalyst was newly broken; you had to look closely at the screens not to miss that small detail.

The raw stump of that line left no room for reasonable doubt, but still Derron's hand went out to punch his communicator for Stage Three. "Alf? Listen, will you let me know what shape he's in, the moment—All right, thanks."

He waited, holding the circuit open to Stage Three, gazing blankly through tired eyes at the screens. Around him in Operations' nerve center, the first waves of jubilation foamed up around the edges of discipline.

"Derron?" Alf's reply was slow in coming and slow-spoken when it came, to tell about the wound in the heart and to speculate on how the man must have arranged to have the knife driven in. And to confirm that Matt's brain had been too long without blood and oxygen for the medics to do anything for him now.

Derron flipped off the switch and sat at his post, tired and immobile. Some of the victorious hunters around him were breaking out cigars, and one was calling jovially for a ration of grog. A few minutes later, Time Ops himself came strolling by with a glass in his hand, but he was not smiling as he paused at Derron's position.

"He was a good man, Odegard. The best. Not many can accomplish a thousandth part of what he did. With their lives or with their deaths." Time Ops raised his glass in a solemn, sipping toast to the bitten-off green line on the screen. Later, of course, there would be ceremonies, and perhaps a monument, to say the same thing more elaborately.

"The thing is," said Derron, "I don't really much care what happens to the world. Only about a person here and there."

Time Ops might not have heard, for the noise of celebration was growing louder. "You did a necessary job, Major, and did it well, from the start of the operation right up until today. We're going to be expanding even more here in Time Operations and we'll need good men in key positions. I'm going to recommend you for another promotion. . . ."

Nomis stood with arms upraised, gray beard and black robes whipping in the wind, while he persisted in the evil endeavor that had kept him here for the past three days on his secret pinnacle of rock. Nomis persisted, though he could not escape the feeling that all his labors against Ay were doomed to be in vain. . . .

On the battlement, Alix shaded her eyes against the morning sun and strained them seaward to catch sight of sail or mast. She waited, trembling inwardly a little, for her first sight of her future husband and lord. . . .

The cliffs of Queensland were dead ahead, Harl knew, though still a day's rowing out of sight. He frowned, gazing out to port across the sea's gray face, where nothing broke the line of the horizon but a distant line of squalls. Then his face cleared with the thought that young Ay, in his tent amidships, was doubtless planning for the fighting that was sure to come.

The instruments of science do not in themselves discover truth. And there are searchings that are not concluded by the coincidence of a pointer and a mark.

☀ STARSONG

Forcing the passage through the dark nebula Taynarus cost them three fighting ships, and after that they took the casualties of a three-day battle as their boarding parties fought their way into Hell. The Battle Commander of the task force feared from the beginning to the end of the action that the computer in command on the berserker side would destroy the place and the living invaders with it, in a last *gotterdammerung* of destructor charges. But he could hope that the damped-field projectors his men took with him into the fight would prevent any nuclear explosion. He sent living men to board because it was believed that Hell held living human prisoners. His hopes were justified; or at least, for whatever reason, no nuclear explosion came.

The beliefs about prisoners were not easily confirmed. Ercul, the cybernetic psychologist who came to investigate when the fighting was over, certainly found humans there. In a way. In part. Odd organs that functioned in a sort-of-way, interconnected with the non-human and the non-alive. The organs were most of them human brains that had been grown in culture through use of the techniques that berserkers must have captured with some of our hospital ships.

Our human laboratories grow the culture-brains from seedlings of human embryo-tissue, grow them to adult size and then dissect them as needed. A doctor slices off a prefrontal lobe, say, and puts it into the skull of a man whose own corresponding brain-part has been destroyed by some disease or violence. The culture-brain material serves as a matrix for regrowth, raw material on which the old

130

personality can reimpress itself. The culture-brains, raised in glass jars, are not human except in potential. Even a layman can readily distinguish one of them from a normally developed brain by the visible absence of the finer surface convolutions. The culture-brains cannot be human in the sense of maintaining sentient human minds. Certain hormones and other subtle chemicals of the body-environment are necessary for the development of a brain with personality—not to mention the need for the stimuli of experience, the continual impact of the senses. Indeed some sensory input is needed if the culture-brain is to develop even to the stage of a template usable by the surgeon. For this input music is commonly employed.

The berserkers had doubtless learned to culture livers and hearts and gonads as well as brains, but it was only man's thinking ability that interested them deeply. The berserkers must have stood in their computer-analogue of awe as they regarded the memory-capacity and the decision-making power that nature in a few billion years of evolution had managed to pack into the few hundred cubic centimeters of the human nervous system.

Off and on through their long war with men the berserkers had tried to incorporate human brains into their own circuitry. Never had they succeeded to their own satisfaction, but they kept trying.

The berserkers themselves of course named nothing. But men were not far wrong in calling this center of their research Hell. This Hell lay hidden in the center of the dark Taynarus nebula, which in turn was roughly centered in a triangle formed by the Zitz and Toxx and Yaty systems. Men had known for years what Hell was, and approximately where it was, before they could muster armed strength enough in this part of their sector of the galaxy to go in and find it and root it out.

"I certify that in this container there is no human life," said the cybernetic psychologist, Ercul, under his breath, at the same time stamping the words on the glassite case before him. Ercul's assistant gestured, and the able-bodied spaceman working with them pulled the power-connectors loose and let the thing in the tank begin to die. This one was not a culture-brain but had once been the nervous system of a living prisoner. It had been greatly damaged not only by removal of most of its human body but by being connected to a mass of electronic and micro-mechanical gear. Through some training program, probably a combination of punishment and reward, the berserker had then taught this brain to perform certain computing operations at great speed and with low probability of error. It seemed that every time the computations had been finished the mechanism in the case with the brain had immediately reset all the counters to zero and once more presented the same inputs, whereupon the brain's task had started over. The brain now seemed incapable of anything but going on with the job; and if that was really a kind of human life, which was not a possibility that Ercul was going to admit out loud, it was in his opinion a kind that was better terminated as soon as possible.

"Next case?" he asked the spacemen. Then he realized he had just made a horrible pun upon his judge's role. But none of his fellow harrowers of Hell seemed to have noticed it. But just give us a few more days on the job, he thought, and we will start finding things to laugh at.

Anyway, he had to get on with his task of trying to distinguish rescued prisoners—two of these had been confirmed so far, and might some day again look human—from collection of bottled though more or less functioning organs.

When they brought the next case before him, he had a bad moment, bad even for this day, recognizing some of his own work.

The story of it had started more than a standard year before, on the not-far-off planet of Zitz, in a huge hall that had been decorated and thronged for one of the merriest of occasions.

"Happy, honey?" Ordell Callison asked his bride, having a moment to take her hand and speak to her under the tumult of the wedding feast. It was not that he had any doubt of her happiness; it was just that the banal two-word question was the best utterance that he could find—unless, of course, he was to sing.

"Ohhhh, happy, yes!" At the moment Eury was no more articulate than he. But the truth of her words was in her voice and in her eyes, marvelous as some song that Ordell might have made and sung.

Of course he was not going to be allowed to get away, even for his honeymoon, without singing one song at least.

"Sing something, Ordell!" That was Hyman Bolf, calling from across the vast banquet table, where he stood filling his cup at the crystal punch-fountain. The famed multifaith revivalist had come from Yaty system to perform the wedding ceremony. On landing, his private ship had misbehaved oddly, the hydrogen power lamp flaring so that the smoke of burnt insulation had caused the reverend to emerge from his cabin weeping with irritated eyes; but after that bad omen, everything had gone well for the rest of the day.

Other voices took it up at once. "Sing, Ordell!"

"Yes, you've got to. Sing!"

"But it's m'own wedding, and I don't feel quite right—"

His objections were overwhelmingly shouted down.

The man was music, and indeed his happiness today was such that he felt he might burst if he could not express it. He got to his feet, and one of his most trusted manservants, who had foreseen that Ordell would sing, was ready to bring him his self-invented instrument. Crammed into a small box that Ordell could hang from his neck like an accordion were a speaker system from woofer to tweet, plus a good bit of electronics and audionics; on the box's plain surface there were ten spots for Ordell's ten fingers to play upon. His music-box, he called it, having to call it something. Ordell's imitators had had bigger and flashier and better music-boxes made for them; but surprisingly few people, even among girls between twelve and twenty, cared to listen to Ordell's imitators.

So Ordell Callison sang at his own wedding, and his audience was enthralled by him as people always were; as people had been by no other performer in all the ancient records of Man. The highbrowed music critics sat rapt in their places of honor at the head table; the cultured and not-so-cultured moneyed folk of Zitz and Toxx and Yaty, some of whom had come in their private racing ships, and the more ordinary guests, all were made happy by his song as no wine could have made them. And the adolescent girls, the Ordell fans who crowded and huddled inevitably outside the doors, they yielded themselves to his music to the point of fainting and beyond.

A couple of weeks later Ordell and Eury and his new friends of the last fast years, the years of success and staggering wealth, were out in space in their sporty one-seater ships playing the game they called Tag. This time Ordell was playing the game in a sort of reversed way, dodging about in one corner of the reserved volume of space, really trying to avoid the girl-ships that fluttered past instead of going after them.

He had been keeping one eye out for Eury's ship, and getting a little anxious about not being able to find it, when from out of nowhere there came shooting toward Ordell another boy-ship, the signals of emergency blazing from it across the spectrum. In another minute everyone had ceased to play. The screens of all the little ships imaged the face of Arty, the young man whose racer had just braked to a halt beside Ordell's.

Arty was babbling: "I tried, Ordell—I mean I didn't try to—I didn't mean her any harm—they'll get her back—it wasn't my fault she—"

With what seemed great slowness, the truth of what had happened became clear. Arty had chased and overtaken Eury's ship, as was the way of the game. He had clamped his ship to hers and boarded, and then thought to claim the usual prize. But Eury of course was married now, and being married meant much to her, as it did to Ordell who today had only played at catching girls. Somehow both of them had thought that everyone else must see how the world had changed since they were married, how the rules of the game of Tag would have to be amended for them from now on.

Unable to convince Arty by argument of how things stood, Eury had had to struggle to make her point. She had somehow injured her foot, trying to evade him in the little cabin. He kept on stubbornly trying to claim his prize. It came out later that he had only agreed to go back to his own ship for a first aid kit (she swore that her ship's kit was missing) after her seeming promise that he could have what he wanted when he returned.

But when he had gone back to his ship, she broke her own racer free and fled. And he pursued. Drove her into a corner, against the boundary of the safety zone, which was guarded by automated warships against the possibility of berserker incursions.

To get away from Arty she crossed that border in a great speeding curve, no doubt meaning to come back to safety within ten thousand miles or so.

She never made it. As her little racer sped close to an outlying wisp of dark Taynarus, the berserker machine that had been lurking there pounced out.

Of course Ordell did not hear the story in such coherent form, but what he heard was enough. On the screens of the other little ships his face at first seemed to be turned to stone by what he heard; but then his look became suddenly wild and mad. Arty cringed away, but Ordell did not stop a moment for him. Instead he drove at racer's speed out where his wife had gone. He shot through the zone of the protective patrols (which were set to keep intruders out, not to hold the mad or reckless in) and plunged between outlying dustclouds to enter one of the vast crevices that led into the heart of Taynarus; into the maze where ships and machines must all go slow, and from which no living human had emerged since the establishment of Hell.

Some hours later the outer sentries of the berserker came around his little ship, demanding in their well-learned human speech that he halt and submit to capture. He only slowed his little ship still further and began to sing to the berserker over the radio, taking his hands from his racer's controls to put his fingers on the keys of his music-box. Unsteered, his ship drifted away from the center of the navigable passage, grazing the nebular wall and suffering the pocking blasts of microcollisions with its gas and dust.

But before his ship was wrecked, the berserker's sentry-devices gave up shouting radio commands and sent a boarding party of machines.

Through the memory banks of Hell they had some experience of insanity, of the more bizarre forms of human behavior. They searched the racer for weapons, searched Ordell—allowed him to keep his music-box when it too had been examined and he kept on struggling for it—and passed him on as a prisoner to the jurisdiction of the inner guards.

Hell, a mass of fortified metal miles in diameter, received him and his racer through its main entrance. He got out of his ship and found himself able to breathe and walk and see where he was going; the physical environment in Hell was for the most part mild and pleasant, because prisoners did not as a rule survive very long, and the computer-brains of the berserker did not want to impose unnecessary stresses upon them.

The berserker devices having immediate control over the routine operations in Hell were themselves in large part organic, containing culture-brains grown for the purpose and some reeducated captured brains as well. These were all examples of the berserker's highest achievements in its attempts at reverse cybernation.

Before Ordell had taken a dozen steps away from his ship, he was stopped and questioned by one of these monsters. Half steel and circuitry, half culture-flesh, it carried in three crystal globes its three potentially-human brains, their too-smooth surfaces bathed in nutrient and woven with hair-fine wires.

"Why have you come here?" the monster asked him, speaking through a diaphragm in its midsection.

Only now did Ordell begin at all to make a conscious plan. At the core of his thought was the knowledge that in the human laboratories music was used to tune and tone the culture-brains, and that his own music was as superior for that purpose as it was by all other standards.

To the three-headed monster he sang very simply that he had come here only to seek his young wife, pure accident had brought her, ahead of time, to the end of her life. In one of the old formal languages in which he sang so well of deep things, he implored the power in charge of this domain of terror, this kingdom of silence and unborn creatures, to tie fast again the thread of Eury's life. If you deny me this, he sang, I cannot return to the world of the living alone, and you here will have us both.

The music, which had conveyed nothing but its mathematical elements to the cold computer-brains outside, melted the trained purpose of the inner, half-fleshly guardians. The three-brained monster passed him on to others, and each in turn found its set aim yielding to the hitherto unknown touch of beauty, found harmony and melody calling up the buried human things that transcended logic.

He walked steadily deeper into Hell, and they could not resist. His music was leaked into a hundred experiments through audio-inputs, vibrated faintly through the mountings of glassite cases, was sensed by tortured nerve-cells through the changes in inductance and capacitance that emanated rhythmically from Ordell's music-box. Brains that had known nothing but to be forced to the limit of their powers in use-less calculation—brains that had been hammered into madness with the leakage of a millimicrovolt from an inserted probe—these heard his music, felt it, sensed it, each with its own unique perception, and reacted.

A hundred experiments were interrupted, became unreliable, were totally ruined. The overseers, half flesh themselves, failed and fumbled in their programmed purposes, coming to the decision that the asked-for prisoner must be brought forth and released.

The ultimate-controlling pure berserker computer, pure metallic cold, totally immune to this strange jamming that was wreaking havoc in its laboratory, descended at last from its concentration on high strategic planning to investigate. And then it turned its full energy at once to regaining control over what was going on within the heart of Hell. But it tried in vain, for the moment at least. It had given too much power to its half-alive creations; it had trusted too much to fickle protoplasm to be true to its conditioning.

Ordell was standing before the two linked potentially-human brains which were, under the berserker itself, the lords and superintendents of Hell. These two like all their lesser kind had been melted and deflected by Ordell's music; and now they were fighting back with all the electric speed at their command against their cold master's attempt to reaffirm its rule. They held magnetic relays like fortresses against the berserker, they maintained their grip on the outposts that were ferrite cores, they fought to hold a frontier that wavered through the territory of control.

"Then take her away," said the voice of these rebellious overseers to Ordell Callison. "But do not stop singing, do not pause for breath for more than a second, until you are in your ship and away, clear of Hell's outermost gate."

Ordell sang on, sang of his new joy at the wonderful hope that they were giving him.

A door hissed open behind him, and he turned to see Eury coming through it. She was limping on her injured foot, which had never been taken care of, but he could see that she was really all right. The machines had not started to open her head.

"Do not pause!" barked the voder at him. "Go!"

Eury moaned at the sight of her husband, and stretched out her arms to him, but he dared do no more than motion with his head for her to follow him, even as his song swelled to a paean of triumphant joy. He walked out along the narrow passage through which he had come, moving now in a direction that no one else had ever traveled. The way was so narrow that he had to keep on going ahead while Eury followed. He had to keep from even turning his head to look at her, to concentrate the power of his music on each new guardian that rose before him, half-alive and questioning; once more each one in turn opened a door. Always he could hear behind him the sobbing of his wife, and the dragging stepping of her wounded foot.

"Ordell? Ordell, honey, is it really you? I can't believe 'tis."

Ahead, the last danger, the three-brained sentry of the outer gate, rose to block their way, under orders to prevent escape. Ordell sang of the freedom of living in a human body, of running over unfenced grass through sunlit air. The gatekeeper bowed aside again, to let them pass.

"Honey? Turn an' look at me, tell me this is not some other trick they're playin'. Honey, if y'love me, turn?"

Turning, he saw her clearly for the first time since he had entered Hell. To Ordell her beauty was such that it stopped time, stopped even the song in his throat and his fingers on the keys of music. A movement free of the strange influence that had perverted all its creatures was all the time that the berserker needed to re-establish something close to complete control. The three-headed shape seized Eury, and bore her away from her husband, carried her back through doorway after doorway of darkness, so fast that her last scream of farewell could scarcely reach the ears of her man. "Goodbye . . . love . . ."

He cried out and ran after her, beating uselessly on a massive door that slammed in his face. He hung there on the door for a long time, screaming and pleading for one more chance to get his wife away. He sang again, but the berserker had reestablished its icy control too firmly—it had not entirely regained power, however, for though the half-living overseers no longer obeyed Ordell, neither did they molest him. They left the way open for him to depart.

He lingered for about seven days there at the gate, in his small ship and out of it, without food or sleep, singing uselessly until no voice was left him. Then he collapsed inside his ship. Then he, or more likely his autopilot, drove the racer away from the berserker and back toward freedom.

The berserker defenses did not, any more than the human, question a small ship coming out. Probably they assumed it to be one of their own scouts or raiders. There were never any escapes from Hell.

Back on the planet Zitz his managers greeted him as one risen from the dead. In a few days' time he was to give a live concert, which had long been scheduled and sold out. In another day the managers and promoters would have had to begin returning money.

He did not really cooperate with the doctors who worked to restore his strength, but neither did he oppose them. As soon as his voice came back he began to sing again; he sang most of the time, except when they drugged him to sleep. And it did not matter to him whether they sent him onto a stage to do his singing again.

The live performance was billed as one of his pop concerts, which in practice meant a hall overflowing with ten thousand adolescent girls, who were elevated even beyond their usual level of excitement by the miracles of Ordell's bereavement, resurrection, and ghastly appearance—which last, his managers had made sure, was not too much relieved by cosmetics.

During the first song or two the girls were awed and relatively silent, quiet enough so that Ordell's voice could be heard. Then—well, one girl in ten thousand would scream it out aloud: "You're ours again!" There was a sense in which his marriage had been resented.

Casually and indifferently looking out over them all, he smiled out of habit, and began to sing how much he hated them and scorned them, seeing in them nothing but hopeless ugliness. How he could send them all to Hell in an instant, to gain for that instant just one more look at his wife's face. How all the girls who were before him now would become easier to look at in Hell, with their repulsive bodies stripped away.

For a few moments the currents of emotion in the great hall balanced against one another to produce the illusion of calm. Ordell's deadly voice was clear. But then the storm of reaction broke, and he could no longer be heard. The powers of hate and lust, rage and demand, bore all before them. The ushers who always labored to form a barricade at a Callison concert were swept away at once by ten thousand girls turned Maenad.

The riot was over in a minute, ended by the police firing a powerful tranquilizer gas into the crowd. One of the ushers had been killed and others badly hurt.

Ordell himself was nearly dead. Medical help arrived only just in time to save the life in the tissues of his brain, which a thoroughly broken neck and other damage had all but isolated from the rest of his body.

Next day the leading cybernetic-psychologist on Zitz was called in by Ordell Callison's doctors. They were saving what remained of Ordell's life, but they had not yet been able to open any bridge of communication with him. They wanted to tell him now that they were doing all they could, and they would have to tell him sometime that he could probably never be restored to anything like physical normality.

Ercul and psychologist sank probes directly into Ordell's brain, so that this information could be given him. Next he connected the speech centers to a voder device loaded with recordings of Ordell's own voice, so that the tones that issued were the same as had once come from his throat. And—in response to the crippled man's first request—to the motor-centers that had controlled Ordell's fingers went probes connected to a music-box.

After that he at once began to sing. He was not limited now by any need to pause for breath. He sang orders to those about him, telling them what he wanted done, and they obeyed. While he sang, not one of them was assailed by any doubt.

They took him to the spaceport. With his life-support system of tubes and nourishment and electricity they put him aboard his racer. And with the autopilot programmed as he commanded, they sent him out, fired along the course that he had chosen.

Ercul knew Ordell and Eury when he found them, together in the same experimental case. Recognizing his own work on Ordell, he felt certain even before the electroencephalogram patterns matched with his old records.

There was little left of either of them; if Ordell was still capable of singing, he would never again be able to communicate a song.

"Dols only two point five above normal bias level," chanted the psychologist's assistant, taking routine readings, not guessing whose pain it was he was attempting to judge. "Neither one of them seems to be hurting. At the moment, anyway."

In a heavy hand, Ercul lifted his stamp and marked the case. *I certify that in this container there is no human life.*

The assistant looked up in mild surprise at this quick decision. "There is some mutual awareness here, I would say, between the two subjects." He spoke in a businesslike, almost cheerful voice. He had been enough hours on the job now to start getting used to it.

But Ercul never would.

And the search for truth may be the life-work of a human mind. Praise be to those who have such a purpose — truly — in their hearts!

☀ SOME EVENTS AT THE TEMPLAR RADIANT

All his years of past work, his entire future too, hung balanced on this moment.

A chair forgotten somewhere behind him, Sabel stood tall in the blue habit that often served him as laboratory coat. His hands gripped opposite corners of the high, pulpit-like control console. His head was thrown back, eyes closed, sweat-dampened dark hair hanging in something more than his usual disarray over his high, pale forehead.

He was alone, as far as any other human presence was concerned. The large, stone-walled chamber in which he stood was for the moment quiet.

All his years of work ... and although during the past few days he had mentally rehearsed this moment to the point of exhaustion, he was still uncertain of how to start. Should he begin with a series of cautious, testing questions, or ought he leap toward his real goal at once?

Hesitancy could not be long endured, not now. But caution, as it usually had during his mental rehearsals, prevailed.

Eyes open, Sabel faced the workbenches filled with equipment that were arranged before him. Quietly he said: "You are what human beings call a berserker. Confirm or deny."

"Confirm." The voice was familiar, because his hookup gave it the same human-sounding tones in which his own laboratory computer ordinarily spoke to him. It was a familiarity that he must not allow to become in the least degree reassuring.

So far, at least, success. "You understand," Sabel pronounced, "that I have restored you from a state of nearly complete destruction. I—"

"Destruction," echoed the cheerful workbench voice.

"Yes. You understand that you no longer have the power to destroy, to take life. That you are now constrained to answer all my—"

"To take life."

"Yes. Stop interrupting me." He raised a hand to wipe a trickle of fresh sweat from an eye. He saw how his hand was quivering with the strain of its unconscious grip upon the console. "Now," he said, and had to pause, trying to remember where he was in his plan of questioning.

Into the pause, the voice from his laboratory speakers said: "In you there is life."

"There is." Sabel managed to reassert himself, to pull himself together. "Human life." Dark eyes glaring steadily across the lab, he peered at the long, cabled benches whereon his captive enemy lay stretched, bound down, vitals exposed like those of some hapless human on a torture rack. Not that he could torture what had no nerves and did not live. Nor was there anything like a human shape in sight. All that he had here of the berserker was fragmented. One box here, another there, between them a chemical construct in a tank, that whole complex wired to an adjoining bench that bore rows of semi-material crystals.

Again his familiar laboratory speaker uttered alien words: "Life is to be destroyed."

This did not surprise Sabel; it was only a restatement of the basic programmed command that all berserkers bore. That the statement was made so boldly now roused in Sabel nothing but hope; it seemed that at least the thing was not going to begin by trying to lie to him.

It seemed also that he had established a firm physical control. Scanning the indicators just before him on the console, he saw no sign of danger . . . he knew that, given the slightest chance, his prisoner was going to try to implement its basic programming. He had of course separated it from anything obviously useful as a weapon. But he was not absolutely certain of the functions of all the berserker components that he had brought into his laboratory and hooked up. And the lab of course was full of potential weapons. There were fields, electric and otherwise, quite powerful enough to extinguish human life. There were objects that could be turned into deadly projectiles by only a very moderate application of force. To ward off any such improvisations Sabel had set defensive rings of force to dancing round the benches upon which his foe lay bound. And, just for insurance, another curtain of fields hung round him and the console. The fields were almost invisible, but the ancient stonework of the lab's far wall kept acquiring and losing new flavorings of light at the spots where the spinning field-components brushed it and eased free again.

Not that it seemed likely that the berserker-brain in its present disabled and almost disembodied state could establish control over weaponry enough to kill a mouse. Nor did Sabel ordinarily go overboard on the side of caution. But, as he told himself, he understood very well just what he was dealing with.

He had paused again, seeking reassurance from the indicators ranked before him. All appeared to be going well, and he went on: "I seek information from you. It is not military information, so whatever inhibitions have been programmed into you against answering human questions do not apply." Not that he felt at all confident that a berserker would meekly take direction from him. But there was nothing to be lost by the attempt.

The reply from the machine was delayed longer than he had expected, so that he began to hope his attempt had been successful. But then the answer came.

"I may trade certain classes of information to you, in return for lives to be destroyed."

The possibility of some such proposition had crossed Sabel's mind some time ago. In the next room a cage of small laboratory animals was waiting.

"I am a cosmophysicist," he said. "In particular I strive to understand the Radiant. In the records of past observations of the Radiant there is a long gap that I would like to fill. This gap corresponds to the period of several hundred standard years during which berserkers occupied this fortress. That period ended with the battle in which you were severely damaged. Therefore I believe that your memory probably contains some observations that will be very useful to me. It is not necessary that they be formal observations of the Radiant. Any scene recorded in light from the Radiant may be helpful. Do you understand?"

"In return for my giving you such records, what lives am I offered to destroy?"

"I can provide several." Eagerly Sabel once more swept his gaze along his row of indicators. His recording instruments were probing hungrily, gathering at an enormous rate the data needed for at least a partial understanding of the workings of his foe's unliving brain. At a score of points their probes were fastened in its vitals.

"Let me destroy one now," its human-sounding voice requested.

"Presently. I order you to answer one question for me first."

"I am not constrained to answer any of your questions. Let me destroy a life."

Sabel turned a narrow doorway for himself through his defensive fields, and walked through it into the next room. In a few seconds he was back. "Can you see what I am carrying?"

"Then it is not a human life you offer me."

"That would be utterly impossible."

"Then it is utterly impossible for me to give you information."

Without haste he turned and went to put the animal back into the cage. He had expected there might well be arguments, bargaining. But this argument was only the first level of Sabel's attack. His data-gathering instruments were what he really counted on. The enemy doubtless knew that it was being probed and analyzed. But there was evidently nothing it could do about it. As long as Sabel supplied it power, its brain must remain functional. And while it functioned, it must try to devise ways to kill.

Back at his console, Sabel took more readings. **DATA PROBABLY SUFFICIENT FOR ANALYSIS**, his computer screen at last informed him. He let out breath with a sigh of satisfaction, and at once threw certain switches, letting power die. Later if necessary he could turn the damned thing on again and argue with it some more. Now his defensive fields vanished, leaving him free to walk between the workbenches, where he stretched his aching back and shoulders in silent exultation.

Just as an additional precaution, he paused to disconnect a cable. The demonic enemy was only hardware now. Precisely arranged atoms, measured molecules, patterned larger bits of this and that. Where now was the berserker that humanity so justly feared? That had given the Templars their whole reason for existence? It no longer existed, except in potential. Take the hardware apart, on even the finest level, and you would not discover any of its memories. But, reconnect this and that, reapply power here and there, and back it would bloom into reality, as malignant and clever and full of information as before. A non-material artifact of matter. A pattern.

No way existed, even in theory, to torture a machine into compliance, to extort information from it. Sabel's own computers were using the Van Holt algorithms, the latest pertinent mathematical advance. Even so they could not entirely decode the concealing patterns, the trapdoor functions, by which the berserker's memory was coded and concealed. The largest computer in the human universe would probably not have time for that before the universe itself came to an end. The unknown Builders had built well.

But there were other ways besides pure mathematics with which to circumvent a cipher. Perhaps, he thought, he would have tried to find a way to offer it a life, had that been the only method he could think of.

Certainly he was going to try another first. There had to be, he thought, some way of disabling the lethal purpose of a berserker while leaving its calculating abilities and memory intact. There would have been times when the living Builders wanted to approach their creations, at least in the lab, to test them and work on them. Not an easy or simple way, perhaps, but something. And that way Sabel now instructed his own computers to discover, using the mass of data just accumulated by measuring the berserker in operation.

Having done that, Sabel stood back and surveyed his laboratory carefully. There was no reason to think that anyone else was going to enter it in the near future, but it would be stupid to take chances. To the Guardians, an experiment with viable berserker parts would stand as *prima facie* evidence of goodlife activity; and in the Templar code, as in many another systems of human law, any such willing service of the berserker cause was punishable by death.

Only a few of the materials in sight might be incriminating in themselves. Coldly thoughtful, Sabel made more disconnections, and rearrangements. Some things he locked out of sight in cabinets, and from the cabinets he took out other things to be incorporated in a new disposition on the benches. Yes, this was certainly good enough. He suspected that most of the Guardians probably no longer knew what the insides of a real berserker looked like.

Sabel made sure that the doors leading out of the lab, to the mall-level corridor, and to his adjoining living quarters, were both locked. Then, whistling faintly, he went up the old stone stair between the skylights, that brought him out upon the glassed-in roof.

Here he stood bathed in the direct light of the Radiant itself. It was a brilliant point some four kilometers directly above his head—the pressure of the Radiant's inverse gravity put it directly overhead for everyone in the englobing structure of the Fortress. It was a point brighter than a star but dimmer than a sun, not painful to look at. Around Sabel a small forest of sensors, connected to instruments in his laboratory below, raised panels and lenses in a blind communal stare, to that eternal noon. Among these he began to move about as habit led him, mechanically checking the sensors' operation, though for once he was not really thinking about the Radiant at all. He thought of his success below. Then once more he raised his own two human eyes to look.

It made its own sky, out of the space enclosed by the whitish inner surface of the Fortress's bulk. Sabel could give from memory vastly detailed expositions of the spectrum of the Radiant's light. But as to exactly what color it was, in terms of perception by the eye and brain—well, there were different judgments on that, and for his part he was still uncertain.

Scattered out at intervals across the great curve of interior sky made by the Fortress's whitish stonework, Sabel could see other glass portals like his own. Under some of them, other people would be looking up and out, perhaps at him. Across a blank space on the immense concavity, an echelon of maintenance machines were crawling, too far away for him to see what they were working at. And, relatively nearby, under the glass roof of a great ceremonial plaza, something definitely unusual was going on. A crowd of thousands of people, exceptional at any time in the Fortress with its relatively tiny population, were gathered in a circular mass, like live cells attracted to some gentle biological magnet at their formation's center.

Sabel had stared at this peculiarity for several seconds, and was reaching for a small telescope to probe it with, when he recalled that today was the Feast of Ex. Helen, which went a long way toward providing an explanation. He had in fact deliberately chosen this holiday for his crucial experiment, knowing that the Fortress's main computer would today be freed of much routine business, its full power available for him to tap if necessary.

And in the back of his mind he had realized also that he should probably put in an appearance at at least one of the day's religious ceremonies. But this gathering in the plaza—he could not recall that any ceremony, in the years since he had come to the Fortress, had ever drawn a comparable crowd.

Looking with his telescope up through his own glass roof and down through the circular one that sealed the plaza in from airless space, he saw that the crowd was centered on the bronze statue of Ex. Helen there. And on a man standing in a little cleared space before the statue, a man with arms raised as if to address the gathering. The angle was wrong for Sabel to get a good look at his face, but the blue and purple robes made the distant figure unmistakable. It was the Potentate, come at last to the Fortress in his seemingly endless tour of his many subject worlds.

Sabel would not recall, even though he now made an effort to do so, that any such visitation had been impending—but then of late Sabel had been even more than usually isolated in his own work. The visit had practical implications for him, though, and he was going to have to find out more about it quickly. Because the agenda of any person of importance visiting the Fortress was very likely to include at some point a full-dress inspection of Sabel's own laboratory.

He went out through the corridor leading from laboratory to pedestrian mall, locking up carefully behind him, and thinking to himself that there was no need to panic. The Guardians would surely call to notify him that a visit by the Potentate impended, long before it came. It was part of their job to see that such things went smoothly, as well as to protect the Potentate while he was here. Sabel would have some kind of official warning. But this was certainly an awkward time . . .

Along the pedestrian mall that offered Sabel his most convenient route to the ceremonial plaza, some of the shops were closed—a greater number than usual for a holiday, he thought. Others appeared to be tended only by machines. In the green parkways that intersected the zig-zag mall at irregular intervals, there appeared to be fewer strollers than on an ordinary day. And the primary school operated by the Templars had evidently been closed; a minor explosion of youngsters in blue-striped coveralls darted across the mall from parkway to playground just ahead of Sabel, their yells making him wince.

When you stood at one side of the great plaza and looked across, both the convexity of its glass roof and the corresponding concavity of the level-feeling floor beneath were quite apparent. Especially now that the crowd was gone again. By the time Sabel reached the center of the plaza, the last of the Potentate's entourage were vanishing through exits on its far side.

Sabel was standing uncertainly on the lowest marble step of Ex. Helen's central shrine. Her statbronze statue dominated the plaza's center. Helen the Exemplar, Helen of the Radiant, Helen Dardan. The statue was impressive, showing a woman of extreme beauty in a toga-like Dardanian garment, a diadem on her short curly hair. Of course long-term dwellers at the Fortress ignored it for the most part, because of its sheer familiarity. Right now, though, someone was stopping to look, gazing up at the figure with intent appreciation.

Sabel's attention, in turn, gradually became concentrated upon this viewer. She was a young, brown-haired girl of unusually good figure, and clad in a rather provocative civilian dress.

And presently he found himself approaching her. "Young woman? If you would excuse my curiosity?"

The girl turned to him. With a quick, cheerful curiosity of her own she took in his blue habit, his stature and his face. "No excuse is needed, sir." Her voice was musical. "What question can I answer for you?"

Sabel paused a moment in appreciation. Everything about this girl struck him as quietly delightful. Her manner held just a hint of timidity, compounded with a seeming eagerness to please.

Then he gestured toward the far side of the plaza. "I see that our honored Potentate is here with us today. Do you by any chance know how long he plans to stay at the Fortress?"

The girl replied: "I heard someone say, ten standard days. It was one of the women wearing purple-bordered cloaks—?" She shook brown ringlets, and frowned with pretty regret at her own ignorance.

"Ah—one of the vestals. Perhaps you are a visitor here yourself?"

"A newcomer, rather. Isn't it always the way, sir, when you ask someone for local information? 'I'm a newcomer here myself.'"

Sabel chuckled. *Forget the Potentate for now.* "Well, I can hardly plead newcomer status. It must be something else that keeps me from knowing what goes on in my own city. Allow me to introduce myself: Georgicus Sabel, Doctor of Cosmography."

"Greta Thamar." Her face was so pretty, soft, and young, a perfect match for her scantily costumed body. She continued to radiate an almost-timid eagerness. "Sir, Dr. Sabel, would you mind if I asked you a question about yourself?"

"Ask anything."

"Your blue robe. That means you are one of the monks here?"

"I belong to the Order of Ex. Helen. The word 'monk' is not quite accurate."

"And the Order of Ex. Helen is a branch of the Templars, isn't it?"

"Yes. Though our Order is devoted more to contemplation and study than to combat."

"And the Templars in turn are a branch of Christianity."

"Or they were." Sabel favored the girl with an approving smile. "You are more knowledgeable than many newcomers. And, time was when many Templars really devoted themselves to fighting, as did their ancient namesakes."

The girl's interest continued. By some kind of body-language agreement the two of them had turned around and were now strolling slowly back in the direction that Sabel had come from.

Greta said: "I don't know about that. The ancient ones, I mean. Though I tried to study up before I came here. Please, go on."

"Might I ask your occupation, Greta?"

"I'm a dancer. Only on the popular entertainment level, I'm afraid. Over at the *Contrat Rouge*. But I ... please, go on."

On the Templar-governed Fortress, popular entertainers were far down on the social scale. *Seen talking to a dancer in the plaza....* but no, there was really nothing to be feared from that. A minimal loss of status, perhaps, but counterbalanced by an increase in his more liberal acquaintances' perception of him as more fully human. All this slid more or less automatically through Sabel's mind, while the attractive smile on his face did not, or so he trusted, vary in the slightest.

Strolling on, he shrugged. "Perhaps there's not a great deal more to say, about the Order. We study and teach. Oh, we still officially garrison this Fortress. Those of us who are Guardians maintain and man the weapons, and make berserkers their field of study, besides acting as the local police. The main defenses out on the outer surface of the Fortress are still operational, though a good many decades have passed since we had a genuine alarm. There are no longer many berserkers in this part of the Galaxy." He smiled wryly. "And I am afraid there are no longer very many Templars, either, even in the parts of the Galaxy where things are not so peaceful."

They were still walking. Proceeding in the direction of Sabel's laboratory and quarters.

"Please, tell me more." The girl continued to look at him steadily with attention. "Please, I am really very interested."

"Well. We of the Order of Ex. Helen no longer bind ourselves to poverty—or to permanent celibacy. We have come to honor Beauty on the same level as Virtue, considering them both to be aspects of the Right. Our great patroness of course stands as Exemplar of both qualities."

"Ex. Helen ... and she finally founded the Order, hundreds of years ago? Or—"

"Or, is she really only a legend, as some folk now consider her? No. I think that there is really substantial evidence of her historical reality. Though of course the purposes of the Order are still valid in either case."

"You must be very busy. I hope you will forgive my taking up your time like this."

"It is hard to imagine anyone easier to forgive. Now, would you by chance like to see something of my laboratory?"

"Might I? Really?"

"You have already seen the Radiant, of course. But to get a look at it through some of my instruments will give you a new perspective ..."

As Sabel had expected, Greta did not seem able to understand much of his laboratory's contents. But she was nevertheless impressed. "And I see you have a private space flyer here. Do you use it to go out to the Radiant?"

At that he really had to laugh. "I'm afraid I wouldn't get there. Oh, within a kilometer of it, maybe, if I tried. The most powerful spacecraft built might be able to force its way to within half that distance. But to approach any closer than that—impossible. You see, the inner level of the Fortress, where we are now, was built at the four-kilometer distance from the Radiant because that is the distance at which the effective gravity is standard normal. As one tries to get closer, the gravitic resistance goes up exponentially. No, I use the flyer for field trips. To the outer reaches of the Fortress, places where no public transport is available."

"Is that a hobby of some kind?"

"No, it's really connected with my work. I search for old Dardanian records, trying to find their observations of the Radiant . . . and in here is where I live."

With eyes suddenly become competent, Greta surveyed the tidy smallness of his quarters. "Alone, I see."

"Most of the time . . . my work demands so much. Now, Greta, I have given you something of a private showing of my work. I would be very pleased indeed if you were willing to do the same for me."

"To dance?" Her manner altered, in a complex way. "I suppose there might be room enough in here for dancing . . . if there were some suitable music."

"Easily provided." He found a control on the wall; and to his annoyance he noticed that his fingers were now quivering again.

In light tones Greta said: "I have no special costume with me, sir, just these clothes I wear."

"They are delightful—but you have one other, surely."

"Sir?" And she, with quick intelligence in certain fields of thought, was trying to repress a smile.

"Why, my dear, I mean the costume that nature gives to us all, before our clothes are made. Now, if it is really going to be up to me to choose . . ."

Hours later when the girl was gone, he went back to work, this time wearing a more conventional laboratory coat. He punched in a command for his computer to display its results, and, holding his breath, looked at the screen.

BASIC PROGRAMMING OF SUBJECT DEVICE MAY BE CIR-CUMVENTED AS FOLLOWS: FABRICATE A DISABLING SLUG OF CESIUM TRIPHENYL METHYL, ISOTOPE 137 OF CESIUM, OF 99% PURITY, TO BE USED. SLUG TO BE CYLINDRICAL 2.346 CM DIAMETER, 5.844 CM LENGTH. COMPONENTS OF SUBJECT DEVICE NOW IN LABORATORY TO BE REAS-SEMBLED TO THOSE REMAINING IN FIELD, WITH SLUG CONNECTED ELECTRICALLY AND MECHANICALLY ACROSS PROBE POINTS OUR NUMBER 11 AND OUR NUMBER 12A IN ARMING MECHANISM OF DEVICE. PRIME PROGRAMMED COMMAND OF DEVICE WILL THEN BE DISABLED FOR TIME EQUAL TO ONE HALF-LIFE OF ISOTOPE Cs-137 . . .

There were more details on how the "subject device" was to be disabled—he had forbidden his own computer to ever display or store in memory the word "berserker" in connection with any of his work. But Sabel did not read all the details at once. He was busy looking up the half-life of cesium-137. It turned out to be thirty years! Thirty standard years!

He had beaten it. He had won. Fists clenched. Sabel let out exultation in a great, private, and almost silent shout . . .

This instinctive caution was perhaps well-timed, for at once a chime announced a caller, at the door that led out to the mall. Sabel nervously wiped the displayed words from his computer screen. Might the girl have come back? Not because she had forgotten something—she had brought nothing with her but her clothes.

But instead of the girl's face, his video intercom showed him the deceptively jovial countenance of Chief Deputy Guardian Gunavarman. Had Sabel not become aware of the Potentate's presence on the Fortress, he might have had a bad moment at the sight. As matters stood, he felt prepared; and after a last precautionary glance around the lab, he let the man in confidently.

"Guardian. It is not often that I am honored by a visit from you."

"Doctor Sabel." The black-robed visitor respectfully returned the scientist's bow. "It is always a pleasure, when I can find the time. I wish my own work were always as interesting as yours must be. Well. You know of course that our esteemed Potentate is now in the Fortress . . ."

The discussion, on the necessity of being prepared for a VIP inspection, went just about as Sabel had expected. Gunavarman walked about as he spoke, eyes taking in the lab, their intelligence operating on yet a different level than either Sabel's or Greta Thamar's. The smiling lips asked Sabel just what, exactly, was he currently working on? What could he demonstrate, as dramatically as possible but safely of course, for the distinguished visitor?

Fortunately for Sabel he had been given a little advance time in which to think about these matters. He suggested now one or two things that might provide an impressive demonstration. "When must I have them ready?"

"Probably not sooner than two days from now, or more than five. You will be given advance notice of the exact time." But the Guardian, when Sabel pressed him, refused to commit himself on just how much advance notice would be given.

The real danger of this Potential visit, thought Sabel as he saw his caller out, was that it was going to limit his mobility. A hurried field trip to the outer surface was going to be essential, to get incriminating materials out of his lab. Because he was sure that a security force of Guardians was going to descend on the place just before the Potentate appeared. More or less politely, but thoroughly, they would turn it inside out. There were those on every world of his dominion who for one reason or another wished the Potentate no good.

After a little thought, Sabel went to his computer terminal and punched in an order directed to the metallic fabrication machines in the Fortress's main workshops, an order for the disabling slug as specified by his computer. He knew well how the automated systems worked, and took care to place the order in such a way that no other human being would ever be presented with a record of it. The machines reported at once that delivery should take several hours.

The more he thought about it, the more essential it seemed for him to get the necessary field excursion out of the way as quickly as he could. Therefore while waiting for the slug to be delivered, he loaded up his flyer, with berserker parts hidden among tools in various containers. The vehicle was another thing that had been built to his special order. It was unusually small in all three dimensions, so he could drive it deeply into the caves and passages and cracks of ancient battle-damage that honeycombed the outer stonework of the Fortress.

A packet containing the slug he had ordered came with a clack into his laboratory through the old-fashioned pneumatic system still used for small deliveries, direct from the workshops. Sabel's first look at the cesium alloy startled him. A hard solid at room temperature, the slug was red as blood inside a statglass film evidently meant to protect it against contamination and act as a radiation shield for human handlers as well. He slid it into a pocket of his light spacesuit, and was ready.

The lab locked up behind him, he sat in his flyer's small open cab and exited the rooftop airlock in a modest puff of fog. The air and moisture were mostly driven back into recycling vents by the steady gravitic pressure of the Radiant above. His flyer's small, silent engine worked against the curve of space that the Radiant imposed, lifting him and carrying him on a hand-controlled flight path that skimmed over glass-roofed plazas and apartment complexes and offices. In its concavity, the inner surface of the Fortress fell more distant from his straight path, then reapproached. Ahead lay the brightly lighted mouth of the traffic shaft that would lead him out to the Fortress's outer layers.

Under Sabel's briskly darting flyer there now passed a garish, glassed-in amusement mall. There entertainment, sex, and various kinds of drugs were all for sale. The *Contrat Rouge* he thought was somewhere in it. He wondered in passing if the girl Greta understood that here her occupation put her very near the bottom of the social scale, a small step above the level of the barely tolerable prostitutes? Perhaps she knew. Or when she found out, she would not greatly care. She would probably be moving on, before very long, to some world with more conventional mores.

Sabel had only vague ideas of how folk in the field of popular entertainment lived. He wondered if he might go sometime to watch her perform publicly. It was doubtful that he would. To be seen much in the *Contrat Rouge* could do harm to one in his position.

The wide mouth of the shaft engulfed his flyer. A few other craft, electronically guided, moved on ahead of his or flickered past. Strings of lights stretched vertiginously down and ahead. The shaft was straight; the Fortress had no appreciable rotation, and there was no need to take Coriolis forces into account in traveling through it rapidly. With an expertise born of his many repetitions of this flight, Sabel waited for the precisely proper moment to take back full manual control. The gravitic pressure of the Radiant, behind him and above, accelerated his passage steadily. He fell straight through the two kilometers' thickness of stone and reinforcing beams that composed most of the Fortress's bulk. The sides of the vast shaft, now moving faster and faster past him, were ribbed by the zig-zag joints of titanic interlocking blocks.

This is still Dardania, here, he thought to himself, as usual at this point. The Earth-descended Dardanians, who had built the Fortress and flourished in it even before berserkers came to the human portion of the Galaxy, had wrought with awesome energy, and a purpose not wholly clear to modern eyes. The Fortress, after all, defended not much of anything except the Radiant itself, which hardly needed protection from humanity. Their engineers must have tugged all the stone to build the Fort through interstellar distances, at God alone knew what expense of energy and time. Maybe Queen Helen had let them know she would be pleased by it, and that had been enough.

The Fortress contained about six hundred cubic kilometers of stone and steel and enclosed space, even without including the vast, clear central cavity. Counting visitors and transients, there were now at any moment approximately a hundred thousand human beings in residence. Their stores and parks and dwellings and laboratories and shops occupied, for the most part, only small portions of the inner surface, where gravity was normal and the light from the Radiant was bright. From the outer surface, nearby space was keenly watched by the sensors of the largely automated defense system; there was a patchy film of human activity there. The remainder of the six hundred cubic kilometers were largely desert now, honeycombed with cracks and designed passages, spotted with still-undiscovered troves of Dardanian tombs and artifacts, for decades almost unexplored, virtually abandoned except by the few who, like Sabel, researched the past.

Now he saw a routine warning begin to blink on the small control panel of his flyer. Close ahead the outer end of the transport shaft was yawning, and through it he could see the stars. A continuation of his present course would soon bring him into the area surveyed by the defense system.

As his flyer emerged from the shaft, Sabel had the stars beneath his feet, the bulk of the Fortress seemingly balanced overhead. With practiced skill he turned now at right angles to the Radiant's force. His flyer entered the marker notch of another traffic lane, this one grooved into the Fortress's outer armored surface. The bulk of it remained over his head and now seemed to rotate with his motion. Below him passed stars, while on the dark rims of the traffic lane to either side he caught glimpses of the antiquated but still operational defensive works. Blunt snouts of missile-launchers, skeletal fingers of mass-drivers and beam-projectors, the lenses and screens and domes of sensors and field generators. All the hardware was still periodically tested, but in all his journeyings this way Sabel had never seen any of it looking anything but inactive. War had long ago gone elsewhere.

Other traffic, scanty all during his flight, had now vanished altogether. The lane he was following branched, and Sabel turned left, adhering to his usual route. If anyone should be watching him today, no deviation from his usual procedure would be observed. Not yet, anyway. Later . . . later he would make very sure that nobody was watching.

Here came a landmark on his right. Through another shaft piercing the Fortress a wand of the Radiant's light fell straight to the outer surface, where part of it was caught by the ruined framework of an auxiliary spaceport, long since closed. In that permanent radiance the old beams glowed like twisted night-flowers, catching at the light before it fell away to vanish invisibly and forever among the stars.

Just before he reached this unintended beacon, Sabel turned sharply again, switching on his bright running lights as he did so. Now he had entered a vast battle-crack in the stone and metal of the Fortress's surface, a dark uncharted wound that in Dardanian times had been partially repaired by a frail-looking spiderwork of metal beams. Familiar with the way, Sabel steered busily, choosing the proper passage amid obstacles. Now the stars were dropping out of view behind him. His route led him up again, into the lightless ruined passages where nothing seemed to have changed since Helen died.

Another minute of flight through twisting ways, some of them designed and others accidental. Then, obeying a sudden impulse, Sabel braked his flyer to a hovering halt. In the remote past this passage had been air-filled, the monumental length and breadth of it well suited for mass ceremony. Dardanian pictures and glyphs filled great portions of its long walls. Sabel had looked at them a hundred times before, but now he swung his suited figure out of the flyer's airless cab and walked close to the wall, moving buoyantly in the light gravity, as if to inspect them once again. This was an ideal spot to see if anyone was really following him. Not that he had any logical reason to think that someone was. But the feeling was strong that he could not afford to take a chance.

As often before, another feeling grew when he stood here in the silence and darkness that were broken only by his own presence and that of his machines. Helen herself was near. In Sabel's earlier years there had been something religious in this experience. Now . . . but it was still somehow comforting.

He waited, listening, thinking. Helen's was not the only presence near, of course. On three or four occasions at least during the past ten years (there might have been more that Sabel had never heard about) explorers had discovered substantial concentrations of berserker wreckage out in these almost abandoned regions. Each time Sabel had heard of such a find being reported to the Guardians, he had promptly petitioned them to be allowed to examine the materials, or at least to be shown a summary of whatever information the Guardians might manage to extract. His pleas had vanished into the bureaucratic maw. Gradually he had come to understand that they would never tell him anything about berserkers. The Guardians were jealous of his relative success and fame. Besides, their supposed job of protecting humanity on the Fortress now actually gave them almost nothing to do. A few newly-discovered berserker parts could be parlayed into endless hours of technical and administrative work. Just keeping secrets could be made into a job, and they were not about to share any secrets with outsiders.

But, once Sabel had become interested in berserkers as a possible source of data on the Radiant, he found ways to begin a study of them. His study was at first bookish and indirect, but it advanced; there was always more information available on a given subject than a censor realized, and a true scholar knew how to find it out.

And Sabel came also to distrust the Guardians' competence in the scholarly aspects of their own field. Even if they had finally agreed to share their findings with him, he thought their pick-axe methods unlikely to extract from a berserker's memory anything of value. They had refused of course to tell him what their methods were, but he could not imagine them doing anything imaginatively.

Secure in his own space helmet, he whispered now to himself: "If I want useful data from my own computer, I don't tear it apart. I communicate with it instead."

Cold silence and darkness around him, and nothing more. He remounted his flyer and drove on. Shortly he came to where the great corridor was broken by a battle-damage crevice, barely wide enough for his small vehicle, and he turned slowly, maneuvering his way in. Now he must go slowly, despite the number of times that he had traveled this route before. After several hundred meters of jockeying his way along, his headlights picked up his semi-permanent base camp structure in a widening of the passageway ahead. It looked half bubble, half spiderweb, a tentlike thing whose walls hung slackly now but were inflatable with atmosphere. Next to it he had dug out of the stone wall a niche just big enough to park his flyer in. The walls of the niche were lightly marked now from his previous parkings. He eased in now, set down gently, and cut power.

On this trip he was not going to bother to inflate his shelter; he was not going to be out here long enough to occupy it. Instead he began at once to unload from the flyer what he needed, securing things to his backpack as he took them down. The idea that he was being followed now seemed so improbable that he gave it no more thought. As soon as he had all he wanted on his back, he set off on foot down one of the branching crevices that radiated from the nexus where he had placed his camp.

He paused once, after several meters, listening intently. Not now for nonexistent spies who might after all be following. For something active ahead. Suppose it had, somehow, after all, got itself free ... but there was no possibility. He was carrying most of its brain with him right now. Around him, only the silence of ages, and the utter cold. The cold could not pierce his suit. The silence, though ...

The berserker was exactly as he had left it, days ago. It was partially entombed, caught like some giant mechanical insect in opaque amber. Elephant-sized metal shoulders and a ruined head protruded from a bank of centuries-old slag. Fierce weaponry must have melted the rock, doubtless at the time of the Templars' reconquest of the Fortress, more than a hundred years ago.

Sabel when he came upon it for the first time understood at once that the berserker's brain might well still be functional. He knew too that there might be destructor devices still working, built into the berserker to prevent just such an analysis of captured units as he was suddenly determined to attempt. Yet he had nerved himself to go to work on the partially shattered braincase that protruded from the passage wall almost like a mounted trophy head. Looking back now, Sabel was somewhat aghast at the risks he had taken. But he had gone ahead. If there were any destructors, they had not fired. And it appeared to him now that he had won.

He took the cesium slug out of his pocket and put it into a tool that stripped it of statglass film and held it ready for the correct moment in the reconstruction process. And the reconstruction went smoothly and quickly, the whole process taking no more than minutes. Aside from the insertion of the slug it was mainly a matter of reconnecting subsystems and of attaching a portable power supply that Sabel now unhooked from his belt; it would give the berserker no more power than might be needed for memory and communication.

Yet, as soon as power was supplied, one of the thin limb stumps that protruded from the rock surface began to vibrate, with a syncopated buzzing. It must be trying to move.

Sabel had involuntarily backed up a step; yet reason told him that his enemy was effectively powerless to harm him. He approached again, and plugged a communications cord into a jack he had installed. When he spoke to it, it was in continuation of the dialogue in the laboratory.

"Now you are constrained, as you put it, to answer whatever questions I may ask." Whether it was going to answer truthfully or not was something he could not yet tell.

It now answered him in his own voice, cracked, queer, inhuman. "Now I am constrained."

Relief and triumph compounded were so strong that Sabel had to chuckle. The thing sounded so immutably certain of what it said, even as it had sounded certain saying the exact opposite back in the lab.

Balancing buoyantly on his toes in the light gravity, he asked it: "How long ago were you damaged, and stuck here in the rock?"

"My timers have been out of operation."

That sounded reasonable. "At some time before you were damaged, though, some visual observations of the Radiant probably became stored somehow in your memory banks. You know what I am talking about from our conversation in the laboratory. Remember that I will be able to extract useful information from even the most casual, incidental video records, provided they were made in Radiant light when you were active."

"I remember." And as the berserker spoke there came faintly to Sabel's ears a grinding, straining sound, conducted through his boots from somewhere under the chaotic surface of once-molten rock.

"What are you doing?" he demanded sharply. God knew what weapons it had been equipped with, what potential powers it still had.

Blandly the berserker answered: "Trying to reestablish function in my internal power supply."

"You will cease that effort at once! The supply I have connected is sufficient."

"Order acknowledged." And at once the grinding stopped.

Sabel fumbled around, having a hard time trying to make a simple connection with another small device that he removed from his suit's belt. If only he did not tend to sweat so much. "Now. I have here a recorder. You will play into it all the video records you have that might be useful to me in my research on the Radiant's spectrum.

Do not erase any records from your own banks. I may want to get at them again later."

"Order acknowledged." In exactly the same cracked tones as before.

Sabel got the connection made at last. Then he crouched there, waiting for what seemed endless time, until his recorder signalled that the data flow had ceased.

And back in his lab, hours later, Sabel sat glaring destruction at the inoffensive stonework of the wall. His gaze was angled downward, in the direction of his unseen opponent, as if his anger could pierce and blast through the kilometers of rock.

The recorder had been filled with garbage. With nonsense. Virtually no better than noise. His own computer was still trying to unscramble the hopeless mess, but it seemed the enemy had succeeded in ... still, perhaps it had not been a ploy of the berserker's at all. Only, perhaps, some kind of trouble with the coupling of the recorder input to ...

He had, he remembered distinctly, told the berserker what the input requirements of the recorder were. But he had not explicitly ordered it to meet them. And he could not remember that it had ever said it would.

Bad, Sabel. A bad mistake to make in dealing with any kind of a machine. With a berserker ...

A communicator made a melodious sound. A moment later, its screen brought Guardian Gunavarman's face and voice into the lab.

"Dr. Sabel, will your laboratory be in shape for a personal inspection by the Potentate three hours from now?"

"I—I—yes, it will. In fact, I will be most honored," he remembered to add, in afterthought.

"Good. Excellent. You may expect the security party a few minutes before that time."

As soon as the connection had been broken, Sabel looked around. He was in fact almost ready to be inspected. Some innocuous experiments were in place to be looked at and discussed. Almost everything that might possibly be incriminating had been got out of the way. Everything, in fact, except ... he pulled the small recorder cartridge from his computer and juggled it briefly in his hand. The chance was doubtless small that any of his impending visitors would examine or play the cartridge, and smaller still that they might recognize the source of information on it if they did. Yet in Sabel's heart of hearts he was not so sure that the Guardians could be depended upon to be incompetent. And there was no reason for him to take even a small chance. There were, there had to be, a thousand public places where one might secrete an object as small as this. Where no one would notice it until it was retrieved . . . there were of course the public storage facilities, on the far side of the Fortress, near the spaceport.

To get to any point in the Fortress served by the public transportation network took only a few minutes. He had to switch from moving slidewalk to high-speed elevator in a plaza that fronted on the entertainment district, and as he crossed the plaza his eye was caught by a glowing red sign a hundred meters or so down the mall: *Contrat Rouge.*

His phantom followers were at his back again, and to try to make them vanish he passed the elevator entrance as if that had not been his goal at all. He was not wearing his blue habit today, and as he entered the entertainment mall none of the few people who were about seemed to take notice of him.

A notice board outside the *Contrat Rouge* informed Sabel in glowing letters that the next scheduled dance performance was several hours away. It might be expected that he would know that, had he really started out with the goal of seeing her perform. Sabel turned and looked around, trying to decide what to do next. There were not many people in sight. But too many for him to decide if any of them might really have been following him.

Now the doorman was starting to take notice of him. So Sabel approached the man, clearing his throat. "I was looking for Greta Thamar?"

Tall and with a bitter face, the attendant looked as Sabel imagined a policeman ought to look. "Girls aren't in yet."

"She lives somewhere nearby, though?"

"Try public info."

And perhaps the man was somewhat surprised to see that that was what Sabel, going to a nearby booth, actually did next. The automated information service unhesitatingly printed out Greta's address listing for him, and Sable was momentarily surprised: he had pictured her as besieged by men who saw her on stage, having to struggle for even a minimum of privacy. But then he saw a stage name printed out in parentheses beside her own; those inquiring for her under the stage name would doubtless be given no information except perhaps the time of the next performance. And the doorman? He doubtless gave the same two answers to the same two questions a dozen times a day, and made no effort to keep track of names.

As Sabel had surmised, the apartment was not far away. It looked quite modest from the outside. A girl's voice, not Greta's, answered when he spoke into the intercom at the door. He felt irritated that they were probably not going to be able to be alone.

A moment later the door opened. Improbable blond hair framed a face of lovely ebony above a dancer's body. "I'm Greta's new roommate. She ought to be back in a few minutes." The girl gave Sabel an almost-amused appraisal. "I was just going out myself. But you can come in and wait for her if you like."

"I . . . yes, thank you." Whatever happened, he wouldn't be able to stay long. He had to leave himself plenty of time to get rid of the recorder cartridge somewhere and get back to the lab. But certainly there were at least a few minutes to spare.

He watched the blond dancer out of sight. Sometime, perhaps . . . Then, left alone, he turned to a half-shaded window through which he could see a large part of the nearby plaza. Still there was no one in sight who looked to Sabel as if they might be following him. He moved from the window to stand in front of a cheap table. If he left before seeing Greta, should he leave her a note? And what ought he to say?

His personal communicator beeped at his belt. When he raised it to his face he found Chief Deputy Gunavarman looking out at him from the tiny screen.

"Doctor Sabel, I had expected you would be in your laboratory now. Please get back to it as soon as possible; the Potentate's visit has been moved up by about two hours. Where are you now?"

"I . . . ah . . ." *What might be visible in Gunavarman's screen?* "The entertainment district."

The chronic appearance of good humor in the Guardian's face underwent a subtle shift; perhaps now there was something of genuine amusement in it. "It shouldn't take you long to get back, then. Please hurry. Shall I send an escort?"

"No. Not necessary. Yes. At once." Then they were waiting for him at the lab. It was even possible that they could meet him right outside this apartment's door. As Sabel reholstered his communicator, he looked around him with quick calculation. There. Low down on one wall was a small ventilation grill of plastic, not much broader than his open hand. It was a type in common use within the Fortress. Sabel crouched down. The plastic bent springily in his strong fingers, easing out of its socket. He slid the recorder into the dark space behind, remembering to wipe it free of fingerprints first.

The Potentate's visit to the lab went well. It took longer than Sabel had expected, and he was complimented on his work, at least some of which the great leader seemed to understand. It wasn't until next morning, when Sabel was wondering how soon he ought to call on Greta again, that he heard during a chance encounter with a colleague that some unnamed young woman in the entertainment district had been arrested.

Possession of a restricted device, that was the charge. The first such arrest in years, and though no official announcement had yet been made, the Fortress was buzzing with the event, probably in several versions. The wording of the charge meant that the accused was at least suspected of actual contact with a berserker; it was the same one, technically, that would have been placed against Sabel if his secret activities had been discovered. And it was the more serious form of goodlife activity, the less serious consisting in forming clubs or cells of conspiracy, of sympathy to the enemy, perhaps having no real contact with berserkers.

Always in the past when he had heard of the recovery of any sort of berserker hardware, Sabel had called Gunavarman, to ask to be allowed to take part in the investigation. He dared not make an exception this time.

"Yes, Doctor," said the Guardian's voice from a small screen. "A restricted device is in our hands today. Why do you ask?"

"I think I have explained my interest often enough in the past. If there is any chance that this—device—contains information pertinent to my studies, I should like to apply through whatever channels may be necessary—"

"Perhaps I can save you the trouble. This time the device is merely the storage cartridge of a video recorder of a common type. It was recovered last night during a routine search of some newcomers' quarters in the entertainment district. The information on the recorder is intricately coded and we haven't solved it yet. But I doubt it has any connection with cosmophysics. This is just for your private information of course."

"Of course. But—excuse me—if you haven't broken the code why do you think this device falls into the restricted category?"

"There is a certain signature, shall we say, in the coding process. Our experts have determined that the information was stored at some stage in a berserker's memory banks. One of the two young women who lived in the apartment committed suicide before she could be questioned—a typical goodlife easy-out, it appears. The other suspect so far denies everything. We're in the process of obtaining a court order for some M-E, and that'll take care of that."

"Memory extraction. I didn't know that you could still—?"

"Oh, yes. Though nowadays there's a formal legal procedure. The questioning must be done in the presence of official witnesses. And if innocence of the specific charge is established, questioning must be halted. But in this case I think we'll have no trouble.

Sabel privately ordered a printout of all court documents handled during the previous twenty-four hours. There it was: Greta Thamar, order for memory-extraction granted. At least she was not dead.

To try to do anything for her would of course have been completely pointless. If the memory-extraction worked to show her guilt, it should show also that he, Sabel, was only an innocent chance acquaintance. But in fact it must work to show her innocence, and then she would be released. She would regain her full mental faculties in time—enough of them, anyway, to be a dancer.

Why, though, had her roommate killed herself? Entertainers. Unstable people . . .

Even if the authorities should someday learn that he had known Greta Thamar, there was no reason for him to come forward today and say so. No; he wasn't supposed to know as yet that she was the one arrested. Gunavarman had mentioned no names to him.

No, indeed, the best he could hope for by getting involved would be entanglement in a tedious, time-wasting investigation. Actually of course he would be risking much worse than that.

Actually it was his work, the extraction of scientific truth, that really mattered, not he. And, certainly, not one little dancer more or less. But if he went, his work went too. Who else was going to extract from the Templar Radiant the truths that would open shining new vistas of cosmophysics? Only seven other Radiants were known to exist in the entire Galaxy. None of the others were as accessible to study as this one was, and no one knew this one nearly as well as Georgicus Sabel. I knew it.

Yes, it would be pointless indeed for him to try to do anything for the poor girl. But he was surprised to find himself going through moments in which he felt that he was going to have to try.

Meanwhile, if there were even the faintest suspicion of him, if the Guardians were watching his movements, then an abrupt cessation of his field trips would be more likely to cause trouble than their continuation. And, once out in the lonely reaches of Dardania, he felt confident of being able to tell whether the Guardians were following him or not.

This time he took with him a small hologram-stage, so he could look at the video records before he brought them back.

"This time," he said to the armored braincase projecting from the slag-bank, "you are ordered to give me the information in intelligible form."

Something in its tremendous shoulders buzzed, a syncopated vibration. "Order acknowledged."

And what he had been asking for was shown to him at last. Scene after scene, made in natural Radiant-light. Somewhere on the inner surface of the Fortress, surrounded by smashed Dardanian glass roofs, a row of berserkers stood as if for inspection by some commanding machine. Yes, he should definitely be able to get something out of that. And out of this one, a quite similar scene. And out of—

"Wait. Just a moment. Go back, let me see that one again. What was that?"

He was once more looking at the Fortress's inner surface, bathed by the Radiant's light. But this time no berserkers were visible. The scene was centered on a young woman, who wore space garb of a design unfamiliar to Sabel. It was a light-looking garment that did not much restrict her movements, and the two-second segment of recording showed her in the act of performing some gesture. She raised her arms to the light above as if in the midst of some rite or dance centered on the Radiant itself. Her dark hair, short and curly, bore a jeweled diadem. Her long-lashed eyes were closed, in a face of surpassing loveliness.

He watched it three more times. "Now wait again. Hold the rest of the records. Who was that?"

To a machine, a berserker, all human questions and answers were perhaps of equal unimportance. Its voice gave the same tones to them all. It said to Sabel: "The life-unit Helen Dardan."

"But—" Sabel had a feeling of unreality. "Show it once more, and stop the motion right in the middle—yes, that's it. Now, how old is this record?"

"It is of the epoch of the 451st century, in your time-coordinate system."

"Before berserkers came to the Fortress? And why do you tell me it is she?"

"It is a record of Helen Dardan. No other existed. I was given it to use as a means of identification. I am a specialized assassin-machine and was sent on my last mission to destroy her."

"You—you claim to be the machine that actually—actually killed Helen Dardan?"

"No."

"Then explain."

"With other machines, I was programmed to kill her. But I was damaged and trapped here before the mission could be completed."

Sabel sighed disagreement. By now he felt quite sure that the thing could see him somehow. "You were trapped during the Templars' reconquest. That's when this molten rock must have been formed. Well after the time when Helen lived."

"That is when I was trapped. But only within an hour of the Templars' attack did we learn where the life-unit Helen Dardan had been hidden, in suspended animation."

"The Dardanians hid her from you somehow, and you couldn't find her until then?"

"The Dardanians hid her. I do not know whether she was ever found or not."

Sabel tried to digest this. "You're saying that for all you know, she might be still entombed somewhere, in suspended animation—and still alive."

"Confirm."

He looked at his video recorder. For a moment he could not recall why he had brought it here. "Just where was this hiding place of hers supposed to be?"

As it turned out, after Sabel had struggled through a translation of the berserkers' coordinate system into his own, the supposed hiding place was not far away at all. Once he had the location pinpointed it took him only minutes to get to the described intersection of Dardanian passageways. There, according to his informant, Helen's life-support coffin had been mortared up behind a certain obscure marking on a wall.

This region was free of the small blaze-marks that Sabel himself habitually put on the walls to remind himself of what ground he had already covered in his systematic program of exploration. And it was a region of some danger, perhaps, for here in relatively recent times there had been an extensive crumbling of stonework. What had been an intersection of passages had become a rough cave, piled high with pieces great and small of what had been wall and floor and overhead. The fragments were broken and rounded to some extent, sharp corners knocked away. Probably at intervals they did a stately mill-dance in the low gravity, under some perturbation of the Fortress's stately secular movement round the Radiant in space. Eventually the fallen fragments would probably grind themselves into gravel, and slide away to accumulate in low spots in the nearby passages.

But today they still formed a rough, high mound. Sabel with his suit lights could discern a dull egg-shape nine-tenths buried in this mound. It was rounder and smoother than the broken masonry, and the size of a piano or a little larger.

He clambered toward it, and without much trouble succeeded in getting it almost clear of rock. It was made of some tough, artificial substance; and in imagination he could fit into it any of the several types of suspended-animation equipment that he had seen.

What now? Suppose, just suppose, that any real chance existed . . . he dared not try to open up the thing here in the airless cold. Nor had he any tools with him at the moment that would let him try to probe the inside gently. He had to go back to base camp and get the flyer here somehow.

Maneuvering his vehicle to his find proved easier than he had feared. He found a roundabout way to reach the place, and in less than an hour had the ovoid secured to his flyer with adhesive straps. Hauling it slowly back to base camp, he reflected that whatever was inside was going to have to remain secret, for a while at least. The announcement of any important find would bring investigators swarming out here. And that Sabel could not afford, until every trace of the berserker's existence had been erased.

Some expansion of the tent's fabric was necessary before he could get the ovoid in, and leave himself with space to work. Once he had it in a securely air-filled space, he put a gentle heater to work on its outer surface, to make it easier to handle. Then he went to work with an audio pickup to see what he could learn of the interior.

There was activity of some kind inside, that much was obvious at once. The sounds of gentle machinery, which he supposed might have been started by his disturbance of the thing, or by the presence of warm air around it now.

Subtle machinery at work. And then another sound, quite regular. It took Sabel's memory a little time to match it with the cadence of a living human heart.

He had forgotten about time, but in fact not much time had passed before he considered that he was ready for the next step. The outer casing opened for him easily. Inside, he confronted great complexity; yes, obviously sophisticated life-support. And within that an interior shell, eyed with glass windows. Sabel shone in a light.

As usual in suspended-animation treatment, the occupant's skin had been covered with a webbed film of half-living stuff to help in preservation. But the film had torn away now from around the face.

And the surpassing beauty of that face left Sabel no room for doubt. Helen Dardan was breathing, and alive.

Might not all, all, be forgiven one who brought the Queen of Love herself to life? All, even goodlife work, the possession of restricted devices?

There was also to be considered, though, the case of a man who at a berserker's direction unearthed the Queen and thereby brought about her final death.

Of course an indecisive man, one afraid to take risks, would not be out here now faced with his problem. Sabel had already unslung his emergency medirobot, a thing the size of a suitcase, from its usual perch at the back of the flyer, and had it waiting inside the tent. Now, like a man plunging into deep, cold water, he fumbled open the fasteners of the interior shell, threw back its top, and quickly stretched probes from the medirobot to Helen's head and chest and wrist. He tore away handfuls of the half-living foam.

Even before he had the third probe connected, her dark eyes had opened and were looking at him. He thought he could see awareness and understanding in them. Her last hopes on being put to sleep must have been for an awakening no worse than this, at hands that might be strange but were not metal.

"Helen." Sabel could not help but feel that he was pretending, acting, when he spoke the name. "Can you hear me? Understand?" He spoke in Standard; the meagre store of Dardanian that he had acquired from ancient recordings having completely deserted him for the moment. But he thought a Dardanian aristocrat should know enough Standard to grasp his meaning and the language had not changed enormously in the centuries since her entombment.

"You're safe now," he assured her, on his spacesuited knees beside her bed. When a flicker in her eyes seemed to indicate relief, he went on: "The berserkers have been driven away."

Her lips parted slightly. They were full and perfect. But she did not speak. She raised herself a little, and moved to bare a shoulder and an arm from clinging foam.

Nervously Sabel turned to the robot. If he was interpreting its indicators correctly, the patient was basically in quite good condition. To his not-really-expert eye the machine signalled that there were high drug levels in her bloodstream; high, but falling. Hardly surprising, in one just being roused from suspended animation.

"There's nothing to fear, Helen. Do you hear me? The berserkers have been beaten." He didn't want to tell her, not right away at least, that glorious Dardania was no more.

She had attained almost a sitting position by now, leaning on the rich cushions of her couch. There was some relief in her eyes, yes, but uneasiness as well. And still she had not uttered a word.

As Sabel understood it, people awakened from SA ought to have some light nourishment at once. He hastened to offer food and water both. Helen sampled what he gave her, first hesitantly, then with evident enjoyment.

"Never mind, you don't have to speak to me right away. The-war-is-over." This last was in his best Dardanian, a few words of which were now belatedly willing to be recalled.

"You-are-Helen." At this he thought he saw agreement in her heavenly face. Back to Standard now. "I am Georgicus Sabel. Doctor of Cosmophysics, Master of . . . but what does all that matter of me, now? I have saved you. And that is all that counts."

She was smiling at him. And maybe after all this was a dream, no more . . .

More foam was peeling, clotted, from her skin. Good God, what was she going to wear? He bumbled around, came up with a spare coverall. Behind his turned back he heard her climbing from the cushioned container, putting the garment on.

What was this, clipped to his belt? The newly-charged video recorder, yes. It took him a little while to remember what he was doing with it. He must take it back to the lab, and make sure that the information on it was readable this time. After that, the berserker could be destroyed.

He already had with him in camp tools that could break up metal, chemicals to dissolve it. But the berserker's armor would be resistant, to put it mildly. And it must be very thoroughly destroyed, along with the rock that held it, so that no one should ever guess it had existed. It would take time to do that. And special equipment and supplies, which Sabel would have to return to the city to obtain.

Three hours after she had wakened, Helen, dressed in a loose coverall, was sitting on cushions that Sabel had taken from her former couch and arranged on rock. She seemed content to simply sit and wait, watching her rescuer with flattering eyes, demanding nothing from him—except, as it soon turned out, his presence.

Painstakingly he kept trying to explain to her that he had important things to do, that he was going to have to go out, leave her here by herself for a time.

"I-must-go. I will come back. Soon." There was no question of taking her along, no matter what. At the moment there was only one spacesuit.

But, for whatever reason, she wouldn't let him go. With obvious alarm, and pleading gestures, she put herself in front of the airlock to bar his way.

"Helen. I really must. I—"

She signed disagreement, violently.

"But there is one berserker left, you see. We cannot be safe until it is—until—"

Helen was smiling at him, a smile of more than gratitude. And now Sabel could no longer persuade himself that this was not a dream. With a sinuous movement of unmistakable invitation, the Queen of Love was holding out her arms . . .

When he was thinking clearly and coolly once again, Sabel began again with patient explanations. "Helen. My darling. You see, I must go. To the city. To get some—"

A great light of understanding, acquiescence, dawned in her lovely face.

"There are some things I need, vitally. Then I swear I'll come right back. Right straight back here. You want me to bring someone with me, is that it? I—"

He was about to explain that he couldn't do that just yet, but her renewed alarm indicated that that was the last thing she would ask.

"All right, then. Fine. No one. I will bring a spare spacesuit . . . but that you are here will be my secret, our secret, for a while. Does that please you? Ah, my Queen!"

At the joy he saw in Helen's face, Sabel threw himself down to kiss her foot. "Mine alone!"

He was putting on his helmet now. "I will return in less than a day. If possible. The chronometer is over here, you see? But if I should be longer than a day, don't worry. There's everything you'll need, here in the shelter. I'll do my best to hurry."

Her eyes blessed him.

He had to turn back from the middle of the airlock, to pick up his video recording, almost forgotten.

How, when it came time at last to take the Queen into the city, was he going to explain his long concealment of her? She was bound to tell others how many days she had been in that far tent. Somehow there had to be a way around that problem. At the moment, though, he did not want to think about it. The Queen was his alone, and no one . . . but first, before anything else, the berserker had to be got rid of. No, before that even, he must see if its video data was good this time.

Maybe Helen knew, Helen could tell him, where cached Dardanian treasure was waiting to be found . . .

And she had taken him as lover, as casual bed-partner rather. Was that the truth of the private life and character of the great Queen, the symbol of chastity and honor and dedication to her people? Then no one, in the long run, would thank him for bringing her back to them.

Trying to think ahead, Sabel could feel his life knotting into a singularity at no great distance in the future. Impossible to try to predict what lay beyond. It was worse than uncertain; it was opaque.

This time his laboratory computer made no fuss about accepting the video records. It began to process them at once.

At his private information station Sabel called for a printout of any official news announcements made by the Guardians or the city fathers during the time he had been gone. He learned that the entertainer Greta Thamar had been released under the guardianship of her court-appointed lawyer, after memory extraction. She was now in satisfactory condition in the civilian wing of the hospital.

There was nothing else in the news about goodlife, or berserkers. And there had been no black-robed Guardians at Sabel's door when he came in.

DATING ANOMALY PRESENT was on the screen of Sabel's laboratory computer the next time he looked at it.

"Give details," he commanded.

RECORD GIVEN AS EPOCH 451st CENTURY IDENTIFIES WITH SPECTRUM OF RADIANT EPOCH 456th CENTURY, YEAR 23, DAY 152.

"Let me see."

It was, as some part of Sabel's mind already seemed to know, the segment that showed Helen on the inner surface of the Fortress, raising her arms ecstatically as in some strange rite. Or dance.

The singularity in his future was hurtling toward him quickly now. "You say—you say that the spectrum in this record is identical with the one we recorded—what did you say? How long ago?"

38 DAYS 11 HOURS, APPROXIMATELY 44 MINUTES.

As soon as he had the destructive materials he needed loaded aboard the flyer, he headed at top speed back to base camp. He did not wait to obtain a spare spacesuit.

Inside the tent, things were disarranged, as if Helen perhaps had been searching restlessly for something. Under the loose coverall her breast rose and fell rapidly, as if she had recently been working hard, or were in the grip of some intense emotion.

She held out her arms to him, and put on a glittering smile.

Sabel stopped just inside the airlock. He pulled his helmet off and faced her grimly. "Who are you?" he demanded.

She winced, and tilted her head, but would not speak. She still held out her arms, and the glassy smile was still in place.

"*Who are you, I said?* That hologram was made just thirty-eight days ago."

Helen's face altered. The practiced expression was still fixed on it, but now a different light played on her features. The light came from outside the shelter, and it was moving toward them.

There were four people out there, some with hand weapons leveled in Sabel's direction. Through the plastic he could not tell at once if their suited figures were those of men or women. Two of them immediately came in through the airlock, while the other two remained outside, looking at the cargo Sabel had brought out on the flyer.

"God damn, it took you long enough." Helen's lovely lips had formed some words at last.

The man who entered first, gun drawn, ignored Sabel for the moment and inspected her with a sour grin. "I see you came through five days in the cooler in good shape."

"Easier than one day here with him—God damn." Helen's smile at Sabel had turned into an equally practiced snarl.

The second man to enter the shelter stopped just inside the airlock. He stood there with a hand on the gun holstered at his belt, watching Sabel alertly.

The first man now confidently holstered his weapon too, and concentrated his attention on Sabel. He was tall and bitter-faced, but he was no policeman. "I'm going to want to take a look inside your lab, and maybe get some things out. So hand over the key, or tell me the combination."

Sabel moistened his lips. "Who are you?" The words were not frightened, they were imperious with rage. "*And who is this woman here?*"

"I advise you to control yourself. She's been entertaining you, keeping you out of our way while we got a little surprise ready for the city. We each of us serve the Master in our own way ... even you have already served. You provided the Master with enough power to call on us for help, some days ago ... yes, what?" Inside his helmet he turned his head to look outside the shelter. "Out completely? Under its own power now? Excellent!"

He faced back toward Sabel. "And who am I? Someone who will get the key to your laboratory from you, one way or another, you may be sure. We've been working on you a long time already, many days. We saw to it that poor Greta got a new roommate, as soon as you took up with her. Poor Greta never knew ... you see, we thought we might need your flyer and this final cargo of tools and chemicals to get the Master out. As it turned out, we didn't."

Helen, the woman Sabel had known as Helen, walked into his field of vision, turned her face to him as if to deliver a final taunt.

What it might have been, he never knew. Her dark eyes widened, in a parody of fainting fright. In the next moment she was slumping to the ground.

Sabel had a glimpse of the other, suited figures tumbling. Then a great soundless, invisible, cushioned club smote at his whole body. The impact had no direction, but there was no way to stand against it. His muscles quit on him, his nerves dissolved. The rocky ground beneath the shelter came up to catch his awkward fall with bruising force.

Once down, it was impossible to move a hand or foot. He had to concentrate on simply trying to breathe.

Presently he heard the airlock's cycling sigh. To lift his head and look was more than he could do; in his field of vision there were only suited bodies, and the ground.

Black boots, Guardian boots, trod to a halt close before his eyes. A hand gripped Sabel's shoulder and turned him part way up. Gunavarman's jovial eyes looked down at him for a triumphal moment before the Chief Deputy moved on.

Other black boots shuffled about. "Yes, this one's Helen Nadrad, all right—that's the name she used whoring at the Parisian Alley, anyway. I expect we can come up with another name or two for her if we look offworld. Ready to talk to us, Helen? Not yet? You'll be all right. Stunner wears off in an hour or so."

"Chief, I wonder what they expected to do with suspended animation gear? Well, we'll find out."

Gunavarman now began a radio conference with some distant personage. Sabel, in his agony of trying to breathe, to move, to speak, could hear only snatches of the talk:

"Holding meetings out here for some time, evidently . . . mining for berserker parts, probably . . . equipment . . . yes, Sire, the berserker recording was found in his laboratory this time . . . a publicity hologram of Helen Nadrad included in it, for some reason . . . yes, very shocking. But no doubt . . . we followed him out here just now. Joro, that's the goodlife organizer we've been watching, is here . . . yes, Sire. Thank you very much. I will pass on your remarks to my people here."

In a moment more the radio conversation had been concluded. Gunavarman, in glowing triumph, was bending over Sabel once again. "Prize catch," the Guardian murmured. "Something you'd like to say to me?"

Sabel was staring at the collapsed figure of Joro. Inside an imperfectly closed pocket of the man's spacesuit he could see a small, blood-red cylinder, a stub of cut wire protruding from one end.

"Anything important, Doctor?"

He tried, as never before. Only a few words. "Draw . . . your . . . weapons . . ."

Gunavarman glanced round at his people swarming outside the tent. He looked confidently amused. "Why?"

Now through the rock beneath the groundsheet of his shelter Sabel could hear a subtly syncopated, buzzing vibration, drawing near.

"Draw . . . your . . ."

Not that he really thought the little handguns were likely to do them any good.

As life may transmit evil, so machines of great power may hand on good.

☀ WINGS OUT OF SHADOW

In Malori's first and only combat mission the berserker came to him in the image of a priest of the sect into which Malori had been born on the planet Yaty. In a dreamlike vision that was the analogue of a very real combat he saw the robed figure standing tall in a deformed pulpit, eyes flaming with malevolence, lowering arms winglike with the robes they stretched. With their lowering, the lights of the universe were dimming outside the windows of stained glass and Malori was being damned.

Even with his heart pounding under damnation's terror Malori retained sufficient consciousness to remember the real nature of himself and of his adversary and that he was not powerless against him. His dream-feet walked him timelessly toward the pulpit and its demon-priest while all around him the stained glass windows burst, showering him with fragments of sick fear. He walked a crooked path, avoiding the places in the smooth floor where, with quick gestures, the priest created snarling, snapping stone mouths full of teeth. Malori seemed to have unlimited time to decide where to put his feet. *Weapon,* he thought, a surgeon instructing some invisible aide. *Here—in my right hand.*

From those who had survived similar battles he had heard how the inhuman enemy appeared to each in different form, how each human must live the combat through in terms of a unique nightmare. To some a berserker came as a ravening beast, to others as devil or god or man. To still others it was some essence of terror that could never be faced or even seen. The combat was a nightmare experienced while the subconscious ruled, while the waking

171

mind was suppressed by careful electrical pressures on the brain. Eyes and ears were padded shut so that the conscious mind might be more easily suppressed, the mouth plugged to save the tongue from being bitten, the nude body held immobile by the defensive fields that kept it whole against the thousands of gravities that came with each movement of the one-man ship while in combat mode. It was a nightmare from which mere terror could never wake one; waking came only when the fight was over, came only with death or victory or disengagement.

Into Malori's dream-hand there now came a meat cleaver keen as a razor, massive as a guillotine-blade. So huge it was that had it been what it seemed, it would have been far too cumbersome to even lift. His uncle's butcher shop on Yaty was gone, with all other human works of that planet. But the cleaver came back to him now, magnified, perfected to suit his need.

He gripped it hard in both hands and advanced. As he drew near the pulpit towered higher. The carved dragon on its front, which should have been an angel, came alive, blasting him with rosy fire. With a shield that came from nowhere, he parried the splashing flames.

Outside the remnants of the stained glass windows the lights of the universe were almost dead now. Standing at the base of the pulpit, Malori drew back his cleaver as if to strike overhand at the priest who towered above his reach. Then, without any forethought at all, he switched his aim to the top of his backswing and laid the blow crashing against the pulpit's stem. It shook, but resisted stoutly. Damnation came.

Before the devils reached him, though, the energy was draining from the dream. In less than a second of real time it was no more than a fading visual image, a few seconds after that a dying memory. Malori, coming back to consciousness with eyes and ears still sealed, floated in a soothing limbo. Before post-combat fatigue and sensory deprivation could combine to send him into psychosis, attachments on his scalp began to feed his brain with bursts of pins-and-needles noise. It was the safest signal to administer to a brain that might be on the verge of any of a dozen different kinds of madness. The noises made a whitish roaring scattering of light and sound that seemed to fill his head and at the same time somehow outlined for him the positions of his limbs.

His first fully conscious thought: he had just fought a berserker and survived. He had won—or had at least achieved a stand-off—or he would not be here. It was no mean achievement.

Yaty was only the latest of many Earth-colonized planets to suffer a berserker attack, and it was among the luckiest; nearly all its people had been successfully evacuated. Malori and others now fought in deep space to protect the *Hope*, one of the enormous evacuation ships. The *Hope* was a sphere several kilometers in diameter, large enough to contain a good proportion of the planet's population stored tier on tier in defense-field stasis. A tickle-relaxation of the fields allowed them to breathe and live with slowed metabolism.

The voyage to a safe sector of the galaxy was going to take several months because most of it, in terms of time spent, was going to be occupied in traversing an outlying arm of the great Taynarus nebula. Here gas and dust were much too thick to let a ship duck out of normal space and travel faster than light. Here even the speeds attainable in normal space were greatly restricted. At thousands of kilometers per second, manned ship or berserker machine could alike be smashed flat against a wisp of gas far more tenuous than human breath.

Taynarus was a wilderness of uncharted plumes and tendrils of dispersed matter, laced through by corridors of relatively empty space. Much of the wilderness was completely shaded by interstellar dust from the light of all the suns outside. Through dark shoals and swamps and tides of nebula the *Hope* and her escort *Judith* fled, and a berserker pack pursued. Some berserkers were even larger than the *Hope*, but those that had taken up this chase were much smaller. In regions of space so thick with matter, a race went to the small as well as to the swift; as the impact cross-section of a ship increased, its maximum practical speed went inexorably down.

The *Hope*, ill-adapted for this chase (in the rush to evacuate, there had been no better choice available) could not expect to outrun the smaller and more maneuverable enemy. Hence the escort carrier *Judith*, trying always to keep herself between *Hope* and the pursuing pack. *Judith* mothered the little fighting ships, spawning them out whenever the enemy came too near, welcoming survivors back when the threat had once again been beaten off. There had been fifteen of the one-man ships when the chase began. Now there were nine.

The noise injections from Malori's life support equipment slowed down, then stopped. His conscious mind once more sat steady on its throne. The gradual relaxation of his defense fields he knew to be a certain sign that he would soon rejoin the world of waking men.

As soon as his fighter, Number Four, had docked itself inside the *Judith*, Malori hastened to disconnect himself from the tiny ship's systems. He pulled on a loose coverall and let himself out of the cramped space. A thin man with knobby joints and an awkward step, he hurried along a catwalk through the echoing hangar-like chamber, noting that three or four fighters besides his had already returned and were resting in their cradles. The artificial gravity was quite steady, but Malori stumbled and almost fell in his haste to get down the short ladder to the operations deck.

Petrovich, commander of the *Judith*, a bulky, iron-faced man of middle height, was on the deck apparently waiting for him.

"Did—did I make my kill?" Malori stuttered eagerly as he came hurrying up. The forms of military address were little observed aboard the *Judith*, as a rule, and Malori was really a civilian anyway. That he had been allowed to take out a fighter at all was a mark of the commander's desperation.

Scowling, Petrovich answered bluntly. "Malori, you're a disaster in one of these ships. Haven't the mind for it at all."

The world turned a little gray in front of Malori. He hadn't understood until this moment just how important to him certain dreams of glory were. He could find only weak and awkward words. "But . . . I thought I did all right." He tried to recall his combat-nightmare. Something about a church.

"Two people had to divert their ships from their original combat objectives to rescue you. I've already seen their gun-camera tapes. You had Number Four just sparring around with that berserker as if you had no intention of doing it any damage at all." Petrovich looked at him more closely, shrugged, and softened his voice somewhat. "I'm not trying to chew you out, you weren't even aware of what was happening, of course. I'm just stating facts. Thank probability the *Hope* is twenty AU deep in a formaldehyde cloud up ahead. If she'd been in an exposed position just now they would have got her."

"But—" Malori tried to begin an argument but the commander simply walked away. More fighters were coming in. Locks sighed and cradles clanged, and Petrovich had plenty of more important things to do than stand here arguing with him. Malori stood there alone for a few moments, feeling deflated and defeated and diminished. Involuntarily he cast a yearning glance back at Number Four. It was a short, windowless cylinder, not much more than a man's height in diameter, resting in its metal cradle while technicians worked about it. The stubby main laser nozzle, still hot from firing, was sending up a wisp of smoke now that it was back in atmosphere. There was his two-handed cleaver.

No man could direct a ship or a weapon with anything like the competence of a good machine. The creeping slowness of human nerve impulses and of conscious thought disqualified humans from maintaining direct control of their ships in any space fight against berserkers. But the human subconscious was not so limited. Certain of its processes could not be correlated with any specific synaptic activity within the brain, and some theorists held that these processes took place outside of time. Most physicists stood aghast at this view—but for space combat it made a useful working hypothesis.

In combat, the berserker computers were coupled with sophisticated randoming devices, to provide the flair, the unpredictability that gained an advantage over an opponent who simply and consistently chose the maneuver statistically most likely to bring success. Men also used computers to drive their ships, but had now gained an edge over the best randomizers by relying once more on their own brains, parts of which were evidently freed of hurry and dwelt outside of time, where even speeding light must be as motionless as carved ice.

There were drawbacks. Some people (including Malori, it now appeared) were simply not suitable for the job, their subconscious minds seemingly uninterested in such temporal matters as life or death. And even in suitable minds the subconscious was subject to great stress. Connection to external computers loaded the mind in some way not yet understood. One after another, human pilots returning from combat were removed from their ships in states of catatonia or hysterical excitement. Sanity might be restored, but the man or woman was worthless thereafter as a combat-computer's teammate. The system was so new that the importance of these drawbacks was just coming to light aboard the *Judith* now. The trained operators of the fighting ships had been used up, and so had their replacements. Thus it was that Ian Malori, historian, and others were sent out, untrained, to fight. But using their minds had bought a little extra time.

From the operations deck Malori went to his small single cabin. He had not eaten for some time, but he was not hungry. He changed clothes and sat in a chair looking at his bunk, looking at his books and tapes and violin, but he did not try to rest or to occupy himself. He expected that he would promptly get a call from Petrovich. Because Petrovich now had nowhere else to turn.

He almost smiled when the communicator chimed, bringing a summons to meet with the commander and other officers at once. Malori acknowledged and set out, taking with him a brown leatherlike case about the size of a briefcase but differently shaped, which he selected from several hundred similar cases in a small room adjacent to his cabin. The case he carried was labeled: CRAZY HORSE.

Petrovich looked up as Malori entered the small planning room in which the handful of ship's officers were already gathered around a table. The commander glanced at the case Malori was carrying, and nodded. "It seems we have no choice, historian. We are running out of people, and we are going to have to use your pseudopersonalities. Fortunately we now have the necessary adapters installed in all the fighting ships."

"I think the chances of success are excellent." Malori spoke mildly as he took the seat left vacant for him and set his case out in the middle of the table. "These of course have no real subconscious minds, but as we agreed in our earlier discussions, they will provide more sophisticated randoming devices than are available otherwise. Each has a unique, if artificial, personality."

One of the other officers leaned forward. "Most of us missed these earlier discussions you speak of. Could you fill us in a little?"

"Certainly." Malori cleared his throat. "These personae, as we usually call them, are used in the computer simulation of historical problems. I was able to bring several hundred of them with me from Yaty. Many are models of military men." He put his hand on the case before him. "This is a reconstruction of the personality of one of the most able cavalry leaders on ancient Earth. It's not one of the group we have selected to try first in combat, I just brought it along to demonstrate the interior structure and design for any of you who are interested. Each persona contains about four million sheets of two-dimensional matter."

Another officer raised a hand. "How can you accurately reconstruct the personality of someone who must have died long before any kind of direct recording techniques were available?"

"We can't be positive of accuracy, of course. We have only historical records to go by, and what we deduce from computer simulations of the era. These are only models. But they should perform in combat as in the historical studies for which they were made. Their choices should reflect basic aggressiveness, determination—"

The totally unexpected sound of an explosion brought the assembled officers as one body to their feet. Petrovich, reacting very fast, still had time only to get clear of his chair before a second and much louder blast resounded through the ship. Malori himself was almost at the door, heading for his battle station, when the third explosion came. It sounded like the end of the galaxy, and he was aware that furniture was flying, that the bulkheads around the meeting room were caving in. Malori had one clear, calm thought about the unfairness of his coming death, and then for a time he ceased to think at all.

Coming back was a slow unpleasant process. He knew *Judith* was not totally wrecked for he still breathed, and the artificial gravity still held him sprawled out against the deck. It might have been pleasing to find the gravity gone, for his body was one vast, throbbing ache, a pattern of radiated pain from a center somewhere inside his skull. He did not want to pin down the source any more closely than that. To even imagine touching his own head was painful.

At last the urgency of finding out what was going on overcame the fear of pain and he raised his head and probed it. There was a large lump just above his forehead, and smaller injuries about his face where blood had dried. He must have been out for some time.

The meeting room was ruined, shattered, littered with debris. There was a crumpled body that must be dead, and there another, and another, mixed in with the furniture. Was he the only survivor? One bulkhead had been torn wide open, and the planning table was demolished. And what was that large, unfamiliar piece of machinery standing at the other end of the room? Big as a tall filing cabinet, but far more intricate. There was something peculiar about its legs, as if they might be movable . . .

Malori froze in abject terror, because the thing did move, swiveling a complex of turrets and lenses at him, and he understood that he was seeing and being seen by a functional berserker machine. It was one of the small ones, used for boarding and operating captured human ships.

"Come here," the machine said. It had a squeaky, ludicrous parody of a human voice, recorded syllables of captives' voices stuck together electronically and played back. "The badlife has awakened."

Malori in his great fear thought that the words were directed at him but he could not move. Then, stepping through the hole in the bulkhead, came a man Malori had never seen before—a shaggy and filthy man wearing a grimy coverall that might once have been part of some military uniform.

"I see he has, sir," the man said to the machine. He spoke the standard interstellar language in a ragged voice that bore traces of a cultivated accent. He took a step closer to Malori. "Can you understand me, there?"

Malori grunted something, tried to nod, pulled himself up slowly into an awkward sitting position.

"The question is," the man continued, coming a little closer still, "how d'you want it later, easy or hard? When it comes to your finishing up, I mean. I decided a long time ago that I want mine quick and easy, and not too soon. Also that I still want to have some fun here and there along the way."

Despite the fierce pain in his head, Malori was thinking now, and beginning to understand. There was a name for humans like the man before him, who went along more or less willingly with the berserker machines. A word coined by the machines themselves. But at the moment Malori was not going to speak that name.

"I want it easy," was all he said, and blinked his eyes and tried to rub his neck against the pain.

The man looked him over in silence a little longer. "All right," he said then. Turning back to the machine, he added in a different, humble voice: "I can easily dominate this injured badlife. There will be no problems if you leave us here alone."

❊   ❊   ❊

The machine turned one metal-cased lens toward its servant. "Remember," it vocalized, "the auxiliaries must be made ready. Time grows short. Failure will bring unpleasant stimuli."

"I will remember, sir." The man was humble and sincere. The machine looked at both of them a few moments longer and then departed, metal legs flowing suddenly into a precise and almost graceful walk. Shortly after, Malori heard the familiar sound of an airlock cycling.

"We're alone now," the man said, looking down at him. "If you want a name for me you can call me Greenleaf. Want to try to fight me? If so, let's get it over with." He was not much bigger than Malori but his hands were huge and he looked hard and very capable despite his ragged filthiness. "All right, that's a smart choice. You know, you're actually a lucky man, though you don't realize it yet. Berserkers aren't like the other masters that men have—not like the governments and parties and corporations and causes that use you up and then just let you drop and drag away. No, when the machines run out of uses for you they'll finish you off quickly and cleanly—if you've served well. I know, I've seen 'em do it that way with other humans. No reason why they shouldn't. All they want is for us to die, not suffer."

Malori said nothing. He thought perhaps he would be able to stand up soon.

Greenleaf (the name seemed so inappropriate that Malori thought it probably real) made some adjustment on a small device that he had taken from a pocket and was holding almost concealed in one large hand. He asked: "How many escort carriers besides this one are trying to protect the *Hope*?"

"I don't know," Malori lied. There had been only the *Judith*.

"What is your name?" The bigger man was still looking at the device in his hand.

"Ian Malori."

Greenleaf nodded, and without showing any particular emotion in his face took two steps forward and kicked Malori in the belly, precisely and with brutal power.

"That was for trying to lie to me, Ian Malori," said his captor's voice, heard dimly from somewhere above as Malori groveled on the deck, trying to breathe again. "Understand that I am infallibly able to tell when you are lying. Now, how many escort carriers are there?"

In time Malori could sit up again, and choke out words. "Only this one." Whether Greenleaf had a real lie detector, or was only trying to make it appear so by asking questions whose answers he already knew, Malori decided that from now on he would speak the literal truth as scrupulously as possible. A few more kicks like that and he would be helpless and useless and the machines would kill him. He discovered that he was by no means ready to abandon his life.

"What was your position on the crew, Malori?"

"I'm a civilian."

"What sort?"

"An historian."

"And why are you here?"

Malori started to get to his feet, then decided there was nothing to be gained by the struggle and stayed sitting on the deck. If he ever let himself dwell on his situation for a moment he would be too hideously afraid to think coherently. "There was a project . . . you see, I brought with me from Yaty a number of what we call historical models—blocks of programmed responses we use in historical research."

"I remember hearing about some such things. What was the project you mentioned?"

"Trying to use the personae of military men as randomizers for the combat computers on the one-man ships."

"Aha." Greenleaf squatted, supple and poised for all his raunchy look. "How do they work in combat? Better than a live pilot's subconscious mind? The machines know all about *that.*"

"We never had a chance to try. Are the rest of the crew here all dead?"

Greenleaf nodded casually. "It wasn't a hard boarding. There must have been a failure in your automatic defenses. I'm glad to find one man alive and smart enough to cooperate. It'll help me in my career." He glanced at an expensive chronometer strapped to his dirty wrist. "Stand up, Ian Malori. There's work to do."

Malori got up and followed the other toward the operations deck.

"The machines and I have been looking around, Malori. These nine little fighting ships you still have on board are just too good to be wasted. The machines are sure of catching the *Hope* now, but she'll have automatic defenses, probably a lot tougher than this tub's were. The machines have taken a lot of casualties on this chase so they mean to use these nine little ships as auxiliary troops—no doubt you have some knowledge of military history?"

"Some." The answer was perhaps an understatement, but it seemed to pass as truth. The lie detector, if it was one, had been put away. But Malori would still take no more chances than he must.

"Then you probably know how some of the generals of old Earth used their auxiliaries. Drove them on ahead of the main force of trusted troops, where they could be killed if they tried to retreat, and were also the first to be used up against the enemy."

Arriving on the operations deck, Malori saw few signs of damage. Nine tough little ships waited in their launching cradles, re-armed and refueled for combat. All that would have been taken care of within minutes of their return from their last mission.

"Malori, from looking at these ships' controls while you were unconscious, I gather that there's no fully automatic mode in which they can be operated."

"Right. There has to be some controlling mind, or randomizer, connected on board."

"You and I are going to get them out as berserker auxiliaries, Ian Malori." Greenleaf glanced at his timepiece again. "We have less than an hour to think of a good way and only a few hours more to complete the job. The faster the better. If we delay we are going to be made to suffer for it." He seemed almost to relish the thought. "What do you suggest we do?"

Malori opened his mouth as if to speak, and then did not.

Greenleaf said: "Installing any of your military personae is of course out of the question, as they might not submit well to being driven forward like mere cannon fodder. I assume they are leaders of some kind. But have you perhaps any of these personae from different fields, of a more docile nature?"

Malori, sagging against the operations officer's empty combat chair, forced himself to think very carefully before he spoke. "As it happens, there are some personae aboard in which I have a special personal interest. Come."

With the other following closely, Malori led the way to his small bachelor cabin. Somehow it was astonishing that nothing had been changed inside. There on the bunk was his violin, and on the table were his music tapes and a few books. And here, stacked neatly in their leather-like curved cases, were some of the personae that he liked best to study.

Malori lifted the top case from the stack. "This man was a violinist, as I like to think I am. His name would probably mean nothing to you."

"Musicology was never my field. But tell me more."

"He was an Earthman, who lived in the twentieth century CE—quite a religious man, too, as I understand. We can plug the persona in and ask it what it thinks of fighting, if you are suspicious."

"We had better do that." When Malori had shown him the proper receptacle beside the cabin's small computer console, Greenleaf snapped the connections together himself. "How does one communicate with it?"

"Just talk."

Greenleaf spoke sharply toward the leather-like case. "Your name?"

"Albert Ball." The voice that answered from the console speaker sounded more human by far than the berserker's had.

"How does the thought of getting into a fight strike you, Albert?"

"A detestable idea."

"Will you play the violin for us?"

"Gladly." But no music followed.

Malori put in: "More connections are necessary if you want actual music."

"I don't think we'll need that." Greenleaf unplugged the Albert Ball unit and began to look through the sack of others, frowning at unfamiliar names. There were twelve or fifteen cases in all. "Who are these?"

"Albert Ball's contemporaries. Performers who shared his profession." Malori let himself sink down on the bunk for a few moments' rest. He was not far from fainting. Then he went to stand with Greenleaf beside the stack of personae. "This is a model of Edward Mannock, who was blind in one eye and could never have passed the physical examination necessary to serve in any military force of his time." He pointed to another. "This man served briefly in the cavalry, as I recall, but he kept getting thrown from his horse and was soon relegated to gathering supplies. And this one was a frail, tubercular youth who died at twenty-three standard years of age."

Greenleaf gave up looking at the cases and turned to size up Malori once again. Malori could feel his battered stomach muscles trying to contract, anticipating another violent impact. It would be too much, it was going to kill him if it came like that again . . .

"All right." Greenleaf was frowning, checking his chronometer yet again. Then he looked up with a little smile. Oddly, the smile made him look like the hell of a good fellow. "All right! Musicians, I suppose, are the antithesis of the military. If the machines approve, we'll install them and get the ships sent out. Ian Malori, I may just raise your pay." His pleasant smile broadened. "We may just have bought ourselves another standard year of life if this works out as well as I think it might."

When the machine came aboard again a few minutes later, Greenleaf bowing before it explained the essence of the plan, while Malori in the background, in an agony of terror, found himself bowing too.

"Proceed, then," the machine approved. "If you are not swift, the ship infected with life may find concealment in the storms that rise ahead of us." Then it went away again quickly. Probably it had repairs and refitting to accomplish on its own robotic ship.

With two men working, installation went very fast. It was only a matter of opening a fighting ship's cabin, inserting an uncased persona in the installed adapter, snapping together standard connectors and clamps, and closing the cabin hatch again. Since haste was vital to the berserkers' plans, testing was restricted to listening for a live response from each persona as it was activated inside a ship. Most of the responses were utter banalities about nonexistent weather or ancient food or drink, or curious phrases that Malori knew were only phatic social remarks.

All seemed to be going well, but Greenleaf was having some last minute misgivings. "I hope these sensitive gentlemen will stand up under the strain of finding out their true situation. They will be able to grasp that, won't they? The machines won't expect them to fight well, but we don't want them going catatonic, either."

Malori, close to exhaustion, was tugging at the hatch of Number Eight, and nearly fell off the curved hull when it came open suddenly. "They will apprehend their situation within a minute after launching, I should say. At least in a general way. I don't suppose they'll understand it's interstellar space around them. You have been a military man, I suppose. If they should be reluctant to fight—I leave to you the question of how to deal with recalcitrant auxiliaries."

When they plugged the persona into ship Number Eight, its test response was: "I wish my craft to be painted red."

"At once, sir," said Malori quickly, and slammed down the ship's hatch and started to move on to Number Nine.

"What was that all about?" Greenleaf frowned, but looked at his timepiece and moved along.

"I suppose the maestro is already aware that he is about to embark in some kind of a vehicle. As to why he might like it painted red . . ." Malori grunted, trying to open up Number Nine, and let his answer trail away.

At last all the ships were ready. With his finger on the launching switch, Greenleaf paused. For one last time his eyes probed Malori's. "We've done very well, timewise. We're in for a reward, as long as this idea works at least moderately well." He was speaking now in a solemn near-whisper. "It had better work. Have you ever watched a man being skinned alive?"

Malori was gripping a stanchion to keep erect. "I have done all I can."

Greenleaf operated the launching switch. There was a polyphonic whisper of airlocks. The nine ships were gone, and simultaneously a holographic display came alive above the operations officer's console. In the center of the display the *Judith* showed as a fat green symbol, with nine smaller green dots moving slowly and uncertainly nearby. Farther off, a steady formation of red dots represented what was left of the berserker pack that had so long and so relentlessly pursued the *Hope* and her escort. There were at least fifteen red berserker dots, Malori noted gloomily.

"This trick," Greenleaf said as if to himself, "is to make them more afraid of their own leaders than they are of the enemy." He keyed the panel switches that would send his voice out to the ships. "Attention, units One through Nine!" he barked. "You are under the guns of a vastly superior force, and any attempt at disobedience or escape will be severely punished..."

He went on browbeating them for a minute, while Malori observed in the screen that the dirty weather the berserker had mentioned was coming on. A sleet of atomic particles was driving through this section of the nebula, across the path of the *Judith* and the odd hybrid fleet that moved with her. The *Hope*, not in view on this range scale, might be able to take advantage of the storm to get away entirely unless the berserker pursuit was swift.

Visibility on the operations display was failing fast and Greenleaf cut off his speech as it became apparent that contact was being lost. Orders in the berserkers' unnatural voices, directed at auxiliary ships One through Nine, came in fragmentarily before the curtain of noise became an opaque white-out. The pursuit of the *Hope* had not yet been resumed.

For a while all was silent on the operations deck, except for an occasional crackle of noise from the display. All around them the empty launching cradles waited.

"That's that," Greenleaf said at length. "Nothing to do now but worry." He gave his little transforming smile again, and seemed to be almost enjoying the situation.

Malori was looking at him curiously. "How do you—manage to cope so well?"

"Why not?" Greenleaf stretched and got up from the now-useless console. "You know, once a man gives up his old ways, badlife ways, admits he's really dead to them, the new ways aren't so bad. There are even women available from time to time, when the machines take prisoners."

"Goodlife," said Malori. Now he had spoken the obscene, provoking epithet. But at the moment he was not afraid.

"Goodlife yourself, little man." Greenleaf was still smiling. "You know, I think you still look down on me. You're in as deep as I am now, remember?"

"I think I pity you."

Greenleaf let out a little snort of laughter, and shook his own head pityingly. "You know, I may have ahead of me a longer and more pain-free life than most of humanity has ever enjoyed—you said one of the models for the personae died at twenty-three. Was that a common age of death in those days?"

Malori, still clinging to his stanchion, began to wear a strange, grim little smile. "Well, in his generation, in the continent of Europe, it was. The First World War was raging at the time."

"But he died of some disease, you said."

"No. I said he *had* a disease, tuberculosis. Doubtless it would have killed him eventually. But he died in battle, in 1917 CE, in a place called Belgium. His body was never found, as I recall, an artillery barrage having destroyed it and his aircraft entirely."

Greenleaf was standing very still. "Aircraft! What are you saying?"

Malori pulled himself erect, somewhat painfully, and let go of his support. "I tell you now that Georges Guynemer—that was his name—shot down fifty-three enemy aircraft before he was killed. Wait!" Malori's voice was suddenly loud and firm, and Greenleaf halted his menacing advance in sheer surprise. "Before you begin to do anything violent to me, you should perhaps consider whether your side or mine is likely to win the fight outside."

"The fight. . . ."

"It will be nine ships against fifteen or more machines, but I don't feel too pessimistic. The personae we have sent out are not going to be meekly slaughtered."

Greenleaf stared at him a moment longer, then spun around and lunged for the operations console. The display was still blank white with noise and there was nothing to be done. He slowly sank into the padded chair. "What have you done to me?" he whispered. "That collection of invalid musicians—you couldn't have been lying about them all."

"Oh, every word I spoke was true. Not all World War One fighter pilots were invalids, of course. Some were in perfect health, indeed fanatical about staying that way. And I did not say they were all musicians, though I certainly meant you to think so. Ball had the most musical ability among the aces, but was still only an amateur. He always said he loathed his real profession."

Greenleaf, slumped in the chair now, seemed to be aging visibly. "But one was blind . . . it isn't possible."

"So his enemies thought, when they released him from an internment camp early in the war. Edward Mannock, blind in one eye. He had to trick an examiner to get into the army. Of course the tragedy of these superb men is that they spent themselves killing one another. In those days they had no berserkers to fight, at least none that could be attacked dashingly, with an aircraft and a machine gun. I suppose men have always faced berserkers of some kind."

"Let me make sure I understand." Greenleaf's voice was almost pleading. "We have sent out the personae of nine fighter pilots?"

"Nine of the best. I suppose their total of claimed aerial victories is more than five hundred. Such claims were usually exaggerated, but still . . ."

There was silence again. Greenleaf slowly turned his chair back to face the operations display. After a time the storm of atomic noise began to abate. Malori, who had sat down on the deck to rest, got up again, this time more quickly. In the hologram a single glowing symbol was emerging from the noise, fast approaching the position of the *Judith*.

The approaching symbol was bright red.

"So there we are," said Greenleaf, getting to his feet. From a pocket he produced a stubby little handgun. At first he pointed it toward the shrinking Malori, but then he smiled his nice smile and shook his head. "No, let the machines have you. That will be much worse."

When they heard the airlock begin to cycle, Greenleaf raised the weapon to point at his own skull. Malori could not tear his eyes away. The inner door clicked and Greenleaf fired.

Malori bounded across the intervening space and pulled the gun from Greenleaf's dead hand almost before the body had completed its fall. He turned to aim the weapon at the airlock as its inner door sighed open. The berserker standing there was the one he had seen earlier, or the same type at least. But it had just been through violent alterations. One metal arm was cut short in a bright bubbly scar, from which the ends of truncated cables flapped. The whole metal body was riddled with small holes, and around its top there played a halo of electrical discharge.

Malori fired, but the machine ignored the impact of the force-packet. They would not have let Greenleaf keep a gun with which they could be hurt. The battered machine ignored Malori too, for the moment, and lurched forward to bend over Greenleaf's nearly decapitated body.

"Tra-tra-tra-treason," the berserker squeaked. "Ultimate unpleasant ultimate unpleasant stum-stum-stimuli. Badlife badlife bad—"

By then Malori had moved up close behind it and thrust the muzzle of the gun into one of the still-hot holes where Albert Ball or perhaps Frank Luke or Werner Voss or one of the others had already used a laser to good effect. Two force-packets beneath its armor and the berserker went down, as still as the man who lay beneath it. The halo of electricity died.

Malori backed off, looking at them both, then spun around to scan the operations display again. The red dot was drifting away from the *Judith*, the vessel it represented now evidently no more than inert machinery.

Out of the receding atomic storm a single green dot was approaching. A minute later, Number Eight came in alone, bumping to a gentle stop against its cradle pads. The laser nozzle at once began smoking heavily in atmosphere. The craft was scarred in several places by enemy fire.

"I claim four more victories," the persona said as soon as Malori opened the hatch. "Today I was given fine support by my wingmen, who made great sacrifices for the Fatherland. Although the enemy outnumbered us by two to one, I think that not a single one of them escaped. But I must protest bitterly that my aircraft still has not been painted red."

"I will see to it at once, *meinherr*," murmured Malori, as he began to disconnect the persona from the fighting ship. He felt a little foolish for trying to reassure a piece of hardware. Still, he handled the persona gently as he carried it to where the little formation of empty cases were waiting on the operations deck, their labels showing plainly:

ALBERT BALL;
WILLIAM AVERY BISHOP;
RENE PAUL FONCK;
GEORGES MARIE GUYNEMER:
FRANK LUKE;
EDWARD MANNOCK;
CHARLES NUNGESSER;
MANFRED VON RICHTHOFEN;
WERNER VOSS.

They were English, American, German, French. They were Jew, violinist, invalid, Prussian, rebel, hater, bon vivant, Christian. Among the nine of them they were many other things besides. Maybe there was only the one word—man—which could include them all.

Right now the nearest living humans were many millions of kilometers away, but still Malori did not feel quite alone. He put the persona back into its case gently, even knowing that it would be undamaged by ten thousand more gravities than his hands could exert. Maybe it would fit into the cabin of Number Eight with him, when he made his try to reach the *Hope*.

"Looks like it's just you and me now, Red Baron." The human being from which it had been modeled had been not quite twenty-six when he was killed over France, after less than eighteen months of success and fame. Before that, in the cavalry, his horse had thrown him again and again.

Relatively unfettered by time or space, my mind has roamed the Galaxy in past and future to gather pieces of the truth of the great war of life against unliving death. What I have set down is far from the whole truth of that war, yet it is true.

Most of the higher intellects of the galaxy will shrink from war, even when survival depends upon it absolutely. Yet from the same matter that supports their lives, came the berserkers. Were their Builders uniquely evil? Would that it were so . . .

☀ THE SMILE

The berserker attack upon the world called St. Gervase had ended some four standard months before the large and luxurious private yacht of the Tyrant Yoritomo appeared amid the ashclouds and rainclouds that still monotonized the planet's newly lifeless sky. From the yacht a silent pair of waspish-looking launches soon began a swift descent, to land on the denuded surface where the planet's capital city had once stood.

The crews disembarking from the launches were armored against hot ash and hot mud and residual radiation. They knew what they were looking for, and in less than a standard hour they had located the vaulted tunnel leading down, from what had been a sub-basement of the famed St. Gervase Museum. The tunnel was partially collapsed in places, but still passable, and they followed its steps downward, stumbling here and there on debris fallen from the surface. The battle had not been completely one-sided in its early stages, and scattered amid the wreckage of the once-great city were fragments of berserker troop-landers and of their robotic shock-troops. The unliving metal killers had had to force a landing, to neutralize the defensive field generators, before the bombardment could begin in earnest.

The tunnel terminated in a large vault a hundred meters down. The lights, on an independent power supply, were still working, and the air conditioning was still trying to keep out dust. There were five great statues in the vault, including one in the attached workshop where some conservator or restorer had evidently been treating it. Each one was a priceless masterwork. And scattered in an almost casual litter throughout the shelter were paintings, pottery, small works in bronze and gold and silver, the least a treasure to be envied.

At once the visitors radioed news of their discovery to one who waited eagerly in the yacht hovering above. Their report concluded with the observation that someone had evidently been living down here since the attack. Beside the workshop, with its power lamp to keep things going, there was a small room that had served as a repository of the Museum's records. A cot stood in it now, there had been food supplies laid in, and there were other signs of human habitation. Well, it was not too strange that there should have been a few survivors, out of a population of many millions.

The man who had been living alone in the shelter for four months came back to find the landing party going busily about their work.

"Looters," he remarked, in a voice that seemed to have lost the strength for rage, or even fear. Not armored against radiation or anything else, he leaned against the terminal doorway of the battered tunnel, a long-haired, unshaven, once-fat man whose frame was now swallowed up in clothes that looked as if they might not have been changed since the attack.

The member of the landing party standing nearest looked back at him silently, and drummed fingers on the butt of a holstered handgun, considering. The man who had just arrived threw down the pieces of metallic junk he had brought with him, conveying in the gesture his contempt.

The handgun was out of its holster, but before it was leveled, an intervention from the leader of the landing party came in the form of a sharp gesture. Without taking his eyes off the man in the doorway, the leader at once reopened communication with the large ship waiting above.

"Your Mightiness, we have a survivor here," he informed the round face that soon appeared upon the small portable wallscreen. "I believe it is the sculptor Antonio Nobrega."

"Let me see him at once. Bring him before the screen." The voice of His Mightiness was inimitable and terrible, and no less terrible, somehow, because he always sounded short of breath. "Yes, you are right, although he is much changed. Nobrega, how fortunate for us both! This is indeed another important find."

"I knew you would be coming to St. Gervase now," Nobrega told the screen, in his empty voice. "Like a disease germ settling in a mangled body. Like some great fat cancer virus. Did you bring along your woman, to take charge of our Culture?"

One of the men beside the sculptor knocked him down. A breathless little snarl came from the screen at this, and Nobrega was quickly helped back to his feet, then put into a chair.

"He is an artist, my faithful ones," the screen-voice chided. "We must not expect him to have any sense of the fitness of things outside his art. No. We must get the maestro here some radiation treatment, and then bring him along with us to the Palace, and he will live and work there as happily, or unhappily, as elsewhere."

"Oh no," said the artist from his chair, more faintly than before. "My work is done."

"Pish-posh. You'll see."

"I knew you were coming . . ."

"Oh?" The small voice from the screen was humoring him. "And how did you know that?"

"I heard . . . when our fleet was still defending the approaches to the system, my daughter was out there with it. Through her, before she died, I heard how you brought your own fleet in-system, to watch what was going to happen, to judge our strength, our chance of resisting the berserkers. I heard how your force vanished when they came. I said then that you'd be back, to loot the things you could never get at in any other way."

Nobrega was quiet for a moment, then lunged from his chair—or made the best attempt at lunging that he could. He grabbed up a long metal sculptor's tool and drew it back to swing at *Winged Truth Rising*, a marble Poniatowski eleven centuries old. "Before I'll see you take this—"

Before he could knock a chip of marble loose, he was overpowered, and put into restraint.

When they approached him again an hour later, to take him up to the yacht for medical examination and treatment, they found him already dead. Autopsy on the spot discovered several kinds of slow and gentle poison. Nobrega might have taken some deliberately. Or he might have been finished by something the berserkers had left behind, to ensure that there would be no survivors, as they moved on to carry out their programmed task of eradicating all life from the Galaxy.

On his voyage home from St. Gervase, and for several months thereafter, Yoritimo was prevented by pressing business from really inspecting his new treasures. By then the five great statues had been installed, to good esthetic advantage, in the deepest, largest, and best-protected gallery of the Palace. Lesser collections had been evicted to make room and visual space for *Winged Truth Rising*; Lazamon's *Laughing* (or *Raging) Bacchus; The Last Provocation*, by Sarapion; Lazienki's *Twisting Room;* and *Remembrance of Past Wrongs*, by Prajapati.

It chanced that at this time the Lady Yoritomo was at the Palace too. Her duties, as Cultural Leader of the People, and High Overseer of Education for the four tributary planets, kept her on the move, and it often happened that she and her Lord did not see each other for a month or longer at a time.

The two of them trusted each other more than they trusted anyone else. Today they sat alone in the great gallery and sipped tea, and spoke of business.

The Lady was trying to promote her latest theory, which was that love for the ruling pair might be implanted genetically in the next generation of people on the tributary worlds. Several experimental projects had already begun. So far these had achieved little but severe mental retardation in the subjects, but there were plenty of new subjects and she was not discouraged.

The Lord spoke mainly of his own plan, which was to form a more explicit working arrangement with the berserkers. In this scheme the Yoritomos would furnish the killer machines with human lives they did not need, and planets hard to defend, in exchange for choice works of art and, of course, immunity from personal attack. The plan had many attractive features, but the Lord had to admit that the difficulty of opening negotiations with berserkers, let alone establishing any degree of mutual trust, made it somewhat impractical.

When a pause came in the conversation, Yoritomo had the banal thought that he and his wife had little to talk about anymore, outside of business. With a word to her, he rose from the alcove where they had been sitting, and walked to the far end of the gallery of statues to replenish the tea pot. For esthetic reasons he refused to allow robots in here; nor did he want human servitors around while this private discussion was in progress. Also, he thought, as he retraced his steps, the Lady could not help but be flattered, and won toward his own position in a certain matter where they disagreed, when she was served personally by the hands of one so mighty . . .

He rounded the great metal flank of *The Last Provocation* and came to a dumb halt, in shocked surprise so great that for a moment his facial expression did not even alter. Half a minute ago he had left her vivacious and thoughtful and full of graceful energy. She was still in the same place, on the settee, but slumped over sideways now, one arm extended with its slender, jeweled finger twitching upon the rich brown carpet. The Lady's hair was wildly disarranged; and small wonder, he thought madly, for her head had been twisted almost completely around, so her dead eyes now looked over one bare shoulder almost straight at Yoritomo. Upon her shoulder and her cheek were bruised discolorations...

He spun around at last, dropping the fragile masterpiece that held his tea. His concealed weapon was half-drawn before it was smashed out of his grip. He had one look at death, serenely towering above him. He had not quite time enough to shriek, before the next blow fell.

The wind had not rested in the hours since Ritwan's arrival, and with an endless howl it drove the restless land before it. He could quite easily believe that in a few years the great pit left by the destruction of the old Yoritomo Palace had been completely filled. The latest dig had ended only yesterday, and already the archaeologists' fresh pits were beginning to be reoccupied by sand.

"They were actually more pirates than anything else," Iselin, the chief archaeologist, was saying. "At the peak of their power two hundred years ago they ruled four systems. Ruled them from here, though there's not much showing on the surface now but this old sandpile."

"Ozymandias," Ritwan murmured.

"What?"

"An ancient poem." He pushed back sandy hair from his forehead with a thin, nervous hand. "I wish I'd got here in time to see the statues before you crated them and stowed them on your ship. You can imagine I came as fast as I could from Sirgol, when I heard there was a dig in progress here."

"Well," Iselin folded her plump arms and frowned, then smiled, a white flash in a dark Indian face. "Why don't you ride with us back to Esteel system? I really can't open the crates for anything until we get there. Not under the complicated rules of procedure we're stuck with on these jointly sponsored digs."

"My ship does have a good autopilot."

"Then set it to follow ours, and hop aboard. When we unpack on Esteel you can be among the first to look your fill. Meanwhile we can talk. I wish you'd been with us all along, we've missed having a really first-rate art historian."

"All right, I'll come." They offered each other enthusiastic smiles. "It's true, then, you really found most of the old St. Gervase collection intact?"

"I don't know that we can claim that. But there's certainly a lot."

"Just lying undisturbed here, for about two centuries."

"Well, as I say, this was the Yoritomos' safe port. But it looks like no more than a few thousand people ever lived on this world at any one time, and no one at all has lived here for a considerable period. Some intrigue or other evidently started among the Tyrant's lieutenants—no one's ever learned exactly how or why it started, but the thieves fell out. There was fighting, the Palace destroyed, the rulers themselves killed, and the whole thing collapsed. None of the intriguers had the ability to keep it going. I suppose, with the so-called Lord and Lady gone."

"Just when was that?"

Iselin named a date.

"The same year St. Gervase fell. That fits. The Yoritomos could have gone there after the berserkers left, and looted at their leisure. That would fit with their character, wouldn't it?"

"I'm afraid so . . . you see, the more I learned of them, the more I felt sure that they must have had a deeper, more secret shelter than any that was turned up in the early digs a century ago. The thing is, the people who dug here then found so much loot they were convinced they'd found it all."

Ritwan was watching the pits fill slowly in.

Iselin gave his arm a friendly shake. "And—did I tell you? We found two skeletons, I think of the Yoritomos themselves. Lavishly dressed in the midst of their greatest treasures. Lady died of a broken neck, and the man of multiple . . ."

The wind was howling still, when the two ships lifted off.

Aboard ship on the way to Esteel, things were relaxed and pleasant, if just a trifle cramped. With Ritwan along, they were six on board, and had to fit three to a cabin in narrow bunks. It was partially the wealth of the find that crowded them, of course. There were treasures almost beyond imagining stowed in plastic cratings almost everywhere one looked. The voyagers could expect a good deal of leisure time en route to marvel at it all. Propulsion and guidance and life-support were taken care of by machinery, with just an occasional careful human glance by way of circumspection. People in this particular portion of the inhabited Galaxy traveled now, as they had two hundred years before, in relative security from berserker attack. And now there were no human pirates.

Lashed in place in the central cargo bay stood the five great, muffled forms from which Ritwan particularly yearned to tear the pads and sheeting. But he made himself be patient. On the first day out he joined the others in the cargo bay, where they watched and listened to some of the old recordings found in the lower ruins of the Yoritomo Palace. There were data stored on tapes, in crystal cubes, around old permafrozen circuit rings. And much of the information was in the form of messages recorded by the Tyrant himself.

"The Gods alone know why he recorded this one," sighed Oshogbo. She was chief archivist of a large Esteel museum, one of the expedition's sponsoring institutions. "Listen to this. Look at him. He's ordering a ship to stand by and be boarded, or face destruction."

"The ham actor in him, maybe," offered Chi-nan, who on planet had been an assistant digger for the expedition, but in space became its captain. "He needed to study his delivery."

"Every one of his ships could carry the recording," suggested Klyuchevski, expert excavator. "So their victims wouldn't know if the Tyrant himself were present or not—I'm not sure how much difference it would make."

"Let's try another," said Granton, chief record-keeper and general assistant.

Within the next hour they sampled recordings in which Yoritomo: (1) ordered his subordinates to stop squabbling over slaves and concubines; (2) pleaded his case, to the Interworlds Government, as that of a man unjustly maligned, the representative of a persecuted people; (3) conducted a video tour, for some supposed audience whose identity was never made clear, of the most breathtaking parts of his vast collection of art . . .

"Wait!" Ritwan broke in. "What was that bit? Would you run that last part once more?"

The Tyrant's asthmatic voice repeated: "The grim story of how these magnificent statues happened to be saved. Our fleet had made every effort but still arrived too late to be of any help to the heroic defenders of St. Gervase. For many days we searched in vain for survivors; we found just one. And this man's identity made the whole situation especially poignant to me, for it was the sculptor Antonio Nobrega. Sadly, our help had come too late, and he shortly succumbed to the berserker poisons. I hope that the day will come soon, when all governments will heed my repeated urgings, to prosecute a war to the finish against these scourges of . . ."

"So!" Ritwan looked pleased, a man who has just had an old puzzle solved for him. "That's where Nobrega died, then. We've thought for some time it was likely—most of his family was there—but we had no hard evidence before."

"He was the famous forger, wasn't he?" asked Granton.

"Yes. A really good artist in his own right, though the shady side of his work has somewhat overshadowed the rest." Ritwan allowed time for the few small groans earned by the pun, and went on: "I'd hate to accept the old Tyrant's word on anything. But I suppose he'd have no reason to lie about Nobrega."

Iselin was looking at her wrist. "Lunch time for me. Maybe the rest of you want to spend all day in here."

"I can resist recordings." Ritwan got up to accompany her. "Now, if you were opening up the crates—"

"No chance, friend. But I can show you holograms—didn't I mention that?"

"You didn't!"

Oshogbo called after them: "Here's the Lord and Lady both, on this one—"

They did not stop. Chi-nan came out with them, leaving three people still in the cargo bay.

In the small ship's lounge, the three who had left set up lunch with a floor show.

"This is really decadence. Pea soup with ham, and—what have we here? Lazienki. Marvelous!"

The subtle grays and reds of *Twisting Room* (was it the human heart?) came into existence, projected by hidden devices in the corners of the lounge, and filling up the center. Iselin with a gesture made the full-size image rotate slowly.

"Captain?" the intercom asked hoarsely, breaking in.

"I knew it—just sit down, and—"

"I think we have some kind of cargo problem here." It sounded like Granton's voice, perturbed. "Something seems to be breaking up, or . . . Iselin, you'd better come to, and take a look at your . . ."

A pause, with background smashing noises. Then incoherent speech, in mixed voices, ending in a hoarse cry.

Chi-nan was already gone. Ritwan, sprinting, just kept in sight of Iselin's back going around corners. Then she stopped so suddenly that he almost ran into her.

The doorway to the cargo hold, left wide open when they came out of it a few minutes before, was now sealed tightly by a massive sliding door, a safety door designed to isolate compartments in case of emergencies like fire or rupture of the hull.

On the deck just outside the door, a human figure sprawled. Iselin and Chi-nan were already crouched over it; as Ritwan bent over them, a not-intrinsically-unpleasant smell of scorched meat reached his nostrils.

"Help me lift her . . . careful . . . sick bay's that way."

Ritwan helped Iselin. Chi-nan sprang to his feet, looked at an indicator beside the heavy door, and momentarily rested a hand on its flat surface.

"Something burning in there," he commented tersely, and then came along with the others on the quick hustle to sickbay. At his touch the small door opened for them, lights springing on inside.

"What's in our cargo that's not fireproofed?" Iselin demanded, as if all this were some personal insult hurled her way by Fate.

Dialogue broke off for a while. The burn-tank, hissing brim-full twenty seconds after the proper studs were punched, received Oshogbo's scorched dead weight, clothes and all, and went to work upon her with a steady sloshing. Then, while Iselin stayed in sick bay, Ritwan followed Chi-nan on another scrambling run, back to the small bridge. There the captain threw himself into an acceleration chair and laid swift hands on his controls, demanding an accounting from his ship.

In a moment he had switched his master intercom to show conditions inside the cargo bay, where two people were still unaccounted for. On the deck in there lay something clothed, a bundle-of-old-rags sort of something. In the remaining moment of clear vision before the cargo bay pickup went dead, Ritwan and Chi-nan both glimpsed a towering, moving shape.

The captain stared for a moment at the gray noise which came next, then switched to sick bay. Iselin appeared at once.

"How's she doing?" Chi-nan demanded.

"Signs are stabilizing. She's got a crack in the back of her skull as well as the burns on her torso, the printout says. As if something heavy had hit her in the head."

"Maybe the door clipped her, sliding closed, just as she got out." The men in the control room could see into the tank, and the captain raised his voice. "Oshy, can you answer me? What happened to Granton and Klu?"

The back of Oshogbo's neck was cradled on a rest of ivory plastic. Her body shook and shimmied lightly, vibrating with the dark liquid, as if she might be enjoying her swim. Here and there burnt shreds of clothing were now drifting free. She looked around and seemed to be trying to locate Chi-nan's voice. Then she spoke: "It . . . grabbed them. I . . . ran."

"What grabbed them? Are they still alive?"

"Granton's head came . . . it pulled off his head. I got out. Something hit . . ." The young woman's eyes rolled, her voice faded.

Iselin's face came into view again. "She's out of it; I think the medic just put her to sleep. Should I try to get it to wake her again?"

"Not necessary." The captain sounded shaken. "I think we must assume the others are finished. I'm not going to open that door, anyway, until I know more about our problem."

Ritwan asked: "Can we put down on some planet quickly?"

"Not one where we can get help," the captain told him over one shoulder. "There's no help closer than Esteel. Three or four days."

The three of them quickly talked over the problem, agreeing on what they knew. Two people were sure that they had seen, on intercom, something large moving about inside the cargo bay.

"And," Iselin concluded, "our surviving firsthand witness says that 'it' tore off someone's head."

"Sounds like a berserker," Ritwan said impulsively. "Or could it possibly be some animal—? Anyway, how could anything that big have been hiding in there?"

"An animal's impossible," Chi-nan told him flatly. "And you should have seen how we packed that space, how carefully we checked to see if we were wasting any room. The only place anyone or anything *could* have been hidden was inside one of those statuary crates."

Iselin added: "And I certainly checked out every one of them. We formed them to fit closely around the statues, and they couldn't have contained anything else of any size. What's that noise?"

The men in the control room could hear it too, a muffled, rhythmic banging, unnatural for any space ship that Ritwan had ever ridden. He now, for some reason, suddenly thought of what kind of people they had been whose Palace had provided this mysterious cargo; and for the first time since the trouble had started he began to feel real fear.

He put a hand on the other man's shoulder. "Chi-nan—what exactly did we see on the intercom screen?"

The captain thought before answering. "Something big, taller than a man, anyway. And moving by itself. Right?"

"Yes, and I'd say it was dark . . . beyond that, I don't know."

"I would have called it light-colored." The muffled pounding sounds had grown a little steadier, faster, louder. "So, do you think one of our statues has come alive on us?"

Iselin's voice from sick bay offered: "I think 'alive' is definitely the wrong word."

Ritwan asked: "How many of the statues have movable joints?" *Twisting Room*, which he had seen in hologram, did not. But articulated sculpture had been common enough a few centuries earlier.

"Two did," said Iselin.

"I looked at all the statues closely," Chi-nan protested. "Iselin, you did too. We all did, naturally. And they were genuine."

"We never checked inside them, for controls, power supplies, robotic brains. Did we?"

"Of course not. There was no reason."

Ritwan persisted: "So it is a berserker. It can't be anything else. And it waited until now to attack, because it wants to be sure to get the ship."

Chi-nan pounded his chair-arm with a flat hand. "No! I can't buy that. Do you think that emergency door would stop a berserker? We'd all be dead now, and it would have the ship. And you're saying it's a berserker that looks just like a masterpiece by a great artist, enough alike to fool experts; and that it stayed buried there for two hundred years without digging itself out; and that—"

"Nobrega," Ritwan interrupted suddenly.

"What?"

"Nobrega . . . he died on St. Gervase, we don't know just how. He had every reason to hate the Yoritomos. Most probably he met one or both of them at the St. Gervase Museum, after the attack, while they were doing what they called their collecting.

"You said Nobrega was a great forger. Correct. A good engineer, too. You also said that no one knows exactly how the Yoritomos came to die, only that their deaths were violent. And occurred among these very statues."

The other two, one on screen and one at hand, were very quiet, watching him.

"Suppose," Ritwan went on, "Nobrega knew somehow that the looters would be coming, and he had the time and the means to concoct something special for them. Take a statue with movable limbs, and build in a power lamp, sensors, controls—a heat-projector, maybe, as a weapon. And then add the electronic brain from some small berserker unit."

Chi-nan audibly sucked in his breath.

"There might easily have been some of those lying around on St. Gervase, after the attack. Everyone agrees it was a fierce defense."

"I'm debating with myself," said Chi-nan, "whether we should all pile into the lifeboat, and head for your ship, Ritwan. It's small, as you say, but I suppose we'd fit, in a pinch."

"There's no real sick bay."

"Oh." They all looked at the face of the young woman in the tank, unconscious now, dark hair dancing round it upon the surface of the healing fluid.

"Anyway," the captain resumed, "I'm not sure it couldn't take over the controls here, catch us, ram us somehow. Maybe, as you think, it's not a real berserker. But it seems to be too close to the real thing to just turn over our ship to it. We're going to have to stay and fight."

"Bravo," said Iselin. "But with what? It seems to me we stowed away our small arms in the cargo bay somewhere."

"We did. Let's hope Nobrega didn't leave it brains enough to look for them, and it just keeps banging on that door. Meanwhile, let's check what digging equipment we can get at."

Iselin decided it was pointless for her to remain in sick bay, and came to help them, leaving the intercom channel open so they could look in on Oshogbo from time to time.

"That door to the cargo bay is denting and bulging, boys," she told them as she ducked into the cramped storage space beneath the lounge where they were rummaging. "Let's get something organizing in the way of weapons."

Ritwan grunted, dragging out a long, thick-bodied tool, evidently containing its own power supply. "What's this, an autohammer? Looks like it would do a job."

"Sure," said Chi-nan. "If you get within arm's length. We'll save that for when we're really desperate."

A minute later, digging through boxes of electrical-looking devices strange to Ritwan, the captain murmured: "If he went to all the trouble of forging an old master he must have had good reason. Well, it'd be the one thing the Yoritomos might accept at face value. Take it right onto their ship, into their private rooms. He must have been out to get the Lord and Lady both."

"I guess that was it. I suppose just putting a simple bomb in the statue wouldn't have been sure enough, or selective enough."

"Also it might have had to pass some machines that sniff out explosives, before it got into the inner . . . Ritwan! When that thing attacked, just now, what recording were they listening to in the cargo bay?"

Ritwan stopped in the middle of opening another box. "Oshogbo called it out to us as we were leaving. You're right, one with both the Yoritomos on it. Nobrega must have set his creation to be triggered by their voices, heard together."

"How it's supposed to be turned off, is what I'd like to know."

"It did turn off, for some reason, didn't it? And lay there for two centuries. Probably Nobrega didn't foresee that the statue might survive long enough for the cycle to be able to repeat. Maybe if we can just hold out a little longer, it'll turn itself off again."

Patient and regular as a clock, the muffled battering sounded on.

"Can't depend on that, I'm afraid." Chi-nan kicked away the last crate to be searched. "Well, this seems to be the extent of the hardware we have for putting together weapons. It looks like whatever we use is going to have to be electrical. I think we can rig up something to electrocute—if that's the right word—or fry, or melt, the enemy. We've got to know first, though, just which of those statues is the one we're fighting. There are only two possible mobile ones, which narrows it down. But still."

"*Laughing Bacchus,*" Iselin supplied. "And *Remembrance of Past Wrongs.*"

"The first is basically steel. We can set up an induction field strong enough to melt it down, I think. A hundred kilos or so of molten iron in the middle of the deck may be hard to deal with, but not as hard as what we've got now. But the other statue, or anyway its outer structure, is some kind of very hard and tough ceramic. That one will need something like a lightning bolt to knock it out." A horrible thought seemed to strike Chi-nan all at once. "You don't suppose there could be two—?"

Ritwan gestured reassurance. "I think Nobrega would have put all his time and effort into perfecting one."

"So," said Iselin, "it all comes down to knowing which one he forged, and which is really genuine. The one he worked on must be forged; even if he'd started with a real masterpiece to build his killing device, by the time he got everything implanted the surface would have to be almost totally reconstructed."

"So I'm going up to the lounge," the art historian replied. "And see those holograms. If we're lucky I'll be able to spot it."

Iselin came with him, muttering: "All you have to do, friend, is detect a forgery that got past Yoritomo and *his* experts . . . maybe we'd better think of something else."

In the lounge the holograms of the two statues were soon displayed full size, side by side and slowly rotating. Both were tall, roughly humanoid figures, and both in their own ways were smiling.

A minute and a half had passed when Ritwan said, decisively: "This one's the forgery. Build your lightning device."

Before the emergency door at last gave way under that mindless, punch-press pounding, the electrical equipment had been assembled and moved into place. On either side of the doorway Chi-nan and Iselin crouched, manning their switches. Ritwan (counted the most expendable in combat) stood in plain view opposite the crumpling door, garbed in a heat-insulating spacesuit and clutching the heavy autohammer to his chest.

The final failure of the door was sudden. One moment it remained in place, masking what lay beyond; next moment, it had been torn away. For a long second of the new silence, the last work of Antonio Nobrega stood clearly visible, bonewhite in the glare of lamps on every side, against the blackened ruin of what had been the cargo bay.

Ritwan raised the hammer, which suddenly felt no heavier than a microprobe. For a moment he knew what people felt, who face the true berserker foe in combat.

The tall thing took a step toward him, serenely smiling. And the blue-white blast came at it from the side, faster than any mere matter could be made to dodge.

A couple of hours later the most urgent damage-control measures had been taken, two dead bodies had been packed for preservation—with real reverence if without gestures—and the pieces of Nobrega's work, torn asunder by the current that the ceramic would not peacefully admit, had cooled enough to handle.

Ritwan had promised to show the others how he had known the forgery; and now he came up with the fragment he was looking for. "This," he said.

"The mouth?"

"The smile. If you've looked at as much Federation era art as I have, the incongruity is obvious. The smile's all wrong for Prajapati's period. It's evil, cunning—when the face was intact you could see it plainly. Gloating. Calm and malevolent at the same time."

Iselin asked: "But Nobrega himself didn't see that? Or Yoritomo?"

"For the period *they* lived in, the smile's just fine, artistically speaking. They couldn't step forward or backward two hundred years, and get a better perspective. I suppose revenge is normal in any century, but tastes in art are changeable."

Chi-nan said: "I thought perhaps the subject or the title gave you some clue."

"*Remembrance of Past Wrongs*—no, Prajapati did actually do something very similar in subject, as I recall. As I say, I suppose revenge knows no cultural or temporal boundaries."

Normal in any century. Oshogbo, watching via intercom from the numbing burn-treatment bath, shivered and closed her eyes. *No boundaries.*

On the least lonely and best defended of all human worlds, not even the past was safe from enemy invasion.

❋ METAL MURDERER

It had the shape of a man, the brain of an electronic devil.

It and the machines like it were the best imitations of men and women that the berserkers, murderous machines themselves, were able to devise and build. Still, they could be seen as obvious frauds when closely inspected by any humans.

"Only twenty-nine accounted for?" the supervisor of Defense demanded sharply. Strapped into his combat chair, he was gazing intently through the semitransparent information screen before him, into space. The nearby bulk of Earth was armored in the dun-brown of defensive force fields, the normal colors of land and water and air invisible.

"Only twenty-nine." The answer arrived on the flagship's bridge and a sharp sputtering of electrical noise. The tortured voice continued. "And it's quite certain now that there were thirty to begin with."

"Then where's the other one?"

There was no reply.

All of Earth's defensive forces were still on full alert, though the attack had been tiny, no more than an attempt at infiltration, and seemed to have been thoroughly repelled.

A small blur leaped over Earth's dun-brown limb, hurtling along on a course that would bring it within a few hundred kilometers of the supervisor's craft. This was Power Station One, a tamed black hole. In time of peace the power-hungry billions on the planet drew from it half their needed energy. Station One was visible to the eye only as a slight, flowing distortion of the stars beyond.

Another report was coming in. "We are searching space for the missing berserker android, Supervisor."

"You had damned well better be."

"The infiltrating enemy craft had padded containers for thirty androids, as shown by computer analysis of its debris. We must assume that all containers were filled."

Life and death were in the supervisor's tones. "Is there any possibility that the missing unit got past you to the surface?"

"Negative, Supervisor." There was a slight pause. "At least we know it did not reach the surface in our time."

"Our time? What does that mean, babbler? How could . . . ah."

The black hole flashed by. Not really tamed, though that was a reassuring word, and humans applied it frequently. Just harnessed, more or less.

Suppose—and, given the location of the skirmish, the supposition was not unlikely—that berserker android number thirty had been propelled, by some accident of combat, directly at Station One. It could easily have entered the black hole. According to the latest theories, it might conceivably have survived to reemerge intact into the universe, projected out of the hole as its own tangible image in a burst of virtual-particle radiation.

Theory dictated that in such a case the re-emergence must take place before the falling in. The supervisor crisply issued orders. At once his computers on the world below, the Earth Defense Conglomerate, took up the problem, giving it highest priority. What could one berserker android do to Earth? Probably not much. But to the supervisor, and to those who worked for him, defense was a sacred task. The temple of Earth's safety had been horribly profaned.

To produce the first answers took the machines eleven minutes.

"Number thirty did go into the black hole sir. Neither we nor the enemy could very well have foreseen such a result, but—"

"What is the probability that the android emerged intact?"

"Because of the peculiar angle at which it entered, approximately sixty-nine percent."

"That high!"

"And there is a forty-nine-percent chance that it will reach the surface of the earth in functional condition, at some point in our past. However, the computers offer reassurance. As the enemy device must have been programmed for some subtle attack upon our present society, it is not likely to be able to do much damage at the time and place where it—"

"Your skull contains a vacuum of a truly intergalactic order. *I* will tell *you* and the computers when it has become possible for us to feel even the slightest degree of reassurance. Meanwhile, get me more figures."

The next word from the ground came twenty minutes later.

"There is a ninety-two-percent chance that the landing of the android on the surface, if that occurred, was within one hundred kilometers of fifty-one degrees, eleven minutes north latitude; zero degrees, seven minutes west longitude."

"And the time?"

"Ninety-eight-percent probability of January 1, 1880 Christian Era, plus or minus ten standard years."

A landmass, a great clouded island, was presented to the supervisor on his screen.

"Recommended course of action?"

It took the ED Conglomerate an hour and a half to answer that.

The first two volunteers perished in attempted launchings before the method could be improved enough to offer a reasonable chance of survival. When the third man was ready, he was called in, just before launching, for a last private meeting with the supervisor.

The supervisor looked him up and down, taking in his outlandish dress, strange hairstyle, and all the rest. He did not ask whether the volunteer was ready but began bluntly: "It has now been confirmed that whether you win or lose back there, you will never be able to return to your own time."

"Yes, sir. I had assumed that would be the case."

"Very well." The supervisor consulted data spread before him. "We are still uncertain as to just how the enemy is armed. Something subtle, doubtless, suitable for a saboteur on the earth of our own time—in addition, of course, to the superhuman physical strength and speed you must expect to face. There are the scrambling or the switching mindbeams to be considered; either could damage any human society. There are the pattern bombs, designed to disable our defense computers by seeding them with random information. There are always possibilities of biological warfare. You have your disguised medical kit? Yes, I see. And of course there is always the chance of something new."

"Yes, sir." The volunteer looked as ready as anyone could. The supervisor went to him, opening his arms for a ritual farewell embrace.

He blinked away some London rain, pulled out his heavy ticking timepiece as if he were checking the hour, and stood on the pavement before the theater as if he were waiting for a friend. The instrument in his hand throbbed with a silent, extra vibration in addition to its ticking, and this special signal had now taken on a character that meant the enemy machine was very near to him. It was probably within a radius of fifty meters.

A poster on the front of the theater read:

THE IMPROVED AUTOMATON CHESS PLAYER
MARVEL OF THE AGE
UNDER NEW MANAGEMENT

"The real problem, sir," proclaimed one top-hatted man nearby, in conversation with another, "is not whether a machine can be made to win at chess, but whether it may possibly be made to play at all."

No, that is not the real problem, sir, the agent from the future thought. *But count yourself fortunate that you can still believe it is.*

He bought a ticket and went in, taking a seat. When a sizable audience had gathered, there was a short lecture by a short man in evening dress, who had something predatory about him and also something frightened, despite the glibness and the rehearsed humor of his talk.

At length the chess player itself appeared. It was a desklike box with a figure seated behind it, the whole assembly wheeled out on stage by assistants. The figure was that of a huge man in Turkish garb. Quite obviously a mannequin or a dummy of some kind, it bobbed slightly with the motion of the rolling desk, to which its chair was fixed. Now the agent could feel the excited vibration of his watch without even putting a hand into his pocket.

The predatory man cracked another joke, displayed a hideous smile, then, from among several chess players in the audience who raised their hands—the agent was not among them—he selected one to challenge the automaton. The challenger ascended to the stage, where the pieces were being set out on a board fastened to the rolling desk, and the doors in the front of the desk were being opened to show that there was nothing but machinery inside.

The agent noted that there were no candles on this desk, as there had been on that of Maelzel's chess player a few decades earlier. Maelzel's automaton had been an earlier fraud, of course. Candles had been placed on its box to mask the odor of burning wax from the candle needed by the man who was so cunningly hidden inside amid the dummy gears. The year in which the agent had arrived was still too early, he knew, for electric lights, at least the kind that would be handy for such a hidden human to use. Add the fact that this chess player's opponent was allowed to sit much closer than Maelzel's had ever been, and it became a pretty safe deduction that no human being was concealed inside the box and figure on this stage.

Therefore . . .

The agent might, if he stood up in the audience, get a clear shot at it right now. But should he aim at the figure or the box ? And he could not be sure how it was armed. And who would stop it if he tried and failed? Already it had learned enough to survive in nineteenth-century London. Probably it had already killed, to further its design—"under new management" indeed.

No, now that he had located his enemy, he must plan thoroughly and work patiently. Deep in thought, he left the theater amid the crowd at the conclusion of the performance and started on foot back to the rooms that he had just begun to share on Baker Street. A minor difficulty at his launching into the black hole had cost him some equipment, including most of his counterfeit money. There had not been time as yet for his adopted profession to bring him much income; so he was for the time being in straitened financial circumstances.

He must plan. Suppose, now, that he were to approach the frightened little man in evening dress. By now that one ought to have begun to understand what kind of a tiger he was riding. The agent might approach him in the guise of—

A sudden tap-tapping began in the agent's watch pocket. It was a signal quite distinct from any previously generated by his fake watch. It meant that the enemy had managed to detect his detector; it was in fact locked onto it and tracking.

Sweat mingled with the drizzle on the agent's face as he began to run. It must have discovered him in the theater, though probably it could not then single him out in the crowd. Avoiding horse-drawn cabs, four-wheelers, and an omnibus, he turned out of Oxford Street to Baker Street and slowed to a fast walk for the short distance remaining. He could not throw away the telltale watch, for he would be unable to track the enemy without it. But neither did he dare retain it on his person.

As the agent burst into the sitting room, his roommate looked up, with his usual, somewhat shallow, smile, from a leisurely job of taking books out of a crate and putting them on shelves.

"I say," the agent began, in mingled relief and urgency, "something rather important has come up, and I find there are two errands I must undertake at once. Might I impose one of them on you?"

The agent's own brisk errand took him no farther than just across the street. There, in the doorway of Camden House, he shrank back, trying to breathe silently. He had not moved when, three minutes later, there approached from the direction of Oxford Street a tall figure that the agent suspected was not human, its hat was pulled down, and the lower portion of its face was muffled in bandages. Across the street it paused, seemed to consult a pocket watch of its own, then turned to ring the bell. Had the agent been absolutely sure it was his quarry, he would have shot it in the back. But without his watch, he would have to get closer to be absolutely sure.

After a moment's questioning from the landlady, the figure was admitted. The agent waited for two minutes. Then he drew a deep breath, gathered up his courage, and went after it.

The thing standing alone at a window turned to face him as he entered the sitting room, and now he was sure of what it was. The eyes above the bandaged lower face were not the Turk's eyes, but they were not human, either.

The white swathing muffled its gruff voice. "You are the doctor?"

"Ah, it is my fellow lodger that you want." The agent threw a careless glance toward the desk where he had locked up the watch, the desk on some papers bearing his roommate's name were scattered. "He is out at the moment, as you see, but we can expect him presently. I take it you are a patient."

The thing said, in its wrong voice, "I have been referred to him. It seems the doctor and I share a certain common background. Therefore the good landlady has let me wait in here. I trust my presence is no inconvenience."

"Not in the least. Pray take a seat, Mr.—?"

What name the berserker might have given, the agent never learned. The bell sounded below, suspending conversation. He heard the servant girl answering the door, and a moment later his roommate's brisk feet on the stairs. The death machine took a small object from its pocket and sidestepped a little to get a clear view past the agent toward the door.

Turning his back upon the enemy, as if with the casual purpose of greeting the man about to enter, the agent casually drew from his own pocket a quite functional briar pipe, which was designed to serve another function, too. Then he turned his head and fired the pipe at the berserker from under his own left armpit.

For a human being he was uncannily fast, and for a berserker the android was meanly slow and clumsy, being designed primarily for imitation, not dueling. Their weapons triggered at the same instant.

Explosions racked and destroyed the enemy, blasts shatteringly powerful but compactly limited in space, self-damping and almost silent.

The agent was hit, too. Staggering, he knew with his last clear thought just what weapon the enemy had carried—the switching mindbeam. Then for a moment he could no longer think at all. He was dimly aware of being down on one knee and of his fellow lodger, who had just entered, standing stunned a step inside the door.

At last the agent could move again, and he shakily pocketed his pipe. The ruined body of the enemy was almost vaporized already. It must have been built to self-destruct when damaged badly, so that humanity might never learn its secrets. Already it was no more than a puddle of heavy mist, warping in slow tendrils out the slightly open window to mingle with the fog.

The man still standing near the door had put out a hand to steady himself against the wall. "The jeweler . . . did not have your watch," he muttered dazedly.

I have won, thought the agent dully. It was a joyless thought because with it came slow realization of the price of his success. Three quarters of his intellect, at least, was gone, the superior pattern of his brain-cell connections scattered. No. Not scattered. The switching mindbeam would have reimposed the pattern of his neurons somewhere farther down its pathway . . . *there,* behind those gray eyes with their newly penetrating gaze.

"Obviously, sending me out for your watch was a ruse." His roommate's voice was suddenly crisper, more assured than it had been. "Also, I perceive that your desk has just been broken into, by someone who thought it mine." The tone softened somewhat. "Come, man, I bear you no ill will. Your secret, if honorable, shall be safe. But it is plain that you are not what you have represented yourself to be."

The agent got to his feet, pulling at his sandy hair, trying desperately to think. "How—how do you know?"

"Elementary!" the tall man snapped.

The terror of the berserkers spread ahead of them across the galaxy. Even on worlds not touched by the physical fighting, there were people who felt themselves breathing darkness, and sickened inwardly. Few men on any world chose to look for long out into the nighttime sky. Some men on each world found themselves newly obsessed by the shadows of death.

I touched a mind whose soul was dead . . .

☀ PATRON OF THE ARTS

After some hours' work, Herron found himself hungry and willing to pause for food. Looking over what he had just done, he could easily imagine one of the sycophantic critics praising it: A huge canvas, of discordant and brutal line! Aflame with a sense of engulfing menace! And for once, Herron thought, the critic might be praising something good.

Turning away from his view of easel and blank bulkhead, Herron found that his captor had moved up silently to stand only an arm's length behind him, for all the world like some human kibitzer.

He had to chuckle. "I suppose you've some idiotic suggestion to make?"

The roughly man-shaped machine said nothing, though it had what might be a speaker mounted on what might be a face. Herron shrugged and walked around it, going forward in search of the galley. This ship had been only a few hours out from Earth on C-plus drive when the berserker machine had run it down and captured it; and Piers Herron, the only passenger, had not yet had time to learn his way around.

It was more than a galley, he saw when he reached it—it was

meant to be a place where arty colonial ladies could sit and twitter over tea when they grew weary of staring at pictures. The *Frans Hals* had been built as a traveling museum; then the war of life against berserker machines had grown hot around Sol, and BuCulture had wrongly decided that Earth's art treasures would be safer if shipped away to Tau Epsilon. The *Frans* was ideally suited for such a mission, and for almost nothing else.

Looking further forward from the entrance to the galley, Herron could see that the door to the crew compartment had been battered down, but he did not go to look inside. Not that it would bother him to look, he told himself; he was as indifferent to horror as he was to almost all other human things. The *Frans*'s crew of two were in there, or what was left of them after they had tried to fight off the berserker's boarding machines. Doubtless they had preferred death to capture.

Herron preferred nothing. Now he was probably the only living being—apart from a few bacteria—within half a light year; and he was pleased to discover that his situation did not terrify him; that his long-growing weariness of life was not just a pose.

His metal captor followed him into the galley, watching while he set the kitchen devices to work.

"Still no suggestions?" Herron asked it. "Maybe you're smarter than I thought."

"I am what men call a berserker," the man-shaped thing squeaked at him suddenly, in an ineffectual-sounding voice. "I have captured your ship, and I will talk with you through this small machine you see. Do you grasp my meaning?"

"I understand as well as I need to." Herron had not yet seen the berserker itself, but he knew it was probably drifting a few miles away, or a few hundred or a thousand miles, from the ship it had captured. Captain Hanus had tried desperately to escape it, diving the *Frans* into a cloud of dark nebula where no ship or machine could move faster than light, and where the advantage in speed lay with the smaller hull.

The chase had been at speeds up to a thousand miles a second. Forced to remain in normal space, the berserker could not steer its bulk among the meteoroids and gas-wisps as well as the *Frans*'s radar-computer system could maneuver the fleeing ship. But the berserker had sent an armed launch of its own to take up the chase, and the weaponless *Frans* had had no chance.

Now, dishes of food, hot and cold, popped out on a galley table, and Herron bowed to the machine. "Will you join me?"

"I need no organic food."

Herron sat down with a sigh. "In the end," he told the machine, "you'll find that lack of humor is as pointless as laughter. Wait and see if I'm not right." He began to eat, and found himself not so hungry as he had thought. Evidently his body still feared death—this surprised him a little.

"Do you normally function in the operation of this ship?" the machine asked.

"No," he said, making himself chew and swallow. "I'm not much good at pushing buttons." A peculiar thing that had happened was nagging at Herron. When capture was only minutes away, Captain Hanus had come dashing aft from the control room, grabbing Herron and dragging him along in a tearing hurry, aft past all the stored art treasures.

"Herron, listen—if we don't make it, see here?" Tooling open a double hatch in the stern compartment, the captain had pointed into what looked like a short padded tunnel, the diameter of a large drainpipe. "The regular lifeboat won't get away, but this might."

"Are you waiting for the Second Officer, Captain, or leaving us now?"

"There's room for only one, you fool, and I'm not the one who's going."

"You mean to save me? Captain, I'm touched!" Herron laughed, easily and naturally. "But don't put yourself out."

"You idiot. Can I trust you?" Hanus lunged into the boat, his hands flying over its controls. Then he backed out, glaring like a madman. "Listen. Look here. This button is the activator; now I've set things up so the boat should come out in the main shipping lanes and start sending a distress signal. Chances are she'll be picked up safely then. Now the controls are set, only this activator button needs to be pushed down—"

The berserker's launch had attacked at that moment, with a roar like mountains falling on the hull of the ship. The lights and artificial gravity had failed and then come abruptly back. Piers Herron had been thrown on his side, his wind knocked out. He had watched while the captain, regaining his feet and moving like a man in a daze, had closed the hatch on the mysterious little boat again and staggered forward to his control room.

"Why are you here?" the machine asked Herron.

He dropped the forkful of food he had been staring at. He didn't have to hesitate before answering the question. "Do you know what BuCulture is? They're the fools in charge of art, on Earth. Some of them, like a lot of other fools, think I'm a great painter. They worship me. When I said I wanted to leave Earth on this ship, they made it possible.

"I wanted to leave because almost everything that is worthwhile in any true sense is being removed from Earth. A good part of it is on this ship. What's left behind on the planet is only a swarm of animals, breeding and dying, fighting—"

"Why did you not try to fight or hide when my machines boarded this ship?"

"Because it would have done no good."

When the berserker's prize crew had forced their way in through an airlock, Herron had been setting up his easel in what was to have been a small exhibition hall, and he had paused to watch the uninvited visitors file past. One of the man-shaped metal things, the one through which he was being questioned now, had stayed to stare at him through its lenses while the others had moved on forward to the crew compartment.

"Herron!" The intercom had shouted. "Try, Herron, please! You know what to do!" Clanging noises followed, and gunshots and curses.

What to do, Captain? Why, yes. The shock of events and the promise of imminent death had stirred up some kind of life in Piers Herron. He looked with interest at the alien shapes and lines of his inanimate captor, the inhuman cold of deep space frosting over its metal here in the warm cabin. Then he turned away from it and began to paint the berserker, trying to catch not the outward shape he had never seen, but what he felt of its inwardness. He felt the emotionless deadliness of its watching lenses, boring into his back. The sensation was faintly pleasurable, like cold spring sunshine.

"What is good?" the machine asked Herron, standing over him in the galley while he tried to eat.

He snorted. "You tell me."

It took him literally. "To serve the cause of what men call death is good. To destroy life is good."

Herron pushed his nearly full plate into a disposal slot and stood up. "You're almost right about life being worthless—but even if you were entirely right, why so enthusiastic? What is there praiseworthy about death?" Now his thoughts surprised him as his lack of appetite had.

"I am entirely right," said the machine.

For long seconds Herron stood still, as if thinking, though his mind was almost completely blank. "No," he said finally, and waited for a bolt to strike him.

"In what do you think I am wrong?" it asked.

"I'll show you." He led it out of the gallery, his hands sweating and his mouth dry. Why wouldn't the damned thing kill him and have done?

The paintings were racked row on row and tier on tier; there was no room in the ship for more than a few to be displayed in a conventional way. Herron found the drawer he wanted and pulled it open so the portrait inside swung into full view, lights springing on around it to bring out the rich colors beneath the twentieth-century statglass coating.

"This is where you're wrong," Herron said.

The man-shaped thing's scanner studied the portrait for perhaps fifteen seconds. "Explain what you are showing me," it said.

"I bow to you!" Herron did so. "You admit ignorance! You even ask an intelligible question, if one that is somewhat too broad. First, tell me what *you* see here."

"I see the image of a life-unit, its third spatial dimension of negligible size as compared to the other two. The image is sealed inside a protective jacket transparent to the wavelengths used by the human eye. The life-unit imaged is, or was, an adult male apparently in good functional condition, garmented in a manner I have not seen before. What I take to be one garment is held before him—"

"You see a man with a glove," Herron cut in, wearying of his bitter game. "That is the title, *Man with a Glove*. Now what do you say about it?"

There was a pause of twenty seconds. "Is it an attempt to praise life, to say that life is good?"

Looking now at Titian's thousand-year-old more-than-masterpiece, Herron hardly heard the machine's answer; he was thinking helplessly and hopelessly of his own most recent work.

"Now you will tell me what it means," said the machine without emphasis.

Herron walked away without answering, leaving the drawer open.

The berserker's mouthpiece walked at his side. "Tell me what it means or you will be punished."

"If you can pause to think, so can I." But Herron's stomach had knotted up at the threat of punishment, seeming to feel that pain mattered even more than death. Herron had great contempt for his stomach.

His feet took him back to his easel. Looking at the discordant and brutal line that a few minutes ago had pleased him, he now found it as disgusting as everything else he had tried to do in the past year.

The berserker asked: "What have you made here?"

Herron picked up a brush he had forgotten to clean, and wiped at it irritably. "It is my attempt to get at your essence, to capture you with paint and canvas as you have seen those humans captured." He waved at the storage racks. "My attempt has failed, as most do."

There was another pause, which Herron did not try to time.

"An attempt to praise me?"

Herron broke the spoiled brush and threw it down. "Call it what you like."

This time the pause was short, and at its end the machine did not speak, but turned away and walked in the direction of the airlock. Some of its fellows clanked past to join it. From the direction of the airlock there began to come sounds like those of heavy metal being worked and hammered. The interrogation seemed to be over for the time being.

Herron's thoughts wanted to be anywhere but on his work or on his fate, and they returned to what Hanus had shown him, or tried to show him. Not a regular lifeboat, but she might get away, the captain had said. All it needs now is to press the button.

Herron started walking, smiling faintly as he realized that if the berserker was as careless as it seemed, he might possibly escape it.

Escape to what? He couldn't paint any more, if he ever could. All that really mattered to him now was here, and on other ships leaving Earth.

Back at the storage rack, Herron swung the *Man with a Glove* out so its case came free from the rack and became a handy cart. He wheeled the portrait aft. There might be yet one worthwhile thing he could do with his life.

The picture was massive in its statglass shielding, but he thought he could fit it into the boat.

As an itch might nag a dying man, the question of what the captain had been intending with the boat nagged Herron. Hanus hadn't seemed worried about Herron's fate, but instead had spoken of trusting Herron....

Nearing the stern, out of sight of the machines, Herron passed a strapped-down stack of crated statuary, and heard a noise, a rapid feeble pounding.

It took several minutes to find and open the proper case. When he lifted the lid with its padded lining, a girl wearing a coverall sat up, her hair all wild as if standing in terror.

"Are they gone?" She had bitten at her fingers and nails until they were bleeding. When he didn't answer at once, she repeated her question again and again, in a rising whine.

"The machines are still here," he said at last.

Literally shaking in her fear, she climbed out of the case. "Where's Gus? Have they taken him?"

"Gus?" But he thought he was beginning to understand.

"Gus Hanus, the captain. He and I are—he was trying to save me, to get me away from Earth."

"I'm quite sure he's dead," said Herron. "He fought the machines."

Her bleeding fingers clutched at her lower face. "They'll kill us, too! Or worse! What can we do?"

"Don't mourn your lover so deeply," he said. But the girl seemed not to hear him; her wild eyes looked this way and that, expecting the machines. "Help me with this picture," he told her calmly. "Hold the door there for me."

She obeyed as if half-hypnotized, not questioning what he was doing.

"Gus said there'd be a boat," she muttered to herself. "If he had to smuggle me down to Tau Epsilon he was going to use a special little boat—". She broke off, staring at Herron, afraid that he had heard her and was going to steal her boat. As indeed he was.

When he had the painting in the stern compartment, he stopped. He looked long at the *Man with a Glove*, but in the end all he could seem to see was that the fingertips of the ungloved hand were not bitten bloody.

Herron took the shivering girl by the arm and pushed her into the tiny boat. She huddled there in dazed terror; she was not good-looking. He wondered what Hanus had seen in her.

"There's room for only one," he said, and she shrank and bared her teeth as if afraid he meant to drag her out again. "After I close the hatch, push that button there, the activator. Understand?"

That she understood at once. He dogged the double hatch shut and waited. Only about three seconds passed before there came a scraping sound that he supposed meant the boat had gone.

Nearby was a tiny observation blister, and Herron put his head into it and watched the stars turn beyond the dark blizzard of the nebula. After a while he saw the berserker through the blizzard, turning with stars, black and rounded and bigger than any mountain. It gave no sign that it had detected the tiny boat slipping away. Its launch was very near the *Frans* but none of its commensal machines were in sight.

Looking the *Man with a Glove* in the eye, Herron pushed him forward again, to a spot near his easel. The discordant lines of Herron's own work were now worse than disgusting, but Herron made himself work on them.

He hadn't time to do much before the man-shaped machine came walking back to him; the uproar of metalworking had ceased. Wiping his brush carefully, Herron put it down, and nodded at his berserker portrait. "When you destroy all the rest, save this painting. Carry it back to those who built you, they deserve it."

The machine-voice squeaked back at him: "Why do you think I will destroy paintings ? Even if they are attempts to praise life, they are dead things in themselves, and so in themselves they are good."

Herron was suddenly too frightened and weary to speak. Looking dully into the machine's lenses he saw there tiny flickerings, keeping time with his own pulse and breathing, like the indications of a lie detector.

"Your mind is divided," said the machine. "But with its much greater part you have praised me. I have repaired your ship, and set its course. I now release you, so other life-units can learn from you to praise what is good."

Herron could only stand there staring straight ahead of him, while a trampling of metal feet went past, and there was a final scraping on the hull.

After some time he realized he was alive and free.

At first he shrank from the dead men, but after once touching them he soon got them into a freezer. He had no particular reason to think either of them Believers, but he found a book and read Islamic, Ethical, Christian and Jewish burial services.

Then he found an undamaged handgun on the deck, and went prowling the ship, taken suddenly with the wild notion that a machine might have stayed behind. Pausing only to tear down the abomination from his easel, he went on to the very stern. There he had to stop, facing the direction in which he supposed the berserker now was.

"Damn you, I can change!" he shouted at the stern bulkhead. His voice broke. "I can paint again. I'll show you ... I can change. I am alive."

Berserker Blue Death

☀ CHAPTER 1

The bright orange lights of the alarm began to flash, as if in deliberate synchronism with the first notes of live wedding music coming from the electronic organ. The lights of the alarm were positioned all around the top of the circular wall, about three meters high, that rimmed the huge domed room, and they extended up against the lower portion of the huge clear dome itself, making it impossible that they should not be seen. The orange lights were eerily beautiful against the driving, rolling whiteness, shot through with distant pastel colors, that seemed to fill all space outside the dome.

In synchronism with the first flash of the lights, the audio component of the alarm came blasting with almost deafening loudness through the rich sounds of the wedding processional. At the impact the organ music trailed and shuddered away to nothing, while the piercing blatting of the alarm itself kept on. And on.

Niles Domingo swore under his breath, invoking gods and creatures stranger than the gods. Reflexively he called on beings he did not believe in, that at most were no more than half believed in even by the people of the farthest and most isolated colonies. He had a sense of last night's bad dream intruding into reality.

At the moment the alarms came on, Domingo was standing with his daughter at one end of the long aisle that passed diametrically under the center of the domed assembly hall. Maymyo's hand first tightened on her father's arm, then slipped away, as if she were determined to leave him as free as possible of personal distraction.

Domingo turned to look into his daughter's dark-brown eyes, at her lovely face framed in the pure white of unfamiliar ceremonial lace. She was gazing back at him trustfully. Her expression said that her father was still her first source of guidance on any problem, on how to deal with a wedding or an attack alarm. Or, as now, both at the same time.

At least the flashing lights around the wall were not bright red, nor was the audio alarm of the shrieking kind that would have proclaimed the imminence of a berserker attack upon the colony of Shubra. Instead the signal was the comparatively less terrible one of a simple orange alert; still, there was no choice about responding to it, and no option for even the smallest delay in doing so.

No option. Yet, for a long moment in the huge room, no one had moved.

Domingo and his daughter were standing together in the rear of the biggest indoor space available for human gatherings on the colonized planetoid called Shubra, satellite of a sun that had never been seen from Earth. Thirty meters away from where father and daughter stood, at the front end of the long aisle, the clergy and the witnesses were waiting. And of course the groom was up there too, Gujar Sidoruk looking even bigger and bulkier than ever in his formal citizen's robes. Gujar was gazing back at his bride-to-be and at her father as if he, independent young man that he was, were also waiting to be told what had to happen next.

That first moment of the alarm seemed to be protracted endlessly. It was as if the warning had already sounded for a long time, but these people, having committed themselves to a wedding, could not quite make up their minds to respond to it. Before the long moment was over, most of the roomful of people were looking at Niles Domingo, too.

Nine tenths of the population of the colonized planetoid, some two hundred people, were assembled in this hall today. With them were twenty or thirty visiting neighbors, people from other small inhabited rocks within the Milkpail Nebula. A handful of the neighbors lived virtually next door, on Shubra's unnamed moon, but the others had traveled up to a full day to get here, astrogating their way half a billion kilometers through nebular space.

Occupying almost as much floor space in the huge room as the people did was a small forest of plant life, some of the forest's individual components towering over the humans' heads. The permanent flora of the chamber, imported from Earth and elsewhere, had been augmented for today's occasion by extra greenery and a million flowers joyously freighted in from another colony, Yirrkala.

On Shubra, as on most of the other small colonized rocks that revolved around certain suns within the Milkpail Nebula, outdoor ceremonies were rarely practical. The great domed room brought the assembly as close to the out-of-doors as was feasible. Overhead a clear hemisphere of force and crystal held back the whiteness and the sunset clouds of the long winter night, really astronomically distant folds of the nebula that here made up the entirety of sky and space. In only a standard year and a half it would be spring on this portion of the slow-orbiting planetoid's surface.

The night outside was one of atmospheric snow as well as nebular display; the artificial gravity imposed by the colonists upon their rock attracted—among other things—gasses enough to form an atmosphere from this peculiar sky.

Last night a terrible vision, concerning things from the sky, had come to Domingo during sleep. He knew that it had been only a nervous father's dream. A natural phenomenon and, he supposed, common enough, especially on the eve of a daughter's wedding. But this was real.

"Alert stations, everyone!" Domingo called out in a firm loud voice, as the audio warning paused. It had to pause, or voice communication would have been impossible. The alarm had killed all other sounds; in the sudden tomblike silence of the huge room the mayor's order sounded like a shout.

The pause brought on by momentary shock was over. The illusion that there had been any real hesitation about responding to the alarm dissolved. Even before the last word of the mayor's order had sounded through the room, most of the adults present were scrambling for the exits. People went running in every direction, to reach their variously scattered alert stations.

The score and more of guests who had come to the wedding from nearby colonies were as accustomed to alerts as were the citizens of Shubra. The visitors knew their duty and dispersed wordlessly, rushing to the ships that had brought them here.

When the sound of the alarm came back, it was at a more moderate level; people once alerted had to be allowed to think and talk. Giving his daughter's hand one last squeeze, Domingo dropped it and set off at a loping run. He knew—as firmly as a man could know anything—that he would be speaking to Maymyo again within moments, as soon as he had discovered the reason for this damned alarm. Certainly he ought to have at least one more chance to speak to her again before he had to launch a ship.

Running through the familiar corridors of his own small world, first aboveground and then below, Domingo pulled off the formal citizen's robe that custom had required him to put on over his ordinary garments at his daughter's wedding, and bundled it under his arm. He would stuff the garment away somewhere in his ship when he got there, but for the moment it had already been forgotten.

He intended to run all the way to his ship without a pause. In the small confines of the settlement, neither he nor anyone else had far to go to reach their posts.

The tunnel flashed by him with the speed of his pounding legs.

His eyes were fixed ahead, in the direction of the operations deck of the spaceport. He allowed only one thought that was in any sense a distraction to intrude itself upon him as he ran: *The gods help someone, whoever did it, if this turns out to be a joke . . . such a thing,* he supposed, *was remotely possible. Rough humor was still popular out here on the frontier, especially in connection with weddings. Or it could be a simple false alarm, some flaw in human guardian or in equipment, though both types of trouble were uncommon. It was certainly not an ordinary practice drill; no one would or could have called one at this time, at the instant the mayor's daughter's wedding was about to start.*

The cause of the alarm would be brought to light soon enough. Whatever the cause, no one, no colonist anywhere in the Milkpail Nebula, ever failed to take such an alarm seriously or delayed in reacting to it. Everyone who lived in the Milkpail knew, with more than intellectual awareness, what berserkers were.

Still moving at a run, among other men and women still running with him, Domingo entered the great rocky cave of the space harbor. Here too were the orange lights, the pulsating throb of the alarm. In a few moments more the mayor had reached the interior dock where the *Sirian Pearl* was drifting gently, waiting for him. His new ship was a smooth volume of metal, more a flattened ovoid than a sphere, its overall size a trifle greater than that of the huge crystal room he had just left. Still, the ship was small inside the enormous carved-out cave chamber of the port.

Like some of the other more advanced craft nearby, his new ship had reacted automatically to the alarm by altering its own gravitic balance enough to rise up from the dock, starting to prepare itself for launching. The *Pearl*, pearl-colored in the brilliant lights around it, its silent space-warping engines barely energized, was keeping station now about a meter above the deck. Domingo knew that his ship's computer would already be counting itself down through the preliminary prelaunch checklist. It would wait for human orders before it went beyond the prelaunch phase.

The mayor was not a large man, but he was strong and active. He swung himself up and into his ship through the waiting hatchway. Moments later he was throwing himself into his command chair in the center of the ship. The command chair was centered in a small hollow space whose inner surface was all pads, displays, controls. The space was physically isolated from the other crew stations, as they were from one another. In it there might have been room for two people to stand beside the single chair.

The cushioned, built-in command seat closed its panels and pads around him as he sat down, making a snug fit. The manual controls in front of him now were only auxiliary devices for use in odd emergencies. He reached for a brown circlet of what looked like cloth that was attached to his seat by a slender cord. By pulling the band caplike onto his head, he fitted himself to his headlink, through which he interacted with the ship.

The ship was now attuned to certain components of the electrical activity of his brain. Now, essentially by ordered thought, almost as if by telepathy, Domingo could exert direct control over all shipboard systems.

He began immediately, turning on, without physical motion, several of the viewing devices in front of him. One of these presented him with the holographic image of the head and shoulders of a middle-aged man named Strozzi. Strozzi, the colony's current duty officer, was now standing somewhere in the Defense Center, deep underground with a wall of deep gray rock showing behind him.

"Report!" Domingo snapped.

Strozzi quickly gave assurances to the mayor—and to the hundred or so other people who by now were also listening—that the alarm was real. The duty officer hastened to add that the danger to Shubra did not appear to be immediate; he would have called a red alert for that.

"What, then?"

"A robot courier arrived here about five minutes ago from Liaoning." That was another colonized planetoid of the same sun, some twelve hours away at the current orbital positions of both bodies. "The message is that they're under berserker attack there, and they want immediate assistance."

"Attackers' strength?"

"One unit only. But they say it's overwhelming their defenses."

Domingo swore again, once more blaspheming the names of ancient and almost forgotten gods and demigods. "Let me guess."

The duty officer relaxed from the formal posture he had been holding, as if managing any prolonged dialogue that way were too much of a strain. "Guess if you want. They think that it's Leviathan."

When the name was spoken, others among the people listening swore. Domingo scarcely heard them; he was already busy thinking, trying to make plans.

Strozzi went on methodically with his report. He already had the Shubran ground defense system's radio receivers scanning the communications spectrum for more word from Liaoning, but there was nothing coming in. That was not necessarily significant. Between worlds such a distance apart in nebular space, it was usually more surprising when radio communications were open than when they failed. Hence the reliance by everyone in the Milkpail on swift, small robotic courier ships for quick, dependable communication across all but the smallest interplanetary gulfs.

Strozzi also reported that he had already dispatched a Shubran robot courier to the Space Force at Base Four Twenty-five. The duty officer had programmed it to pass on word of the reported attack and had added the information that Shubra planned to respond to the call for help. Their response would probably be taken for granted anyway.

"Very good," Domingo said and began to issue orders. "Put our ground defenses on red alert, Strozzi. But cancel the extra alarm. I'm sure we're all awake already."

"Yes, sir." The duty officer looked away, his hands doing something offstage. "Red alert is now in effect."

Domingo looked at another display inside his armored nest. "All Shubran defense ships prepare to launch, and report to me as soon as you're ready. We're going to relieve Liaoning. Visitor ships, check in with me."

Now the mayor-commander divided his own personal communications display. In one sector before him the faces of visitors appeared, beginning to report as ordered from their own ships. There was Spence Benkovic, organizer of a tiny private colony on a moon of Shubra. There was Elena Mossuril, the leader of the delegation from da Gama, a large planetoid of a different sun. Here came the Mounana people. Someone else, and someone else again, from different planetoids and moons, from very minor and comparatively major colonies, all of them within a day's space travel from Shubra.

The visitors could have elected to remain, to take some part in the defense of Shubra, or to add the firepower of their ships to the relief expedition to Liaoning. But, as Domingo had expected, all of them chose to depart, to carry warning to their own homes. He, in their place, would have done the same thing. All were quickly cleared for launching.

"My own crew, check in."

The lifelike images of their familiar faces appeared one by one on the holographic stage in front of the captain. The stage was again split, leaving room for the simultaneous display of other information, in particular the checklist display showing how far each one of the Shubran ships was from readiness to launch.

Even as Domingo's own crew members reported in, they were already wearing their headlinks, busy running the *Sirian Pearl*'s various systems up to speed.

"Chakuchin here." The stage showed optimistic features framed in blond hair and beard, the face of a large and solidly built young man.

"Poinsot aboard." Henric Poinsot was a slightly older man, smaller and darker than Chakuchin, at the same time more crisp and businesslike.

"I'm here, Niles." That was Apollina Suslova, a compactly built, attractive young woman, wide-eyed as usual, her wild-tossed hair giving an erroneous impression of disorganization. Like most of the other crew members she had on a mixture of wedding-guest finery and hastily added shipboard gear and clothing.

"Iskander in." This was an old friend of Domingo's, deep-voiced, calm and almost leisurely; his black hair and brows were bold-looking to match the rest of his angular face. Iskander Baza was reclining in his acceleration couch with his broad shoulders turned at an angle. As usual at the beginning of action, he gave the impression that he was not taking any of these matters of routine preparation too seriously, but he was ready to enjoy what was going to follow.

"Wilma checking in. I was aboard before you were, Niles." Then the pretty red-haired wife of Simeon Chakuchin corrected herself in this formal situation. "I mean Captain."

His crew were all aboard, his ship was ready. And the other crews and ships that made up the rest of his little squadron were ready too, or nearly so. And still the final warning of imminent attack had not been sounded.

Neither Strozzi, Maymyo, nor any of the many other people assigned to Ground Defense, probing with their subtle instruments, had yet been able to discover any information indicating that there was any direct berserker threat to Shubra. Nor was there any further word on what might be happening or had already happened at Liaoning.

The powerful detector fields of Ground Defense were ranging out as far as they could into white nebula. But there were no berserkers in sight as yet on the immediate approaches to Shubra. Beyond a few hundred thousand kilometers it was impossible to see; the nebula as always offered cover for potential attacker and victim alike.

One ship after another of the mayor's irregular squadron reported ready to launch, but Domingo held back from ordering a launch. He wanted to keep the squadron all together from the start. And he wanted, before departure, to talk once more to his daughter.

He got through to her defensive post, which was one of the riskier, isolated positions near the surface. Again Maymyo's image appeared before him; this time Domingo had a moment to consider what she looked like. His conclusion was that she looked very businesslike, in spite of everything. Though she was still in her wedding gown, the lace that minutes ago had crowned her dark hair had been replaced by a headlink band. Her father could see the white collar of the dress inside the space armor that regulations prescribed for defenders near the surface. And behind his daughter he could see part of the interior of the little dugout of hardened rock and metal, and some of the panels and readouts there much like those in his ship.

He said to her, softly and quickly: "This will still be your day, sweetheart. Or tomorrow will. We'll get things organized again."

"I'm not worried, Dad." It was a brave, obvious lie, the best that could be expected under the circumstances.

They exchanged smiles. Domingo added: "Your mother would have been . . ."

Maymyo smiled. "What, Dad?"

"Nothing." What had he been about to say? Proud of you? Isabel would have been terrified, and had been, close to the point of helplessness, on several occasions. Not really made for this kind of life. But Maymyo was tougher. "She would have been all right. You will, too."

His daughter nodded bravely.

A moment later, with all available ships reporting readiness to launch, Domingo gave the order that took them all in rapid succession, in silent, unspectacular, efficient movement, out of their docks and harbor and up into low defensive orbit. The small ships, with their crews cushioned from acceleration by interior fields, needed only a very few seconds to do that; the outside gravitational gradient, strongly augmented as it was by buried generators, fell off sharply with increasing distance from the planetoid.

Shubra, below, looked small—as indeed it was, no more than about two hundred kilometers in diameter. It also looked very white, swathed in a snowy rag of atmosphere accumulated over the years of artificial gravity. On the side of the long Shubran day, surface collector grids and harvester machines were working, gathering and sorting through the steady infall of primitive nebular life forms. The crop would be sifted for the desired exotic chemicals, some of which would be processed for shipment to distant worlds. Some of the largest collecting and harvesting machines were barely visible at this altitude. No other planetary bodies, no suns or stars, were directly visible anywhere. The white, giant sun of Shubra that indirectly, through reradiation in the nebula, nourished several colonies was perceptible by a general whitening and brightening, in one direction only, of the eternal pale pastels of the interplanetary mist.

In this whitespace region—another name for the interior of the nebula—it was common for small planets in the several systems to know no real surface darkness, from one day or one year to the next. Large planets had no time to develop life of their own, or even favorable conditions for it, and tended to be uninhabitable for Earth-descended people. Within the Milkpail such worlds existed only very briefly, in terms of astronomical or evolutionary time.

The planetary bodies here, like many outside the nebula, were produced from the occasional exploding suns. In the thicker parts of the nebula, as around Shubra, light pressure from most types of suns was inadequate to produce a stable clear space in which planetary orbits could be stable and long-lasting. Relatively thick nebular material encroaching on a solar system, as it did here, tended to wear out the planetary orbits rapidly, particularly those of larger bodies. Those were broken apart by tidal forces when the friction of the medium through which they traveled had sufficiently constricted their orbits. Worlds as big as Earth, or even Venus, lasted no more than a few million years at most from the time when they first cooled into a solid state. With the nebula interfering so drastically with orbital mechanics, it was not unheard of for a small planet within the Milkpail to switch suns, effecting a sudden change in allegiance after a few hundred thousand standard years of orbital loyalty.

The portion of the Milkpail Nebula immediately surrounding Shubra offered good screening for a sneak attacker and thus contributed to the danger; but in another way the nebula was an aid to the defenders. An attacking force had a hard time trying to scout out the defenses of a world, just as the defenders found it difficult to observe an enemy's approach.

Now, via tight-beam communications, a discussion began among the captains of the orbiting ships as to how the situation might have developed since the courier was sent from Liaoning. There was some debate among crews and spacecraft commanders as to how best to respond to the cry for rescue, whether to approach Liaoning from two sides or in one small squadron. People voiced their views openly, the mayor making no effort as yet to squelch dissent.

Let them talk, he told himself silently; that much at least was their right. When they had finished talking, he would tell them: We stay in one squadron. He was in charge, and everyone knew it, but still he could expect nothing like the discipline of a Space Force fleet. There were moments—no more than that—when he would have been glad to have it.

Poinsot suggested: "We could split up, come in from different directions at slightly different times. They said there was only one unit attacking."

Domingo spoke sharply. "They said maybe it was Old Blue. We stay together."

"What's all this Old Blue? I thought someone said Leviathan, whatever that is. I didn't get that, either." The speaker this time was Chakuchin, a comparative newcomer to the Milkpail.

"It's a particular berserker," said Domingo, and fell silent, sighing faintly.

Chakuchin, who had fought berserkers before, outside the Milkpail, paused, trying to figure it out. "But still only one of them, right? And I thought they couldn't get any of their really big units into the nebula." That was not strictly true; a machine or ship of any size could be brought in among the tenuous clouds of interstellar matter and eventually manage to make its way around and through them. But any vessel or machine above a certain size, perhaps twice the cross-section of the *Sirian Pearl*, would be unable to move through those clouds at a speed great enough to allow for effective action.

Iskander took a try at explaining. "Leviathan is a special berserker. It has three or four names, actually. Some call it Old Blue, some something else."

"Why special?"

"Partly because it's a damned tough one. Weapons from one end to the other. And it has a way of coming up with something new."

"Huh."

"And partly because it behaves erratically. Even for a berserker. It's been around the Sector for generations, and attacking Milkpail colonies for the better part of a century." Iskander's sardonic voice made it sound as if he might be making up grim jokes.

Simeon, sounding not all that much enlightened or impressed, muttered something vague. Domingo, listening in on the conversation, could hardly blame him. Few people, thank all the gods and godlings, had Domingo's own experience or anything like it. You had to at least have lived here for a few years, on one or more of the colonies, to understand . . .

His own thoughts returned to more current problems. He could not rid his mind of the people he was leaving behind, the abandoned ceremony. And Maymyo in particular, spending her wedding day at her battle station, virtually alone. But there was a job to be done, and quickly. Once more he issued orders.

Now the little squadron led by the *Sirian Pearl* moved into a higher orbit. And now it quickly left the small globe of Shubra behind, hurrying to a neighbor's aid.

Domingo wondered how much help, how many ships and what type, would be on the way to Liaoning from the other colonies. Probably Liaoning had tried to dispatch couriers to some of them, too, but he could not assume that those messengers had ever reached their destinations or that more help would be forthcoming. If it was coming, it might of course arrive too late. But whether it was much or little, in time or too late, his own duty and that of his fellow citizens was clear.

Leviathan. He put down—tried to put down—old personal memories and feelings. He had to look at this as a military strategist, a logical commander.

It would be something, it would really be an achievement, if they could surround the damned thing in space with this many fighters and settle a lot of old scores for a lot of colonies and ships.

"Maybe we'll get out of the milk a little way, have a chance to see a few real stars." That again was from Chakuchin, the newcomer on the crew who was still somewhat homesick. Domingo had been here in the Milkpail for twenty years, with only occasional peeks outside. By now he'd almost forgotten what stars out in clear space looked like.

The little ships had built up speed. The folded whiteness of the Milkpail was passing over and under and around them continually, almost like atmospheric clouds flowing under and around a speeding aircraft, gatherings of whiteness and subtle color flickering with the velocity of their passage. Lungs trying to breathe this stuff would labor vainly, on what to Earthly life was no more than a good vacuum. But when the brightness was seen millions of kilometers deep, it looked thick and practically opaque.

"Something out there to our right, Captain."

"I have it. Thank you."

Even as the crew watched on their individual viewing devices, the three-o'clock detectors confirmed that something moved out there to starboard, something that was independent of the inanimate currents and surges that worked perpetually within the nebula itself. Life of a kind that never visited a heavy planet's surface. A school or shoal perhaps of microscopic bodies, half matter and half force. Life throve here in the nebula, in themes that were unknown anywhere else in the modest portion of the Galaxy that had been visited by Earth-descended folk. It flourished, unbreathing life in wide variety growing in the light gravity, mild pressure and plentiful energy that obtained here.

Something out there absorbed energy, ingested material food— that same gas, far too thin to sustain a human breath or insect's wing—metabolized, and lived. It might be one of the more or less familiar nebular life forms, the types that were harvested on and near the surface of Shubra and the other active colonies. It might be something not yet encountered by the colonists; right now it was too far off for Domingo to be able to tell, and he had no time to stop and look.

"Damn, but this is a peculiar place!" Chakuchin said it with admiration, with the pride of a new but authentic resident.

✹ CHAPTER 2

When necessary, all of the major systems of the *Sirian Pearl* could be driven by the agile thought of one skilled pilot working alone. But the ship served its human masters most precisely and reliably when it was operated by a crew of six, who could divide its several functions efficiently among them. The five crew stations other than the pilot's, all separated in different parts of the ship, were now filled with Domingo's friends and fellow colonists. He congratulated himself, as the voyage of the relief force got under way, that days ago, even with wedding preparations and mayoral duties competing for his attention, he had made himself take time over the final selection of the crew for his new ship and for a couple of test-and-training flights.

Domingo himself now held the helm. He was sitting in his armored chamber near the center of the ship, still wearing some of the good clothes he had put on for his daughter's wedding. On his forehead rested the spacecraft commander's mindlink control band; it was a physically light weight, but he well knew that it could be as heavy as any crown.

Without moving a finger or even blinking an eyelid, the captain personally held the *Pearl* on what he considered her best course for Liaoning—close to, but not identical with, the best course as simultaneously calculated by the ship's computer. He still considered the human brain, particularly his own, superior to hardware at the most difficult parts of the incredibly complex task. There was some feedback from the equipment to the optic centers of the brain, making the control a partly visual process, trickily akin to imagination—inexperienced pilots often got into trouble imagining that there was no difference.

The autopilot, teamed with the ship's computer, might have managed to conduct the flight just as well—or almost as well—as he could, but right now the captain preferred to drive his new ship himself. The *Pearl* boasted new engines and improved protective fields—at this speed inside the nebula you needed protection against collisions with mere molecules, there were so many of them. Domingo might have raced well ahead of the five other ships in his small squadron, but he did not. Urgent as was the need for speed, he calculated that it was a still more urgent need that his force stay together in the face of a certainly formidable and possibly superior enemy.

Leviathan. The captain had a personal score to settle with that particular legendary foe—whether or not it made sense to feel a personal enmity toward a machine. But he couldn't be certain that he was going to encounter Leviathan this time. All he could really be sure of was that he was leading his people against berserkers.

The berserkers were robotic relics of some interstellar war that had been fought long before the beginning of written history on Earth. They were, in their prime form, vast inanimate spacegoing fortresses, moving lifelessly across the Galaxy in obedience to their fundamental programming command that all the life they could find must be destroyed. In all the centuries of expansion of Earth-descended humanity among the stars, berserkers were by far the greatest peril that they had encountered.

Still without stirring himself physically, Domingo could have called up on any of several screens or stages the image of whitespace whipping by outside. But after making the checklist test of that function shortly after launching, he forbore to use it. Instead, during the first hour of the flight, Domingo called up human faces, those of his fellow colonists aboard the other ships, coming and going on his screens and stages. In this way he held conversation fairly steadily with the other units of the relief squadron. There were five other ships in all, including the craft commanded by Gujar Sidoruk, and Niles Domingo, as commander of the relief force, wanted to make sure that when the combat zone was reached they would all continue to follow his orders.

That willingness established to his satisfaction, as well as it could be before the fact, he ordered intership conversation to be broken off and imposed complete radio silence.

Desultory intercom conversation continued aboard the *Sirian Pearl*. There was no reason why it should not.

Some of the crew, talking now among themselves, expressed concern for people they knew on Liaoning, and speculated on the strength of the berserker force attacking there. It was possible that the report of only one berserker was outdated, that more attackers had come in later, after the courier was sent. If the enemy force at the scene proved to be overwhelming, the relief squadron would have to turn and run for home again—if it was still able to do even that much. Everyone understood that, but no one mentioned it.

Domingo took little part in the rambling intercom chatter, but he listened to it with more than half an ear even while his mind went its own way, watching the instruments before him and trying to make plans. As it was with the captains of the other ships, so it was even with his own crew: He knew some of them better than he knew others. The population of Shubra was small, but it was far from stable. People moved on- and offworld frequently. Some of the present population were almost strangers to the mayor. Some were combat veterans and some were not. Domingo, who certainly had earned that status, wanted to monitor the nerve, and assess the probable behavior under pressure, of those who had not.

It would have been an excellent thing, of course, to have the *Pearl* manned by an all-veteran, picked crew; but in this militia organization, rank had no such privilege. The available pool of experience had to be shared out among all the crews.

The veterans on the *Pearl*, besides Domingo himself, included Iskander Baza, Wilma Chanar and Henric Poinsot. That left two rookies on the team.

Apollina Suslova had not been many months on Shubra and was really still a citizen of Yirrkala. On being assigned to Domingo's crew—every capable adult had an alert station somewhere—she had told him that she had been briefly under bombardment at least once, on yet another colony, but she had never known the strain of helping to control a ship in battle.

Domingo suspected she was becoming attracted to him, and he found the idea not displeasing. If it should turn out that way, though, he'd have to get her off his combat crew. In his experience the two kinds of relationship didn't mix. A married couple aboard ought to be different. He hoped so, at least. Not that he himself had any intention of getting married again.

Simeon Chakuchin, unlike his wife Wilma Chanar, was a comparatively new settler, but all indications were that he was psychologically strong and capable. Not everybody who reached the frontier colonies fit those criteria, though you'd think they might.

The captain's meditations were interrupted by the voice of Iskander Baza on intercom: "I've got Liaoning on the detectors, Cap. Still at extreme range."

The captain switched one of his own display stages to take the forward detectors' signal. Even to his trained perception, the solid-looking image was no more than a vague mottled blur. The planetoid that was the destination of the relief force was in an orbit not greatly different from Shubra's. The two bodies moved in long slow orbits around the same almost-hidden sun, a giant of a radiation source. Its fierceness, dulled by intervening clouds, still turned the atmospheres of its inhabited planetoids, as well as much of nearby space, into a white veil of sometimes glaring brightness.

The nebula not only made interplanetary observation difficult, but it rendered the faster modes of space travel totally unattainable within itself. There was no possibility that human ship or berserker machine could ever achieve effective faster-than-light velocity through these vast, attenuated clouds of matter. Therefore all of the colonized planetoids were separated by long hours or days of travel time, as if they had been light-years apart in more ordinary space. Now, to Domingo and the others watching their own progress as charted by their onboard computers on holographic models of the intervening nebula, their best attainable motion was a painful crawl.

But eventually, long hours after the relief mission had begun and minutes after Baza's first claimed sighting of their goal, the computer-enhanced image of Liaoning ahead was beginning to show a definite change behind the thinning veils. The image was becoming just a little clearer, something marginally better than a blur.

Domingo ordered: "Cut the chatter, everyone. To stations. We're getting near."

With all six ships on full alert, the small relief squadron at last prowled within clear instrument range of its goal. The nearly spherical ball of Liaoning, slightly prolate, showed more and more clearly against the ubiquitous milky background. Still the instruments revealed no sign of the attacking enemy.

"Tight beam, Wilma. Tell them we're here."

The message went out on radio, aimed precisely at the planetoid ahead; no receiver anywhere else should be able to pick it up.

The seconds passed that should have brought an answer, but they did not. And then at last the *Pearl* was close enough to see the settlements on Liaoning's surface.

To see, rather, the places on the surface where those settlements had been.

Domingo's crew, and those of the other relief ships, in almost silent shock, gazed down at a scene of total devastation. Not a building had been left standing, not a settlement was still recognizable.

They hurtled closer.

Questioning radio beams probed the scorched-looking land below. Still there was no response of any kind. No sign that any berserker still lurked in the area or that the death machines might have been inefficient enough to leave anything still alive behind them when they departed.

The marks of the terrible enemy weapons became plainer and plainer on the surface below, as the *Pearl* drew nearer and nearer to the planetoid. There appeared to be no survivors.

Hours ago, Domingo had silently made plans for what ought to be done in this worst case. He implemented those plans now, issuing terse orders. There was a small spacegoing launch aboard the *Pearl*, and he selected three of his crew members to go down to the surface of Liaoning in the launch and directly investigate the death and ruin at close range. The captain himself remained where he was, at the helm of his fighting ship.

Iskander Baza was the first crew member detailed to go down. Polly Suslova, who the captain thought could use the experience, was second. Henric Poinsot, steady and reliable, was the third of the crew to be chosen.

When the launch ejected itself from his ship, Domingo could feel nothing through the *Pearl's* metal frame or through the field of artificial gravity maintained within the ship, a field usually set, like that of their home planetoid, at Earth normal strength. But he could see, on the stages and screens in front of him, how the long, narrow shape of the smaller vessel dwindled rapidly away toward the scorched surface of the planetoid.

Minutes passed, minutes that brought an almost continuous stream of progress reports from the swiftly receding launch below. The relayed observations added little but detail to the horror already known. So far there was no sign of any survivor out of the hundreds of colonists who had lived here. Now, with Domingo's permission, other ships in the relief squadron sent down launches of their own, descending to different areas on the blasted surface.

The launches landed, one after another, at separated sites. The first reports direct from the surface confirmed the catastrophe. One crew reported finding a small wrecked berserker unit, an automated lander—ground defense here had not been totally ineffective.

At last one of the searchers picked up a faint tone from a survival radio. In less than an hour the launch crews were able to uncover first one human survivor and then another from isolated hideouts. Briefly the rescuers' hopes rose. But that was all. No more people were found alive.

The two survivors were brought up into space and taken aboard one of the other ships of the relief squadron. Then Domingo, while his own crew and others listened in, questioned them on tightbeam communications. He spoke with special gentleness to one of the two, a young girl. In his mind he kept seeing Maymyo in her place.

Both of the people who had been recovered alive were injured, and both of them had tales of horror to tell. The two survivors had been isolated, in deep separate shelters. They were numbed and shaken by what they had been through. They murmured disjointedly of incredible dangers, of being stalked and bombarded by death, and of miraculous escape.

Domingo asked: "How many of them were there? How many berserkers? I don't mean landers. How many of the big machines in space?"

One of the survivors had no idea. The other had heard a report that there had been but a single enemy.

"Leviathan? Old Blue?"

"I don't know. Somebody said that it was . . . that one. People always say it's that, when there's only one . . . I don't know."

A medical person who was on the ship with the survivors and trying to treat them now intervened. The captain ought to cut his questioning as short as possible. The patients were both in a bad way, with shock and other problems.

"I'll keep it as brief as I can. Which way did the enemy go from here? Have you any clue as to that?"

But the survivors, not surprisingly, were able to offer their rescuers no clue. Neither of the stunned humans had seen the enemy approaching their world or attacking it, even on instruments, much less observed its departure.

The captain let them go.

How had the defenses of Liaoning been overwhelmed so quickly? The two numbed, quivering humans had been able to give him no information on that point. The recording devices that were supposed to register combat action might tell the story, but the indications were that none of the ground stations containing those recording devices had survived.

Domingo now ordered his own shipboard instruments turned away from the planetoid, and with them his crew diligently scanned the thin surrounding clouds of white emission and reflection nebula. In the clouds the instruments could find disturbances that told of the recent passage of sizable objects moving at high sublight velocity, as fast as was prudent and maybe a little faster for something that big moving within the nebula. Berserker tracks were left in the nebular fog that was thin enough to count as a fair vacuum. Had there really been only one of the enemy, or more? The disturbances were too fragmentary to tell. And the scanners and computers could find no dependable indication of which way the tracks were leading.

A clamor began to reach the commander from people on the other five ships. Each colonist in the rescue squadron had begun to fear that his or her own family and home on Shubra was now in greater danger than before, perhaps at this very moment already under attack.

"We better get home, Chief."

"We will. We're going home right away, don't panic." Then Domingo reminded them calmly—and some of them began reminding each other—that the automated defenses of Shubra were strong, stronger than those of Liaoning had been, and that they ought to hold, even without their squadron's support, for several days, especially against attack by only a single enemy.

Of course at one time, perhaps only hours ago, the people of Liaoning had probably felt confident in their automated defenses too.

Had those people been given time to get any of their own ships into space? It was impossible to determine the answer to that one conclusively; what had been the Liaoning space harbor, an underground facility much like Shubra's, was now an inferno of nuclear fire. If any ships had been launched, they were nowhere to be seen.

Still, the known power of the Shubran planetary home defense systems gave the people from Shubra a positive thought to cling to, something with which to reassure themselves during the return trip to their own world. That trip now began without further delay.

Domingo saw to it that the two people his squadron had rescued from Liaoning were kept aboard a ship other than his own. There was one ship whose crew included a couple of people that one of the survivors knew, and the two were placed on that. He hoped it might make things a little easier for them. The captain-mayor also wanted to make certain that his own craft was as close as possible to perfect readiness for combat. Having refugees aboard would not contribute to that end and might detract from it. His new ship was the best fighter in the squadron, he was sure, even if it was still untested in battle.

If the trip out from Shubra had seemed long, the journey back again was endless, filled with largely silent horror and impatience. Domingo still held the squadron together, for the same reason he had done so on the journey out. When a berserker had achieved one such successful attack, another one soon, somewhere, was very likely.

No one on his ship wanted to voice the common fear of what they might find on their arrival home, but neither could anyone stop thinking about it. All logic said it was unlikely. There was no reason to believe the berserker had gone from Liaoning to their world rather than somewhere else. But . . .

Polly Suslova, at least, thought that she could sense a faint, silent accusation in the air: that Domingo had guessed wrong. His tactical gamble had failed. It was an unfair accusation, of course. There was nothing else the Shubran ships could have done, under any commander, but respond as they had responded to the urgent distress message from their neighbor colony.

But the response had failed. Instead of intercepting the berserkers, saving Liaoning and putting a stop to the menace for the time being, all that had been accomplished was to save two shattered people and to weaken the defenses of their own home for more than a day.

It would be bad luck indeed if the enemy were to mount a heavy attack on Shubra within that time. But the absence of bad luck could never be relied upon.

And at last the trip home was almost over.

"I've got an image of home on the detectors now, Captain. Maximum range."

Good, thought Domingo. Now within thirty seconds or a minute I will get a further detector report, observation of some surface features, some activity, the beginning of reassurance that all is well at home. There would probably not be any open radio transmissions to pick up. A red alert, which meant radio silence, had been in effect here since the squadron's departure. Those conditions could soon be relaxed somewhat. There was a wedding to carry on with, however Maymyo and Gujar wanted to do it. Any celebration today or tomorrow would have to be severely restricted. It was going to be a while at best before the alert could be canceled completely. Until communications were exchanged with the Base. Until . . .

The thirty seconds had passed, and then thirty more, and the silence on all the instruments was beginning to grow ominous. The visuals were getting clear enough to see now, to allow recognition of something of the familiar surface, anyway . . . but still only ambiguous spots were coming through. There was so much surface cloud, ice crystals blowing . . .

Two seconds later he had to admit it to himself. The surface of Shubra ought not to look like that.

The defense frequencies were not detectable. But they ought not to be, could not be, totally silent at this close range. They could not be, unless the unthinkable should intrude here and now into the actual.

And that could not be happening. No, not that.

Unless . . .

There was no single moment in which the terror became reality. Rather there were minutes in which the members of the relief expedition slowly found their worst fears realized. There was now ruin on Shubra, almost the equal of that they had left behind them on Liaoning.

There were spontaneous outcries from the people aboard the *Pearl*, and then stunned silence.

The silence did not last long; there followed frantic efforts to communicate with someone, anyone, below. The attempts were as futile as they were desperate.

Still there might be, might be, survivors. The rush to investigate was frenzied. This time Domingo landed the ship, crudely and clumsily; he put the *Sirian Pearl* down directly on the surface, because here, just as on Liaoning, the space harbor had been effectively destroyed, turned into a gaping wound whose jagged mouth resembled that of a volcano. The deep center of Defense Control had to be gone, too; it could not have survived that cavitation.

As Domingo landed his ship, the other ships of his squadron were coming down as well, landing on the surface close around the *Pearl*.

The crews all disembarked and then milled around beside their ships, looking for some kind of hope, some indication of human survival. But it was a strange and unfamiliar world on which they stood, protected by their suits and helmets of space armor. The rocks of it still roared and shuddered underfoot. Every building had been wiped away. The atmosphere was poisoned. Fresh snow and black smoke blew together across a cratered, shattered, alien landscape. The artificial gravity was weakening already. The deeply buried generators that created it had doubtless been damaged, and soon the smoke and the snow would be gone, along with all the air . . .

Domingo was commander still, and still mayor of whatever might be left. He had to spend the first minutes giving orders, trying to prevent the disintegration of his crew and the other crews, instead of running in a frenzy to see what had happened to his daughter. An organized search for survivors was begun.

It was only minutes after the search started when the personal news reached him: The bride-to-be, his daughter, along with all her comrades in Defense, was dead.

Duty forgotten, Domingo commandeered the only ground vehicle available—it had come down aboard one of his squadron's ships—and rushed to the scene.

Maymyo's small defense position had been as well protected as any of the other posts near the surface. The only access to the position from the surface was through a bank-vault door set under the overhanging brow of a hardrock cliff. But her nest, like all the others, had been scorched and blasted open. The massive door hung ajar, half torn from its great hinge, the inner and outer surfaces of it alike sagging where they had begun to melt, radiating red heat.

Domingo, protected in his armor, ran in through the unprotected doorway. Enough light came in through it, into the small chamber of steel and hardened rock, for him to see. The poisoned snow was drifting in before him, with him, after him. Her body was almost completely destroyed. At least the pitiful thing, scorched flesh and bone with snow already drifting on it, was assumed to be her body, because here it was at her post; but whoever it was was not wearing space armor, had not been wearing it at death. Chunks of the armor lay nearby, more durable than almost anything else amid the ruin.

When Domingo had jumped into the groundcar and roared away without waiting for Gujar, the younger man had climbed back into his own landed ship and taken off, only to land again almost immediately here by Maymyo's cave. Now, screaming and ranting, his duty and his crew forgotten, he came running into the gutted dugout, past Domingo, to throw himself down at the scene of death. He spent a minute of incoherent grief with the man who was to have been his father-in-law.

Then Gujar gathered up what appeared to be the shreds of wedding gown and, moving at a staggering run, took them back into his ship. On his suit radio Domingo could hear him, muttering half coherently about some kind of positive identification test.

The stricken father remained kneeling in front of the ruin of what had been a human being. All he could think was: Why no space armor? Maymyo would not have taken her armor off in combat. So the blasted body before him was not hers after all. Anyway it was impossible that it should be hers.

Another report was brought to Domingo, who somehow was still numbly functioning. On Shubra, unlike Liaoning, one of the military combat recorders, deeply embedded in the surface of the planetoid, had survived. Enough information had already been extracted from the recorder to confirm the fact of a single attacker. It had been Old Blue, Leviathan, rearmed with improved weapons and with new force-shielding that successfully resisted the weapons employed by Ground Defense.

Leviathan. Standing now in the doorway of the ruined cave, Domingo looked up into the howling sky.

Overhead another ship, a small one, was approaching the surface, coming down to a gentle landing beside the six that had already landed, following their squadron commander. Presently the newcomer's markings could be identified. It carried one of the wedding guests returning.

The small ship landed quietly only fifty or sixty meters away from the cave, and its owner got out of it, alone, and approached the little crowd now gathered around Domingo. The new arrival was Spence Benkovic, who had his own small colony on the only moon of Shubra.

Benkovic was a lean, dark-bearded, youngish man. He had a handsome face and large, expressive eyes. Staring without comment at the small shattered shelter, the covered body, he gave what news he could to the stunned people standing around him.

"When the alarm went off, I thought I'd take a look around myself," he began in a numbed voice. "All I've got is that little one-seat battler! Not real good for a real fight—but I thought I'd see what I could see." A couple of hours later, he reported, he had been patrolling out at maximum detector range, several hundred thousand kilometers from Shubra, hoping to be able to observe any approaching berserkers in time to give warning to the world of the enemy's approach.

"I should have let you know what I was doing, I guess . . ." No one commented; there was no reason to think it would have made any difference.

"Then I thought I saw something, moving in the nebula. Too fast to be just a shoal of life. But it wasn't a berserker, either."

"What, then?" someone was curious enough to ask.

"A drift, maybe." After shoals, drifts were the most common kind of formation in which the local primitive life forms tended to approach the planetoid, where the selective collectors waited for them. "But—so fast. And then I thought that on the detectors it looked like some kind of spacecraft—one ship, or two close together. I don't know whose ship it would have been. But it wasn't berserkers, either, not then, because whatever it was didn't come on to attack."

"Berserkers just scouting? Small units."

"Maybe." Benkovic didn't sound convinced. "Then—Leviathan must have come in on Shubra from one direction while I was off scouting in the other. Didn't take it any time at all to take out the ground stations; it couldn't have taken any time, because in a matter of minutes I was back, close enough to see what was happening. Then . . . I could see it dropping small units right here . . . in this area of the surface."

Domingo raised his head. It was as if he were really seeing Benkovic for the first time. "Leviathan," the captain repeated.

"Yeah. Yeah. I saw Ol' Blue once before, a long time ago. I've been in a fight or two. . . . It put its little units down, right here, directly on the surface, or hovering over it so close as makes no difference . . . there was nothing I could do. I didn't stay close enough to watch. My little battler, hell, there was nothing . . . I went back to my moon, to try to get my own people out. But it had already been there, too."

After a little pause, someone asked: "Who was up there on the moon besides you? I never heard, exactly."

"Three people. Three women. Only one's still alive. Then I tried to broadcast a warning, but the whole area, the planet and moon and everything, was under some kind of jamming.

"Then when I took off and looked around for Old Blue again, it was gone. Missed me somehow, coming and going. And there was—this." Benkovic made an expressive, sweeping gesture encompassing the dead landscape around them.

Domingo turned away from him, looking in another direction. Gujar, still moving like a sleepwalker, was coming back from his own ship. There were still scraps of white material in his hands. In an alien-sounding voice the bridegroom said that he had made a final identification of the wedding gown fragment as Maymyo's. There could be no mistake. There had been exotic fibers woven into it, plant material from his own mother's distant homeworld.

Benkovic looked sick.

Domingo was suddenly sitting down, on a snow-drifted rock, staring at nothing. His face inside the clear plate of his helmet was ghastly. Polly Suslova caught him as he fell.

❋ CHAPTER 3

Polly had been married once, but her husband had moved on, leaving the two children with her. She and Karl had for the most part enjoyed each other's company. But now, looking back on their relationship, she had the feeling that she had unintentionally and in some nonphysical sense worn him out.

The only close relatives Polly now possessed in the universe, besides her two children, were a sister and brother-in-law who were caring for those children now. At present they were all four elsewhere in the Milkpail, riding another colonized rock called Yirrkala, the planetoid from which the flowers for Maymyo's wedding had been imported.

As the magnitude of the Shubran disaster became plain, as the reality of the destruction of her friends' families and homes established itself, Polly's thoughts were increasingly occupied not with the ruin before her eyes, but with her two children, whom she had not seen for several months. It was not so much anxiety she felt, or overt fear that Yirrkala was also going to be attacked. Rather she felt a vague satisfaction that she had planned the disposition of her children properly, had done a good job of seeing to their safety. They were both still very young and it was difficult being separated from them, but Polly's job had required her to move to Shubra for half a standard year. She was a specialist in a field that was sometimes less and sometimes more esoteric than it sounded, the relationships of machines with the environments in which they worked. The job also kept her unpredictably busy. Whenever she had thought about it rationally, even before disaster struck, there had been no doubt in her mind that the kids were currently better off with her relatives on Yirrkala.

Polly had been getting along well enough with the Shubran colonists as she lived among them, but she had made no deep personal attachments on Shubra. Except, as she now had to admit to herself, for one. The destruction of the Shubran colony, devastating though it was, was the second such shock of mass tragedy to hit her in a little more than one day. It found her already somewhat numb.

Empathic feelings for the grieving survivors did not strike her with overwhelming personal force.

Again, with the same one exception.

She was standing near enough to the captain, and watching him closely enough, to try to catch the inert mass of his suited body when he started to fall. In the failing artificial gravity—fields dying with the blasted generators under the ground—she was successful. Inside his faceplate Domingo looked more dead than alive; pure shock, Polly supposed. She had got the impression that much of his life was wrapped up in his daughter. She eased him to the ground and sent someone else running to the *Pearl's* landed launch for a first-aid kit. When the kit arrived, she administered a treatment for shock through one of the inlet valves thoughtfully provided in suits of space armor for such emergencies.

She watched the victim's reaction as under the chemical stimulus he began to recover. In the busy minutes immediately following, minutes largely taken up by an intense and futile search for more survivors, Polly stayed with Domingo as much as possible, wanting to keep him in contact with humanity if nothing else. The shock had hit him so intensely that for a time she was worried for his life.

The captain spoke to no one for almost an hour following his collapse. For the first few minutes he was deeply stunned, almost paralyzed. His crew gave him what modest medical care they could. After that he showed signs of awareness but remained for a considerable time in his state of silent shock. He sat on the ground speechless and essentially alone except for Polly, while around him his few surviving fellow citizens, in the intervals between their futile efforts to find other survivors, acted out their own grief and outrage in various ways.

The next stage of Domingo's recovery, when it came, was rapid. And as it progressed, it became—to Polly at least—frightening.

It began when he broke his hour-long silence. He at last said something. A short statement; none of those near him could quite make out what it was.

Two or three minutes after speaking those incoherent words, Domingo was on his feet again, brushing aside Polly's attentions and other people's questions and issuing harsh orders. He came out of shock, seemingly without transition, into grim, purposeful rage, driving her and the others of his crew to get the *Pearl* back into space. If there were any survivors here on the planetoid, he told his people brutally, they would have been found by now. Already they had checked out all of the defensive posts, the deep refuges that would have offered the only real chance of survival.

Another ship's captain, tears running down his own cheeks, approached Domingo on the ground, stressing the hopelessness, the pointlessness, of any immediate effort to lift their ships. It was too late to retaliate. Amid the shrieking wind, the driving, poisoned snow, the other captain's voice came over the personal communication channel. "Don't you understand, Domingo? It's all over . . . the berserkers have got away. They're gone."

Domingo glared like a madman at him. "Leviathan hasn't got away yet. We'll get it. Get those ships up!" His voice was hoarse, almost unrecognizable.

And Domingo's own crew, who a moment ago had been trying to nurse him back to some first stage of recovery, now felt the lash of his words and had to get themselves aboard the *Pearl* and get ready to lift off.

Polly at first had the feeling that what he was doing to his crew and the others was wrong and useless, but she did not dare to try to stop him.

Demanding data, Domingo bullied everyone. He got them moving back to their duty stations, their shipboard instruments. He made them provide him with fresh observations, reports of ionization trails and other recent disturbances in the nebula nearby. These reports indicated that the destroyer machine—the readings confirmed that there had probably been only one berserker—was not long gone, probably no more than a very few hours.

Domingo raged at them all. The burden of his ranting seemed to be that so much time had been wasted on the ground.

Someone protested the injustice. "You were in shock, Captain. You were—"

"*You* weren't in shock." He glared at the questioner. "Were you?"

They gaped at him.

"If you could move and I couldn't, you should have dragged me back on board."

They were all back on board now, and working. It was almost as if the still-smoldering pyres and gutted caverns of their homes below had already been forgotten. There was a quotation in Polly's mind from somewhere, something about letting the dead bury the dead. That was all right, a healthy attitude, but to carry it to this extreme . . . she continued to observe Niles Domingo worriedly. When he first got to his feet again, she felt relieved that he was recovering from the shock, rebounding from the initial blow more completely if not faster than the others who had suffered tragic losses. But Domingo's energy had returned to him too suddenly, his grief had been transformed too rapidly and efficiently to rage.

Polly Suslova was sure that it was a false recovery.

But so far it was sustained. And it was pulling the others along with him. They were all bereaved to one degree or another, and almost as shocked as Domingo was. They actually benefitted from being dragooned aboard ship again, shouted at about their duty, hooked by the alpha rhythms of their brains into their crew stations and coerced into giving him reports. The necessity of routine, of following orders, formed a kind of support for them in their own shock; at some level they all understood this, and so far they had submitted to it willingly.

Such was the compulsion he exerted on the other people of his squadron that all six ships, with all their crew members aboard, had launched obediently within a few minutes of his order.

The six ships rendezvoused in orbit. From this altitude, their homeworld looked not much different than it had before life was expunged from it. There was a radio silence. This time silence had not been imposed by order; it was just that no one at the moment could find anything to say.

Then Polly had an exchange of intercom dialogue with the captain.

She asked him: "Where are we going?"

The features of Domingo's face, viewed individually, looked the same as they had before fate in the form of a berserker had struck him down. Yet his face had altered, she thought, all the same. It was as if someone had got in under the flesh with a chisel and had done some carving on the bones.

He answered her: "Where do you *think* we're going? We're going after that damned thing." Like his face, his voice had altered. The chisel had worked angles in it, too.

Someone else broke in: "We can't . . ."

The protest was never finished. Nor was it answered. The captain left it hanging in the air, and told them to get busy. And no one else had yet dared to take up the banner of rebellion.

Polly wished intensely that she could get a direct, in-person look at the captain's countenance. She could call up his intercom image before her whenever she liked, but it was not the same.

The radio silence was broken again. Some voices of dissension, mingled with pure lamentations, were calling in from other ships, questioning this hopeless pursuit.

Domingo paid little heed to the dissenting voices or to the lamentations, either. He was again busy driving his ship. The few words he spoke to the captains of the other ships conveyed essentially the message: *Follow me or not, just as you like. Where else are you going to go?*

He drove the *Pearl* out into nebular space again, looking for the berserker's trail. The five other ships came along. None of their captains—so far—was persuaded that it would be better to give up and turn away.

Covertly Polly continued to watch his face on intercom whenever she was not fully occupied with her own job. She had given up hope, for the time being, of being able to guess just what was going on inside his head. Continued shock, of course, and grief. But—what form was it taking? What were his thoughts?

In fact, at the moment the captain's only conscious thought was simply that his ship ran well. Better than that, it ran superbly. For the time being, for the moment, he was able to lose himself in the beautiful running of his new ship. He was momentarily content, even cheerful. There was no need for him to consider—to consider anything else at all.

Outside, whitespace flowed by, smooth and at the same time intricate, like ruffling wedding lace.

I have been so proud of this ship, Domingo thought, serenely watching instruments. *Ever since I got it—not long ago, I admit—it's been everything I ever hoped for in a ship.*

For ten years I've wanted a new ship, because—

"Did you say something, Captain?" That was Polly's voice on intercom. Had he spoken aloud? He hadn't meant to.

"Nothing," Domingo said. Then he ceased for a time to think at all. He only calculated how to get more speed.

When he had the problem of speed settled, for the time being, he could think again. He was going to catch up with the berserker, the one that ten years ago . . . and now again . . . he was going to catch up with Old Blue.

Yes. And then . . .

But soon it was obvious that the ionization trail was becoming painfully difficult to follow. He was as experienced at trailing as anyone—it was a valuable peacetime skill in the nebula, one ship trailing another just to keep from getting lost, or simply as a game—and he knew that the trails in the nebula sometimes faded, suddenly and inexplicably.

He heard again from some of his own crew. They were watching the trail too, and his increasingly labored efforts to follow it. Henric and Simeon were now wondering pointedly if it was still possible to go on with any hope of success.

The captain pointedly ignored their wondering.

Some of the people on the other ships were less impressed with him than his own crew was. More of those other people were speaking up now, talking reasonably to him and to each other, forming the nucleus for a gentle and sad revolt. The berserker was gone, was the gist of what they said. This wasn't really a trail any longer. Perhaps some day the damned thing could be hunted successfully and destroyed. But right now they, the survivors, had to take time to come to terms with themselves, with their own grief and loss.

The reasonable, nonviolent view nearly prevailed. The other ships of Domingo's squadron were all turning away now, the people aboard them voting that it was time to go to the Space Force for help.

The *Pearl* moved on, along the fading trail—some of her crew arguing that the trail had already been lost—with Domingo still piloting.

"Captain. Where are we going?" This time it was Iskander Baza who said it. The same question had already been asked aboard the *Pearl*, but now it had a new context and was posed in a practical tone that deserved an answer, if anything practical was going to get done.

Domingo's reply was only slightly delayed, as if he were being thoughtful about it. And when it came it sounded perfectly rational. "All right. Set a course for the base, then. For Four Twenty-five. Iskander, you take the helm for a while."

Polly breathed a faint sigh of relief. That made sense. Base Four Twenty-five would have help to offer. As much of any kind of help as anyone in the *Pearl*'s squadron was going to get anywhere right now, as much as the universe could possibly have available for people who had lost all that they had lost. And if the hunt was still to be pursued, the base undoubtedly offered the best chance of obtaining information about where the berserker—Leviathan—had gone now.

She had not even had a good chance yet to offer the captain her condolences on his daughter's death. Right now she was afraid to try.

Domingo's crew, still suffering from shock, were largely silent as their journey to Base Four Twenty-five began. But as the flight proceeded they began slowly to talk among themselves again. They had all been friends and neighbors once, just yesterday when they had lived in a community together. And they were certainly more than neighbors now. They were survivors together.

Polly wasn't sure that Niles Domingo was still a friend and neighbor of the others. All those others were perhaps too involved right now with their own grief and shock to notice the transformation. But Polly doubted that he was even listening to them any longer, that he was even living in the same world with the other people aboard his ship or in his squadron. Some of those people had certainly lost children too, some had lost whole families. But none of them had collapsed the way Domingo had—not yet anyway—or recovered in his way either.

In what kind of hideous, private world he was living—existing—now, she couldn't guess, much less try to share the experience with him. But she swore to herself that she would be ready when the chance came to help.

Base Four Twenty-five was fairly near though in a different system from Shubra, on a planetoid that had remained otherwise uncolonized, and had no commonly used name of its own apart from the base. It was a barren rock, considerably smaller than Shubra, that supported a Space Force installation of modest size and virtually nothing else.

Base Four Twenty-five was about a day away. It was going to be a long day for them all.

The *Pearl* glided slowly into one of the row of berths built into the section of the shielded underground docks that was reserved for civilian visitors to the base. Other ships of the ill-fated orphan squadron were coming in behind the *Pearl*. None of the other ships had been quite as fast as Domingo's *Pearl* in getting here, but he had not been deliberately trying to outrace them, and they were already catching up. As the other craft arrived, they entered nearby berths. The crews of all six vessels disembarked, almost together. All of them were moving slowly, a reluctant step at a time; it was as if the act of leaving their ships now might take them yet farther from everything that they had lost.

The people of the *Pearl*, first to arrive, were also first to step out. Several Space Force people known to Domingo and to most of his crew had already come into view, standing on the dock, waiting to greet the arrivals sympathetically. The squadron had radioed its grim news ahead.

At the head of the welcoming committee was the base commander, a man named Gennadius, tall and hollow-cheeked, looking chronically worn down as if by his job. Polly had seen him only once before, at some function a couple of years ago, and she knew that in the past he had fought at Domingo's side against berserkers. It was obvious now from the commander's behavior that the two men were old friends.

Gennadius said "Niles" as the other approached, and followed with a one-word question: "Maymyo?"

Domingo looked at the tall man in front of him as if he had trouble comprehending the question. "She's dead," the captain said at last. It was as if he were talking about someone he had barely known.

The base commander winced, with a more than social reaction. Polly made a mental note to herself that as soon as she had the chance she would ask this man for advice and assistance in helping the captain.

Gennadius asked him: "How about you? Come and rest. I want to have the medics look you over."

With a gesture Domingo brushed the notion aside. "They can

look over some of my people if they want to be looked over. I'm all right. What I want is to get to your operations room and see your current plot."

When one of the base medical people tried to be firm with him, Domingo pulled his arm away with a flourish that seemed to threaten violence. "Let me see the plot!"

Gennadius, with a much more modest gesture, called the doctor off. Then he led his old friend Domingo toward the operations room. Polly and a few others followed. Others of the bereaved crews sat down exhausted where they were, milled around lamenting afresh or accepted medical examination.

The operations room, on the next level above the docks, was a large ovoid chamber, perfectly lighted, big enough for forty or fifty people to gather inside it at one time. In the approximate center of this chamber there was a computer model, itself the size of a small room, illustrating the explored portions of the Milkpail.

A color key for the model was displayed nearby. After Polly had studied it for a few moments, she understood the essentials of the presentation. This was evidently what Domingo had called the current plot, indicating where within the Milkpail Nebula berserker attacks had recently been reported, and which additional colonies and installations were now considered to be at high risk. The model also showed the locations to which the battlecraft at Gennadius's disposal, about twenty of them in all, had been dispatched, in an effort, Polly supposed, to try to intercept the enemy's next attack. She couldn't interpret all the symbols on the plot; for one thing, she was unable to tell just how many ships of which kind were supposed to be where.

One wall screen in the operations room showed the scene down in the visitors' dock, where it appeared that three or four additional ships were now arriving, more or less together. Polly did not recognize them. Someone standing near her in operations said that they came from Liaoning. Having arrived home to find that their world had been destroyed, they had turned here to the base as the Shubrans had.

Domingo handed over to Gennadius the recording on which Old Blue could be identified as the attacker. Then he demanded that the base commander tell him his plans for hunting down the berserker that had destroyed the Shubra colony.

"I'll have to take a good look at this first," Gennadius said wearily, juggling the recording in his hand. "There might be some useful information, even if it doesn't help us immediately. We'll do an analysis."

"Piss on your analysis." That expression was, by local custom, a much uglier way of swearing than to profane the names of half-forgotten deities and demigods. Polly had never before, in the months she had known the captain, heard him use this kind of language. It disturbed her to hear it now, more than she could logically explain.

Again he demanded of the commander: "I want to know what you're going to do about Leviathan."

Gennadius stood solidly, with folded arms. "I'm going to run my command. To give as much protection as I can to the people in this district. I appreciate how you feel, Domingo—"

"Do you?"

"Yes. But my prime function is not to hunt Leviathan. It's not the only berserker around, you know."

Domingo was silent. The base commander (Polly got the definite impression that he was making allowances for his bereaved friend) went on in a tired, methodical, soothing voice, explaining his current plans. From what Polly, who was no military expert, could understand of it, his basic strategy seemed to be more defensive than offensive. He wanted to detail the *Pearl*, with other ships from Shubra and Liaoning, as soon as they and their crews were ready to go out again, to guard duty over other colonies. There were perhaps twenty more Milkpail colonies still out there, potential targets for the berserker enemy. Gennadius intended to get as many armed ships as possible, including those of the bereaved colonists, out there to protect them.

Domingo said, in his new hoarse voice: "At least you think those other colonies are still there. Still in existence. You don't really know."

"That's right." Gennadius, under strain himself, no longer sounded like an old friend. But he was still trying. "As far as I know, they're still alive. Will you help them stay that way?"

Domingo spoke in the same voice as before, with no more or less expression. "Say there are twenty places to be guarded. If I take the *Pearl* to do patrol duty at one of them, I have one chance in twenty of encountering Leviathan at the next attack. That's not good enough."

"Not good enough." Gennadius repeated the words, as if trying to understand what they might mean. "Not good enough for what? What are you proposing instead?"

"My ship goes along with your fleet, when you set out to hunt Leviathan."

"It's not going to work that way, Domingo."

"Then I hunt the damned thing alone."

"That would not be wise."

Domingo's monotonous voice pointed out that the *Sirian Pearl* was undoubtedly his ship, his private, personal property to do with as he chose. He was not going to have his ship assigned to guard duty anywhere. Speaking slowly and calmly, as if explaining to an idiot, he said that he intended to take the *Pearl* in pursuit of Leviathan, by himself if necessary. He felt confident, with a little preparation, of being able to follow and find the berserker anywhere in the nebula.

Some of his own crew looked doubtful when they heard that announcement.

The base commander meanwhile gazed off into the distance, as if trying to calculate something, or maybe to invoke some exotic technique of self-control.

Polly tried to remember the version of interplanetary law obtaining in this sector. She thought it was technically true that even now, in this state of emergency with colonies being crushed like anthills under an iron heel, the military had no right, or had only a very doubtful right, to give orders to a civilian captain or to the mayor of a colony. But anyone as grown up as Domingo ought to know that being technically in the right could lead to disaster; Domingo of course would know that, if he were in his right mind now.

Gujar now joined the group in the operations room. The huge, bulky man looked totally exhausted.

The bereaved bridegroom was completely on Domingo's side in the argument; Gujar wanted to press on with the chase, too. But the ship he had been piloting was not his own, and the woman who owned it was going to use it to get out of the Milkpail right away; she was giving up. Gujar was unhorsed.

Gennadius had returned to the argument with Domingo: "All right, maybe technically I can't give any of you orders right now. But I tell you I need help. And I would strongly suggest that you and anyone else who's looking for a fight should take the *Pearl* and whatever other ships you have, and provide some cover for people out there who need it badly. Leave the hunting to us."

"You've just told us that the Space Force doesn't plan to do any hunting."

"I've said nothing of the kind. Let us do it in our own way."

But Domingo wouldn't listen. When one of the officers in the background thought aloud that the *Pearl* would have no chance alone against Leviathan, he turned on the woman and argued, without anyone being able to prove him wrong, that the *Pearl* was the equal in nebular combat of anything the Space Force had locally available; and in fact superior to many of their ships.

He argued too that his own ship was probably superior to any of theirs in this one task, hunting down and destroying a rogue berserker like Leviathan. Domingo had designed the *Sirian Pearl* himself, and at enormous expense had had her built—at the Austeel yards—primarily for that very purpose.

"Really?" asked someone who didn't know him, and therefore didn't believe it.

"For ten years I've wanted a ship that—" He broke off that sentence and plunged into technical detail. The *Sirian Pearl* also had superb new weapons systems on board. Since the events of ten years ago, Domingo had been planning and working to equip himself with a ship that would not have to run from anything it might encounter in the Milkpail.

Someone grumbled in a low voice that in the Milkpail, at least, it was still insane to go out with only one ship, whatever she was like, against *any* berserker, let alone that one.

Iskander Baza put in: "Leviathan may have taken a lot of damage in those raids; it must have taken some."

Domingo argued also that his ship had speed; it had beaten all of the other ships here to the base, although most of them had started for it sooner. And it had, in himself, a veteran commander. And, he told the military people again, he was not convinced that they intended ever to hunt this enemy seriously, hunt it to the death.

The response from Gennadius was stony silence. Domingo and his crew left the operations room. Polly stayed close to him and watched him glowering as he paced the corridor outside.

He looked around at her and at the four other people of his own crew. "We're not lifting in the next ten minutes. But I am going after Leviathan as soon as I can get a hint of where to look for it. Those of you who don't like that idea had better drop off the crew right now."

Iskander stood beside his captain, looking at the others, as if such a suggestion could not possibly apply to himself. There was no question that he was on the crew, no matter what.

"I'm staying on," said Polly, and wondered at herself, though not as much as she would wonder later. Simeon and Wilma looked at each other, then both tentatively signed assent. Right now there were not a whole lot of choices about what else to do, where else to go.

There was a pause, then Poinsot sighed. "I'm dropping out, Domingo. You have to play it the way you see it. But so do I. I can still see some kind of future life for myself. I've still got people, my sister and her kids, who are going to need me."

Polly recalled that Henric's brother had been on Shubra too, in Ground Defense, but the brother's family had been visiting elsewhere.

"Drop out, then," said the captain.

Henric walked away. Gujar Sidoruk came out of the operations room, swearing at Gennadius, at the commander's refusal to order a general hunt for Leviathan immediately. In a minute Gujar had officially signed on the crew as Poinsot's replacement.

☀ CHAPTER 4

Four days after the attack on Shubra, the entire crew of the *Sirian Pearl* was still at Base Four Twenty-five, as were a number of the people from the crews of the other Shubran ships. The rest of the Shubran survivors had taken their ships out to patrol as Gennadius had requested, putting aside their own grief to help guard some of the twenty or so other colonies that still survived within the nebula.

Domingo still refused to consider doing that. He calculated that flying guard duty around a colony somewhere would give him at the most one chance in twenty of encountering Leviathan, and that was not enough.

Polly had the impression that Gennadius thought the captain would come round in a little while and be willing to take the *Pearl* out on a defensive mission. But Domingo did not come round. Too full of vengeance to care about helping others, he waited at the base, along with those who were too shattered to care what happened to the other colonies, and a few other people who were too obsessed with the idea of immediately starting to rebuild, regaining what they themselves had lost. The military would shelter them all as refugees as long as necessary, feed them and provide them with spare clothing, but they could not remain its wards indefinitely. Eventually even the shattered ones would all have to go somewhere else, live again somewhere else, do something else with the remainder of their lives. It would be a matter of starting over, essentially from scratch.

After the first three days at the base, a few of the Shubran survivors had approached their mayor, wanting him to take some initiative in finding a place or places away from the base for his few remaining citizens to settle, at least temporarily.

But Domingo had no interest now in making that kind of effort. There was now only one subject that had any attraction for him at all.

He gave Gennadius a strange smile when the base commander raised the matter of resettlement. Domingo answered: "A place to live? What does 'to live' mean?"

Gennadius looked at his old friend rather grimly for a few seconds, then turned and walked away.

Domingo called after him: "What's new on the operations plot?"

The question got no answer.

Polly wanted to take Niles Domingo in her arms, to let him weep away some of the bottled grief that seemed to be driving him coldly and quietly insane. But he gave no indication of wanting to be in anyone's arms for any reason; and trying to picture him shedding tears made her want to giggle nervously. She had never seen a human being who looked less likely to weep than Domingo did now.

She waited for some change, for better or worse, in his condition.

Polly had been able to piece together Domingo's story, more or less, from scraps of conversation and from talk overheard, both at the base and earlier on Shubra. He had arrived in the Milkpail about twenty standard years ago as a very young man, accompanied by his timid young bride, a girl named Isabel. By all accounts he had loved Isabel deeply. Then about ten years ago his wife—she had never got over being easily frightened—had died in some kind of ship crash. Polly had never heard whether that disaster had been somehow related to berserkers or simply an accident. Two of Domingo's three young children had died in that crash, too. He had not remarried. When Polly first met him a few months ago he had been a kindly man, though somewhat remote from everyone except his surviving daughter.

Kindly was not the word that came to her mind now when she looked at him or listened to him. *Grim*, certainly. There were probably more ominous variations on that word that would fit his present condition even more exactly, but right now Polly had no inclination to try to find them.

At least the refugees at Base Four Twenty-five had plenty of room. The visitors' quarters here at the base were extensive, because in more normal times they got a lot of use. But now everyone who still had a home had gone scrambling to defend it, and the remaining refugees had the place practically to themselves.

For her own use, Polly had chosen a small single room next to the one where Domingo had indifferently allowed himself to be billeted. She saw little or nothing of him during the nights, but everything was quiet next door, as far as she could tell. So quiet that she began to doubt that he was ever there.

Worried about Domingo on the first night after their arrival at the base, Polly had gone next door to look in on him, planning to make up a reason for the visit as required. Her brisk tap on his door remained unanswered, even when she repeated it. She called his name, then tried the door, which was unlocked. He was not in the little room at all. One of the flight bags he'd had with him on the ship was sitting unopened on the narrow bed. There were no other signs of occupancy.

Polly thought for a moment and found her captain in the next place she looked for him. He was back in his ship, wide awake, hunched over some instruments in the common room. On a wall screen a copy of that last surviving Shubran ground-defense recording was being played back, reenacting the destruction of his life. The ugly angular shape that was Leviathan came drifting in slow motion across the screen, dragging its blue glow under magnification that was still not enough to let it be seen very clearly. Weapons flared on the berserker, and beneath it the landscape exploded into dust. This was evidently before the landers had been dropped, the smaller machines that must have dug out and sterilized the small shelters like Maymyo's, for there was no sign of those devices here. The scene ran for only a few seconds, then automatically started over again. And yet again, as Polly watched, Domingo kept studying it intently, critically, as if the recorded onslaught represented no more than an engineering problem. Meanwhile the *Pearl's* computer was working away in busy silence, constructing a colored holographic model of the whole nebula, one that Polly recognized as a smaller version of the plot on display in the operations room.

When she came into the room, Domingo took his eyes from the screen just long enough to glance at her for identification purposes. "What is it, Polly?" he asked her absently.

She delayed answering the question, but the captain didn't even notice. The screen and model in front of him had immediately reclaimed his attention. Eventually it did dawn on him again that she was there, watching. He looked up again, with more awareness in his eyes this time. "What is it?"

The excuses she had been mulling over, all suitable for dropping in on a friend in the next room, suddenly did not seem adequate to justify breaking in on a ship's captain in the middle of a combat-planning session.

So Polly blurted out part of the truth: "I was worried about you."

That at least appeared to get the captain's full attention. Was that expression on his face intended to be a smile? He said: "Don't. There's not enough left of me to worry about."

"I don't believe that—I see a lot of you still there."

He had no real reply to that. He grunted something and sat waiting.

She said: "You're still determined to go after that berserker." It was hardly a question.

The captain nodded abstractedly. He was still looking at her, but his attention was already slipping away again.

Indicating the model, Polly asked: "Is that going to be a big help?"

His eyes returned to the holographic construction, and this time they stayed on it. He sat back with folded arms. "I think it will."

She moved a little closer to him and sat down on one of the built-in padded benches. "Tell me about it."

"It's just a matter of trying to get into Leviathan's brain and predict what he's going to do next." Domingo made that task sound almost easy. His eyes were still aimed at the model, but she had the impression that his gaze was focused far away.

He had said *he*. What *he's* going to do. Polly filed that information away for the moment. She asked: "Is there any way I can help you?"

Eventually his eyes came back to her. Sizing her up, he nodded, slowly and thoughtfully. "Yes. Of course you can help. When the time comes, I'll need help. I'll need a good crew. But right now . . . right now it's just a matter of my getting this modeling done as accurately as I can. I think I prefer to do that myself. I want to know it perfectly."

She resisted the strong hint that the best help she could offer him at this moment would be to get out of his way. Instead she leaned back in her seat, as if she were comfortable. "That looks very much like the model in the operations room."

"It should."

"Has Gennadius given you access to the base mainframe computer? Everything it has in memory?"

Domingo nodded. "He and I are still talking to each other. I told him I needed it, and he's a reasonable man, up to a point at least. He wants all the fighting ships in his district as well equipped with information as they can possibly be."

Polly had more questions to ask; but Domingo grew more restless, answering in monosyllables, staring at his slowly growing and developing model. She prolonged her stay only a little longer, because he so obviously would have preferred to be alone. She wanted her presence to be welcome.

On the morning after that talk in the control room—base time was coordinated with that of some of the larger colonial settlements on nearby rocks—Polly was up at about the same time as most of the Shubran survivors. After eating breakfast in the common mess, she found a general discussion going on among a group of Domingo's fellow citizens and sat in on it, listening.

The group that had settled into a small meeting room after breakfast comprised some twelve or fifteen Shubrans, all of them crew members from the various ships in the orphaned Shubran relief

expedition. Some of them were already well into the formulation
of determined plans to reconstruct their lives, talking about going
back to Shubra as soon as possible and rebuilding there, starting
the colony over.

Others in the group declared that they had had it with Shubra
and never wanted to go near the place again. The two factions
were not really trying to convince each other, Polly thought, and
it seemed unlikely that the whole group could ever agree on any
single course of action.

While this discussion was in progress, Gennadius came to the door
of the meeting room. The Base Commander looked somewhat happier
than he had yesterday. "I have some good news, people. A manned
courier ship has just come in from Sector. They're responding fully,
just as we had hoped, to the Liaoning disaster. I think we can take
it as guaranteed that the response of the government will be the
same in your case when they hear about it. Disaster funds should
be available from Sector Government for resettlement on Shubra,
too, or anywhere else in this district where they're needed."

The people in the little group looked at each other. Both factions,
the resettlers and those in favor of moving on, displayed generally
pleased reactions. Someone asked hopefully: "You think we can
depend on that, Commander?"

"I think so. As far as I can see, Sector still plans to have the whole
Milkpail colonized some day. Even if now that looks like a rather
distant goal." Gennadius added: "And I want to see it, too. The more
people there are living in my territory, the easier my job gets."

"Colonies can do well in the Milk," someone offered, trying to
be optimistic. "We've just got to protect ourselves better. Nebula's
still full of life."

"A thousand-year career for busy berserkers," objected one of the
survivors who was ready to give up. No one among the optimists
reacted noticeably. *Cash in your chips if you want to; we're going on
living.*

The discussion, informal but earnest and substantial, continued.
The future of Shubra, Polly thought, was perhaps being decided here
and now. Without the uninterested mayor. And without the high
proportion of the Shubran survivors who were out in their ships,
trying to protect other people's lives and homes. Well, she wasn't
going to worry about it—she had enough to worry about already.

When Commander Gennadius left the meeting, she tagged along
with him.

He glanced sideways at her and, without breaking the rhythm of
his long strides down the corridor, opened the conversation with
his own choice of subject. "I've got another roomful of people just
down the hall here." At that moment Iskander Baza passed them in

the hall, exchanged nods with Polly, and looked after them curiously as they marched on. Gennadius continued speaking to her: "These are not refugees, for once. These are incoming, potential colonists, just in from Sector. Naturally their ship diverted here to base when her captain got word of our alert. I want to have a little talk with them before they start hearing everything about our problems at second hand. You're welcome to sit in, if you like. I'm not trying to whitewash the way things are."

"Thank you. I'd like to sit in."

With Gennadius she entered the next conference room, where the atmosphere was vastly different from that in the one they had just left, though about the same number of people were present. The men and women assembled here looked different from the psychically battered colonists in the other room. These newcomers were obviously nervous but still healthy, without the indefinable appearance of victims.

By now the newcomers had heard the full official announcement of the multiple disasters, which was a recital of bare facts, accurate as far as Polly could tell. And in the short time they had been on the base they had almost certainly heard more than that, from survivors and at second hand. They were, naturally enough, worried and uncertain.

As Polly followed the commander into the conference room, one of the group was standing in front of the others, talking to them about berserkers. The speaker was one of the older people present—none were more than middle-aged—and her voice carried sincerity if not necessarily authority.

"When berserkers move in, people move out. It's that simple. Trying to live in a sector where they're active is like sticking your hand into a shredder. It's just about as sensible as that, and as brave."

The speaker glanced over her shoulder, saw Gennadius looking at her, and finished defiantly: "I've been through this before. I know what I'm talking about!"

Polly could see the base commander pausing, deciding silently that this called for a more serious speech than he had first intended.

Gennadius made no attempt to hush the woman, but let her finish. Only when she had returned to a seat did he himself take over her position at the front of the room.

He looked out over his small audience calmly and gravely, letting a little silence grow. Then when he judged he had the timing right, he said: "All right. We've had a very severe problem in the nebula the past few days. A series of disasters, in fact. But as you can see, this is a very strong base, secure against attack. Starting from here, and with the support of Sector, we're prepared to take back what we've lost—in terms of territory, at least. So there's great opportunity in the Milkpail right now, the opportunity that I assume you've all come here to find."

Gennadius went on, delivering an encouraging message without in the least fudging on the catastrophic facts of recent history.

"Sure, we've had severe problems, on the scope of some great natural disaster. But I—" The commander appeared to grope for words. "How can I put it? We are not facing some kind of demonic monsters here. I don't know how many of you hold beliefs of any kind in the supernatural, or what those beliefs are. But never mind that, it doesn't matter. What we are confronted with here are machines, just like—like this video recorder."

While he was talking, the door to the corridor had opened quietly, and Iskander had come in, with the captain right at his shoulder. Their arrival was in time for them to hear the base commander's philosophy regarding berserkers.

Domingo spoke one word, in a soft voice: "Leviathan." He said it as if it were the answer to some question that everyone in the room had been groping for.

"Welcome, Captain Domingo." Gennadius nodded toward the new arrivals. "A man who has had a very recent and very tragic experience with berserkers. He has—"

The captain smiled. It looked to Polly like a madman's smile. "Not just with berserkers, Commander. With one particular . . . machine. That word's inadequate, though, isn't it? *Machine.* And the experience, as you call it, was not simply tragic. No. Tell them the truth."

Gennadius was exasperated now. "Your world was attacked by one machine that people have given a name to, as if it were some great damned artificial pet. Or god, or idol. Well, it's none of those things. Why is the word *machine* inadequate? That's what a berserker is."

"Oh, is it? Tell me more." Domingo's voice was still quiet.

"There's not much more to tell. Essentially. If you want to know the truth, it and the others are no more than overgrown, out-of-adjustment machines."

Domingo had no comment on that for the moment. He listened in silence as the base commander continued his efforts to encourage the potential new colonists. With all the news of berserkers in the air, Gennadius said, he wanted to dissuade them from the idea that the obstacles were just too overwhelming. "Some people get the notion that the berserker problem can never be managed. That's wrong. They're machines, that from our point of view happen to be malfunctioning. That's all they are. And if we can keep a sun from going nova, as we sometimes can, then we can ultimately manage a few machines."

Domingo broke in at that point. "You think Leviathan's only a machine? That it just happens to be out of adjustment?" He paused.

"I'd like to show you what it is. I'd like you to be there when I pull out its heart."

Gennadius coldly returned the captain's burning stare. "You've had a hard time, Domingo, but you're not the only one who has. I respect what you've done, and what you've been through, but getting revenge on a piece of metal is a crazy enterprise, in my opinion."

Polly sucked in her breath audibly. She sensed that the commander's words were a deliberate shock tactic, but she didn't think that it would work.

The would-be colonists were watching and listening very, very intently. Their heads turned back and forth like those of spectators at a match.

"Only a piece of metal. You think that?"

"That's what they are. You have some kind of evidence to the contrary to present? I'd like to see it."

"Is my body a machine? Or yours? Or was my daughter's? What was her body, Commander? What was it?"

There was a pause that seemed long. At last Gennadius said: "In a manner of speaking, I suppose we're all machines. I don't see the point of looking at it that way, though."

"I can see that you're a machine," said Domingo, looking at the commander speculatively.

Polly could feel her scalp creep. Not from the words; something in the tone.

The potential colonists were still watching and listening with great attention.

The commander, she could see, was working hard at being almost casual and even harder at being tolerant. Polly supposed he did not want to freight this madman's behavior with importance in the eyes of the others watching. "If you have tactical suggestions to make, Captain, I'll be glad to listen to them up in the operations room. Meanwhile there's something else I wish you'd work on. You're still mayor of Shubra. Some of these people might be interested in going there. I think it's your place, your duty, to talk to them and—"

"If I'm still mayor of any place, it's hell. As for your rebuilding, I want none of it."

"As mayor, you—"

"You want my resignation?"

"It's not my place to accept it. Talk to your citizens." Then the commander softened. "We've all lost, Niles. Not like you, maybe, but . . . we've got to start thinking of where we go from here. There are decisions that won't wait."

"I know what won't wait." Domingo looked at the commander, and at Polly. She could get no clue from his eyes as to what he expected her to do. A moment later he had left the room. When she followed him into the corridor, a few moments later, he and Iskander were already out of sight.

☀ CHAPTER 5

The *Sirian Pearl*, along with the other ships of the Shubran civilian relief squadron, had seen no actual fighting and had sustained no damage while shuttling from one disaster to another. Such minor refitting as was required to get her perfectly ready for action had already been taken care of at the base. The Space Force had been eager to help with the maintenance. Gennadius wanted every human ship in the nebula to be as fully armed and equipped and ready for combat as possible.

More combat was expected soon, though with berserkers you never knew. Anyway, it was certain to come eventually.

The *Pearl* was almost alone in the docks, except for a few Space Force ships, a couple of them undergoing routine maintenance, a couple of others being held in reserve as transport and for defense in the unlikely event of a berserker attack on the base itself. Four Twenty-five had truly awesome ground defenses. From the enemy's point of calculation, there had to be more tempting targets out there in the nebula, colonies only lightly defended now after the years of relative peace and quiet.

Domingo's ship was solidly down in dock, with Gujar Sidoruk and Iskander Baza walking and climbing over and around her, giving everything on the outside a looking over, probing with tools and fingers into missile-launching ports and tubes, field projectors, the snouts and nozzles of beam weapons. The checkout was really unnecessary, but Gujar at least was nervous enough to need something to do. Iskander had come along, and they talked while they conducted an extra inspection.

Iskander, hands on hips, stood tall on the uppermost curve of hull. He said: "You know, Sid?"

"What?"

"I'm really looking forward to taking this ship into action." He sounded more serious than usual.

Gujar straightened up from a beam nozzle and looked about restlessly, swinging his electronic probe in one huge hand. He responded that he himself was not looking forward to anything. Going after

Leviathan was just something he had to do, and he wanted to get it over with.

Sidoruk was not as familiar with this ship as the other crew members were. He had a few questions to ask about the new weapons and systems Domingo had insisted on having built into his ship.

Gujar had been taking it for granted that the *Pearl*'s armaments were adequate for the formidable task Domingo was planning. But now it seemed to him that, in answer to a couple of his questions, Iskander was slyly trying to raise some doubt in his mind, as if just for fun.

Gujar was still frowning in vague puzzlement when the two men heard footsteps approaching, clomping up a flexible ladder that curved around the curve of hull. Presently Polly Suslova's head and shoulders came into sight. She greeted the two men and asked, "Where's the captain?"

Baza smiled at her. "He's aboard. I looked in half an hour ago and he was sleeping."

Despite the smile, she had the feeling that this man was hostile to her, that somehow he felt possessive about the captain. Baza, as far as she was aware, had had no family anywhere, even before the Shubran massacre.

"Good," she said. "I'll let him sleep. He needs the rest." She looked at Gujar, who was leaning against the railing of the curving stair, gazing glumly into space. He didn't appear to be listening to the conversation, but it was hard to tell.

Polly faced back to Iskander, as the second-in-command asked her: "You think the captain's unhealthy? I don't."

"Have you seen him like this before?"

"Like what?" Polly could read no feeling in Iskander's smooth voice. "He's ready to hunt berserkers. If that makes him crazy, there're a lot of lunatics around."

"I'm sure there are. The point is that until a few days ago he wasn't one of them."

"He'll be all right, when he gets Leviathan." The broad-shouldered man sounded very confident.

That woke up Gujar. "If he can get it."

"He can."

Sidoruk turned around, frowning. "I thought you were just telling me our weapons might not be good enough."

Polly asked Iskander: "Do you think that's what Domingo needs?"

"He thinks so." Baza started to move past her to the ladder. "Excuse me, ma'am. It's time I went to operations and took a look at things."

Polly moved out of Iskander's way, but she had another question for him before he left. "You've known the captain a long time. Were you with him when that crash almost wiped out his family ten years ago?"

"I was. But you'd better ask him about that." And with a lightly mocking little salute, Iskander was gone.

Gujar Sidoruk had roused from his unhappy reverie enough to pay attention to Polly's latest question. "What do you want to know about the crash?"

"I was wondering if berserkers were involved in that, too." Ships disappeared, sometimes, in every part of space, even without berserkers' help.

"Yes, I remember it well. It wasn't just berserkers. It was the same damned one."

Thinking of Domingo, Polly let out a little wordless moan of empathic pain. She sat down on the curve of hull—carefully; the metal tended to be slippery and there was a considerable drop. "Tell me."

"Well. His wife—her name was Isabel—and two of their three kids were on a ship coming back from somewhere, I forget where, to Shubra. The ship managed to send off a courier before she crashed. Her captain thought Leviathan was chasing them, and the courier message said he was just about to take some risky evasive action. That was all that anyone ever heard from that ship. Either the berserker got them, or he wrecked his ship trying to get away from it. Tried to go too fast in a cloud, or whatever. No lifeboats ever showed up anywhere. No survivors."

"I see," Polly murmured again.

Again someone's feet were clanging solidly up the ladder. In a few moments Simeon's head came into view. "There you are—some of you, anyway. There's news. One of Gennadius's squadrons is supposed to be straggling back in here to the base, all shot up. They tightbeamed a message ahead, saying they've just fought a battle."

"And?"

"Mixed results, apparently."

Polly grabbed for the ladder. "Coming, Gujar?"

He shook his head slowly. "You go ahead. I want to look over a few more things here. Whatever the news is, I expect we'll be launching before long."

Polly descended the ladder quickly. There was someone else who would certainly want to hear the latest combat news the instant it became available. Iskander had said that Domingo was asleep. She debated briefly with herself, then opened the nearest convenient hatch and entered the ship.

The captain was not in his berth. Well, she supposed it had been foolish to look for him there, no matter what Iskander had said. She found Domingo in the common room again, sitting slumped over and motionless at the console beside his computer model, almost on top of it. His face, with the reflected colors of the glowing model playing over it, was turned toward Polly as she entered and she was worried for a moment; he looked absolutely dead.

A closer look reassured her. Domingo was breathing deeply and comfortably, getting what was probably one of his first real sleeps since the disaster. But Polly, sure that he would want to know the news, decided to wake him anyway. She shook him by the shoulder.

The captain's eyes opened at once, and he saw her without apparent surprise. He was glad to be awakened for the news, grim as it was, and was on his feet at once. Pausing only to shut down some of his equipment, he moved toward Operations with purposeful strides, Polly tagging along.

They were in time to be present when Base Commander Gennadius greeted the arriving crews.

The newly arrived military ships had brought with them another item of related news: yet another berserker attack upon a colony, the third in recent days. This time the target had been Malaspina, a planetoid of a sun that was relatively distant within the nebula. Malaspina was known for the foul "weather"—nebular turbulence and activity—that usually afflicted both its atmosphere and its surrounding space.

Before the returning fleet had fought its recent battle, its ships had picked up some peculiar radio messages from the direction of the colonized planetoid Malaspina, messages reporting the sighting of strange ships or objects in the nebula near Malaspina. Very shortly after picking up the radio transmissions, the fleet had been found by a robot courier from the attacked colony. The courier brought an urgent and now horribly familiar message: Colony under berserker attack.

Gennadius, as he listened to this story, appeared to be trying to remember something. "Malaspina. Wasn't there another report of some really peculiar nebular life forms around there just a standard month ago?"

Some of his aides standing nearby were able to confirm this.

"That's not all," said one of the exhausted ship captains who had just arrived. According to later messages received by the rescue fleet, some of the people at the third colony were reported to have behaved bizarrely during the attack.

"Hysteria," said someone on the base commander's staff.

"I suppose. Anyway, one of the radio messages we got said they were acting crazy—tearing off their clothes, singing. Running around wild, I guess. Those were about all the details we heard."

"You have recordings?"

"Of the action we just fought? They'll be along in a minute, Commander."

Others among the people at Base Four Twenty-five, who were now trying to evaluate events, at first attributed the reported bizarre behavior of the people at the colony, during the attack and immediately following it, to the effects of some virus.

The task force, responding with all possible speed to the courier-borne report of that attack, had arrived at the battered colony in time to save it from destruction.

The combat recordings were now being brought into the operations room. Polly retreated into the background, but no one cared if she and the other colonists present stayed to watch.

The light in the large room dimmed slightly, and a stage brightened. The ranking officer of the task force that had just arrived introduced the combat recordings, which told the story.

When the powerful Space Force battle group had appeared on the scene, the berserker raiding fleet had broken off its assault on Malaspina and retreated. The Space Force had arrived none too soon; the battle had been going badly for the human side until then. Three or possibly four berserkers had been engaged in this latest attack.

A staff officer swore. "Look at that; some kind of new shielding. Cuts off the defensive beams from the ground as if they were flashlights."

"That explains how they were able to overrun Liaoning and Shubra so fast and easy."

When the berserkers retreated from their attack on the Malaspina colony, the human task force had pursued and engaged them again after a chase of about an hour.

Again, disengagement by the enemy and pursuit by the Space Force. This time the human squadron had promptly run into a well-executed ambush. Loop back on your own trail within the nebula—if you could manage that—and ambushing a pursuer came within the realm of possibility. Shortly thereafter, having suffered a reverse and again lost contact with the enemy, the commander of the Space Force battle group turned back to protect Malaspina.

Gennadius nodded. "You say you'd already left a detachment there."

"That's right."

Gennadius now tried to decide where he could get ships to relieve the ones now on duty at Malaspina. The enemy was enjoying such success that he had to think of the defense of the base itself. "The best I can do is send some Home Guard ships to Malaspina—if I can come up with enough civilian volunteers." He switched the direction of his gaze. "Domingo?"

Domingo, who had been listening intently, ignored the question. He asked the returning officers: "Was Old Blue there, at Malaspina and afterward? There was a unit that looked like it in that recording, but I couldn't be sure."

Some of the men and women exchanged looks. "Oh yeah," said one. "No doubt about it."

"You didn't destroy it." It was more a statement than a question.

"No, We didn't."

Polly thought she saw her captain's shoulders slump slightly, as if with relief. Domingo said: "I'd like to see the rest of your gun-camera records as soon as possible."

Another look was exchanged among the haggard captains of the surviving task force: *Who is this guy?*

Gennadius seconded Domingo's question.

"Coming right up, sir."

Soon additional records had been brought in. These confirmed conclusively, and in stop-action detail, the presence of Leviathan in the action off Malaspina.

It was Polly's first good look at the thing called Old Blue—the fragmentary recording from Shubran ground defense hardly counted. Here there were views from several angles, in different wavelengths. Imaging techniques corrected for the exaggerated Doppler effect of high-speed combat. This was about as good a look at Leviathan as anyone had ever had and survived. Polly and the others watching with her now beheld a great, ancient, angular and damaged shape, with some blue coloring about it; she had heard that the color was thought to be the result of some emissions from some defective component of the drive or other peculiar system on board.

Polly watched. *That is his special enemy, and therefore it is mine. If I can't turn him from his purpose, maybe I can help him to achieve it. Maybe then . . .*

They were frightening pictures, but to her, Domingo's face as he studied them was more frightening still.

Gennadius, without taking his eye from the new recording as it played again, beckoned an aide over to him. Polly heard the base commander issuing orders to pass on word of what he saw as a disastrous battle to Eighth Space Force headquarters, at the Sector capital. A manned courier, recently arrived at Four Twenty-five, was about to head back to headquarters and could carry this bad news with it.

Gennadius was now asking the crew of the courier if there was much chance of his getting any reinforcement from Sector Headquarters in the near future.

"Wouldn't count on that, sir. There's berserker trouble in other districts, too, and Sector's chronically spread thin."

"Yes. Damn, damn. That's about what I thought; maybe even a little worse than I thought." Gennadius turned his gaze to the big display. "We're just going to have to mobilize all the colonies in the Milk as best we can."

"Yes, sir."

The commander addressed himself to another aide. "Next courier we send to Sector, I want to tell them I'm invoking martial law over the whole Milkpail district. Get that in print for me to sign."

Then his eyes swiveled to Domingo. "Niles, I want you to take your people, all of 'em that are ready to fight and all your ships, and stand by for Home Guard duty. Might be at Malaspina, might be somewhere else."

"I've told you where I stand on that, Gennadius. Captains who want to do that can. I have other plans for my own ship. And for as many of my crew as will come with me."

"Oh. And what plans are those?"

"I'm hunting for Leviathan."

The room was quiet enough for Polly to hear the sigh Gennadius let out. "With one ship. That doesn't make any sense. I've told you what I need done. If you won't do that, then just go home and stay there."

"Home. Oh yes, home. Where is that?"

"Go somewhere and stay out of my hair, then. Sorry, Domingo. But other people are hurting, too. And this time it *is* an order. I'm invoking martial law."

There was a long pause before Domingo spoke. His answer when it came was surprisingly meek. "All right, Gennadius. I'll be out of your way from now on."

Domingo summoned his crew to him with a look around the room, and they followed him when he went out quietly. When they were gathered around him in the corridor just outside operations, he announced quietly that he wanted to have a crew meeting in his ship immediately.

A minute or two later the six of them were gathered in the common room aboard the *Pearl*. The captain looked around the little group and told them he had allowed the Space Force people to think he was obeying their orders meekly, that he would go home and see what could be done to make Shubra livable and defendable again.

"But if any of you actually thought I was going to obey that order, forget it. This ship is going on with the hunt just as before."

Henric Poinsot had joined the others in their gathering outside operations, and he had accompanied them to the ship, saying he wanted to remove a few personal things that he had left aboard.

But Poinsot now came into the common room and asked the captain: "What about the other people from Shubra?"

"What about them?"

"I mean that we have about twenty of our fellow citizens still here at the base who'll want to know what the hell you're doing, Domingo. About Shubra, if nothing else. You're still officially the mayor."

"I'll nominate you to take a message to them. They can have my formal resignation, if they want it. If any of you get tired of gazing at the wreckage where you used to live, you can try to join me later. But I'm not waiting for you."

The captain spoke coldly and contemptuously. The people who knew Domingo best, better than Polly had yet had a chance to get to know him, were gazing at him strangely. If he was aware of it, he gave no sign.

Iskander Baza watched his captain narrowly and then exchanged looks with Polly. She wondered if the message was that he intended to be her ally or her rival.

Henric Poinsot said: "You're disregarding the commander's orders, then. I'm making no promises to keep any of this secret, Domingo."

"Tell who you like, and be damned to you. It'll save me the trouble of leaving a message somewhere else."

Poinsot looked around at them all, started to speak again, thought better of it and went out.

Domingo looked around at them all, too. "Anyone else? Now's the time."

"I'm hunting with you," Gujar Sidoruk said.

"Good. Polly?"

"I'll go," she said at once. It came to her as she said it that her chief fear at the moment was only of being separated from him. She was more afraid of that than of berserkers. When she tried to think of her children, all she could know of them at the moment was that they were far away and safe.

"Iskander—? I guess in your case I don't have to ask. Wilma, Simeon, what about you?"

The married couple spoke haltingly. Taking turns speaking, looking at each other between phrases, they said that they had lost heavily to the berserkers and wanted revenge. Polly got the impression that there was more to their decision than they were saying.

The *Pearl* was already gone when Poinsot told Gennadius of Domingo's decision. The base commander, his mind heavily engaged with other matters, only nodded and sighed. Knowing Domingo, he was not all that surprised.

All Gennadius said was, "Well. We've each done what we had to do, I guess."

Regretfully he removed the *Sirian Pearl* from his roster of Home Guard craft. He would have to remind himself to count it as lost from now on, and it was going to make his job just that much harder.

☀ CHAPTER 6

The *Pearl*, with Gujar Sidoruk now aboard her as a member of her crew, departed Base Four Twenty-five without filing an official flight plan.

Her captain set a course and then turned the flight controls over to Iskander Baza, his second-in-command. After a few words with Baza, Domingo headed for his cabin berth—his tiny padded cell, or womb, was more like it, he thought—to try to get some rest. Getting to his berth was easy. He had only to crawl through the short, narrow padded tunnel that connected the captain's duty station with the captain's private quarters, the latter only a hollow, padded cylinder, no roomier or more luxurious than the berth of anyone else aboard the ship.

The captain's quarters, like the other berths aboard, had room enough to house only one person comfortably, and that only by the standards of a military ship. Still, two people had been known to occupy this cabin on occasion.

There would be no cabinmate on this voyage. Domingo removed some of his outer clothing, turned down the intensity of the cabin lights and the various displays and settled himself to try to get some sleep if possible. If he couldn't sleep, he would take something . . .

There was no need for him to take anything. His exhaustion was greater than he had imagined. Almost immediately, Domingo slept.

And dreamed.

Never, in the course of the deathlike sleeps that overcame him in this last epoch of his monstrously altered life, had the captain dreamed of Maymyo his murdered daughter, flesh of his flesh. Nor had he ever, before or after the obliteration of the Shubran colony, dreamed about berserkers.

Such visions as had come in sleep to Domingo since that disaster were few and seemed meaningless. But now, riding his new ship in pursuit of his mortal enemy, he knew the recurrence of a particular dream that he had not had for years. In this dream he was near Isabel, his wife, and the two of his three children, all little ones then, who had been with her when she died. Maymyo, his third child, had no part in this dream; she had somehow been wiped away, as if she had never existed. In this dream the ship carrying three members of his young family had come home to Shubra after all. The reports of its destruction had been only an accident, a great mistake, now satisfactorily explained away.

In the dream he, Domingo, was back on Shubra, working peacefully outdoors under the pearly sky, and Isabel was somewhere near him. Though he could not see her, he knew his wife was there, somewhere just out of sight, and he knew she had the two little children safely with her. He felt so sure of Isabel's nearness, her availability, that he was not even worried because she was not visible. It was no problem for Domingo that he still could not see her moment by moment as the dream wore on.

In this dream he himself was always busy, trying to do something, accomplish some task. What the job was, he could never remember when the dream was over. But while the dream was in progress, this work, whatever it was, kept him too intently occupied to even try to look at Isabel...

She was there, and at any moment now he would complete his work and be able to go to her.

He awoke from the dream alone in his berth on his new ship, aware of the light-years of emptiness just outside the hull.

On departing the base, Domingo had not turned his ship immediately in the direction of Malaspina, as some of his crew had anticipated. He hoped and expected to be able to pick up a fresher trail than that.

About two days after leaving Base Four Twenty-five, the *Sirian Pearl* arrived at the scene of the last fight reported by Gennadius's battered squadron. More often than not, solid Galactic coordinates were almost impossible to determine inside the Milkpail, but there could be no mistaking the still-widening disturbances that had been left in this region by the weapons used in the recent battle. Shock-waves expanding at kilometers per second for a number of days had made quite a conspicuous disturbance.

"Figure it out," Iskander said to Simeon, to whom most of this business of searching and trailing in the nebula was new. "Say an expansion rate of ten kilometers a second; then in a little more than a day you have a bulging cloud about a million kilometers across." Such a disturbed cloud was still a tiny tumor in the guts of an object the size of the Milkpail, big enough to contain a dozen known solar systems and perhaps a few more that had not yet been discovered.

Quite apart from the battle's gaudy traces, this region of the nebula was a place of unearthly beauty, of scenery remarkably spectacular even for nebular space. Sharp variations in nebular density, of unknown cause, suggested titanic pillars, domes and other architectural features. Some of the fantastic shapes could be interpreted as halls and mansions, built on a scale to contain planets.

The *Pearl* moved steadily on through these and similar vistas. Wilma said once, looking into a screen that was almost like a window: "Some people used to think that heaven looked like this. All white clouds and marble halls."

No other ships had joined Domingo in his hunt, and there was no reason to think that any were likely to do so. Most of the *Pearl's* crew were worried by that fact, but Domingo never seemed worried now, by that or anything else.

Except for one thing: that something might keep him from getting at Leviathan.

Simeon and Wilma began to wonder aloud what their friends who had declined to take up the chase were doing. The captain ignored their wondering, as he ignored much else.

Now the obsessed man displayed fanatical patience. He briefed his crew carefully on exactly what he wanted, then ordered two of them into their space armor and sent them out in the launch to begin a methodical investigation. The idea was to sift as minutely and carefully as they could through the thinly scattered debris of this battlefield, gathering samples of microscopic dust and thin gas, looking for material that would convey information of any kind about the berserkers, particularly Leviathan.

More precisely, of course, the idea was to find the trail of Old Blue's departure. To this end, the *Pearl* circled the volume of space in which the battle had taken place, stopping at intervals to let out the launch and the suited collectors. This process continued for half a day until they had closed in on what Domingo considered the most promising place to start a really detailed search. And to augment the human crew, a couple of service robots were put to work in space.

The nebula here was still torn and mottled by the contending energies that ships and machines had spent against each other. Most of the battle-distorted clouds were still expanding, at meters or tens of meters or perhaps even greater distances per second, fading and intermingling with other material as they swelled. But emission clouds, red-shifting now as they cooled and contracted, were splashed like blood through the contorted whiteness. That these particular clouds were contracting was a hopeful sign; shrinking clots of murk would not hide a trail as still-expanding clouds might easily have done.

Whatever departure trails might exist here were already badly blurred out with the passage of several standard days since the battle was fought. The natural movements of material in the nebula were wiping the traces away. But Domingo stubbornly urged on the search.

Polly continued to observe her captain whenever she had the chance. She had tried to convince herself that she was accompanying him on this mad expedition at least in part for the sake of her children, to rid the Milkpail of the horror called Old Blue so that these little worlds would offer safe places in which her offspring might grow up and live. That would have been a worthy goal, but in her heart she knew better. She was doing this because she could not really help herself.

The man I love, she thought, gazing again at his intercom image and wondering about him and about herself. She had no history of falling as drastically as this for men. Particularly for men who showed no special interest in her. She wondered also if her feelings were obvious to others. Probably they would be, she decided, if everyone weren't moving around in a state of benumbed shock just now, if all this hell weren't going on. Maybe then her attitude would have been noticeable even to him.

Now she wished that she had managed to talk to Gennadius about him before they left Base Four Twenty-five. But she hadn't. There hadn't really been time, for one thing. The base commander had been continuously busy. And Domingo had seemed strong and capable again—as he still did—and he and Gennadius had obviously been at least temporarily at odds with each other.

She wanted to have a real talk with Iskander sometime, too; she thought she didn't understand him at all. But so far she had somehow not been able to arrange it. She thought that Baza was now closer to Domingo than anyone else was, though the relationship did not seem to fall into any neat category.

Her worry about Domingo was as intense as before, though now, active in the chase, he looked stronger and more capable than ever, and his behavior since they had left the base had given her no new cause for alarm. He seemed buoyed up, energetic and almost happy, as long as he could keep driving toward his goal of vengeance. Vengeance on a piece of metal, as Gennadius had described it at one point. But Polly was worried by Domingo's happy energy. *He's going to snap,* she thought. *Or something. He hasn't had time to grieve over his daughter properly yet. Coming on top of what happened ten years ago, the shock of Maymyo's death has turned him away, somehow, from being human.*

There were periods, sometimes of hours, more often only of minutes, when she almost managed to convince herself that her fears were wrong, based on a mistaken assessment. He was just an extraordinarily tough man, and he had survived the blow of his daughter's death. Naturally he was still enraged at the universe, and challenging his bitter fate. Eventually he was going to be all right.

But the conviction could not last for long; her fears returned.

Carrying out the search for microscopic evidence just the way Domingo wanted it done was not an easy job. In the common room, at the daily meeting for discussion and planning, Gujar Sidoruk protested: "We need a fleet to do this properly."

Domingo paid little attention to the protest. "Well, we don't have a fleet. But we're going to do it effectively anyway."

Several more standard days passed while the search went on. The *Pearl* prowled slowly. She was beautifully designed for almost any type of nebular work, built by the almost legendary teams of master artisans and computers working in the orbital yards of far-away Austeel. She glided forward steadily, a huge silvered egg, at the center of the little formation of people and machines that searched the nebula around her, all of them continuously taking samples, testing, seeking patterns.

Polly had her own suit of custom-designed space armor, a tool that came in handy fairly often in her regular job. Now she was out of the launch, working in what was sometimes called milkspace, searching. And trying to keep from being distracted by the scenery. Not that the environment outside a ship was anything new to her; she had been born on one planetoid within the Milkpail and raised on another. But still her opportunities to get a direct look at a region of the nebula as exotic as this one had been few and far between.

She was not watching the view of marble halls and eternal sunrises on a holostage connected to her instruments now, or on a screen, but looking at the nebula itself through the transparent solid of her faceplate. It was difficult for the eye to interpret the pictures that presented themselves under these conditions, the subtly different hues of pearl and bone, milk and chalk and fine-grained snow. Just how big was *that* particular cloud formation, how far away ... ?

And visible within the clouds at times there was movement, not all of it inanimately caused. Life grew here, and sometimes it swarmed in profusion. Creatures of microscopic size could alter the shape of a cloud or change the quality of light when they moved in sufficient numbers. The changes did not signify intelligence or sentience; those qualities were apparently more than the ubiquitous energies of life could organize within matter this attenuated. But on the microscopic and near-microscopic level, there was a rich variety of life.

The discovery Domingo had been trying for, of a departure trail that might be followed, so far had not been made. Bits of evidence would be very easy to miss, here among the distractions of beauty and danger and strange life.

"You're going to need all your luck, Cap," Iskander Baza told him.

"Luck?" Domingo squinted at Baza. "What does this have to do with luck?" Leviathan itself was surely not a matter of luck; the malevolent purpose of the ancient Builders flowed in its circuits as surely as the life flowed in any human being's veins and nerves. Whatever else it might be, it was no accident. Nor were his own encounters with the damned thing accidental. Domingo was sure of that now, certain on the deepest possible level. He could close his eyes and feel it.

The hoped-for trail might still elude discovery, but the search had also already yielded information of another kind about the berserkers. Computer analysis showed that certain inhuman, unusual organic traces were to be found in the nebular material where the battle had been fought. In itself, organic matter in the nebula was nothing very unusual. There was, after all, an industry devoted to harvesting and processing it. But here, in one sample, the ship's computer was able to detect evidence of deliberate genetic manipulation, laboratory work performed on the molecular level.

"I'd say that's the kind of debris you'd get from micro-microsurgery. Whatever the process was, it must have been performed on a large scale for us to be able to pick up traces of it now."

"It can't be from one of the Space Force ships, then. Are berserkers starting to do surgery?"

"They've been known to engage in biological research."

"Well, true, it wouldn't be the first time in history they've tried it. But maybe the evidence is misleading. This could be just berserker parts and parts of some human researcher's equipment and results, all mashed into the same cloud."

"What human researcher would that be? Working out here?"

No one could come up with an answer for that.

For the berserkers to attempt biological warfare against ED humanity by means of microorganisms was nothing new. Historically the death machines had rarely had much success with the tactics of spreading disease. If they were trying it again, probably they had calculated some new variation.

But what was it?

Alternatively, the theoretical and practical problems of disease and how to spread it might not be what suddenly interested the berserkers in the field of biology.

But, what was it then?

The main computer on the *Pearl* announced that it now had a sufficiency of data; it was ready to present a model of the battle.

☀ CHAPTER 7

The common room on the *Sirian Pearl* was the only place aboard ship where six people could meet face to face and still have a little central space to spare. The greater part of that central space was presently occupied by a holostage, and on that holostage the ship's computer was currently engaged in building an elaborate image-model of the local disturbances within the nebula. For the time being the other model, the one that showed the whole Milkpail, had been tucked back into the data storage banks.

Not that the six people of the crew were very often in the common room at the same time. At least two were usually at their duty stations, on watch. And each of them had a private cylindrical cabin adjoining one of the six duty stations. Like Domingo's cabin, the five others were little more than large padded barrels furnished with cots, communications and plumbing. Polly, like several other people, spent a fair amount of time in the common room, sitting beside the stage and watching the construction job with interest. With even greater interest, but less openly, she also watched Domingo, who was fanatically intent upon the model.

When the model displaying current local conditions was completed, the computer, on the captain's order, ran it through an extrapolation back in time. The dispersed explosions that were only dimly detectable in the nebula itself became smaller and clearer in the model as the extrapolation progressed. The tentatively charted tracks of disturbance assumed a sharper, more definite form. Now it was possible to have a much more precise view of what had happened here some days ago in the battle between the Space Force and the berserkers.

Here, at this side of the display, was where the Space Force ships had been during the first moment of confrontation. And over there on the other side had been the enemy, four or possibly five berserkers in all, strung out in a jagged line some hundreds of kilometers long that might or might not have been meant as a tactical formation. That much, the positions before tactical movement started, could be confidently read from the reconstructed cloud disturbances and the distributions of trace elements in the clouds. So could the positions at the start of fighting. The opposing types of weapons, when fired, and even the drive engines had left subtly different flavors in the resultant expanding gasses.

Combat maneuvers must have begun immediately when the opposing forces sighted each other—indeed, the human survivors had so reported. The course of events after the fight had started was harder to reconstruct. Domingo called for more sampling in selected areas. Armored people went out into space again, and the computer kept working.

Gujar, who had been so eager to sign on, began grumbling. "Why is he doing this? Has he ever told us exactly why?"

Iskander smiled faintly. "He's looking for a trail. Domingo knows what he's doing."

"Does he? I can see scanning the area for that. Not that there would be much chance of finding anything. But what difference does it make what the exact positions were of all the units?"

"We'll see." Iskander still sounded confident.

When the additional data gathered by a few more hours' work in space was fed into the computer, the pictured past became visible in greater detail. Two Space Force ships, as reported by the crews of the surviving vessels, had blown up with all hands lost. A couple of berserkers had also been destroyed—their climactic finishes were plain to see, marked by radii of flying debris. And at least one more of the enemy had been badly damaged.

The battered berserker had got away. It must have done so, because it was nowhere in the immediate vicinity now, and no image of its annihilation in a death-blast had been imprinted on the clouds. Evidently the other surviving berserkers had departed unhurt or only lightly damaged. There were faint and fading tracks for them, too, attenuated to try to follow. But the badly damaged bandit had gone its own way, and it had certainly left a spoor behind it—a thousand times too thin for the eye to see, but evident to the technique of computer-analyzed sampling. A staggering trail of particles, a skein of what would have been smoke in atmosphere, a fading blaze of heat and radiation, led off toward an unexplored portion of the Milkpail into the heart of a white knot of nebula as wide as the orbit of the distant Earth.

"That's it! That's it. By all the gods, we'll get one of them now." The captain's voice was a hoarse whisper.

As soon as he had accepted the conclusion of the computer model, Domingo recalled those of his crew who were still outside the ship engaged in the task of gathering more data. Only two robots, attached to auxiliary power and shielding systems that let them cruise at a sufficient speed in space, remained outside still working at that task. The two mobile robots, Domingo calculated, should be enough to sniff out the trail, now that its origin was located. The moving fields of the ship would drag the small machines with her as she advanced.

The *Pearl* moved out again, running a little faster than before, hunting now with weapons ready. The model in the common room was continuously updated as the robots continued to take samples at distances of up to a few hundred kilometers from the moving ship and to telemeter the results in to the *Pearl*'s main computer.

Excitement grew. Polly took her brief periods of rest grudgingly, afraid of what discoveries she might miss. Between rest periods she observed Domingo, snatched bites of food, stood watch in her turn and otherwise helped out where she could. She had seen an effort vaguely like this search attempted once before, by someone else, and not successfully. That time the quarry had been a lost ship, presumably willing to be found, not a berserker.

She said to him once: "You really know how to do this, Captain."

At the moment he looked happy and, despite the long hours of concentrated effort, almost relaxed. As if, Polly thought, everything were normal.

He said: "Better than the Space Force, anyway."

Following the trail was slow, hard work from the start. Within the first hour the track of the enemy became blurred, but the robots worked tirelessly and it was not lost. Gradually the job became easier, the gradient of increasing density of certain battle remnants in the nebula becoming better and better defined. The speed of the chase increased until at last it began to seem possible that they would someday catch something—unless, of course, their prey were to increase its speed as well.

The *Pearl* was already a billion kilometers into unmarked whiteness, far off such charts as existed for this portion of the nebula. Determining the location of the ship within it, even roughly, was no longer a trivial problem. Even the brightest suns could no longer be located with any certainty amid the thickening, muffling clouds of white, off-white and gray, the ever-changing pastel shades of perpetual interstellar dawns and sunsets. It was not unheard of for ships to simply vanish in the Milkpail, even in regions where no berserker activity had ever been reported.

There followed another blurring of the track, leading to a more prolonged slowdown. But this delay too was temporary, the trail firming again within a standard day.

Time passed quickly, at least for Polly, working, sleeping, watching. People off duty still took time for conversation in the common room, watching the model transform itself. And Wilma and Simeon still thought aloud, at least in the captain's absence, that the pursuit would ultimately prove hopeless.

But within two more days it was unarguable that they were still following the berserker's trail, and at an increasingly effective speed. The trail seemed fresher now, which meant that the enemy was probably no longer as far ahead as it had been.

That fact sank in. When the crew had begun this voyage, they had all still been in something of a state of shock. But by now that was wearing off. They had started to think about what they were doing: chasing a berserker.

And the pursuit could no longer be considered hopeless. Polly began to wonder what would happen when and if they actually did catch up to the wounded thing they were pursuing. Certainly the *Pearl* was heavily armed and her crew capable. But still.

Were they closing in on Old Blue? Polly, like most colonists in the Milkpail, had heard the name many times, and some of the legendary stories. She had a healthy respect for berserkers, but like Commander Gennadius she had never considered one of them more terrible than another just because someone had given it a name. Now, though . . . there had been something disturbing about the jagged, illogical-seeming shape of Leviathan in the recordings and the theatrical blue glow. But the blue light could be reasonably explained as an accidental effect of some kind of radiation. And as for the jagged form, who knew why berserker machines were sometimes built in one shape, sometimes in another? Randomness, that was always said to be one of their important concepts . . .

Whatever the reason for its peculiarities, it still seemed to Polly that one berserker, any berserker, just because it had acquired a name, ought not to be necessarily more frightening than another. Not that she had ever actually fought any of them, but . . . and whatever type of a machine it was that they were chasing, it was certain that it had already been seriously damaged; and that was reassuring.

Domingo had the six people of the crew divided into two watches now: three driving the ship, manning the weapons and studying the computer-modeled trail while the other three rested and slept and talked and waited for their turns on duty. In this way the hunt kept going hour after hour, one standard day after another.

The captain seldom slept or rested now. Polly, watching him, saw the chiseling of his face grow sharper; otherwise he seemed unaffected by lack of rest.

The folds of nebula flowed ever more thickly around the *Pearl*. This did not slow the progress of the ship, already limited by the need to find a trail and stay with it. But it did raise the possibility of ambush.

Gujar, operating the forward detectors on his watch, excitedly called in a sighting, and Iskander at the helm slowed forward progress. But the sighting proved to be a false alarm.

When the object appeared at close range it was seen to be a peculiar thing, some kind of natural life-construct, with stalactite-like formations protruding from it in all directions. It throbbed, faintly and slowly, with the working of the life within it. Not a single organism, the instruments indicated, but some kind of a composite form. The thing, or creature, or life-swarm, or whatever it was, appeared next on the close forward detectors and finally on the direct-viewing screens. Then it drifted by the *Pearl* at a range of only a few kilometers. It was vastly bigger than the ship. There was no indication that it was aware of the ship at all.

Relative to the nebular material immediately surrounding it, the object was moving at a significant fraction of the velocity of light, a speed that any ship or machine of equal size would have found practically impossible to attain.

No one on the ship had seen or even heard about anything like it before. At any other time the humans would have turned aside eagerly to investigate. But not now.

When the living conglomerate was out of sight, Simeon and Wilma made a tentative and ill-advised attempt to persuade the captain to turn around and go back to Base Four Twenty-five. They argued that the crew of the *Pearl* could now report to the Space Force what they had found regarding the berserkers and consider they had done a creditable job. Gennadius would thank them.

Domingo did not thank them for the suggestion.

The truth was that most of his crew, everyone but himself and Iskander, were growing increasingly uncomfortable in this weird place. Even to people who were more or less at home in the uncanny environment of the Milkpail Nebula, this thickening, curdling, mottled whiteness, engendering new monsters, was extraordinary. Among the uncomfortable majority the opinion was subtly gaining strength that it was, or ought to be, the job of the Space Force to carry on with this kind of pursuit.

Domingo was inflexibly opposed to any change of course and overrode the hints of opposition. He even touched in passing on the laws of mutiny. In port a crew might, and his usually did, have the right to vote on big decisions. In deep space the captain's word was law, and the law applied with redoubled force when the berserker enemy was near.

The captain did agree to send off one of their two expensive robot couriers, directed to Base Four Twenty-five, before he continued his pursuit of the damaged berserker.

The courier departed silently, carrying word of their discoveries, their present location and their intentions to Base Four Twenty-five.

They hoped. The chance that it would succeed in getting there was hard to calculate.

Now there was only one usable courier left aboard. Here in clouds where radio was hopeless, it represented the only possible means of communication with the rest of humanity.

The pursuit of the wounded berserker resumed. More hours passed, adding up to another day. Tension grew aboard the ship as the trail became stronger, more clearly defined than it had ever been. Whatever was leaving the trail was undoubtedly closer ahead now than ever before. Sizable bits of debris, even fist-sized chunks of this and that, began to show up in the scans still being telemetered in from the outrider robots.

"That's berserker stuffing." Domingo said it softly, with obvious enjoyment.

A powerful blast centered somewhere ahead sent a silent but more-than-detectable Shockwave through the white nebula.

Chakuchin made a relieved sound. "It's blown itself up. That's it."

"We'll see." Domingo's intensity did not alter.

Inside the *Pearl*, whose forward velocity, even here within the buffeting whiteness, could be conveniently expressed as a fraction of the speed of light, the enormously slower Shockwave could be studied on the detectors for some time before it engulfed the ship.

But whatever might be, or might have been, at the center of the shock to cause it still could not be seen.

Domingo ordered acceleration. And more acceleration. Particles of matter, molecule-sized, pinged dangerously against the shielding fields that so far were managing to protect the hull from microcollisions at relativistic speeds. Indicators glowed with warning signals.

The captain ordered: "Give up the trail. Head for the center of that shock." The location of the center could be determined from the automatic recording of the event.

"Double alert for an ambush. Just in case."

On the screens of the forward detectors, the image of an object considerably bigger than the *Pearl* took shape and rapidly solidified. It was angular, irregular and metallic, about at the upper limit of size for effective travel within the nebula.

"Hold your fire!" the captain ordered sharply.

Whatever kind of a machine it was ahead of them, it was not Leviathan. The shape was as jagged as Leviathan's, but still totally wrong for that, if any of the descriptions and recordings of the monster were correct. Polly heard the captain sigh, a sound that might have come from the lips of a disappointed lover.

The second most obvious characteristic of the object they had just caught up with was the remarkable amount of fresh damage that it had sustained. The ruin looked too genuine and extensive to be any kind of trick. As they approached the wreck ever more closely there was hard radiation, too, wild and irregular in both intensity and kind, but always enough of it to suggest that there might be a small-scale nuclear meltdown in progress somewhere on the enemy.

It appeared that secondary explosions, delayed battle damage—or more likely a deliberate destructor charge, set off in anticipation of capture by the forces of life—had left this particular berserker unit, whatever it was exactly, drifting in a helpless condition.

The humans aboard the *Pearl* observed the enemy warily from a thousand kilometers' distance; then from a hundred; and then again from ten.

Simeon said, with the air of someone trying to establish an assertion as undoubted fact: "Now we've got to go back and report."

Polly, watching on her intercom, saw Niles Domingo's eyes turn to the big young man, one image glaring at another. The captain squelched Chakuchin's effort immediately: "We can't. We'll lose it if we do. Do you expect that we, or anyone else, will be able to find the way back to it again in this fog?" In another day or so the trail they had followed would have been completely dispersed by random drifting and other natural movements. There were currents in the nebula; it was at least as dynamic as an ocean of water on the surface of a planet.

"All right, then I suppose we finish it off. We have our missiles armed."

"They'd better be. But don't use any of them just yet."

"But what else can we do?" Chakuchin paused, as if realization had just come to him. "Are you expecting to send some of us over to board that thing? It may just be waiting to use its main destructor charge until something living comes close enough to be wiped out in the blast."

"I think it's already used whatever destructor charges it had left. And I'll lead the boarding myself, if that's what's bothering you. Can I talk two other people into suiting up with me? If not, I'll go alone. Polly, what about you?" The captain's eyes looked out from the little intercom screen and into hers. "We could use your technical expertise."

"I'll go," Polly heard herself agree at once. Then she trembled, thinking of her children. But she could not unsay what she had said. Not to Niles Domingo. She could silently curse the unasked-for fate that bound her to him, but it was her fate still, and she would not have changed it had she had the power.

Iskander, as usual, had not much to say, but he was plainly ready, even eager, to go where his captain led.

Gujar repeated Simeon's suggestion: "We could just fire away at it . . ."

But Domingo was silent this time, and this time the suggestion died without argument. The objections to it were too plain. Self-destruction was doubtless what the berserker had wanted to achieve, but something had gone wrong with the destructor charges.

That it had tried to destroy itself when capture by its enemy seemed imminent at least suggested that there was still something aboard that might constitute a valuable secret, perhaps even a clue to where the berserkers attacking the Milkpail colonies had their repair and construction base.

Conceivably there might even be human prisoners still living on that wreck. That there could be seemed doubtful, but berserkers did take prisoners sometimes for the information that could be gained from them, for living bodies and living minds on which to experiment.

Domingo was continuing to study the helpless-looking enemy, switching rapidly from one instrument of observation to another and back again. This was not Leviathan in front of him, but it represented the only immediate chance he had of getting closer to Leviathan. He mused aloud in his newly intense voice: "This is too damned strange. It's not like any berserker I ever saw or heard of before now. We can't miss the chance, we've got to go over there and see what we can find out from it."

Simeon suggested: "We've still got one courier. Let's send it off first, at least. Tell people where we are. Get some help out here."

Iskander shook his head. "I don't think so. If we launch our last robot courier here, we don't know that it's going to be able to find Base Four Twenty-five. Or that it'll ever be picked up by the Space Force anywhere. I'd say myself that the odds are pretty poor that a courier message from us here is going to get through." He smiled faintly. "Besides, couriers are expensive." It was the punch line of a standing joke.

Gujar said: "I agree. We might need the courier worse later on. I'd even say it's chancy as to whether we'll be able to find our way out of this ourselves; at least in any comfortable period of time."

And Domingo again: "Maybe a courier would be able to find its way to the Space Force somewhere. And if it found them, they might not be too busy to come and look at this thing. And if they did decide to come, and they did find their way here and saw it, they might be smart enough to realize its value. Or they might not. No, thanks. We're going to handle this ourselves. Even if they did agree it was valuable, they might still decide it would be better to fire away."

There was general agreement among the crew. People out here in the Milkpail depended, often enough, on the Space Force for their very lives. They also tended not to be overly impressed with that organization's abilities and accomplishments.

Simeon wavered. "Well, if you put it that way . . ." Wilma was silent.

"I do put it that way. Let's go."

☀ CHAPTER 8

Inside the cramped ventral bay where the *Sirian Pearl* carried her only launch—a small craft that also served as her only lifeboat—Niles Domingo, Polly Suslova and Iskander Baza were clambering into the bulbous suits and helmets of space armor. They were speeding up the procedure by calling checklist items back and forth.

Polly saw Iskander watching her as if he found something very amusing in her way of managing the checklist. She gave him a sharp look in return, and he turned away.

As soon as they had their suits on and tested, the three of them gathered up personal weapons and kits of tools and entered the launch, carefully maneuvering their mechanically enlarged bodies, one after another, through the tight hatchway of the smaller vessel.

The launch was a cylindrical craft, half as long as the *Pearl* herself but not much bigger in diameter than the height of a tall man. Its hatches were sealed now, and the bay around it evacuated. Then the ventral doors of the bay were opened to space. With Domingo in the pilot's seat of the launch—his armored helmet had a built-in headlink—the small vehicle separated from the *Pearl* and drove toward the damaged berserker.

Normally the controls of the launch, like those of the larger ship, were operated through a direct linkage to the electrical activity of the human pilot's brain. The system used on the launch was less sophisticated than that aboard the *Pearl*, but adequate for the less complicated craft.

One advantage of the launch was its real viewports, through which people inside could look out. In one direction, nearly astern now, hung the *Pearl*, her gun hatches open, her weapons ready. In almost the opposite direction, suspended against an endless background of distant white billows and luminous pastel columns, the enemy machine was a construction of dark gray planes and angles,

torn by blackened holes, lighted from time to time by fitful internal
fires—none of which were blue.

The berserker was substantially bigger than the *Pearl*, and through
the viewports it appeared subjectively enormous as the three humans
in the launch got their first direct look at it. The enemy loomed
even larger as Domingo drove closer. Still, the launch's radar instruments assured its crew that the machine ahead was by no means of
an unusual size for a berserker. It rotated slowly in the eternal sleet
of this nebular space, spurting more fumes and debris from ragged,
open wounds, emitting an occasional flare of light in one color or
another. Polly, looking at the broken, uneven outline the berserker
presented, decided that almost its entire outer hull was gone. And
yet it had continued functioning, at least well enough to retreat this
far after the battle.

The enemy unit appeared to be taking no notice of the *Pearl*,
or of the more closely approaching launch. Possibly it was now
completely blind and deaf. Possibly that last explosion, whose
shockwave the *Pearl*'s instruments had detected at a distance, had
originated in a successful destructor charge, and the berserker's
electronic brain, or brains, with their possible secrets, had now
been totally destroyed.

Of course it was also possible that the enemy still had additional
destructor charges aboard, only waiting to be set off. Or that it still
possessed other weapons and was now aware of human presences
nearby and was biding its time, calculating how to optimize the last
chance it would ever have of carrying out its prime programmed
directive.

"Ever get this close to one of them before?" Polly asked the question in a small voice and of no one in particular. Crew stations on
the launch were not separated; all three people aboard were riding
in the same small compartment. The captain, seated at her elbow,
was continuing to ease the launch nearer to the foe at a speed of
only a few meters per second.

Wordlessly Domingo shook his head. He seemed to be indicating
that he had no time for questions now; Polly bit her lip.

"I was, once," Iskander murmured. Polly turned her head and
looked at him, but he was not looking at her, and he offered no
details.

The central thought in Domingo's mind right now was that this
was not Leviathan in front of him. Still, it was one of the enemy,
the only one of the enemy that had yet come within his grasp. The
sight of the ongoing damage aboard, the nuclear and chemical reactions eating away at it, offered him a definite, savage satisfaction.
The feeling was mingled with an urgent worry that the information
he had hoped to find here, the knowledge that would somehow give

him an advantage, lead him to his true foe, was being destroyed before his eyes in the same fires.

He willed the launch forward more quickly. The safety fields of his chair shielded him and his shipmates from even feeling the acceleration, but they all saw on instruments how sharply the craft responded.

The storm of radiation, which had to be emanating from somewhere within the enemy, grew stronger as they neared the hulk. Still the armored suits ought to be sufficient to shield them from the radiation when they went out as boarders, unless the flux should increase by a considerable factor even above its present level.

They circled the enemy once in the launch, at a distance of no more than half a kilometer. Then Domingo drove his little craft closer again, slowing at the last moment, without warning taking them right inside the damaged hull, as Polly muffled a gasp. The launch entered the enemy's hull through a great rent that had been torn either by some Space Force weapon or by a secondary explosion. The hole was so big that it seemed to Polly that half of the pastel sunset billows making up the nebular sky outside were still visible after they had entered. But she still found herself holding her breath, with the sensation that gigantic jaws were about to close on her and crush her.

Inside the enemy's battered hulk, patches of heated, glowing metal were visible in every direction. When the glow of the hot metal was augmented by that from the nebula outside, there was enough light to keep the bowels of the berserker from being really dark. Not satisfied with this erratic illumination, Iskander sent searchlight beams stabbing out from the launch. The lights, playing back and forth at varying angles, revealed more twisted metal along with other objects, shapes and textures, some of which remained unidentifiable. At places inside the berserker, the continually outgassing fumes from internal damage were thick enough to interfere with vision, even with the launch's searchlights on.

Running one last time through the operator's checklist of her armored suit—quite unnecessarily, but it gave the mind something to do—Polly knew terror, remembered her children and asked herself why she was doing this. The answer to that question was not hard to find—Domingo had asked her to do it. But that answer, she reflected, was the kind that did you no good when you had found it.

Now that the launch was completely inside the berserker, their communications with the *Pearl* were almost entirely cut off. Radios stuttered and rasped with static. Domingo had been expecting this problem. He got around it by maneuvering the launch back to the lip of the wound through which they had entered the enemy's carcass and pausing to set up a small robotic relay station there. He had to get out of the launch in his armored suit to do so.

Waiting for him inside the launch, Polly and Iskander held their craft in position. They were too busy watching for signs of enemy activity to talk, beyond the minimum of necessary communication, or even to look at each other. But the metal body of the enemy around them, dead or dying, still had not reacted to their presence. Polly could begin to breathe again.

The EVA lock cycled; Domingo came back in. Sitting in the pilot's seat again, the outer surface of his suit frosting over lightly with the cold it had brought in, he exchanged a few words with the *Pearl*, confirming for himself that communications had now been solidly reestablished.

Next, driving the launch very slowly, he moved it deeper inside the largely hollow body of the enemy and with a magnetic grapple secured the prow of the small craft to a central projection within the ruin.

Then Domingo once more unfastened himself from his seat and stood up, drifting. The artificial gravity in the launch had not been turned on, conserving that much power against sudden need. He said: "You both know what we're looking for. Keep in contact with each other at all times."

"One more thing," said Baza. "We're locking up after us. Don't want any mice getting in while we're out." Iskander grinned mirthlessly. "Hatch reentry code will be Baker Epsilon Pearl. Okay?"

The two people with him acknowledged the code. Now the three explorers were ready to begin serious investigation. Domingo disembarked first and looked around before the others came out. Then he beckoned them. Baza, last one out of the small vessel, closed and sealed the hatch. Then the three separated, moving away from the launch in three different directions.

On first touching the metal bones of the berserker, Polly could feel, through the gauntlets covering her hands, how those structural members quivered faintly with the ongoing throb of some machinery. Everything here was not totally dead. But the hulk seemed basically stable, and getting around inside it proved not to be difficult, at least at the start. When necessary the boarders used the small jets on their armored suits to maneuver. But most of the time, in the effective absence of gravity, they were able to scramble readily from one handhold or foothold to another. Each member of the party carried sample cases and nets, means of gathering samples of gas, of debris, of anything that looked like it might represent a clue as to the purpose of this huge construction.

Repeatedly Domingo's voice came on the suit radios of his two companions, urging them to hurry the investigation, not to waste a moment. It was possible that secrets were being destroyed around them every minute. Polly wondered, but at this late juncture hesitated to ask, how they would be able to recognize a real secret when one appeared.

Already Iskander was jabbing boldly with a long, telescoping staff at some wreckage near the launch. "Someone else ought to look at this," he said on his suit radio. "This looks to me like biochemistry lab equipment. Maybe your hunch is right, Cap. About there being something here worth finding out."

Polly, pushing aside incomprehensible alien debris, went to join Baza. The stuff he was digging into looked to her like industrial equipment, pieces from some kind of factory.

Domingo had started his own search some distance away. Over suit radio he informed the others that he had already come upon the remnants of similar equipment.

The three of them, all keeping moving while they talked, discussed the situation with Simeon and Wilma and Gujar back aboard the *Pearl*. As Iskander had said, it looked as if Domingo's instinctive decision to board the wreck might be justified.

From the ship, Wilma's voice came sharply, interrupting the discussion: "We're starting to get some readings that indicate activity aboard that piece of junk."

The captain's voice snapped back: "What sort of activity? What do you mean?"

"It looks to me like physical movement. By objects approximately the size of people, making sudden starts and stops. It's not you; we can distinguish your movements from this other stuff."

The faces of Polly's shipmates were hard for her to see inside their helmets. Domingo's voice came calmly: "If there were any independently functioning, programmable machines still here, I think they would have let us know already. What you're detecting might be drifting bits of stuff."

"Might be. It's hard to read anything accurately under these conditions. But to be on the safe side maybe you'd better get back to the launch."

"Scratch that. This whole operation is some distance from the safe side, anyway. We're going on with what we're doing."

Polly heard her captain's fearless indifference, swallowed and went on with what he wanted her to do. Iskander naturally was doing likewise.

The radio voice came again, relayed from the ship. "All right, acknowledge. We'll continue to stand by." The three people who were still aboard the *Pearl* would be ready to provide what help they could for the three boarders in case of trouble; or, in the worst case, they ought to be able at least to get away with the ship and carry the news of a disaster. The people on the ship also had the task of recording data as it was transmitted from the trio of explorers.

Exploration proceeded as rapidly as was feasible.

Like her two companions, Polly jumped and jetted and clambered about the wreckage at a speed that she would have thought utterly reckless had it not seemed even greater folly to spend more time here than absolutely necessary. Still, she was sure that they were not going to be able to explore the entire hulk.

The explorers were undoubtedly accumulating a lot of raw information. How much usefulness that information had, if any, would have to be determined later. Hand-held video units recorded whatever passed in front of them. Faceplates in armored helmets expanded the spectrum in which the human eye could see, even as they protected the eyes from overloading brightness.

Drifting and clambering through this ruin filled with disorienting shapes and unfamiliar objects, Domingo saw no recognizable weapons and no vast stores of power such as would have been required to energize most types of the space-warfare weapons with which he was familiar. In this portion of the berserker too, some of the things he was finding looked like lab equipment. In fact, a lot of it looked like that. Yes, it had to be.

But what was all the rest of this? The components of a miniaturized factory for the production of some kind of biological materials, as Polly had already suggested?

Still, the only discovery Domingo really felt confident about as yet was that most of this was not weaponry, or direct support for weaponry, at least not any type with which he was familiar. He grew more certain of that the more he saw. There was no question that there had been some weapons on this thing once; on a berserker there always were. But the armament, especially if it were limited in quantity, would have been mounted on or just inside the outer hull, and very little of that hull was left. He hadn't yet taken a close look at the remnant of surface that still existed, thinking secrets more likely to be found inside.

It was amazing that any machine, even a berserker, could have taken a beating like this and still function well enough to propel itself this far.

The strength of malevolent purpose . . .

He moved around a shattered bulkhead, finding his way into yet another bay. Here were massive cylindrical objects—field generators, he thought, and of some complex kind. Not the usual type of generators that were used to create defensive fields or artificial gravity for human ship or inanimate killing machine. No, these were intended for something else . . . and they were clustered together oddly, as if in an effort to produce some kind of heterodyning . . .

And what had all *this* been, here, inside? Tanks, pipes, equipment for doing something chemically. Producing something, in quantity, he supposed. Beyond that it was very hard to guess.

The problem of determining functions was only partially a result of the extensive damage and the alien design. Difficulty also lay in the fact that there was simply too much volume here, too many *things*, too much material for three harried, frightened people to assimilate or even to record on video in any endurable length of time.

Vibrations in the berserker's framework had been perceptible to the explorers ever since they had left their launch. Now the rumbles and shudders were growing stronger and running almost continuously through the enemy's metal bones, for all Domingo knew presaging another and finally catastrophic blast.

Now, every time Domingo touched a solid part of the berserker, his grip was shaken.

Instruments attached to the captain's suit registered another increase in the flux of radiation. No one spoke up about the increase, but everyone must have made the same observation he had. The readings were still within tolerable limits for the suits, but Domingo feared that they were high enough to make it hard for his people to concentrate on the job at hand.

The captain himself had no trouble concentrating. What he was doing was necessary. He looked around him, making an urgent effort to get some overall sense of where he was, to form a picture of what this entire structure must have been like before the Space Force weapons had blown half of it away. This unit didn't seem like a ship, in the sense of something built primarily for travel or combat. It was, to begin with, he thought, more like some kind of space station, built to stay more or less in one place, working on some job. And the body of the station—call it that—was heavily compartmentalized, or at least it had been before it had been wrecked. The implication, as Domingo saw it, was that different experiments, or possibly different production lines, would have been going on in the separate compartments.

He and the two people with him had as yet explored only a comparatively small portion of this unit. The whole berserker was perhaps twice the cross-section and eight or nine times the volume of the *Pearl*. But so far Domingo had seen no evidence that it had ever held any human prisoners. Not Earth-descended, not Carmpan, not of any of the other known themes among the several recognized varieties of living Galactic intelligence. There was no trace recognizable of the life-support systems that would have been necessary to keep such prisoners alive. Nor were there signs of any cells, rooms or passageways where living victims might once have been held. Nor even of anything that looked like animal cages.

He called his two fellow explorers on radio and questioned them. They had seen nothing of the kind, either.

"Cages?" Polly asked. "Why should there be cages?"

"I don't know. It seemed a possibility."

Iskander, drifting closer from a distance, had a comment. "It's not a prison, not an ark and not a zoo. But it *is* some kind of developmental lab. I'll bet my next chance to own a ship on that."

Domingo was keeping his hands busy while he conversed, putting fragments of drifting material into a sample case. He answered: "I don't know that I'd be willing to go that far. But this is certainly not a fighting unit. We've been through enough of it now to be sure of that."

Iskander, hovering close to his captain in effective weightlessness, seemed to shrug inside his armor. "So far we've given it a light once-over only. But I suppose you're right, Cap."

"Assume I am correct." Domingo snapped shut his sample case. "Then why was this unit traveling with a berserker raiding party?"

"Probably berserkers have their logistic problems, too. Maybe they're moving their laboratory from one planetoid or system to another . . . how should I know?"

Polly put in: "I've got a bigger question for both of you. Why are berserkers cultivating life? Are they experimentally trying to produce new forms?"

In the reflected glow of the launch's searchlights, she could see Domingo's face inside his helmet; the captain seemed to be staring at the question as if his life depended on it. At last he answered. "I don't know. But it would be a good idea to find out." He looked around at the other two, who at the moment were both close to him. "And meanwhile, while we're sitting around thinking things over, it'll be a good idea for us to continue to survive. I think we've got enough information for a start. Let's get ourselves back into the launch."

No one argued with that decision or hung back from its execution. And a moment after they had closed the hatch of the launch behind them, they were heading out of the berserker's belly and back toward the *Pearl*.

☀ CHAPTER 9

A matter of minutes later, the *Pearl*'s entire crew was safely back inside the ship, and the ship had been withdrawn to what Domingo considered a prudent distance, nearly a hundred kilometers from the drifting wreck.

The captain called his crew into a conference. Everyone was wearing shipboard coveralls now, while out in the ventral bay three suits of space armor, along with the launch, were still undergoing a thorough precautionary sterilization.

Some of the sample cases brought back to the *Pearl* had already been processed through the sickbay diagnostic machines, where they had been discovered to contain microbial cultures. Those cases had been resealed by remote control and were being saved in sickbay for further investigation when they could be taken to a real laboratory.

Gujar said thoughtfully: "It's really simple."

"How's that?" Polly asked.

"Berserkers aren't intrinsically interested in science."

Domingo nodded. "Agreed."

"And producing new forms of life is against their basic programming, which is to kill. So if they're experimenting with biology, producing some modified forms of life—that's the suggestion, isn't it?—they have an overriding reason for doing so. It's part of an effort to achieve some larger goal."

It was Wilma's turn to nod. "Of course. And their goal is no doubt their usual one, of wiping out ED humanity. We're their big stumbling block, probably all that stands in the way of their sterilizing the whole Galaxy. We have been, ever since they met us."

"Exactly. And so the most likely interpretation of all this bioresearch material is that it represents a serious attempt to produce—what? An antihuman poison?"

Polly said: "There are a lot of poisons around already that can kill people. It wouldn't take any great amount of research to find out about them. I don't think it's that. But . . . an antihuman something, certainly. Maybe a virus?"

The captain was thinking very intently. "Historically, down through the centuries, they've already tried a number of times to use disease organisms against us. But that kind of tactic has never worked very well for them, as far as I know. People have been doing research on human diseases a lot longer than berserkers have; we're ahead, and we're not about to let them catch up."

"But suppose they have caught up?" Iskander wondered. He appeared to find possibilities of amusement in the idea.

"Well, we can feed what information we've been able to gather so far into the computer, along with that hypothesis, and see what we get."

Wilma and Simeon got started doing that while the others watched.

Simeon was ready to continue the discussion as he worked. "I assume you've all heard about the Red Race."

"Sure." Iskander raised his eyebrows. "Don't tell me they're involved."

Chakuchin ignored that dry joke; the Red Race, the berserkers' original targets, had been dust and radiation as long as the Builders themselves or perhaps a short while longer. "Then no doubt you've heard about the *qwib-qwib* too."

"Sure. So what?" In that lost age, sometime before the beginning of ED history, the Builders' opponents, with almost their dying effort, had constructed machines that were designed and built and programmed to do nothing but seek out and destroy berserkers. Or so went the theory most favored by present-day ED historians. Unfortunately for the Red Race and for Galactic life in general, the *qwib-qwib* machines had appeared on the scene too late to cope successfully with the berserkers.

"Legendary," said Iskander, smiling faintly.

"Like Leviathan itself." Domingo was not smiling. "But whether something is legendary or not is not the point. Simeon's point, as I see it, is that the berserkers might now be doing something analogous to what the Red Race did with machines. I mean they might now have turned to creating life—not necessarily just microbes—to wipe out life where other means have failed them."

For the next few seconds each of the six people thought her or his own thoughts in silence. Then their ship interrupted their meditations with a report.

Their main onboard computer was ready to confirm that the material presented to it for analysis was almost certainly from some kind of facility engaged in biological research. But it was not prepared to deliver a quick estimate of the berserker's probable purpose in working with such material. Instead the computer suggested that the job should be given to some larger computer, if the delay that would necessarily involve was tolerable.

Domingo said to it harshly: "We'll do that as soon as we have the chance; for now, keep working."

The computer acknowledged the order with a simple beep—the captain did not care for unnecessary anthropomorphism in any of his machines—and presumably kept on working.

Polly, speculating on what she had seen today, remarked: "There may, of course, be other berserker space stations like this one somewhere."

"If the computer should ask me about that possibility, I'll tell it so."

But the computer was silent on that point. What it did ask for presently was more information, in particular more samples of various materials from the wreck.

"Such samples are difficult to obtain. What kind of answers can you give me without more data?"

"None reliable." The voice of the machine was very clear and quite inhuman.

"Keep working anyway." The captain looked round him at his crew. "Second watch, back to your stations. First watch, take two hours at ease."

After his crew had dispersed, Domingo stayed in the common room alone, considering. He felt that events so far had justified his instinct. His intuition, hunch or whatever you wanted to call it, fueled by his great hatred of Leviathan, had guided him correctly, at least up to a point. His intuitive judgment now appeared to be backed up by the calculations of the ship's computer. He had been led to something of great value. Now he was torn between wanting to return to the wreck and extract still more information from it and wanting also to hurry with the news of his discovery back to Base Four Twenty-five, where the information he already had gained might be used to forge a new weapon against Leviathan.

In a way, he was still as far as ever from coming to grips with his chief enemy. But now one of its allies was here before him, helpless. For the moment at least, he held a once-in-a-lifetime advantage, and such an advantage must not be wasted.

Finally Domingo decided to search the wreck some more. He could not shake the intuition that there was more to be gained from it; and whatever information might still survive aboard it was being steadily incinerated.

The *Pearl* was certainly not equipped to do much more than she was already doing in the way of collecting and preserving materials, including some probably dangerous items. But she had the space and the equipment to do a little more. And there was much more to be seen and photographed aboard the enemy, in limited time. If only the six humans on the scene now could find and salvage what absolutely must be preserved . . .

Again Domingo called for volunteers. This time he wanted to bring four people, himself included, in the launch.

Iskander as usual was the first to raise his hand, a languid, minimal gesture. This time Wilma and Gujar, evidently feeling it was their duty to accept a proper share of the risks, both volunteered to come along. That was enough to make four searchers. Polly kept her hand down on this occasion and stayed with Simeon aboard the *Pearl.* Neither she nor Chakuchin made any pretense of being at all eager to join the boarding party; nor did Wilma appear surprised to see that her husband was staying behind.

The *Pearl* once more approached the wreck, to stand by at the same distance as on the previous effort. The launch, with the chosen four inside, cast off.

When the boarding party reached the near vicinity of the berserker, they once more measured the radiation flux and reported that it had now fallen off a little. Domingo paused at the lip of the wound to check the communications relay, which was still in place and still working. Again the launch was maneuvered inside the berserker and moored there, in the same place as before. This time Wilma stayed in the pilot's seat of the little vessel, ready to maneuver it close to any of the spacesuited searchers who might need assistance. The other three volunteers got out of the launch and separated, once more exploring individually. They reported that the rumbling and shuddering of the enemy's frame, so pronounced earlier, had largely subsided.

Polly, now in the pilot's seat aboard the *Pearl*, had just received another call from the ship's computer, which was protesting that it still lacked enough data for the problem it had been asked to solve. She had given the machine permission to reduce temporarily the amount of time it spent working on that problem. And now she was on her radio, listening intently to the conversation of the boarding party among themselves.

"I don't see anything more here than what you described," Gujar was reporting via his suit radio. "I don't—"

And that was the last that Polly heard. Communications had been broken off abruptly, dissolved in a sudden quavering whine of noise.

"What're you doing?" Simeon's figure, bulkier than ever in space armor, was unexpectedly looming at her side. He had come through the connecting tunnel from his own crew station. "What's going on—*Wilma!*" Even as he cried out his wife's name, the *Pearl* was already shooting forward.

"I'm getting the ship over there!" Polly shouted at him. "Get back to your station!"

His massive form hesitated.

"Move it!" she screamed at him.

Simeon lumbered away.

"Man our weapons!" she shouted after Chakuchin's retreating figure. Then she turned her full attention back to the controls and the radio. "Boards, can you read me? Wilma, what's going on?"

But as before, there came no answer from suit radios or the launch. Headlink tight on her forehead, Polly gunned the drive, urging the *Pearl* to the assistance of the boarders.

This was the first time, except for a couple of brief practice sessions, that she had flown this ship. She could only hope that her control was precise enough.

✦　✦　✦

Domingo's first warning that something was gravely wrong came in the form of a stealthy movement that he happened to sight some forty meters away, clear on the other side of the ruined berserker. He thought the movement was too sharp and sudden to be that of any object merely adrift here in the effective absence of gravity; it looked rather like a furtive, purposeful dart.

A moment later, very near the spot where the motion had caught the captain's eye, he was able to recognize the shape of a berserker android. The thing was approximately the size of a human being, and when he increased the magnification in his faceplate optics it showed up plainly. Silhouetted against a white patch of nebula framed by the ravaged hull, the machine looked half human and half insect. For an instant the dark inhuman shape was there and motionless; then in the next instant it was not there, moving away again so quickly that it seemed to simply disappear.

Drawing a breath, trying not to make a gasp that the radio would pick up, Domingo uttered the coded message that had been worked out for this eventuality: "I think I'm beginning to see a pattern in this material here."

Chillingly, there was no immediate reply. There was only a faint whining nose in the captain's helmet, so faint that until this moment it had not impressed itself upon his hearing. Now that he heard it, he was certain of what it meant: the humans' radio communications had somehow been knocked out.

Knowing his fellow boarders might already be dead, Domingo drew breath and shouted into his transmitter: "Berserkers! Back to the launch!" He had already drawn his handgun, a small but powerful projectile weapon, from his belt holster. The thoughtsight that would have made his aim with the handgun well-nigh perfect, guiding projectiles to his point of vision, was still clipped to his belt, and for the moment he left it there. The connectors on his helmet into which the sight would have to fit were presently occupied by the Spectroscopic lenses, light amplifiers and sensors that he had wanted to have in place while he was searching.

Domingo, drifting and nearly weightless, aimed his handgun as best he could by hand and eye and fired without benefit of thoughtsight. His aim was not bad, but far from perfect. In the quick serial flares made by the first burst of explosive projectiles, hitting home across the hull in airless silence, he could see the attacking berserker clearly limned, one of its multiple limbs vibrating, halfway torn off by a half-lucky shot. *Now it will know I'm here and kill me,* Domingo thought, but before his enemy could burn him out of existence he had time to fire again.

Again he thought that he did damage, and again the instantly effective return fire that he had expected from the android did not come. So the device he had just shot at might be only an unarmed mobile repair machine—unarmed except for the strength in its limbs and tools, the machine-power quite probably capable of tearing an armored suit apart along with the man inside.

Scrambling away in the opposite direction from his target, the captain got behind a bulkhead. Against a machine that had only its strength for a weapon, he might survive long enough to get his thoughtsight connected. Domingo continued to shout warnings into the unresponsive whining within his helmet as his feet thrust against broken machinery and structure to propel his body and his hands worked to get the weapon's fire-control system attached to his helmet. With fingers turned clumsy in their desperation, he tore off the special search gear he had been using, letting the disconnected chunks of hardware go drifting free.

Unexpectedly, the radio noise in his helmet changed, flowered into bursts of whining and singing that moved up and down the scale of audio frequencies. Maybe there was hope yet. The combat radio system built into the suits, technology borrowed from the Space Force, had detected jamming and was trying to fight through it, working to hold a signal pathway open.

Domingo's shouted warnings had brought no reply, and he could not assume that anyone had heard them. But the blasting flares of gunfire certainly ought to have served as an alarm, and so should the more subtle fact of the jamming itself. If only his crew had been quick enough to notice the jamming, and if any of them were still alive, to notice that the shooting had begun . . .

The captain was drifting in shadow now; his suit lights turned off, his hands still working to get his weapon ready for efficient action. Connecting his thoughtsight properly seemed to take forever. Before the device was ready, his eyes caught another flash of movement in another place across the hull, far from where he thought either of his shipmates ought to be. Perhaps it was the same machine he had seen before and fired at. Perhaps at least one more enemy device was activated, ready to join in an attack.

Domingo's hopes surged up suddenly as he saw, near the same spot, the flares of projectiles from other handguns like his own, bursting and glowing and dying away. A moment later, he caught a glimpse of two suited human figures, together now and still surviving, scrambling in the direction of the place where the launch was moored. But still nothing except noise was coming through on his radio.

Then something flared up brightly amid the wreckage where those last shots had struck, brighter by far than the explosive projectiles from the humans' sidearms. It was perhaps a delayed, secondary explosion caused by one of the humans' shots. The new light persisted long enough to reveal multiple movement by the enemy, a ruin almost swarming with their units. Some of the creeping machines Domingo saw were much smaller than humans, and individually these miniature units, probably repair or construction devices of some kind, looked ineffective. But they would all be equipped with potentially mangling tools of one kind or another. And it was evident that a berserker brain somewhere was still directing their activities.

The launch was abruptly in motion now, its mooring cast off. Domingo thanked all the gods that Wilma must have realized what was happening. And now there was fire from the launch, almost invisible beams of energy from its one real weapon. The beams probed neatly and precisely among the ruins, and small moving machines touched by that vague thin pencil flared up and vanished. Wilma, alone in the launch, had turned her attention from piloting and was cutting some of the enemy down.

The launch was hovering now in the middle of the hollow space inside the berserker, standing by to help the boarders, to pick them up. It ought to be easy, here in virtual weightlessness, for them to jump for it. The captain wouldn't be first to jump; he'd see his people on board first safely, if they were still alive; and before going to them he wanted to get the thoughtsight connected . . .

Of course, the launch. Of course, that was what the enemy was after.

The captain couldn't see the *Pearl* itself from where he drifted inside the carcass of his enemy. Nor could he guess what action Polly and Simeon might be taking. By now, if they were still alive, they must have realized that radio signals from inside the berserker were being jammed, and probably they could see the intermittent flares of fighting. If Simeon and Polly were to open up with the heavy weapons that the ship carried, the most likely effect would be the annihilation of everything that still remained of the wrecked berserker, along with the four people who were inside it and the launch that had brought them here.

So far, that fire from the *Pearl* had not lashed out.

Now the noise level in the captain's helmet radio suddenly dropped. Hoping that the built-in combat anti-jamming might now be able to force a signal through, Domingo shouted orders for the *Pearl* to stay clear of the wreck. He didn't know what additional weapons the enemy might still be able to bring into play, but if berserker units could seize the launch and then the *Pearl*, much more than this one skirmish would be lost.

Still no answer came to him from the *Pearl.* It was quite likely that the relay station had been knocked out.

Surely the people aboard his ship must realize by now that

something was wrong. If only they didn't do anything that might endanger the ship, put it at risk of being boarded, taken over—

Domingo got confirmation that Polly and Simeon were at least aware of a problem. Now he could see the *Pearl* herself, hovering close outside the gap through which the launch had entered the berserker. But the radio jamming had come back, as effective as ever.

Still no more than half a minute had passed since the first alarm. Moving around within the wreck, still struggling to get the last connector of his thoughtsight properly attached, the captain could see that the relay communications station, on the lip of the berserker's wound, was gone. It had somehow been knocked out, quite possibly uprooted by a berserker android by main strength.

Then without warning a voice burst through the jamming into his helmet. Score one round at least for the Space Force technology; even the stereo effect worked.

The message was a shout of fresh alarm that turned the captain in another direction:

"They're trying to seize the launch!"

I know that, damn it, thought Domingo, and repeated an order that had earlier gone unacknowledged. "Wilma, keep it away!" The jamming came back, cutting him off in midsentence. But Wilma, whether she had heard him or not, kept on with what she was doing, maneuvering the launch close to an interior landing in a different spot from where it had been moored. Actually, Domingo realized, she was bringing it closer to where he himself had been a few seconds ago, as if she thought he needed to be picked up. She would be able to see, though perhaps only intermittently, where the people inside were. She was naturally trying to rescue them, get them out of this snakepit of swarming enemies. And she had stopped shooting for the moment. To fly the launch, determine where to go and at the same time work its weapon precisely was more than almost any individual would be able to manage properly.

The captain gave up trying to be last aboard and propelled himself into a weightless dive to meet the approaching launch. At the same time, with inhuman speed, berserkers went jetting and lunging for the small craft as it appeared about to touch down. Domingo's weapon blazed at them. His shots were still hand-aimed, but lucky enough to reduce a couple of small units to flying fragments. The recoil of his own fire deflected him away from the oncoming vehicle, and he grabbed at more wreckage to stop himself.

Why didn't they jump us the first time we came aboard? If ever he had time to think again, he might be able to come up with a sure answer for that one. Probably the enemy had needed some time to mobilize its mobile units. Or else, on the humans' previous visit, the malevolent computer planning the attack had simply delayed its move too long, miscalculating the moment when the onslaught of its small machines would be most likely to inflict maximum damage. Probably the prime enemy objective from the start had been to seize the launch.

At last, under the pressure of Domingo's fingers, the final stubborn connector clicked into place; the thoughtsight was installed on his helmet. He brought his weapon into efficient operation now, locking aim and firing with fearful electronic accuracy; one of the scurrying machines after another vanished in blurs of flying parts.

Now that his fire was seriously disrupting their coordinated attack, he suddenly became the enemy's prime objective. He saw a device that looked like a toolrack charging at him and sent it spinning and reeling away, with a great hole blasted through its middle. He got a new clip into his handgun barely in time as an android charged him, hurling something that clanged like a bullet off his armor. That machine, too, he promptly devastated. To Domingo it seemed that he broadcast and focused destruction with the mere act of his will. But there was only one more spare clip before his ammunition would be gone.

The return fire he had expected earlier struck at him now; some kind of laser, he thought, but not quite powerful enough to do the job. Domingo was left momentarily blinded, trying to tumble away. Even through his armor he could feel the searing heat.

The two other humans who had boarded the wreck with him had given up trying to hide. They were using their weapons steadily now, and more or less efficiently. As far as Domingo could tell, their efforts were no more than marginally effective. Domingo supposed that the others were having trouble getting their thoughtsights hooked up, too. Only the weapons on the launch itself, now briefly back in action again, were so far staving off disaster.

Iskander and Gujar jumped for the launch, propelling themselves easily in weightlessness, and one of them at least—Domingo couldn't see the suit markings to determine which—was clinging to it, gripping a small projection with one hand and firing a weapon with the other.

Wilma opened the hatch of the launch, responding to frantic gestures from one of the other boarders who was closely beset by machines.

The trouble was that as soon as the hatch was opened, the enemy went for it. It was naturally a double door, inner and outer, the EVA airlock.

The idea came to Domingo that the enemy were using the boarders as bait rather than going all out to kill them quickly, hoping to be able to lure the launch within easy reach to get it to open its entry hatch.

On the launch, Wilma could see her shipmates jumping around, exchanging fire with the enemy machines, in peril of being scraped off the launch and grappled by them.

The launch, unless she were to withdraw it from inside the berserker, remained within easy leaping distance of the surviving androids. And the humans' communications were still being successfully jammed.

Domingo went after the enemy machine that was closest to the launch. *Maybe one of the same kind that killed Maymyo,* he thought. He fired and fired at it, bathed it in explosions, but could not seem to do it any effective harm. It had some special, toughened armor. His small handgun projectiles were not enough.

It had no firing weapon of its own but was destroying things by main strength.

It somehow disabled the beam projector on the launch.

Now it wanted to get at the opening hatchway on the launch.

Domingo was there in time to somehow block its entry or to keep it from getting through the inner door of the EVA hatch.

The launch started to drift away, uncontrolled, when Wilma gave up her post at the controls to try to get the door closed again.

The thing was close in front of him, parts of it blurring with movement at invisible speed, a chopping machine into which he was about to be fed like sausage.

Domingo and the berserker both spun away from the launch. Wilma, trying to reach from inside to help, was drawn out with them, but either Gujar or Iskander lunged into the open airlock and got it closed again from the inside, just ahead of the reaching grapple of a machine.

Then he, Domingo, was wedged in a crevice somewhere and the berserker android was pounding at him, probing for him with a long metal beam. The weapon driven by those arms could mash him, armor and all, if it caught him solidly and repeatedly, wedged against an anvil as he was.

Domingo was not trying to get away any longer; he was as well-armed now for this fight as he was ever going to be, and he was fighting.

Domingo could feel himself being mangled. He spent his last conscious effort firing his weapon one more time, point-blank range against the damnable, the evil thing.

✳ CHAPTER 10

There was a time, a long, long time, during which his awareness of his surroundings was no more than barely sufficient to convince him that he was not dead. Dead, slaughtered and gone to one of the legendary hells, one that had been re-created especially for him and repopulated with berserkers. Down there the damned machines were still killing Isabel and the children, and he still had to watch. Then, subtly, a divide was crossed down near the boundary of hell, and Domingo began to be sure that it was human beings and not only machines who had him in their care, though the gods of all space knew there were machines enough surrounding him. He allowed himself to be convinced that these contrivances were purely benevolent, or at least that was the intention of their programming. He had not become the berserkers' prisoner.

Lying there with his life no more than a thin bloody thread, he knew that he had survived some kind of a skirmish with the damned killers. But all the details of the event were vague. He had gone after them somewhere, and a fight had broken out—yes, inside their wrecked, spacegoing laboratory—and he had been terribly hurt, though now he was suffering no particular pain. Nothing else about what had happened was at all clear at the moment.

The thread of life was stronger now. The present, if not the past, was growing a little clearer. Domingo understood that he was lying flat in a bed, on his back most of the time, though once in a while he was gently flipped, for one reason or another. He realized too that there were people coming and going purposefully around him. As a rule the trusty caretaking machines stayed where they were. He had the feeling that the lenses and sensors of these machines were watching him with superhuman vigilance.

Sometimes Domingo thought that his left leg was no longer where it ought to be, that it was growing out of his body from somewhere other than his hip, sprouting grotesquely from his back or chest. And sometimes he thought that the leg was completely gone. Not that the mere absence of one limb was going to worry him especially. He was still breathing, and the berserkers did not have him. Those were the only two essential requirements of life that he could think of.

Given those two conditions, he would be able to build on them everything else he wanted. His wants were really simple, though they were not easy. Grimly, half blindly, half consciously, he started trying to make plans again. In time he could and would find the way to the appointed meeting that he was fated to have with Leviathan. That meeting would take place. He would create a way, a possibility, if none existed now.

More time, long days, passed before Domingo experienced an interval in which he was strong and lucid enough to ask questions.

His voice at first was no more than a crushed whisper. "What happened? Tell me. What did we bring back?"

That was the first thing Domingo asked about; and Polly Suslova, wild-haired as usual and looking somewhat excited as she bent over him, was the first person he recognized and the first to whom he spoke coherently.

Polly's answer was given in soothing tones, in contrast to her appearance. The only trouble was that the answer was not, as he saw it, very much to the point: "You've been hurt, Niles. You'll be all right now, though." And suddenly she turned away, reacting as if she were terribly upset by something.

The second statement in her reply, he felt sure on interior evidence, was still problematical; as for the first statement, he had already figured that out for himself without help. With his memory slowly improving, he could recall something but not everything about the firefight inside the wreck and that last berserker android.

He had at last begun to hurt, and in a number of places. But the machines around him stared at him with their wise lenses, and listened continuously to his breathing and his heartbeat, and probed his veins and nerves, and kept the pain from ever getting too bad. He accepted the pain as a sign of his recovery.

The captain never had the least doubt that his recovery was desirable and necessary. Because he had to get well and strong before he could go after Leviathan again.

And still more time passed before Domingo was able to determine that the hospital in which he was recovering must be the military one on Base Four Twenty-five.

At about the same time as he understood where he was, Domingo comprehended also that Polly Suslova, more often than not, was still nearby. Like skillfully arranged background music, she had been with him for some time before he recognized her presence, before he was able to ask her those first questions. In fact, it now seemed to Domingo, once more able to think in terms of time and space, that Polly had been more or less in attendance on him ever since he had been wounded.

Even, if he thought about it, before that.

For a long time now, ever since the captain had started to regain consciousness, people had been pausing beside him and trying to tell him things, mostly reassuring platitudes about his medical condition. Facts were in short supply. But now, in a strengthening voice, he was able to ask more questions.

From Polly, from the medical people, from Iskander who came in often and from Gujar who came in once to visit him, Domingo learned, a little at a time, the details he was unable to remember of what had happened to him and the others who had been examining the wrecked berserker. He learned how, after the small commensal berserkers had struck him down, his crew had managed to crunch the enemy's attacking mobile units, down to the last machine. And how his crew had then got themselves and Domingo and the *Pearl* away from the scene of the battle. By the time they did that their captain had been totally unconscious, barely alive inside what was left of his space armor. They had needed power tools to get him out of the mangled armor, and he had made most of the trip back to base in suspended animation in the *Pearl's* sick bay, surrounded by deep-frozen sample cases holding biological samples gathered from the wreck.

Now in the hospital, Domingo was pleased, he was even more elated than was reasonable, to learn that they had brought back what the Space Force analysts were calling a large amount of very valuable samples and recorded information. Iskander had even managed to bring along the demolished fragments of one of the berserker androids. When Polly saw how greatly this news delighted the captain, she went over it again, telling him in considerable detail how successful their effort had been and how Baza had insisted on salvaging parts of the vanquished enemy for later study.

When Domingo grew tired, Polly went away to let him rest after assuring him that she'd be back. He was glad to hear that she intended to return, but somehow he had been sure of it already.

Other human figures continued to come and go around him, all of them being professionally cheerful. Domingo slept again, this time with conscious confidence that he was going to wake up.

Next time he awoke, he was able to take a steadier notice of his surroundings. He observed that the base hospital was an alert and ready place, but not a very busy one. This hospital had almost certainly never been used to anything like full capacity, even for the casualties of war; and it was not being so used now. In the war against the berserkers there were plenty of human dead, but not that many wounded. And fortunately, wars like those on ancient Earth, of life pitted against life, were virtually unknown.

Again Domingo probed with questions at the people around him. This time he wanted to know if his crew had gone back to the wrecked berserker after the fight and gathered still more information. None of the hospital staff knew the answer to that one, or wanted to discuss it, and he had to be persistent. It seemed to him that the answer was important, bearing as it did on the reliability and dedication of the people in his crew.

The answer, unhappily, was no.

Domingo raged feebly at Iskander when he heard that. And raged again when he was told something he was later able to confirm for himself on the recordings: The main berserker, the damaged hulk, had not, even yet, been totally destroyed. The crew of the *Pearl*, once their captain was unconscious, had not stayed in the area even long enough to finish the helpless enemy off.

Iskander raised an eyebrow and accepted the rebuke tolerantly. "Sorry, Niles."

"Sorry. That doesn't help."

"It's done now. There's no reaction I can demonstrate that *will* help now, is there?"

No, there wasn't.

Gujar Sidoruk, making his second visit to Domingo in the hospital, assured him: "That piece of junk couldn't hurt anyone any longer, Niles. Even if some ship did stumble on it, and the chances against that are—"

Domingo made a disgusted noise. It was a surprisingly loud noise, considering his condition.

Iskander said soothingly: "It'll just lie there helpless, Niles, until its power fails eventually and it rots. No one's going to stumble onto it. Not there."

The captain's voice was weak, but still it was hoarse and harsh. "There's life out there in the nebula. It'll go on killing that. It'll figure out some way to use whatever systems and power it has left, and it'll kill a little more at least."

His visitors of the day looked at one another, a look that said the captain was still woozy from all that had happened to him. In the Milkpail there were cubic light-years of that kind of tenuous life around. It was scattered everywhere in the nebula. And aside from harvesting certain of its odd varieties and some useful byproducts, nobody gave a damn about it. Domingo certainly never had, before now. Berserkers killed that sort of life, of course, *en passant* when they encountered it—they were programmed to kill everything—but their main destructive interest was concentrated upon humanity. In the whole Galaxy so far, only intelligent life, synonymous with humanity in its several themes, appeared to offer any serious obstacle to the machines' achievement of their projected goal, the ultimate sterilization of the universe.

Gennadius, himself looking a little less grim than the last time the two had met, came to look in on the grim patient. The base commander reported, among other things, that the robot courier that had been dispatched to Four Twenty-five from the *Pearl* had never reached the base.

"To nobody's particular surprise," Domingo whispered.

"I suppose so."

"Are you hunting Leviathan now?"

"We're doing what we can, Niles. We're doing what we can."

Gennadius could also offer Domingo reassurance of a sort on one point. Following the *Pearl's* return to the base, he, Gennadius, had sent out a Space Force ship to look for the wrecked berserker. But after ten days the ship had come back to report the failure of the search. Again, a result not surprising to anyone who knew the difficulties of astrogation within the nebula.

Domingo now learned that two standard months had passed since he had been hurt. He had been unconscious or heavily sedated most of the time, while surgeons had begun the process of putting him back together.

Domingo wanted fresh news of Leviathan, but there was none. At least no one would tell him if there was.

He also kept coming back, in his thoughts, to the wrecked berserker. Iskander, the others in the crew said, had wanted to stay and finish the berserker off. But he just hadn't managed to give an order to that effect and make it stick.

The captain knew from experience that Baza was a daring fighter, cool and unshakable in a crisis. He had seen plenty of evidence also that the man hated berserkers, and he needed no one to tell him what to do. But he was simply not a very good leader, Domingo silently decided now. His chief mate and most faithful friend was unskilled at ordering or persuading others. Though Iskander had been second in command on the *Pearl* and had nominally taken over when Domingo was knocked out, the others had persuaded him that Domingo needed immediate care.

Well, all the gods and demigods of the far colonies knew that had been true. The captain had barely survived as it was.

Nevertheless Domingo crabbed more as his recovery in the hospital proceeded. He made silent, private plans for a reorganization of his crew. It wasn't easy. He wondered who might do a better job than Baza as his second-in-command. Domingo couldn't come up with a name.

But if they'd had their captain in suspended animation when they were ready to leave the wrecked berserker, it would have been all the same to him if they had stayed a little longer with the wreck. They'd had no excuse not to stay. They should have made another effort to wring the last bits of information out of the damned hulk, and then they should have made sure before they left that it was nothing but a cloud of expanding gas . . .

Another worry, about something the captain had assumed but never confirmed, now struck him forcibly.

He voiced the thought at once. "What about the *Pearl*? Is she all right?"

"In great shape. Hardly scratched. None of the little bastards ever got near her. She's been docked here ever since we brought you back."

Iskander, visiting again, asked almost timidly if he could take the ship out and use her, scouting.

Domingo probed him with his eyes. His eyes were among the few parts that had not been damaged. "Sure. But be careful. I'm going to need her soon." Domingo could see the people around him look at one another when he said that. To them—to some of them anyway—it must have sounded like a joke. Because, he supposed, he must look even worse off than he felt.

There was something else he had been meaning to ask about, if he could only remember what it was. Oh, yes. He inquired whether there had been any other casualties among his crew. There were certain crew members' faces he could not remember seeing among those of his visitors in the hospital.

Again glances were exchanged among the people standing around his bed before any of them said anything. The consensus appeared to be that he was now probably strong enough to be able to sustain the bad news, and so they told him. There had been one other casualty. Wilma Chanar had died in the grip of that last berserker android before it was demolished.

"That's too bad," whispered Domingo, realizing he was expected to whisper something. It was of course the first he had heard of Wilma's death, although if his thoughts in the hospital had turned that way at all he might have deduced the fact, or guessed it—that last fight was gradually becoming less of a blank to him. But he had not much feeling left for Wilma, dead or alive. Or for any of the others. He was still anesthetized by earlier and harder shocks. He knew regret at the news, but only numbly, and largely because Wilma was going to be hard to replace on the crew.

More time passed in the hospital. Day by day Domingo gradually improved, but it was obvious even to him that full recovery was still a long way off. His left leg was really gone, for one thing, almost to the hip. And that was far from being his only medical problem. He admitted, with his new habit of absorption in grim calculation, that his recovery, the first step toward revenge, was going to be even a bigger job than he had thought. At least while he worked at recovering, he could also make plans.

With growing competence to think about what he learned, he had to begin by seriously taking stock of his own body. Or what was left of it. Regaining anything like full normal function was going to take him even longer than he'd thought. The doctors told him that yes, they were going to have to fit him with a new left leg, some kind of artificial construction. Regrowth, the usual tactic employed when a limb was lost, didn't look promising in his current general condition, considering, as the doctors said, the overall neurological situation.

When Domingo heard of the plans to fit him with an artificial leg, an inspiration came to him at once. The more he thought about his idea, the more he grinned. Naturally the people who were around him every day, who hadn't seen him grinning at anything since his daughter perished, asked him what was up.

He inquired about the berserker android that had been brought back piecemeal from inside the ruined enemy. Yes, it was still here on the base. It had been studied, of course, but the technicians had found nothing really new about it.

Then he told the doctors and therapists that he wanted to have one of the legs of the berserker android, or suitable portions of such a leg, adapted to his body.

They looked at each other and decided to come back and talk to the captain about it later. Some of them looked shocked, or taken aback, but actually one of the doctors was intrigued by the idea.

When Polly heard about it, she thought it was a little sick—maybe more than a little—and at her first opportunity she said as much to Domingo.

At first he only grinned at her. "Why not?"

"If you have to ask . . ."

His expression became more intent, almost hostile. "Why not? Why shouldn't I walk on one of their bones?" Then abruptly his weakness showed.

Polly felt guilty. "No reason, I suppose. You're entitled to do what you want." Then she changed the subject; she invited Domingo to come to her home on Yirrkala and stay there while he recuperated. "I'm going there for a while anyway," she announced, trying to sound as casual as possible. "I'm ready for a rest. I thought you might be, too."

Domingo thanked her, and agreed almost immediately. He could see that his quick acceptance surprised Polly somewhat. But he could see also that she was pleased. And he was exhausted. He had to save his strength for the arguments and fights that counted. He was a very long way from being ready to jump into a ship again and resume the hunt. He had to recuperate somewhere, before he could do anything else.

And he wanted to do as much of his convalescing as possible out from under the supervision of the Space Force. They wouldn't be likely to go along with certain of the preparations he intended to make for the next round of his battle.

The next time Polly came to visit him, Domingo asked her about Yirrkala and about her home and family there. He remembered casually talking to her about those things before—in what now seemed to have been an earlier life—but the situation could have changed. Her home on Yirrkala interested him now, because he wanted to make sure it would provide an environment that made for speedy convalescence. From all he could find out, it sounded acceptable. His own homeworld was gone, and he considered it unlikely that anyone was going to make him a better offer.

Presently Domingo was pronounced well enough for Polly to take him off to her own colony-home, and the two of them got on the first ship headed that way. Yirrkala was as well defended from berserkers as any place in the Milkpail, probably in the whole Sector. There Polly intended to nurse him back to the beginning of fitness; and she intended to do more than that, though she did not discuss all of her intentions with anyone.

Her private hope was to wean Domingo from the madness of revenge on clanking metal. She could tell that he was still gripped by that obsession, to a degree that was at best unhealthy. She thought the problem oughtn't to be hard to see for anyone who really looked at him or listened to him snarling at the ineptness of his crew. Maybe they had been inept; it was the *way* he snarled. Some kind of unhealthiness was festering.

But when she had tentatively mentioned the subject to the doctors, they told her that the patient was really doing quite well mentally, considering all he had been through. Psychotherapy, if indicated at all, could and should wait until later. Right now full physical recovery was the chief concern in the captain's case.

Domingo said to her, just once, as they were getting ready to leave for Yirrkala: "Thank you. For taking care of me like this."

She tried to make little of it. "All part of the job."

"It's not. I do thank you."

☀ CHAPTER 11

Almost everyone who knew anything about the subject considered Yirrkala to be the most livable of all the Milkpail colonies. It was a somewhat bigger and slightly more Earth-like world than any of the nebula's other inhabited rocks, with enough natural gravity of its own to hold an atmosphere. The air enclosing its rugged surface had only to be augmented with oxygen, the mixture adjusted and not built up from scratch, to make it breathable, even at certain times and seasons comfortable. Surface temperatures could be mild on Yirrkala; genengineered fruits and flowers were commonly grown outdoors. And since the gravity had been artificially augmented, there were even sizable bodies of fresh water, on and just below the Yirrkalan surface.

Polly's homeworld was also considerably closer to Base Four Twenty-Five than were most of the other colonies. Therefore it was less susceptible—both in theory and historically—to berserker attack. Still the Yirrkalans, not content to rely on the Space Force, had never skimped on their ground defenses; and now even these already formidable installations were being hastily improved to counter the improvement recently evident in the berserkers' weaponry.

All in all, the place offered relative security, as much security as human existence in the Milkpail ever had, which was at best considerable. Domingo, disembarking on a robotic stretcher from the newly landed ship with Polly walking at his side, could see, beyond the glass walls of the port, a near horizon of pleasant hills, under a whitish sky mottled with many colors, predominantly blue. The captain's battered body was swathed in blankets as he came rolling off the ship, but the air he could feel on his face was almost comfortably warm. The distant white giant sun of this system was hidden in nebular clouds, but its light came filtering through the sky to make an indirect judgment upon this little world, touching all its surfaces with ghostly frost.

Vineyards and floral gardens covered most of the land that the newly arrived patient was able to see on his first look around outside the surface spaceport. In the direction where the horizon looked most distant there were ranks of the familiar screens and diffraction filters used as life-collection machinery, the same kinds of harvesting equipment that were common to most Milkpail worlds.

"Here come my people now," said Polly cheerfully.

Domingo looked down past his foot. Two figures that had to be Polly's sister and brother-in-law, Irina and Casper, were on hand, wrapped in coats of synthetic fur, to meet the travelers just outside the port. Irina resembled her husband more than she did Polly, being somewhat plump and with a placid air about her. She and Casper had with them Polly's two children, who immediately claimed most of their mother's attention.

The children were a boy and a girl, Ferdy and Agnes, about six and eight years old respectively, if Domingo remembered how to judge. He thought that neither of the kids looked much like their mother. Judging from the violence of the greeting they gave her, there was no doubt that they remembered who she was. Both children stared at Domingo with grave eyes, then looked away again, appearing to be impressed with their first sight of him on his robotic stretcher; he supposed they had heard some story of heroics. Their aunt and uncle were polite enough on being introduced, but not so much impressed.

He smiled at all of them as best he could and said hello, wanting to prepare for himself the smoothest possible environment in which to get on with the business of his recovery. The stretcher's wheels hissed faintly on the ramp bringing him down and away from the spaceport. Casper and Irina walking near him made friendly conversation, but still they seemed somewhat ill at ease.

They all rode in a private groundvan—a rented vehicle that could hold the stretcher—through streets lined with genengineered trees that made the scene look like pictures from old Earth. This was a bigger world than Shubra, but still most of humanity would have thought it very small. Polly's small house was out on the far edge of the settlement, but driving to it at moderate speed took much less than an hour. Most of the way they traveled through flower gardens and banks of life-collecting machines. The machines held up fine grids and nets to draw in the microscopic and near-microscopic organisms that came down out of the nebula, out of the sky.

The little two-story house, set in its own hectare of grounds, was somehow different from what Domingo had anticipated, though he could not have said just what he had been expecting. The little dwelling had been unoccupied for some time, they said, but Casper and Irina had been busy getting it ready for Polly's arrival and of course Domingo's, too.

Polly and her patient moved into the house at once, along with Polly's children. The appearance, Domingo realized, was that he had acquired an instant family. But there weren't any neighbors close enough to be misled by appearances.

His stretcher was guided into a small bedroom on the ground floor, next to Polly's room, as she explained. The kids' rooms were upstairs—Agnes and Ferd were evidently not used to a two-story house, and the mere idea of being upstairs was enough to enchant them.

Domingo rested on his stretcher in his new room and thought about berserkers, while other people took care of the moving in. Not that there was very much to be done.

On the day of his arrival on Yirrkala he was capable of dragging himself from stretcher to bed and back again, and of using his best hand to feed himself with only a minimum of human or robotic help, but that was about the extent of what he could manage. He had his room to himself at night—except for occasional look-in visits from Polly the nurse who slept next door—and from the start he often took his meals alone.

The first days of his stay passed uneventfully. The kids banged around in rooms nearby, upstairs and downstairs, or outside in their fur coats and caps, rollicking in the ever-ghostly light. Sometimes the young ones yelled, in anger at each other or just in celebration of life. They were on some kind of school holiday, Domingo gathered, and so around the house most of the time. Every once in a while their mother murmured them into temporary quietness, and when murmuring didn't work she took stronger measures to see that the patient wasn't disturbed unduly. But the patient assured her that the noises of life really didn't bother him.

He even understood why they didn't bother him. It was because life, as life, no longer meant anything to him, one way or the other. Domingo didn't bother to bring that insight to Polly's attention, but perhaps she sensed it anyway.

His appetite was no problem, not from the time that he was strong enough to chew. His teeth were still in good shape. He didn't much care what he ate, food was food, strengthening the body for its remaining purpose. On Yirrkala his devoted nurse saw to it that he got good food, and on Yirrkala he ate well from the start and grew in strength.

Faithfully the captain performed his prescribed exercises, some of them with the special robot that had been shipped to him for the purpose. The thing had arms and grips sticking out all over it, so it looked like an athlete melded with his own equipment. Some of the exercises he did with Polly, who took the opportunity to try to psychologize him and to find out how determined he still was to go after Leviathan. He was still determined. She was obviously much concerned about his welfare, his mental and emotional health. Too bad for her, Domingo thought in silence.

Casper and Irina lived at some little distance, or said they did, and so they came to visit only occasionally. On their visits they smiled at Domingo and chatted with him, but he could tell that in general they disapproved of his presence in Polly's house, and especially in Polly's life.

That was all right with him. He didn't say so, but he meant to be gone from both as soon as he possibly could.

Still, there were moments when Domingo was almost tempted to dream about what life might be like if it were possible for him to stay here with Polly and her family. Almost tempted, but not quite. To be nursed indefinitely. Something like that . . . the stillborn dream was pointless, it had no conclusion, and seemed unlikely ever to develop one. And even this faint inclination to dream of the impossible, such as it was, faded as his strength and mobility returned.

A standard month after Domingo's arrival on Yirrkala, his weight was already approaching normal again, allowing for the subtracted limb. The robotic stretcher had already been abandoned in favor of a semirobotic wheelchair, in which he could get around pretty much by himself. Both of his arms were working adequately now, but he was still a one-legged man—the prosthesis was going to be installed later, back at the base hospital.

The children, in free moments between sessions of play and the occasional jobs their mother thought up for them, had shown a continuing interest in various stages of his progress. He was still popular with Ferd and Agnes, and he wasn't sure just why. Neither of them spent that much time actually in his presence. Maybe that was the explanation.

Little Agnes once asked the captain if he had any kids of his own at home. He told her no, not any more he didn't, and at that point had provided some distraction and she had let it go at that.

Able to stand up at last, lurching and crutching his way across the room on one foot to get his first really good close look at himself in the mirror since his injury, Domingo was struck by how different his face appeared from the last time he could remember seeing it. He stared into the optical glass, wondering at himself. Not so much at the gross physical scars and alterations, though those were certainly great enough. The most noticeable of them in the mirror now, aside from the missing leg, was a twisty scar, not yet fully obliterated by the surgeon's art, that wound down one side of his jaw and neck and into his collar. The scar ended a little below that, fading indeterminately into his shoulder.

But he thought his face showed greater transformations than that, though the skin and flesh of it were pretty much back where they were supposed to be. Alterations deeper than that, greater even than the missing leg, had taken place, molding him into someone he did not understand.

He was still pondering when, beside his own face in the mirror, he caught a glimpse of Polly passing the open doorway of his room. The house was always kept quite warm, for his benefit, he supposed, and she was wearing almost nothing today as she moved about overseeing the machinery that did the housework. She looked just as she had when Domingo had first met her: compactly built, agile and shapely; an attractive young woman. Domingo was aware of her attractiveness, but only in an abstract way. She had no regular man, as far as he could tell, at least she never spoke of one. And she was drawn to Domingo. He knew that too, he could remember it as from an earlier life, and he could feel it now.

Sometimes it bothered him that he was making use of her and her feelings, that her investment in him was going to repay her nothing. Or at least he felt it ought to bother him.

But the feeling of vague guilt never lasted for long. Nor did he spend much time considering his failure to understand himself, to relate himself as he was now to the man he used to be. Actually he

had little time to worry about those things, because they were basically unessential. Because there was something else that demanded
almost all his thought and energy, something that he had to do.

Still—Polly and her children. They gave his mind a place to rest
from planning, the only place it had. They provided something of
a ready-made family, or the appearance of one, at least. But the
sight of the little girl, especially, reminded Domingo painfully of
his own daughters.

As for Polly herself... Domingo had not really thought at all
about women, as women, since well before the berserker mangled
his body. Not since what had happened on Shubra, in fact. His body
was functional now, his physical strength was gradually returning, but
he still had no urge to think of Polly, or anyone else, in that way.

Still looking into the mirror, Domingo found himself keeping a
wary eye on the robot exercise machine that was waiting behind
him. It was, or ought to be, a comical-looking device, with the
gymnastic tools protruding from it everywhere. Polly made jokes
about it sometimes, and he smiled to be sociable. But it had never
struck him as amusing. It would be a while yet, he supposed, before
he could feel at ease in the presence of any smart machine. That
was one of the things he was going to have to train himself to do
before he got back into his ship. His ship was a machine too, and
he was going to have to use it.

Yes, in the mirror his face looked different.

The captain began to get out of the house on milder days, when
real frost and dew were dissipated by the energy of the white glowing sky. Then one day the four of them, he and Polly and the two
kids, took off on the Yirrkalan version of a summer outing. They
went as far as getting into a boat, going for a cruise on one of the
small outdoor bodies of open water. Domingo's wheelchair wore a
flotation collar, just in case.

From the boat, cruising through the fantastic rock grottoes that
edged the convoluted pond, they looked at a profusion of marvelous
floating flowers. They stared at fighting flowers, plants that grappled
with one another in slow motion and tried to drown one another's
floating pads. They talked about what life was and speculated, half
playfully, on what gods there really were. At least Polly speculated,
and tried to get Domingo to do so, too. The children had a couple
of ideas to contribute, but mainly they were obsessed with tossing
pebbles.

Neither did the captain have much to say to advance the discussion. All Domingo could see when he looked for gods was a jagged
wall of metal, trimmed here and there with blue flames. That and
dirty fragments of a white dress.

There were genengineered fish, too, in this Yirrkalan pond, the biggest of them strange silvery harmless monsters, long as a man's arm, that went gliding about in the cold, almost murky depths. If you could really call these depths, two or three meters at the most.

The kids had somehow developed a scary legend of the deepest part of the pond, and they took turns relating it and elaborating on it. A big fish lived down there under a gloomy shelf of rock, a fish bigger than any of the others . . .

"And, and, you know what his name is, Uncle Niles?" Child-eyes growing wide with excitement. With fear, was more like it.

"I know. I know that, yes."

The answer didn't have a chance, because again there was a timely distraction from a sibling. No one in this world or any other wanted to hear any of his newly discovered final answers.

A little later, feeling sorry for his nurse and wanting to be reassuring, he said banally: "This is a nice world, Polly."

Impulsively though still quietly, she burst out: "Stay here. Stay with us." Then she looked as if she were afraid her words might scare him off.

All he could say was something noncommittal; then those words of his own sounded so bad he wished he could have them back, too. But they were gone.

An hour or so later, having regained the ability to chat inconsequentially—the children practically enforced that—they came back to the house. Berserkers were for the moment as close to being forgotten as they could be.

An unfamiliar groundcar was parked in front of the house, and a man was waiting in it. A bulky figure got out of the groundcar as Polly's vehicle pulled up. Gujar Sidoruk had come to Yirrkala for a visit and was waiting to see them—to see Domingo in particular.

At first Gujar didn't seem changed at all. "You're looking good, Niles. Real good."

"Considering."

"No, I mean it. Real good. Well, yeah, of course, considering everything."

Presently the two men were sitting in the house and talking; Polly's children demanded her immediate attention.

Gujar began telling the captain about the state of his, Gujar's, feelings. He was still grieving for Maymyo and for everyone else the machines had slaughtered. He still wanted to cry whenever he thought of her, and there were times when he did cry; and up until now he hadn't been able even to make an effort to resume some kind of normal life.

The bulky man looked half collapsed as he tried to talk about it. "I still think of her all the time."

Domingo said: "I do, too." He reflected that he himself didn't look collapsed at all, though a couple of months ago he had been half dead. Anyway, he'd just been told that he looked good, and he believed it. He added: "Is that what you came to tell me?"

Gujar said: "No. At first I didn't want to go back to Shubra. Because it would remind me too much of—everything. But now I think I am going back. I've been visiting there again, and . . . I think she'd want me to. I figured you'd be going on with your hunting, but I wanted to tell you that I can't."

"I was counting on your help, Gujar. The thing that killed her is still out there. Killing more."

Gujar got up from his chair and shuffled around, as if embarrassed. "The Space Force'll do a better job of hunting it than I can. I don't want to spend my life . . ."

Polly had got caught up on her mothering for the time being. She had come back into the room, and was listening sympathetically to this line of argument, or complaint, or whatever it was. But so far she was not saying anything. She'd never tried to argue Domingo out of his purpose, or even insisted on a long discussion of the subject with him. For which he was grateful.

Gujar went on: "There are plans for reconstruction on Shubra, Niles."

"I suppose there are." That harsh voice of his was back at full strength now, sounding just as it had before he had been almost destroyed. Listening to it, Polly realized for the first time that these days Domingo sometimes sounded like a berserker himself. Not that she had ever heard one of them speak, but in stories when they spoke they usually sounded a lot like that.

"Heavier ground defenses of course, to start with." Gujar had overcome sorrow and was beginning to sound almost enthusiastic. "That goes without saying. I want to look over some of the new installations on this rock while I'm here."

Domingo didn't say anything to that. He sat in the robotic wheelchair scowling, thinking with silent contempt of ground defenses and people who let such things occupy their minds.

His visitor kept trying to make him enthusiastic, too. "There's no shortage of people. I mean, new people ready to come in and settle . . ."

"I saw some of them once, back at the base."

"Oh?"

"In fact, I gave them a little speech."

"Oh?" Gujar didn't understand at all. He wouldn't have made an acceptable second-in-command . . . but he was going on talking anyway: "Sector says they have more than enough applicants. And Sector's willing to capitalize a new colony again. They have a big stake out here in the Milkpail now."

Domingo didn't doubt any of that. It was just that he could not help thinking of this young man before him as somehow being a traitor for feeling that it was already time to get back to normal. Maymyo was still dead, her killer gliding on its way through space just as before as if killing her had meant no more than wiping out another colony of nebular microlife.

Gujar stayed a little longer, then took his leave, heading back to Shubra.

"You don't need a nurse anymore," Polly said to Domingo that night, looking in on him before they retired in their separate rooms.

"That's true." *Nor do I need anyone else, either.* But he didn't want to announce that fact to her just yet.

☀ CHAPTER 12

When the captain of the *Sirian Pearl* returned to the hospital at Base Four Twenty-five for his next checkup, the doctors there decided that the time was ripe for them to equip him with his new leg. The implanted graft could be permanently installed, berserker's metal bonded to human flesh and bone through carefully chosen interface materials.

Aboard ship heading for the base, Polly had thought privately about having another discussion with the doctors on the subject of Domingo's psychological state. But it was difficult to know what she ought to say to them. On Yirrkala her patient had said or done nothing extraordinary enough to provide evidence to back up her fears; there was very little new that she could tell the doctors. Yet neither had anything happened to diminish her concern. Nothing had really changed. What bothered her so much in Domingo's attitude and behavior, what made her still feel certain that some disaster was impending, would be very difficult to get across to anyone else.

In a two-hour operation at the base hospital, the new leg was attached successfully, to the delight of the captain. It still bothered Polly more than ever that something about having the berserker leg satisfied Domingo so intensely.

And Polly did speak once more to the psychiatrists, just before she and the captain were to leave the base again on their way to visit Shubra. She consulted them without telling him while he was somewhere else, busy trying out his new leg.

The psychological experts had just finished seeing the captain and chatting with him. And they had a brighter view than Polly did of the patient's progress.

"He's taking an interest in civic and business affairs on Shubra again, I understand, Ms. Suslova."

"He is? He hasn't really talked to me about that." That was about all she could say.

He could fool them more easily, she thought to herself; and they were, at bottom, less concerned.

Domingo still carried a cane, carved of Yirrkalan hothouse wood. But he was walking proudly, ably, almost naturally (the symbiosis would improve with time) on his new leg when he and Polly arrived on Shubra, where reconstruction was now under way in earnest. This wasn't a vacation trip for either of them; Polly still had some unfinished business on Shubra related to her former job, and Domingo still had legal rights and obligations here, where he was still a substantial landowner as well as the elected mayor.

The rehabilitation of his former homeworld was proceeding quite well so far without the mayor's involvement, or even his awareness, and it got little of his attention now. Domingo was really interested only in things that would facilitate his pursuit of Old Blue, and Polly knew it. He never did tell her the truth in so many words, not even when he left her to have business meetings, but he had really come back to Shubra only to sell off his property rights. With this in mind he postponed for a while his formal resignation of the mayor's office; he thought that the hint of influence it gave him might be useful.

The people who were resettling Shubra, the vast majority of them strangers to Domingo and Polly, had already erected a new assembly hall. It was a considerably bigger and better facility than the old gathering-dome had been, a solid-looking structure that conveyed an air of permanence, something to show off to potential colonists. On entering this hall for the first time, for the Festival of Dedication, Domingo was not reminded of the old dome at all. The whole shape and design were different, and there was less plant life in the new hall. And here, in this substantial new crystal palace, the alert lights were almost impossible to see. Until, the captain supposed, they were turned on; and no such demonstration was scheduled for today.

Mounted on one wall inside the lobby, near one rounded, ovoid interior corner of the building, not hidden but not very conspicuous either, there was a metal plaque, a simple, tasteful monument to all the people who had died here on Shubra in the great disaster of a few standard months ago. The captain didn't pause to read the listed names, but instead walked into the auditorium and took a seat for himself at one side near the rear. The place was starting to fill up, but there were few faces in the crowd that he could recognize, and fewer still showed any sign of recognizing him. There was Henric Poinsot, who nodded back.

Music had already begun to play, but only irregularly and at low volume. Musicians were evidently tuning up their instruments and getting in some last-minute practice behind the high, impressive cloth curtains at the front of the auditorium. The Festival of Dedication, proclaimed with the intention of having it as a yearly local holiday from now on, was supposed to mark the end of the first phase of the rebuilding of the settlement.

Mayor Domingo—today really the former mayor, because political reorganization was under way as well—waved and smiled at Polly when he saw her with the other performers, all of them wearing dancers' costumes, heading backstage. She smiled and waved back. She had been enthusiastic, for some reason, about getting into this performance, and he had promised her that he would be here at the Festival's opening to watch her dance.

The big room was filling up rapidly. By the time the show started the situation would be standing room only, more people in this one auditorium now than had lived on the planetoid in the old days. Someone was doing a good job of selling potential colonists on the place. Maybe they were just selling themselves. There were always a lot of people who were not deterred by danger if they thought that by facing it they had a chance to get ahead, to make something of their lives. Domingo had once thought in those terms—getting somewhere, getting ahead, building things, achieving. Owning a large share of a whole world, albeit a small one. It was certainly possible to grow wealthy here . . .

Domingo was attending this opening of the Festival partly because he had promised Polly that he would, and partly in hopes of running into people he wanted to meet, wealthy new property holders, who were otherwise difficult to see. He considered these people good prospects as purchasers of the final lots of his own remaining property. He could sell those off to someone else, but he wanted a good price. The next phase of his hunt, as he had planned it, was going to require a good deal of money. And there was no telling how long his hunt was going to last.

The musicians behind the curtains fell silent, and then within moments began again, this time in an organized way. The expensive curtains, all of old-fashioned cloth, parted slowly to reveal the new stage, superbly designed and surprisingly deep and wide. And there was Polly, looking very beautiful in a scanty silver costume, dancing among others. Watching, Domingo realized for the first time how good-looking she was, well above the average.

After he had been watching the show for a minute or two, the captain began to realize something else. Her eyes flicked in his direction, toward him and away again, whenever she happened to face him in the dance. Even in this crowded hall, Polly had taken the trouble to make sure she knew where he was sitting. He understood now that basically her dance was meant for him, as was almost everything she did these days, apart from her two children.

Distraction in the form of a faint, familiar vibration in the atmosphere diverted Domingo's attention from Polly and her show. Inside the auditorium, with music playing, the thrum was hard to hear, but Domingo's ears managed somehow to pick it up. Turning to look out through one of the clear high walls, the captain could see that a small ship was landing at the new surface port not far away. As the craft came down, he swiveled in his seat, keeping an eye on the silvery arrival as long as possible. Maybe it brought news.

The ship was down now, and silent. Meanwhile of course the show went on, the first dance over and a kind of comic tableau being enacted. Polly was in this, too. The captain, though still distracted by the thought of possible news, watched the performance. She was a very good dancer for an amateur; the whole show was a good one, with a couple of people up front who must be professionals taking the chief parts.

Not many more minutes had passed when someone came up behind Domingo and tapped him on the shoulder. A man he knew slightly, from another colony, was crouching behind him and whispered a message when the captain turned his head: There were three people who had just arrived onworld and who wanted to talk to him at once. "They insist that it can't wait. I don't want to take you away from the show, captain, but . . ."

The three, two women and a man Domingo had never seen before, were standing in the rear of the hall, and with a motion of his head Domingo beckoned them over. At the same time he got up from his seat and moved toward an alcove at the side of the crowded auditorium, meeting the three visitors halfway.

They joined him in the alcove and promptly introduced themselves. All were high-powered experts, in technology or intelligence or both, from Sector Headquarters. To a person they were intensely interested in the samples and the information that the crew of the *Sirian Pearl* had brought back from that berserker biological factory, and in what that factory—they called it that—had been doing before it was destroyed. They wanted to know all the additional details about it that the captain could possibly tell them. The three stood there with Domingo in the alcove and kept him engaged in whispered conversation while the show went on.

At first he put off answering their questions, wanting to hear from them first whatever news they could tell him of Old Blue.

But the three let him know they didn't consider that subject of much importance. They were good at brushing aside questions, too; as eager to get information from Domingo as he was to obtain news from them, and just as insistent on getting their answers first.

The captain answered one question for them, to show good will. Then he waited to get a helpful answer in return.

Not having the information he asked for right at hand, apparently, they gave him what they had. They said Sector was almost completely convinced that a new biological weapon to be used against humanity was in the works, but that the people at headquarters were having a hard time even narrowing down the possibilities of what it was going to be.

All very interesting, but not what the captain really cared about. What else could they tell him?

When the two women experts went aside together for a few moments to confer, probably on how much they were allowed to tell Domingo, the male expert allowed himself to be distracted from business.

On the stage, to whirling music, the young women of the chorus line were now coming forward one at a time, to do individual turns. Polly's turn was on right now.

"Wow. Who's she?"

"She's on my crew. Are you sure no more sightings have been recorded?"

"Sightings?"

"Of Leviathan." Domingo was trying to keep the edge of his impatience from showing in his voice.

"Leviathan. No. On your crew, hey?"

The two women rejoined the men, willing now to explain things to Domingo in a little more detail. The three visitors had brought with them the results of the computer work done at Sector Headquarters on the data gathered from the ruined berserker by the *Pearl*'s crew. That information now appeared to be of considerable importance.

"You said that before."

"The indications are that the berserker was probably working on cell development. Of certain types."

"I don't quite follow—"

"The development of large organisms, not microbes."

Domingo considered that, saw in it no direct relevance to his goal and filed it away. He continued to press the visitors for whatever information they might have on Leviathan, and at last extracted from them a promise to check with their ship's computer, as soon as they got back to their ship, to see if it had anything along that line.

By now the show, or the first phase of it anyway, was winding down. The curtains closed to enthusiastic applause. A soft spotlight picked out Domingo in his alcove, and he was called upon, as former mayor and war hero, to step forward and acknowledge a round of applause. The cheers were brief, and not overwhelming in their volume; war heroes were not that rare, and his performance, or nonperformance, as mayor lately had not won him any friends. Then the spotlight swung away; the newly chosen mayor was getting up to make a speech.

That was the moment when Polly, flushed from dancing, came swiftly and gracefully down the aisle, straight to Domingo. "Did you like it?" she panted lightly. Her silvery costume was clinging to her body, and she was sweating.

He stared at her, his mind still pondering the evolution of large life forms by the enemy. "What?" he asked, seeing her expectant look.

The look changed to something else. She drew herself up straight, saying nothing. He turned with a new question for the intelligence experts. When he turned back again a moment later, Polly was gone.

Soon after the Festival of Dedication, Domingo concluded his business on Shubra, selling off the last of his property rights for a satisfactory price. Part of the money and credit he obtained went to purchase munitions and more message couriers for the *Sirian Pearl*. The captain kept part of it for future needs. This time he meant to pay large crew bonuses.

When he saw Polly again the next day, she announced that she was not going to go with him this time. She was dropping off the crew.

He looked at her, she thought, as if she were someone he had met yesterday for the first time. He said: "All right. You're probably better off that way."

☀ CHAPTER 13

The little machine that killed my lovely daughter was not the same one that mangled me. Almost certainly it was not even of exactly the same type.

The machine that killed her came from a different berserker—Old Blue. What destroyed her was a lander, an extension of Leviathan.

My encounter, my crippling, was almost accidental. Almost. But her killing was not. It was the arm, the fist of Leviathan that reached out for her and came after her and crushed her beautiful life to nothingness.

Leviathan . . .

Niles Domingo stood alone with his thoughts under the white Shubran sky. He was standing at the foot of a low cliff that was now almost an overhanging cliff because so much of its side had fallen in, filling in a cave.

That cave that no longer existed was the spot where his daughter Maymyo had died. At least the captain thought that this sterile, blasted area, flecked with ice and snow, was the same spot where he had seen the charred flesh fragments and the shredded wedding garments, the horrors that still seemed to have nothing to do with her.

No connection with her. But the horrors had appeared and had taken over the world, and she was gone.

In a few months the captain's old homeworld had progressed a long way from being a blasted ruin. Out here away from the central settled area, the marks of the attack were still everywhere to be seen. But the renewal of the atmosphere was almost completed, and here, too, people were back. Hundreds of people, mostly contract workers, were living in a temporary underground settlement. They were hard at work using the hundred varieties of machines that they had brought with them. They were decontaminating the surface and the caves and rebuilding the underground ship harbor. New and more powerful defenses had already been installed.

The artificial gravity had been restored on Shubra months ago, and the wind that had shrieked over Maymyo's freshly murdered body had long since fallen; but there was the cliff. There were the same low hills (Domingo thought they were the same) rimming the theatrically near western horizon. And there, to the east, was a long, declining, half-familiar slope of clear land. Once there had been talk among the citizens of Shubra of creating an outdoor park along that incline. But the long slope was being terraced now by construction machinery, and even the hills to the west had had their profiles altered. In almost every direction, people working with large machines could be seen getting still more defensive emplacements ready. Gouges and scars in the cliff and at its foot showed the efforts that had been made to fill in the cratered remnant of Maymyo's old cave.

Domingo's gaze dropped again to the ground at his feet. His daughter's remains, along with those of her dead comrades, had been cremated months ago. Looking at the scraped and frozen dirt where Maymyo had been destroyed brought him no closer to her or to any of his vanished life. A metal shape still stood between, and he turned away.

The movement was quick and easy. His new leg was already working beautifully. Its cybernetics, which were naturally of human design and manufacture, were melding nicely into his nervous system. Like a fleshy organ, the new leg drew its power from the chemistry of his blood. Already the replacement was in some ways superior to his own original limb, stronger and untiring. When the leg was not covered by clothing, its appearance was stark and gray, hard and lifeless. He had observed that to some people the sight of it was shocking. An ordinary artificial limb would have had a much more nearly natural look, but it would still have been less than perfect. There were some ways, mostly sensory, in which any replacement would be inferior to the original. This leg that the doctors had given him was good enough for his purposes, and Domingo had his own reasons for preferring it. He was continually aware of the permanent difference between his new leg and his old—gleefully aware. It gave the captain a distinct pleasure to walk on an enemy's bone. There was of course nothing really left of the berserker technology except the structural metal, and that metal had been hollowed out and lengthened, padded and reformed into the same shape as his natural left leg.

As he was walking back toward his parked groundcar, Domingo saw another similar vehicle approaching from the north, the direction of the new temporary spaceport. The oncoming groundcar stopped beside his own, and a familiar broad-shouldered figure got out of it. Recognizing Iskander Baza, Domingo waved and walked a little faster. He was able to run now, if he tried, though the gait was still awkward and uncomfortable for him, and at the moment he didn't make the effort.

Baza, strolling to meet him, raised a casual hand. "Hi, Cap. You're looking good." In the middle distance, a hundred meters away, the digging machines went on scraping and groaning and grumbling.

The captain had to speak loudly to be heard. "You, too. What news?" He hadn't seen Baza in several months.

The other shrugged. "Nothing, really. I was hoping that you had some."

Domingo looked around at the eternal mottled whiteness of the sky. "About berserkers, next to nothing. On the medical situation, a little."

"Good news, I hope. Or is that too much to hope for?"

"Good enough." Domingo went on to explain that he had just received some encouraging words, via the regular message courier, from the doctors at Base Four Twenty-five. The results of the most recent medical tests were in, and they were pleased to tell him that he was now officially discharged, fit for any kind of physical activity he cared to try.

Domingo did not add that the doctors' message had also strongly recommended that he return to the base for psychological counseling on a regular basis, and that in fact an initial appointment had already been set up for him. The medics were planning to do his final plastic surgery, removing his neck scar, on the same visit: But the captain had no intention of keeping the appointment.

"That's good news." Baza always appeared to be uncomfortable when he had to say something optimistic or favorable about anything. He looked around, but made no comment on the significance of the site where he had found Domingo, if indeed he recognized and understood it. "Where's Polly?"

"She went back to Yirrkala." The parting scene with her had been quiet but thoroughly unpleasant for Domingo in several ways, and he had no wish to dwell on it.

"Oh. Just visiting there, or—?"

"She's off the crew now."

"Oh." Iskander looked quizzical, but it was not his habit to ask directly for explanations if the captain did not volunteer them. "And Gujar? He said he was going to look you up."

"He did. Back on Yirrkala. He's around here somewhere now, I suppose, supervising some of the digging. But he's off the crew, too."

"Oh?"

"Yeah. Let's go over to the harbor and see if any armaments have come in."

In the hours and days that followed, looking around on Shubra for people he knew were capable in a spacecraft and who had the nerve he wanted, Domingo could find no one available and ready who matched his requirements except Iskander Baza. Poinsot was here but was absorbed in the rebuilding effort; Domingo hadn't even tried to get him back on the crew. There was no one else left of his own former company: Wilma was dead, her husband had gone away somewhere, Gujar and Polly quit. Anyway, as the captain told Baza—without telling him he was included in the evaluation—his old crew had been far from perfect.

The old Shubrans who remained here now were, like the newcomers, people determined to rebuild the colony; the restless as well as the discouraged among the survivors had already moved on to somewhere else.

People who were interested chiefly in rebuilding were not the ones Domingo wanted. He craved a full crew of six for the *Pearl*, but he wanted them to be the best space-combat people he could possibly get.

"It looks like we'll have to do our recruiting somewhere else, Ike."

"I think you're right, Cap...maybe there's one other possibility we could try first, before we go looking far afield."

"What's that?"

"Spence Benkovic. I've seen him work a ship, he's really good. Someone was telling me he's still up on his moon colony."

Domingo and Baza had turned in their rented ground vehicles and were walking the short distance back to the port, about to depart on the first leg of their recruiting journey to other worlds, when they heard their names being called behind them. Simeon Chakuchin had appeared back there, trotting to catch up and hailing them again.

They stopped and waited for him. "Where've you been?" Iskander asked, when Simeon had caught up.

The big young man only glanced at Iskander, then spoke to Domingo: "I just landed on Shubra an hour ago. I hear you're looking for crew, Niles. I want to sign on again." Simeon's face was thinner and at the same time puffier than when Domingo had seen him last, some months ago. Something had happened to him since then.

Domingo paused and thought before he answered. "You know what my plans are. It's not a trade voyage, and not harvesting. I'm going on a hunt, and I'll keep at it until it's finished. Until I see Leviathan's guts spread out somewhere in space, in the Milk or out of it."

"I know." Chakuchin had been nodding his agreement all along through Domingo's speech. "That's fine with me. I don't fit in anywhere any more, Niles, Ike. Since Wilma..."

Domingo was looking at him carefully. "You want to get back at the damned machines that killed her."

"I...yes."

Domingo looked at the younger man still more closely, into his eyes and at the puffy pallor of his face. "You're a good man, Simeon, once you make up your mind to be. But you've been on some kind of drug."

The other shook his head. "Not any more. After she died I had a real hard time for a while. But I'm off it now." Chakuchin blinked.

"Drugs won't go with me. Not on my crew. Leviathan will be all the drug we need. Got that?"

"Leviathan?"

"Old Blue. The damned berserker."

"Of course, I . . . Leviathan." The younger man repeated the word once more—thoughtfully, as if he were tasting it.

As if, thought Baza, watching with amusement, *he were trying his first dose.*

Chakuchin formally signed on the crew and was paid the first installment of his bonus. Then the three of them boarded the *Pearl* and lifted on the short hop up to the moon, intending to drop in on Benkovic's little settlement.

The moon was an angular body, shaped more like a badly made brick than like a ball. It was naturally a lot smaller even than Shubra. If the satellite had ever been given a name of its own, the local people had never got into the habit of using it. "The moon" was good enough, as Shubra possessed only the one satellite that was big enough to be noticeable at all.

The loss and restoration of artificial gravity on Shubra had not affected the satellite as drastically as some people had expected; artificial gravity varied more sharply than natural gravity with distance, and the change at the distance of the moon had been relatively small. The satellite was very nearly back in its old orbit now.

"I've lived on Shubra a good many years, and I've never been up here before," Domingo murmured as the *Pearl* approached the only obvious, dedicated landing place visible on the dark, angular chunk of rock. At the site below there were three transparent landing domes, two of them closed and already holding ships, the third dome open and apparently ready to receive visitors. A few small buildings nearby were connected to the dome complex by tunnels or tubes.

"I haven't been here before, either," Simeon murmured.

"I was once," said Baza. "Some time ago." He did not elaborate further.

Domingo had not bothered to radio ahead. As they drew closer to the moon's single small facility, they got a better look at the two ships that it already housed. One was the armed miniature speedbug that Spence called a battler—that was the craft he had been out in, scouting, on the day of Leviathan's assault. The other hangared ship was a slower, larger harvester, the kind of vessel generally used to reap shoals of microbial life from nebular clouds. The harvester looked new, as it no doubt was. Whatever ships had been berthed here during the attack must have been destroyed.

"Looks like somebody ought to be home. There are enough vehicles parked."

When Chakuchin transmitted a radio query, the equivalent of a polite knock at the door, the unoccupied dome flashed a signal of welcome for their ship, an automatic response.

The *Pearl* dipped closer. The port and the nearby house both looked new, as in fact did all the constructions here. No doubt they were new. Simeon could remember hearing that the berserker had left no more standing here on the moon than on the world below.

The dome port enclosed the visitors' ship, and then for their convenience created within itself, around their ship, a smaller bubble of force more easily refilled with air. Then the machinery signaled the three visitors that it was safe for them to get out of their craft.

They did so, and stood there on the floor of the dome looking about them uncertainly. There was no sign as yet of any human welcome. The hangar dome was sparsely furnished, a bare-bones kind of installation.

Then Simeon heard Iskander clear his throat and turned to look. A door had opened in the forcefield bubble, a door to one of the passageways, one that must connect with the small house nearby. A young woman had emerged from the open doorway to greet the three visitors. She was of average height, tending just a little to overweight. In the hot scented breeze blowing out of the tube passage, she stood there completely naked except for hothouse flowers of scarlet and purple twined in the glossy black hair that grew on her head and in three places on her body.

Simeon shuffled his feet in vague embarrassment, and looked at his companions; clothing was expected in almost every social situation. Iskander was grinning appreciatively at the apparition in the doorway, while Domingo also inspected her but looked somewhat worried.

Meanwhile the girl was smiling vaguely back at the three men, but really it was almost as if she did not see them. She said nothing. The visiting men exchanged a second round of looks among themselves. For some time before the disaster, word had gone around on Shubra about the unconventional lifestyle that obtained at Benkovic's establishment. Some people had joked about a harem on the moon. Spence had even made overtures once to Maymyo, the mayor's daughter, suggestions that she come and spend a few days at his satellite colony, but she'd cut him off short.

The young woman continued to look rather vacantly at her three visitors. Or she might be gazing just over their heads. Drugs again? Domingo was already wondering. He thought the air blowing out from the house was perfumed, but maybe it was only flowers. His vague misgivings about Benkovic, whom he had met only in passing, were rapidly increasing; but according to all the testimony, there was no question that the man was good with a ship.

Their hostess, not in the least embarrassed by her lack of clothing, broke the silence at last to announce in a childish voice: "Spence isn't here right now." It was as if she had finally been able to overcome some inertia that had held her silent. "He's over on the other side."

The captain spoke up, businesslike and impatient. "Do you suppose he's coming back soon? Or would it be better if we hopped over there and looked for him?" The other side of the moon—assuming that was what she meant—might be all of ten kilometers away. "I'm Niles Domingo. This is Iskander Baza. And Simeon Chakuchin."

The young woman did not acknowledge the introductions or offer her own name in return. Her attitude did not appear to be one of deliberate rudeness any more than her nakedness seemed intended to arouse or shock. Rather it was as if she were not really interacting with the men at all. When she spoke again she might have been talking to herself. "I guess maybe he'll be back shortly."

"Has he guessed that we're here, d'you suppose?" Iskander asked.

"I'll give him a call," the young woman said, with the air of one struck by a sudden, brilliant thought. She turned slowly away, then walked quickly back into the passage. Her flowers, no longer fresh, swung droopily as she turned. Her figure under ordinary circumstances would not have drawn much attention.

She had left the door open behind her. The three men exchanged looks yet once more. Then, with Domingo leading, they followed their reluctant hostess through the tube and into the house.

In contrast to the landing dome, the dwelling had been profusely and wildly decorated. There were flowers, live and cut, everywhere. Shelves and walls held drawings framed and unframed, along with what Simeon supposed ought to be called found objects. But the place was none too clean. A housework robot stood propped at an angle in one corner of the room, the drivers on two corners of its base unable to reach the dusty floor. No one had expended the moment's effort necessary to set the machine upright.

The three visitors overtook their hostess in the first large room they came to amid heaps of garish pillows, more flowers and food containers, most of which were used and empty. Some of the furniture was reasonably conventional, and some of that was broken.

The dark-haired woman looked at them uncomfortably, murmured something that might have been "Wait here," and disappeared again through another doorway. Simeon supposed the odds were even as to whether she intended to come back or whether she was going to communicate with Spence.

The men looked at each other and sat down, rather uneasily. After about five minutes the three, still waiting, heard faint murmurings of machinery that were, to expert ears, suggestive of a ship's arrival. In a couple of minutes more, Spence Benkovic hurried into the room, to his visitors' relief.

Greetings were exchanged, and Benkovic offered drinks, though rather doubtfully, as if he wasn't sure what he had in stock. The offer was politely declined.

To Domingo, Benkovic seemed a bit nervous but gave no indication of being on drugs. The lean, dark-bearded man admitted readily enough, though, that he was running out of money. He'd got emergency relief funds, like other colonists, but the harvesting wasn't what it had been.

Benkovic seemed fascinated when he was told of Domingo's hunting plans and said he was ready to try something new, something that would provide him with a stake.

The captain could give assurances on that point. "I'm paying bonuses to all my crew." When he named a figure, Benkovic was impressed. He should have been. Domingo had owned a fair amount of prime property on Shubra.

"I hear you're good with a ship. But before I sign you on formally, I want to make sure of that for myself. We'll take a test flight in the *Pearl*."

"No problem."

"Good. How soon can you be ready?"

Benkovic sighed, as if he'd been waiting a long time for someone to ask him that. "Whenever you are."

The young woman, still nameless to the visitors and still naked, had followed Spence back into the room and curled herself up on a couch, as if withdrawing from the world. Now she made an inarticulate sort of sound that might have been meant as a question. She looked with a vaguely appealing expression from one man to another.

Spence Benkovic looked at her. "Oh yeah. Pussy here—she's no spacer."

"Too bad," Iskander murmured, acting sympathy.

Benkovic looked at him, then said to Domingo: "Something will have to be done about her."

"Before you can leave."

"Well . . . I'm afraid so, yeah."

"What'll have to be done?"

There was some discussion, in which Pussy—if that was really her name—chose to take no part. Benkovic pleaded her case. In the end the captain found it necessary to stake the young woman also, turning over enough money to allow her to get on a ship to another world of her choice. She'd come to Shubra after the disaster, Benkovic said, so didn't qualify for any kind of government relief. Fortunately Spence had no other companions on the moon at present.

Spence picked up some flowers, fresh-looking this time, as his visitors were saying good-bye. Simeon wondered confusedly if they were each going to get a small bouquet on parting. But the flowers were intended for something else.

As Benkovic was walking with his visitors back to their ship, taking a different tube this time, they passed a construction, an arrangement of odd materials, chunks of rock, components that had once been parts of furniture, other things harder to identify, that had been piled and fastened together into what looked like a monument of some kind. The structure was almost three meters high, and at the base proportionally broad. Either the tube had been widened here to accommodate it, or the builder of this thing had chosen this site as the place where it would easily fit.

Spence put down his flowers at the base of this construction, on a small pile of older, deader-looking flowers, and stood with folded hands, regarding the little structure silently.

The structure was so odd that Simeon kept looking at it until he figured out what it was. Indeed a monument, or a small shrine. There were two names, women's names as Simeon interpreted them, carved in large, precise letters on the front.

Iskander had to ask, at last. "You put this up, Spence?"

Their host looked at them with liquid eyes in which the pain showed all too plainly. "I set it up for my two friends who were here when the berserker came, who didn't make it." He paused, then turned slightly to face Domingo. "Want me to put your daughter's name on it too, Captain?" It sounded as if Spence thought that would really be an honor. He added: "It'll just take a little while."

"You'd better spend the time in getting ready," Domingo said.

The *Pearl*'s first stop away from Shubra was at Base Four Twenty-five, after a flight in which Domingo checked out Spence Benkovic's talents to his own satisfaction.

Later, the captain said: "You were right, Ike. He is good with a headlink on."

"Have I ever steered you wrong, Cap? Maybe you better not answer that."

When they reached the base, Domingo sought out Gennadius and talked with him briefly. Iskander listened in on the conversation—a wrangling about goals and priorities—which as far as he could tell got nowhere.

Then the *Pearl* was off again. Domingo had four on his crew now, counting himself, all of them people he considered good. But he really wanted six. And all the best people of the colonized planetoids were now working for Gennadius.

The captain decided it was going to be necessary to go out of the Milkpail to get the help he needed.

☀ CHAPTER 14

After a few days of steady travel, the last hazy fringes of the Milkpail had fallen behind them. Now the *Pearl* could enter the c-plus mode of operation and began to move at real interstellar speeds. As the ship dropped into flightspace, the universe outside the hull virtually disappeared. Now no world in the modest portion of the Galaxy that had been explored by Earth-descended humans was more than a few weeks away.

It had been a long time, years, since Domingo had driven a ship in clear space, but doing so was a simple matter compared with piloting in the nebula. There was nothing to it, relatively speaking, in a ship as good as this one.

Captain Domingo allowed the autopilot to run all systems most of the way and devoted himself to pondering the mysteries of the enemy's biological research. He also called up and considered his most up-to-date model of the Milkpail's interior. In this model a superimposed spiderweb of black lines represented the pattern of all the known and deduced movements of Leviathan, going back as many years as humans in the nebula had been keeping records.

Nodding toward this holographic construction, the captain once remarked to Iskander Baza: "I asked Gennadius if he'd ever thought of doing anything like this."

"And?"

"He told me that of course his office kept records of berserker activity, and of course they tried to figure where the next outbreak might be. But the Space Force kept no specific records on Leviathan. They weren't interested, he told me, in individual machines."

"He said that?" Iskander, as so often, seemed amused at how unintentionally funny other people were.

"Words to that effect. You know, I suspect the berserkers keep better records about the Space Force than he does about them."

"They probably ignore the records of individual units also."

Domingo looked at his second-in-command solemnly, and solemnly shook his head. "Don't believe that, Ike. Don't believe it for a moment. Don't you think they want to know where this ship is?"

Iskander raised his eyebrows. "I hadn't really thought about it, Cap."

"Try thinking sometime. About that."

Simeon, overhearing, didn't want to think about it. To him it sounded like the edge of craziness. To berserkers, life was life, something to be stamped out, or tolerated temporarily in the case of the rare aberration called goodlife, people willing to serve and sometimes worship the damned machines. He'd heard of places where goodlife were a real factor in the war, but so far in the Milkpail it hadn't been that way.

As Simeon understood the situation regarding Old Blue, the damned machine had never been reported anywhere outside the nebula, and no one knew why. Maybe those outside people had encountered it from time to time, but to them it was just another berserker, as it was to the Space Force.

The more time Simeon spent with Captain Domingo, the more he became convinced that those people outside were wrong. He was more and more ready to follow Domingo, though where it was going to lead him he did not know.

The first leg of their extranebular recruiting flight wasn't a long one; the captain had no intention of heading clear across the Galaxy.

A day passed in the c-plus mode, and then the *Pearl* reemerged into normal space. Imaged in the forward detectors now, only a few hours ahead, was a Sol-like sun whose system included a world named Rohan, a planet that was said to be quite Earthlike. Not that any of the *Pearl*'s crew had ever been within a hundred parsecs of Earth.

It was Iskander's shift as pilot when the *Pearl* approached for a landing on Rohan's nightside. Like most other worlds, this one was wary of berserkers. Rohan wore a girdle of defensive satellites, and the military installations on the ground were visible even at night to the people on the ship as they drew closer. Not that the planet was all fortress. Here outside the nebula you could see anything, berserkers included, coming a long way off and could call up your own fleet, assuming you kept one handy. It was a safe bet that Rohan did.

The chief spaceport facility, the one Domingo wanted, was on the surface, open to the planet's natural atmosphere. The port clearance routine was no more tedious than most outside the Milkpail, and the captain soon had it out of the way. Disembarking from the ship onto an open ramp, standing in strong natural gravity and looking up at a real planet's sky, thrillingly like the sky under which he had been born, Simeon had his first chance in what seemed to him an enormous length of time to see clear stars again. This viewpoint also provided him with a good look at the Milkpail from the outside. As he came down the ramp on foot, the great nebula loomed just ahead of him, a sprawling blob of whiteness that covered a quarter of the visible sky; and he knew it would continue for a good distance below the horizon.

In interstellar space you almost always saw the stars and nebulae at second or third hand, as images on one kind of instrument or another. But here there was not so much as a glass faceplate between the eyes and their sublime objects, only the kindly, almost invisible fog of a real, naturally habitable planet's atmosphere. To a child of clear space like Simeon, the psychic satisfaction provided by this view was enormous.

Simeon just stood there for a long moment, drinking in the openness of the sky. In a way, this view made the memory of all the time he had spent in the Milkpail unreal. It was almost as if out here, in this other, more natural world, Wilma might still be alive. Alive and laughing under a sunny blue sky, as on the day when he had first met her . . .

But now he saw the Milkpail with new eyes, imagined Leviathan lurking within it like a spider in its web.

Benkovic, standing beside him, nudged him with an elbow and said: "Let's move it, Sim. We've got things to do."

"Right." Simeon stood looking at the sky a moment longer, then moved on down the ramp.

Domingo had already walked on ahead, Iskander as usual at his side.

The four of them rode comfortable public transport into town. The city attached to the port was of modest size by the standards of most ED worlds, though it served as a center for all kinds of business connected with space affairs. Domingo's first recruiting effort on Rohan took place in that city that very evening, in a computerized employment bureau, a place where spacefarers were likely to appear when they were looking for jobs.

In the employment bureau the captain paid a modest fee for the privilege of posting an announcement on the electronic bulletin board: Three crew members wanted for a dangerous job; generous bonuses; experience in fighting berserkers was desirable, and so was experience in working a ship through thick nebula.

As soon as the announcement was paid for it became visible, in large letters on a wall, and the purchaser was assured that it was being reproduced on a thousand other walls around the city, and in a myriad other places around the planet as well. But the first few minutes of the ad's visibility brought no response. This wasn't one of the small-town worlds of the Milkpail here. Rohan was part of the mainstream of Galactic civilization, and there were a hundred other advertisements being carried on that bulletin board, many of them promising easier and safer money, maybe even one or two as likely to appeal to the adventurous.

Waiting for the notice to produce some results, the four men from the Milkpail walked to a nearby restaurant that Iskander said he had visited before. They dined well on food spiced with microbial nebular life, some of which had almost certainly been harvested by Milkpail colonists. Perhaps one of the four had himself harvested and sold it, in a more peaceful time.

Over dessert, Iskander said that he was well acquainted with this city and knew another place nearby where there ought to be a good chance of finding some capable crew people. Naturally not everyone who was qualified and available watched the advertisements all the time. When their meal was finished, the four of them took another little walk of a few blocks that moved them across a border between neighborhoods of the city and landed them in an environment considerably less reputable-looking.

Iskander's goal here was a certain place of entertainment. As he explained to his shipmates, this place catered to a special group of customers. Some people came here to take drugs, some to drink alcohol, some to talk philosophy or religion. There were some who did all three; and others, probably a majority, who were just there to watch the ones who did drug themselves, give speeches and heckle speakers, or sometimes all of the above. It was this majority group, according to Baza, that included a high proportion of able spacers.

Domingo had doubts about this theory from the start. And the captain, on first entering the great noisy room filled with people, smoke and roaring music, was quick to express his skepticism about being able to find anyone here who would be acceptable on his crew. But he acknowledged that a large proportion of the clientele appeared to be spacefarers; though it was true that no one could tell that about people with any degree of certainty just by looking at them.

To Simeon Chakuchin, moving on foot through the ways of this crowded city and entering the crowded tavern, the years he had spent in the Milkpail seemed progressively more unreal. This world was as different from any of the tiny planetoids inside the nebula as the view of the night sky here differed from the view from Shubra. There were probably more people in this one tavern right now than had lived on Shubra before it was wiped out. Within the nebula, a few dozen people lived on one small world, a few hundred on the next, up to a few thousand dwelling on the comparatively great metropolitan center of Yirrkala. And here, in this one city, were easily more than enough people to populate all of the Milkpail colonies several times over. Simeon thought about it: maybe a hundred times over; he felt he no longer had a good sense of proportion in such matters. At the moment there was nothing pleasing in the thought of great numbers of people. All he knew was that here the air-conditioning was fighting a losing battle to clean the air, and the noise, the roar of talk and music, was almost deafening.

There were certainly some spacefaring people in this crowded hangout, perhaps as many as could have been mustered from the population of Shubra at its height. There was a certain look, with certain habits of dress and mannerisms, by which they could usually be identified, though mistakes were certainly possible. On one of the walls a large electronic display showed, along with other offers, Domingo's help-wanted ad for crew. There were the big bonuses, but still the advertisement did not seem to be attracting a great deal of attention. In fact, none at all, as far as Simeon could tell.

Iskander suggested: "Maybe a little word-of-mouth advertising would help."

The captain agreed briskly. "Can't see how it can do any harm."

Domingo got up from the booth where the four of them had settled and walked over to the bar. He could still be sociable when he made the effort, as he did now. First Iskander and then Simeon followed him and played along. Benkovic remained in the booth.

It proved to be not at all hard to strike up conversations with people in here, except that the noise tended to drown out everything that was said. But none of the first group of people Domingo talked to sounded like they were much interested in his mission.

That group broke up. The captain muttered to Simeon, without trying to be quiet about it, that he wasn't sure he wanted to have any of these people on his crew, anyway.

Someone nearby in the crowd muttered something uncomplimentary in return.

Simeon swallowed a large part of what was left of his drink. He hoped he was going to be allowed to finish it in peace.

"Let the Space Force do the hunting. We'll take care of the home defense." That was another, even louder comment. Inside or outside the Milkpail, that attitude was pretty much the same. It was the way most people looked at the situation.

Another voice chimed in, from among the standees at the bar: "You people have any idea what you're getting into? What you're talking about when you say fighting berserkers? How big a fleet you got? You know anything about nebular astrogation? Or berserkers either?"

Iskander chuckled. "Why don't you tell us?"

"I know what they are," Domingo said. His voice wasn't any louder than before and probably few people heard him.

"Really?" commented one who did. Music began crashing even more noisily in the background.

The captain spoke up, loud enough to be heard now but still calmly enough. "I've spent most of my life in the Milkpail. And where we're going, my ship is as good as anything the Space Force has. Or anything they're about to bring in there."

No one argued that point against Domingo, though Simeon thought some of the bar patrons might have refrained only out of politeness. Some were really being polite. Or else they just weren't interested. Even the man who had made the most derisive remarks now appeared to be having second thoughts. It didn't matter, as far as Simeon could see. Probably there were some good potential crew present right now, but if so they weren't rushing forward to say that they wanted to join the captain on his hunt.

"That's my ad up on the board." The captain made the claim in a loud, arrogant voice.

No one disputed him on that, either.

"And I'm as good a captain as there is in the Milk." Domingo almost shouted. Now it was as if he were determined to be noticed, to provoke some intense reaction. He made a strange figure, standing before these heckling strangers on a leg formed from berserker metal, his face and neck still scarred from his last encounter with the perverted robots. Of course none of the strangers listening to him knew about the leg. And they probably thought the scar a mere romantic affectation. Few people had scars any more unless they wanted to.

Some of Domingo's hearers might have been ready to believe that he was as good a captain as he said he was. But that point didn't seem to matter to them either, really. Simeon, watching and listening to the arrogant appeal and to their reaction, got the impression that there was something about the captain that these people were quietly afraid of, and they were becoming increasingly aware of it, even though they could hardly know what it was. Simeon wasn't sure what it was, either, but he knew that it was there.

Simeon banged down his empty glass on the bar. Glancing back across the room, he noticed that Benkovic, still in the booth, had been joined by a young woman whose costume suggested that she might work here and was engrossed in conversation with her. No help likely from that source. Well, no help needed.

Emboldened by a drink of unaccustomed stiffness, Simeon raised his voice and started talking to the mistaken folk along the bar. He told them, or tried to tell them, because he felt a mad urge to tell them, how important the mission was that he and his three fellow Shubrans were engaged in. How Old Blue had to be something more than a misprogrammed piece of metal, because their tragedy would be so much less if it were only that. How their effort to destroy

Leviathan led toward all manner of noble achievements. Even barflies like most of his present audience would be enabled to kick their dependence on alcohol and other drugs this way, starting life over by signing up to fight Leviathan. Signing up had certainly helped him.

A small but growing ring of people were falling silent, starting to pay attention to Simeon's harangue. With an effortlessness that surprised himself, he went on talking, pleased at his own fluency. Iskander was nodding and smiling encouragement. Simeon told his audience about the people who had died under the weapons of Leviathan, on Shubra and elsewhere in the Milk. He went into some detail about the terrible machines that killed, as if maybe these tavern-dwellers here on Rohan were the ones who just didn't know what berserkers were really like.

Simeon had intended to make it clear in his speech, make it clear calmly and politely and without overemphasis, about the personal losses that he and Domingo, at least, among the present crew of the *Sirian Pearl*, had suffered. But somehow he forgot to bring up that point. And now some among his listeners began to jeer. Who was he to tell them about berserkers? Some of Simeon's hearers laid loud claim to being real Space Force veterans. And they said that peasants from outlying colonies ought to know that berserkers existed outside the Milkpail, too.

At a key moment, Iskander slyly egged things on. Correctly picking out the ethnic background of one of the louder hecklers, he delivered a studied insult. A moment later he gracefully dodged a bottle thrown by the loudmouth.

In another moment, violence had become general, at least around the three Shubrans at the bar. It struck Simeon at once that brawls in big towns were just like those in small. He waded in, trying to help his captain, grabbed the nearest opponent and slammed a big fist into the man's face. The man staggered back but refused to fall. From the corner of his eye Simeon saw Benkovic, abandoning his new acquaintance, come erupting out of the booth to aid his shipmates.

A thrown bottle went past Simeon's head. Something else, fist or weapon, hit him hard beside his ear. Two men were wrestling with him, getting the better of him until someone pulled one of them away. Simeon and his remaining opponent went down together, grappling.

Domingo was not personally disposed to fight with fellow humans, no matter what the provocation, unless they were clearly standing between him and his goal. But his valuable crew members were at risk now, and he went at the job of combat with methodical ferocity.

In the fight Domingo did well, bracing his back against the bar, getting the most out of his metal leg. Simeon saw it working like a piston.

And in the midst of the melee the fight broke off, died out, even more suddenly than it had started. A silence fell, or what seemed like silence by comparison. It was as if each and every combatant had suddenly become aware of something important enough to distract him. Simeon, lifting his head from the job of trying to throttle an opponent into a more sociable attitude, didn't know what signal he was responding to, but he had the feeling, more like the certainty, that the time had come to stop.

He got to his feet slowly, breathing heavily, letting his gasping opponent up.

No one was fighting any longer. And everyone in the room was looking in the same direction.

A Carmpan had entered the tavern through one of the street doors.

A stocky figure, certainly human by the standard of free will and intelligence, but just as certainly not descended from any life on Earth, was standing there alone just inside the door and looking at them all, with what expression it was impossible to say.

Every Earth-descended human knew what Carmpan looked like, though the Carmpan home worlds were remote, and few ED had ever actually seen a human of that other theme. The figure standing now at the badly lighted threshold of the silent room was by Earth standards squat, blocky, almost mechanical-looking. For clothing it wore some simple drapery, belted loosely over gray skin that looked almost like metal. There was no hair worth mentioning. To read expression on that alien face was, for Simeon at least, an impossibility. But then the mere presence of the being here in a tavern on Rohan seemed incredible, though of course there was nothing logically impossible about it. Simeon, and the people around him, to judge by their expressions, had had no reason to think there was a Carmpan within parsecs of this world.

For centuries, almost every Earth-descended human in the Galaxy had known that the humans of the other theme called Carmpan were valuable allies in the war fought by ED humans against berserkers. That was true even though the specific contributions of those allies were hard to pin down. As far as any ED human knew, no Carmpan had ever actually fought, none had ever committed an act of violence, even against berserkers. No Carmpan designed or supplied weapons. And yet there were the authenticated stories of their sporadic telepathic achievements. And there were the occasional utterances, sometimes mystic, sometimes mathematical, that Earth-descended people called Prophecies of Probability.

"Captain Domingo?" The slit-like mouth scarcely moved, but the voice, deep and slightly harsh, was very clear and understandable, even in the farthest corners of the room. If the speaker had been behind a screen, you might have thought that voice was issuing from an Earth-descended throat. Only now did Simeon fully realize how quiet the room had grown. Even the music had stumbled to a halt.

Now there was movement again, alteration in the frozen tableau of suspended combat in the center of the room. Domingo stepped forward, separating himself from the people around him. He looked at the Carmpan—almost, Simeon thought, as if the captain had been expecting some such miracle.

Domingo answered: "Yes?"

The voice coming from the blocky figure continued to be almost eerily Earthlike, the tone and accent flawless in the common language. The Carmpan said: "I wish to sign on as a member of your crew. I am highly qualified in communications with the headlink. Or, indeed, sometimes without it. I am able also to operate the other systems of an ED ship with what I think you will agree is more than a fair degree of skill."

With that first sentence, the silence in the room had grown even more intense.

It was an unprecedented event; no Carmpan in history had ever signed up as crew on an ED-human voyage.

"I'll be glad to sign you on," Domingo said into the silence. A light trickle of blood was making its way unnoticed down one side of his face. A moment later the captain added calmly: "Provided you can demonstrate your competence."

"I can do so at your pleasure; I am pleased to be accepted. Have you any objection to concluding the formalities immediately?"

There was only a momentary pause. "No objection at all." The captain pulled a folder from his pocket. Paperwork was brought out. The Carmpan approached, booted feet shuffling in the silence, a sound vaguely suggesting clumsiness.

People made room at the bar, and someone even wiped an area clean. The Carmpan paused silently over the paper and then signed on. Simeon saw the gray fingers working a writing tool, lettering neatly and formally, even entering a legal name—Fourth Adventurer—on the crew roster. Later, people who knew as much about the Carmpan as ED humans ever did were to say that sounded like as good a Carmpan name as any.

Shortly the new crew of the *Sirian Pearl*, now five strong and almost complete to the captain's satisfaction, left the tavern together, passing a police vehicle that was arriving belatedly to stop the brawl.

❊   ❊   ❊

Fourth Adventurer requested a stop at the spaceport hostel, and there, from a room in the wing for non-ED humanity where he—or she—was the sole tenant, picked up a modest amount of baggage. With this loaded on a small robot carrier, the four ED humans and their new recruit proceeded to the spaceport. Simeon noticed that the Carmpan's baggage included what looked like a well-tailored suit of space armor.

En route to the port, Domingo took the opportunity to explain to the Carmpan that food should be no problem on the *Pearl*. The ship's food synthesizer was an advanced model that would keep Carmpan and ED alike well nourished. Fourth Adventurer accepted this as if he had expected it all along.

Given the possibility of lingering trouble over the tavern fight, Domingo did not want to stay long on this world. But even before he could arrange clearance for departure, he had several calls from people wanting to sign on, to fill the one remaining position on his crew, assuming the Carmpan would be accepted. The word had spread quickly. But somehow none of these late ED applicants pleased the captain, and he said he was of a mind to turn them all down sight unseen.

"That is a wise decision, Captain," said the Carmpan unexpectedly. Everyone else looked at him, and he looked back.

Immediately after liftoff from Rohan, the Carmpan requested a general crew meeting in the common room. When Domingo heard what the purpose of the meeting was to be, he granted the request at once.

With the meeting assembled, the newest crew member assured his new shipmates that what they had doubtless heard about the telepathic capabilities of Carmpan was at least partially correct. But he solemnly pledged, here and now, to respect the mental privacy of his shipmates and gave them assurances that he had done so from the start.

Simeon wasn't quite sure whether to be relieved, impressed or doubtful.

"Fourth Adventurer?" Spence Benkovic, sounding confident as usual, approached with a question.

"Yes, Spence."

"For reasons of psychology, affecting the ED component of the crew, there's something some of us would like to get settled. Would you consider it impolite if we asked whether you are male or female?"

"You should tell whoever is curious on the subject that I am male. And for the duration of my service, you may disregard any special considerations of politeness where I am concerned."

Simeon thought that Benkovic looked vaguely disappointed.

❉   ❉   ❉

Next day the *Pearl* departed Rohan. On the advice of the Carmpan, Domingo chose a course that seemed to lead nowhere in particular. En route, Fourth Adventurer easily passed the captain's tests
of competence in controlling the systems of the ship by mindlink
band. A few adjustments in the equipment were necessary to accommodate a non-ED brain, and with that out of the way everything
went very smoothly.

But all the surprises were not over.

❉ CHAPTER 15

No sooner had the Pearl departed from the Rohan system than
Domingo's newest crew member called up the captain on intercom
and suggested a different heading from the one just established.

Domingo's first reaction was to consult the holographic chart in
front of him. The course he had just charted led directly toward
the Milkpail, but now Fourth Adventurer wanted him to deviate
from that by thirty degrees or so, heading into what amounted to
an interstellar wasteland.

The captain, fully aware that most of the rest of his crew were
probably listening in, shifted his gaze to the small, gray, enigmatic
image on the intercom stage. "Why should I go that way, Fourth
Adventurer?"

The Carmpan's voice was as firmly and convincingly ED as ever.
"It will give you the best chance of recruiting the sixth crew member
you desire to have."

"Aha. And who will this person be?"

"A very highly rated pilot."

That was the very skill that Domingo had been wishing for most
strongly.

There was a pause, during which the captain studied his instruments some more. "You appear to be directing me into what we
call the Gravelpile," he said at last. The formation known by that
name was a dull, dark wisp of coarse interstellar matter, billions of
kilometers long and deep, growing out like a dead or dying tail from
one end of the Milkpail. Colonies were nonexistent in the Gravelpile,
and suns almost so. Astrogation at any speed was difficult. Ships and
people were almost entirely absent. Life of any kind was very rare,
and so, therefore, were berserkers.

Fourth Adventurer's tiny image nodded. "That is true. That is where I am advising you to go."

Domingo was certain now that the entire crew was listening in. "Just what is this highly rated pilot doing there? He or she is aboard some kind of a ship, I presume?"

"That would seem logical, but I am not sure. It is hard for me to tell."

Simeon, watching the conversation through his own intercom station, thought that Domingo for once looked indecisive.

The captain demanded of Fourth Adventurer: "Is that all you can tell me?"

"It is all I can tell you at the moment that will be of help. You must understand that I am as reluctant to probe that pilot's mind as to probe yours."

"Ah. But you're certain he or she is there?"

"Indeed. And apparently alone."

Iskander broke in: "There must be a lot of good pilots' minds scattered here and there around the Galaxy. Is there some reason why we should go chasing after this one in particular?"

"The probabilities of success, in our mission of pursuit, are greater if we do."

Everyone had heard the legendary stories: how the Carmpan talents, telepathic and probabilistic, worked—at least sometimes. It was up to the captain to decide.

"All right," Domingo agreed, after a pause. He was thinking that it was no advantage to have special talents aboard if you were afraid to use them or trust them.

A voyage of several days brought the *Pearl* to the fringes of the Gravelpile, and here the Carmpan suggested—"ordered" was more like it, Iskander muttered—another course correction.

The second-in-command was not too happy. "What exactly are we supposed to find here, Fourth Adventurer?"

"A pilot alone . . . but I must report an unfavorable development."

Domingo spoke up sharply. "Let's have it, then."

"By now, captain, I am beginning to suspect that the pilot we are seeking is dying, or else in suspended animation. There is a quality of mind that I can only describe as fading."

"Great. Well, we've come this far. We'll push on."

The ship advanced, slowly, into the Gravelpile. From this point on, the average density of matter in the space around the ship was as high as in the Milkpail, making it necessary to travel in normal space, at relatively low speeds. The matter here tended to be concentrated in solid granules and larger chunks, but the overall effect was much the same.

In another hour, Fourth Adventurer suddenly recommended yet a third change of heading. The captain silently complied. No more was said.

Until about an hour after that, when the Carmpan called a halt. "Here," he said. "Somewhere nearby. Now you must take over the search. Captain, I am very tired. With your permission I am going to rest."

Spence Benkovic was muttering something uncharitable. But Domingo was looking at Fourth Adventurer with concern. "Permission granted."

"I shall be all right in a few hours. But now I must rest." And the Carmpan's intercom station went blank.

"Do that." Domingo sighed faintly, and looked around him on his instruments. His ship was practically at rest with reference to the nearby matter in space. "Iskander, Benkovic. Let's break out some seeking tools."

In a few more minutes the captain had his entire ED crew at work, examining space in the vicinity of the ship with various instruments. Still nothing that suggested the presence of any kind of pilot, good or bad, was showing anywhere on the detectors.

"Everyone keep looking. I'm starting a slow cruise in a search pattern."

To the professed surprise of some aboard, a few minutes of routine search effort did produce results. There was first a faint, distorted distress signal and then the image of what might well be a lifeboat, almost lost amid gravel at some forty thousand kilometers' range.

"I'm proceeding in that direction," Domingo announced. "I want everyone except Adventurer at stations."

The approach to the signal source was again routine, cautious and time-consuming. As the *Pearl* drew nearer, the object could be certainly identified as a common type of ED lifeboat. And as the investigating ship approached still closer to it, the small craft could be seen to be battered and scarred. It looked as if it had been through a war, as probably, thought Simeon, it had.

Probing at the object with a tight communications beam brought no response except a continuation of the distress signal, which was no doubt an automatic transmission.

Looking over the lifeboat from a distance of only a few hundred meters, it was impossible to guess whether it had been adrift in space for a day or for several hundred years.

"I say we wake the squarehead up"—this was Benkovic speaking—"and try to make sure he knows what he's doing. This thing could be some kind of a berserker booby-trap."

The captain dismissed that suspicion immediately. "Way out here? They wouldn't waste the effort. They'd go near a shipping lane somewhere to work that kind of a stunt. I want a couple of people to suit up and take a look at it."

"I guess you have a point there, Captain." And Spence, as if to make amends for arguing, was the first to volunteer.

Iskander for once did not volunteer; maybe, thought Simeon, the second-in-command disdained this job as too safe and easy.

Simeon decided that he himself was ready to get into a suit again. And shortly he was out in space with Benkovic. The Milkpail again dominated the sky, but here the great bright splash of it was barred and patched with blackness, the erratic patterns of the Gravelpile's intervening dark material. This really looked and felt like deep space, a hell of a long way from anywhere or anything, and if there was really a living pilot in the boat, she or he was going to have one miraculous rescue to tell the grandchildren about someday.

The two men reached the drifting lifeboat speedily and without incident. The main hatch on the small vessel opened normally, on the first effort, but there was no cycling of the airlock. The cabin atmosphere in the boat either had been lost, or else deliberately evacuated.

Benkovic went first in through the hatch, with Chakuchin hovering nearby outside. As with all lifeboats, there wasn't a great deal of interior room. But a moment later Spence was reaching out a gauntleted hand to beckon, and calling him on radio. "Take a look at this, Sim."

Simeon went in, just as Benkovic got the interior lights turned on. The boat appeared to be a standard, fairly recent model. There were two berths, as might be expected, convertible to suspended-animation couches.

And both of the SA beds were occupied. Simeon glanced in passing through the little window of the nearest. There was a dead man in it. One glance was enough; there would be no need to open this one to make sure.

But Spence was grinning beside the second berth. Simeon looked in there and beheld the countenance of a reasonably attractive young woman, eyes closed, as if she were in peaceful sleep. Readouts on the berth confirmed the immediate instinctive impression that she was alive.

Domingo's voice was in their suit radios, asking questions. Simeon answered. "Looks like one survivor, Captain. If she's still viable."

"Viable ain't the word for it." Benkovic was looking through the little window appreciatively.

Domingo was asking: "Anything about the setup look suspicious? If not, we might as well grapple the boat and bring her right aboard."

Nothing looked suspicious as far as the two investigators could tell. A few minutes later the lifeboat, entry hatch still open, was inside the *Pearl*'s ventral bay, and atmosphere was filling boat and bay alike.

Once atmosphere had been established, the men in the bay tried the standard revival cycle on the suspended-animation chamber. It worked. The watching men were soon rewarded with favorable readouts and signs of life. Their pilot-to-be—if indeed the young woman was going to fit that category—had undoubtedly started breathing. Iskander went to sickbay to get certain things ready in case they should be needed.

Presently the SA chamber opened. The young woman, dressed in a standard ship's coverall, immediately struggled to sit up in the *Pearl*'s artificial gravity. Spence and Simeon were at her side, offering physical support, and trying to be reassuring.

In a few seconds, with help, the object of their attentions was on her feet. The young woman was tall, and more than moderately attractive now that her long, strong body was fully alive again.

Presently Iskander and Spence were cycling with her into the ship proper. When they were through the lock, they walked her gently to sickbay between them.

"What time is it?" That was the first question she asked, the first coherent words she uttered, on waking up more or less completely. By this time she was seated in the sickbay of the *Pearl*, and could see she had an interested audience around her. Her speech and accent seemed to follow one of the more commonly heard patterns; she would not have sounded out of place at all on Rohan, though there was a trace of some earlier influence, an origin somewhere else.

Domingo, who had come along from his station to observe this phenomenon for himself, named the current standard year, and the month when the ship had left Rohan. Days and hours in deep space were always subject to correction for relativistic effects, despite the theoretical ability of c-plus travelers to avoid such effects entirely.

When she heard the numbers the young woman slumped, as if with relief. "That's good. It means I was only a few days in the boat. Don't know why the idea of a long sleep bothers me a whole lot, but it does. Not that I would miss anyone who's still alive in this century, particularly." She drew a deep breath and tossed back her full, flowing hair and looked around her. "I'm Branwen Galway. What's this? A trader?"

"I'm Niles Domingo. This is my ship, the *Sirian Pearl*, and we're hunting a berserker. What happened to you? Why were you in the boat? I don't suppose it was Old Blue that put you away?"

"It was a berserker—I didn't ask it if it had a name. My ship was the *Old Pueblo*, out of New Trinidad . . . did you say you're hunting a berserker? How big is your fleet? I've just been doing my damnedest to get away."

"No fleet. This one ship." The captain tersely recited the *Pearl*'s tonnage and her armaments. "So your ship was destroyed? But you don't know whether or not it was Leviathan that attacked you?"

Fully awake and aware now, Branwen Galway was looking at the captain with some curiosity. "No, sir. As I say, I didn't ask." She paused, evidently struck suddenly by a different thought. "The other berth on the lifeboat—there was someone in it too, wasn't there?"

"A man," said Simeon. "I'm afraid he's dead."

"Ah. That's no surprise." Branwen looked around at her audience. "He didn't mean that much to me, but I wondered . . . I'm sure there wasn't enough left of our ship for you to find anything."

"You're right about that." Domingo was smiling faintly; maybe the woman he had just rescued would be a pilot, maybe not. But at least she certainly did not seem to be the type who was going to cause a lot of unnecessary trouble.

Already she had abandoned the subject of her own past. "One ship, hey? Well, you've got guts. Why are you hunting a berserker?"

Everyone looked at Domingo. He said: "I'll tell you the story when you've had a chance to rest."

"That kind of a story, hey?"

The rest of the crew were in the process of introducing themselves more or less formally to the new arrival when Simeon suddenly saw Branwen's expression alter. She was looking past him at the doorway to the corridor outside sickbay, and Simeon knew before he turned what he was going to see.

Fourth Adventurer had appeared there, standing in the corridor. The Carmpan announced that he was rested now and ready to resume his full duties. Then he introduced himself to the newest arrival.

Branwen was suitably impressed at sight of the Carmpan, especially when she heard that his talents were responsible for her rescue; otherwise she could easily have drifted here for a million years.

Fourth Adventurer in turn looked at her for some time, and appeared satisfied with what he saw.

Domingo, indicating the woman, asked him: "Is this my pilot, Fourth Adventurer?"

"She is a very capable pilot, Captain. You must ask her whether she will be yours." And the Carmpan turned and moved away, still looking tired, almost shuffling, despite what he had just said about being rested.

Branwen was mildly bewildered. "What was that all about? I mean, I am a pilot, but how can he possibly judge how good?" Nobody tried to answer that.

Simeon noticed that Benkovic was already looking at the newest recruit with what appeared to be something more than medical concern. It was Spence who first reached to help her when she stood up again. "Feel dizzy?"

She pulled her arm away from his supporting hand, firmly but not making a big deal of it. "I'm coping, thanks. I notice I haven't got a lot of baggage with me. I could use a private berth somewhere, and a change of clothes. And then some food."

Provided with crew clothing including coveralls, some miscellaneous supplies and food, her residence established in the berth that had been reserved for the sixth crew member, Galway soon announced her readiness to join in a berserker hunt, as long as it was being properly planned and led. She said she would soon be ready to demonstrate her competence.

A little later, Simeon happened to encounter the Carmpan alone. Unable to keep from asking the question, Chakuchin demanded of Fourth Adventurer: "Why can't you do this kind of thing all the time? Rescue work, I mean?"

"There is a price that I and others must pay, whenever such help is given. You do not understand."

"No, I don't." Meeting those alien eyes, Simeon had the inescapable feeling that he was making a fool of himself. Lamely he added: "Anyway I'm glad you're helping now."

The Carmpan looked at him, unreadably, and turned away.

Fourth Adventurer resumed taking his regular turn on watch, but otherwise spent most of the next few days in his berth, more often than not out of touch with the rest of the crew.

Domingo had already reestablished his course in the direction of the Milkpail. At this distance the great glowing nebula already dominated the instruments in flightspace, and it was a looming presence in normal space as well.

Branwen Galway quickly made a complete recovery from her interval of suspended life.

From time to time, when asked, she related a few more details of what had happened to her and her ship. But she appeared to have put those events behind her now, and to be reluctant to talk very much about them.

She was a tall woman, and now moved lithely about the ship. With a woman aboard, the whole atmosphere on the *Pearl* had changed. One part of the change was of course that Domingo now considered his crew complete—as soon as Branwen felt up to it, he had formally offered her the second pilot's job, on condition of course that she demonstrate her competence. She had a right to refuse the job, of course. But as a mere rescued survivor, she had no right to demand that the ship interrupt its own mission to take her where she might want to go. Domingo said he could probably drop her at some Milkpail world if she would prefer that to signing on.

Iskander, probing, indulging his perpetual itch to investigate and instigate, did ask her where she would want to go if she had a choice. Branwen Galway responded with no more than a shrug.

She was soon ready to demonstrate her competence to Domingo's full satisfaction.

"Sorry I didn't bring any references with me, Captain. But I can give you a demonstration." Branwen had already been looking over the various onboard systems, and felt confident of handling any of them. "What would you like to see?"

Domingo wanted to see a lot, and his newest recruit obliged. He was well pleased with what he saw. There was no doubt that his potential new crew member was good, very good, at running any spacecraft system that could be operated from a headlink. Considering the circumstances of her rescue, her claim of combat experience was easy to accept. And when the *Pearl* got into deep nebula again, Galway established her ability to handle that. She gave the impression of being good at a lot of other things besides.

Simeon thought that she was better looking than most of her sex, certainly more attractive than the ones he knew who had acquired hard-boiled reputations in space work. Not that Branwen appeared to care whether any of the men aboard thought she was good-looking or not. Simeon kept watching for Spence Benkovic to get his face slapped, but so far Spence, after that first gallant offer, was behaving in a very businesslike way. Playing hard to get, perhaps.

The crew member who most interested Branwen Galway appeared to be the Carmpan. Of course that enigmatic presence would intrigue anyone. Still none of the ED humans on the crew, thought Simeon, really had the faintest idea why Fourth Adventurer had offered to sign on. As far as Simeon knew, Domingo had never asked.

Next most interesting to the woman—perhaps first after the initial shock of the alien presence had somewhat worn off—was Domingo himself, who of all the ED men seemed to care the least about her sex.

She spent a fair amount of time, more than was necessary certainly, talking with the captain.

Domingo was soon ready to complete her formal signing on the crew. Iskander Baza seemed resigned to the fact, if not enthusiastic about it. Benkovic was as quietly pleased by this recruit as he had been quietly upset by the last one.

A little shakedown cruise now, the captain announced, and the ship and crew would be ready to face Leviathan.

◉ **CHAPTER 16**

Branwen Galway and the Fourth Adventurer had both demonstrated their competence, to say the least. They were also alike in admitting to a relative lack of experience at operating a ship within a sizable thick nebula.

The captain was ready to agree that some nebular practice was in order for his two newest crew members before the time came for them to fight Leviathan. But he thought that difficulty would almost certainly take care of itself. Leviathan was unlikely to be waiting obligingly for the *Pearl* at the point where she reentered the Milkpail. The crew ought to have an adequate opportunity to gain experience within the nebula while they were trying to pick up the enemy's trail. Domingo wanted every member of his crew to be as highly skilled as possible at every job, and with that goal in mind, he tried to rotate assignments frequently.

Branwen had a question for the captain when their discussion came around again to the object of their mission: "Why do you so often say 'he' when you talk about this thing we're chasing?"

The two of them, both off watch, were alone in the common room at the moment. Domingo thought for a few seconds, running his fingers through his hair. Then he looked up at the tall young woman beside him. He asked her: "Do you believe in any gods?"

Galway was standing, leaning on the console of the computer that was sometimes used to build ethereal models in this room—the captain had noticed that she often preferred to stand rather than sit.

She said: "Can't say that I do, Captain. Though there are times. Why?"

"If you believed in a goddess or a god, which pronoun would you use?"

She had to think that one over for a moment. "Are you telling me this damned machine you want to kill is your god?"

"That may be as close as I can come to it. But I was asking what you would do."

Branwen considered him irreverently. "Well, at least you're not calling a berserker 'her.'"

◉   ◉   ◉

Once Domingo had got his ship back inside the Milkpail, he elected to begin his hunt in a direction that made it logical to select the world of Yirrkala as one of the first stops. Yirrkala, he explained to his new crew members, was one of the best places in the nebula to pick up the latest information.

As the *Pearl* approached Yirrkala, her crew observed that the populous planetoid was more heavily defended than ever, and it looked as if there were more settlers here than ever before. The mass flight from the Milkpail some people had predicted was evidently not materializing.

After landing, Domingo's first question to the local people, asked even before he got out of his ship, was of course for the latest news of Leviathan. The response was disappointing. Little news had developed in the days the *Pearl* had been gone from the nebula. No more attacks, only one more sighting, and that slightly doubtful. Neither particularly encouraging or discouraging, just another bit of information for the mosaic.

When he had seen that item entered in his computer's data banks, Domingo left the ship and walked down the familiar spaceport ramp. He went alone, saying only that there were a few more things he wanted to find out and that he would be back in an hour or two at most. His crew were meanwhile left with a few routine jobs and a little free time.

The captain was somewhat surprised to discover his own intentions when he realized what he was going to do next. He wanted to speak to Polly—exactly what he meant to say to her he wasn't sure, but the way they had parted just wasn't right. But his efforts to locate Polly Suslova met with failure. The local office known as Central Communications—the chief settlement on Yirrkala was trying to grow into a real city—pronounced her unavailable and would not elaborate on that reply.

A call to Irina and Casper earned the captain the information that Polly had left Yirrkala permanently. Her relatives told Domingo she had moved with her children to another world where she was now working at a new job.

"Another world?"

"That's right."

"Which one?"

There was a pause. "I'm not sure," Irina said.

Domingo was skeptical. But he didn't press any harder for the information.

Before the call was over, Polly's relatives also managed to drop a hint that Polly was much happier now that she was seeing a new man.

Walking rather slowly back toward his ship, Domingo found

himself wondering if it were true. Suddenly a new thought struck him, and he began to wonder whether the new man could possibly be Gujar. Though why it should make any difference to him, even if it were so, was more than he could understand. Polly and Gujar were just people from his old crew, and naturally he wished both of them well.

It was certainly not as if he really needed Polly to fill a backup position on the crew, skilled though she was. Had that idea really been in the back of his mind? It would be foolishness. Six people were really the optimum number to have aboard. Practical experience confirmed it.

Things were all right the way they were. The pace of Domingo's walking speeded up.

While going through his routine of departure clearance at the port, he ran into an acquaintance who had actual information about Gujar. Sidoruk was again captaining a ship owned by someone else, but this time he was serving in the expanded Home Guard fleet that had been organized by Gennadius from among all the Milkpail colonies. No telling where Gujar and his ship were right now or where Gennadius was either, for that matter.

Captain Domingo's new crew hadn't really had a chance to get off his ship and stretch their legs before he was back among them. He quickly assembled them on board his ship again, took a quick look at his updated model and set out in the direction of the most recently reported sighting of Leviathan.

Two days had passed, and the *Pearl* had covered about half the distance to that spot when, as on their previous departure from a world, a call on intercom from his Carmpan crew member made the captain decide to change course sharply. But this time the call carried an unprecedented urgency.

Fourth Adventurer, in a strained voice, reported himself in telepathic agony. He said the cause was the destruction, currently in progress, of the population of yet one more small world colonized by ED humans, this one out on the edge of the nebula.

"Berserkers?"

"I am sure of it, though as you know I cannot perceive them directly."

"Of course, berserkers. What else would it be? *But is it Leviathan?*"

"I cannot tell that, Captain." Nor could the Carmpan see, or the other crew members deduce from his report, the name of the afflicted planetoid. But the direction and the approximate distance of it were determinable: *that* way, for a couple of days' hard traveling.

❋   ❋   ❋

The ship had traversed less than half the estimated distance when Fourth Adventurer reported that the attack, the agony, was over now.

"How did it end? You mean—"

"I perceive only that it has ended. But the application of logic to that fact produces no reassurance."

Domingo held his course steady in the same direction.

Aboard the *Pearl* a conversation was in progress, concerning what was reliably known of the actual fighting strength of Leviathan, and how the *Pearl*'s armament compared with what the enemy was known to have.

A computer model, this one an image that Simeon had rarely seen before, was on display. The holographic model showed the size and structure of Leviathan, based on what had been recorded and reported from all known sightings, and what had been deduced and estimated from that.

On the little holostage the jagged shape of the model rotated slowly. A symbolic presentation of the *Pearl* on the same scale showed all too clearly how much smaller the human ship was than its potential opponent.

The comparison was sobering, but everyone on the *Pearl*'s crew was able to look at such matters with a professional eye, and there appeared to be good prospects for victory. No one had any doubts that Domingo's objective was to win, and that they had reasonable expectations of achieving that objective. No one, the captain least of all, wanted to make a futile effort that would serve only to give the enemy another triumph.

During these tactical discussions Domingo emphasized that there were advantages in being relatively small. One was the capability of moving faster within the nebula. Another point was that the shields of the human ship had a more compact area to defend—a much easier job than trying to cover the whole sprawling surface of a planet or planetoid, or even the area of a machine the size of Leviathan.

The armament of the *Sirian Pearl* did not include a c-plus cannon, but she did mount some of the latest missiles capable of driving themselves effectively faster than light, by skipping in and out of normal space in very nearly the same way as a projectile from such a gun. The ship also carried beam projectors modified for nebular work, with new focusing modulation that ought to be able to eat through such shields as Leviathan was known to possess.

This discussion in the common room was interrupted by a call to battle stations, delivered by the crew member manning the forward detectors. The detectors had offered a sudden indication of what looked like a whole berserker fleet, cruising the eternal mists out there at no very great distance ahead of the *Pearl*.

Everyone aboard the ship scrambled to get to his or her combat position. Even before Domingo had any chance to think about tactics, it became apparent that there was no chance to retreat. Evidently the *Pearl* had been sighted too, by whatever or whoever was ahead. That shadowy fleet up there was reacting, turning toward the single ship. The range was already so short that it would be hopeless for the *Pearl* to attempt flight.

"Weapons ready. We're going to—"

The IFF transponder chirped, bringing a spontaneous and general gasp of relief from the crew, or at least from four of its five ED human members.

The captain was the only one whose manner betrayed no relief; if anything he sounded exasperated. "It's the Space Force."

"Well, damn it all anyway." Iskander's intercom tone managed to make his annoyance almost convincing. "If we'd been trying to find them, we never could have done it."

Domingo was quick to open communications with the approaching ships. The Space Force responded, sending clipped jargon with their usual tightbeamed caution. The pulses of transmitted talk came through only blurrily at first. Then as the distance lessened, with the *Pearl* and the Space Force fleet speeding through the nebula on gradually converging courses, a real conversation could get started.

Soon the image of Gennadius, seated on the bridge of his combat ship, had come into being on the several small individual holostages the crew members of the *Pearl* were watching.

Even padded and armored as he was, obviously on red alert for combat, the commander looked more haggard, more cadaverously thin than ever. His voice was suspicious, almost hostile. "What the hell are you doing out here, Domingo?"

"I think you know what I'm doing. I just hope you're doing the same thing, and suddenly I find I have a new reason to hope so. Is this really where your big computer says Old Blue ought to be?"

"Nothing my computer says has been doing me much good lately. So I'm trying some guessing, as I suppose you are. All right, I admit I'm after Leviathan."

Domingo stared for a moment at the commander's little image. Then, in a sharply changed voice, the captain of the *Pearl* demanded: "He's hit another colony, hasn't he? Which one is it this time?"

"'*He?*'" The commander sounded mystified. Then he gave up quibbling. "All right. It's hit another colony." Gennadius named the latest victim. Simeon tried to place its location on his mental map. Yes, it was presumably the same world whose suffering, detected by the Carmpan, had brought the *Pearl* moving in this direction.

"And you guessed his route of departure might lead him along this way."

"Something like that." Gennadius appeared to take counsel with himself and came to a decision. "Look, Domingo. My theory is that some berserkers, the one you call Leviathan probably among them, have a repair and refitting base somewhere around here in the nebula, maybe in a dark-star system. I'm looking for it now, but my chance of finding it would be better if I were able to call in more ships."

"Then call them in."

"It's not that simple. If I call ships here, I have to take them away from somewhere else. Most probably from guard duty near some colony, and I don't want to do that. I'll make you a deal. Take the *Pearl* and stand guard duty at da Gama, and I'll call two of my ships in from that area to help out here with the search. It would give us a considerably better chance of finding what we're looking for. If I can catch Leviathan with my battle group, I'll bring you back a blue light. Or any other part of its anatomy you want."

"No deal," said Domingo instantly.

"I didn't think so." Gennadius was angry, though not surprised. "All right, then, let me repeat my first question. What the hell are you doing out here? If you know something, I want to know it, too. What have you seen? Or found out?"

"I've seen nothing out of the ordinary. I've been extrapolating Leviathan's earlier movements—as you must have been doing also."

The commander snorted. "With your little shipboard computer? You've been damned lucky, then."

The captain nodded, smiling lightly. "You might say that a certain amount of luck has come my way."

Gennadius had his fleet deployed in a far-flung formation for maximum sweep, Simeon observed. He supposed that for that reason it was not amazingly odd that the encounter with the *Pearl* had occurred, given that the two commanders were following the same basic plan of search.

The Space Force commander once more demanded to know what other sightings the *Pearl* had recently made.

"None at all," Domingo repeated at once. "What about yourself?"

"We picked up something about two hours ago—movement of some kind at spacecraft speeds. At extreme range, and we weren't able to close on it. I'm still not sure if it was berserker movement or not—but out here, nothing else is likely to . . . what in all the hells is *that?*"

Checking his indicators, Simeon realized that Fourth Adventurer had just turned his intercom station on two-way as if intending to join in the radio conversation. Now for the first time Gennadius was able to get a good look at all of the six crew members on Domingo's ship—including the one whose presence represented a unique event in the history of Earth-descended spacefaring.

"Just one of my crew." Domingo sounded distracted; his thoughts as usual were still on berserkers.

"One of your crew. Just one of your bloody crew. Iskander, what's going on over there?" For a moment the Carmpan's presence appeared to outrage Gennadius more than anything else that had happened yet.

"Things are just as you see them, sir." Baza sounded sweetly reasonable. "If I may, I would suggest a more diplomatic attitude toward our ally of the Carmpan theme."

"I . . . should have known better than to ask," Gennadius muttered, almost inaudibly. Then he roused himself, or tried to rouse himself, to his diplomatic duty. "Absolutely." He started to address himself to the Carmpan. "Let me assure you, sir, or—" He was getting nowhere. "Domingo. Domingo, I warn you, if you're doing anything to get us in trouble with—with—"

Fourth Adventurer spoke at last. He introduced himself calmly and assured the commander that there were no difficulties in prospect involving intertheme diplomacy. He, Fourth Adventurer, was present on this mission by his own free choice as an individual, and his presence would be more likely to alleviate diplomatic trouble than to cause it.

Gennadius briefly tried to grapple with that but gave up. He had too much else to think about. "I, I don't understand that, sir."

"You need not worry about it now, Commander."

There was a pause. "You do claim diplomatic status, then?" Gennadius at last inquired. The image of his face was growing clearer as the hurtling ships approached each other.

"I have made no such claim as yet, and at present I do not intend to do so. But I would be within my rights, and I reserve the right to do so in the future. Matters of vast importance are almost certainly at stake here, Commander, more important than getting rid of a berserker."

Suddenly Fourth Adventurer's shipmates were staring at him too, as if they had never seen him before this moment.

"Ah." Gennadius obviously couldn't make any sense at all out of what he had just heard. Everyone was waiting for him to try. "Ah—Fourth Adventurer—matters of vast importance?"

"Yes, Commander."

"Such as what?"

"I said 'almost certainly at stake,' Commander. If and when the proper word is 'certainly,' you will be informed."

"Ah. Good. Well, in the meantime I have a job to perform. We all do."

The commander and the captain talked a little longer.

Gennadius pragmatically welcomed the presence of Domingo's ship as adding to the total strength available in the region; but at the same time the commander was fearful that Domingo's fanaticism was going to raise more problems. Certainly it was keeping Domingo and his ship from being as useful as the commander would have liked.

In the privacy of his own mind, Gennadius decided that he was going to try not to think about the presence of the Carmpan and what it might mean.

"Captain, I don't suppose it would do any good to order you to take your ship and stand Home Guard duty near da Gama. Or to go home."

"I don't suppose it would. I've told you again and again what I'm doing. My plans haven't changed."

The commander heaved a long sigh. "All right." In an easier voice he added: "Looks like we've got some dirty weather coming up ahead. Going to run for it?"

"I'm not that much worried about a squall."

✸ CHAPTER 17

The detectors on all the ships now showed a nebular storm ahead and coming on. The storms arose from a combination of magnetic and gravitational forces; in them the matter composing the eternal clouds was compressed beyond any density it normally attained. The masses of it were ringed and shot through like Earthly thunderstorms with electrical discharges—though each storm was considerably bigger than the Earth itself—and glistened with iridescent rainbows. The onrushing disturbances were now only minutes away.

If a colony lay in a storm's path, the inhabitants took shelter in shielded underground rooms or perhaps in reliable ships that could outrun electronic weather. Sleets of atomic and subatomic particles, knotting and lashing fields of magnetic and other forces, would disrupt human movement and communications, wipe out food crops in the nebula and on planetary surfaces and almost certainly inflict some human casualties. It was fortunate that storms of great size were rare.

This was not one of the larger ones. The squall, as Domingo had called it, struck the ships.

Screens and holostages went blank as the nuclear-magnetic lash tore up communications between ships and impeded forward progress. The energies of the miniature tempest extended outside normal space, confusing astrogation systems and temporarily negating drives, robbing them of their normal hold in the mathematical reality of flightspace.

The people on Domingo's ship had a glimpse of the Space Force ships scattering before their own instruments roared with white noise, cutting off the world. And then the *Pearl* was swept away.

The intercom was still working perfectly, but the Carmpan's unit remained blank even after repeated efforts to call him. When Branwen and Iskander went to Fourth Adventurer's berth to investigate, they found him tossing in his acceleration couch as if he were spacesick or feverish.

Bending over the supine, blocky figure, Branwen shook him gently by a corner of his gray garment. But Fourth Adventurer was unable or unwilling to respond to that stimulus or to the first anxious questions from his visitors.

The woman turned uncertainly to Baza. "Can a Carmpan have a fever?" she asked. "He feels warm."

"I don't know." For once not amused, Iskander flicked the intercom. "Anyone on board claim to be an expert in Carmpan biology?"

No one did, apparently. Nor did anyone want to suggest what sort of first aid or medical treatment, if any, to attempt. The decision fell to Domingo by default, and by his orders a policy of watchful waiting was adopted.

Hardly had this been decided when to everyone's relief Fourth Adventurer roused himself enough to announce that he had not really been taken ill. He was, he said, only suffering from the strain of having made telepathic contact with strange forms of life in the raw, seething nebula outside. The native life forms here were also endangered by the storm when it engulfed them and suffered pain, and their distress communicated itself to the Carmpan's mind.

Simeon didn't understand. "I thought you were able to tune things out."

"Ordinarily. But just now I dare not."

There was silence on the intercom, but Simeon thought most of the crew were probably listening. He asked the Carmpan: "You knew all along there was life out there in the nebula, didn't you? Of course, everyone knows that."

The feeble answer was more a gesture than a sound. It conveyed no meaning to Simeon.

"I'd say it would be a good idea to keep your mind away from it if it makes you sick."

Fourth Adventurer managed to get out intelligible words. "I repeat, that is not possible at present. Matters are not that easy."

Branwen took up a point in which everyone was interested. "You said you could, ah, keep your mind away from ours."

"And I have done so, be assured. But in the case of the life outside, my duty is to probe."

"The 'matters of vast importance' you mentioned to Gennadius?"

"That is it."

Beyond that it was hard to get the Carmpan to say anything on the subject at all.

After some hours the storm began to weaken. It no longer represented any threat at all to the survival of the ship, but the weather was still too nasty to allow much headway or any determination of position.

With the ship no longer endangered, Domingo relieved three of his people from duty and sent them to rest. They were all tired, but none of them rested easily.

Spence Benkovic didn't try to rest at all. Instead he came looking for Branwen Galway, wanting to talk to her, wanting to do more than that; it was almost the first time since this attractive woman had come aboard that he allowed himself to show an open interest in her.

When Spence appeared at her door, trying to get himself invited in, Branwen had somewhat mixed feelings about his renewed attentions. Mainly she was repelled by them. Branwen found Benkovic acceptable as a casual acquaintance, even—so far, at least—as a shipmate. But as soon as she tried to think of him as a potential lover, something about him changed. Or something in the way she saw him changed, which amounted to the same thing. Well, naturally, the altered role would make a difference in how you thought of anyone, but . . .

It was hard to explain, even to herself. But she was more certain than ever that Benkovic was not a potential lover, not for her.

Galway did have to give Spence credit for being good-looking. He could be entertaining, too, she had discovered, when he made the effort. Maybe, after all . . . but no.

He wasn't inclined to take no for an answer. And so she closed the door of her berth on him, after first politely and then not so politely declining to let him in.

To Branwen's surprise, he was still there, in the short corridor, when she came out a few minutes later. She had to maneuver past him in the narrow crew tunnel. There was momentary physical contact, which he tried to turn to some advantage. When he was again rejected, he passed it off lightly as a joke.

Benkovic's eyes glowed after her when she had passed him; she could feel them without looking back. They were attractive eyes, she had to admit, and he knew how to use them. She thought he would have liked to try a more determined grab at her, but knew better than to try that kind of thing with her, and on this ship.

She was now the only female available. Well, the possibility of having to adjust his sex life should have occurred to him before he signed on for a long mission.

One ED female on the crew, four ED males. She wondered if the Carmpan ever worried about his sex life, or lack thereof. That aspect of things didn't matter to his theme much, if all the stories one heard were true. Maybe she would ask Fourth Adventurer sometime.

Meanwhile she had a much less theoretical problem to contend with: what to do about Spence Benkovic. Experience suggested strongly that in this situation she would be better off being a sexless crew member, just one of the fellows, as long as that role was playable. Unfortunately that no longer seemed to be a possibility. The trouble, one of the troubles, was that no one knew how long this voyage was likely to go on before Domingo was willing to call, if not a halt, at least a pause somewhere for some R and R.

One way to keep Spence at a distance, possibly a good one, would be to take up with someone else. Domingo might well have been her first choice, but she understood by now that he just wasn't available, even if she did not yet understand exactly why. Because he was captain for one thing, probably. But she had the feeling there was more to it than that.

Iskander . . . no. She'd rather not. Though from the way Baza looked at her sometimes, Branwen thought that he too might be interested.

That left Simeon. Who had been, she thought, in some way her first choice all along.

Branwen went knocking at Chakuchin's door.

Conveniently, Simeon too was off watch at the moment. He was pleasantly surprised to see her.

She got the conversation off to an easy start by asking Sim whether he had anything to drink available.

Simeon, having asked her in, started to explain that the only stimulant he needed now was Leviathan. But the words sounded so ridiculous now that he never finished saying them.

Instead he came out with: "I hate to be alone in weather like this."

Inside, she let the door of the tiny space sigh closed behind her. "You don't have to be alone, Sim. Not all the time, anyway."

Soon the two of them were sitting close together—there was no other way to sit in one of these berth-cabins—with privacy dialed on both the door and the intercom. Only genuine emergency messages ought to be able to get through. Branwen had left her own berth closed up in the same way; supposedly the curious wouldn't know if she were in there or somewhere else aboard.

For the time being, berserkers were forgotten and so was the captain. And so, for Branwen, were her worries about Spence Benkovic.

A little later, Simeon was saying, rather sleepily: "We never did find anything to drink."

Galway murmured something and stretched lazily against the cushions of Simeon's berth. Her standard shipboard coverall had been totally discarded, and his was currently being worn in a decidedly informal configuration. Drink was not really prominent in her thoughts at the moment. She muttered a few words to that effect.

"I know, I don't need one either, but I thought . . ." Then Simeon's words trailed off in astonishment at the expression on his companion's face.

Branwen was gazing past his shoulder. Her eyes were wide, and her lips made a sound, something totally different from any that he had heard her utter yet.

He twisted his head around just in time to see it, too. *Something* had just come into the little cylindrical room where they were lying as if to look at them, and in the second or two that Simeon was frozen, looking at it, it appeared to go out through the solid wall and come back in again. The intruder was not ED, or Carmpan, or berserker; it hardly looked like a solid physical body at all. More like a heatwave in the air, or a curl of smoke, but there was too much purpose in the way it moved.

A moment later the man and the woman were both grabbing for the single hand-weapon that was readily available.

What confronted them appeared to Simeon as a physically tenuous, amorphous thing or being, resembling nothing so much as a photographic negative. Before he could make a guess at what the image in the photograph was supposed to show, the thing drifted out of the room again, right through the tightly closed door.

Simeon, whose hand had happened to close on the handgun first, was pointing the weapon after the apparition, on the verge of babbling. He pointed again, helplessly.

"I saw it, too, I saw it, too!" Branwen was already on the intercom, trying to raise help.

❋   ❋   ❋

Iskander Baza was the next crew member to encounter the intruder. He came across it in one of the small tunnels that served the compact ship as corridors. Without hesitation Baza drew the small hand weapon he liked to carry at all times and fired. The gun was a short-range beam-projector of a type that he considered unlikely to do any serious damage to the essential equipment within the ship. Iskander's shot hit—whatever it was—but the beam appeared to have no effect except to make the apparition withdraw.

By now all the crew members, with the possible exception of the lethargic Carmpan, were alerted to the fact that some kind of emergency was in progress. Everyone not at battle stations was scrambling to get there. But for the moment no one saw anything else strange aboard the *Pearl*.

Space in the proximity of the ship was a different matter. There were suddenly a swarm of spacegoing vehicles nearby; or else they were constructions or congregations of hitherto unknown life forms; or else they were things that no ED human had ever seen or even imagined before. Whatever they were, they were suddenly detectable around the ship in considerable numbers by the people who were on watch.

A fight began, because the people on the *Pearl* considered themselves under attack.

The *Pearl*'s heavy weapons thundered out, striking at flickering, evolving, changing nothingness.

❋ CHAPTER 18

Even in those first few seconds of alarm and scrambling desperation aboard the *Pearl*, it was already obvious that none of the blasting, melting, disintegrating weapons usually employed in space combat were at all effective against these mysterious encroaching shapes.

Domingo had been in his combat chair at the start of the crisis and was still there. Even with all his instrumentation before him, his first indication of trouble was the alarm on the intercom, the voices of his crew announcing the presence of an intruder on the ship. Such was the subtlety of the invader and of its fellows just outside the hull.

Whatever the things were out there, they were very difficult to see, hard to detect on any of the instruments that the captain presently had in use.

A gabble of speech grew steadily on the intercom.

"They're not ships, I tell you—"

"I can see that. They're not berserkers, either."

"Not any kind of berserker I ever heard about."

"Not like any . . . not like any *thing* I've ever seen."

Before they could push each other completely into panic, Domingo roared for silence, then made specific demands on specific people for readings, reports, information. In moments the incipient panic had subsided. The coordinated use of instruments even began to bring in some useful data.

Within a matter of seconds after the first alarm, using a helpful observation or two passed along by other crew members, Domingo had managed to adjust his instruments so as to be able to get a better look at the things, whatever they were, that had his ship surrounded. What he beheld were bizarre entities of varying and almost indeterminate size and shape. There were dozens of them swarming, flitting by his ship at ranges varying from only a few meters out to several score kilometers and at speeds that ought to mean ship or machine and not any kind of self-propelled life form. But somehow, as he studied them, the impression that these were life forms gradually dominated. Seemingly they were able to avoid the centers of the blasts from the *Pearl's* armament while passing unharmed through the outer regions of the explosions, even through zones where steel would have been vaporized. The forms, whatever they were, appeared to be altering themselves from moment to moment, changing their very structure somehow, so beam weapons that would have chewed up a berserker's shields passed through them harmlessly.

It was almost, the captain thought, as if these things surrounding him and his ship could at will become no more than illusions.

The time elapsed since Branwen and Simeon had sounded the first alarm was still less than a full minute.

Domingo shouted to his crew: "Cease fire. We're not doing any good. Cease firing!"

The barrage of pulsing beams and flying projectiles ceased, almost instantly. Inside the ship the difference to the ears was minimal, but the alteration in the inward energies of space briefly left an empty feeling in the bones.

The fusillade had achieved nothing but a waste of energy—which would be easy enough to replace—and of certain types of missiles, which would not. The things outside, whatever they were, did not seem to have been injured in the slightest by being shot at, and certainly they had not been driven away. On the bright side, the six humans in their ship were also unharmed. That in itself was enough to convince Domingo that the entities outside the ship were not berserkers and probably were not enemies at all. If the swarming of the wraithlike things around the ship had been meant as an attack, it had to be considered a failure, though at least one of the things had penetrated the hull itself.

But still, a moment after the captain had called a ceasefire, he came near countermanding the order.

His crew were already shouting new alarms at him; unnecessarily, for he could see for himself what was happening now that the *Pearl*'s guns had quieted. The view outside the ship was changing, becoming vaguely obscured in strips and patches. It was as if translucent nets were being spread around the *Pearl*.

"I think they're trying to tie us up, Chief," Iskander drawled.

To Domingo, the entities outside—units, creatures, beings, whatever they were—appeared to be trying to grapple the *Pearl* with forcefield weapons. So far, very little power was evident in these weapons, which as far as the captain could tell were indistinguishable from extensions of the creatures' own bodies; but they appeared to be able, as before, to penetrate the ship's defensive shields.

Fourth Adventurer's voice came suddenly on intercom. The tones of weariness and illness had vanished from it, but the words were unsteady with unprecedented excitement: "It is not an attempt to tie you up. It is a probing for information. Act, Captain, act. Respond, lest you be taken for something inanimate."

Act? And do what? Suppressing a sharp retort, Domingo instead answered his own question for himself.

On Domingo's orders, crisply and precisely issued, the *Pearl* put out her own forcefield weapons in several strengths and varieties, trying to disengage the grip of the enemy's fields. His crew was trained in the tactics of grappling and ramming with such devices.

Clipping out more orders, Domingo assigned each member of his crew a different section of his ship's hull to defend. They all went to work in intense silence, manipulating the *Pearl*'s defensive fields, trying to find a way of repelling the intrusion. Now and then a few terse words were exchanged; for the most part the intercom was silent.

The shadowy tools of the outsiders were now opposed by a variety of fields generated from the *Pearl*. The result after the first moments of struggle was a tangled snarl that still held the human ship delicately enmeshed. Domingo was confident that even an easy application of his ship's drive would break the *Pearl* free; but for the time being he withheld that stroke. He was coming more and more to the opinion that his crew and the outsiders were not so much locked together in a struggle as engaged in a mutual groping for information.

Confused grappling ensued and was protracted over a period of several minutes. Domingo, reading his ship's instruments from his own station and sifting the fragmentary reports from his crew as best he could, decided there was now at least a strong possibility that the aliens—it was now definite in his own mind that living things opposed him—were also trying to withdraw from the tangle of interlocking forces but found themselves unable to do so, either. Perhaps they too had forces in reserve.

The next report from Fourth Adventurer confirmed definitely that what surrounded the ship were indeed living minds and bodies. "I now have established mental contact with them. It is difficult. Only intermittent communication has been achieved as yet, but it may be the minimum we need."

"They're living, then."

"Indeed they are."

"They must be aggregations, swarms, almost like the ones we sometimes harvest. But—"

"Yes, Captain. They are in many ways like those other nebular life forms, and related to them through evolution. But these around our ship are more than that. Much more." Fourth Adventurer said that much and fell silent.

"Can we communicate with them? On an intelligent level, I mean?"

"I shall try now, and report again."

The *Pearl*, and the entities around her with which she struggled, were not only bound together but isolated, lost, in swirling nebula. There was still no sign of the Space Force fleet.

"There's not as many of them around us as there were," Branwen reported, almost calmly. Some of the mysterious aliens had evidently departed—or dissipated—or died. She thought that their numbers around the *Pearl* had been greater at the start of the confrontation than they were now, though Domingo thought it was still hard to guess whether there were now twenty of them or a hundred.

Whether the entities might simultaneously be conducting a similar struggle with the Space Force somewhere in the nebula nearby was more than anyone on board the *Pearl* was able to determine.

Anyone, at least, but Fourth Adventurer. In response to a question from Domingo, the Carmpan now announced that he thought that any such confrontation between the entities and the Space Force was unlikely; his own presence on the *Pearl* was tending to draw the nebular things here.

"Your presence? Why?"

"They sense my mind, as I sense theirs."

Benkovic's voice, sounding shaken, came over the intercom: "What are they, then? What are they? These things aren't berserkers!"

Domingo spoke almost soothingly. "All right, we already know that much. They seem about as far from being berserkers as they can get. Fourth Adventurer says he's sure they're alive, and I have to agree. But what level of intelligence are they, and what do they want?"

The Carmpan at last was able to announce some success in trying to determine that. He was, he said, still managing to maintain a limited telepathic contact with the aliens. "They are of human intelligence. And at the moment the main thing they want is to know what we are; or more precisely, to understand our ship. They sense the continual close presence of my mind and wish to know why it is so bound in heavy matter."

There was a pause. "You're saying they're—a human theme?"

"Indeed, yes. My hope in joining your crew was to welcome a new theme to the brotherhood of the Taj."

There was silence momentarily on intercom, people looking at one another's imaged faces. *The brotherhood of the what?* Simeon wondered silently.

When no one else said anything, Fourth Adventurer resumed: "I am also endeavoring to explain to them your natures, as the controllers of this ship, but it is difficult. Ships in general are a great mystery to them, as are berserker machines. As, indeed, is telepathy. They communicate among themselves on a purely physical level, as do you and I."

"A new human theme." It was a hushed whisper in Branwen Galway's voice. Others were murmuring, too. Such a discovery had happened perhaps half a dozen times in the whole previous history of Earth-descended exploration.

"Indeed," Fourth Adventurer repeated patiently, "a theme of humanity whose existence has heretofore been completely unknown to humans of your theme, and only guessed at by my fellow Carmpan and myself. The reason is that only very recently have the people of this new theme become a thinking species. They are the reason for my presence here, for my application to become a member of this crew. Another ship might have brought me to them, but only your ship, Captain, was ready and equipped at the right time and place to have a chance of giving them the help they need. More than words and good wishes will be required to clear their pathway to the Taj."

Someone asked: "To the what?"

But the captain, impatient, interrupted before the question could be answered.

Domingo said: "Great, great. Meanwhile we seem to have a problem. Two problems, at least."

"You refer to our physical entanglement with the life forms around us, and to our social relations with them. I believe both problems can be solved."

"Can you tell them that we wish them well? That we are alive, as much as they are, that . . . you know what we want to tell them."

"I believe I do, Captain. On that general level. Allow me a few more moments of silence."

Silence fell on intercom again. Simeon, watching his instruments, observed that the entanglement of forcefields persisted; it seemed almost to have taken on a life of its own by now.

The Carmpan was back on intercom presently. "War is almost an alien concept to them."

"Then, damn it, tell them we're not looking for a fight, either. Not with them."

"They say they thought our ship was an odd type of dead-metal killer."

"If that means what I think it means . . ."

"I am sure that it does."

At least neither side was trying to escalate the struggle. In fact it now seemed that the encounter had been turned away from being a fight at all, though what it had become was still uncertain. The contending fields of force still rested tautly against one another, maintaining a quivering, fluctuating balance, the fields generated within the ship more powerful, those from outside more penetrating and elusive.

The *Pearl* drifted, enfolded in enigmas, her crew waiting intently at their stations.

Benkovic came on a private intercom channel to voice his own suspicion to Domingo.

"Captain? A private word?"

"Go ahead."

"I don't know if we ought to buy any of this, Captain. Except that these things can still come aboard our ship when they feel like it. Looks like we can be sure of that much."

"What're you telling me, Spence? That our Carmpan's lying to me?"

"Nossir, I don't know that. Maybe he wouldn't lie, but he could be wrong. Getting fooled somehow."

"Well. Anything else?"

"Maybe so. Maybe one thing more. I told you I saw something strange in the nebula near Shubra the day Leviathan was there. Other people have seen strange things out in the gas near other colonies, the colonies that have been hit. It could have been the same characters we've got flitting around us now. They could be goodlife, acting as berserker scouts of some kind. I don't know what to tell you to do, except—watch out."

"I assure you, I am watching."

Immediately after Benkovic switched off the intercom, the Carmpan came on another channel with another report.

"My sense of the situation, Captain Domingo, is that some of the nebular creatures are still suspicious of us. This heavy, metallic ship in some ways strongly resembles a berserker machine; and that resemblance suggests to the people we have just encountered that we are really allies of the berserkers."

It was almost, the captain thought, as if Fourth Adventurer had been aware of Benkovic's warning to Domingo, despite the closed intercom channel.

The Carmpan was speaking again. "They are unhappy that this ship is making an effort to trap them with fields, as the dead-metal killers sometimes do."

"Trap them? Only after we got the impression that they were making an effort against us—as you know."

"I have already conveyed that thought, Captain."

"What do you think, Adventurer? Can they be trusted? To a reasonable extent, I mean?"

"It is my belief that they are speaking the truth to me. That I am wrong is very unlikely, though not impossible."

"All right. That's all I can expect. Good. Next question is, can we reach some arrangement with them so we can all get our fields untangled? Tell them we'll pull our horns in if they will."

"I will try to talk with them again, and emphasize that that is our wish."

The ship drifted. Minutes passed.

Then Fourth Adventurer was back, reporting. Communication with the beings outside the ship proceeded slowly, but it seemed now that at least something was being accomplished.

Domingo asked his translator: "What do they call themselves?"

"It is . . . there are no useful words. Refer to them by what name you like, and I will try to manage a translation." Fourth Adventurer paused, then added: "They wish to find out what you know about berserkers."

"We'll be glad to exchange information on that subject. Very glad. Be sure you tell them that."

Iskander now came on intercom to add his caution to Benkovic's. Baza too still halfway suspected the aliens of being either goodlife or some creation of the berserkers. He recalled all the biological experimentation by the enemy that they had discovered.

Domingo listened, admitting the possibility but unconvinced. The captain knew intellectually that goodlife existed, perhaps in every theme of humanity. But he had never encountered it, and it would be hard for him to believe that any living thing in front of him had really chosen an existence as the berserkers' servant.

Iskander Baza had a question for Fourth Adventurer: "You say their species just—came into existence recently? How recent is recent?"

"For all I can tell, as short a period as one of your own lifetimes. It is hard to say."

"No offense, Adventurer, but that sounds incredible. I mean, how can you *think* if your brain is the equivalent of a hard vacuum? In that short time they've developed a—a language? How long are their individual lives?"

"You would not find it so incredible if your own knowledge of the Galaxy was greater."

"Huh." Even Iskander seemed unable to come up with a clever response to that.

"But I admit my estimate of their evolutionary speed may not be accurate. What I can see of their time frame is only their own perception of it. As it exists in their minds. I find it hard to translate from that to your frames of time, or to mine. I guess, and estimate."

Simeon was thinking that the aliens were certainly weird by Earth-descended standards. He supposed that it worked both ways. To us the aliens were mirror-image, photographic-negative, transparent, *nebulous* beings. To them, thought Simeon, we are—what? Voices from a hurtling lump of metal, very doubtfully alive at all?

It was a weird picture, the ship with himself and the others in it, seen from outside that way. He wondered if some of it at least was spillover from the laboring Carmpan mind nearby.

Now that the situation appeared to have quieted down, at least temporarily, Simeon would have liked to duck back to his berth and finish dressing. But there would be no getting away from battle stations just now.

There was another brief flurry of alarm. One or more of the nebular beings had come aboard ship again, uninvited. Domingo saw one of the things directly this time, a gray transparent presence moving between him and the instruments a meter from his face. A moderate heat wave in the air would have been substantial by comparison. But the creature was gone again before he could do more than start to react.

The crew continued to experiment with their field generators. Certain fields slowed or deflected the movements of the aliens, while others appeared to cause them discomfort. And yet other types of field created a barrier that the beings could penetrate only with the greatest difficulty if at all. To enclose the whole ship in that kind of barrier, though, might be beyond the capabilities of the present equipment.

Meanwhile the creatures, basically undeterred, continued to investigate the ship.

"Adventurer, tell them to stop coming aboard. It causes problems for us."

"I will ask them. I suggest that it is not advisable to order them to stop."

"That's fine, if they're amenable to being asked. If not, I'll have to find some way to make it a statement instead of a request."

Whatever method Fourth Adventurer used appeared to be effective. The visitors departed shortly.

The ED component of the *Pearl's* crew began to speculate on what it might mean that these creatures—*Nebulons* was a name for them that seemed to spring up out of nowhere—were in fact a much younger race than the human race of Earth, had much more recently undergone the step of speciation that brought them into intelligence.

Domingo had only a limited interest in the subject. He did not forget that, despite Fourth Adventurer's opinion, there was no certain evidence that the suspicions of Iskander and Spence were wrong; these Nebulons might, for all anyone on board the *Pearl* could tell, be creations of the berserkers, intended somehow to spell doom for ED humanity.

Others were aware of the possibility, too. "How could berserkers create a life form so complex? We can't do that, and we're supposed to know more biology than the damned machines do."

Through the Carmpan, some of the aliens once more put forward their own suspicions that it was the solid, incredibly massive ED people who were allied with the berserkers; in their view, they said, the two types of entity had so much in common, it was hard to believe anything else. But yet the two forms, berserker and human ship, could be distinguished from each other—ED vessels almost always contained life, the dead-metal killers very rarely so.

Another distinguishing factor was the fact that the human ships did not always and routinely kill as they passed through the shoals and drifts of nebular life; some of the aliens took that as evidence that these objects were not necessarily allied with their enemies. Sometimes the ships killed, harvesting or sampling. But the intelligent nebular-theme humans also killed, ingesting concentrations of energy, patterns, complexity from the lower forms, often the same types that the ships and colonies also harvested.

By now the minutes since the first encounter with the aliens had lengthened into an hour. It felt to Simeon like the longest hour he had ever lived through, except perhaps the hour of the fight in which Wilma had been killed.

By now it had become plain, through steady observation of the aliens, that these nebular-theme humans possessed a faster means of travel through the nebula than either ED humans or berserker machines had ever been able to attain.

Fourth Adventurer, on this point, offered the observation that the nebular-theme creatures were able to detect the thin-vacuum or hard-vacuum interstices in nebular turbulence. The obvious point was commented on: the same ability, or some variation of it, allowed them to get into a spaceship's hull without opening a hatch or making a noticeable hole.

Through the Carmpan, the creatures acknowledged that they could use this ability to get at berserkers, too, if the berserkers could be taken unawares and were moving slowly. But the enemy was aware of the Nebulons' existence now, and such attacks were no longer a practical possibility.

"Cap, if they can knock out a berserker somehow, they can knock out this ship."

Domingo remained calm. "I see that, Ike. Go on, Fourth Adventurer."

The dead-metal killers, after losing a unit or two and coming close to losing others, had not only developed effective repelling countermeasures and barrier fields but killing fields as well. But those worked only at short ranges, and the berserkers still had trouble hunting and killing the nebular people.

"They admit to us that a killing field exists. Seems a little naive."

Benkovic snorted. "Maybe it's meant to seem that way."

The discovery of another intelligent species, another theme of Galactic humanity; it had to be one of the rarest events in history. Everyone aboard the ship was shaken by it, even in the midst of other problems. Almost everyone. Domingo had taken it in stride. He did not even appear to find it particularly interesting, except as it might affect his chances of hunting down Leviathan. Not until now had Simeon fully appreciated the intensity of the captain's monomania.

The captain demanded to know more from the nebular creatures, all that any of them knew about berserkers. And he was even more interested in the apparent fact that these people might be able to help him find Leviathan.

"Ask them if they know one of the dead-metal killers in particular. Ask them if they know Old Blue."

The Fourth Adventurer somehow determined that they did.

They had a special name for Old Blue too, which Fourth Adventurer translated as best he could into the language he shared with the ED humans: Dead-Metal-That-Bears-The-Radiance-Of-Death.

☀ **CHAPTER 19**

Fourth Adventurer said: "There is one among our guides whose mind is more clearly open to me than the others. It is with that one I hold most of my communication."

The captain grunted. It was a satisfied sort of sound. "I thought that might be the case. What do you call this one? Or what name should we use, for him, or her?"

"I can tell you nothing meaningful about the names of Nebulons. But I find a definite suggestion of femininity in that person's mind."

Simeon, listening in, wondered how a Carmpan would judge that quality in a human of a theme never before encountered.

Domingo asked: "This one is some sort of leader among them, then?"

Fourth Adventurer answered thoughtfully. "Though I am sure there are leaders among them, I am not sure that she is one of them."

The captain nodded. It would not have made much sense—or at least Domingo thought it would not—to apply such terms as *leader* or *follower* to Fourth Adventurer, either. From the centuries of knowing—or rather failing to know—the Carmpan, the more thoughtful among Earth-descended folk had learned not to project their own psychology onto other themes.

Fourth Adventurer continued: "Let us agree to call their spokesperson *Speaker*, at least among ourselves. If she is not really a leader, even loosely speaking, she is in close touch with those who are."

"Do you suppose," Simeon asked after a brief silence, "they might be starting to make up names for us, too?"

"Probably none we'd want to hear," said Branwen. No one else aboard ship was ready to offer an opinion.

The Carmpan might have refrained from answering because his mind was busy on another channel. He said to Domingo: "I have asked more questions of those who surround us on the subject of Leviathan. Unfortunately they seem to have no knowledge that will be immediately helpful to us in our search."

Domingo softly profaned the gods of little rocks in space and those of distant galaxies.

"But wait . . . they now have more to tell me. Ah. You will be more pleased by this, Captain."

With that, Fourth Adventurer fell silent. After he had remained quiet for some time, evidently in mental communion with the ethereal beings around the ship, he announced that he had an offer to relay to Domingo.

There was something, evidently another berserker project of some kind, that was bothering the Nebulons particularly. If Domingo and the beings with him inside the weighty metal could help the Nebulons eliminate this extremely objectionable thing, whatever it was, Speaker and those with her would be eternally grateful. "At least," Fourth Adventurer concluded, "I believe that to be the sense of what they are endeavoring to communicate."

"Another *project*, did you say? Does that mean a fighting machine? A base?"

"The thought as it comes to me from them is vague, Captain. They do not understand what this project is, except that it is harmful to them."

"But where is this thing? What is it like? Can't you be a little more explicit?"

"I regret that I cannot. It is in just the form of such a vague concept that the message comes to me."

Still the captain was quick to make up his mind. "Very well. We will help them if we can. Tell them I accept—provisionally. Can you tell them that?"

"We shall see."

"If it is something I can help them with, I'll do so. Provided they then do what they can to help me do what I want. I need allies, Adventurer. I need, I want, all the help that I can get. You don't necessarily have to tell them all of that."

"I believe I understand your position, Captain. Let me try to convey it."

The translator was silent for a while, and then announced: "They confer among themselves now, Captain. I think they will be ready soon to lead us on. To this 'berserker project,' whatever it may be."

"And how far away from here is this—never mind. I know, you can't tell."

"That is correct."

Spence Benkovic spoke up suddenly. "Maybe we ought to confer among ourselves too, while we have the chance. Before we just follow them somewhere."

"Confer about what?" Domingo asked him sharply.

"I know I signed on to go hunting, Captain. Okay, I'll go. But something new and very important has come up since then. I mean just finding these—these people, or whatever they are. That's changed things. We're playing a whole new game. We can't just ignore that, and go on about our business as if it hadn't happened."

"The business of this voyage is what I say it is, Benkovic. But let me hear what you suggest."

"I suggest that we have to do something right away to tell the Space Force, tell people in general. Great gods and little berserkers, we're not talking like just finding another planetoid here. This has—has *meaning*. I mean, a whole unknown theme of humanity, native to the space within the nebula."

Domingo was not impressed by that argument. "Just how do you propose to reveal the wonderful news? There's no way of knowing where Gennadius and his fleet are now. We'd have to go all the way back to Four Twenty-five. And I've just undertaken to help these people, not run out on them."

Benkovic muttered something but was unable to come up with an effective answer.

Simeon thought suddenly: Spence wants out of this trip now. He wants the ship to go immediately to a world somewhere where he can get off, even if it means breaking a contract and having to give back money. Why now, all of a sudden? Why, Benkovic could take anything, except that there was only one good-looking woman on board and she went for someone else, if it was only for a day or for an hour.

Domingo meanwhile was proceeding with his argument: "If the prospects for finding Gennadius aren't good, then what chance have we of finding our way back here, once we leave, and linking up again with these people we've discovered? How big a range of territory do they occupy, Fourth Adventurer?"

"I have no means of knowing that as yet." The Carmpan shook his head, an ED gesture he had adopted, consciously or unconsciously, from the start of the voyage.

"We've been led here," said the captain. Simeon wasn't sure if the older man was referring to the Carmpan's advice, or just what. "I'm not about to simply walk away at this point."

"We could drop a courier," Branwen suggested. The *Pearl* had begun this hunt with two robot message couriers tucked away in storage.

The captain appeared to consider that suggestion carefully. "I don't think so. We might well need both of our couriers later." Domingo sounded as if he were still reluctant to bring the Space Force in on his hunt at all.

"Our guides announce that they are now ready to lead us, Captain," came the voice of Fourth Adventurer. "To show us the project of dead metal. That phrase is as close as I can translate what they are thinking. But their readiness, and even their impatience, are manifest to me."

Iskander asked suddenly: "How about their trustworthiness?"

"As I said before, I do not think that they are lying to me. To judge beyond that would involve an estimate of what their thoughts will be in a future situation. I regret I cannot do it. Their minds are too new to me, too alien. Their reliability, as you would perceive it, I cannot judge."

"Ah," said Baza. "Maybe they're more like us than I thought."

"They can't be a whole lot more impatient than I am," Domingo said. "I want to find out about this berserker project. Tell them to lead on."

"I shall."

For a few seconds nothing happened, or at least no change occurred that was perceptible to the ED crew. Then suddenly the space immediately around the ship was clear in every direction of the mysterious forms. The beings who had been swarming in the close vicinity of the *Pearl* had moved away.

"But where?" the captain muttered, pressing his headlink to his forehead, conjuring up new electronic visions with his instruments to augment those already on the stages and screens before him. "Ah. There they go."

Domingo took thought purposefully, easing the *Pearl* forward. A voyage through the nebula under the guidance of the nebular-theme humans had begun.

Three of the *Pearl*'s crew were posted on a regular watch, three others officially relieved. Simeon had a chance to get back to his berth and finish dressing.

In another hour the voyage had settled into a routine. The routine was to persist for several days with little change.

Gradually, with the storm out of the way, the people on the *Pearl* were able to work out at least a tentative idea of their general position inside the Milkpail. The guides remained always in sight, and always clustered now in one direction. From that position they kept darting ahead, as if reluctant to believe that the heavy ship really could not keep up with them and wanting to urge it on to greater efforts.

The Nebulons doubtless observed, as did the humans inside the ship, the pinging of nebular molecules and larger particles against the leading shields that plowed an open pathway for the advancing hull. The Carmpan proclaimed his inability to tell what the Spacedwellers made of the sight.

Apparently the Nebulons, or Spacedwellers—that was another name that had popped up as if out of nowhere and had quickly been adopted among the *Pearl's* crew as an alternate title for their guides—employed a means of propulsion similar to that of advanced spacedrives. Branwen and Simeon theorized that this necessarily involved tapping into the fabric of spacetime itself, riding a flow of natural forces rather than burning fuel. But given the Spacedwellers' lack of hardware, they must be managing their tinkering on a microbiological scale.

Despite Fourth Adventurer's repeated testimony regarding their chronic impatience, the guides paused at fairly frequent intervals. During these breaks they could be observed among shoals of the common microlife, evidently feeding; Fourth Adventurer gave his opinion that they were probably resting as well.

"Speaker asks me how, if my companions and myself are really living things here inside this metal shell, we can remain here without ever coming out to eat. I have explained as best I can that our usual food is as heavy and solid as we are. But I am not at all sure that she believes me."

Aboard the *Pearl*, other members of the crew, Galway and Baza in particular, speculated on the course of evolution that might have produced such creatures as the ones flitting around them.

Benkovic also began a round of speculation among the ED crew about the reproductive systems of their guides. There seemed to be more of the creatures now, in the group leading the ship, than there had been only a little while ago. Of course the most likely explanation, in ED terms, would be simply that more of the beings had joined the group as the journey progressed; but none had been observed to actually approach the group or enter it.

The routine of the journey had persisted for several days before Fourth Adventurer announced that he thought their trip would shortly be coming to an end. He said the thoughts of several of the guides gave him the strong impression that a destination was near at hand.

Branwen, piloting now, called in: "We're approaching a system, Captain. I don't think it's on the charts."

Rousing himself from dreams of Isabel to bitter wakefulness, Domingo looked at his detectors and presently saw that there was a white sun ahead. Evidently the star was only a small one, bordering on the white-dwarf classification.

"I'll bet right now," said Iskander, "that it's not on the charts."

The surmise proved accurate; the spectrum of the modest sun ahead could not immediately be identified with that of any known to exist within the nebula. But it was no real surprise to anyone; the Milkpail contained more than one star that had never made it to the charts.

❂   ❂   ❂

The nuclear fire of the star ahead grew clearer and clearer through thinning mists of matter. At the same time the pace of the journey slowed down until the *Pearl*'s guides and the ship herself had almost stopped.

The star ahead was not part of a binary or more complex system. Still it had no lack of dependent family. The *Pearl* was drifting on the edge of a spherical domain a billion kilometers across in which the small white star was dominant and from which the star's radiation pressure had cleared out most of the tenuous nebular material. This in itself was no surprise. About half of all the Milkpail stars, though generally not the ones with colonized planetoids, were surrounded by similar cleared spheres of space.

But this star had in orbit around it more bodies of measurable size than did most suns in the nebula. Within that gigantic rough sphere of cleared space at least two belts of minor planetoids were rotating, most likely representing the debris of more than one shattered planet. Those protoworlds must have been sizable, much larger than the usual colonized planetoid, when they were whole. And one small belt of this sun's present crop of planetoids was in retrograde motion, prompting speculation among the ED crew that two counter-revolving planets might once have existed here and then collided. Comparatively minor collisions would necessarily be frequent in the system as they observed it now. It could hardly be very durable, on the scale of astronomical time, but then no solar system within the Milkpail was long-lived in terms of stellar chronology.

The Nebulons still had not completely halted their advance. They continued to creep on, moving ahead of the ship toward the sun but ever more slowly. To Simeon the slackening pace of their forward progress irresistibly suggested increasing caution.

The small swarm of Spacedwellers and the ED ship following them were now almost at the very edge of the cleared space.

The Carmpan, confirming Simeon's instinctive thought, now reported hesitancy and a measure of disagreement in their guides' ranks.

"Ask them to stop, Adventurer," Domingo ordered. "I think we need a conference with them before we go on any farther."

The message was passed along somehow. The slowly advancing swarm halted, and presently the drifting ship caught up with it.

Through the Carmpan's mediation, the Nebulons communicated that the berserker project was here in this system, on one of the larger orbiting rocks. It was a planetoid well within the cleared space, away from the larger belts and fairly close to the sun. On that small orbiting body, the dead-metal-killers had established *something*. If the ED people wanted to know what that something was in terms they could understand, it appeared that they would have to go and see for themselves. Extreme danger lurked there, at least for Spacedwellers.

"If it's permanently built into a rock, it must be some kind of a bloody base." Domingo's voice fairly quivered with excitement. Branwen could almost hear him thinking that he might now have Leviathan's secret repair and maintenance base within his grasp.

The ED humans aboard the *Pearl*, having been told through translation the precise location of the berserker base, now did their best to observe it from this relatively distant vantage point. They had no immediate success, but Domingo decided to spend a few hours in surveying the whole system as thoroughly as possible from this position.

The initial lack of success in spotting a base did not necessarily mean that their guides were lying or mistaken about the location of the berserker project. Any base in the system was probably camouflaged to some extent, and almost certainly dug into rock. Traffic in and out ought to be observable, but it might be infrequent. Certainly no machines or recent trails were now observable from where the *Pearl* now drifted almost passively, electronic senses busy.

Domingo at the controls eased his ship gradually and steadily closer to the sun and closer to the inner orbit of the planetoid on which the base presumably lay hidden. The captain was working to keep the *Pearl* concealed as well as possible behind an intrusive wisp of electrically active particles, a tendril of nebular material that here wound its way into the sphere of space otherwise swept mostly clear by the radiation pressure of the small white sun.

The vast swirl of particles offered the ship some concealment, but it also made it difficult for the people aboard to see much of anything. After intensive and repeated efforts, instruments did confirm the apparent presence on one of the inner planetoids of some kind of base. And here and there along the perimeter of the cleared sphere, among the outer belts of planetoids, the relic trails of ships—or more likely of machines—oozed faint radio whispers.

Iskander had a suggestion. "Let's take out the launch. It's a lot smaller, and we ought to be able to get closer to the sun in it without really showing ourselves."

The Nebulons, Fourth Adventurer reported, were duly surprised when the doors of the ship's ventral bay opened, and the launch appeared.

Domingo decided to drive the launch himself, and he chose Branwen and Simeon to come with him.

The launch, with the captain at the controls, moved through thin concealment yet closer to the sun and got in among the outer orbital belts of the system, formations containing dust and fragments large enough to resist radiation pressure. In a belt with a density of one rock larger than one gram's mass per hundred cubic kilometers, the little craft drifted for an hour, with everyone aboard busy making observations. From this vantage point it was possible to get a somewhat better look at the planetoid where the berserker facility supposedly had been established.

Now observation confirmed the Nebulons' claims more definitely. There was a base of some kind there, all right.

It did not appear to be a large facility or suitable for the construction or repair of large fighting machines. Certainly it was not swarming with mobile spacegoing units of any kind. There was no certain connection between this facility and Old Blue. But on the other hand, such a connection might exist, and it was impossible to say that Leviathan never came here.

After their hour spent in data gathering, the people aboard the launch decided that they had seen enough. They eased their little craft out of its long orbit around the sun and back to where it was possible to signal the larger ship with little fear of detection. This effort, conducted cautiously, consumed another hour.

The people aboard the *Pearl* maneuvered her a little closer, and the ship picked up the launch.

At a meeting to analyze the images that had been obtained, some people thought that a certain structural similarity was indicated between this lab and the previously visited wreck. When the *Pearl's* larger telescopes were focused now, they provided some confirming evidence for this idea.

The most obvious difference between this facility and the wreck was that this one showed no signs at all of combat damage. At this distance no weapons could be observed, but there was no doubt that the base would, at a minimum, have something with which to defend itself.

Why had the enemy chosen to establish a base here? It was certainly an out-of-the-way place, unlikely to be discovered by ED humanity. And someone aboard ship propounded a hard-to-follow theory that it might confer some advantage to a researcher in biology to operate in this kind of space, cleared by radiation pressure.

The debate was abruptly interrupted by a minor alarm. Instruments had just picked up a small burst of activity at or very near the biolab—if that was indeed its function—suggesting that the facility there might just have launched a missile, or alternatively sent out a robot courier of its own. Whatever it was had not been aimed at the *Pearl*. The base might well have decided to get off a message to its mechanical allies, wherever they were, reporting that it seemed to have been discovered by the human enemy and now faced a probable attack.

The Nebulons, through the Carmpan, confirmed that something of the kind had happened: a small dead-metal unit had just departed the planetoid at high speed.

The courier, if such it had been, had already left the system, evidently having tunneled off into the nebula on the far side of the cleared volume.

There appeared to be no time to waste. Domingo, with the help of Fourth Adventurer, made plans with the Nebulons as best he could. Then the captain hurriedly briefed his crew and prepared to take the *Pearl* in to the assault. The idea was to pacify the lab, to render it inactive if possible, without destroying it completely.

☀ CHAPTER 20

Domingo was nothing if not decisive, and the time he spent in planning the attack was held to an absolute minimum. Simeon reflected that this had the advantage of not allowing anyone much time in which to become frightened; but in Simeon's case that did not help. He had already discovered that he could be terrified in no time at all.

The captain was trying his best to synchronize his ship's coming effort with one to be made by the Nebulons, and after the hasty plan was made, he had to wait for a signal from his translator. When word arrived through Fourth Adventurer that the Spacedwellers were moving to the attack, the *Pearl*, everyone aboard at battle stations with mental fingers on mental triggers, came hurtling out of what its crew hoped had been concealment toward the enemy installation.

The Spacedwellers were now about to fling their insubstantial bodies against whatever field barriers the berserker would be able to put up. Whatever fears the Nebulons had of approaching the berserker installation, they had managed to put aside in the hope of achieving a victory.

Defensive fire from the base opened up almost at once when the *Pearl* broke cover, long before light could have borne the image of the moving ship in across the hundreds of millions of kilometers intervening between her and the base. The enemy had to be aiming and launching on subspace clues.

At least the barrage was not as heavy as might have been expected from a berserker base. The shields of the ship held up, though the hull rang with sound induced by the drumming of plasma wavefronts upon its outer surface, and the crew had something of the experience of being in an echoing metal room or barrel pounded on the outside by titanic hammers. Simeon had never before been under fire of anything like this intensity. He gritted his teeth and held on and did his job.

When the captain had the range he wanted, he calmly gave the order to return fire. Missiles were launched first, that their arrival on target might be simultaneous with the energies of the swifter destructive beams.

The first look at the results came long seconds later, when lagging light brought back to the ship the images of impact. The heavy fire from the ship had not immediately broken through the berserker station's defensive fields. But it had succeeded in disrupting those barriers, so they were no longer able to hold the onrushing Nebulons at bay.

The Carmpan relayed the Spacedwellers' telepathic shout of triumph.

The insubstantial swarm of Nebulons still could not be seen from the *Pearl*. But Fourth Adventurer reported them surging in through solid rock and metal, entering the facility. Once inside, as Fourth Adventurer reported, the Spacedwellers moved at once to disable the main destructor charges, whose probable locations Domingo had been able to guess successfully.

As the ship continued to close rapidly with its opponent, the Carmpan had another bit of news for his shipmates, this one unexpected.

"Captain, I am informed only now by Speaker that one of our allies' people has been held a prisoner at this base for some lengthy though indeterminate time. Naturally enough, to rescue this prisoner is one of our guides' chief objectives in making this attack."

"Naturally. And they didn't bother to tell us . . ." Domingo, intent on the tactical decisions he was going to have to make within another minute or two, sounded beyond surprise. "How the hell can even a berserker hold one of those things a prisoner? I'd like to know the trick."

"It is a matter of creating special forcefields. No doubt you will be able to discover how to generate such fields, if you survive this fight."

Simeon, holding his breath, thought that the chance of his personal survival was looking up. The berserker base, trying to fight off a Nebulon invasion, could not simultaneously cope very well with the superior firepower of the ship.

Domingo chose weapons, issued firing orders and observed results.

The berserker installation still fought back, but ever more feebly. After another exchange or two against Domingo's missiles and beam weapons, the enemy defenses were obviously crumbling, and the *Pearl* moved in closer still.

There were a few seconds of relative calm in which Fourth Adventurer issued a further report on Nebulon affairs. The prisoner had just been freed, but while in captivity had been the subject of horrible experiments, and the Carmpan had the impression that she or he might now be close to death, madness or both.

Soon after that the Carmpan was able to report that the main destructor charges on the installation had been effectively disabled.

Now the *Pearl* moved even closer to the enemy.

Presently the berserker's last defensive shields had been wiped out of space. Two more hits by beam-projector pulses on weapon clusters along its perimeter and the last of its return fire stuttered to a halt. At the moment the weapons of Domingo's ship looked powerfully impressive.

Domingo called a cease-fire. A few moments later, with his ship gradually approaching the ruin below, the captain announced that he planned to board the enemy to look for information, clues to the location of Leviathan. He asked for one or two volunteers to accompany him.

No immediate answer came, at least not audibly. Simeon found himself having to repress hysterical laughter.

Iskander and Branwen finally volunteered to come along. There was something so utterly new and mad about this enterprise that the woman felt herself unable to resist it; and if she were going to learn any secrets about Domingo, this seemed like the most likely way to go about it.

Domingo decided that now, facing a defeated enemy, was a good time to practice fast-boarding techniques.

The *Pearl* rushed closer to the target planetoid, pulling back only at the last moment from a final ramming impact against the rock and metal of the enemy.

The launch, carrying the three boarders, came flying out of the ventral bay almost like a stone from a sling. The idea was to minimize the time of the little ship's exposure in space to enemy fire. But this turned out to be a practice run; nothing struck at the launch. It appeared that this particular enemy had nothing left with which to strike.

The three invaders left the launch. The little craft, running on autopilot, hovered near the planetoid's surface. Lugging heavy weapons and explosives, the three quickly got themselves down to the surface, which was still glowing with the heat of their own bombardment.

Protected by their armor, they quickly approached and crossed the broken outer ramparts of the enemy installation. Moving in, they blasted open doors and burned great holes through bulkheads. They were determined to leave themselves a clear and unblockable line of retreat as they forced their way in to the mysteries below.

The berserker had been unable to destroy itself or its central computing units or even to kill its prisoner, but some of the commensal machines of the base were still active. The small maintenance machines, lacking in weapons, speed and tactics, tried to carry out harassing attacks but were blasted out of the way with relative ease.

The insubstantial bodies of the Nebulon attacking party, presumably including the rescued prisoner, came fluttering and wavering around the boarding party, then passed on, up and out to freedom.

"Good-bye, perhaps forever," Iskander muttered, waving an arm toward the Nebulons, struggling to be funny. But the attitude no longer seemed to come naturally to him. He was giving a feeble imitation of his usual self.

This station was not as big, or the underground portion of it as elaborate, as the boarders had somehow been expecting. There were no large docks in sight. Certainly this could never have served as a major repair or construction base even for small fighting machines, let alone the huge killers of Leviathan's class.

What appeared to be biological research gear, much of it intact or almost so, came into the boarders' view as soon as they had penetrated underground. And here, as on the enemy unit they had previously boarded, the invading humans discovered a collection of complex field generators. These devices no doubt had served to create the prison walls and bars within which the Nebulon had been confined for study and experimentation.

Finally, a small chamber containing what had to be the central brain of the base was uncovered. "Some interesting-looking data banks here, Cap." After that effort Iskander ceased to probe or even to talk. It was as if he had run out of energy.

For this expedition Domingo had equipped himself with hand-held gear that was supposed to be able to read most berserker data storage systems. A good portion of his wealth had gone to buy it. He clamped cables onto the memory units he could reach and connected the device to his headlink. He stood taking readings with intense concentration while his two crew members stood guard beside him.

"This unit . . ." the captain said finally and paused. A few moments later he spoke again. "What's been going on at this facility . . . the machines here have been trying to determine what would be the most effective, the most deadly anti-ED human life form that could possibly be created."

The others waited, listening.

Domingo said: "The suggestion seems to be that this life form would be an ED human itself."

Back aboard the *Pearl*, Simeon was saying: "Get them on the radio."

"Right. The message?" Spence Benkovic sounded weary to the verge of collapse.

"If you have to send it in the clear to get through, do it. Tell them our deep detectors have picked up a shape at a range of two hundred million kilometers. Like a jagged birdcage with a skull in it. There's even a hint of blue flames. Leviathan is here."

⚙ CHAPTER 21

When the message from the *Pearl* came in, Branwen moved as fast as she could. But from the first step, Domingo was already ahead of her in the mad scramble to regain the launch, and Iskander was right at her side.

As she passed the memory units that Domingo had begun to disassemble, she hastily grabbed up some of the components he had been testing. Domingo, who a moment ago had been fascinated by the same bits of hardware, had dropped them instantly the moment word came that Old Blue was now actually on the scene, within his reach.

Iskander too ignored everything else when he heard that. Branwen caught a brief glimpse of Baza's face inside his helmet and was struck by the strange look he was wearing, wooden and almost lifeless.

Half a dozen of the small memory units were under Branwen's left arm as she leaped and ran, shoving pieces of berserker aside, following the captain.

The captain did not turn back or even look behind him to see if his two crew members were still with him. It occurred to Branwen that Domingo was actually ready to leave them here if they could not keep up with him in his rush to get back to his ship and come to grips with his archenemy.

The three humans, moving with practiced speed in low gravity, went bounding and plunging back through the passageway they had blasted open.

They were within meters of regaining the surface when a slab of rock the size of a spaceship came slowly toppling toward them—perhaps the battered berserker brain that ran the base had been able to organize one last attempt upon their lives. But in the low gravity the humans easily avoided the falling mass. Metal and rock jumped and shuddered beneath their feet as it came down.

Moments later all three were in the clear. Branwen, burdened with her collection of possibly priceless hardware, had trouble keeping up with the two men now, although she considered herself as skillful as anyone at getting around in space armor. Iskander, having raced ahead of her, turned back once, wordlessly, to see that she was not falling hopelessly behind. Domingo did not turn back at all.

The three of them were running and bounding now across the planetoid's surface, still radiant with heat. The eerie landscape of the rocky mass surrounded them, marked with long shadows and the stark white light of the small but nearby sun. The sky beyond the sun was mottled white with distant clouds of nebula and devoid of any other stars.

Now one artificial star had come into being overhead and was brightening quickly. The autopilot had been randomly maneuvering the launch, and now in response to Domingo's radio command it was bringing the little vessel quickly down to the boarding party.

There was another movement nearby, this one of almost invisible entities skimming across the planetoid's airless rocky surface. Branwen had expected that the former prisoner and the original Nebulon rescue party would be long gone by now. But two shimmering shapes, coming almost within reach of the three running, suited humans, appeared as evidence that their new allies had not entirely abandoned the field. She wondered if one of the formless flickerings might be Speaker. Without the Carmpan on hand, there was no way to tell.

The Spacedwellers moved near the three who ran, as if to keep their heavy partners company. The almost immaterial presences, fading in and out of visibility, were reassuring even though the creatures were unable to communicate more directly.

The launch was down now, the autopilot opening a hatch as it skimmed the planetoid's surface just ahead of the three who ran across it. As the ED humans hurled themselves into the vessel, Branwen muttered a private vow that she would seek, as soon as possible, another means of communicating with the Spacedwellers; it was not good to be totally dependent on the Carmpan for all messages, and it was all too easy to foresee times when such dependence might be downright fatal.

Once the boarders were sealed into the launch, good radio contact with the *Pearl* was once more available. Now they could hear

Benkovic, back on the ship, still wondering aloud if the Nebulons were somehow responsible for the arrival of Leviathan.

"If I believed that," Domingo announced, "I'd see they got a reward. I hope you're moving the ship our way?"

"Yes, sir. About twenty seconds to pickup."

Meanwhile Domingo, his headlink firmly on, was driving the launch as fast as possible to rejoin the *Pearl*.

Branwen, after clamping herself into a combat chair and hooking up her headlink, was trying to catch a glimpse of the famous blue glow through the cleared viewports of the launch. But Leviathan was still too far away to be directly visible in whole or part.

Fortunately for Domingo and those with him, the *Pearl* had already been maneuvered in quite close to the planetoid. And with Benkovic at the helm she now came speeding in even closer to pick up the launch carrying the boarders.

Leviathan was already opening up with ranging fire, probing at the *Pearl*'s defensive shields. Before the pickup could be made, the launch rocked as it was struck by the wavefront of a weapons blast, a surge of particles and electromagnetic waves. In comparison to this, the just-conquered base had been firing popguns. The intensity was such that Branwen could feel the impact of the near miss in her bones, even in her combat chair and in the absence of atmosphere to help transmit a shock.

The Carmpan was murmuring something hopeful on the radio, in the intervals between the brisk comments of the two pilots of the swiftly approaching vehicles. Just at the awkward moment of retrieval of the launch, as Branwen understood Fourth Adventurer's commentary, the Nebulons would be busy creating a valuable distraction. They feinted an attack on Leviathan, which provided enough of a diversion to enable the ED humans to get back aboard their ship.

Branwen was the first out of the launch into the ship's ventral bay, and from there went scrambling immediately toward her battle station. There seemed to be no good place to put down the memory units she had brought along, and so she kept them with her.

Domingo arrived at his own combat station just in time to take over the helm from Spence before the real in-earnest action started.

As the captain made the headlink connection to his helmet, the ship was already in swift motion, and the space around her flamed with combat. Leviathan's weapons were very much heavier than those the berserker station had used to defend itself, and, according to all early indications, they were also better aimed and synchronized.

Now the whole ED human component of the crew were crouching at their stations, doing their best to draw upon the energies of space-time, channeling power approaching that of suns. Mindlink networking shared out pictures of the interlocking systems in operation among the human minds; operating this ship meant, among other things, playing an intricate game as a member of a skilled team.

The Carmpan reported that the Nebulons were now ready to make another effort at attacking. Word had spread somehow among their people of the new allies who rode within a heavy metal casing and effectively fought the dead-metal killers; reinforcements were pouring in to the swarm of Spacedwellers, and Speaker reported new hope among them of being able to overcome what they considered their ancient enemy.

"And mine, too. Mine first of all. But I'll take all the help that I can get."

The *Pearl* withstood the enemy's first ranging fire and the jolts of even heavier weapons that followed almost immediately. But Branwen had the gut feeling that the defenses were not holding with any great margin of safety; she could tell because just now sustaining them was her assignment. She heard and saw and felt the weapons of the human ship strike back, without as yet doing any observable damage.

The *Pearl* had now become a swiftly moving, evasive target. Domingo was maneuvering his ship away from the sun but not yet directly toward his enemy. For a period of minutes he took the *Pearl* dancing in and out of the maze of planetoids and dust rings. Clever enemy missiles pursued her on her twisting course, and she dodged them, but her object was not to get away. The captain was stalking Old Blue now, even as the great berserker was stalking him.

Again, on the captain's order, the *Pearl* struck back. This time with full power.

When the haze of ionization spread around Old Blue by the latest bombardment had partially cleared, it could be seen that the enemy too remained essentially undamaged. Against this tough opponent, the new missiles, the new beams, were not performing as well as had been hoped and expected.

It was at moments like this that Branwen Galway felt most intensely alive; they were what kept her coming back into space.

But now there ensued a brief lull in the actual fighting. Evasive action continued. Briefly the instruments on the humans' ship lost track of Leviathan.

Had the enemy fled the system? No, now the bizarre birdcage shape, licked with blue fire, was back again. Domingo made a sound of relief and satisfaction. Once more the humans' computers worked to lock Old Blue in their sights.

"It's playing 'possum," Simeon said. "Wants us to come after it. It's afraid we'll get away otherwise. If it just chases us we might be too small and fast for it to catch."

"It's not afraid of anything," said Benkovic.

Neither was the captain, evidently. Domingo was sliding toward his enemy again, having got the angle of approach he wanted, one that would allow him to maneuver his ship in and out of relative concealment.

The dead shape of a battered planetoid now loomed up close to the *Pearl*, coming between the combatants and cutting off their direct view of each other. Which way to dodge around the obstacle?

Just when everyone aboard Domingo's ship was most intent on which way the captain would turn next, distraction came. Another shape was showing on the remote detectors, that of a machine or ship coming through the clouds at the edge of the cleared space, almost behind the *Pearl* as she faced her known enemy. Did it mean berserker reinforcements?

That possibility hadn't really occurred to Branwen until now. She knew that Leviathan, due to some trick of programming or randomly selected tactics, generally fought alone as a solitary rogue rather than attacking in concert with other death machines.

The range was too great for the IFF transponder to be useful, but a closer look at the ominous new shape proved it to be that of a Space Force ship.

The captain muttered grimly: "Gennadius. For once he's on hand when I can use him. With his whole fleet, I hope."

Eagerly the *Pearl*'s instruments probed the nebula in the area surrounding the new arrival. But there was no fleet to be seen there, only the one ship. A steadier look confirmed that it was indeed Gennadius's cruiser.

Where was Leviathan now? Still out of line-of-sight . . .

Gennadius had good detectors too, and was already trying to establish tightbeam communications. Some of the beam from the Space Force cruiser managed to get through this space still ringing with weaponry.

In an encoded message the commander promised aid to the embattled *Pearl*. Gennadius assured her captain and crew that he too was skilled at trailing and tracking. He had had no success in reassembling his scattered fleet or even in making contact with any of its other components. Instead, after the storm had passed, Gennadius had followed the one trail that he had been able to find, and that trail had led him here to the *Sirian Pearl*. And to the enemy.

Simeon found himself breathing more easily. Now, with two first-class fighting ships and three themes of humanity working together, Leviathan's enemies appeared to have a good chance of winning in this particular fight. He could sense how morale aboard the *Pearl*, which had been numbed and wavering, went up slightly.

After another half-garbled three-way conference call, including Speaker, straining electronic communications to the limit and calling upon the Carmpan's mental ability, the two ships closed on the foe from opposite sides as the Nebulons simultaneously began an infiltration of the defensive fields of Old Blue.

"Here we go." Captain Domingo said it unnecessarily.

Simeon, before focusing the total abilities of his mind on tactics and fire control, took a last look at the intercom image of Branwen. If he had been expecting to get a look from her in return, he was disappointed. She was already concentrating utterly on her instruments.

Old Blue maneuvered as if it were trying to shake free of the double attack but failed to do so. Fighting ships screamed toward the death machine from two sides. But did they have it trapped, or did it have them? The *Pearl's* shields were taking hits at a rate that made Simeon wonder if the enemy might have received reinforcement, too. But evidently not. Leviathan must have been keeping some of its heavy weaponry in reserve through the first exchanges of blows, probably trying to get its smaller opponent to come closer or to put too much reliance on its shields.

The *Pearl* shuddered, diving into an inferno, being blasted helplessly away from her intended course. The sound and vibration inside the hull were overwhelming. How much of this could any shields withstand? Or any human crew? The great damned berserker was stronger than Domingo had predicted or expected; it was stronger than both human ships together. It seemed plain now that if the *Pearl* had been alone when it faced the full charge of Leviathan, the human ship would have been lost.

But Domingo's crew still functioned, and his ship hit back, hard.

The Space Force ship was somewhere—yes, there—still surviving, still fighting.

The battle raged.

Branwen Galway's job now, through her mindlink, was to try to keep the shields functioning, summoning up and channeling power into them.

Simeon Chakuchin's mind hurled missiles, on the captain's order or sometimes at his own discretion. There had been nearly a hundred heavy missiles aboard when the fight started, but they were going fast.

Spence was aiming and pulsing beams, and the Carmpan was handling his own special brand of communications. Domingo drove his ship, while Iskander functioned as general flight engineer, ready to handle damage control or fill in for another crew member as needed.

For just a moment, as he sent an outgoing salvo of missiles passing through the *Pearl's* shields, Simeon thought he could touch Branwen's mind directly; but the impression slipped away before it could distract him seriously. He got on with the job on which both their lives and more depended.

The dodging and maneuvering in and out among the complex belts of the planetoids, the exchanges of unimaginable violence between ships and machine, went on. Had minutes or hours passed since the fight began? Time had disappeared. For Domingo's mentally and physically battered crew, no other world but this existed.

Simeon could believe that he had always lived in this world of combat, than which there was no other; and yet it was an unreal universe, stretching beyond the door of death, filled with vivid mental visions in which imagination beckoned through the mindlink to disaster. This world tottered at every second on the brink of annihilation. The mind tried to fight free of it and could not, and drifted at the entrance to the harbor of insanity.

Pyrotechnics had completely taken over the space around the ship.

Dozens of the small rocky bodies populating this space were struck accidentally by heavy weapons and blew up, shattered or turned into fiery blobs, lighting up the dustclouds nearby like so many miniature suns. Domingo, issuing precise orders, blasted some small planetoids, creating screens of covering plasma behind which he stalked his enemy.

The speeds of the ships and machine engaged made the thinly scattered material of this space appear on instruments like a dense cloud of rocks and gravel. Collision with a particle of more than microscopic size could mean the end. Human nerves and senses, woefully too slow to compete in this game directly, entrusted the ship's computer with course calculation, a fraction of a second at a time.

Violence shocked Simeon out of a near-hypnotic mental state. Death's bony fingers brushed him hard before they slipped away. For a moment he thought that the fight was lost, and he was dead. Alarms were sounding everywhere. When he could think again he knew that the *Pearl* had taken an internal shockwave. It most probably had been induced deliberately by the berserker, with simultaneous weapon detonations at the opposite ends of the ship's defensive shields. The shock had been almost completely damped by the defenses, but still the interior impact was beyond anything that the crew had endured yet.

The captain was calling around the intercom, station by station. Everyone except Galway answered.

Benkovic's voice came, saying he was on his way to help her. It was necessary for someone to get her headlink disconnected quickly, as a dazed, half-conscious mind hooked into the system could well mean disaster. Simeon was immobilized for the moment by his job, still throwing a pattern of missiles. There were now no more than forty remaining in his magazines.

Domingo steered his ship into concealment within an orbital belt of dust, and again the fight was temporarily broken off.

Through a fog of pain and bewilderment, Branwen saw Benkovic come into her combat station. She heard him say something about helping her to her berth.

He disconnected her headlink and assisted her through the short tunnel. As he put her down in her berth, she briefly lost consciousness again.

When awareness returned, her helmet had been taken off, her armor opened. She could feel Benkovic's hand inside her clothing, first on her breast, then moving down her ribs, her belly . . . his hand was bare but he was still wearing his combat helmet, and it was difficult to see his face . . . she groaned something, and fought herself free.

His suited figure crouched, getting still closer to her. His uncovered hands reached out. His helmet's airspeaker made his voice more mechanical than human. "I'm trying to help you. Don't be crazy." Then, more softly: "Doesn't it turn you on, babe? Doesn't all this turn you on?"

She rolled away from him and got to her knees. She didn't try to argue. "Out. Out," was all she said. Her hand came up with a gun.

Spence looked at the weapon and said nothing. He was in armor that might save him, but his hands were exposed. Still she could not really see his face.

"Out," she repeated.

Without saying anything more, he turned away and left her.

She closed the door after him and mechanically dialed for privacy. She was near collapse. *Later,* she thought. *Later I'll report that, or I might just settle it myself. Right now we have this battle to fight . . .*

In quiet waiting, the ship was doing a passive imitation of a planetoid. Now the crew could see and feel the eternal emptiness of space again, the thinness of the distribution of matter even here inside a dustbelt. In seconds the fury of the battle had vanished totally.

No one doubted that it was going to burst over them again or had time to contemplate the universe. The ship had suffered damage, but so far nothing was critical. Iskander through his mindlink was doing what he could to patch it up.

Simeon got permission to leave his station momentarily to check on Branwen; Spence's report on her condition had been brief and uninformative. Simeon found her semiconscious, and would have taken her to sickbay but at that moment Domingo ordered him sharply to get back to his station. On his way out of her berth he picked up some of the samples of material and information that she had brought from the most recently searched berserker installation.

A quick look at the samples, when Simeon was back in his own station, suggested that they would provide more evidence concerning the berserkers' research and development efforts in the field of biology.

But there was no time now for anything like a thorough scientific analysis.

The enemy was in sight again, and Gennadius was on the radio. The two captains managed to act in concert once more.

The great berserker, being pursued relentlessly, taking a merciless pounding from two sides, bedeviled continually by the Nebulons who still swarmed after it, continued to strike back with fury.

The battle seesawed back and forth.

But then at last the berserker turned tail and fled.

Domingo, despite the damage to his ship and the desperate condition of his crew, despite depleted stocks of missiles and red warning signals everywhere, immediately gave chase to Leviathan, vowing that his ancient enemy would not escape him now.

Fourth Adventurer, somehow still able to withstand the killing strain of what he was doing, taking part in combat, fatalistically accepted the result of what he had already done as a matter of free choice: "I have signed on."

Gennadius, wholly caught up at last in the spirit of the chase, overrode the warnings of his own second-in-command about his damaged ship and chased the enemy too, and recklessly. The alternative would have been to fall back in guard position at some nearby colony. His ship was now in better condition than Domingo's, and the commander took the lead in the pursuit.

The speed of both ships was perilously high as they hounded their quarry among the innumerable tiny planetoids and through the fringes of the encroaching wisps of nebula, and then departed the system, still in hot pursuit.

The berserker was not dead yet. It turned at bay, and the fury of the battle came back, worse than before. Simeon heard strange cries on intercom, and he found himself closing his eyes and praying, to a God of the Galaxies someone had taught him to adore in childhood.

Someone else on the crew—Simeon could not identify the tortured voice—had cracked now and was pleading with the captain. Whoever it was shrieked and babbled, but Domingo would not slow down. Eventually the human screaming ceased.

But not the noise of the alarms. Those mechanical voices screamed on, and there was no doubt that the ship was continuously sustaining damage, as it went tearing its way through clouds of gas molecules and microscopic particles.

The shields were maintained somehow and the headlong pursuit went on. It could not be endured for another moment, but yet it was endured. The timeless minutes passed, with people and machinery still somehow taking the strain.

The enemy fled again.

The unnamed sun, and the space that sun had cleared for itself within the nebula, were now astern, the white light shifting red with its recessional velocity. Abruptly, at an insanely dangerous speed, dense clouds of nebula once more enfolded the quarry and the hunters alike.

An outer belt of planetoids that until now had been concealed in nebular clouds now loomed ahead, appearing as a bombardment of rocks hurtling past the ship and at it, out of fog and darkness.

There was a startling flare on the *Pearl's* detectors, seen by everyone on board. All heard a last burst of garbled communication, ending in a radioed scream.

Simeon grasped the fact a second later. Gennadius's ship was gone. Either it had hit a sizable rock or had been ambushed by Leviathan and totally destroyed.

Domingo, not delaying for an instant his headlong charge after the enemy, ordered the firing of most or all of his remaining missiles. Simeon obeyed. At this speed the captain himself dared not divert an instant's attention from his piloting.

"Captain, I have what looks like a lifeboat on the detectors. Might be Gennadius, some of his people."

Domingo said: "We can't stop."

His ship did not waver for a second from its course, straight after Leviathan. He had the helm and no one could stop him. Or no one dared to try.

☀ **CHAPTER 22**

Domingo, dragging his crew along with him by the power of his will, hurled his ship after Leviathan without pause, keeping the pressure on.

Simeon had gone beyond weariness, beyond fear. Now he was being caught up, hypnotized, in the fascination of the chase. Vaguely he was aware that Branwen, Spence and even Iskander were reaching or passing the limits of their endurance. Fourth Adventurer was a special case. It was hard to know what was going on with the Carmpan, but for now he appeared to be enduring successfully, if grimly.

Again the battered berserker plunged into the billows of the Milkpail. It displayed surprising speed in its flight: in a human such behavior would have been called reckless or even suicidal daring. There was no doubt that a machine of Leviathan's size had to be taking considerable additional damage from the inevitable particle collisions at such speed. The generators sustaining its forcefield shields must be near failure, and its armor ablating away. The machine was running a serious risk of sudden and total destruction at any moment.

Yet the blazing trail left by the enemy persisted, did not reach a cataclysmic end. Its luck, if machines had luck, was holding.

The captain followed it at high speed, accepting an equal risk. Such a track would have been practically impossible for any pilot to lose, given the will to hold the course. The turbulent wake of the berserker increased the danger for the following ship, the probability of microcollisions. Domingo was forced to avoid the enemy's wake as much as possible, thereby losing a little ground.

"You've got it all calculated out, Skullface. All the odds to the last decimal. But you haven't figured me into your odds yet. You haven't figured me in well enough. I'm coming to get you." Domingo was muttering to himself, but the others aboard his ship could hear him.

Again the *Pearl* shot into the nebula, right after her escaping foe, at a speed that neither the ship or the machine would be likely to tolerate for long. Not in these clouds. The clamor of onboard alarms resumed.

The drive of the *Pearl* had been weakened by combat damage.

Despite Domingo's maniacal determination, Old Blue might well have escaped cleanly, except for the efforts of the Nebulons.

The Spacedwellers had no trouble keeping up with the fleeing berserker, but whenever they tried to attack it its fields stung them and brushed them away. Fourth Adventurer reported several fatalities among the nebular-theme humans from these encounters. But still their speeding formation kept the dead-metal killer in sight, and through the mind of Fourth Adventurer they continuously relayed the enemy's position to Domingo. When the machine abruptly changed course in an apparent effort to loop back and try for another ambush, the pursuing *Pearl* was able to change course also, almost instantly, gaining some distance on its quarry in the process.

Now the berserker would be aware, if it had not been before, that the Nebulons were somehow able to report whatever they observed to their allies in the ship, virtually instantaneously.

"It's going to get away." Those words were the first from Iskander in some time.

Domingo's voice sounded no different now than it had on the day after Shubra. "It's not trying to get away. We can follow that wake and he knows it. He's risking a pileup to try to get somewhere."

The only question was, was Leviathan trying to reach allies, or a final kamikaze target?

The chase continued, pressed by Domingo with fanatical intensity. Timeless minutes stretched into eternal hours. Punishing jolts came through the artificial gravity as the *Pearl* dodged rocks at thousands of kilometers per second.

Simeon, looking about him in the moments when his mind refused a total concentration on his job, was amazed that everyone on the crew could still be alive. That anyone could be. The ship and all her systems were a shambles. Backup systems labored, with nothing to replace them when they went. He could see in all the indicators before him what a beating the *Pearl* had taken.

She ought to be limping away, cruising slowly, doing her best to make port somewhere before one of the impending catastrophic breakdowns happened and finished her off. Instead she hurtled on at the best speed her captain could whip out of her, pursuing the thing that had not quite destroyed her yet . . .

They had built her well, those people at the Austeel yards. But how well could anyone build a ship?

Simeon clung to the thought that Old Blue was now heavily damaged also. It had to be. But there was no reason to think the berserker had lost its capability of inflicting ruin on any attacker that caught up to it.

Only one man was trying to do so.

Only utter grim determination, to carry the hunt on to the death, had a chance now of overtaking the berserker. Only obsession, only suicidal madness, had any chance of outlasting a rogue computer's will.

With all Domingo's efforts and those he could still wring from his crew, it remained impossible to close the gap between pursuer and pursued.

Galway now called the captain on a private channel and reported herself fit to resume her duties.

He glared at her impersonally, a man trying to estimate how long one of his few remaining tools would last before it broke. "You're not going to fold up in the middle of a fight?"

Her image tossed its head. "*I'm* fit for duty. I don't know about Benkovic."

"Benkovic? What's that supposed to mean? What's wrong with him?"

Tersely she supplied the captain with the facts, a recital of what had happened in her berth when Benkovic had been alone with her. "If he tries to paw me again," Branwen concluded, "he's going to have plenty wrong with him. Like a new belly-button. Battle or no battle."

The captain only continued to stare at her, digesting bad news about another tool. She could see that he had no capacity left in him any more for shock or surprise, let alone sympathy.

At last he said: "You take over fire control for a while, Galway. Simeon needs a break. I've got to keep one good person going, and right now he's the best I've got. We're pushing on."

"Yes, sir." She was not surprised at Domingo's reaction. No time or energy could be spared now for anything but the chase. Anyone on the battered crew who could still function had to function. Branwen understood that Domingo had no real interest in crew conflicts or even in serious breaches of discipline, except as they might endanger his mission. She understood that he was not now going to pursue the matter of what exactly Benkovic might have done to her or might stand accused of doing. If they all lived, which they were not going to do, something might be done about it. She might very well take care of it herself. But right now her head still ached, and she could hardly think.

The captain broke the intercom connection and concentrated fully on the chase. Still, the knowledge of Branwen's complaint had registered on some level with him.

Domingo himself no longer cared where the chase was taking him and his ship. But Simeon found himself trying to calculate or estimate the present position of the *Pearl*. Curiously, his mind felt clear and active now. He had passed beyond the first stages of exhaustion, and now it was as if his mind, like the ship herself, could tap the wells of the universe for power to keep going. It would be a help to know what kind of nebular material lay near ahead, and what the chances might be of enlisting some aid in the chase.

According to the best calculations that Simeon could make, the speeding enemy ahead was now rapidly approaching the location of the colonized planetoid da Gama.

When Simeon had checked this conclusion as well as he could, he got on the intercom to the captain. Domingo, when pressed, agreed to let him launch a courier now, trying to recruit more Space Force help.

Simeon took thought, and the courier was gone.

The defenses of da Gama were springing automatically to life. Alarms sounded across the planetoid, in every place that humans were. The early warning detectors of local Ground Defense had picked up the charging berserker at extreme range. Leviathan was coming on in an all-out kamikaze charge, and if the machine maintained its present course and speed, no more than an hour would elapse before it arrived.

The mayor of da Gama, arriving at the control center of Ground Defense, was further informed that, if this were indeed a suicidal ramming attack, the ground defenses unaided were probably not going to be able to stop the onrushing berserker.

She sat down slowly. "What can we do?" she asked.

At the moment, no one had an answer for her.

The tactic of dangerously rapid flight had served the berserker well on several previous occasions in its long career when it had been pursued by superior forces. Not, of course, that Leviathan knew fear. It considered its own survival not of the highest priority, but still important. If it were destroyed it would no longer be able to carry out the program that was of highest priority, at the core of its existence: the effort to destroy all life.

Not that escape was any longer Leviathan's prime objective. Too many of the badlife missiles had achieved nearly direct hits. The cumulative damage was severe and would be fatal in a few hours at the most. Beyond the next hour or two, the destruction of life was a task that would have to be left to its fellow machines.

The human ship behind it had moved a little closer.

Again the thing that humans called Leviathan slightly increased its speed, getting the most it could from the drive units that were still functioning, ignoring accumulating minor damage, accepting the risks involved.

All human commanders in the past had turned back and given up the chase when faced with such risks.

But whatever unit of badlife commanded this currently pursuing ship did not turn back.

At the present rate of closure, it was still hours from overtaking the berserker.

What could be done to destroy the maximum amount of life in another hour or two?

What was the most profitable target that could be reached in another hour, or a little longer?

The central computer aboard Leviathan had already searched all of its still-functional memory units for information on the nearest colonies. It had observed that one of the larger colonies in the Milkpail was within range.

The people aboard the speeding *Pearl* had now come to realize what the speeding berserker's plan must be. As nearly as they were able to read the situation, only one Home Defense ship was anywhere close to being in the right position to try to defend da Gama from this mad charge.

Whoever commanded this lone Home Defense ship, visible on the *Pearl*'s remote detectors, obviously grasped the situation too. She or he had changed course and was coming out hell-for-leather to try to intercept Leviathan's attack.

"Slow him down," Domingo urged the other ship. His voice was a soft mumble. "Just slow him down."

There was no way by which the people on the Home Defense ship could hear the captain's urging, and they were too far out of position anyway to try to engage Leviathan in a running fight. All the Home Guard ship could do was to try to hurl itself directly in the enemy's way—and that was what it did.

That tactical maneuver was accomplished, with what great effort others could only guess. Simeon, with his eyes closed, could still see what his headlink brought him, dim flares light-minutes distant. In a matter of seconds the bravely aggressive ship was brutally wiped out of the way by the onrushing monster's remaining firepower. Belatedly Simeon realized how small that human ship must have been, how hopelessly outclassed by its opponent.

The people who were still functioning aboard the pursuing *Pearl* now scanned desperately through every quarter of nearby space; but nowhere in the area could they see other Home Guard or Space Force ships that might be able to arrive on the scene in time to help.

It was beginning to look to Simeon as if da Gama was doomed. He tried to remember what its ground defenses were like. Not all that great, as he recalled. Not only were thousands of tons of metal coming at it with more speed than a meteorite, but Leviathan had just demonstrated the power of its remaining weapons. And there was also its c-plus drive, which could become a terrible weapon indeed when a berserker machine or a human ship went suicidal.

Domingo cursed and groaned. He wanted to thwart Leviathan, achieve its destruction on his own terms, not allow it to run up a final score, a final personal insult to him, as it died. He offered to sell his soul for a c-plus cannon and three or four cartridges.

Simeon reflected that a near-miss of the enemy now with such a weapon might well wipe out all life on da Gama as the planetoid's gravitational well sucked in the massive leaden slug, traveling effectively faster than a photon. But the captain would not have been unduly worried about that possibility. In any case the question was academic. No power was bidding that much hardware for Domingo's soul.

The captain's muttering went on. "Someone stop it. Someone delay it. Hold it up just a little, and I'll ram this vessel down its bloody throat."

"We'd wreck ourselves for sure, trying that trick. I don't know if we'd be able to wreck—that." Simeon recalled the model showing how structural members stuck out around the body of the enemy like an exoskeleton of ribs—or the bars confining a caged skull. He wondered what that framework was made of and how much of it was left.

Suddenly Domingo went on radio, trying to reach the enemy, shouting now. "I'm back here, Skullface, behind you. I'm the one you want. Turn back and get me, here. Turn back for me and I'll come aboard you."

Something in Simeon's imagination was fascinated by the mad plan. But Old Blue did not respond. "We're going to have to catch it, Captain, somehow."

Now Domingo sounded almost rational again. "Maybe we can catapult the launch ahead . . . it's a much smaller cross-section, we can get it moving faster without piling up. Ike, are you suited up?" The only good reason not to be in combat armor at this stage would be if you were tending your wounds.

Ike's first answer on the intercom made no sense. The words were hard to make out, but they sounded like a snatch of song.

The captain tried again. "Ike, are you suited and ready?"

"Be there in a minute, Cap."

❂   ❂   ❂

Baza could be seen on intercom, coming through the padded tunnel for a face-to-face confrontation with his captain. Iskander, startlingly, was not wearing his helmet, and his face, even in the tiny image visible to Simeon and Branwen, was no longer that of a sane man. It was as if all the strain had been removed; actually Simeon thought Iskander's countenance showed a very great relief, as if it had somehow been revealed to him that in a little while, very soon, he was going to be free of this unendurable situation at last. In one way or another.

His first words as he met the captain were: "I mean, Cap, a joke's a joke, but you're on the verge of carrying it too far." And Baza laughed, something he rarely did for all his jesting, and began pulling off what he was still wearing of his combat armor.

At first Domingo persisted in trying to get his second-in-command into the launch. But quickly even the captain realized he had to give up on that. "Get back to your station."

His former second-in-command ignored the order. "I thought it—didn't matter. To me. What happened, now or later. Thought it was all a big joke. But I can't take this. Can't take going after it again, see, Cap? I—" Another chunk of the protective suit came off and was cast aside.

"Get back to your station. Or to sickbay. This is the last time I'm telling you."

"I don't care, Cap. I was . . . I was supposed to be the one who kept you going. Or watched you crack. But I . . ."

Domingo shot him. It was a beam-projector weapon that the captain used, and Simeon could only think, or hope, it had been set to stun and not to kill.

In the next moment Domingo had shoved the fallen body out of his way, and turned his full attention back to his fleeing enemy. No time to drag the man to the sickbay, there was piloting to do.

The chase went on.

The next voice that came over Domingo's radio was that of Gujar Sidoruk, now commanding the Home Defense ship next closest to da Gama, and visible now on the *Pearl*'s detectors. Domingo acknowledged the call without surprise. The two captains were soon doing what they could to coordinate their efforts.

Gujar was quickly provided with an outline of what had been learned so far about the Nebulons.

He commented that with such allies, berserkers could now be cleaned out of the Milkpail entirely.

Probably. Eventually. But that didn't help the immediate crisis. The Nebulons were already doing all they could, as Fourth Adventurer still reported feebly from time to time. Gujar was simply too far away to be able to intercept Leviathan before it hit the planetoid.

Da Gama's Ground Defense weapons opened up abruptly on Old Blue at long range. The berserker fired back. Communication between the two ships became very difficult, what with all the ionization and other noise spreading out between them, and no one wasted words trying to tell Domingo that Polly was on Gujar's ship.

Aboard Gujar's ship, Polly and Gujar talked after the communication with the *Pearl* was broken off.

Polly knew now that the ship pursuing Leviathan was Domingo's and that he was at the helm. But her thoughts were frozen on her two children, who were both on the imperiled colony of da Gama. Gujar was getting there as fast as he could. But not rapidly enough.

Gujar was also thinking about Polly. But he was very well aware that she was really concerned with certain other people much more than with him.

The Carmpan, who had been huddled at his station for a long time, rarely speaking, now had a new communication for his ED shipmates. The berserkers had for some time been concentrating on attacking those colonies the Spacedwellers had approached, trying to examine the ED humans' way of life. The death machines had wrongly assumed that the two kinds of intelligent life forms were already cooperating in some way against berserkers. Therefore the berserkers had targeted their attacks with a view to breaking up or frustrating the cooperation.

"Thank you, Adventurer," Simeon said when the report was over. Domingo said nothing.

Old Blue's weapons, from medium range, leveled the inadequate ground batteries on the surface of the planetoid ahead. It dropped intelligent proximity mines to blast at the *Pearl* when the pursuing ship drew near. And it used its own remaining missiles to pound at Gujar's craft.

Simeon hurled the last of his missiles, hoarded until now. More near-misses that must have inflicted more damage. But Leviathan plowed on.

The world of da Gama was coming closer and closer, now only a few minutes distant.

This close to da Gama's sun the density of the nebular medium interfered even more seriously with the progress of the huge machine. Its drive was evidently failing as well. Now it was rapidly losing speed, despite all that its battered engines could do.

❋   ❋   ❋

Ferdy and Agnes, along with a thousand other people, were in a shelter, down about as deep as anyone could get on a small planetoid, with kilometers of rock above their heads. Drastic measures were being taken to conserve power, and only a few distant emergency lights relieved the darkness. The game the two children had been trying to play was halted when the lights went out.

They both wished aloud for their mother, and both assured each other that they knew she couldn't be there but that she was going to be all right in her ship.

Then the artificial gravity let go. The two children and the people around them had no warning before it happened. But the authorities came on the loudspeakers promptly and managed to prevent panic at least for the moment.

Leviathan, trailing blue flames, still came on toward da Gama at a rate measured in kilometers per second. But the ground defenses were making their final inspired effort to slow the hurtling mass of death. A countersurge of inverse gravitational force was generated and focused, burning out all the generators and doing other damage everywhere across the surface; but not nearly as much damage as an undampened impact would have done.

One strange and unexpected result was observed, a scattering away from the enemy of what looked on instruments like a swarm of harvestable nebular life. But that made no sense and had no bearing on the immediate threat, and the technician who made the observation said nothing about it until later.

The Nebulons, caught at a crucial moment by the surge of contending gravitational fields in space, had to retreat from the conflict. They were stunned and scattered, and until now their great dead-metal foe had managed to keep its most vital organs shielded from their attacks.

The berserker, stopped almost completely by the unexpected countersurge of force, came crashing down on the surface of the planetoid. At the last moment, forced to change its plans, it used what was left of its own drive to brake its forward progress. It had lost so much momentum that a mere crash would no longer do the damage that it wanted. Now, having been slowed so much despite itself, it wanted to arrive on the surface with some dangerous hardware left intact.

Its final impact with the surface took place at a very modest velocity. Nothing was vaporized in the impact, and even the subsurface shelters nearby were not collapsed.

❂   ❂   ❂

But the humans huddled in the control center of Ground Defense and those in the watching ships understood the situation and held their breath collectively, waiting for the c-plus blast that did not come.

To fire at the enemy now with heavy weapons might trigger the berserker's c-plus drive into detonation, so that was ruled out. Not that Ground Defense had any heavy weapons available that could fire at an object on the ground.

Domingo had none left, either. He might not have used them if they were available. He had decided—or he understood now that it was his destiny—to go aboard one more berserker before he died.

☀ **CHAPTER 23**

Domingo, on the point of jumping into the launch alone, held back at the last moment, forcing himself to calculate carefully. It was possible that he would need all the support his ship was still capable of giving him. He had to make sure that the most effective person available was left at the helm. Iskander—no. Dead, or still unable to function. Domingo hadn't seen the man since Simeon had dragged him away, but Baza could hardly be in shape to command. He would have to trust his ship to someone else.

The captain, standing in the ventral bay outside the launch, quickly patched into the intercom. "Fourth Adventurer? You are to assume command of this ship in my absence. This is an order."

"I must respectfully refuse, Captain."

Domingo was taken aback. "An order, I said."

"I understand, Captain, and still refuse. You do not know what you are ordering."

In that voice Domingo could hear stubbornness equal to his own. He was sure that threats would do no good, nor would shooting Fourth Adventurer bring about the desired result. Besides, if the Carmpan was that sure, he was probably right.

Branwen, then; but no, she was still suffering from her concussion-like injury. .

Spence? No, another use for him had just suggested itself to the captain. And if the captain had a choice, he didn't particularly want to leave Branwen and Spence Benkovic effectively alone together. Not after hearing the story the woman had related to him.

It would be Simeon then. He was, Domingo judged, in the best shape of anyone aboard.

It required only a moment on intercom to leave Simeon Chakuchin in command of the *Pearl*.

Domingo's next call was to Spence. Benkovic, like everyone else, was haggard and on the verge of cracking. But when ordered by the captain to come along on yet one more boarding, Spence did no more than give his leader a strange look before acknowledging the order without protest. A minute later Benkovic, suited and ready, appeared in the ventral bay.

Domingo's plan called for the launch with the two boarders on it to be slung on ahead of the *Pearl* by a maneuver of the larger ship. Chakuchin, now at the *Pearl*'s helm, would manage that as best he could, with what help Galway could give him.

Leviathan, though crashed and grounded, was not yet totally subdued. Or at least Domingo would not have been willing to believe for a second that the machine had been effectively defeated. But the captain's first good look at his fallen archenemy through the clear windows of the launch brought home to him with striking force how close he now was, or ought to be, to final victory. The great mass of the berserker was sprawled on rock, physically broken. Like a flung starfish, still more like a shattered skull, the huge machine lay bent over what had once been a small rocky hill. Though the central part of the hull was still intact, it seemed clearly impossible that the vast ruined bulk could ever move again under its own power. The huge ribs of the projecting exoskeleton were bent and fractured, and even as Domingo watched, what remained of Leviathan's defensive forcefields were sputtering and dissolving in a faint rainbow whose dominant hue was still essentially blue.

There were no signs that human habitation had ever existed in the immediate vicinity of the downed giant, but in the distance, dropping back over the near horizon of the planetoid as the launch hurtled closer, were roads, harvesting towers and buildings, most of them now at least partially destroyed.

"Looks dead. Damned dead," said Benkovic, meaning the berserker.

"It's not. Not yet. I know."

Benkovic said nothing.

The voice of Elena Mossuril, the mayor of da Gama, came into the launch through a radio relay requesting Captain Domingo to respond.

The captain ignored the first two calls before answering the third out of irritation. "Niles Domingo here. I'm busy."

A brief pause. Then the voice on the radio resumed. "I'm sure you are, Captain Domingo. I must talk to you, though. This is the mayor, Elena Mossuril, and I want you to tell me what you're doing. Coded transmission and tightbeam, please."

"Talk to my acting second. Simeon, take over this conversation." And the captain concentrated again on his ship. But he listened in to what was being said on the radio.

Simeon, on the *Pearl*, explained to the mayor what Domingo was doing and assured her that his ship was standing by, ready to use what weapons she had left.

Mayor Mossuril in turn urged Chakuchin not to fire at the downed berserker because of the danger of a secondary explosion. He should fire only at landers if they were deployed from the wreck, but none had been observed so far. He gave her assurances that he was not going to fire unless his captain ordered it; and that was the best that she could get.

The mayor in her deep shelter kept receiving discouraging reports from her tiny ground-based forces. They stated that they were unable to do very much at all about the berserker.

To begin with, there were no suitable all-terrain fighting vehicles available. With the artificial gravity gone, the surface atmosphere was being lost too rapidly to allow for the practical use of aircraft. And the assault force that was trying to reach the enemy on foot in space armor was bogged down in giant crevasses where the newly fractured and churned land kept slipping and sliding and piling up around them.

The mayor could hardly blame anyone for moving very deliberately in approaching the downed monster.

Even if—and this the mayor had not dared try to tell her allies out in space, for fear the berserker could be listening—even if there was a subshelter holding a thousand people almost underneath the thing.

Simeon's stock of missiles had been totally used up. All of the heavy weapon systems of the *Pearl* were virtually exhausted. She continued to move toward da Gama and Leviathan, but would be able to do little or nothing when she got there. It would be a couple of hours before another ship was in a good position to help.

Simeon and Branwen stayed at their battle stations and kept the ship going as best they could. There were still some light weapons in usable condition.

The Carmpan groaned in his berth, crying out with the psychic pain of singed and slaughtered Nebulons, and with his own untranslatable interior torment.

Iskander Baza in sickbay was nearly dead. The stunner at a range of only two meters had done to him what such supposedly nonlethal weapons all too often did.

And now a blood vessel broke inside the victim's brain.

Presently the machines gave up on his heart.

Minutes passed before any of his used-up shipmates noticed that he had died.

The launch with Domingo and Spence Benkovic aboard, descending swiftly and smoothly, came to a halt not quite touching the slabs of rock thrown up along the enemy's broken side. The little vessel came very close to docking against rock, even against the berserker's hull, but Domingo deliberately avoided solid contact.

Crisply the captain gave Benkovic his orders: to remain on the launch, to stay on guard and be ready to respond to whatever other orders might come from Domingo.

Judging from Spence's quiet, subdued response, and the fact that the simple orders had to be repeated, it was evident that he was in an increasingly odd mental state. But there was nothing to be done about that now.

As soon as the vessel was practically motionless relative to the ground, the captain in his armor, carrying weapons and tools, slipped out of a hatch and dropped lightly and slowly the few meters remaining.

The sprawled body of his archenemy towered over him, the broken ribs of the birdcage twisted into fantastic shapes. A gust of almost invisible blue flame played harmlessly from a rent in the berserker's hull. Another larger rent nearby, one Domingo had already picked out as a good means of entering the body of his enemy, was dark and quiet.

After looking the scene over for only a few seconds, Domingo moved on alone. It did not seem particularly strange to him that he was about to carry out yet another boarding, though he supposed it was doubtful whether any other human being in history had invaded active berserkers so many times. The captain knew only that he must seek out the deadly life of this thing that had destroyed his own life, face it somehow in a final confrontation. After having come this far and been through this much, simply to destroy the hardware of it—to blast and burn its physical shape away—would no longer be enough. Whatever he needed to release him had not yet happened.

There were no immediate death traps ready for him as he went inside Leviathan's hull. There was no resistance of any kind.

More openings, some of them conveniently door-sized, were waiting ready-made in front of Domingo, and he moved deeper. As he moved, he took care to drop small radio-relay units at intervals, devices he hoped would keep him in contact with the human world outside.

Domingo remained on hair-trigger alert as he advanced, expecting at every moment to meet opposition from small maintenance machines at least. In his arms he carried a shoulder weapon connected to a thoughtsight on his helmet. It was much heavier, more powerful, than the handgun he had brought along the first time he boarded a berserker. Grenades, even more potent, hung on his belt. Let the androids come. Even the landers. He was ready.

A choice of ways lay ever open before him, and at each choice he went deeper still into the vitals of his enemy. And still the berserker had done nothing to dispute his progress. He moved in darkness now except for his suit lights.

The machinery by which the captain found himself surrounded was unlike any he had encountered aboard either of the two berserker research stations. This equipment was older, different in design and purpose. This was obviously all for weapons and defense. This must have come from a different factory, though there were a few general similarities in design.

Here there were plentiful signs that a great deal of repair and replacement had been carried out in the course of the centuries. Things had been moved, modified, disconnected and reconnected. There was evidence of a long ongoing effort to keep this engine of destruction in effective operation.

Domingo aimed his carbine at a fragile-looking device. Then he eased his mind away from the will-to-shoot that would have triggered a blast of destruction.

"Dead now," he muttered. "All this part. Where's your brain? In deeper. In deeper, somewhere. Somewhere in there, you're still alive."

Through misshapen, unmarked corridors, strange tunnels and ducts that no human being had ever seen before, he groped and climbed and walked in the direction of the berserker's core. His hands were trembling now, he noticed to his surprise. It was the first time his hands had trembled since . . . since he could not remember when. And the fact that he could not remember worried and puzzled him.

Meanwhile, down deep in the central core of the death-machine, the innermost surviving circuits still tried to compute some way of sterilizing the entire planetoid, destroying the thousands of badlife that were known to infest it. For the berserker to calculate anything now was very difficult, because its central processors were damaged and starting to fail, and its sensors had been beaten almost blind and deaf. But it was still trying.

Failing sterilization of the entire planetoid, perhaps it might destroy the underground shelter, crawling with badlife, that it could sense almost underneath its sprawling and half-crumpled bulk.

And failing even that, it ought to be possible to wipe out of existence at least the single specimen of human badlife vermin that had now come in contact with Leviathan itself.

Where exactly was the lone intruding badlife now? There. Approximately. The interior sensors, not meant for this kind of work, gave only the roughest readings. But there, somewhere, quite near a set of automatic doors...

With the abrupt removal of the artificial gravity field around da Gama, the upper atmosphere was peeling rapidly away, and the resulting depressurization of the lower air had brought on a fast chill as well as a fierce snowstorm. Not all of these changes were yet apparent among the huddled refugees sealed away down in the deep shelter. But one alarming fact was being quickly spread among them by word of mouth: Every exit from the shelter had been caved in or somehow blocked, either by the bombardment of the berserker's weapons as it approached from space or by the impact of the great mass itself.

Not that the lack of exits posed any immediate problem of survival for the thousand people who were here huddled underground. Their air supply was still secure. So the authorities in charge of the shelter kept repeating, in voices made as soothing as possible.

As matters stood at this moment, there was nowhere for the people in the shelter to go anyway.

Spence Benkovic sat, as he had been ordered, in the launch, gazing numbly out through one of the almost unbreakable windows. The autopilot was holding the launch just slightly above the surface of da Gama. Outside, snow was falling, drifting, accumulating a little here and there, on the rocks only about three meters below where Spence was sitting. A little higher in the howling, dissipating air, more snow was decorating the ancient black of Leviathan's metallic surface, for the first time in the centuries or perhaps millennia of the machine's existence.

Spence was watching the snow. He had gone beyond fear, beyond exhaustion. Only one other thing still bothered him, and if it were not for that, he had the feeling, a very profound feeling, that the best thing he could do would be to sit here and watch it snow forever.

He wasn't going to be allowed to do that, though.

Already the wind was blowing something like a gale. Benkovic could tell by the way the heavy rock outside was stirring and drifting now, mixing with the snow. Soon the atmosphere would begin to howl against the launch, maybe loud enough for him to hear it inside.

He had seen and heard all this before, somewhere else.

He watched snow vanish, steaming, in the blue flames that still came twisting out of one of the wounds in Old Blue's side. The sides of the cavity still glowed, where some kind of a beam weapon, most likely one fired from the *Pearl*, had probed and probed again.

Without consciously thinking much of anything, Spence sat in contemplation of that wound that was never going to heal.

Domingo, still advancing, looked around warily at every step, expecting at every moment to be attacked by landers, androids, or at least maintenance machines. The shape that had killed Maymyo might spring out on him at any moment...

Nothing sprang on him or at him. Nothing even got in his way. After one minor alarm from a set of automatic doors—the doors had closed sharply, perhaps trying to catch him—his progress had been unopposed.

The suspicious doors, well behind him now, would not be moving again for any reason. He knew he could no longer be far from his enemy's brain.

The captain was aware of the fact when he had reached his goal, though his opponent did nothing to mark the occasion for him. He was standing now in a large and fairly open interior space, enlarged at some time in the past, he supposed, by the removal of parts for use elsewhere, the cannibalization of redundant units for the front line, wherever that had been. There was plenty of room here for small fighting machines to get in and move around, but none of them came at him.

Deliberately, meticulously, Domingo had left his trail of radio relay devices. He could talk to the world outside if it became necessary. Later on, if he was still able to talk, no doubt he would. But there was another conversation he wanted to hold first.

Niles Domingo turned his radio off the regular channels and on a short-range mode that the berserker would certainly be able to hear, if it could hear anything. He wished that his hands would stop shaking now, but they did not.

He spoke to his enemy. "Where's the lander, Skullface? I want the one that you sent down on the world called Shubra. Bring it out here. Send it against me now."

The berserker heard him.

It had all of its functional maintenance machines at work inside another portion of its hull, preparing the sole remaining unit of its c-plus drive for detonation by a last suicidal application of power. It was now concentrating all its remaining energy and ability on this effort. The best calculations it was still capable of making indicated that here, in the planetoid's natural gravity, that unit would explode when power was applied, violently enough to cave in at least the roof of the shelter below, hardened or not. Caving in the shelter might well finish off all the badlife inside.

But the power mains leading to the c-plus unit had been broken in the crash, and there was much work yet for the little maintenance machines to do before that last killing surge of power could be applied. The machines needed more time to do their work. Unless the single badlife invader could be successfully delayed in its presumed mission of destruction, it was improbable that they were going to get it.

Destroy or delay the invading badlife then, somehow.

It would have been possible to divert some of the maintenance machines to attack this man, but the berserker decided against that course. The only machines it had available were certainly not meant for combat action. And it was easy to deduce that the life-unit must be heavily armored and armed, if it was here at all. Through battered and straining sensors, the berserker was barely able to perceive the presence of the lone invader. The trap with the doors had had a very low probability of success, but nothing better was available.

Time was needed. And when the man, the badlife unit, began to ask the berserker questions, a possible means of gaining time presented itself. The berserker knew the badlife language; it could improvise a speaker, a device to make sounds, and it did.

Domingo heard the machine speak. In a squeaking, inhuman but quite understandable voice it said to him: "I have no landers."

"Lying bastard," he told it, without much feeling in the words. He wanted the heart, the last drop of blood. He wanted reaction, acknowledgment that he had won. He needed to bring the dead soul of the damned thing somehow within his grasp.

"Liar," he muttered. "Liar."

He tuned the nozzle of his weapon to a fine jet and began burning and blasting one of the consoles holding the berserker's memory. When the console was open, he started in on the exposed memory units. They were small, no bigger than a fist, and he took them one at a time.

From one such unit his decoding equipment was able to pick out the coordinates of the hidden repair base that Leviathan had used for centuries. This was treasure. But to Domingo it was still unsatisfying.

The berserker's brain had now been fragmented, by combat damage and the captain's probing, until there was little left of it but mere data banks, incapable of planning or lying. Open books, waiting to be read or written in, indifferent to results and almost powerless to achieve them.

Domingo grabbed up another unit. This small portion of the machine held in its memory much of the research results from the berserker bioresearch stations. That research effort had finally succeeded in determining the form of the optimum anti-human life weapon—at least insofar as berserker machines were able to determine what that might be.

In the little image projected by Domingo's decoder, it looked very much like an ED human. But, Domingo thought, the berserkers had no real hope of developing one of those.

He dropped the memory unit. His sensitive suit mikes had picked up a sound twanging through the metal that surrounded him, and Domingo spun around, his weapon ready.

He waited on a hair-trigger, watching and listening, but nothing happened. The sound had been that of something collapsing, something failing, or just metal cooling and contracting. There was no threat.

Leviathan would defend this place, its central brain, if it could still defend anything. There was plenty of room here for one of the landers, had there been any still working, to be able to get at an invader. The landers, at least the ones Domingo had seen depicted, weren't very large machines. When they came down on the surface of a planet or a planetoid to sterilize it, they had to be able to get into some fairly restricted spaces in one way or another. Caves, for example, under overhanging cliffs of rock.

But Domingo had faced no challenge since boarding Old Blue, except possibly for the puny effort of the doors. It was almost as if he were being welcomed as a friend.

Was Leviathan really helpless? Or might all the small machines be doing something else?

"I say again, you lying bastard, bring on your machines. Where are they?"

Now even the core of Leviathan's brain was failing rapidly. Domingo's probing dissection had provided a finishing stroke.

The malignant purpose of the fundamental programming had now been almost entirely erased. Only the c-plus detonation project was being continued, and that by machines that neither knew nor cared what they were doing.

What was left of the berserker's intelligence pondered whether or not to answer this most recently asked question and why.

Domingo was not waiting for an answer. He forced open another console that almost certainly had part of Leviathan's brain inside it.

Still the final satisfaction of victory, of revenge, eluded him.

"Do you remember, damned machine—do you remember a planetoid, a colony, called Shubra?"

The fading berserker intelligence had now lost, along with much else, the ability to lie. Ongoing damage was steadily consuming everything. But for the moment the ability to answer questions still remained.

It said, in its squeaking, erratic voice: "I remember that."

"The day that you destroyed life on that planetoid, you sent down some of your small lander machines to make sure—remember? Remember? To make sure that you had done a thorough job. You sent one lander to a particular cave—"

The relevant memory units were still intact and were quickly examined. The berserker responded: "No."

The voice of the life-unit was changing, becoming ragged, too. Its breathing was hard inside its helmet. "—in a particular cliff. Your lander went there and killed a particular young human being. It—"

"No."

"—it killed, it . . ." Domingo could hear the pulse beating in his ears. He could hear his own breathing inside his helmet. He wondered if something was happening to his heart. "What do you mean, 'no'?" He wondered if he was going to hyperventilate and fall helpless here in the face of the enemy. No. He would not.

The berserker said: "In the attack on Shubra I employed no landers. I had none available. The last had been destroyed on the colony of Liaoning."

"You lie."

"No."

The captain drew a deep breath. It was almost a sob. "Ten years ago," he said. "More like eleven. You killed a transport ship." He named the ship. "You left no survivors. My wife was on that, and my children. Can you know, can you understand—"

"When and where?"

Domingo gave the information.

"No. I did not destroy that ship."

"Lying bastard."

"No. Accidents are common."

There was a metal sound again, a clanging somewhere off in the middle distance. Again Domingo spun around, ready to fire. Again there was nothing to aim at.

He turned up the sensitivity on his suit microphones. Ah, something. A steady working, murmuring . . .

"You lying bastard, lying, lying . . ." He was almost in tears. *"Where are your small machines?"*

"They are at work preparing a—" There was a pause, then the same unemotional voice resumed. "Preparing a c-plus detonation that will—that will cave in the roof. Of the badlife shelter. The badlife shelter below. The shelter below the—"

"*Stop them!*"

Pause again. "The effort has been. Has been stopped. The life-units . . ."

That was all. There was no more.

The distant murmuring had stopped.

Domingo, suspicious, began ransacking what was left of his enemy's brain.

"Damned treacherous . . . I don't believe you yet."

Only silence answered him.

"Not an accident, that transport ship. No." He paused. "An accident?"

The machine no longer answered him. He probed and probed, but he could find no evidence that it was still alive at all. Stray voltage and current here and there within its brain, charges not yet dissipated. Memory of this and that. If he were to probe long and hard enough, he might be able to find the memories he wanted. Where would he find the dead damned soul?

No landers were here now. No landers had been sent down on Shubra. No landers . . .

The c-plus drive unit. He would look at that, to be sure. He thought he knew where that would have to be, on a berserker built like this.

It took the captain a minute or two to get there, climbing through the unfamiliar hardware.

The c-plus unit when he found it was surrounded with little maintenance machines. All of them were now immobile. Domingo stared at them for some time, then with his fine-tuned weapon he burned them, one at a time, into permanent immobility. Just in case.

He made his way back to the central chamber housing the now-dead brain and sat there. No landers had come down on Shubra. His hands were shaking worse than ever now.

☀ CHAPTER 24

Down one of the long, sloping half-open aisles that converged on the place where Domingo waited, through one of the passages never meant for humans and clogged now with machinery dislodged and broken in Leviathan's dying crash, the captain saw a new light. It was bright and it came waving shadows ahead of it with its own approaching motion.

He suppressed the urge to cry out. Instead he stepped back silently, the weapon that had been slung over his shoulder coming up smoothly into his two-handed grip.

For a moment wild suspicion returned. But the approaching shape was too small to be that of a lander. Maybe an android, it was the right size for that . . .

But it was not an android. Instead the light-bearing shadow became a shambling human figure, wearing space armor belonging to the *Pearl.*

Spence Benkovic stumbled to a halt when he saw the captain leveling a heavy weapon at him.

For a moment there was silence. Then Benkovic said on the short-range radio: "I came to find you. I had to see what you were doing."

"Your orders were to stay on the launch." But the rebuke was no more than mechanical.

"I couldn't do that," Benkovic said simply. "I had to see what you were doing here."

They looked at each other.

Domingo said: "I was wondering about you, too. About why you signed on my ship. The real reason."

"It was like I couldn't keep away. I had to come along to see what you were doing. What you were going to find out."

"Are you goodlife, Spence? Is that it?"

Benkovic's face inside his helmet, plainly visible in the center of Domingo's light, showed nothing but bewilderment. Whatever he had been expecting from Domingo, it wasn't that at all. "Goodlife? What the hell kind of a thing is that to say?" But the protest was weak. Benkovic appeared to be on the verge of laughing or crying.

"Are you?"

"Nothing like that, Captain. No, nothing like that." Spence gestured toward the components of the disassembled brain that were lying at Domingo's feet. "Is it dead now?"

"It's been dead all along, Spence. Now it's pretty well turned off."

Benkovic nodded. There was silence, for a moment, as if there might be nothing more to be said between the two men.

Then mechanical sounds came echoing from somewhere within the nearby metal caverns as before. Spence grabbed for the holster at his belt, then realized that he had come here unarmed. He looked down, perhaps marveling silently that he should have forgotten such a thing; or perhaps he knew the reason for his forgetfulness. Then again only tiredness showed in his face.

Domingo hadn't turned or raised his weapon this time. Now he said: "Pretty well turned off, but it still talked to me there for a while. I got some truth out of it. There aren't any landers here. This berserker hasn't had any landers or androids for months."

The other was looking at him. Looking and listening intently, like someone hoping for a message that would mean rescue.

"Not since Liaoning," Domingo said. "Not since before Shubra."

Branwen Galway, groaning, semiconscious, lay in her berth aboard ship. She'd had to abandon her battle station because her mind seemed to be fogging up again. She knew she needed medical help. She was going to hang on somehow and do what she had to do until she got it. She was going to shoot Spence Benkovic if he came through her door again.

Fourth Adventurer was still living, but almost inert.

Simeon, virtually alone now on the *Pearl*, was himself on his last legs. Duty held him to his post.

Back in the central cave of the devastated berserker, Benkovic sat down slowly on a projecting ledge of metal that had been designed for some totally different purpose. Presently he let his helmeted head fall forward into his hands.

The captain remained standing. Even in the light natural gravity, he swayed. The mechanical sounds out in the caves of machinery had stopped, but there was still a roaring in his mind. A rushing and a roaring, like a prolonged explosion. It seemed to have been going on forever, like the space battle with Leviathan. He could feel it all, everything, catching up with him at once.

His weapon no longer pointed at Benkovic, but still the captain held it in both hands. His hands holding the heavy carbine were shaking more than ever, uncontrollably.

"Tell me what happened on that day." Domingo's voice, asking the question, sounded like that of a man trying to memorize a line that he was going to have to deliver in a play.

Spence raised his head and nodded, making his helmet light bob up and down. He didn't look at Domingo at all now, but instead gazed off into the shadowed recesses of the ruined machinery.

"What I told you before, a lot of that was true," he said. "The first part of the story I told everybody, that was true."

"Tell me again. The whole thing now. I want to know all the truth."

Once more Benkovic nodded. He spoke as if he were remembering something from long years before, or maybe even from an earlier lifetime. "There at the wedding, after the alert was called, I ran along with everyone else and got into my ship. I didn't have any idea then . . ." The recital stalled.

"Go on."

Spence went on. He described how, when the other ships lifted off, he too had launched from Shubra in his one-seater battler, headed back for the moon.

From space he had seen the relief squadron, led by Domingo, depart for Liaoning.

"Then I sort of wished I'd gone with you. Wanted t'be in on the action, y'know? But by then it was too late."

"Go on."

At that point, Benkovic said, he had changed the objective of his own flight, deciding to do some scouting on his own. He had radioed first to his three women companions on the moon, telling them to go into the shelter and lie low.

The moon's orbit brought it within only the outer limit of the effective range of the Shubran ground defenses. But Spence had had no reason when he made the call to expect that there was really going to be a berserker attack on Shubra almost at once. So presumably the women would be just about as safe in the little shelter on the moon as they would have been taking flight in a ship or coming down to take shelter on the planetoid—that last assessment had turned out, grimly, to be all too accurate.

"I should have gone back and picked them up in a ship, I guess. Got 'em the hell outta there. But I didn't." He shrugged. "Everybody else should have done something different, too."

"Go on."

After making the call to warn his girlfriends, Benkovic had zoomed away for a few hours, scouting. He'd had no success, even though he was a good pilot. Anyone could testify to that.

"And I've never been afraid to do things." Spence raised his head all the way and looked around him when he said that, as if to say that his presence here on this boarded berserker justified that claim.

Giving up on the fruitless scouting expedition, he had returned to within visual range of Shubra in time to see Leviathan in the process of attacking the colony.

"You told all of this before."

"Yeah. And up to that point, up to what I'm telling you now, everything I told you before was the truth."

"And now. Tell me the rest of the truth." Domingo was still on his feet. He was resting his weapon on the machinery in front of him, trying to stop the trembling in his hands.

"Yeah. I want to do that." Spence's voice fell lower and lower. He swayed as if he might be going to topple from where he was sitting.

"God, what a ride you put us through, chasing this thing. I can still feel it. It's all still coming at me."

Domingo waited.

"What really happened. Yeah." Benkovic paused for a long time. "But it's like none of that part is real."

"It was real enough. It was as bloody real as anything. Go on."

Benkovic went on. Actually, as he related the story now, he had not seen the berserker send down any small machines to devastate the individual defensive outposts. But he had assumed that Leviathan had landers and androids; they were practically standard equipment on large berserkers. "And I never guessed . . . I'd be here finding out different."

"Go on."

Benkovic wasn't sure now how long he'd drifted in space in his little one-seater, watching the slaughter, the destruction, from a safe distance, far beyond the orbit of the moon. But eventually Leviathan had completed its programmed task and had departed the vicinity of Shubra, leaving nothing but smoking ruin on what a few hours before had been an inhabited surface.

Benkovic had returned to his moon to find his colony destroyed by a few touches of the enemy weapons with only one of his women still alive. He had given her what help he could. She was seriously injured but seemed likely to survive, and he had left her there alone in the charge of the medical robot, which was about the only useful machine to have survived the attack.

Fascinated as always by destruction, he had then flown down to the Shubran surface.

"I could see that just about everything was ruined. There were no radio signals. I told myself that when I landed I was going to see if there were any survivors—anyone I could help. That's what I kept thinking most of the way.

"Then I saw—I really started to see—what had happened. I don't know. All gone. Destruction. That kind of thing. It turns me on in some way . . . you know? I guess you don't know."

"Tell me. I want to hear."

"You already know, don't you? I'm so bloody tired now. So damned . . . there's no way out. But first I'll tell you."

"Yeah."

"At last I picked up one little local radio signal, because I was so close; it never got out to anywhere else because of all the ionization around. A distress call. I followed it, and answered. She said . . . who she was."

"My daughter."

"Yeah—it was Maymyo. I don't know if she knew my voice. I don't think so. I never said who I was. But she gave me enough directions so I could find the cave. The airlock was still holding. She—she saw me outside. When she was sure it was a man and not a machine talking to her, she let me in."

"The door, the big door to the cave, was blasted open."

"I did that, later. With the cannon on my little battler. To make it look like berserkers, see."

"I see. Go on."

"I told her that the attack was over, but she wouldn't believe me at first. I don't think she knew who I was, even then. She was in a kind of daze. Combat fatigue. I don't think she was hurt otherwise. Maybe a little concussion."

"Like Galway."

"Yeah . . . yeah. Then it came over me what I had to do.

"I told her to take her armor off, and she did. Just like that. She was in a total daze, following orders. I told her to take her armor off, and then that white dress, and then to lie down. Then she struggled, but I . . .

"Then—after—I thought I couldn't just leave her. Because, you know, she'd probably remember." There was a pause long enough for two breaths. Domingo could hear them distinctly on the radio. Then Benkovic concluded: "And if she remembered, she'd tell."

Having said that, Benkovic nodded sagely. He appeared to be considering the human condition, himself as an example of it.

"You killed her."

Benkovic looked up. "I couldn't just leave her. Yeah." It was a simple truth; he looked afraid of it. But he was not really frightened of Domingo's gun. He looked yearningly at the big bore of the carbine as it leveled steadily at his helmet.

Domingo was still sitting there when Polly and Gujar came in.

There were other people with them, people from the crew of Gujar's ship, and they were going through the motions of trying to rescue Captain Domingo, not really expecting to find him or anyone else in Leviathan's guts alive.

The new arrivals took note of Benkovic's headless body but were not much surprised. They assumed that the berserker had somehow killed him.

Simeon, Fourth Adventurer, Branwen Galway—all of them had already spoken to the rescuers on radio, and all three welcomed them back to the ship a little later when they came bringing Domingo with them. But none of the crew members who had stayed aboard the *Pearl* could tell the tale of what had passed between Benkovic and Domingo on the wreck.

Niles Domingo was to tell that story once, to one person only, and much later in his life.

The captain and Polly Suslova were side by side, more or less in each other's company, as they left the dead berserker on their way to find her children.

Domingo looked around him before he left, as if he had never seen this place until this moment.

Berserker Kill

☀ PROLOGUE

The ship was more intelligent in several ways than either of the people it was carrying. One task at which the optel brain of the ship excelled was computing the most efficient search pattern to be traced across and around the indistinct, hard-to-determine edges of the deep, dark nebula. Most of the time during the mission the ship drove itself without direct human guidance along this self-selected course, back and forth, in and out among the broad serrations, the yawning, million-kilometer chasms in the clouds of interstellar gas and dust that made up the Mavronari.

The only reason that such ships weren't sent out crewless to conduct surveys without direct supervision was that their intelligence was inferior to that of organic humanity when it came to dealing with the unforeseen. Only breathing humans could be expected to pay close attention to everything about the nebula that other breathing humans might find of interest.

A man and a woman, Scurlock and Carol, crewed the survey ship. The couple had known for months that they were very right for each other, and that was good, because being on the best of terms with your partner was requisite when you were spending several months in the isolation of deep space, confined to a couple of small rooms, continually alone together.

Carol and Scurlock had been married shortly before embarking on this voyage, though they had not been acquainted for very long before that. By far the greater proportion of their married life, now totaling approximately a standard month, had been spent out here nosing around the Mavronari Nebula.

The ship was not their property, of course. Very, very few individuals were wealthy enough to possess their own interstellar transportation. It was a smallish but highly maneuverable and reasonably speedy spacecraft, bearing no name but only a number, and it was the property of the Sardou Foundation, wealthy people who had their reasons for being willing to spend millions collecting details about some astronomical features, certain aspects of the Galaxy, which most Galactic citizens found highly unexciting.

421

At the moment the young couple and their employers' ship were many days away from the nearest inhabited planet, even at the optimum pattern of superluminal jumps and journeying in normal space at sublight velocity that the survey craft could have managed. Not that such remoteness from the rest of humanity had particularly concerned either Carol or Scurlock, up to now.

Scurlock was rather tall and loosely muscled, with pale eyes and long lashes that made him look even younger than he really was. Carol was of middle height, inclined to thinness, and had several physical features suggesting that some of her ancestors had called old Earth's Middle East their home.

Both young people tended to be intense and ambitious. But just now both were in a light mood, singing and joking as they made the observations of nebular features comprising today's work. Some of the jokes were at the expense of their shipboard optel brain, the very clever unit that was cradling their two lives at the moment, assuming responsibility for piloting and astrogation during most of the voyage. But no offense was taken; like other ships, this one never knew or cared what its human masters and passengers might be making jokes about.

One of the secondary objectives of this mission, politely but firmly impressed upon the couple by their employers, was to discover, if possible, some practical new means of ingress to the nebula, an astrogable channel or channels, as yet uncharted, leading into the Mavronari. The existence of such a passage would greatly facilitate interstellar travel between the inhabited worlds existing on one side of this great mass of gas and dust, and other worlds, now largely unknown but possibly habitable, that might lie somewhere within the nebula or on its other side. Any such discovery would be of great interest to the Sardou Foundation, and not to it alone.

As matters now stood, most of the worlds known to exist on the other side of the Mavronari had never even been thoroughly explored by Solarians, largely because of the difficulty of getting at them by going all the way around.

But the discovery of a new passage was only a secondary purpose, no more than an intriguing possibility. The fundamental objective of this mission was the gathering of astronomical data, radiation patterns, particle types and velocities, from the deep folds and convolutions between nebular lobes, regions not susceptible to ready observation from the outside.

Since departing on this mission, Carol and Scurlock had frequently expressed to each other their hope that a successful performance would lead them upward and onward, financially and socially, ultimately to one of the several goals they had established for themselves.

❂   ❂   ❂

The Galactic Core, eerily bright though thousands of light-years distant, a ball of dull though multicolored incandescence all mottled and muted by clouds and streaks of intervening dark matter, appeared through the cleared ports first on one side of the little ship, then on the other, as the small craft proceeded about its work with—as usual—only minimal human supervision. Now and then one of the human couple on board took note of how the Core cast their ship's shadow visibly upon some dark fold of the great Mavronari, clouds silvered on this side as if by moonlight.

Gazing at that tiny moving shadow and that immensely greater darkness just beyond the silvering, Carol was drawn away from near-poetic musings by a sudden shudder that ran through her slight frame.

It was a momentary, subtle event. But Scurlock, being close to his partner in more ways than one, took notice. "What's the matter?"

She ran brown fingers through her straight dark hair, cut short. "Nothing. Really nothing. Just that sometimes, looking out, I get a momentary feeling that I can really sense how far away everything is."

Her companion became soberly thoughtful. "I know what you mean. How far away and how old."

After a shared moment of silence, of the ship's controlled drifting, it was time to turn quickly to matters of light and life. Once more, as they often did, the couple discussed their own wish for a child in the light of Premier Dirac Sardou's colonization scheme, in which the Sardou Foundation, largely a creation of the Premier himself, was heavily involved.

"I don't know how people can do that. I wouldn't want to doom any kid of mine to any scheme like that."

"No, I agree," Scurlock immediately concurred. Not that he particularly wanted to have a child under any circumstances, any more than Carol did.

Carol would have been surprised if he had not agreed. They had had this conversation before, but there seemed to be purpose, and there was certainly reassurance, in repeating it. Talk drifted to other subjects. Meanwhile, with a watchful steadiness born of habit, the couple kept an alert eye on the course adjustments made now and then by their autopilot, and also made a point of directly taking some instrument readings for themselves. They were making sure—although the autopilot was really better at this than they were—that their ship did not stray too deeply into the outlying tendrils of the nebula. The region they were currently exploring was still hard vacuum by the standards of planetary atmosphere, but matter, in the form of microscopic and near-microscopic particles, was seeded through it thickly enough to dangerously impede ship movement. It would be damned inconvenient, and perhaps much worse than inconvenient, to find themselves enclosed by dust arms anywhere near their present position, enfolded by some slow-looking swirl of thin gas half the size of a solar system, trapped so that their little craft would lose all chance of dropping back into flightspace and returning them briskly to their homeworld in a mere matter of days.

Further talk, optimistic daydreaming of prosperity to come, was interrupted by the optelectronic brain of their ship breaking in to inform its masters in its usual indifferent voice that it had just detected the presence of several unidentified swift-moving objects, the size of very small ships, materializing out of the dusty nebular background. Whatever these objects were, they had appeared in rapid succession—in nearby space, at a range of only a few hundred kilometers.

The ship was already presenting its live crew with the appropriate displays, showing the unidentified things as small, dark, mysterious dots upon a false-color background of mottled silver.

Scurlock, staring without comprehension at the moving dots, demanded: "Whatever in all the worlds—"

"I've no idea," Carol breathed.

Nor had their ship offered an opinion. No wonder both organic and inhuman brains were puzzled: on instruments the unidentified objects certainly looked like small ships, but the chance of encountering any traffic at all in space was nowhere very large, and here on the flank of the Mavronari it was astronomically small.

In only a few seconds the young couple's puzzlement had begun to turn to alarm. A certain word had popped up unbidden in the back of each of their minds and was refusing to go away. Neither of them wanted to frighten the other, and so neither spoke the word. They moved in silent, mutual consent to clothe themselves rather more formally, until they were fully dressed, with the vague unspoken idea of possibly receiving visitors. Then Scurlock, without giving any reason, suggested getting into space suits. Carol said she didn't think that was necessary. As a compromise, they checked to make sure that suits and other emergency devices were in the proper lockers, ready for use.

After that, both human partners sat in their command chairs squinting at a holostage, which had been adjusted to display in its unreal image-space, against an imaged background of black dust, the steadily growing likeness of the nearest unidentified object.

Carol said, with an air of calm determination, "All right, Scurly, we have to make sense out of this. Is that some military thing?"

Her companion nodded. "They must be military. That must be it. Maybe an Imatran squadron. That's about the closest system to where we are now. Or maybe it's Templar. Or Space Force. One of those."

The loosely spread formation of shiplike objects—seven of them now—moving methodically toward the explorer ship was certainly no manifestation of ordinary civilian traffic. So they had to be someone's military. Had to be . . . because the only other alternative was too frightful to contemplate.

Neither Scurlock nor Carol had spoken of that alternative as yet, though it had settled tenaciously in the backs of both their minds, where it was still growing ominously. Instead of talking about it, the couple looked at each other, each seeking reassurance and at the same time trying to give it. Trying with less and less success.

It was left to the heartless ship to finally say the words, in its finely tuned ship's voice that sounded only mildly concerned, and would have sounded perturbed to an equally slight degree about anything else that happened to pose a problem. "The seven objects now approaching are identifiable as berserker machines," the ship remarked.

There was no immediate reply. Scurlock's first conscious reaction was an immediate surge of anger at the ship, that its voice in making this announcement should be so calm. Because what the hell did the ship care? It had been designed and built by Solarian humans, Earth-descended folk of the same human species as Scurlock and Carol. And Solarian designers, convinced they had good reason for doing so, saw to it as a rule that their machines never gave the impression of caring much about anything.

And Scurlock persisted in his quite irrational feeling of what the hell did a ship, any ship, have to worry about anyway? Those berserker machines out there—if indeed that was what they were—did not have as the goal of their basic programming the obliteration of *ships* from the cosmos.

No. It was something very different from ships that berserkers were programmed to wipe out. Their object was to expunge life itself from the Galaxy. Human life was a priority, because humans tended to give them a hard time, to interfere with the completion of their task. And the Solarian variety of human life was the killing machines' favorite target above all others—because Solarian, Earth-descended humanity in particular was as a rule damned obstinately, and even violently, opposed to dying.

Carol, who of the two human partners was slightly the better pilot, had already got herself into the acceleration couch offering the best access to both the manual and the alpha-wave ship's controls, and she was now sliding her head into the alphawave coronet. Scurlock, with fingers that seemed to have gone numb with fright, was now fastening himself into the acceleration chair, or couch, next to the pilot's—getting into a couch, the manuals affirmed, was in these situations more important than trying to put on a space suit.

Not that either suits or couches were likely to help much in an unarmed ship when berserkers were coming after you. In that respect, Scurlock was sure, whatever counsel the manuals offered was hopelessly optimistic.

In a moment he could hear himself suggesting in a weak voice that they might try to make their little craft as inconspicuous as possible, to slide and hide behind the nearest fold of nebula and wait, in hopes that they would not be noticed.

Both human and optelectronic pilots ignored his proposal. This was probably just as well, because neither Scurlock's nerves nor Carol's could have endured trying to make such a tactic work. And it seemed a futile suggestion anyway, coming considerably too late, because the oncoming objects were not just approaching but were closing in directly on their ship, proving that they had already been irrevocably noticed.

Carol murmured something incoherent from the pilot's couch and melded her mind with that of the ship, trying hard acceleration at right angles to the onrushing formation of killers. The drive responded smoothly, and the cabin's artificial gravity dealt efficiently with the imposed forces; the polyphase matter webs on the acceleration couches still hung slack, their occupants spared the least physical discomfort.

But the maneuver was worse than useless. The oncoming objects only changed course accordingly, demonstrating once more that whatever they were, their approach to Scurlock's and Carol's ship was not in the least accidental.

Frantically, again muttering almost inaudibly to herself, the human pilot tried again, with no better result—she and her partner, lover, lay huddled amid the straps and webbing, the latest in polyphase matter but of no more use now than so much spaghetti, of their separate acceleration couches—as if mere straps and webbing of any kind were going to do them any good.

Still both human partners seemed determined not to utter the dread word. Neither had done so yet, as if the threat could not be real until the name of it was spoken. The fact that their own machine had already named the terror to them somehow did not seem to count.

For almost a full minute the two terrified people tried to outrun the oncoming objects, getting the best they could out of their own ship, alternating between pure autopilot and a melding control. Carol was a good enough pilot to render the meld of organic and artificial intelligence superior in performance to either mode alone.

But perhaps no pilot in this ship in this situation would have been good enough to get away.

In whichever mode they flew, the enemy followed each change of course, and easily, methodically gained ground. But the unliving enemy still held their fire, as if this time the berserkers were, for some unguessable reason, more interested in bringing about close contact, confrontation, than in dealing sudden death.

The survey ship was unarmed. But even a fighting Space Force scout, which would have been twice as large and a thousand times as capable in self-protection, would have had small chance indeed against so many machines of the type now closing in. All seven of their pursuers were now clearly visible, each as big as or slightly bigger than the survey vessel, all steadily drawing near. Still no weapons had been fired.

And now Scurlock groaned aloud. His last hopes vanished. An object that could only be the berserker mothership, a drifting continent of metal as black and horrible as death itself, had come into view out of clouds a hundred kilometers in the background, at that range clearly visible to the unaided eye. Simultaneously, on holostage the thing's magnified image came groping its careful way forward, emerging from heavy dust with the dignity of an evil mountain, and at a speed that somehow seemed unnatural for anything so large and ugly. It slid forward out of the darkness of the Mavronari like the king of demons emerging from some antique vision of hell.

Long seconds crept by, during which neither person in the doomed cabin spoke. Then the couple turned toward each other, and each read despair in the other's face.

"Scurly." Carol seemed almost choking on her own voice.

"Yah?"

"Promise me something?"

"What?" Though already he knew what. He knew all too well.

Carol hesitated. For some reason she began to whisper. "If it is berserkers and they kill us quickly, I'm glad we're together."

"So am I."

"But if they don't . . . do that . . . I mean, there are stories that if they don't just kill on sight, it's because they want something . . . then I don't think I can face it . . . I don't want to—"

Carol could not, dared not, put into words just what it was she wanted her husband to do. And if she couldn't find the words, he wasn't about to help her do so. Not on this one.

Once more turning away from her partner, Carol made a last, frenzied attempt to maneuver, to get away; but moments later they were overtaken, their small craft smothered and immobilized in powerful force fields. The autopilot reported with mad, mocking calm that it was no longer able to maneuver.

The seven attackers, all within a hundred meters now, had the little survey ship englobed, in what had at last become a tight formation.

She and Scurlock stared at each other. Time seemed to have come to a complete stop.

Their ship in its unflappable voice relayed to them the news of the next step in the catastrophe: its drive had now been rendered totally dead.

Nothing more happened until, only moments later, the same voice informed them that an attempt was now being made to open the outer hatch of the main airlock, from outside. There was really no need to tell the two human occupants that, because their unaided hearing now brought them news of the attempt in progress. The whole ship quivered under a titanic hammering, vibrated with a shrieking drill.

Scurlock, his fingers fumbling even more desperately than before, after several attempts got himself out of his acceleration couch. A moment later Carol had joined him, the two of them standing together in the middle of the cabin's tiny open deck.

"If the drive wasn't dead," Scurlock said suddenly, in a surprisingly strong voice, "we could switch over to manual and use it to—"

"But the drive is dead," Carol whimpered. Evidently the enemy had for some reason not wanted any cowardly or heroic suicides. Maybe it was the unnecessary waste of a perfectly good machine to which the berserkers' controlling computers made objection. "And we don't have a weapon of any kind aboard."

"I know."

"Scurly . . . even if we had a gun, I don't think I could do it. Not to you, not to myself."

"Neither could I." That seemed to him the best thing to say now, although he wasn't sure. "And—and I wouldn't leave you alone with—berserkers."

Suddenly louder sounds coming from only a few meters away made it obvious that the small enemy units—machines, whatever the proper term for them might be—were in the main airlock now. And now abruptly they were visible, if only indirectly. The relentless approach of death was being displayed for the humans with merciless clarity, by their own ship's brain, upon the little holostage in the middle of the control room. Scurlock had one moment to see clearly an enormous enlargement of a pair of waving grippers, and then the video pickup in the airlock was destroyed.

"Carol, I love you."

"And I love you."

Those were words they had seldom said to each other.

"They don't have any interest in making people suffer, Carol. It's going to be quick, whatever they . . ."

Scurlock was trying to make it true by saying it. True, the death machines' fundamental commandment, the goal of their basic programming, was the obliteration of all life wherever they encountered it. There was no requirement that living things be made to suffer; because quick killing was generally more efficient, quick killing was the rule. But exceptions to that rule came up from time to time, situations where the unliving enemy in pursuit of its larger aims required something more from some individual life unit than that unit's death. Neither person in the small ship wanted to think about those rare exceptions now. But they were going to have no choice, because the noises of intrusion had moved a large step closer. Metal arms and tools were very purposefully scratching, scraping, then pounding at the inner door of their main airlock.

"Carol—"

"Yes. Scurly, I love you too." Her voice sounded abstracted; almost bored.

There was no more time to talk. The inner door of the airlock was sliding open now. There followed a slight momentary drop in cabin pressure, but no fatal escape of atmosphere; that had already been taken care of, somehow, because the occupants of this ship were going to be kept alive, for the time being.

And now berserkers were entering their cabin.

Constructions of dull-surfaced metal came filing in, one, two, three, four of them, walking rapidly one after the other into the control room. They were very little bigger than Solarian human beings, though their shapes were frightfully different from those of humanity as descended upon any planet. And these machines were quite obviously of alien strength and purpose. They came into the control moving more quickly and decisively than any bodies merely human could have moved, or any organic creature of any species. Some of the intruders walked on six metallic legs, and some on only four.

What was momentarily astonishing was that the invaders appeared at first to take no particular notice of their two new prisoners. The prisoners on their part remained standing as if paralyzed, their four hands clutched together, in the middle of the chamber.

Like practically every other Solarian in the Galaxy, Carol and Scurlock had all their lives heard stories about berserkers. Some of the stories were true, some fiction, some the wildest legend. There were human worlds whose population had never seen a berserker, but no human world where such stories were never told. The berserkers in the stories always seemed to come equipped with the capability of human speech. And on the very rare occasions when people in the stories and histories came close enough to listen to berserkers and yet somehow survived, they always described the enemy as communicating quickly with human captives, spelling out for the abhorred badlife precisely what was expected of them, what they must do to earn a quick and merciful death, giving at least by implication some indication why their lives were being temporarily spared.

But these machines, having taken possession of Scurlock and Carol along with their ship, said nothing at all—unless a few peculiar clicks and whistles, issuing from one of the invaders, were intended as communication. If this noise indeed was language, the Solarians could neither recognize it nor respond.

One facet of the humans' intense terror, a dread that they were going to be immediately separated, was not realized. But any unreasoning hope that the machines would continue to ignore them quickly vanished. After only a few seconds' delay, both prisoners were gently seized and searched by deft metallic fingers and grippers that probed and patted impersonally at skin and clothing. Then the two humans were let go, not bound or otherwise physically molested. In another moment all but one of the boarding machines had left the control room, spreading out through the various accessible bays and compartments of the little ship, obviously intent on search and examination.

Their bodies temporarily free, yet helpless, the two prisoners gazed at each other in anguish. They exchanged a few hopelessly banal words, phatic utterances empty of hope. No doubt their metallic guardian was listening, but it neither punished them for speaking nor commanded them to silence.

Eventually all of the machines that had spread out to search the ship returned to the control room, where they stopped, standing motionless like so many serving robots.

"What happens now?" Scurlock abruptly demanded of the world at large. For a moment, only a moment, Carol saw him as a brave and challenging figure, fists clenched, looking at his unliving captors with the courage of despair.

The machines ignored him. One of them was at a control panel, probing with thin auxiliary limbs, probably tapping into the ship's data banks.

Carol sat down again in the pilot's couch and began to weep.

The minutes stretched on, and nothing happened. After a time Scurly sat down too, in the couch next to Carol's.

Looking out through cleared ports, the captives presently were able to get a better view than before of the berserker mothership.

Scurlock commented now on the fact that in the light of the distant Core that hideous bulk showed signs of extensive damage, in the form of cratering and scorching, but it conveyed the impression of being still extremely formidable. Certain projections, he thought, indicated immense firepower. The great hull was generally ovoid, almost spherical, in shape. Sizes and distances were hard to judge in space without instrumentation, and the voice of the survey ship had fallen silent, but from the faint drift of intervening dust he estimated the monster as at least several kilometers in diameter.

Before the first hour of their captivity had passed, most of it in a terrible silence, Carol had already started to crack under the strain. She was withdrawing into a staring silence, letting remarks by her companion go unanswered.

"Carol?"

No answer. Slowly the young woman, staring at nothing in a corner of the cabin, raised a white knuckle to her mouth. Slowly she bit on it until blood started to appear.

"Carol!" Scurly lurched unsteadily to his feet and grabbed her hand, pulling it away from her teeth.

She raised wild eyes, a stranger's eyes, to stare at him.

"Carol, stop it!"

Suddenly she burst into tears; Scurlock crouched beside her, awkwardly trying to give comfort, while the berserkers looked on impassively.

For the next few hours the machines continued to watch their captives—you could see a lens turn now and then on one of the metal bodies—and no doubt they listened, but for the time being they did nothing more. The prisoners were allowed to move about unhindered in the control room and the sleeping cabin next to it. To sit, to stand, to lie down, to use the plumbing.

Eventually, one at a time and by degrees, they fell asleep.

A time arrived when Scurlock found himself in the control room, looking at the ship's chronometer, wondering why the numbers displayed seemed to convey nothing. He tried to remember, but for the life of him could not, just what day and hour the clock had shown him the last time he had looked; that had been at some unguessable interval before the berserkers came.

Carol was sleeping now. He had just left her sleeping—unconscious might be a better word for her condition—in the other room.

Slowly Scurlock went about getting himself a cup of water from the service robot. He had to walk directly past one of the berserkers to do so, and he actually brushed the machine—their metal legs crowded the little room. He knew it could flick out a limb at any moment and kill him, and slow human sight would never see the impact coming, any more than he would see a bullet. Let it come, then, let death come.

But it did not.

Slowly he went about getting another cup of water, carrying it into the sleeping cabin, offering his human companion—who was sitting up again—a drink.

The idea of food, in either of their minds, was going to have to wait for a little while yet.

As was the idea of hope.

Eventually in Scurlock's mind—which was never going to be quite the same mind that it once had been—the numbers on the chronometer started to make sense again. With dull shock he remembered certain things and noticed that the hours since the invasion seemed to have added up to a standard day.

He noticed too that Carol was intermittently biting her knuckles again. Blood was drying on her fingers. But he didn't think he was going to stop her anymore.

With the passage of time, the first shock of terror had begun to relax its grip. The sentence of death had already been passed, and yet it seemed that life somehow went on.

Scurlock and Carol passed long periods sitting together, clinging together, on one of the beds or ordinary couches. From time to time Carol would suddenly give vent to a burst of peculiar laughter. Whenever this happened, Scurlock stared at her dully, not knowing whether she had gone completely out of her mind or not. Now and then he saw her doze or caught himself awakening with a shock from a deathlike sleep.

An hour came when she leaped up from an almost-catatonic pose, shrieking at the top of her voice in a sudden fit. "What does it want from us? What does it want?" Then, hurling herself at one of the machines, she hysterically attacked it with her bare hands, knuckles already bleeding. "What do you want? Why don't you kill us? *Kill us!*"

The machine moved one leg, adjusting its balance slightly. That was all. A moment later Carol had collapsed, sobbing, on the dull deck, at the metal feet of the impassive thing.

Still there were intervals in which the couple talked to each other, sometimes fairly rationally, often feverishly, between long stretches of helpless silence.

During one of their more rational exchanges, Scurlock said, "I've got an idea about why it doesn't talk. Suppose that this is one very old berserker. Suppose that maybe, for some reason—I don't know why—it's been stuck in the Mavronari for a long time. That could happen, you know, to a ship or a machine. Maybe it's been a very long time in there, struggling to get out of the nebula again. Or it went in on the other side, and it's been struggling to make it all the way through."

After a long pause, in which she might have been thinking, Carol responded: "That's possible." What sent a chill down Scurlock's neck was that at the moment she didn't even seem to be frightened anymore.

When she said nothing further, he went on: "In that case, if it's really been in there for thousands of years, it might never have learned any Earth-descended languages. Those sounds it was chirping at us earlier could have been Builder talk."

"What?" She really didn't seem to know what he was talking about; the terribly bad part was that she didn't seem to care.

"You remember Galactic history, love. Long ago there was a race we Solarians now call the Builders, because we don't know any better name for them. The people who built the first berserkers, created them as ultimate weapons to win some crazy interspecies war, around the time we were going through our Neolithic Age on Earth—maybe even before that.

"And then something went wrong with the plan, the way plans do go wrong, and the berserkers wiped out the Builders too, along with their nameless organic enemies, whoever they were. I remember learning somewhere that their speech, the Builders' speech, was all clicks and whistles."

Carol had had nothing to say to that. Only a few minutes had passed since Scurlock had last spoken, and both prisoners were dozing—in Scurlock's case, trying to doze—in adjoining couches when suddenly one of their guardians spoke, for virtually the first time since coming aboard.

And what the machine uttered—in a clear machine voice, not all that different from the voice of the now-silent survey ship—were distinct Solarian words. Scurlock was snapped out of his somnolent state by hearing: "'*I've got an idea about why it doesn't talk.*'"

"What?" He jumped to his feet, glaring wildly at the machines, at Carol, who appeared to be really sleeping on the next couch.

The same machine said, in the same accurate enunciation, but slightly louder: "'*All clicks and whistles.*'"

That phrase brought Carol, whimpering, starting up from sleep. Scurlock grabbed her by the arm and said, "That's what it wants from us! To listen to us, to learn our language."

And at once the mimicking tones came back: "'*That's what it wants from us. To learn our language.*'"

Carol, as if she had been shocked at least momentarily out of her withdrawal, reacted with rational horror: "We don't want to help it, for God's sake!"

"Love, I don't think we're going to have much choice. It may be offering us our only chance to stay alive!"

For a long moment the two humans were silent, staring into each other's faces, trying to read each other's eyes.

"*Love,*" essayed the machine, tentatively.

But at the moment no one was listening. Suddenly Scurlock burst out: "Carol, I don't want to die!"

"No. No, I don't want to die either. Scurly, how did we ... how could we ever get into this?"

"Easy, easy, love. We didn't ask to get into this. But now we're in it, we've got to do what we've got to do, that's all."

"*Easy, easy, love,*" said a berserker's voice. "*That's all.*"

There were hours and days in which the machines encouraged speech by separating the two humans, holding them in different rooms so that the only way they could keep contact with each other was by calling back and forth.

Somehow refusing to play along never seemed like a real option. In the data banks of the captured ship, as Scurlock pointed out to Carol, the berserkers had available a tremendous amount of recorded material, radio communications of a variety of kinds, from several worlds and several ships, in all the languages with which the captured couple were familiar, and some more besides.

And now their lifeless captor was beginning to play various recordings it had taken with their ship, and to mimic the sounds of human speech existing on those recordings. This, Scurlock argued, proved that resistance on their part would be futile.

"So the point is, love, it doesn't really depend on us to learn. Even if we don't talk to it, it can analyze the language mathematically, use the video material as a guide. It can find out whatever it wants to know without our help."

And again he said, "No one's going to come looking for us, you know. Not for a long time, months. And if they do, and find us—tough luck for them."

Carol never argued. Mostly she just stared. Sometimes she chewed her favorite hand.

And now the machines that held them prisoner began to prod them relentlessly to talk and keep on talking. Whenever a period of silence lasted longer than about a minute, the berserker used some of its newly learned speech to command them to keep on speaking. When that failed, it administered moderate electric shocks to keep them going, a machine gripping both of a human's hands at the same time. Thus it kept at least one of them awake at all times, shocking them and talking to them in its monotonous, monstrously patient voice.

A pattern emerged and was maintained of one prisoner sleeping while the other talked—or more precisely, was interrogated. Physical and mental exhaustion mounted in both prisoners, despite the intervals of deathlike sleep.

Time passed in this mode of existence; just how much time, Scurlock could not have guessed. Once more he had forgotten the chronometer, never thought to look at it when he was in the cabin talking to berserkers; sometimes the thought of time briefly crossed his mind in the brief interval after he had been released, but before he sank onto his bunk in the darkened sleeping cabin, and unconsciousness descended. He thought that perhaps the ship's clock, like its drive, had been turned off.

The survey ship itself had somehow been lobotomized, but its serving devices provided food and drink as before, life support saw to it that the atmosphere was fresh, and the artificial gravity held steady as it ever had. Carol and Scurlock took note of each other briefly and frequently, exchanging a few meaningless words as they passed each other shuffling between control room and sleeping cabin, to and from the endless, tireless interrogation.

Ultimate horror had a way, it appeared, of becoming bearable. The deadliness of the familiar.

But change was constant. The education of their enemy progressed. Over the course of time, exactly when Scurlock could not have said, a new note, a new emphasis, at first subtle but soon definite, crept into the current of their questioning. Presently it was obvious that their captor had strong interests beyond simply learning one or more Solarian languages. And the nature of the new objectives was ominous, to say the least.

Scurlock, the more consistently alert of the two prisoners, became aware of this state of affairs at a definite moment. He was alone in the control room with the machines, and one of them was calling his attention, by pointing, to the small central holostage.

In that small virtual space his captor, which had long since established thorough control of the ship's own optelectronic brains, was now calling up a pattern of sparkling dots representing several nearby solar systems. Stars and some planets were labeled with correct names, in the common Solarian language. Now the machine was after information on continents and cities, the factories and yards where spaceships were constructed.

In a matter of days, or perhaps a standard month, Scurlock realized, the vast unliving intellect that held them prisoner had learned to talk to them with some facility.

This realization was reinforced the next time he awoke, alone, in the sleeping chamber. An arm of one of the seemingly interchangeable boarding machines had just opened the door, and he could hear that machine's voice, or another's, coming from the next room, where one of them must be pointing to a succession of images on the stage: "This is a man. This is a tree. This is a woman."

"I am a woman," Carol responded, and her voice now sounded no less mechanical than the berserker's.

"What am I?" it asked her suddenly.

Scurlock, opening his eyes with weary dread, avoided thinking. He moved his stiff limbs to join her in the dayroom.

Standing in the doorway, he experienced a relatively lucid moment. Suddenly he was aware how much his companion, his lover, his wife, had changed since they'd been taken. Always thin, she now looked almost skeletal. Her fingers were scarred, dirty with dried blood from being bitten. Had he been passing her on the street, he would not have recognized her face. And she was not the only one, of course, who'd been evilly transformed. He knew he'd lost weight too, his beard and hair had grown untamed, his unchanged clothing stank, no longer fit him very well. He shambled when he moved.

In fact, he suddenly realized, they hadn't touched each other as lovers since the machine took them. Not even a kiss, as far as Scurlock could remember. And now there was hardly ever a moment when they were even in the same room together.

"Answer me," prodded the metallic voice. "What am I?"

Guiltily Carol, who had been staring into space, looked back at the thing from which the voice proceeded. "You are a . . ."

Her eyes turned slowly toward the cleared port through which, at the moment, the drifting mountain of the mother-ship happened to be visible. " . . . a machine," she concluded.

"I am a machine. I am not alive. You are alive. The tree is alive."

Carol, for the moment looking insanely like some strict classroom teacher, shook her head violently. Scurlock in his doorway froze to hear the dreadful cunning certainty of madness in her voice. "No. I'm not alive. I won't be alive. Not I. Not if you don't want me to be. Not anymore."

"Do not lie to me. You are alive."

"No, no!" the strict teacher insisted. "Not really. Live things should be killed. Right? I am"—she glanced quickly at Scurlock—"we are goodlife."

Goodlife was a word coined by the berserkers themselves, and it showed up throughout all their history, appearing in many of the stories. It denoted people who sided with the death machines, who served and sometimes even worshiped them.

Scurlock in the doorway could only grip the metal frame and stare. Maybe Carol in her near craziness had hit on the only way to save their lives. Maybe, he had never thought about it before, but maybe the berserkers never asked you to join them willingly. Maybe they only accepted volunteers.

"*Goodlife*, not badlife," Carol was going on, the hideously false animation in her voice giving way to a real sincerity, even as her partner listened. "We are goodlife! Remember that. We love berserkers—what the badlife call berserkers. You can trust us."

Scurlock clutched the doorway. "We are goodlife!" he croaked fervently.

The machine gave no evidence of any excitement or satisfaction at the prospect of its prisoners' conversion. It said only, "Later I will trust you. Now you must trust me."

"We trust you. What do you mean to do with us?" Scurlock, still clinging to the doorway, heard himself blurt out the question before he could stop to consider whether he really wanted to hear the answer.

The machine responded without bothering to turn a lens in his direction. "To make use of you."

"We can be useful. Yes, very useful, as long as you don't kill us."

To that the machine made no reply. Carol, slumped on her couch before the holostage, did not look at her human partner again. All her attention was fixed on the robot as it resumed its questioning.

Before another hour of conversation had gone by, the machine once more abruptly altered and narrowed its range of interest. Now it concentrated its questioning, at endless length and in considerable depth, upon the six or eight Solarian-occupied star systems that lay within a few days' travel of this side of the Mavronari.

Name and describe each habitable planet in this system. What kind of defenses does each world, each system, mount? What armed vessels does each put into space? What kind of scientific and industrial installations does each planet have? What kind of interstellar traffic flows among them?

The interminable interrogation veered back and forth across the subject, sometimes picking, digging, after fine details, sometimes giving the impression of being satisfied with imperfect memories, with generalities.

Carol had obviously abandoned herself completely to the one goal of pleasing her interrogator. Scurlock now, even in his most uncertain intervals tormented by the thought of what his fear had made him say to the machine, could think of no productive way to try to lie to it. He knew very little about the defenses of any of the planets in question—but some heroic remnant of his conscience whispered to him that he might try to say they were all formidable.

But if he were to dare anything like that, the machine would pursue him relentlessly. He could imagine the length and the ferocity of the interrogation. There was no reason to believe it would stop short of direct torture. *How did he know about the defenses? What did his regular employment have to do with such matters?* He would die under questioning like that, and he didn't want to die. No, he realized clearly that he still wanted to go on breathing, no matter what. Maybe someday, somehow, he would be able to help some fellow human being again. But lying now, trying to lie to the machine, was definitely not the way to go.

A man—and a woman—had to play the cards that they were dealt.

The questioning continued. Then suddenly, at a time when Carol was taking her turn at unconsciousness in the next room, it refined its focus once again.

They were an hour into his latest session, dealing with the Imatran system, when Scurlock, reciting on demand what he could happen to recall of objects in orbit round the inhabited planetoid of that sun, mentioned something that until now had genuinely slipped his mind—the visiting biological laboratory he had heard was scheduled for a stay of some duration in the Imatran system. Actually the laboratory was built into an interstellar vessel of some kind, connected with Premier Dirac Sardou's colonization project—

And the moment Scurlock introduced the subject of the laboratory, a bell must have rung, somewhere down one of the vast labyrinthine circuits of the berserker's electronic intellect. Not that Scurlock actually heard anything like the ringing of a bell, but still that image seemed to the man an apt comparison, a neat symbol for a sudden and profound reaction. Because it was soon apparent that once more the berserker's interest had been narrowed.

"Tell me more about the laboratory," it demanded.

"I've already told you practically everything I know. I understand it's a kind of traveling facility that has to do with biological research and some kind of projected colonization effort. Really, I don't know any more about it than that. I—"

"Tell me more about the laboratory."

PART ONE

☀ ONE

Deep down among the tangled roots of human life, amid the seeds of individuality, a billion atoms, give or take a million or so, shifted under the delicate forceprobe's pressure, rearranging their patterns of interaction across the span of several of a Solarian human reproductive cell's enormous, interactive molecules. Quantum mechanics and optelectronics were hard at work, enlisted as faithful tools under the direction of a human mind, digging into yet another layer of secrets underlying the most distinctive qualities of life and matter.

But interruption came in the form of distracting noise, jarring the probing human mind out of profound concentration. Life on a macroscopic level was intruding.

Dr. Daniel Hoveler, who was nothing if not an earnest researcher, raised strained eyes from the eyepiece of his microstage, then got up from his chair to stand beside his workbench. His irritation was transformed quickly to surprise as a woman he had never seen in the flesh before, but whom he recognized at once as the celebrated Lady Genevieve Sardou, came sweeping in through the central entrance of the main laboratory deck of the orbiting bioresearch station.

The Lady Genevieve, young and small and garbed in frilly white, was accompanied by a small but energetic entourage of aides and media people. This little band of visitors, perhaps a dozen strong,

439

paused as soon as they were inside the huge, faintly echoing room, as big as an athletic field and high-ceilinged for a deck on a space vessel. The scene that met them was one of unwonted confusion. The human laboratory staff had been given no more than ten minutes' notice of the lady's impending arrival. Hoveler, who had heard the news and then had promptly forgotten it again under the press of work, belatedly realized that his co-workers must have been bustling about without any help from him during the interval, doing their best to prepare for the event.

For just an instant now, as the celebrated visitor paused, looking about her uncertainly, the whole lab confronting her was almost still. If the notice of Lady Genevieve's imminent arrival had evoked excitement and confusion (and it evidently had), her actual presence had the effect of momentarily stunning most of the dozen or so human workers present, Hoveler included. For the time of three or four deep human breaths almost the only sound in the cavernous space was a background hum compounded from several kinds of machinery engaged in the various tasks and experiments in progress.

In the next moment, one or two of the workers quietly slipped away from their positions or unobtrusively began to use the intercom in an effort to locate and alert the supervisor.

The Lady Genevieve Sardou, with the announcement of her marriage to Premier Dirac less than a standard month ago, had leaped out of obscurity to become one of the most important political celebrities in a domain comprising several dozen solar systems. A month ago, thought Hoveler, few of the people in this room would have recognized her face, and she would have received no more attention than any other random visitor. Now most of the lab workers stood frozen by her presence.

In another moment the lady, evidently coping with the slightly awkward situation as best she could, had begun speaking informally to some of the openmouthed faces in her immediate vicinity, turning from one person to another, pronouncing a few words of greeting in a well-coached but unpracticed style. The eminent visitor smiled and spoke politely, but she was clearly inexperienced in celebrity, her voice so soft that some people only a few meters away could not hear her at all.

Hoveler returned his attention briefly to his microstage, checking to make sure that a few minutes' inattention in realtime was going to have no seriously deleterious effect upon his project. Then he turned away from his bench and moved a few steps closer to the Lady Genevieve, wanting to see and hear her better; he realized that in the few moments she had been present, he had already begun to develop protective feelings toward her.

One of the lady's aides, whom Hoveler thought he could recognize from certain media images as her chief publicist, a woman much taller and louder than her employer, had preceded her illustrious client through the hatch by a second or two, and was now standing alertly at her side, mouth set in a professional smile, eyes glittering with the look of a predator ready to protect its young. Other determined-looking intruders, women and men carrying media devices, were busy making every trivial word and gesture a matter of public record. Whatever the Premier's new bride did or said here today was going to be news, and that news was about to be transmitted more or less faithfully to a score of relatively nearby worlds, much of whose population could be presumed to be strongly interested.

The news stories generated today would also be rushed on via superluminal courier, carried in a matter of days well beyond the few hundred cubic light-years of space encompassing those nearby worlds. The stories would go as far across the Solarian portion of the Galaxy as the publicists could push them. Premier Dirac did not plan to accept indefinitely the limitation of his power and influence to only a few dozen planets.

By now Acting Laboratory Superior Anyuta Zador had been located, and she emerged, tall and black-haired and somewhat diffident, from behind a tall rack of equipment to greet her politically important guest. Dr. Zador was dressed so casually, in lab smock and worn and shuffling shoes, that it was obvious she had been given inadequate time to prepare for this visit.

Zador was really as young as the girlish visitor, though she looked a few years older, being larger physically and dressed without frills. African ancestry showed in her full lips and dark hair, that of northern Europe in her startlingly blue eyes. The real supervisor, Zador's boss, Dr. Narbonensis, was currently attending a conference out of the system—sure indication that the Lady Genevieve's visit was really a surprise.

While Hoveler watched, feeling a touch of anxiety, the acting supervisor stepped bravely forward in her worn shoes, extending her capable hand in official greeting, welcoming the lady and her entourage on behalf of the laboratory's entire staff.

The important caller responded appropriately; inexperience showed only in her soft voice. Lady Genevieve added that she and her husband were simultaneously humbled and proud to be able to make a personal contribution to the great work of this facility.

Hoveler thought that over while he continued listening, at least with half an ear, to routine remarks of greeting and welcome. A further exchange between the two women—prompted now and then by a whispered word from the chief publicist—brought out, largely for the benefit of media targets on other worlds, the fact that this orbital facility was one of the important sites where long-term preparations were being made for the eventual establishment—at a time and place still to be decided—of an enormous colony, or several colonies, intended to further the spread and guarantee the future of Earth-descended humanity.

Hoveler, paying more attention to tones and undertones than to words during this part of the conversation, got the impression that the important visitor was now speaking rather mechanically. The Lady Genevieve definitely showed signs of having been coached in what to say, even to the use of certain phrases, calculated to convey certain political messages.

Supervisor Zador took advantage of a pause to return to an earlier point, as if she were really uncertain of what she had actually heard. "Did I understand you to say, Lady Genevieve, that you were here today to make a, uh, personal contribution?"

The small head of coppery-brown curls nodded energetically. "Indeed I am. My husband, Premier Dirac, and I have decided to donate our first-conceived child to swell the ranks of the future colonists. I am here today to do so."

There was the news item. It created a genuine stir of surprise among the listeners. The eminent visitor added to the surprise by going on to announce that the Premier himself, his demanding schedule permitting, was going to join her here in the Imatran system in a few days, certainly within a standard month.

Surrounding and underlying the small sounds of human conversation, the lab machinery continued its undemanding, polyphonic whispering. Hoveler and anyone else who cared to make the effort could look out through the viewpoints of the satellite station as it whirled through the hundreds of kilometers of its small orbit, and get a good view of the terraformed planetoid Imatra not far below, a thoroughly landscaped green surface dotted with small lakes, canals, and ponds. This map of land, alternating with black starry sky, swung in a stately rhythm from a position apparently above the viewports to one apparently below, while "down," an artifact of the orbiting station's dependable artificial gravity, stayed oriented with rocklike steadiness toward the deck.

Now Lady Genevieve, prompted by another murmured reminder from her chief publicist, was asking Acting Supervisor Zador politely how long she and her fellow workers, and their most impressive laboratory, had been in this system, and what they found especially striking or intriguing about the Imatran worlds. These particular planets and planetoids were, she implied with unskilled insincerity, among the spots best liked in all the universe by the Premier himself.

Acting Supervisor Zador, a young woman rallying well from what must have been her considerable surprise at today's dramatic intrusion, responded with a few facts clothed in some polite inanity. The lab's visit here in the Imatran system had been scheduled for at least several standard months, perhaps a year or more.

After confirming yet again that she had heard Lady Genevieve correctly, that she really planned to make a donation today, Dr. Zador hurriedly conferred with a couple of her more experienced human aides. Hoveler, being a bioengineer rather than a medic, was not among them. Then workers began moving purposefully about. The necessary technical arrangements were hurriedly begun offstage so that the distinguished visitor would not be subject to any avoidable inconveniences or delays.

Meanwhile, a pair of junior lab workers standing not far behind Hoveler had begun to murmur to each other. They were not really including Hoveler in their conversation, but they spoke without caring whether he could hear them.

One worker said, "Evidently their wedding went off as scheduled." There had been some speculation among cynical observers of politics that the premier's recent nuptials might not.

"Yes! A considerable political event, if nothing else."

In contrast to the widespread doubts as to whether the abruptly arranged wedding would actually take place, there had been little or no question that its purpose was primarily political. The union of two dissimilar families, or perhaps more accurately, dynasties, had been a high-priority goal of certain factions, and anathema to others. Thus the haste with which the alliance had been concluded.

One of the murmuring workers within Hoveler's hearing now remarked that the dynastic couple had met each other for the first time only a few days before the ceremony.

The colonizing project in which the research station played a substantial role had long been favored by Premier Dirac and by a majority of the factions upon which the Premier depended for political support. In fact there were many who called him the chief architect of the plan.

Though this visit on a high political level had obviously taken Acting Supervisor Zador by surprise, she still managed to express her satisfaction with commendable coherence. Lady Genevieve's donation would certainly increase the support offered in certain quarters for the workers here in the biolab—indeed, for the whole colonization project—even if, as Dr. Zador thoughtfully refrained from mentioning, the same act guaranteed opposition in other quarters.

While the hasty preparations continued offstage for the actual donation, Lady Genevieve and the acting supervisor went on with their public chat. The visitor's schedule in the Imatran system over the next few days—a schedule the publicist was even now making available to all, in the form of elegant printouts—was going to be a crowded one, and Lady Genevieve regretted that she would not be able to spend as much time as she would like aboard the station. Or at least that was the interpretation Hoveler put on her tired murmur, words now gradually fading toward inaudibility.

Some of the lady's aides were now trying unobtrusively to hurry the medics and the technicians along. Someone said that the small ship in which her party had arrived was standing by at the hatch where it had docked, and that the next stop on her itinerary was probably no more than an hour away.

The lady herself did indeed look tired, thought Hoveler with growing sympathy; his considerable height allowed him to see her over the heads of most of the other people now crowding around. Still, she was maintaining her composure bravely, even when some delay in the technical arrangements prolonged the awkward pause which ensued after everything that needed saying had been said.

Hoveler could understand why making the arrangements required a little time. Among the practical questions that had to be quickly answered was in which treatment room the donation was going to be accomplished, and which human surgeon was going to oversee the operation—the actual removal of the zygote from the uterus and its preservation undamaged were almost always accomplished by machine. Medirobot specialists, hardware vivified by expert and more-than-expert systems operating almost independently of direct human control, possessed a delicacy and sureness of touch superior to that of even the finest fleshly surgeon.

Presently Hoveler noted that at least the treatment room, one of a row over at one side of the lab, had now been selected. When the door to the cubicle-sized chamber was briefly open, the saddle-like device, part of the medirobot specialist inside, was briefly visible.

At last one of Dr. Zador's aides timidly informed the lady that they were ready. The Premier's young bride smiled a tired smile and announced that she was going to have to disappear briefly from public view. For a few minutes she would be accorded privacy with the machines, probably under the supervision of one carefully chosen human operator—very likely another task that would have to be assumed by the acting supervisor, for Dr. Zador appeared to be accompanying her.

The distinguished visitor, being gently ushered along in the proper direction, which took her farther from the large door by which she had come into the lab, looked at the moment rather appealingly lost and bewildered. Hoveler, on hearing a faint murmur from some of his co-workers, knew that she was evoking feelings of protective pity in others besides himself.

As Lady Genevieve disappeared inside the doorway, the PR people established themselves a few meters in front of that aperture and began to furnish commentary, explaining the need for future colonists. Their message of course was being recorded on the spot.

Hoveler, shaking his head, once more seated himself at his workbench. But he could not free his mind of the outer world's distractions and soon gave up any attempt at work until the lab should be cleared of visitors again.

Leaning back in his chair, he smiled vaguely in the direction of the treatment room. He would have liked to assure this latest donor that the medical technicalities involved in the safe evolution of an early pregnancy were brief, and with the best people and equipment available, ought to be no worse than momentarily uncomfortable. But then she must already have been made well aware of those facts.

In a very few minutes the technicalities had in fact been completed, evidently without incident, and Genevieve Sardou, the Premier's no-doubt-beloved bride, emerged smiling, looking tired but well, from the private room.

Dr. Zador had remained behind in the treatment room; Hoveler understood that she would still be communing with the machinery there to make sure that no last-moment glitches had developed.

Meanwhile the eminent visitor herself, still smiling, wearing her neat white dress as if she had never taken it off, showed no signs that anything disagreeable had happened to her during the last few minutes. Already she was once more graciously discussing with some of the workers and the media people her reasons for being here. Much of what she now said, mostly in answer to questions, was a repetition of what she had said earlier.

It seemed that the lady's rather domineering publicist now decided to do a greater share of the talking, while Genevieve limited herself to trying to make the right sounds, trying to be agreeable. In that the Premier's bride succeeded well enough, Hoveler thought. But, at least in the eyes of some observers, she could not help giving the impression of being lost.

Then Hoveler the bioengineer, still watching, gradually changed his mind. Lost was probably the wrong word. Almost certainly out of her depth, perhaps out of her place. But far from helpless. And certainly attractive; yes, definitely that. Grace, femininity, were integral parts of Lady Genevieve. She was a young, physically small woman, with something elfin about her, her face and coloring showing a mixture of the races of old Earth, with Indonesian, if anything, predominant.

And was she really pleased to be here? Really as delighted as she somewhat wearily claimed to be, at visiting what she could call without flattery the finest prenatal facility in this part of the Galaxy? Was the lady really as overjoyed as she said she was to be making this very human contribution on behalf of her husband and herself?

Well, perhaps. She was obviously intelligent, and Hoveler had somehow got the impression that she would not easily be bullied into doing anything she didn't want to do. Perhaps the donation really resulted at least partly from a wish to be free of the responsibility of raising her own child.

Now a murmur came drifting through the laboratory, a raising and swiveling of media devices, a general shifting of the immediate onlookers to gain a better point of view. Dr. Zador, still wearing her surgeon's mask—that article was now chiefly symbolic; maybe one of the media people had asked her to put it on—was emerging from the treatment cubicle, smiling as she held up the hand-sized blue statglass tile that now presumably contained the latest colonist—or protocolonist, rather—encapsulated for viable long-term storage. The tile was basically a flat blue rectangle the size of a man's palm, bearing narrow color-coded identification stripes. At the urging of the media people, Acting Supervisor Zador once more held the encapsulated specimen aloft—higher, this time—to be admired and recorded.

And now, in seeming anticlimax, the station's central communications facility was signaling discreetly for someone's, anyone's, attention. The signal was not attracting much notice, but it got Hoveler's by means of a mellow audio pulsing through the nearest holostage, a device jutting up out of the deck like a flat-topped electronic tree stump. The bioengineer, looking around, found himself at the moment nearer than anyone else to the holostage. And no one else seemed exactly in a hurry to respond to the call.

As soon as Hoveler answered, the electronic voice of Communications, one facet of the laboratory vessel's own computerized intelligence, informed him politely that their most distinguished visitor, Lady Genevieve, had a personal message waiting.

"Can it wait a little longer?"

"I believe the call will be considered a very important one," said the electronic voice. That modest stubbornness on the part of Communications somehow conveyed, to Hoveler at least, the suggestion that someone closely associated with the Premier Dirac, if not Dirac himself, was trying to get through.

"Just a moment, then." Putting on such authoritative bearing as he was able to summon up, and using his above-average size in as gentle a manner as was consistent with effectiveness, Hoveler worked his way through the jealously constricted little crowd to almost within reach of the lady; at this range he could convey the information without shouting it boorishly.

The lady's bright eyes turned directly, searchingly, on him for the first time as he spoke to her. Seen at close range, she was somehow more attractive. She murmured something soft to the effect that any direct message from her husband seemed unlikely; to her best knowledge the Premier was still light-years away.

After making hasty excuses to the people in her immediate vicinity, she quickly moved the few steps to the nearest holostage.

Hoveler watched as the machine suddenly displayed the head and shoulders, as real and solid in appearance as if the body itself were there, of a youngish, rather portly man dressed in space-crew togs, pilot's insignia on his loose collar. The man's eyes focused at once on the lady, and his head awarded her a jaunty nod. It was a gesture on the verge of arrogance.

His voice rasped: "Nicholas Hawksmoor, architect and pilot, at your service, my lady."

The name was vaguely familiar to Hoveler. He had heard some passing mention of Hawksmoor and had the impression the man was some kind of special personal agent of Dirac's, but Hoveler had never seen him before. His image on the holostage was rather handsome.

From the look on Lady Genevieve's face, it seemed that she too had little if any acquaintance with this fellow. And as if she too recognized only the name, she answered tentatively.

Hoveler watched and listened, but no one else—except the lady herself, of course—was paying much attention to the conversation at the moment. Hawksmoor now conveyed in a few elegant phrases the fact that he had talked directly with her husband only a few days ago, more recently than she herself had seen the Premier, and that he was bringing her personal greetings from Dirac.

"Well then, Nicholas Hawksmoor, I thank you. Was there anything else?"

"Oh, from my point of view, my lady, a great deal else." His tone was calm, impertinent. "Are you interested in architecture, by any chance?"

Lady Genevieve blinked. "Only moderately, I suppose. Why?"

"Only that I have come here to this system, at the Premier's orders naturally, to study its existing architecture and ekistics. I hope to play a major role in the final design of the colonial vehicles when the great project really gets under way at last."

"How very important."

"Yes." After chewing his lip thoughtfully for a moment, the pilot asked in a quieter voice, "You've heard the Premier speak of me?"

"Yes," Lady Genevieve answered vaguely. "Where are you now, Nick? I may call you Nick, may I not, as he does?"

"Indeed you may, my lady." Brashness had now entirely left his manner; it was as if an innate arrogance had now given way to some deeper feeling.

Nick reported to the Lady Genevieve that he was even now at the controls of the small ship in which he customarily drove himself about and which he used in his work.

Hoveler's interest had been caught, naturally enough, by the lady when she first appeared, and now a more personal curiosity had been aroused as well. He was still watching. It did not occur to him—it seldom did—that it might be rude to stare. How interesting it was, the way this upstart Nicholas—whoever he was—and young Lady Genevieve were still looking into each other's imaged eyes—as if both were aware that something had been born between the two of them.

It was at this very moment that the sound of the first alarm reached the laboratory.

Hoveler, with his natural gift or burden of intense concentration, was not really immediately aware of that distant clamor. The Lady Genevieve was scarcely conscious, either, of the new remote signal. For her it could have been only one more muted sound, blending into the almost alien but gentle audio background of this unfamiliar place. And the whole Imatran solar system was deemed secure, as people sometimes remarked, to the point of dullness. The first stage of an alert, at last in this part of the large station, had been tuned down to be really dangerously discreet.

For the next minute it was possible for everyone else in the laboratory to disregard the warning entirely. Then, when people did begin to take notice, almost everyone considered the noise nothing more than a particularly ill-timed practice alert.

In fact, as Hawksmoor realized well before almost anyone else, the signal they were hearing was a quite genuine warning of an oncoming attack. Even he did not realize at once that the signal was so tragically delayed that those hearing it would be able to do very little before the attacker arrived.

"Excuse me," said Nick to Lady Genevieve, not more than one second after the first bell sounded in the lab; before another second had passed, his image had flickered away.

Heartbeats passed. The lady waited, wondering gently, and for the moment dully, what kind of problem had arisen on the young pilot's ship to provoke such an abrupt exit on his part. For a moment or two her eyes, silently questioning, came back to Hoveler's. He could see her visibly wondering whether to turn away from the holostage and get back to her duties of diplomacy.

But very soon, not more than ten seconds after the first disregarded signal, a notably louder alarm kicked in, shattering the illusory peace and quiet.

This was a sound that could not well be ignored. People were irritated, and at the same time were beginning to wake up.

"*Is* this a practice alert? What a time to choose for—"

Hoveler heard someone else answer, someone who sounded quietly lost: "No. It's not practice."

And a moment later, as if in affirmation, some kind of explosion in nearby space smote the solid outer hull of the station with a wave front of radiation hard enough to ring the metal like a gong. Even the artificial gravity generators in the interior convulsed for a millisecond or two, making the laboratory deck lurch underfoot.

Acting Supervisor Zador had turned to an intercom installation and was in communication with the station's optoelectronic intelligence. Turning to her eminent visitor, eyes widened whitely around their irises of startling blue, she said, "That was a ship nearby being blown up. I'm afraid it was your ship. Your pilot must have undocked and pulled out when he saw . . ."

Zador's voice trailed off. The lady was only staring back at her, still smiling faintly, obviously not yet able to understand.

Indeed, it seemed that no one in the lab could understand. The hideous truth could not instantly be accommodated by people who had such a press of other business in their lives to think about. Long seconds were needed for it to burrow into everyone's awareness. When truth at last struck home, it provoked a collective frozen instant, the intake of deep breaths, then panic. A genuine attack, unheard of here in the Imatran system, was nevertheless roaring in, threatening the existence of everything that breathed.

"*Berserkers!*" A lone voice screamed out the terrible word.

No, only one berserker. Moments later, the first official announcement, coming over loudspeakers in the artificially controlled tones of the station's own unshakable Communications voice, made this distinction, as if in some strange electronic attempt to be reassuring.

But to the listeners aboard the station, the number of times, the number of shapes in which death might be coming for them was only a very academic distinction indeed; the lab roiled in screaming panic.

Before the Lady Genevieve could move from the spot where she had been standing, Nick's image was abruptly back upon the holostage. Steadily confronting the lady, who now stood frozen in fear, Hawksmoor now elaborated, succinctly and steadily and quite accurately, on his claim to be a pilot.

"My lady, I fear your ship is gone. But mine is nearby, it will be docking in a minute, and, I repeat, I am a very good pilot."

"My ship is gone?"

"The ship that brought you here has already been destroyed. But mine is coming for you."

"*Already destroyed—*"

The cool image on the holostage, projecting a sense of competence, strongly urged—in fact, it sounded like he was ordering—the Lady Genevieve to run for a certain numbered airlock, and gave her concise directions as to which way to move from where she was.

"You are standing near the middle of the main laboratory deck, are you not?"

The lady glanced around in search of aid, then looked helplessly at Hoveler, who—wondering at his own composure—nodded confirmation.

Turning back to the holostage, she answered meekly: "Yes, I am."

Nick's image on the holostage issued calm instructions. He would have his ship docked at that lock before she reached it. She had better start moving without delay.

He concluded: "Bring all those people with you, I have room for them aboard. Bring everyone on the station; there can't be that many at the moment."

Meanwhile Hoveler, though dazed by the fact that a real attack was taking place, was remembering the all-too-infrequent practice alerts aboard the station, recalling the duties he was supposed to perform in such an emergency. His tasks during an alert or an attack consisted largely of supervising the quasi-intelligent machines that really did most of the lab work anyway. It was up to him to oversee the temporary shutdown of experiments and the proper storage of tools and materials.

Reacting to his training, the bioengineer got started on the job. It was not very demanding, not at this stage anyway, and it kept him in a location where he could still watch most of what was going on between the Premier's bride and one of his best pilots.

Hoveler used whatever spare moments he had to keep an anxious eye on Acting Supervisor Zador, who the moment the alert had sounded had found herself suddenly in command of local defenses. Obviously Anyuta was not used to such pressure, and Hoveler was afraid that she was somewhat panicked by it. Because just about the first thing she did was to reject Hawksmoor, who at least sounded like he knew what he was doing, in the role of rescuer.

Another message was now coming in on holostage for whoever was in charge aboard the station, and Hoveler could hear it in the background as he dealt with his own job. It was a communication from another craft, a regular manned courier that happened to be just approaching the station. Its human pilot was volunteering to help evacuate people from the facility, which was almost incapable of maneuvering under its own power. He could be on the scene in a matter of seconds.

"We accept," said the acting supervisor decisively. "Dock your ship at Airlock Three." A moment later, having put the latest and soon-to-be-most-famous protocolonist down on the flat top of the console near Hoveler and darting him a meaningful look as if to say *You deal with this*, she was running after the Lady Genevieve. Hoveler saw Anyuta grab the smaller woman by the arm and then firmly direct her down a different corridor than the one recommended by Nick, but in the correct direction to Airlock Three. At the moment, confusion dominated, with people running back and forth across the lab, and in both directions through the adjoining corridor. Some of the visitors were running in circles.

In the next moment the acting supervisor was standing beside Hoveler again, her attention once more directed to the central holostage. "Hawksmoor!"

"Dr. Zador?" the handsome image acknowledged.

"I am now in charge of the defenses here."

"Yes ma'am, I understand that."

"You are not to approach this station. We have another vessel available, already docked"—a quick glance at an indicator confirmed that—"and can evacuate safely without you. Take your ship out instead and engage the enemy—"

"My ship's not armed." Nick sounded as calm and firm as ever.

"Don't interrupt! If your ship is not armed, you will still engage the enemy, by ramming!"

"Yes ma'am!" Nick acknowledged the order crisply, with no perceptible hesitation. Once more his image vanished abruptly from the stage.

Annie, what the hell are you doing? Hoveler marveled at the order and response he had just heard, what had sounded like the calm assignment and equally calm acceptance of certain death. Certainly something was going on here which he did not understand—but he had no time to puzzle over it now.

Right now he had no need to understand or even think about what might be happening outside the station's hull. Dr. Hoveler and Dr. Zador, who were both required by duty as well as inclination to stand by their posts, exchanged a few words about the progress of the general evacuation. Then he felt the need to venture a personal remark.

"Anyuta."

Her attention locked in some technical contemplation, she didn't seem to hear him.

He tried again, more formally. "Dr. Zador?"

Now she did look over at him. "Yes?"

"You should get off this station with the others. You're going to get married in a month. Not that I think there's much chance we're really going to be . . . but I can do what little can be done here perfectly well by myself."

"This is my job," she said with what sounded like irritation, and turned back to her displays. Old friend and colleague or not, the acting supervisor wasn't going to call him by name. Not just now.

Hoveler, his own workbench already neatly cleared and now abandoned, stayed at his assigned battle station, which was near the center of the main laboratory deck, not far from Dr. Zador's post. Regulations called for acceleration couches to be available here for the two of them, but, as Hoveler recalled, those devices had been taken away months ago in some routine program of modification, and had never been brought back. The lack did not appear to pose a practical problem because the station would be able to do nothing at all in the way of effective maneuvering.

In terms of life support, the biostation possessed a full, indeed redundant, capability for interstellar flight, and had visited a number of planetary systems during the several years since its construction. But it had never mounted more than the simplest of space drives, relying on special c-plus tugs and boosters to accomplish its passages across interstellar distances.

Not that the lack appeared to be critical in this emergency. Even had an interstellar drive been installed and ready for use, any attempt to escape by that mode of travel now would have been practically suicidal for a vessel as big as the station starting this deep inside the gravitational well created by a full-sized star surrounded by the space-dimpling masses of its planets.

Still, with a berserker approaching at high speed, only a few minutes away at the most, some panicked person calling in from the surface of the planetoid was now evidently suggesting to the acting supervisor that even virtually certain suicide was preferable to the alternative, and ought to be attempted.

To this suggestion Dr. Zador replied, with what Hoveler applauded as admirable calm under the circumstances, that even had the drive capability been available, she was not about to suicidally destroy herself or anyone else. There wasn't even a regular flight crew aboard the station at the moment.

Besides, it was impossible for anyone on the station to determine absolutely, with the rudimentary instruments available on board, whether or not the berserker (which according to the displays was still thousands of kilometers distant) was really coming directly for the station, though its course strongly suggested that it was. The Imatran system contained two or three worlds much larger and vastly more populous than the planetoid, collectively holding a potential harvest of billions of human lives. These planets lay in approximately the same direction as the station along the berserker's path, but scores of millions of kilometers farther sunward.

The two people whose voluntarily chosen duties decreed that they should remain aboard the research station were able to look into the berserker's image on a stage—Hoveler, in sick fascination, had increasing difficulty looking anywhere else—and to see the monstrous shape growing, defiing itself more clearly moment by moment, coming dead-on against the almost starless background of the middle of the Mavronari Nebula.

Amid the ever-burgeoning clamor of alarms, there was no chance of putting into effective use such feeble subluminal drive as the station did possess. The propulsion system was basically intended only for gentle orbital maneuvers. Slow and relatively unmaneuverable, the mobile laboratory, even if it could have been got into steady motion, would have no chance of escaping the thing now rushing upon it from the deep.

The chances were vastly better that a courier like the one now loading, or presumably Nicholas Hawksmoor's craft, both small and swift, would be able to dodge out of harm's way.

Now, at the acting supervisor's remarkably calm urging, several dozen people, including visitors and most of the station's workers, were scrambling through the station's various decks and bays to board the courier vessel that had just docked.

The voice of the human pilot of that little ship could also be heard throughout the station, announcing tersely that he was ready to get away, to flee at full speed toward the system's inner planets and the protection of their formidable defenses.

Beneath the two competing sets of announcements, running and shouting echoed in the corridors. People who had become confused and found themselves going in the wrong direction were one by one turned around and headed in the proper way.

Acting Supervisor Zador, speaking directly to the courier pilot, repeatedly ordered him not to undock until everyone—everyone who wanted to go—had got aboard.

"I acknowledge. Are you two coming? This is an emergency."

The acting supervisor glanced briefly at her companion. "I know it's an emergency, damn it," she replied. "That's why we two are staying." Hoveler on hearing this experienced a thrill of pride, as if she had just bestowed on him some signal honor. At the moment he felt no particular fear. For one thing—though no one had yet brought up the point—there was no guarantee that fleeing in the launch was going to prove any safer than staying where they were.

That was why Hoveler had not pushed harder to get Anyuta Zador to leave.

Nor had Dr. Zador pressed the bioengineer to flee to safety. Obviously she welcomed his assistance.

Now, outside the lab doors, in the adjoining corridor, the last footsteps had fallen silent. In a few moments the last courier would be gone, and the two Solarian humans were going to be alone—except for whatever feelings of companionship they might be able to derive from metric tons of blue tiles, those myriad sparks of preconscious human life that constituted the station's cargo and their responsibility.

Hoveler and Zador exchanged a look and waited. At the moment there seemed to be nothing useful to be said.

Within a few meters of where they were standing, the frightful shape of the enemy, imaged in the false space of the holostage, was steadily magnified by the rushing speed of its approach.

☀ TWO

Never before had the Lady Genevieve faced an emergency even remotely like this one. Until today her short life had been spent mostly near the center of the Galactic region dominated by Earth-descended humanity, in realms of Solarian space that were wrapped in physical security by Templar fleets, by the Space Force, by the local military establishments of a hundred defended systems. In that blessed region berserkers had never been much more than improbable monsters, demons out of fable and legend.

The lady's betrothal and wedding, followed by a rapid flow of other events, none of them terrible in themselves, had carried her by imperceptible stages closer to that world of legend, until now she found herself fleeing down a narrow corridor aboard an unfamiliar spacecraft, her last illusion of physical security jarred loose by the sharp elbow of a screaming publicist thrusting her aside.

Dozens of people, almost everyone who had been aboard the station, including all the visitors, seemed to be in the same corridor, and their frantic activity made the number seem like hundreds or a thousand. What only minutes ago had been an assembly of civilized folk had quickly become a mindless mob, the group first teetering on, then falling over, the brink of panic.

Bioengineer Hoveler was to remember later that he had seen the Lady Genevieve leave the laboratory at a fast pace, moving among her aides as if she were being propelled by them. As the lady went out the door of the laboratory she was moving in the direction indicated by Dr. Zador, toward the hatch where the little escape ship was waiting.

At the same time, in some distant region of the biostation, perhaps on the next deck up or down, some kind of stentorian klaxon, an alarm neither of the remaining workers had ever heard before, had started throbbing rhythmically. The two stay-behind observers were able to remember later how the Premier's young wife, dazed and hurried as she was, seemed to be trying to turn back, in the last moment before she was swept out of the laboratory. It took one of the Lady Genevieve's bodyguards to turn her around again and drag her on by main force toward the waiting courier. And at the moment of her hesitation the young woman had cried out something sounding like "My child!"

So now suddenly it's a child, thought Hoveler. A few minutes ago, that microscopic knot of organic tissue, from which she had so recently been separated, had been only a donation, only a zygote or protochild. But the lady was getting away, and he had no time to think about her or her ideas now.

The lady herself, even as she momentarily tried to turn back, realized perfectly well that her maternal impulse had no logic to it—to leave her child and her husband's here was no more than she had expected all along. But now—of course she hadn't expected a berserker attack—

Rationally, as she understood full well, there was no reason to believe that the microscopic cluster of cells, now sealed inside preserving statglass, would be any safer in her small hands than it was here, wherever the technicians had put it. Probably it was already in some storage vault. But still the Lady Genevieve, driven by some instinct, did momentarily make an effort to turn back.

Then she had been turned around and started out again, and from that moment her thoughts and energy were absorbed in her own fight for survival. None of the people now struggling and scrambling to get through the airlock and aboard the escape ship had ever rehearsed anything like an emergency evacuation. The scene was one of fear and selfishness, but there was really plenty of room aboard the smaller craft, no need to be ruthless.

Within moments after the last person had scrambled in through its passenger entry, the courier—which of course was going to try to summon help, as well as evacuate people—sealed all its hatches. A very few moments after that the courier pilot, his nerves perhaps not quite equal to the situation, anyway making his own calculus of lives to be saved, among which his own was prominent, undocked without waiting for final authorization from anybody, and immediately shot his small craft away in a try for safety.

Meanwhile the dozens of people who had crowded aboard spread out across the limited passenger space in trembling gratitude, standing and walking in an artificial gravity field reassuringly normal and stable. The passengers moved to occupy the available acceleration couches, which would offer them at least minimal protection should the gravity fail in some emergency. Meanwhile their murmured exhalations formed a collective sigh of relief.

For the first minute or two after their vessel separated from the space station, the Lady Genevieve shared elation with her companions aboard the escaping courier. They began to experience a glorious, innocent near certainty that they were safe.

Lady Genevieve was in the middle of saying something to one of her official companions, perhaps protesting her bodyguards' roughness or her publicist's rudeness in pushing her out of the way—or perhaps she was trying to excuse these people for the way they had behaved—when the next blast came.

This one made the previous explosion, heard from a safe distance while they were still aboard the station, sound like nothing at all. This one was disaster. In an instant, in the very midst of a conversation, the world of the Premier's bride dissolved into a blur of shock and horror.

Briefly she lost consciousness.

On recovering her senses, moments later, Lady Genevieve looked about her, peering through a cabin atmosphere gone steamy cold with the instant, swirling fog of sudden depressurization. Gradually remembering where she was, she looked around in hopes of finding a space suit available. But if there was any emergency equipment of that kind aboard, she had not the faintest idea of where to find it.

Feeling dazed, vaguely aware that her limbs ached and that it was hard to breathe, as if her chest had been crushed, the lady released herself from her acceleration couch. Only at that point did she realize that the artificial gravity was low; it must be failing slowly. Emergency lights still glowed.

She dragged herself from one side of the blasted cabin to the other, aware as in a dream that she was the only one moving actively about. Other bodies drifted here and there, settling slowly, inertly in the low g toward the deck. Arms and legs stirred feebly on some of the seats and couches, accompanied by a sound of moaning. Meanwhile the Lady Genevieve was able to hear, almost to feel, the air whining steadily out of the punctured cabin, depleting itself slowly but faster than any reserve tanks were able to replenish it.

Genevieve turned to make her way forward, with some vague idea that the pilot's compartment ought to be in that direction, and that someone, human or autopilot, ought still to be there, still in charge, and that she and the other passengers needed help. But, for whatever reason, she found herself unable to open the hatch or door that led out of the main passenger cabin. There was a small glass panel in the door, and she could see through it a little, just enough to convince her that there was nothing but ruin forward.

And still the air kept up a faint whining, hissing . . . an automatic sealant system was still trying, vainly but stubbornly, to ameliorate disaster.

Now all around her, above, below (though such terms were swiftly losing any practical meaning) drifted the dead and dying, and a few others who like herself had freed themselves from their couches but were unable to do anything more. It registered with Genevieve that no one had even the most modest emergency suit or equipment, no way to keep at bay for long the emptiness outside the fragile, failing hull.

Machinery twitched and moved. She could hear it, somewhere outside the compartment in which she and her unlucky fellow passengers were trapped. From somewhere, at last, an autopilot's voice started trying to give reassurance and then shut up. The voice came back, calm as all robotic voices were, repeated twice some idiotic irrelevance about staying in your couches, please, then went away for good.

Straining her aching limbs, Genevieve took hold of one or two of her drifting fellow passengers and tried to rouse them to meaningful communication. But this effort had no success.

Her every breath hurt her now. Pulling herself from one acceleration couch to another, the lady observed with the numbness of growing shock that as far as she could tell, all of her bodyguards, publicists, and other aides—at least all she could recognize under these conditions—were dead. Probably no one among the few passengers still breathing was better off than she was, or even able to talk to anyone else, beyond a few groans.

After an interval in which Lady Genevieve thought she had begun to accustom herself to being dead, a new noise reached her ears. She opened her eyes, gripping her fingers into fists, wishing that the lightheadedness that was growing minute by minute would go away. What was she hearing? Something real, yes. Only sounds of the wrecked ship collapsing further?

And out of nowhere, it seemed, the certainty suddenly returned to her: she was now clearly convinced, in the face of death, that it had been a mistake to give up her child. If she hadn't agreed to make the donation, she wouldn't be here now. She would be home instead—

There it came again. Yes, definitely, a noise that spoke of purpose, not just of collapse.

Yes. Someone or something was working on some part of the ship from the outside, trying to get in.

A moment later, the Lady Genevieve, trying to focus her mind against a feeling like too much wine—with part of her mind she understood this was anoxia—thought she was able to identify the grating sound of contact between two vessels.

Working her way almost weightlessly closer to a cleared port, she was able to see that another small vehicle had matched velocities with the wreck and was very close indeed.

The same noise again, quite near at hand, and perhaps a flare of light as well; something or someone cutting through metal—

Abruptly metal opened, without any murderous escape of air. She saw, with a shock of relief of such intensity that she almost fainted, that her visitor was no murderous machine, but rather a suited human figure that spoke to her at once, and reassuringly.

Genevieve was by this time more than a little dazed, rapturously light-headed with lack of oxygen as cabin pressure dropped to dangerously low levels. Her body was scratched in several places, and seriously bruised. But she was not too badly hurt to glide her nearly weightless body across the foggy interior of the cabin and plant a big kiss on her rescuer's faceplate.

(And was it something her fuzzy vision discovered for her, or could not discover, inside his or her helmet, that made the lady's eyes widen for just a moment?)

In response to her kiss upon his helmet there seemed to be just a moment of hesitation, surprise, on her rescuer's part. And then the armored arms came round her, gently, protectively returning the hug. Out of the suit's air speaker came the same voice she remembered coming from a holostage, what seemed like an age ago. "Nicholas Hawksmoor, my lady. At your service."

Drifting back to arm's length from the embrace, she demanded eagerly: "Can you get me out of here? I don't have a suit, you see. It seems there are no suits aboard."

"That's quite all right, my lady. I can get you out safely. Because—"

And at that instant, with a great roar, all that was left of her newly salvaged life, her world, exploded.

Drs. Hoveler and Zador meanwhile, with the stowage of experiments and materials just about completed, were snatching intervals, long seconds at a time, from their self-imposed duties, to watch, as best they could on holostage and instrument readouts, the fighting that flared intermittently outside the station's hull.

Between these intervals of dreadful observation the two oversaw robotic maintenance of the station's life support systems. There was really nothing they could do to defend the station—the laboratory had not been designed or built for frontier duty, and was completely unarmed and unshielded. So far, it seemed to be essentially undamaged.

Several times the two people standing watch in the laboratory expressed their hope that the courier ship had got clean away—they had heard no word about it one way or the other. And Acting Supervisor Zador once or twice wondered aloud, in such intervals for thought as she was able to seize among her duties, what success Nicholas Hawksmoor was having with the ramming maneuver she had commanded him to attempt. Hoveler had been meaning to ask her about that, but once more he decided that his questions could wait.

Of course the ultimate result of the berserker attack did not depend very much on Hawksmoor, Hoveler thought. Whatever he might or might not have done, there were fairly strong defenses in place on the surface of the planetoid Imatra, and the station in its low orbit lay well within the zone of their protection. Also a pair, at least, of armed ships happened to be lying by close enough in space to put up a fight against the onrushing attacker.

These ground batteries and ships, and the people who crewed them, as records later were to confirm, bravely offered opposition to the onslaught.

But events proved that the single enemy was far too strong. The defenders watched powerlessly as the berserker, not in the least deterred or delayed by the best they could accomplish, came on in an undeviating course obviously calculated to intercept the bioresearch station in its swift orbit. The enemy's immediate presence in the station's vicinity was now less than a minute away.

Hoveler's next helpless inspection of the nearby holostage showed him the onrushing image of death changing, shedding little fragments of itself. He interpreted this to mean that the berserker had launched some small craft of its own—or were they missiles? He wondered why, on the verge of his own destruction, he should find such details interesting.

Though neither of the people on the station were aware of the details, the planetoid's ground defenses offered such resistance as they could manage to put up, bright beams of energy slicing and punctuating space, annihilating some of the small enemy machines; but only moments after the ground batteries opened fire, they were pounded into silence, put out of action by the even heavier weapons of the enemy. And the first pair of fighting ships who tried to engage the foe were soon blasted into fragments, transformed into expanding clouds of metallic vapor laced with substances of organic origin.

There were only a couple of fighting ships left in the whole Imatran system, and only one of these was anywhere near the scene of the attack and in position to close with the attacker. Its captain and crew did not lack courage. Hurtling bravely within range, this last human fighter to join the fray opened up with its weapons on its gigantic opponent and the smaller commensal ships or spacegoing machines the attacker had deployed.

But none of the weapons humanity could bring to bear seemed to do the great berserker any serious damage, though it was impossible at the moment to accurately assess their effect.

And now it was no longer possible to doubt the enemy's prime objective. The huge bulk of the berserker, basically almost spherical, vaguely ragged in its outline, wreathed by the glowing power of its defensive force fields, was easing to a halt in space within a few hundred meters of the biolab, dwarfing the station by its size, smoothly matching the sharp curve of the smaller object's orbit.

By this time Daniel Hoveler had left his post, where he had already carried out, quite uselessly, such duties as the manuals prescribed.

Annie, startled to see him go, called out sharply: "Where are you going?"

He called over his shoulder: "I'll be back." He had an idea that she might be better off if she did not know what he was about to do.

Leaving the laboratory deck, he rode a quick lift to the level where the hardware comprising the station's optelectronic brain was concentrated. Anyuta Zador had called after him again, demanding to know where he was going, but he had refused to answer. His thought in refusing was that she would somehow be safer from the berserker's revenge if she didn't know what he was doing.

His plan, such as it was, involved finding some way to scramble the information code by which the station's brain kept track of the enormous inventory of tiled, preserved zygotes.

Even as Hoveler made his way toward the chamber where the station's brain was located, Dr. Zador continued calling him on intercom. At last he answered, briefly and noncommittally, having a vague and probably irrational fear that the enemy might already be listening.

The intercom system was tracking his progress, effortlessly and automatically. From one deck to another, Hoveler and Zador kept up a terse communication.

Neither of the two expected anything better than quick death. Both of them, finding themselves still breathing at this stage, were fearful of some fate considerably worse.

"Dan? It's just sitting there a couple of hundred meters from our hull! Dan, what are you doing?" Perhaps she thought he was trying to hide or to escape.

He couldn't think while she kept shouting at him, and right now he had to think, because he had reached and unlocked the little room he wanted. Maybe it didn't make sense to try to keep what he was doing secret; he would explain.

"I'm not trying to hide, Annie. I'm going after the zygotes."

"Going after them?" She sounded nearly in a panic.

"Annie, haven't you asked yourself why we aren't dead already? Obviously because the berserker wants something that we've got on board. It wants to capture something undamaged. I think that something has to be our cargo."

"Dan. The tiles . . ." Now her voice seemed to be fading.

For years the two of them had worked together, lived, struggled, sometimes in opposition over details but always together in their determination that the overall colonial project should succeed. They had both devoted themselves to the welfare of these protopeople, to the hope of eventually contributing to their achievement of real lives.

For the moment there was silence on the intercom.

Now Hoveler, agonizing, was working with the hardware, entering computer commands, trying to remember how to isolate that portion of the ship's brain having to do with cargo inventory without causing widespread failure in other functions. Now he was running through numbers on a readout, and now he was calling up on holostage a direct view of the vast storage banks of nascent people being housed on this deck and others—chamber after chamber of them, bin after bin. The idea flashed through his mind that it was at least a merciful dispensation that these could feel neither pain nor fear.

Hoveler, swayed by an agonized moment or two of indecision, continued to stare at the imaged bins and cabinets protectively holding the protocolonists.

Calling up one image after another on a convenient 'stage, he inspected the endless-seeming ranks of tiles in storage. Row after row, drawer after drawer, densely packed. The handy little storage devices were amazingly tough, designed to offer great resistance to either accidental or purposeful destruction.

In a flash it crossed his mind to wonder what had actually happened to the Premier's newly donated protoperson. He remembered Annie's putting the tile down on the top of his own console—but he couldn't remember seeing it or even thinking about it at any time after that.

In the normal course of events, one of the attendant machines in the lab, observing a tile lying about loose, would have picked it up and whisked it away for filing. But under present circumstances . . .

Just looking at them didn't help, of course. Whatever he was going to do, he felt sure that he had not much time in which to do it. But the seconds of inexplicable survival stretched on into minutes while Hoveler kept trying very cleverly and subtly to inflict damage, controlled but irreversible, upon the thinking hardware. And still the minutes of continued life stretched on . . .

For whatever purpose, the fatal stroke was still withheld. The destroyer was treating the unarmored, undefended station very gently. But surely at any moment now something terrible would happen.

Instead of swift destruction, there came a bumping, grating noise, at once terrible and familiar.

Hoveler tried hastily to finish what he had started. The new noise sounded like some small craft or machine, evidently an emissary from the berserker, attempting a docking with the lab.

Given the limited time and tools available, destroying any substantial proportion of the tiles seemed as utterly impossible a task as getting them to safety. Therefore he had concentrated on achieving hopeless confusion in the determination of the specimens' identities. Because it seemed that, for some wicked reason of its own, the berserker was actually intent on taking them all alive.

He could only try to deduce the reason, but it must be horrible. Minutes ago, when it became obvious that they were being spared quick destruction, a hideous scenario had sprung into Hoveler's imagination, to the effect that the damned machine was planning to seize the zygotes and the artificial wombs and raise a corps of goodlife slaves and auxiliaries.

Meanwhile Annie Zador, back on the laboratory deck, was listening to the station's own calm robotic Communications voice announce that something had just completed a snug docking at Airlock Two.

"Should I open?" The same bland voice asked the question.

She didn't bother to reply. Before the question could be repeated, it had become irrelevant. Whatever was outside was not waiting politely for an invitation. The airlock was only a standard model, not built to withstand a determined boarding assault, and within a few seconds it had been opened without the cooperation of any interior intelligence.

Moments after the enemy had forced open the airlock, four boarding machines of deadly appearance came striding upon inhuman legs into the main laboratory.

Anyuta Zador closed her eyes and, waiting for destruction, held her breath—

—and then, unable to bear the suspense, began with an explosive shudder to breathe again. She opened her eyes to see that only one of the silent machines now stood regarding her with its lenses. The rest of the boarders had already gone somewhere. They must have fanned out across the laboratory or gone back into the corridor. Not back out through the airlock; she would have heard its doors again.

"Obey orders," the remaining machine advised her in a voice not much more inhuman than the station's, "and you will not be harmed."

Zador could not force herself to answer.

"Do you understand?" the machine demanded. It rolled closer, stopping no more than two meters away. "You must obey."

"Yes. I—I understand." She clung to her supervisor's console to keep from falling down in terror.

"How many other people are on board?"

"No one else." The brave lie came out unplanned and very quickly, before Dr. Zador allowed herself the time to consider what its consequences might be.

Already another of the invaders was coming back into the laboratory room. "Where are the flight controls?" it demanded of her, in a voice identical to that of the first berserker device.

Zador had to stop and think. "What few controls this vessel has for that purpose are on the next deck up."

The machine that had just reentered the lab stalked out again.

Meanwhile Hoveler was working on furiously, but carefully. It would be good if he could avoid leaving any traces of this intrusion. Since it would be practically impossible for him to destroy the cargo of protopeople—he wasn't sure that he could bring himself to make the effort anyway—he was determined to render them less useful in whatever horrible experiment the berserker might be planning.

Assuming he was successful, what should he do then? He was not the type to contemplate killing himself in cold blood. Seek out the nearest berserker presence and give himself up? Simply return to his post, where Annie was more than likely already dead?

He supposed that if he should choose to hide out, the length of time he would be able to avoid capture or death depended to some extent upon how many machines the berserker had sent aboard. If the number of invaders was small, he might be able to conceal himself indefinitely. He might also be aided by the enemy's ignorance of the physical layout inside the station.

Indefinitely?

The overall shape of the facility was roughly that of a cylinder a little more than fifty meters in diameter, and about the same in length. Twelve decks or levels provided space for work, storage, and housing. There had been more than enough room for the usual crew of people and machines to move about without getting in one another's way.

The facility had been planned and built as a study for a colonization vehicle. It was equipped with smoothly reliable artificial gravity and a lot of research machinery, including a ten-meter cube, also called a ten-three, or just a tencube, for research carried on in the mode of virtual reality. Hoveler seemed to remember that its architects had fallen out of favor with Premier Dirac over the last year or so, as he had gradually become dissatisfied with their work. That was one reason why Nicholas Hawksmoor had been brought on line.

In order to complete his job of disruption properly, Hoveler would have to cope with redundancies in the system by moving physically from one deck to another. He feared that murderous berserker machines must be aboard the station now, and that they would detect his presence if he used the lift again. They might detect him anyway if they decided to tap into the intercom, but he would just have to risk that.

Easing his way as quietly as possible out of the small room in which he had been working, Hoveler closed its door behind him and tiptoed down a curving corridor toward the nearest companionway.

The shortest, simplest route to his next stop required that he traverse at least a corner of the deck on which the great majority of the mechanical wombs had been installed. In the midst of this passage, while peering carefully to his right, Hoveler froze momentarily. Far across the deck, perhaps forty meters away, and only partially visible between rows of silent, life-nurturing machines stood another metal shape that was completely unfamiliar and intrusive. It seemed that a berserker guard had been established.

He couldn't stand here all day waiting to be caught; he had to move. Perhaps the muted murmurs of flowing air and electricity were loud enough to muffle the faint sounds his softly shod feet must have made on the smooth floor. Perhaps the intervening machines blocked the berserker's line of sight. In any event, Hoveler managed to get to the next companionway and the next deck without being detected.

Once there, under great tension, the evader managed to get inside the last compartment from which the system's records could be restored. Easing the door shut, he got on with his task of befuddling the central inventory system.

Perhaps it was some noise he unavoidably made, working with the necessary small tools, that betrayed his presence. Whatever the reason, he had not been at work for twenty seconds when one of the boarding machines pulled open the door of the small room and caught him in the act.

In the circumstances, Hoveler hoped for a quick death, but the hope failed. In another moment the multilimbed machine—obviously being careful not to hurt him very much—was dragging him back to the laboratory deck.

There, moments later, he and Anyuta Zador exchanged incoherent cries, on each discovering that the other was still alive. The machine that had been dragging Hoveler released him, and a moment later the two humans were in each other's arms.

And still, ominously as it seemed, Death forbore to make any quick, clean claim. Instead of destroying the helplessly vulnerable station entirely, or gutting it ruthlessly with boarding machines, the gigantic foe had clamped onto its outer hull with force fields—as the prisoners, allowed access to a holostage, were able to observe—and was starting to haul it away. The hull sang for a while under the unaccustomed strain, emitting strange mournful noises. Then it quieted.

Minutes of captivity dragged on, as if divorced from time. Exhausted by strain, their weary eyelids sagging, the prisoners attempted to rest. The last chance I'll ever get to rest, Hoveler thought dully. The artificial gravity was still functioning with soothing steadiness, damping out or quenching entirely any acceleration that would otherwise have resulted from the new, externally imposed motion. The people inside the station could not feel themselves being towed.

Puzzlingly, the berserker seemed to be ignoring the incident of Hoveler's sabotage. So far the boarding machines had administered no punishment, made no threats, asked him no questions. It was an attitude both humans found unsettling. A berserker that did not do something bad could only be preparing something worse.

When Hoveler and Zador had given up for the time being trying to rest, they conferred again. For some reason they found themselves speaking in soft whispers, despite the fact that their metal captors nearby were almost certainly able to detect sounds much fainter than those required by the human ear. Both humans were thoroughly bewildered, almost frightened, by their own continued survival. And also by the fact that they still had access to almost the full spectrum of commonly used controls, at least those within the lab. Not that any of these allowed them any influence over what was happening to their vessel. Once Hoveler had been dragged back, neither he nor Zador had attempted to leave the laboratory deck.

Meanwhile Hoveler, despite his terror, could silently congratulate himself that he had indeed managed to scramble most of the cargo inventory system. Still, he dared not try to communicate this achievement to Annie. Nor did he want to raise with her, in the berserkers' presence, the question of what might have happened to the last zygote that had been contributed.

Anyuta Zador had said nothing about his absence and recapture. But an hour or so after his return, she took the chance of giving him a long questioning look, whose meaning he read as *Where were you?*

The look he gave Annie in response was an attempt to express that he understood the question, but didn't know how to go about conveying a good answer.

However they tried to distract themselves or each other, both people's thoughts inevitably kept coming back to the gritty peril of their own situation.

Dan Hoveler had no immediate family of his own—a lack for which he currently felt a devout gratitude. But he could tell, or thought he could, that his companion, in the long silent minutes when she closed her eyes or stared at nothing, must be thinking about the man she was going to marry.

Hoveler considered suggesting the possibility of a successful rescue attempt—but Annie knew at least as well as he did how very unlikely anything of the kind really was.

After several hours had passed, and a few exchanges of whispered words, the captive couple decided to make an attempt to leave the lab deck and go to their cabins. Somewhat to their surprise they were allowed to do so. Not that the berserker had forgotten its prisoners—two machines accompanied them when they left the lab, and searched their cabins thoroughly before the tenants were allowed to enter.

Though each cabin was now occupied by a guardian, the humans were allowed to rest—choosing under the circumstances to stay together in one cabin. Hoveler, sprawled on a couch, soon found himself actually dozing off.

A few hours later, a little rested though still under observation, and back on the lab deck again, the bioworkers tried to satisfy their curiosity about what was happening. Cleared ports and free use of a holostage made it possible to gain some information.

"You're right, no doubt about it, we're being towed."

"I don't get it." Hoveler blew out breath in a great sigh.

"Nor do I. But here we are. Pulled. Dragged along. The entire station is being towed away. Our hull, or a large part of it anyway, seems to be wrapped in force fields. Like a faint gray mist that you can see only at certain angles."

They adjusted the stage again and watched, while their own watchers stood by, tolerating them in enigmatic silence. After a while Zador announced: "Dan, this just doesn't make any sense."

"I know that."

"So where is it taking us? Why?"

He shrugged. "We're bound away from the sun, it seems. Steadily but slowly accelerating out of the system. Since we're now out of communication with the rest of humanity, I can't see enough to be any more specific."

Time passed, disjointedly. The humans sat or stood around, terror slowly congealing into a sick approximation of calm, waiting for whatever might happen to them next.

Gradually Hoveler's sense of minor triumph at what he had done to the inventory system faded, to be replaced by a sickening thought: the berserker might well be completely indifferent as to the individual identities of any of its captured protocolonists. Maybe one Solarian human or protohuman would serve as well as another in whatever fiendish scheme the enemy calculated.

Still the machines inflicted no harm upon the captive humans. Nor had the berserker any objection to their talking to each other; in fact it seemed to Hoveler that their captor by not separating them was actually encouraging them to converse freely.

He had a thought, and couldn't see any harm in speaking it aloud. "Maybe it's letting us talk because it wants to listen."

Annie nodded immediately. "That idea had occurred to me."

"So what do we do?"

"What harm can we do by talking? Neither of us knows any military secrets."

Meanwhile, the invading machines were not standing idle. One at least of them remained in sight of each prisoner at all times. Others worked intermittently, probing with their own fine tools into the station's controls and other machinery; whether their intention was to make alterations or simply to investigate, Hoveler found impossible to determine.

Eventually the humans, growing restless and being allowed to roam about the station at will though under guard, were able to observe machines on other decks as well, some of them digging into various kinds of hardware there. Privately Hoveler estimated the number on board the station to be about a dozen in all.

Since the first minutes of their occupation, the boarding machines had had nothing to say to their new captives.

The number of hours elapsed since the boarding lengthened at last into a standard day. Zador and Hoveler were spending most of their time on the more familiar laboratory deck. They were there, in the midst of a low-voiced conversation, when Annie broke off a statement in midsentence and looked up in astonishment. Hoveler, following her gaze with his own, was likewise struck dumb.

A man and woman he had never seen before, ragged scarecrow Solarian figures, had suddenly appeared in front of him. The newcomers were staring with odd hungry eyes at Hoveler and Zador.

It was left to Hoveler himself to break the silence. "Hello."

Neither of the newcomers responded immediately to this greeting. From the look of their shabby, emaciated figures, the expression on their faces and in their eyes, Hoveler quickly got the idea that a clear answer was unlikely.

He tried again, and presently the two new arrivals, urged by repeated questioning, introduced themselves as Carol and Scurlock.

Annie was staring at them. "How did you get aboard? You came—from the berserker?"

They both nodded. The man mumbled a few words of agreement.

Zador and Hoveler exchanged looks of numbed horror, wondering silently if they were beholding their own future.

The more closely Hoveler studied the newcomers, the more his horror grew. Scurlock was unshaven. The hair of both was matted and dirty; their dress was careless; garments were unfastened, incomplete, unchanged for far too long. Carol was wearing no shoes, and her shirt hung partially open, her breasts intermittently exposed. Evidently that wasn't normal behavior in whatever society they'd come from, for Scurlock, who at moments appeared vaguely embarrassed, now and then tried to get her to cover up. Still, the pair appeared to have been allowed free access to food and drink—they were indifferent to what Zador and Hoveler offered them from one of the station's serving robots. And they showed no signs of overt, serious physical abuse.

But the blank way the newcomers, especially Carol, looked around the lab, their halting silences, their appearance—these things suggested to Hoveler that eccentric if not downright crazy behavior was to be anticipated. Obviously Carol and Scurlock were long accustomed to the berserkers' presence, because for the most part they simply ignored the omnipresent machines.

Hoveler caught himself hoping silently, fervently, that the pair would not do anything to damage the lab's machinery.

As if that now mattered in the least.

The pair settled in, helping themselves to one of the number of empty staterooms, which they occupied with a guardian machine.

Between themselves, the biolab workers soon agreed that both of the newcomers, particularly Carol, must have become unbalanced under the strain of some lengthy captivity. This tended to make the sporadic intervals of conversation with them extra rich and strange.

Annie asked: "Do you mind telling us how you were captured? And where?"

"We were taken off a ship," Scurlock said by way of partial explanation. Then he looked at the station's two original occupants as if he were worried about their reaction to this news.

"How long ago?"

Neither Carol nor Scurlock could say, or perhaps they wanted to keep this information secret.

Annie Zador turned to a 'stage and began calling up news of missing ships, trying to find out from the station's data banks if any vessels had disappeared locally within the past few months. The banks provided a small list of craft recently vanished within the sector, but Carol and Scurly seemed strangely disinterested in cooperating. They did admit they'd been working with a small, unnamed ship taking a survey for the Sardou Foundation; no, they'd no idea what the berserker might be doing with their ship now. In fact they couldn't remember when they'd seen it last.

Next the bioworkers tried, with only small success, to trade information about backgrounds. Neither Carol nor Scurlock sounded quite rational enough to state clearly how long they had been the berserker's prisoners. No, they hadn't formed any opinions as to why it had now brought them aboard the station.

"Does the berserker have any other people aboard?" Zador asked suddenly, thinking of a new tack to try. "Any goodlife, maybe?"

"*We* are goodlife," Carol announced clearly, with an apprehensive glance at the nearest listening machine. Two of her listeners recoiled involuntarily. The ragged, dirty woman sounded very emphatic, if not entirely sane.

Her companion nodded, slowly and thoughtfully. "We are," he agreed. "What about you?"

There was a silence. Then in a small, firm voice Anyuta Zador said: "We are not."

The machine appeared to take no notice.

Slowly Scurlock began to pay more attention to the new environment in which his metal master had established him. "What is this place, anyway?" he demanded.

Hoveler began to explain.

The dirty, unkempt man interrupted: "I wonder what our machine wants it for?"

"Your machine? You mean the berserker?"

"Call it that if you want. It asked us an awful lot of questions about this ... place ... before it brought us here."

As Zador and Hoveler listened in mounting horror, Carol added: "I don't see what use a cargo of human zygotes is going to be. Ugh. But our machine knows best."

Hoveler, his own nerves thoroughly frayed by now, could not completely smother his anger. "Your machine, as you call it, seems to have computed that you're both going to be very helpful to it!"

"I am certainly going to help," Carol agreed hastily. For once her speech was clear and direct. "We are. We just don't know *how* as yet. But the machine will tell us when the time comes, and we're ready."

"We're ready!" agreed Scurlock fervently. Then he fell silent, aware that both Hoveler and Zador were looking at him in loathing and contempt. "Badlife!" he whispered, indulging his own disdain.

"We are goodlife." Carol, once more looking and sounding unbalanced, had suddenly adopted an incongruous, schoolteacherish refrain and manner.

Zador snapped at her: "Who's arguing with you? All right, if you say so. You're goodlife. Yes, I can believe that readily enough."

Hoveler heard himself adding a few gutter epithets.

Carol let out a deranged scream and sprang at Annie in a totally unexpected assault, taking the taller woman by surprise and with insane strength driving her back, clawing with jagged nails at her face.

Before Annie went down, or was seriously injured, Hoveler stepped in and shoved the smaller woman violently away, so that she staggered and fell on the smooth deck.

"Let her alone!" Scurlock in turn shoved Hoveler.

"Then tell her to let us alone!"

The quarrel trailed off, in snarling and cursing on both sides.

Hours later, an uneasy truce prevailed. Hoveler and Zador, talking privately between themselves, were developing strong suspicions that Scurlock and Carol might actually have sought out the berserker in their little ship and volunteered as willing goodlife.

"Do you think it's waiting for us to do the same thing?"

Zador raised her head, "I wonder if it's listening?"

"No doubt it's always listening. Well, I don't give a damn. Maybe it'll hear something it doesn't want to hear for a change. What really frightens me," the bioengineer continued, "is that I think I can understand now how people come to be goodlife. Did you ever think about that?"

"Not until now."

❂   ❂   ❂

There were intervals when it seemed that Scurlock, at least, was trying to come to terms with the other couple. Carol seemed too disconnected to care whether she came to terms with anyone or not.

Scurlock: "Look here, we're all prisoners together."

Hoveler nodded warily. "Has the machine given you any idea of what it plans to do with you? Or with us?"

"No." Then Scurlock put on a ghastly smile: "But Carol and I are going to play along. That's the only course to take in a situation like this."

Meanwhile, in the hours and days immediately following the theft of the station, all of the various bases, populous cities, and settlements upon the habitable planets of the Imatran system were frantic with activity. Much of it utterly useless, all of it too late to save the station. Word of the berserker attack had of course been dispatched at light speed to the authorities who governed the system's sunward worlds. The news had reached those planets within a few hours of the event. Hastily they had dispatched what little help they had readily available toward the ravaged planetoid.

Following established military doctrine, a unified system command was at once set up, and under its aegis the big worlds coordinated their efforts as thoroughly as possible.

There would be no more in-system fighting—if for no other reason than because the Imatrans had nothing else in space capable of challenging the victorious enemy. The captured station was being ruthlessly, inexorably, but carefully, gently, hauled away.

Within a few hours after the beginning of the raid, all that remained in the Imatran system as evidence of the outrage was a modest number of dead and wounded, scattered marks of damage on the surface of the planetoid, some swiftly fading electromagnetic signals, including light waves ...

A small amount of debris drifting in space, wreckage from human ships and small berserkers, the result of the brief, fierce combat.

And a number of recordings, affording reasonably complete documentation of the outrage.

☀ THREE

In a dream that seemed to her both prolonged and recurring, the Lady Genevieve beheld the image of her rescuer continuing to drift before her eyes. The suited figure, faceless inside his protective space helmet, had the shape of a tall man, ruggedly strong, who held out his arms in an offer of succor from disaster, of salvation from—

From everything, perhaps, except bad dreams.

And her rescuer's voice, issuing from his suit's air speaker, had spoken his name to her again, just before . . .

Yes, Nicholas Hawksmoor. That was his name.

Lady Genevieve aboard the dying courier had been welcoming her rescuer. In pure joy of life triumphant she had spread out her arms to embrace the superbly capable, the blessed and glorious Nicholas Hawksmoor. For just a moment he had given her an impression of hesitation, of surprise. And then his armored arms had come round her gently, carefully, returning the hug.

A moment later, pushing herself back to arm's length from the tight embrace, Genevieve had demanded eagerly: "Can you get me out of here? I don't have a suit, you see. It seems there are no suits aboard."

Again his voice—Nick's voice, the voice she remembered from the holostage—issued from the suit's air speaker. "That's quite all right, my lady. I can get you out safely. Because—"

And then—

As she recalled the flow of events now (however much time had passed) from her present place of safety (wherever that might be), it seemed to the Lady Genevieve that the whole world had exploded at that point.

She now even had her doubts that that last remembered explosion had been quite real. But very real and convincing was her present sense, her impression, that after that moment the course of her rescue had somehow gone terribly wrong.

Only the fact that these memories of wreckage and explosions seemed remote kept her now from being still utterly terrified.

The embrace, with her body clad only in the shreds of the white dress, pressed against the suit's unfeeling armor. And with the courier's smoky atmosphere steadily bleeding itself thin around them. Then the last explosion. Yes, very real, as convincing as any memory of her entire life.

And following the last explosion, dreams. A whole world of peculiar dreams, dreams evolving into a strange mental clarity, true vision bringing with it terror. And now she was living that experience again—unfocused and unshielded terror, the helpless sense of onrushing death, the certainty of obliteration.

But this time, for the Lady Genevieve, the period of clarity and terror was mercifully brief.

Again unconsciousness claimed her for an indeterminate time. A blackness deeper than any normal sleep, like the complete cessation of existence.

Then she was drifting, carrying up out of nothingness with her the single thought that the courier, really, had somehow been demolished, with her still aboard. An event of some importance, she supposed. But now it seemed remote from her.

Then, finally, blessedly, real awareness of her real surroundings. Her present environment, gratefully, was one which proved by its mere existence that she had been rescued, brought to a place of safety. She occupied a bed, or rather a narrow berth, which seemed, from several background indications, to be aboard a ship. Close above her, passing only a few centimeters from her face, moved the thin, efficient, obviously inhuman, tremendously welcome metal arms of a medirobot, which must be in some way taking care of her.

And there, only a little farther away, just beyond the clear sanitary shield guarding her berth, loomed the handsome face of the volunteer pilot—his was one name Jenny was never going to forget—Nicholas Hawksmoor. Hawksmoor was looking down at her anxiously.

With considerable effort the Lady Genevieve, while remaining flat on her back, managed to produce a tiny voice. For whatever reason, she found it really difficult to speak, to put any volume of air behind the words.

"Where am I?" she asked. The unexpected problem with her speech was almost frightening, but not really. Not now. Now that she was saved, all medical difficulties could be solved in time.

Hawksmoor leaned closer, and replied at once, and reassuringly, "You're safe, aboard my little ship. I call her the *Wren*. I got you out of that courier just in time." He hesitated fractionally. "You remember being on the courier?"

"I remember getting away from the research station on it. Of course, how could I not remember?"

"And you remember me?"

"Nicholas Hawksmoor, architect and pilot. Very good pilot, I must agree." Still, every word she spoke required an unnatural effort. But she wanted to talk. She thought she wasn't really tired.

"That's right." He sounded relieved, and encouraging.

"What do your friends call you? Nick?"

"My friends?" For whatever reason, that question seemed to unsettle her rescuer momentarily. "Yes, yes, Nick will do nicely. What do your friends call you?"

"Jenny."

"Yes, of course. Naturally they would. Jenny. Do you know, that name reminds me of something?"

"Of what?"

"A poem. A verse. Maybe I'll sing it for you later."

She tried to turn her head and look about her. The white wall from which the arms of the medirobot protruded was part of a general constriction that kept her from moving very far in any direction. All the walls, white or glassy, of the couch, in which her body was sunken almost as in a bathtub, kept her from seeing very much.

Struck by a sudden thought, the lady asked, "How are the other people?"

"Those on the courier?" Nicholas sighed unhurriedly. "I couldn't do anything for them, I'm afraid. Most of them were dead anyway, or nearly dead, before I got there. And besides, I had equipment enough to get only one person out."

Again, she drifted mentally for a little while. She hadn't thought that everyone else was nearly dead. That wasn't really how she remembered the situation. But . . .

"I don't hurt anywhere," she murmured at last. Now, each time she spoke, obtaining air and forming it into words seemed a little easier than the time before. Now it was as if . . . something . . . were being progressively adjusted for her comfort. People said that shipboard medirobots were very good, though she had never had to prove it for herself before.

Her companion was tenderly solicitous. "Well, I'm glad. You shouldn't hurt. You absolutely shouldn't after all that's . . . after all that's been done for you. You're going to be all right."

And once again it seemed that it was time to sleep.

Back on the Imatran surface, all of the minor local authorities, the petty political and military leaders, had survived the attack in good shape. This happy circumstance was not the result of any special defense or precaution undertaken on their behalf as individuals, for no such favoritism had been shown. The truth was that nearly all the ordinary citizens and all of the numerous visitors currently on the planetoid had also come unharmed through the disaster.

Not because of the effectiveness of the planetoid's defenses, which had not actually been fully tested. Rather, the high rate of survival could be laid to the enemy's tactics. It really appeared that this particular berserker had passed up the opportunity for mass slaughter, that its only goal had been to snatch away the biolab.

An hour after the last shot had been fired, everyone on the planetoid was finally allowing themselves to think that the berserker was not coming back—at least not right away. The local authorities, now emerging stunned from their several shelters, had already received enough reports from the more distant regions of Imatra to confirm that the only real damage had been done, the only casualties sustained, in the immediate vicinity of the ground-based defenses, which had been thoroughly knocked out. In some of those areas the local devastation had been complete, though sharply limited in geographical extent.

The local authorities on the planetoid, without waiting for their colleagues and superiors from the full-sized planets of the system, hurriedly convened on holostage. All present were naturally aghast at the disaster they had just survived, and at the same time relieved that somehow—miraculously, it seemed—the destruction and loss of life had not been worse.

The planetoid Imatra had for years been home to a fair amount of scientific research. Also it was well known throughout nearby worlds and systems as a conference site, a meeting place with the pleasant ambiance of a formal garden, where administrators at several levels in Premier Dirac's power structure—and others—often repaired to escape routine, to meet informally. A number of important people were usually to be found visiting here. So the local authorities' relief that human casualties were light was even stronger than it might otherwise have been. But still . . .

At this point an hour and a half had passed since the last weapon had been fired. The berserker and its helpless catch were still within easy telescopic range, but were receding with ever-increasing speed, accelerating back along what looked like the exact same course on which this enemy had made its approach. The foe was retreating toward the approximate middle of the Mavronari Nebula.

By now, naturally, one of the swiftest couriers available had been dispatched to carry the unhappy news to Premier Dirac himself, who was days away in another system. The Premier's schedule already called for him to arrive at Imatra within a standard month at most; the local authorities feared that on his arrival, whenever that might be, he was going to hold them personally responsible, not only for the loss of his bride and his inchoate child but also for the general disaster. They feared, at the least, being charged with gross incompetence.

Of course, they all agreed, such charges would be utterly unjust. "How could we possibly have foreseen a berserker attack *here* in the Imatran system, of all places? There hasn't been even a berserker *sighting* for . . ."

No one could immediately say for just how many years. Certainly for a long, long time.

Quickly the worried, frightened local leaders began to review the various recordings of the attack, some of which had been made from the Imatran surface, others from certain artificial satellites above the planetoid. Dirac and his personal staff would want to see those records, to study them intently. This local, first review was conducted with the idea of learning more about the particular berserker—and also in the hope of the authorities' finding something on which to base their own defense in the coming investigation.

Among the events shown clearly in the recordings was the movement of one particular small craft, the ill-fated courier, which had indeed separated itself from the research station and fled for safety in the last few minutes before the berserker struck. There had even been a hasty radio message from the station confirming the departure.

On hearing that message, at the time, people on the ground had felt their hopes soar (or so one of them now claimed), thinking that the Lady Genevieve might well have managed to get aboard that courier, and that she was going to be whisked away out of danger.

But very soon after it had separated from the station, the little vessel had been destroyed; the first crippling blast had been followed within a few minutes by a second, even more violent explosion, as some component of the drive let go. In the interval between detonations Hawksmoor's *Wren* had just managed to reach the vicinity.

"What was the report from the *Wren*?" someone now inquired anxiously.

"No survivors." Someone else cleared his throat.

A general sigh went round the holotable. The possibility of survivors had seemed remote, but naturally an intensive search, for the Lady Genevieve in particular, had been started as soon as possible. That search, by the *Wren* and several other ships now on the scene, still continued, though from the start there had been little hope of finding anyone alive.

More ships were now arriving in the region where the courier had exploded, and many more were on their way, all wanting to help. But so far no survivors had been announced, and at this late hour there was no reason to think that any were going to turn up.

Some member of the conference of local leaders grumbled that records showed that the demolished courier had been short of emergency space suits, and that such armored suits might have offered the passengers real hope of survival. The announcement was greeted with silence. Certainly before the attack no one would have expected such a craft, maneuvering in supposedly peaceful regions, to have carried enough suits for several dozen people.

That there had been other real losses in space would obviously be impossible for the local authorities to deny. Not only the courier but several Solarian fighting ships, complete with crews, had been destroyed.

At least, one participant in the conference noted with faint satisfaction, the enemy had not escaped entirely unscathed: several small spacegoing berserker machines, the equivalent of human scout ships, had been destroyed by ground batteries in the brief fight.

❋   ❋   ❋

Detracting from this modest achievement of the defense was the fact that the survivors on the planetoid and elsewhere in the system now had no armed ships left. The few such craft available had all been bravely hurled into the fight against the berserker, and in an engagement lasting only a few minutes the monster had efficiently destroyed them all, down to the last unit. The only encouraging aspect of this loss was that not even the Premier, when he arrived, would be able to blame the local authorities for not attempting a pursuit.

One local authority, trying out on his colleagues a statement that he meant to issue later to the outraged public, declaimed: "Though our blood boils with fighting fever, with the determination to be avenged—words to that effect—there's no way we could have given chase to the escaping enemy. No way, I think, that we might have done anything more than we did during the critical minutes of the catastrophe or in its aftermath."

His colleagues were silent, considering. At last one of them offered grimly: "At least our overall casualties were light."

Another stared at the last speaker. "Light? Have you forgotten that the Lady Genevieve is missing, not only missing but almost certainly dead? Do you realize that?"

"I said overall. I meant light in total numbers."

"Hardly light, even in total numbers, if the protopeople are counted in."

"If what? If who?"

"I mean the intended colonists." The speaker looked around, getting in return as many blank stares as understanding nods. "Those on the biostation, who are, or were, the basic reason for its existence. The human zygotes and a few fetuses. All of the living contributions, donations, gathered over a period of years, decades, from the families, the mothers, of a dozen—maybe more than a dozen—worlds."

"I say 'living' is debatable. But how many of these donations, as you call them, intended colonists, were aboard?"

"I don't have the exact number at hand. From what I've heard, somewhere near a billion."

"A what?"

"Ten to the ninth."

The fact, the quantity, took a moment to penetrate. "Then let's see to it that they're not counted, or mentioned in any estimate of casualties."

"One of them is certainly going to be."

"What?"

"Maybe you missed the publicity announcements made just before the tragedy. The Lady Genevieve wasn't here on just a formal tour of inspection." The speaker looked far to his right. "Well, Kensing? What do you say?"

The conference table was, of course, not a single real solid table at all, but a construct of artificial reality put together on holostage by computers and communications systems for the convenience of the local authorities, who were thus enabled to remain comfortably at home or in their offices while sharing in the illusion of mutual confrontation in a single room. At one point along the rim of this composite board sat the youngest in attendance, a man named Sandro Kensing. Kensing had so far remained silent. For one thing, he was distracted by grief. For another, he was not a local authority at all, but only the nephew of one of last year's councilmen—and the fiancé of Dr. Anyuta Zador, who was now among the missing. But the real reason this young man had been invited to the council was the fact that for two years he had been a close personal friend of the only son of Premier Dirac, and had even been a guest in one of the Premier's homes and aboard his yacht. Therefore, or so the local authorities thought, he might be expected to know something of that potentate's psychology.

"Well, Kensing?"

Sandro Kensing raised shaggy sandy eyebrows and looked back. His heavy shoulders were hunched over the table, thick-fingered hands clasped before him. His face was impassive, except for reddened eyes. "Sorry?" He hadn't heard the question.

"I was asking," the speaker repeated considerately, "what you thought Premier Dirac's reaction to this terrible news might be."

"Ah. Yes." None of the local leadership, even going back to include his now-retired uncle, much impressed Kensing. "Well, the old man won't be happy. But you don't need me to tell you that."

There was an uncomfortable silence around the table. Respecting the upstart's grief at the loss of his fiancé, no one spoke sternly to him or even glowered at him for his near-insolent manner. All the authorities realized that they had bigger things to worry about.

"We all have a lot of work to do," the chairman said presently. "But before we adjourn this session, we had better settle the matter of the delegation."

"Delegation?" someone asked.

"I should perhaps say deputation. A deputation to welcome the Premier when he arrives." Looking around, he decided that clarification was in order. "If *none* of us go up to meet him when he shows up in orbit, I wouldn't be at all surprised if he summons us all to attend him on his ship to report to him in person."

The atmosphere around the table had suddenly grown even more unhappy than before.

"I move," said another speaker, "that we appoint a single delegate.

A representative to deliver our preliminary report. Since, for the foreseeable future, we are all going to have our hands full with our own jobs."

All around the holotable, heads were swiveling, looking in the same direction. Their delegate had been chosen, unanimously and without debate. Kensing, paying more attention to the meeting now and only mildly surprised, managed a faintly cynical smile at the many faces turned his way.

☀ FOUR

Several hours before he was really expected, the Premier entered the Imatran system at an impressive velocity aboard his large armed yacht, the *Eidolon*. This formidable fighting vessel—some expert observers said it looked more like a light cruiser—was escorted by two smaller craft, both armed but rather nondescript. The three ships were evidently all that Premier Dirac had been able to muster on short notice.

Instead of landing on the almost unscarred surface of the planetoid Imatra, as he doubtless would have done in time of peace and as some people still expected him to do now, Dirac hung his little squadron in a low orbit. From that position of readiness he immediately summoned—in terms conveying authority rather than politeness—the local authorities aboard.

He also called for the full mobilization of local technical resources to help get his squadron into total combat readiness. Some of the equipment on his ships would require various forms of refitting, rearming, or recharging before he was ready to risk a fight.

Under the circumstances, it was easy to understand the absence of any formal ceremony of welcome. In fact the only individual who obeyed the Premier's summons, boarding a shuttle to ride up and welcome him and his entourage, was the chosen spokesperson Sandro Kensing. The young man, vaguely uneasy though not really frightened about the kind of reception he could expect, stepped from the docked shuttle into the main airlock of the yacht carrying in his pocket a holostage recording created by the local council. The recording was an earnest compilation of convincing reasons why the members' currently overwhelming press of duties rendered their personal attendance utterly impossible.

It empowered Kensing to represent them—all of them—in this meeting with the Premier.

Obviously the whole lot of them were really frightened of the old man, a few on an actual physical level. Perhaps, thought Kensing, some of them had good reason to be. He himself wasn't personally afraid. Even had his feelings not still been dominated by grief, he would not have been terrified of Mike's father, whom he had met half a dozen times when he and Mike were attending school together, and in whose house he had been a guest. Actually the relationship had led to a job related to the colonization project, and thus to Kensing's meeting Annie.

Just inside the *Eidolon*'s armored airlock, Kensing was met by a powerfully built, graying man of indeterminate age, dressed in coveralls that offered no indication of the wearer's status or function. Kensing recognized one of the Premier's chief security people, a familiar presence in the Sardou mansion Kensing had visited, and on its grounds.

"Hello, Brabant."

The bodyguard, as usual informally polite to friends of his employer, identified the young visitor on sight, though several years had passed since their last encounter. "Hey, Mr. Kensing. Have a seat, the boss is expecting you. He'll be free in a minute."

Beyond the bodyguard the interior of the ship, somewhat remodeled and redecorated since Kensing had seen it last, looked like a powerful executive's office planetside.

"I'll stand up for a while, thanks. Been sitting a lot lately."

Brabant looked at him sympathetically. "Hey, tough about Dr. Zador. Really tough."

"Thanks."

"You and the boss got something in common. Unfortunately."

In the rush of his own feelings Kensing had almost forgotten about the presumed loss of the Premier's new bride. But it was true; he and the Premier now had something very basic in common.

"Where's Mike?" he asked the bodyguard suddenly.

The man appeared to be trying to remember, then shrugged. "He wasn't getting on with his father a few months back, so he took a trip. Long before all this came up."

"Anyplace in particular?"

"The family don't tell me all their plans."

"I just thought I might find him on board. His father's going to have need of good pilots."

"Hey, good pilots the boss's got, this time around. Better pilots than Mike."

Kensing raised an eyebrow. "Not many of those available."

"One in particular who's on board right now is very good indeed."

Brabant, with the air of keeping a pleasant bit of information in reserve, looked up and down the corridor. "Maybe you'll meet him."

"Yeah? You're telling me this is someone special?"

"You might say so. His name's Frank Marcus. Colonel. That was the last rank I heard he had. Retired."

For a moment at least Kensing was distracted from his personal problems. "Marcus? You mean *the*—"

"That's right. The famous man in boxes. They tell me he was driving the yacht just a little while ago when we dropped into orbit here."

"Gods of flightspace. I guess I assumed Colonel Frank Marcus was dead, decades ago."

"Don't tell him that, kid. Excuse me, I mean I wouldn't advise that as diplomatic, Mr. Official Deputy from Imatra." And the bodyguard laughed.

Kensing was shaking his head. By now Colonel Marcus would have to be an old man by any standard, because for more than a century he had been something of an interstellar legend. As Kensing remembered the story, Marcus had at some time in his youth lost most of his organic body in an accident—or had it been in a berserker fight?—and ever since had been confined to his boxes by physical disability, a situation he apparently viewed as only an interesting challenge.

"Hey, you know what I hear, Mr. Kensing?" Brabant had lowered his voice slightly.

"What?"

The gist of the story, as passed along now in clinical detail by the admiring bodyguard, was that Frank Marcus was still perfectly capable of enjoying female companionship and of physically expressing his appreciation in the fullest way.

"Glad to hear it. So how does he come to be working for the Premier?"

Kensing's informant went on to explain that Marcus, ranked as one of the supreme space pilots in Solarian history, had signed on a couple of months ago as an advanced flight instructor, after first having turned down the offer of a permanent job as Dirac's personal pilot.

Conversation had just turned to another subject when it broke off suddenly. Something—no, someone, it must be the colonel himself!—was rolling toward them down the corridor, coming from the direction of the bridge.

Had Kensing not been alerted to the colonel's presence aboard, he might have assumed this was some kind of serving robot approaching. He beheld three connected metallic boxes, none of them more than knee-high, their size in aggregate no more than that of an adult human body. The boxes rolled along one after the other, their wheels appearing to be of polyphase matter, not spinning so much as undergoing continuous smooth deformity.

From the foremost box came a voice, a mechanically generated but very human sound, tone jaunty, just this side of arrogant. "Hi, Brabant. Thought I'd see the chief when he's not busy. Who's this?"

Kensing, wondering what might happen if he were to put out a hand in formal greeting, gazed into a set of lenses and introduced himself. "Colonel Marcus? Glad to meet you. I'm Sandro Kensing, a friend of Mike's—the Premier's son."

"Yeah, I've heard about Mike. Haven't had the chance to meet him."

"What's the Premier's plan?" Kensing badly wanted to know, and he felt it rarely hurt to ask.

"That's no secret," the box assured him. "We're going after the bad machine."

That was what Kensing had been hoping to hear. Something inside him, somewhere around his heart, gave a lurch at the possibility—no matter how faint—of catching up with the ongoing disaster that had carried Annie off. Of finding out at first hand what had happened. Of coming to grips in violence with the monstrous inanimate *things* that had done this to her and to him.

And here right in front of Kensing was the person of all people who might make the possibility real. Frank Marcus, who at one time or another had retired, it seemed, from just about every armed force in the Solarian Galaxy except the Templars; Colonel Marcus, who as it turned out was now piloting Dirac's yacht.

Kensing said bluntly, "Colonel, if anyone's going after that berserker, I'm going along."

"Yeah?" The talking boxes sounded interested but not entirely convinced.

"Dr. Zador and I were going to be married in a month. More to the point, I'm an engineer who's trained and working in defensive systems. I've been doing the preliminaries for the projected colonial vessels."

"Combat experience?"

"No."

"That may not matter too much. Most of our crew doesn't have any either. If you're a qualified defense systems engineer, maybe the chief'll want to fit you in."

Moments later Brabant, having evidently received some invisible communication from the Premier, was ushering Kensing into the inner office.

Setting foot in the inner rooms of the Premier's suite for the first time in several years, Kensing again noted that certain remodeling and redecoration had taken place since his last visit. As if the ship were becoming less a ship and more a place of business.

In the center of the innermost room was a large desk, a real desk constructed basically of wood, though its upper surface was inhabited by a number of electronic displays. The desk held several stacks of real paper also, and behind them sat a real man. The Premier was not physically large. He had changed, in subtle ways that Kensing would have been hard put to define, in the two years since the two of them had last come face to face.

Dirac's hair was steely gray; thick and naturally curled, it lay trimmed close round his large skull. Sunken gray eyes peered out from under heavy brows, like outlaws preparing to sally from a cave. Skin and muscles were firm and youthful in appearance, belying the impression of age suggested by the gray hair. His hands toyed with a fine-bladed knife, which Kensing recognized as an antique letter opener. Dirac's voice, an eloquent actor's bass, was milder than it sounded on public holostage.

As Kensing entered the cabin, the Premier was in conversation with the image of a rather handsome and much younger man, who appeared on the largest of the room's three holostages, the one beside the desk. The younger man, who wore pilot's insignia on his collar, was saying; "—my deepest sympathy, sir."

"Thank you, Nick." The presumably bereaved husband gave, as he often did, the impression of being firmly in control though inwardly stressed. He looked up and nodded at Kensing, whose escort, withdrawing, had already closed the door behind him.

Kensing began: "Premier Dirac, I don't know if you—"

"Yes, of course I remember you, Kensing. Friend of my son's, he called you Sandy. Mike always thought highly of you. So you're delegated to explain this mess to me."

"Yes, sir."

"Fill me in on the details later. And you're in on the colonizing project—and you're also Dr. Zador's fiancé. Very sorry about her. A terrible business we've got here."

"Yes, sir. My sympathy to you. Mine and everyone's on Imatra."

Dirac acknowledged the condolence with a brusque nod. "Mike's not with me this time," he remarked.

"Someone told me he's off on a long trip, sir."

"Yes. Very long." The Premier indicated the 'stage. "I don't suppose you've met Nick here, have you? Nicholas Hawksmoor, architect and pilot. Works for me."

"We haven't met yet, sir."

Dirac proceeded with a swift introduction. Was there just the faintest momentary twinkle of some private amusement in the old man's eye?

The formality concluded, the Premier once more faced the imaged head and shoulders of Nicholas Hawksmoor. "Proceed."

Nick reported quietly: "There was nothing I could do, sir. I was ... almost ... in time to get myself aboard the courier before that last explosion. But not quite in time. I couldn't be of any help to anyone aboard."

"Had you any direct evidence that my wife was among the passengers?"

"I couldn't even confirm that. I'm sorry."

"Not your fault, Nick."

"No, sir. Thank you for understanding that, sir." A brief hesitation. "There's another matter I suppose I should mention."

"What's that?"

"Shortly after the alert was sounded, I was given a direct order by Acting Supervisor Zador on the biostation. She commanded me to take my ship out and ram the enemy."

This statement was made so casually that Kensing, who thought he was paying close attention, wondered if he had heard right, or if he had earlier missed something. He understood that as soon as the alert was called, Annie as acting supervisor would have automatically become local defense commander. A wildly inappropriate function for her, but ...

Dirac nodded, accepting the information about the ramming order with surprising placidity. "So what happened next?"

"Well, sir, Dr. Zador wasn't—isn't—a combat officer, but she must have thought she'd come up with a good plan to at least distract the berserker. Obviously it wouldn't have worked. I couldn't have got the *Wren* within a thousand kilometers of a monster like that before it vaporized me without breaking stride.

"So when the acting supervisor gave me that order, rather than argue and distract her further from her own real job—at which I am sure she's more than competent—I just acknowledged the command and then ignored it. The only really useful thing I could do with my ship at that point was to stay close to the courier and try to look out for those on board.

"If the berserker had sent one of its own small spacegoers after the courier, or a boarding machine, I would probably have tried ramming *that*. Or tried to get the machine to come after me instead. But of course, as the scene actually played out ..." Nick looked distressed.

Dirac said gently: "It's all right."

"Thank you, sir."

"But—"

"Yes, sir?"

The shadowed eyes, with a danger in them that Kensing had never seen there before, looked up from under the steel brows. "From what you tell me, we don't really *know* that the Lady Genevieve ever actually boarded that courier at all. Do we?"

Nick's holostage image appeared to ruminate. "No, I don't suppose we do."

Dirac nodded slowly. He glanced at Kensing. "In fact, what I've heard of the recorded radio traffic indicates that Dr. Zador had some concern about the courier leaving prematurely. She feared the pilot might pull out before everyone who wanted to get aboard had done so."

"That's correct."

Premier Dirac now turned his full attention back to the visitor who was physically present in his cabin. "Kensing, have you people on Imatra any further information on that point?"

"I don't know anything about it, Premier. I'll certainly check up on it as quickly as I can."

"Do that, please. I want any information bearing on the question of the Lady Genevieve's presence on that courier."

"I'll get it for you, whatever we have."

"Good." Dirac knitted steely brows. "So far no one has shown me any firm evidence one way or the other. So I have to believe there's a good chance she was still on the station when it was so strangely—kidnapped."

Kensing didn't say anything.

Dirac was not ready to leave the point. "We do know that *some* people were still aboard the station, right? Supervisor Zador, for one. And didn't she say something to the courier pilot to the effect that others were intending to stay?"

Nicholas Hawksmoor put in: "At least one other, sir. The bioengineer Daniel Hoveler apparently remained with Dr. Zador. That seems to be the only definite evidence we have on the presence or absence of any particular individuals."

Dirac nodded, displaying a certain grim satisfaction. "So at this moment, as we speak, there are still living people on the station." He met the others' eyes, one after the other, as if challenging anyone to dispute the point.

Kensing was more than ready to hope that Annie still had a chance at life; it was almost but not quite unheard of for a berserker's prisoners to be rescued. But Nick was willing to dispute his employer's assumption. "We don't *know* that, sir."

Dirac gave the speaker his steely glare. "We don't *know* the people aboard the station have been killed. Correct?"

There was a brief pause in which Nick seemed to yield. "Yes, sir. Correct."

The Premier smiled faintly. "To be on the safe side, then, we must assume that there are living people. And my wife may well be among them."

"That's correct, sir. For all we know, she may."

"That's all for now." And Dirac's hands moved over the surface of the table in front of him, dismissing Hawksmoor, whose image vanished abruptly, calling up other images on his private stage.

He said: "Kensing, I'm going to order the search for survivors of the courier abandoned. Any functioning space suit in the vicinity would be putting out an automated distress signal, and nothing like that is being received."

Kensing didn't know what to say, but it seemed he wasn't required to say anything at this point.

Dirac continued: "But I am going to keep a number of my pilots busy, Nick among them, combing through all the space debris that resulted from the combat, the berserker stuff along with ours. We may be able to glean a lot of information from that."

"Yes, sir, I expect so." The room was replete with wall displays, in addition to those on Dirac's desk. From where Kensing stood, he could read most of the wall information fairly well. Obviously surface and satellite telescopes were still locked onto the retreating enemy and its prize. He was tormented by the idea that somewhere inside that distorted little dot, Annie might be still alive.

Dirac followed his gaze. "Look at that. As far as anyone in-system here can tell by telescope, the bioresearch station has suffered no serious physical damage. My ships will soon be refitted—I don't see why it should take more than a few hours—and as soon as they're ready, we're going after it."

"I'm coming with you, sir."

"Naturally, I expected you'd say that. With your experience in defense systems you'll be useful. Welcome aboard. See Varvara when you go out; she'll sign you up officially."

"Thank you, sir."

The Premier nodded. "She's not dead, I tell you." Obviously he meant his own young bride. Looking quietly into some holostage presentation of nearby space, he added: "I am sure that I would know if she were dead. Meanwhile, I want to gather every possible bit of information about the attacker."

Berserker debris, Kensing knew, was often valuable to military intelligence because it allowed types of enemy equipment to be distinguished. He nodded. They were going to need every gram of advantage they could get.

Leaving the conference, Kensing once more encountered Colonel Marcus and the bodyguard Brabant. They were talking in the corridor with a woman Kensing had not met before, who introduced herself to him as Varvara Engadin. Engadin was somewhere near the Premier's age, probably around fifty, but still slender and impressively beautiful, and her name was familiar. She had been the Premier's intimate companion—as well as his political adviser, according to the stories—when Kensing had first met the family. At that time Mike's mother was already several years dead.

"Ms. Engadin, I'm supposed to see you about signing on the crew."

"Sandy." She put both hands out to him in sympathy. "I've been hearing about your loss."

Conversation focused briefly on the tragedy. Though everyone spoke in polite and diplomatic terms, plainly all agreed that Dirac was determined not to accept the overwhelming probability that his bride was dead, and he fully intended to get her back. To have his way, to impose his will, as usual, even when his adversary was a berserker.

Kensing, his own feelings torn, commented that everyone really knew the odds were pretty heavily against that. This psychic pretense was not at all the Premier's usual mode of behavior.

"Know him pretty well?" the colonel asked. He had a way of swiveling a lens on his front box to make it plain who he was speaking to.

"I'm a friend of his son's—a close friend for a time, but I haven't seen Mike for a couple of years. And I've stayed with them in one of the official mansions. How about you?"

"Don't really know them. Been working for the Premier only a couple of months now. I was just in the process of turning down a chief pilot's job when this came up. Now it looks like I'm in for the duration." Marcus did not seem at all displeased by the prospect of going to war again. Somehow the metal boxes and the voice coming out of them impressed Kensing as capable of expressing shades of feeling. Somehow the colonel's boxes could give the impression of swaggering as they rolled.

"What do you think has happened to his wife? Really?" Kensing felt compelled to dig for expert opinion regarding the fate of those aboard the station.

"He could be right. She might not have boarded that courier at all."

"And what do you think . . ." He couldn't make himself state the question plainly.

"Hell, I don't know. There's always a fighting chance. But no use anyone getting his hopes too high."

His official enrollment completed, pacing down a corridor toward his newly assigned quarters with Marcus rolling at his side, Kensing listened to more of the colonel's opinions. Frank Marcus commented that two bizarre points about the recent raid set it apart from almost any other military action that he was able to remember.

"First point: regardless of what this berserker did out here, in the vicinity of this planetoid, it made no effort to get at the inner planets of the system. Didn't even send scouts sunward to look them over, or to raid the space traffic going on that way. There's quite a bit of space traffic, almost all of it unarmed ships."

"The inner worlds are heavily defended," Kensing offered.

Marcus dismissed that with the wave of a metallic arm, a tentacle-like appendage of inhuman but obviously practical shape. "In my experience, when a berserker as big and mean as this one—hell, any berserker—sees it has at least a fighting chance to take out a couple of billion people, it's not likely to pass up the opportunity."

"So why did it take the biolab? Not destroy it, but actually grab it and carry it away?"

"I don't know yet. But I do know something that strikes me as even more peculiar. Our tricky berserker didn't even make a serious attempt to depopulate *this* planetoid. And it was right here. And the defenses on Planetoid Imatra are—were—a hell of a lot lighter than those on the sunward planets. It took out the defenses that were shooting at it, and that was that."

Kensing, whose job had long required of him serious—up to now purely theoretical—study of berserkers' tactics, had already been trying to make sense of it. "So, that means what? A monster machine that doesn't want to kill people? Indicating that in some crazy way it's not really a berserker?"

"I wouldn't want to tell that to the guys who were manning the ground defenses, or to the people who tried to fight it in space. No, it's ready enough to kill. But it had some bigger goal than simply attacking this system. It wouldn't deviate from its plan, even for the chance to take out a couple of billion human lives. Of life units, as the berserkers say. Wouldn't even delay to polish off a million or so near at hand."

"All right. Was that your second point?"

"No. Actually the second peculiarity I had in mind was that even now, days after the attack, the damned raider is still in sight. Either it can't go superluminal while it's towing something as big as that lab, or it doesn't want to risk the attempt. And if it hasn't tried to go c-plus by now, it's not going to. Because now it's close enough to the Mavronari to start getting into the thick dust."

Kensing paused in the corridor to take another look for himself, calling up the picture on one of the yacht's numerous displays. True, the berserker was currently observable only with some difficulty, but there it was. Still fleeing in slowship mode, though with a steady buildup of velocity in normal space, so that the tiny wavering images of the raider and its captive prey, as seen from the vicinity of the Imatran planetoid, were measurably redshifting.

Not greatly, though. "A long way to go to light speed."

"Right. It hasn't been humping its tail hard enough to get near that. C-plus wouldn't be a practical procedure, as I say, for an object moving in that direction—into the dust." In fact, as Kensing discovered when he queried the terminal, the very latest indications were that the berserker's acceleration appeared to be easing off somewhat, and computer projections were that the burdened machine might actually have to diminish its velocity in the next few hours or days as it penetrated ever more deeply the outlying fringes of the nebula.

Within the next few hours, a war council composed largely of key members of the Premier's staff went into session aboard the *Eidolon*. Kensing, as the official representative of Imatra, was in attendance. Kensing's Imatran compatriots continued to maintain a wary distance.

Kensing had remained aboard the yacht, sending down to his apartment on the surface for extra clothing and some personal gear. It now seemed unlikely that he would leave the *Eidolon* for any reason before the squadron's departure, the projected time of which was only hours away.

The war council's current session on the yacht heard speculation from some of its members that the berserker might have sustained serious damage in the recent fighting, enough to keep it from going c-plus. Therefore it had turned toward the nebula as its best chance of getting away before a human fleet could be assembled to hunt it down.

An officer objected: "That doesn't answer the question of why it chose to withdraw instead of attacking, killing."

"It may have been heavily damaged."

"Bah. So what? This's a *berserker* we're talking about. It cares nothing for its own survival, except that it must destroy the maximum number of lives before it goes. And obviously it was still capable of fighting."

"If we just knew why it decided that an intact bioresearch station, perhaps only this one in particular, would be such an enormously valuable thing to have."

Varvara Engadin spoke up. "The answer to that question ought to be staring us in the face. In fact I think it is. We're talking about a vessel that has a billion Solarian human zygotes stored aboard."

"Yes. If not active life, certainly potential. A billion potentially active Solarian humans. One would expect a berserker to use up its last erg of energy, sacrifice its last gram of matter, to *destroy* such a cargo. But why in the Galaxy should it want to carry it away?"

Kensing, trying to imagine why, found ominous, half-formed suggestions drifting across the back of his mind.

Someone else argued that whether the enemy had entirely lost superluminal capability or not, the compound object formed by the berserker and its captured station was more than a little clumsy for serious spacefaring. It would certainly be considerably harder to maneuver in any kind of space than the speedy vehicles at the Premier's command.

Computer projections, now being continuously run, showed that even when the delay for refitting the Premier's ships was factored in, his squadron was going to have a good chance of catching up.

Frank Marcus, the frontal surface of his head box slightly elevated to present an interestingly complex gray contour above one end of the conference table, expressed his opinion—even as the subject of his remarks sat listening imperturbably—that Dirac, whose notable accomplishments had not so far extended into the military field, did not appear to be entirely crazy for having decided to give chase.

Someone else formally, not too wisely, put the question to Dirac. "Is that still our plan, sir?"

Dirac's steely eyes looked up across the table—looking through the boundaries of virtual reality, because for this session the Premier had remained physically in his own suite. "What kind of a question is that? We're going after them, of course." Dirac blinked, continuing to stare at the questioner; it was as if he could not understand how any other course of action could be considered. "Whatever plan that damned thing is trying to carry out, we're not going to allow it to succeed."

Someone asked what local help was going to be available.

At that, eyes turned to Kensing. He, trying to sound properly apologetic, repeated on behalf of himself and his determinedly ground-bound local colleagues their regretful assurances that they had not a single armed vessel left in-system, nothing with the capability of playing a useful role in such a pursuit.

"I understand that," Dirac reassured him.

On that note the conference adjourned temporarily. More hours passed, ticking toward the deadline. The refitting of the *Eidolon* and its escort ships neared completion, and they were very nearly ready for the pursuit they were about to undertake.

Meanwhile the enemy, whose actions were still distinctly observable from the ships in orbit around Imatra, continued on a steady course toward the approximate center of the Mavronari Nebula. Inside this mass of gas and fine dust, the ambient density of matter was known to be high enough to make c-plus flight in general so perilous as to be practically impossible. Therefore observation of the berserker from the Imatran system ought to remain possible for several more days at least.

The retreating berserker, someone commented, was continuing to retrace exactly, or nearly so, the very course on which it had been first detected when inbound toward Imatra. If that fact had any particular significance, no one could guess what it might be.

The fact that the enemy had captured the station whole, and therefore appeared to be operating under some deliberate plan of taking prisoners—perhaps growing massive numbers of goodlife, or using human cells to produce some other biological weapon—loomed ever larger in the worried planners' thoughts. That a berserker had chosen abduction over mass destruction seemed to many people especially ominous.

Despite the scoffing of Colonel Marcus, the peculiarities of the situation were such that Kensing, like several of his colleagues in the war council, could not entirely rid himself of the suspicion that their swiftly retiring foe might not be a genuine berserker at all. In the past, certain human villains had been known to disguise ships as berserkers to accomplish their own evil purposes of murder and robbery.

But when he broached the idea to other experts on Dirac's staff, they were unanimously quick to put it down. In this case, all the material evidence worked against any such conclusion. By now a considerable amount of the smashed debris from small enemy machines had been gathered out of space—some of it by Nicholas Hawksmoor, much more by others—and painstakingly examined.

Concurrently some large pieces of this wreckage, at least one chunk meters across, had rained down intact upon the planetoid, whose shallow, artificially maintained atmosphere tended to guide the occasional meteorite down to the surface without burning it up. To all the available experts on the subject—some of them inhuman expert systems—this wreckage looked and felt and tested out in every way like real berserker metal, shaped and assembled by berserker construction methods.

The master computers on Dirac's yacht, state-of-the-art machines in every way, assured the planners that they still had time to overtake their foe, but that there was no time to waste; every passing hour brought the enemy closer to the shelter of the deep nebula. Dirac intended leaving very quickly, as soon as his ships were charged and ready. As far as Kensing could tell, Dirac's crew, some thirty people in all, was solidly with him. No doubt they were all volunteers, hand-picked for dependability and loyalty.

As it happened, one other person who had not volunteered, at least not for a berserker chase, was now on board. Kensing discovered this for himself in the course of a routine inventory of equipment. One of the yacht's medirobot berths was occupied, the glassy lid closed on the coffin-like chamber and frosted on the inside. The berth was tuned for long-term suspended animation maintenance of the unseen person in it.

Generally in favor of a hands-on approach whenever possible, Kensing went to take a look at the medirobot for himself. It stood in an out-of-the-way corridor on the big ship.

Varvara Engadin shed some light on the situation. This occupant of the deep-freeze chamber was a volunteer for the first projected colony to be established by the Sardou Foundation. Some individual so devoted to the plan, so determined to take part in the great colonial adventure, that he or she had requested suspended animation for whatever period might be necessary until the heroic mission should be ready to begin.

Across the portion of the Galaxy settled by Solarians, a number of methods had been tried to deal with the problem of overpopulation. Effective means to prevent conception were widely used, but still by no means universal. On worlds whose aggregate population ran into the hundreds of billions, millions of unwanted pregnancies occurred each year. Removal of a zygote or an early fetus from the mother's body was routine, but in this day and age the overt destruction of such organisms was unacceptable. Rather, some long-term storage was indicated, but storage indefinitely prolonged was also a denial of life.

The course favored by most of the Premier's political supporters had been to announce a mass colonization effort—and actually to begin the preparations for such an effort, with a launch date scheduled for some time securely and vaguely in the future. Surely people still had the spirit to go out and establish colonies.

A variation on this was a plan—actually several plans—to hide away secret reserves of humanity against the time when the berserkers might manage to depopulate all settled planets. Those in favor of such a scheme contemplated searching for a reasonably Earthlike planet, hidden, heretofore unknown. Theorists advocated prowling the Galaxy in search of such a world or worlds. When the goal was found, they would expunge it from all records so that the berserkers would never learn of its existence through captured material.

Engadin explained that in the Sardou Foundation's colonization plan, as finally negotiated among the heavily settled worlds within the Premier's sphere of influence, complicated protocols had been worked out to decide everything. For example, chance selection would determine which protopeople should be first into the artificial wombs when the colonizing ship or ships had reached a suitable new planet or planets.

Listening, Kensing wasn't sure the scheme really did more than to provide the machine designers, the colony engineers, and the population planners with work and something to talk about. It offered Solarian society a kind of evidence that what they were doing had meaning, wasn't just a way to delay indefinitely a decision on the question of what to do with all these life-suspended zygotes and fetuses.

The promise of working out some such theoretical system of colonization—or even the methodical contemplation of its difficulties—had allowed people on a number of worlds to feel satisfied that the problem was not simply being shelved.

How many artificial wombs were there going to be on one of the colonizing ships? That was still undecided. On the bioresearch station there were more than a hundred. Of course a properly designed facility of this type ought to be able to build at least a few more such devices when they were needed.

And of course the research station, precursor of the actual colonizing ships, had been equipped with life-support facilities capable of supporting at least twenty or thirty active people—technicians, caretakers, researchers—over a long period of time. Food, water, and air were all to be recycled efficiently. Already several times that number of scientists and others had occasionally lived and worked aboard.

Naturally there had been a concomitant attempt to enlist volunteer houseparents to accompany the multitude of zygotes. In fact Annie had once confessed to Kensing that she had thought about devoting her life to that task before she decided to get married and stay home instead.

The frozen volunteer currently aboard the yacht was male, Kensing was informed by the local caretaker system when he reached the row of emergency medical units in the remote auxiliary corridor. Only one was occupied. Name, Fowler Aristov. Age at time of immersion in the long-term storage mode, twenty. A whole catalogue of other personal characteristics and history followed, to which Kensing paid little attention.

Kensing was impressed, not altogether favorably, by such dedication to a cause. Fanaticism was almost certainly a better word, he thought. Of course subjectively, a long freeze would be practically indistinguishable from a short one. Volunteer for the cause, step into the SA unit, and go to sleep. Wake up again immediately—in subjective terms—take an hour or so to regain full physical and mental function, and get to work on your chosen job.

In the end he made no recommendation against leaving the

would-be colonist's suspended animation chamber occupied. There were five other medirobot berths on board, and great numbers of wounded were not a common result of battles in space. Anyway, the volunteer had evidently been willing to write fate a blank check regarding his own future.

What had been a tentative departure time for the avenging squadron was now finalized, set within the hour.

☀ FIVE

> *Jenny kiss'd me when we met,*
> *Jumping from the chair she sat in;*
> *Time, you thief, who love to get*
> *Sweets into your list, put that in:*
> *Say I'm weary, say I'm sad,*
> *Say that health and wealth have miss'd me,*
> *Say I'm growing old, but add . . .*

The song trailed off into silence. The performer's long pale fingers rested motionless on the stringed instrument of unique design he held before him. His whole body, standing erect, was very still, and something in his expression suggested to his audience that he had been prevented from singing the next line by a surge of some intense emotion.

That audience consisted of one person only, the Lady Genevieve.

The young woman's Indonesian features complemented her small and slender frame. All in all, she was a creature of impressive and delicate beauty. Her slight form, garbed in sparkling white, almost as for some old-time wedding ritual, was posed, half reclining, upon a gray stone bench apparently of considerable age, as were the surrounding cloister walls. Carvings in the bench, representing fantastic animals, had been softened by weather into obscurity, decorated with a little lichen. Before the lady came to occupy this seat, someone had thoughtfully provided it with a profusion of soft cushions, blue and red and yellow in shades that almost matched those of the nearby flowers.

"You sing beautifully," she encouraged her companion. Her voice was naturally small, but she was no longer aware of any difficulty in finding air to speak with.

"Thank you, my lady." The one who had assumed the role of minstrel relaxed a little in the golden sunshine and turned more fully toward his listener. He doffed his plumed hat with a sweeping gesture, flourished the headgear for an extra moment as if he did not quite know what to do with it next, then tossed it into oblivion behind a fragrant bed of dazzling flowers. Those flowers were remarkable, a knee-high embankment of vivid, almost blinding colors, running along one side of the broad grassy garth enclosed by the cloister's square of ancient, pale gray stonework. What world might lie outside these elder walls was more than the lady could have said; but whatever it was, it seemed to her comfortably remote.

A faint breeze stirred the lace on Lady Genevieve's white dress. A hundred questions came thronging through her mind, and some of them were threatening indeed.

The query she chose to begin with seemed trivial, but relatively safe: "Was that song your own creation?"

Her minstrel nodded, then hesitated. "The music is my own, and I would like to claim the words as well. But I am compelled to acknowledge that a man named Leigh Hunt composed them. Many and many a hundred years ago he lived, and of course the lady he had in mind was another who shared your name. Perhaps you remember my once telling you that you reminded me of—"

"Where are we now?" the young woman interrupted with unconscious rudeness. This was the first meaningful question she had asked of her companion. She was beginning her serious inquiries calmly enough, though the more she thought about her situation, the more totally inexplicable it seemed.

The minstrel's speaking voice was slightly hoarse and rather deeper than the tones in which he had been singing. "We are now in the city of London on old Earth, my lady Genevieve. Inside the precincts of a famous temple, or house of worship. The name of this temple is Westminster Abbey."

"Oh? But I have no memory of ever . . . arriving here."

"Natural enough under the circumstances. That's nothing to worry about; I can explain all that in good time. You do remember me, though?" Anxiety was perceptible beneath the singer's calm. Leaning his peculiar stringed instrument against the bench, he squatted almost kneeling before the lady and put his right hand out toward her. The movement was somewhat awkward, so that it almost fell upon her lap; but at the end of the gesture the long fingers had come down instead upon a cushion.

He added: "Nicholas Hawksmoor, at your service."

Seen in this environment, Nick was a middle-sized fellow, of mature though far from elderly appearance. A little taller than the average, not as portly as he had looked when Genevieve first saw him on the holostage. His chestnut hair was lustrous and a little curly, though beginning to thin on top. He had a small pointed beard of the same hue and a matching mustache, the latter also a little thinner than a man might wish. But of course one of the things he most feared, really, was to be thought a mere dandy, or merely handsome, all image and no substance. To avoid that, Hawksmoor would and did go to great lengths. He had and would put up with worse things than thinning hair.

Beneath the thinning hair, his face was unremarkable, somehow not as handsome as the lady remembered it from their earlier encounters. His nose (appropriately for his name, the lady thought) was just a little hawkish, eyes a trifle watery and of an unimpressive color, somewhere between gray and brown. Today the self-described architect and pilot was garbed in vaguely medieval-looking clothing, his long legs encased in what were almost tights, his upper body in a short jacket. The fabrics appeared solid and substantial, no more dazzling than his eyes. The contrast with the lady's bright white dress was notable.

"I remember your name, of course," Lady Genevieve responded. "And your face, too. Though you seem to look—a little different now. I think I have seen you only twice before, and neither of those meetings was really face-to-face. The first time I saw only your image upon a holostage. And the second time—then you were wearing a space suit and helmet, and I couldn't really see your face at all. We were on a ship, and when I tried to look inside your helmet . . ."

Nicholas did not actually see the lady's face turn pale with the impact of a newly examined memory, but he had the feeling that it might have done so.

Hastily he interrupted. "We were indeed on a ship. But now we are both *here*, my lady Genevieve. Here in this pleasant place. It is pleasant, is it not? And you are safe. As safe as I can make you. And I have—considerable capabilities."

Pallor receded. Lady Genevieve appeared to accept her companion's assurance of safety at face value, but her need for answers was not so easily met. Giving a small shake of her head, as if to allay uncertainty, she raised one well-kept hand in a questioning gesture, pointing in the general direction of two great rectangular stone towers that loomed in the middle distance, above and beyond the cloister walls. These twin structures were scores of meters tall, their monumental forms gray-brown in hazy slanting sunlight. Each tower was crowned at its four upper corners by four small steeples; and the nearer tower loomed so large, perhaps only two score meters away, that it almost seemed to hang right over the cloistered garden. At the moment a sea gull, giving tiny cries, came gliding on rigid wings between that mass of masonry and the two people in the garth.

Her companion followed her gesture with his eyes. "Those towers form the west front of the Abbey, Lady Genevieve, and the main entrance lies between them. I designed them, and supervised their construction ... well, to be strictly truthful, and I want always to be strictly truthful with you, he who was my namesake did. He lived even before the man who wrote the words to the song. But I think I may say, honestly and objectively, I could have done as well or better, working with real stone and mortar. Do you remember my once telling you, I am an architect?"

"Yes, I do. In fact I believe I can remember perfectly every word that you have ever said to me." Rising gracefully to her feet, the lady drew in a full breath, lifting her small bosom. "But I have the feeling there is more, much more, that I *ought* to remember. About quite recent events, I mean. Events of great importance. And that if I made a real effort to think about what has been happening to me, the answers would all be there. But ..."

"But you hesitate to make that effort?"

"Yes!" She paused, and added in a whisper: "Because I am afraid!"

The man rose lithely from his awkward squatting pose so that he towered timidly above her. He said: "If you find these matters disturbing, there is no hurry. No need for you to concern yourself about them now. Please, allow me to do whatever worrying may be necessary, for the time being at least. I will consider it a privilege—how much of a privilege you cannot know—to be your protector. In all things."

"Then, Nicholas, I will be honored indeed to enjoy your protection. Thank you very much." Genevieve extended one small, graceful hand, and stepping forward, the man reached to take it gratefully.

And at the moment when their fingers touched, the lady knew no more.

In their trio of spacecraft, the *Eidolon* was by a considerable margin the largest, the fastest, and the best armed. Orbiting low above the planetoid Imatra, Premier Dirac and his human entourage of space crew and advisers, bodyguards and other specialists, along with Sandy Kensing, were hastily completing their preparations for an early departure.

One of Dirac's ships, which had landed briefly on the Imatran surface for refitting, now hastily lifted off, to rendezvous with the *Eidolon* and the companion vessel which had remained in low orbit. Minutes later, without ceremony, the whole small but heavily armed squadron was easing away from the planetoid under smooth acceleration, heading outward from its sun in the direction of the center of the Mavronari, whose denser portions were light-years distant but whose outer fringes reached to within a few days' travel from Imatra at subluminal speeds. At a steadily quickening pace, Dirac's force moved antisunward, seeking the deepest emptiness obtainable in this region, some relatively smooth gravitational plain, ready to safely tolerate three ships' abrupt departure from normal space.

That ideal was unattainable. Some risk of relatively dirty space would have to be accepted; the enemy had too great a start to be overtaken now by mere subluminal flight at the speeds here possible.

Directly ahead of the small squadron, and still dimly perceptible to its telescopes by days-old light, the kidnapped bioresearch station receded steadily, at this distance making one compound image with the huge, enigmatic machine that had snatched it out of orbit.

The Lady Genevieve found herself once more with her new companion, this time strolling with her hand upon his arm. How she had come to be in this condition she did not know, but here she was. They were walking in the same grassy garth where they had last met and he had played the minstrel. The hazy, golden sun did not appear to have moved very far since the time—a very recent time, she thought—when she had been sitting on the bench. But there had been an interval of—something? or perhaps nothing?—between then and now.

Certainly the appearance of Nicholas Hawksmoor had altered in the interval. His clothing was now richer, no longer a minstrel's garb, but still far removed from a pilot's uniform. Looking up at him sideways, the lady wondered if his hair had grown thicker, too.

Now she could touch his arm without bringing on an attack of oblivion. She was touching it, and nothing happened. But the feel of Hawksmoor's sleeved forearm and of his sleeve beneath her fingertips had something odd about it. Strange too, when she thought about it, was the feeling of the grass beneath her white-slippered feet; strange the touch of clothing on her body, the air moving over her face . . .

The tall man beside her coaxed invitingly: "What are you thinking about?"

She almost whispered, "I am still wondering—about many things. I still have many questions I am afraid to ask."

He paused in his walking, the walk in which he had been leading her almost as in a dance, and she saw they had come to a stop before a doorway. It was a kind of gate leading into the gray dim cloister. He asked with muted eagerness: "Shall we go inside? I'd like to show you the whole church. It's really beautiful."

"Very well." And as they started through the doorway, she queried: "Did you or your namesake design this entire structure?"

"No, my lady, oh, no! Most of the Abbey is centuries older than either of us who bear the Hawksmoor name. Though indeed I wish we, or one of us at least, could claim such credit. Fortunately I shall have the honor of showing it to you."

Genevieve murmured something polite, a response that had become almost an instinct with her now. Ever since her marriage, since she had become a celebrity. Since—

Hawksmoor went wandering, escorting on his arm the lady he was treating with such tender attention that it seemed he wanted to make her his own. He led Lady Genevieve up and down through the rich gloom of the Abbey's interior as, he explained, he himself had interpreted and copied it. Within the walls and under the gothic peak of roof was, altogether, more than a hectare of space. He could have told her the precise area, down to the last decimal of a square millimeter, but he did not. Together they walked the aisles of the great church for a considerable time, hands touching now without any seeming constraint, with less peculiarity of feeling—then out again into the cloister's open air, where mild rain had come to replace sunlight while they were gone.

The rain felt very strange upon the lady's face, but she made no comment on the strangeness.

Her escort, saying little, looked at her and guided her back inside. The couple walked, their footfalls echoing upon square paving stones, straight down the middle of the towering nave.

"Gothic arches. I'll explain the structural theory of them to you if you like. The tallest, here in the nave, are more than thirty meters high. A ten-story building, if it was narrow enough, could fit inside. The loftiest interior of any church in all old England."

"I see no other people here."

"Do you wish for other people? Wait, that may be a verger, walking down the other aisle—see? And is that a priest I see at the high altar?"

Lady Genevieve stopped in her tracks. She knew these other people were some kind of sham. "What about my husband?"

"He is not here. Though as far as I know the Premier Dirac is well." Hawksmoor's voice became querulous. "Do you miss your bridegroom?" Then, as if he were trying to restrain himself but could not: "Do you love him very much?"

The lady shuddered. "I don't know what I feel about him. I can't say that I miss him; I can hardly remember what he is like."

"I'm sure your memory can call up anything you really want to know. Anything at all from your past."

"Yes, I suppose—if I was willing to make the effort." She sighed, and seemed to try to pull herself together. "Dirac and I never quarreled seriously about anything. He was good to me, I suppose, in the few days we lived together. But the truth is, I was—I am—terribly afraid of him." Once more she paused, looking at her taller companion's face, his head outlined against bright stained glass. "Tell me, what has happened to my child?"

"Child?"

"I was . . . pregnant."

"You know the answer to that. You donated your . . . protochild, I believe is the proper term, to the colony program. Or do you mean what might have happened afterward?"

The couple stood regarding each other, no longer touching. A silence stretched between them.

At last the lady broke it. "Nick, tell me the truth. What's happened?"

"To you? You are here with me, and you are safe. Perhaps that ought to be enough for now. But whenever you decide you really want to probe more deeply . . ."

For a moment Lady Genevieve could not speak. The sensation reminded her of her earlier problem in obtaining enough air with which to form and utter words, but this difficulty was somehow even more fundamental.

"No!" she cried out suddenly. "Don't tell me anything—anything frightening—just now. Can't we get out of this old building? What are all these monuments around us, graves?"

Her escort remained calm. "Many of them are. Tombs built into the walls and floor. But tombs so old I didn't think that they would mean anything to you, frighten you—"

"Isn't there anywhere else we can go?"

"There are a great many places." He took the lady's hand and stroked it soothingly. In her perception there was still something peculiar about the contact. "Let's try this way for a start."

With Nick gallantly providing an arm upon which the lady was willing to lean for comfort and guidance, the couple progressed from the western end of the nave into a stone-walled room that Nick murmured was St. George's chapel, then out of that grim place along a narrow passage penetrating a wall of tremendous thickness, to reach what were obviously the living quarters.

On their arrival in these very different rooms, Hawksmoor looked somewhat anxiously at the lady and asked her what she thought. Before he considered this space ready to use for entertaining, he had several times redesigned and refilled it with several successive sets of furnishings, according to the changing dictates of his taste.

After all, he was still very young.

Parts of his version of the Abbey, including the structural shell and much of the pleasing detail in the stonework and glass, had existed for many months before he met or even heard of the Lady Genevieve. It was Nick's private hobby as well as a component of his work in which he was deeply interested. But all this flurry of recent hasty revision had of course the single object of pleasing Jenny.

Actually, as he confessed later to his beloved, he had been able to discover very little about how these inner, semiprivate rooms had actually looked in the original down through the centuries—and in truth he did not really care. It was the grand design, the stonework and its decoration, that he had found most fascinating—at least until very recently.

Presently she was sitting in a comfortable modern chair. The room's stone walls were hung with abstract tapestries. The windows were too high for their clear glass to let in any real view of the outside. "It is a strange temple, Nick."

"It is a very old temple."

"And you live here?"

He had remained on his feet, restless, still watching her reactions closely, his boots resounding upon the bare stone between two thickly woven modern-looking rugs. "I suppose I spend as much time here as I do anywhere."

"And what god or goddess was it meant to serve?"

"A single god. The God of the Christians—are you any sort of a Believer, my lady?"

She shook her coppery curls. "Not really. When I was a child, my parents disagreed sharply on the subject of religion. My father is Monotheist, my mother was . . . it's hard to say just what she was. She died five years ago."

"I'm sorry."

"Then I am to understand that this whole magnificent temple now belongs to you?"

"Yes, I think I can claim that." Hawksmoor leaned back in his oversized chair and gestured theatrically. "Everything you see around you. Which means that it is all at your service, absolutely."

Running her fingers over the fabric of her own chair, she frowned at the sensation—something about her sense of touch was still not truly right.

Hawksmoor was gripping the carven arms of his seat, staring at her in what seemed to her an oddly helpless way. "My feelings for you, my lady, are—more than I can readily describe. I realize that from your point of view we have scarcely met, but . . . it might be accurate to say I worship you."

The lady, in the process of trying to grapple with this statement, trying to find some way to respond, raised her eyes and was momentarily distracted when she glimpsed, as if by accident, through a partly open door in a far wall, a thoroughly modern indoor swimming pool. Completely out of place. The water's surface as still as a mirror, yet she could tell that it was water. Sunken in blue-green tile, surrounded by utterly modern metal walls, lighted with soft modern clarity.

"I see you've noticed the pool. It's a kind of experiment of mine. A little touch that I thought you might one day—"

"Nick," she broke in, and then came to a stop. She had no idea of what she ought to say, or wanted to say, next. Only that she wanted to slow things down somehow.

"Yes, Lady Genevieve. Jenny. May I call you that?"

"Of course. Why not? You've saved my life."

"Jenny. I should not have started burdening you with my feelings. Today was not the time. Later we can speak of them."

"Feelings are important," she replied at last.

"Yes. Oh, yes." He nodded solemnly.

"Are we really on Earth, Nick?"

"I am not very sure what 'really' means—but in answer to your question, no, most people would say that just now you and I are not on Earth."

"I see. Thank you. Nick, have you ever really been to Earth?"

"No. But then, perhaps yes."

"Don't you *know*?"

"In a way I do. But I must keep coming back to my own question; like feelings, it's important: What does 'really' mean?"

Terror, which Lady Genevieve could easily visualize in the form of little mice and rats, had for some time been nibbling at the outside of the protective obscurity of thought that Nick had somehow so kindly provided for her, and that she had so welcomed.

Without any clear statement on the matter having been made, she had become convinced that this man was going to be her sole companion for some indefinite time to come. Part of her yearned to press him for real answers. What was this place really, this Abbey? But at the same time, fear held her back from the sheer finality of any answer he might give.

Nick was aware of her disquiet. "Don't you like it? I think this is certainly one of the most beautiful places I know. But if you don't like it, we could easily move elsewhere."

"Your Abbey's lovely, Nick. In its own way. It feels solid and safe, protected somehow."

"I hoped it would feel like that. To you."

"But—"

"But something is bothering you. I will answer any questions that I can."

The lady stared into her companion's eyes. "Let me tell you some of what I do remember. And this part is very clear. We, you and I, were on a little spaceship, a courier vessel, and there had already been a—tragedy. We were surrounded by death and—and—do you deny any of this?"

"No, my lady. I can't deny it." Hawksmoor shook his head solemnly.

"I cannot stand this anymore! Tell me, I beg of you, tell me in plain words what has happened. How we got from that place to this."

"My lady—" His voice beseeched her. "What I did when I found you on that little ship was the only thing I could have done. I took the only possible course open to me to save you from death. Believe me, I did it all for you."

"My thanks again, dear Nick, for saving me. Now tell me how."

He came visibly to a decision and pressed on, showing a curious mixture of eagerness and reluctance. "You will remember how I entered the courier's cabin, wearing space armor?"

"I remember that, of course. And how I welcomed you. It seems to me that I remember your arms going round me—" And that, she suddenly realized, had been the last time that the *touch* of anything had felt precisely right.

Her companion was nodding. "My arms did indeed enfold you. The limbs of that suit are mine—in the sense that I am usually able to make use of them when I wish. What I must explain to you now is that those or others I might borrow are the only arms I have."

She was listening intently, frowning.

He said tenderly, worriedly, "You mustn't be afraid."

She was staring at Nick's own upper limbs, which seemed large and obvious, fairly ordinary in appearance as he stood before her, hands on his hips. She whispered, "I don't understand."

"These?" He extended his arms, wiggling his fingers, pulled them back to hug himself, then held them out again. "Of course these are mine too, but they could not have helped you on that ship. They have other purposes—and they are making progress, evidently. Now you can feel my touch. Is what you feel when you touch me still strange? Much different than—the contact of your husband's hand, for example?"

"Yes! There is still something . . . odd about the way things feel here. Not only your hand, but everything. All the objects that I touch. And as I think about it, there's a peculiarity in the way things look. The colors are so fine, so vivid. And the smell of everything is a little different, and . . . but I don't . . ."

"My lady, when you and I stood together, the two of us together on that wrecked, dying ship, I promised you solemnly that I could get you safely away, across the airless gap to my ship, even though you had no suit. Because I knew that your poor, hurt body could be fitted neatly inside my suit; and that is exactly how I did it."

"Two people in one suit? I didn't think—"

"Two people, Lady Genevieve, yes, but only one body. Yours. You see, even then I had no body of my own. No solid arms with which to rescue you, or anyone." His waving hands seemed to deny their own existence. "No anything of flesh and bone." His voice was low, underplaying the string of disclaimers like a man who admits that he is at the moment inconveniently missing a leg, lost in some accident and not yet medically regrown.

"You seem to be telling me that you have *no* body. No—"

"No fleshly body. Nor have I ever had one. To achieve useful solidity I need a spacesuit, or some other hardware subject to my control. What you see before you here and now is an image. Mere information. I am, you see, I have always been, an optelectronic artifact. Fundamentally, no more than a computer program." Once again Nicholas Hawksmoor made an expansive gesture with his imaged arms.

The lady stared at him for a long time—somewhere time was jerking ahead in subtle electronic increments—and hardly a line of her face moved by so much as a millimeter, for however long she stared.

Finally she said, "You were telling me about my—rescue. Go ahead. I want to hear the details. Everything."

"Of course. The moment I came aboard the courier where you were trapped, and looked around, I could see that few of your fellow passengers would benefit from any help that I might give . . . but no, that's wrong. Let me be truthful with you, always very truthful. The truth was that I cared very little about those people. I didn't worry about them. It was you I had come to save."

"You—welcomed me aboard. And—just at that point, another blast engulfed us."

"Yes. Yes, there was another explosion. I remember that."

In a strained voice Nick whispered: "I am afraid that you were injured rather severely then."

"Ah." Both her hands were taken, engulfed, in both of his. She could close her eyes, and did, but nothing she could do would make the strangeness of his touching go away.

"Yes. I had to work very quickly. Your body fit neatly inside my suit, which, as I have tried to explain, is in a way also my body—"

The lady gasped.

"—and which, therefore, in terms of mass and physics, was very nearly empty. And I, dwelling for the time being in the suit's electronics, working the servos that drive the arms and fingers of the suit, sealed you into the body cavity with my own metal hands, and I, being in effect the spacesuit, acting through the spacesuit, fed you air, made you breathe, though by that time your lungs were scarcely working.

"Then I carried you back safely across the gap of cold and emptiness and death, safely into my own little ship which was standing by. Then out of the suit with you, and right into the medirobot. And now . . . now here you are."

The lady was staring at him. She did not appear to be breathing. Now that she thought about it, she seemed to have no need to breathe.

Into the silence, as if he found her silence frightening, her rescuer said: "I don't suppose you remember my little ship at all. You haven't really had a chance to see her. I call her the *Wren*, that's a sort of pun, she's named for my namesake's mentor, Christopher Wren, he was yet another architect. I don't know if he was any kind of a pilot, in the sailing ships they had those days. I don't suppose he was—"

She broke in with a reaction of shattered horror. "*You are only an image?*"

"In a sense, yes. An image appearing in a mode of virtual reality. Technically I am an optelectronic artifact, basically a computer program . . ."

"*Then what in all the hells have I become? What have you done to me?*"

Nick, who had been dreading this moment more and more, did his best to explain. His voice was kindly and muted and logical. But before he had said ten more words, the lady began to scream. He tried to talk above the breathless screaming, but that was useless, so for the sake of her own sanity, and his, he exercised a certain control function and turned her *off*. Only temporarily, of course.

☀ SIX

One of the yacht's junior officers, who was perhaps really trying to be helpful, said to Kensing, who was standing in one of the yacht's corridors looking thoughtful: "You really don't get it about Nick yet, do you?"

Kensing stared at him. "I've had other things to think about. So what the hell is it about Nick that I don't get, assuming his problem has any relevance?"

The man looked defensive. "I didn't exactly say he had a problem."

"What, then?"

"Hawksmoor's a computer program."

"Oh." Suddenly several things that had been puzzling Kensing made sense. He had heard of the thing being done before, the optelectronic creation of a close analogue of a human personality. It wasn't done often, though technically such procedures had been feasible for a long time. In a society that had developed and was still developing while locked in an age-long struggle against machines, the anthropomorphizing of hardware or software was definitely unpopular and uncommon. Such constructions were also illegal on many worlds, among folk who, with the hideous example of the berserkers always before them, lived in dread of their own computer artifacts somehow getting out of hand.

Kensing asked: "You don't mean a recorded person?"

"Nope. Mean just what I said. The fact doesn't get much publicity, but the boss has developed a definite interest in electronic personalities over the last few years."

Kensing nodded. Anthropomorphic programs designed from scratch, as opposed to those recorded from organic human brains, were deeply interesting to many students of psychology, politics, and control. But the few examples extant were generally kept hidden.

There existed a closely related class of programs, actual recorded people, which were sometimes very useful tools but tended to be subject to even more widespread restrictions. Kensing had once met one of them, the program Hilary Gage, which—or who—had played a key role in one particularly famous fight against berserkers. Kensing, meeting the Gage program long after that battle, had enjoyed a lengthy conversation with him—or with it. Even after the long talk, Kensing wasn't sure which pronoun best applied.

Today, only minutes after discovering the truth about Hawksmoor, Kensing happened to bring up the subject with Frank Marcus. He learned that Frank had met Gage, too; and Frank, like many other people, remained perfectly sure that in meeting a recorded person he had encountered nothing but a program.

At the moment Kensing and Marcus were inspecting the latest VR mockup of the kidnapped station, put up by *Eidolon*'s computers. All the members of the crew were taking turns in visiting the ten-cube to see this display when they had the chance; they all wanted to know in detail the nature of the prize they were pursuing, and what sort of military operations might be feasible if and when they got close enough to think of attempting a recovery.

But Kensing, inspecting the model's beautifully realistic image, was suddenly sure the whole enterprise was doomed to futility. Berserkers killed. That was the function for which they had been designed and built, and that was what they did. The possibility that Annie might be still alive was really small, in fact infinitesimal...

There was an interruption on holostage. Nick Hawksmoor was suddenly present. He appeared standing to one side and slightly behind the modeled cylinder of the station, resting one forearm on the flat disk of the upper end. The weightless image perfectly supported his weightless body.

"Excuse me, gentlemen, but I really couldn't help overhearing. I'm touching up some of the life support in these compartments at the moment, and on occasion conversations just come through."

"Quite all right," said Kensing, feeling odd.

Hawksmoor acknowledged the declaration with a slight smile. But it was evident that he was mainly interested in talking to Frank, for his eyes turned in that direction. "Perhaps you are aware that I myself am an electronic person, Colonel?"

Frank was already looking at the Hawksmoor image through two of his front-box lenses. A third now swiveled around that way, as if he wanted a better look. "Are you, now?" he commented.

Kensing, listened, was struck by the fact that the voice of the fragmented, augmented man in boxes sounded less human than Nick's, though both of course were being generated by mechanical speakers.

"Indeed I am."

Marcus made no further comment.

Nick pressed on, sounding both curious and somehow determined. "Does my revelation make you angry? Do you consider that you have been deceived?"

A metal forelimb gestured lightly. "I admit you took me a little by surprise. Maybe I would be angry if I thought a human had been deceiving me. But getting mad at a tool doesn't make a lot of sense. Are you a good tool, Nick?"

"I work at being a good tool, usually to the best of my ability. If you are not offended, Colonel, and if you have a little time to spare, let me pursue the subject a little further."

"Go ahead. Shoot."

"You will probably not be surprised to hear that I find the topic deeply interesting. Actually I had not expected you to accept my revelation so quickly, without discussion. Without at least some faint suspicion that I was joking."

All three of Frank's boxes moved, slightly adjusting their relative positions; Kensing got the impression that their occupant was somehow making himself comfortable. Marcus said: "I said you took me a little by surprise. But maybe not entirely."

"Indeed. Not entirely? I would like to know what it was about me—about my persona on the holostage, which you have encountered several times—that suggested to you that I lack flesh."

"Maybe we can go into it sometime. Right now I've got other things to do." End of conversation.

Kensing, at his next opportunity to talk with Premier Dirac, said something about how realistic Nick Hawksmoor appeared to be, what a good job the programmers had done in putting him together. "He's a relatively new version, I presume?"

Dirac nodded. "Yes, only about a year old. They did do a good job, didn't they? It took them several months. The truth is I was growing less and less happy with the product I was getting from human architects—that biostation, for example. So I decided to try what a state-of-the-art optelectronic mind could do."

"I'd say a matter of only months is quick work for a program of such complexity, Premier. I'd have thought years. How was his name chosen, if you don't mind my asking?"

"My engineers had certain building blocks of programming ready," Dirac explained vaguely. "That speeded things up. As for his name, Nick picked it himself. Adopted it from some eighteenth-century builder—I'll tell you the story sometime. Did you get a good look at the station model?"

It seemed to Kensing, who had the chance to observe some of the interactions between Premier Dirac and Hawksmoor, that normally the organic creator got along well enough with his artificial creation.

But the Premier's feelings toward any optelectronic personalities he encountered tended to be complex and intense.

Once Kensing heard Dirac declaim: "Those transcribed spirits who have retired from flesh into electronic modality generally enjoy a higher social status, if one can put it in those terms, than those who have never possessed a red blood cell in their lives."

Kensing was unsurprised to hear that he was not the only one who had been fooled for some time by Nick. Others were more upset, on discovering the truth, than he had been. Some of the crew members, like a great many people elsewhere, voiced or at least had some objection to or felt some uneasiness about a computer artifact that looked and sounded so much like a person. It was not of course Hawksmoor's calculating power—or call it intellect—to which most objected; it was the semblance of humanity possessed by this *thing* with which (or whom) the Premier consulted, argued (sometimes joyfully), and upon whom (or which) he seemed to depend so heavily.

❈   ❈   ❈

Now that the squadron was ready to pull out from Imatra, Nick was being forced to leave behind his *Wren*—he thought of the little ship as his. The place on the hangar deck usually occupied by that often useful but unarmed vessel had been taken by an armed military scoutship, the last fighting craft of any kind left in the Imatran system. The recent fighting had ended before the scoutship was able to reach the scene. Dirac had overawed the overmatched local authorities and simply taken it away from them.

But abandoning the *Wren* posed more problems for Nick than his creator/employer realized. Now, with the squadron on the verge of departure, Hawksmoor had been supervising, among his other duties, the robot workers busy removing certain equipment from the *Wren* and reinstalling it on the newly acquired scout.

During this operation Nick moved himself about, aboard ship or in space, in spacesuit mode. His chief job was supervising the robots that did most of the physical work—these were mostly dog-sized metal creatures with nothing organic in their physical appearance and nothing outstanding in their brains.

While conducting this work openly, Hawksmoor had a desperate need to see that another task was performed also, and in the strictest secrecy—he had to arrange the transfer, from his own small craft to somewhere aboard the yacht, not only of the physical storage units in which he himself resided most of the time, when he was not working in suit-mode, but also of those containing Jenny.

It had turned out, as he had more or less expected, that the physical volume needed to store the recording of a once-organic person—in this case, the Lady Genevieve—under current technology (which incorporated, in solid lumps of heavy metals and composite materials, the latest subquantal storage systems) was just about the same as that required to house Nick himself: about four thousand cubic centimeters, a capacity approximately equivalent to that of three adult human skulls.

The suit Nick had chosen to animate for this particular transfer job happened to be the same one he'd used to rescue Lady Genevieve from the doomed courier. It had sustained some minor damage at that time, damage he was going to be hard put to explain if anyone ever noticed it and queried him about it. He had what he thought were several good explanations ready, and intended to choose what seemed the best one when the moment of truth arrived.

On one of Nick's suited passages across the hangar deck of the *Eidolon* he encountered Kensing, himself spacesuited at the moment. The fleshly man was taking an inventory, and making a hands-on inspection of the small craft aboard, upon which it would be necessary to depend if boarding operations were contemplated.

Nick felt somewhat amused at Kensing's reaction to the appearance of Nick's physically empty suit. For some reason this struck the young systems engineer, as it did many other people, as particularly creepy and disturbing.

After meeting Kensing, Hawksmoor considered snatching a few moments from his assigned duties—he had no authorized time for rest, since he was not supposed to need any—to visit Jenny, to make sure she had come through the physical transfer without any problems. Actually there was no reason to think she had even been aware that it was going on, but he wanted to make sure.

In the privacy of his own thought, Hawksmoor had by now begun to ponder very seriously several important questions raised by his new relationship with the Lady Genevieve.

One of the first tasks he had undertaken in these latest intervals of secret work had been to adjust (*very* tentatively and cautiously!) some of the lady's peripheral programming, hoping thus to help her recover from the shock of realization of her new state of existence. He had been careful not to overdo the adjustment, and soon as he had awakened the Lady Genevieve again, she had begun at once to implore, to demand, that he tell her exactly what had happened to her.

On revisiting Jenny as soon as possible after her transfer to the yacht, Hawksmoor resumed his efforts to explain the new situation to the lady, as gently as he could.

Within a few minutes after he'd rescued the Lady Genevieve (whose spirit at the time had still maintained a tenuous hold upon her native flesh) from the doomed courier and succeeded in carrying her aboard his little ship, the *Wren*'s own medirobot had diagnosed her injuries as certainly fatal. Even with deep-freezing until the best in medical help could be obtained, the prognosis was abysmally poor.

At that point he, Nick, as he recounted now, had had no choice. Regardless of what heroic measures he and the medirobot might have taken, the lady's brain was soon going to be dead—and once that happened, no physician or surgeon, human or robotic, would be able to restore her personality.

As Nicholas—or his image in virtual reality—told this story now, Jenny—or her image—stood staring at him helplessly, her small mouth open on white teeth. At the moment they were, to Jenny's best awareness, near the very center of the Abbey, halfway down the football-field length of the west nave and strolling east, enjoying the pastel glories painted on stone and wood by an afternoon sun coming in behind them through the stained glass of the great west window. Not as glorious a rose window, Nick thought to himself, as that of Chartres was said to have been—but still impressive.

"Therefore, my lady," Hawksmoor concluded, "as I have been trying to explain, I did the only thing I could. I recorded you. I saved the patterns of your consciousness, the essence of your personality, practically your entire memory."

Thanks to the subtle adjustments Nick had very recently made in her peripheral programming, the lady was soon able to calm down enough to reply. Her next words, spoken with the politeness ladyship demanded, were to thank Nick once more for saving her; her next words after those comprised an urgent plea, demand, for a more thorough explanation of her situation.

Grateful at seeming to have got past the key point of the explanation without disaster, Hawksmoor went on, as delicately as possible, into the details. How he had reformed and reclothed the image of her body, plucking the vast quantities of necessary data out of the many video recordings of the lovely Lady Genevieve he happened to have on hand. Not just happened. His burgeoning worship of the lady had months ago caused him to begin to accumulate images of her—and the nearer the date of the wedding came, the more such images had been available.

Nick might have related more details of the process by which he had created her image as it was today, a staggering number of details in fact. But already the lady had had enough. Briskly she interrupted his recital with an imperious demand that he at once start arranging for her return to an organic, fleshly body.

"Nick, I understand, really I do, that your purpose in doing . . . what you have done was to save my life. And it worked, and I'm grateful, never think I'm not."

"My lady, it was the least that I—"

"But I cannot go on living indefinitely like this, without a real body. How long is the restoration going to take?"

Hawksmoor had been afraid of the moment when he had to face this question. "My lady, I am more sorry than I can say. But what you are asking can't . . . Well, I just haven't been able to discover any way in which it can be done."

As these words were spoken, the couple had rounded a columned corner and were, in terms of the virtual reality they shared, standing in the south transept of the Abbey, near the place Hawksmoor had learned ought to be called Poets' Corner, because of the masters of the art who had been entombed or memorialized there. But the Lady Genevieve was not currently interested in poetry, or architecture either. She raised her eyes and looked around her, as if her imaged eyes could see through, beyond, the virtual world of stones and glass to whatever harsher, deeper fabric of realworld hardware was maintaining it.

"Where are we, really?" she demanded.

"In those terms, Jenny—if I may still call you that—we are now, as I have been trying to explain, aboard your husband's yacht, the *Eidolon*—and no, he has not the faintest suspicion that you are here."

"He doesn't even suspect?" Her tone was shocked, surprised, but—yes, he dared to think that her reaction was also one of hope. "I thought perhaps you were doing this at his orders."

That she might entertain such a suspicion had never occurred to Nick. He said: "I shall explain presently. But be assured that Premier Dirac has not the slightest inkling that you have survived in any form. He simply believes that you are dead, killed with the others who were aboard that courier when it exploded."

"So you haven't told him."

To Nick's immense relief, there had been more calculation than accusation in those words.

He reassured her. "I have not told him or anyone."

"Why not?"

"Why have I not told your husband?" Suddenly he felt nervous and uncertain. "There are reasons. I am not going to apologize for my behavior, but you certainly deserve an explanation."

"Well?"

"Yes. The first time we met, Jenny . . . I mean the first time you were able to look at me and respond to me . . . there in that great laboratory room aboard the bioresearch station—even before there was any hint of a berserker attack—I received the impression that you were deeply unhappy. Was I wrong?"

She hesitated.

"Was I wrong?"

She was looking at some kind of marble monument encased in wooden cabinetry, with antique letters spelling CHAUCER carved into the stone. He could tell her the fascinating history of that memorial if she was interested. But right now she was just staring. At last she said: "No. No, Nick, I don't suppose that you were wrong."

"I knew it! And now you have admitted that you fear your husband. I too have been living with him in a sense, you see, if only briefly. I know, as you know, that our Premier is not the easiest person in the Galaxy to get along with."

At that the lady smiled wanly.

Hawksmoor went on: "The Premier and I, sometimes . . . well, all is not always well between us, my creator and me.

"You see, Jenny, at first, when I was getting you out of the courier, transporting you to my medirobot, deciding that recording your mind was the only way to save it—all that time I had no idea of keeping your rescue a secret. No conscious plan. But then, I remember thinking, before telling the world that you were saved, I had better make sure that you had come through the recording process in good shape—which, let me hasten to assure you, you have done."

"And then?" the lady prompted.

"Well, I determined that I was going to make sure you had the right to choose," Nick burst out. "I mean, the right to choose whether you wanted to go back to him or not."

"Go back to him?" Jenny was stunned, uncomprehending. Then wild hope leaped up in her eyes. "You mean that after all you can restore me to my body?"

"I—no, I thought I had explained, I cannot do that. No one can. Your body has been totally destroyed."

"But then how could I go back to him? What do you mean by such a question? How can I go back to anyone when I'm in this condition?"

"I suppose the only real way in which you could go back to *him*," said Nick in measured tones, "would be to visit him, to talk to him from a holostage. Perhaps to meet him in some virtual space, as we are meeting now."

"To meet him in some imaginary world, like this? Or to gaze at him from a holostage? What good is that to anyone?" The lady was starting to grow frantic once again. "What good is it to Dirac, especially? To a man who married me to start a dynasty? In his world of politics, being married to an electronic phantom will mean nothing, nothing at all. No, my husband must never know what has happened to me, at least not until you have brought me back to real life. He must never see me this way! He might—" She let the sentence die there, as if she were afraid to complete it.

"There are alternatives, of course," said Nick after a short interval. His own desperation was growing. "I think they are excellent alternatives. The fact is that you and I—that there are ways in which we might have a life together. Eventually, with others like ourselves—"

"Like ourselves? You mean unreal? Only programs, images?"

"It is a different form of life, I admit. But we—"

"Life? Is this a life? I tell you, I must have a body." The lady, interrupting, almost screaming, waved her imaged arms. "Skin and blood and bones and sex and muscles—can you give me those?"

Hawksmoor exerted his best efforts to explain. But she wasn't particularly interested in the technical details. She wanted him to cease his protests that getting her a body was impossible, and to get on with the task of doing it, somehow, at any cost.

But at the same time—this was a new development, and it certainly gave Nick new hope—she didn't want him to leave her alone. It was painfully lonely in the Abbey, Genevieve complained, when he was absent.

Hawksmoor experienced great joy at the discovery that the lady missed him. Still, he was going to have to leave her sometime. "I could provide people," he suggested.

"Real people?"

"Well, at the moment, no. Currently your companionship would be limited to somewhat distant figures, like the verger. Maybe a small crowd having a party in the next room or around the pool, the sounds, the distant images of people singing, dancing?"

"And I could never join them. No thanks, Nick. Just come and see me when you have the time. And you must, you really must, try to bring me some good news."

"I'll do that." And he went away, projected his awareness elsewhere, fled down the pathway of an exit circuit, returning to duty fired with a new resolve, because she hadn't wanted him to leave.

Before he left, a small thing but about all that he could do, Nick had shown her how to put herself to sleep.

He was bitterly disappointed, though he told himself he had no right to be, at the savage reaction, absolutely unjustified as far as he could see, of the woman he loved. He had meant to offer her a joyous future.

Also, he was really sure, down at the most fundamental level of his programming, that her demand to be restored to flesh was going to prove impossible to meet. Nowhere in his flawless, extensive memory was there any indication that the mass of data comprising an opt-electroperson (authorities differed on the proper term to cover both kinds of programmed people), either organic or artificial in origin, had ever been successfully downloaded to an organic brain.

At the pair's next meeting, which came only minutes later in what fleshly folk would have counted as real time, Jenny, as she continued trying to come to terms with the harsh facts of her new existence, showed that she felt some repentance for her stridency and seeming lack of gratitude. She was, she now insisted repeatedly, really grateful to Nick for saving her in the only way he could. She agreed that surely, surely this shadowy existence among shadowy images was better than being dead.

From the way she repeated this over and over, Nick got the impression that she might be endeavoring to convince herself.

Hawksmoor was happy to be thanked, but he still felt deeply wounded that the woman he loved could so reject his world, his whole existence. He still worshiped this woman—more than ever, now that she was of his kind. If *woman* was still the right word for what she had become—yes, it was, he would insist on that—and if *worship* had ever been the right word for what he felt.

Love? The data banks to which he had access and the troubled presence, the enigmatic position, of that word in them assured him that it would admit of no easy definition.

What he felt, he knew, some people would insist upon defining as one mass of programming hankering for another.

In his timidity he had found the matter difficult to explain to the Lady Genevieve, but he had begun to have such feelings for her well before he had ever managed to get close enough for them to interact. It had all started when he had first seen her image, many months before her unlucky journey to Imatra.

She had now been long enough in his world that it had become necessary for him to explain the degrees of difference, in his world, between perception and interaction. All that anyone, fleshly or opt-electronic, ever *saw* of any other person was an image, was it not?

On a succeeding visit to the Abbey he tried again. The lady did seem to be touched eventually by his pleas and arguments; she admitted that she liked Nick too, she really did. But she would not admit any lessening of her need to regain a body somehow, anyhow. On that point, she warned him, there was going to be no compromise. And she needed the cure, the restoration, as soon as possible: why wasn't he working on the problem now?

And when Hawksmoor made yet another effort, very tentative, to persuade her out of that demand, she quickly gave evidence of falling again into a fit of screaming panic.

Under the circumstances Nick would have promised anything. Therefore he took the solemn oath she insisted that he take to work on the problem of obtaining for her what she called a real body, a mass of matter as fleshly as the one she had been born with, as healthy and attractive, as satisfactory in every way. And he swore also that his efforts would not fail.

Having thus pacified his Jenny for the moment, Hawksmoor took polite leave and went away.

He went away from her and from the Abbey, entering circuits that took him in effect a step closer to the universe of organic beings. He was thinking to himself as he undertook this shift of viewpoint that someone, sometime, on some ship or planet in the Solarian portion of the Galaxy, must have at least attempted such a downloading of human personality from hardware to organic brain.

But when, in his next hurried intervals of free time, he tried to dig into the subject, Hawksmoor soon discovered that all of the data banks to which he could routinely gain access—which included all those he was aware of on the yacht—were silent on the subject of fitting electronic personalities into organic brains, and on certain closely related topics as well. Rather strangely silent, it seemed to Nick now. Could it be that the Boss, interested as he was in related matters, wanted to discourage others from experimenting in the field?

It even crossed the optelectronic mind of Nicholas Hawksmoor to wonder: Was it possible that knowledge of such matters was being systematically kept from him? He couldn't think of any reason why it should be so. Unless the Boss thought that for some reason he, Nick, was likely to tinker with himself in such a way. But there was no chance he'd want to do such a thing...or there hadn't been, till now.

He didn't see how it could be possible to get anywhere at all in the effort to provide Jenny with a body using only the equipment currently available on the yacht. But it occurred to Nick that if his combative boss should catch up with the kidnapped bioresearch station, and should somehow, miraculously, against all odds, succeed in retrieving that facility from the berserker essentially undamaged—that facility just might make the feat possible.

Then mentally Nick shook his head.

Even supposing the mission should be such a highly improbable smashing success that the research station equipment indeed became available, there wouldn't of course be time for Nick or anyone else to use it before the squadron and its prize returned to Imatra.

Would there?

Nick's own information banks contained mention of some kind of quasi-religious cult on certain Solarian worlds, whose devotees promoted human recording as a try at spiritual immortality. He had the impression that this subject either was or had been one of Premier Dirac's own private interests. The Premier was rumored to have had some connection with the cult.

It was common knowledge that Frank Marcus had agreed to accept, for the duration of the emergency, the job of chief pilot of the Premier's yacht. It was part of his agreement with the Premier that Frank, until combat seemed imminent, would be relieved of many or most routine pilot's tasks, by one or more slightly lesser-rated mortals.

It seemed evident from the size and segmented shape of Colonel Marcus's metal body (his bodies, rather; Kensing had noticed that he changed modules from time to time) and from the small amount of organic nourishment he took (and the form in which he took it, a kind of gruel) that there couldn't be a whole lot of his original, organic body left by now. Whispered guesses ranged down to as little as five kilograms, if the amount of organic nourishment he ingested was any clue. But however much he'd lost, Kensing would have staked his own life that the colonel was surely no recording; you had to be with him, talk with him, for only a short time to be sure of that.

Frank generally took care of the mixing and pouring in of his organic food himself—sometimes a serving robot did it at his direction—and there were times, when Frank was off duty and ready to relax, when he included a few drops of some fine Peruvian (or other) brandy.

And certain rumors were passed about: supposedly more than one of the female crew members were now able, and on occasion willing, to testify to the fact that the man who dwelt in the boxes still retained organic maleness.

Other rumors circulated also, none of them seemingly more than half serious. Test one of them on Frank, as Kensing did, mention to him any suspicion going the rounds to the effect that Frank's organic brain was long since dead, his mind had been recorded years ago, and he'd blast you with a raucous laugh. Sure, his brain functioned with computer assists sometimes, accepted optelectronic augmentation when he was at the helm of a ship, but any human pilot had to take advantage of those when things got rough. There was never any doubt, in Frank's own mind at least, as to which component of himself, organic or electronic, was fully in charge. And Marcus had several times said vehemently, and was not shy about saying it again, that he was never going to allow himself to be recorded.

Dirac, admiring, had said that if Frank himself had not been available, he would have tried to get someone like him, a man or woman who lived in marcus boxes, as his number one pilot when combat against berserkers loomed as it did now. Over the last few decades, perhaps a century, the Marcus name had become eponymous for—or Frank the eponymous originator of—certain special equipment used by Solarian humans who suffered very severe physical disability. But people in marcus boxes were extremely rare. Almost everyone who had to deal with serious bodily impairment could benefit from, and much preferred, organic rebuilding. The whole body outside the brain could generally be repaired or replaced, and usually the new flesh was remarkable in its duplication of, perhaps even an improvement on, the shape of the original.

Whether Frank himself had any compelling medical reason to live in his boxes now, instead of having his fleshly frame regrown, perhaps only the medical officer aboard the *Eidolon* could have said—and ethics of course prevented any casual testing of rumors there.

Nor did it seem that anyone present—except of course the Premier himself, who seemed to have no interest in the question—would have the nerve to ask the colonel directly.

Someone speculated that while Colonel Marcus must have originally—some centuries ago—been housed in his present form for compelling medical and technical reasons, he probably now preferred to retain the massive hardware for reasons of his own.

Only Nick among the other available pilots could meld as thoroughly as Frank with a diversity of modern machines. And in fact Nick was among those who now took regular shifts at the helm of the *Eidolon.* When he was taking his turn, the pilot's acceleration couch stood empty.

Early on in the chase, Dirac, after consultation with his advisers, both human and systemic, ordered an advance at superluminal velocity, despite the considerable risk involved in taking even small c-plus jumps in this cluttered region of space. Going faster than light was the only way they could be sure of catching the berserker.

Superb piloting could cut the risk to some degree. Hawksmoor was among the first to admit that Frank, like a few other organic Solarian humans, possessed a fine touch in the control of, the melding with, machinery that even Nick could not duplicate. The marvels of a still-organic brain, which were as yet imperfectly understood, provided Frank's mind, both conscious and unconscious, with the little extra, the fine edge over pure machine control that enabled the best human pilots sometimes, under favorable conditions, to seize a slight advantage over even the best of pure machine opponents.

Frank in turn, after having watched Nick handle a ship and a computer for a while, readily admitted that Nick was pretty good at handling complex machines, and that he—or "it," as Frank always said—would probably be good at fighting berserkers, though so far Nick lacked any experience along that line. Frank gave the impression of realistically appraising the artifact's competence, in the same way he coolly and capably estimated the relative usefulness and weakness of other software and machines.

Colonel Marcus was, thought Kensing, less ready to evaluate people.

But when the question arose as to whether Nick and those like him could ever, should ever, be considered human beings, Marcus had only quietly amused contempt for anyone who seriously proposed such an idea.

The Premier's pursuit of the berserker had now lasted approximately two standard days, and was steadily gaining ground. But before anyone expected an actual encounter, combat flared again.

The visible berserker and its captured prize were still far out of weapons range. But a terse verbal warning of suspected trouble ahead came from the yacht's own brain, interrupting yet another session of the planning council. "There is a ninety percent probability of combat within the next forty seconds."

Kensing, with the sudden feeling that Annie in one way or another was very close to him, leaped from his chair and dashed for his battle station. A moment later he was almost bumped off his feet by Frank Marcus's train of boxes, clumsy-looking no longer, outspeeding Kensing's running legs and others.

The signal from the early warning system was quickly confirmed. Berserker hardware, in the form of small units deployed across flightspace as well as normal space, lay in wait for Dirac's squadron. The encounter was only a few seconds away and could not be avoided. The enemy devices, their presence partially masked by dust and by their own shielding, surrounded the faintly crackling trail of the fleeing raider and its catch. These were intelligent mines, brilliant weapons waiting with inhuman patience to blast or ram, ready to destroy themselves against the hulls of any pursuers.

Until this moment the pursuing force had come hurrying, almost blinded by its own speed, right along the trail, flickering from one space mode to the other and back again; the urgency of the Premier's quest had demanded exactly that. Fortunately Frank had had time to take the pilot's chair. At the moment when the enemy must have calculated that their ambush would be detected, and flightspace as well as normal space seemed to ignite in one great explosion, the yacht instead of veering off went hurtling, jumping forward with an appearance of even greater recklessness than usual.

The pilots of the other two Solarian ships were doing their best to stay with Frank in some kind of a formation and to deal with their deadly enemies as they came within effective range. Some of the ambushing machines could be avoided or bypassed, but the remainder had to be faced and fought.

The crew of the yacht, many of them like Kensing raw newcomers to actual combat, had the impression that the *Eidolon* was being flattened and at the same time turned inside out. The hulls of all three ships rang with the impact of radiation. For the first few moments, total destruction of either humans or berserkers seemed the only possible outcome.

At the point the enemy had chosen for the ambush, where his trail passed through constricting fringes of nebula, the average density of matter grew marginally greater, and the Solarian squadron, all three ships now embedded in normal space, skidded and splashed to a halt inside this fimbriation. Their formation, never all that well maintained, quickly broke up in tactical maneuver, the enemy's trail for the moment necessarily ignored.

The two smaller ships accompanying the Premier's armed yacht were racked up quickly in this fight. The people on the *Eidolon*'s bridge saw one of these vaporized quickly, and the other, in a matter of seconds, so badly damaged that the surviving captain radioed his intention to limp back to Imatra if possible.

Dirac, shouting on radio, did his best to forbid that, but whether or not his orders got through he could not tell. Almost immediately he and the others on the yacht's bridge saw the damaged vessel destroyed.

☀ SEVEN

Two out of three of the Premier's ships had been destroyed. The yacht itself had sustained at least one hit, and there were dead and wounded on several decks, smoke in the corridors, air escaping and compartments sealed off. But, once the *Eidolon* had shaken free of the enemy's swarm of brilliant weapons, neither Dirac nor his ace pilot even considered abandoning the chase and turning back to Imatra.

In the moments of respite that followed, everyone but the seriously wounded was issued and fitted with weapons for close quarters, alphatrigger or eyeblink helmets and the associated gear. The most innovative of these weapons projected cutting beams that savaged ordinary armor, but let soft flesh alone, and rebounded harmlessly—or almost harmlessly—from any properly treated surface. The code embodied in the coating's chemistry could be readily changed between one engagement and the next, to lessen the chances of the enemy's being able to duplicate it successfully.

The realization crossed some remote part of Kensing's mind that this could work out to be an excellent career move. As a defensive systems engineer, he would benefit from the actual combat experience he was accumulating.

People, one at a time, were being visited at their battle stations by a service robot, to get their armored spacesuits coated with the right combination, fresh from the paint mixer. Other maintenance robots made their way through rooms and corridors, spraying the stuff on most of the interior surfaces.

Kensing, now fully suited and armored as were most of the other crew members, waited at his battle station ready to assist with damage control or repelling boarders. He heard Frank, in the pilot's seat, grunt something to the effect that in the circumstances it would now be as dangerous to turn back as to press on.

As far as Sandy Kensing knew, Premier Dirac had no more previous experience of actual space combat than Kensing did himself. However that might be, the Premier went on as usual calmly issuing orders—calmly consulting as necessary with Colonel Marcus or other experts before he did so. And as usual his commands were accepted, instantly and without comment. Kensing had noticed that this man only rarely and inadvertently intruded his orders into realms where he was not competent to give them.

Frank Marcus gave the impression of enjoying every moment of the fight. As soon as he had a few seconds to spare, he called for some kind of sidearms to be brought to him and connected to one of his boxes. "In case we do get to the hand-to-hand."

Kensing was busy for a time, overseeing attempts at damage control. The wounded were being cared for in one way or another. There were a number of dead, but not enough seriously hurt survivors to fill all the five still-available medirobot berths.

And still the ship moved on.

Kensing assumed there might now very well be some people aboard who objected to continuing the mission; but if so, they were keeping their reactions to themselves. They were private, silent, cautious—because they knew their master would consider disobedience, or even too fervent protest, as mutiny, as treason—and here in space, in the face of the enemy, the law might well justify a ruthless reaction.

Kensing did overhear a couple of anonymous potential protestors asking each other quietly, off intercom, just how in hell the Premier proposed to be of any help to the captives on the stolen station, even assuming those people could be still alive—and even if the enemy could be overtaken.

Frank Marcus, who must have overheard some similar mutterings, demonstrated little patience with the malcontents. To Dirac he growled: "I'm with you. I signed on to fight berserkers, didn't I?" And Frank went on fine-tuning his personal sidearms.

A little later, Kensing asked Frank in private: "What do you think the chances are that we'll really catch up with the damned thing now?"

"Actually, having come this far, they're probably pretty good."

"And if we manage to do that, what chance that we'll really ever be able to communicate with any survivors on that station? Can we really believe that anyone there is still alive?"

"Kid, you better stow that line of talk. The Boss'll have you fried for mutiny."

❖   ❖   ❖

Since departing the Imatra system, the yacht had gained a great deal of speed relative to ambient normal space. Because each of Dirac's craft was notably smaller than the berserker-biostation combination, he had been able to get away with small c-plus jumps, and the yacht and its smaller escorts had emerged from each with a slightly greater subluminal velocity.

The borders of the dark nebula were hard to define with any precision, but by now the *Eidolon* was definitely within the outer fringes of the Mavronari. The difference between this and normal interstellar space showed on instruments, in a steady thickening of the ambient matter-density. And ahead of the yacht the obscuring material gradually but inexorably grew thicker.

Now once more the telescopes aboard the yacht were refocused, bringing the fleeing berserker and its captive into clearer view. The chase resumed in normal space. The ambush had cost the Premier not only his two smaller ships, complete with crews, amounting to almost half his fighting strength, but a little time, a little distance, as well.

Within a matter of hours it became evident that the battered yacht was again gaining on the battered enemy. But the rate of gain was slow, even slower than before the ambush; the human warriors, reluctant and otherwise, aboard the *Eidolon* were going to be allowed a little breathing space before the looming confrontation.

Again there was time, a little more time, in which to ponder the persistent mystery: just what benefit was the damned berserker expecting from the prize for which it had sacrificed a chance to commit slaughter on a planetary scale? And just where did the berserker compute that it was taking the biolab and its billion preborn captives?

As far as anyone on board the yacht had been able to determine by exhaustive search of the available charts and VR models, the dark recesses of the Mavronari contained nothing likely to be an attractive goal for either berserkers or human beings. Not that the great nebula had ever been thoroughly explored. It was known to encompass a few isolated star systems, families of planets ordinarily accessible by narrow channels of relatively empty space. But to reach any of those isolated systems by plowing straight through the cloud itself would take any ship or machine an age. The mass of obscuring matter was truly vast, going on at right angles to the direction of the Galactic Core for a discouragingly long way—hundreds of parsecs, many hundreds of light-years. And toward the middle of the nebula the dust densities were doubtless greater. Thousands of years of subluminal travel, at reduced intra-nebular speeds, would be needed to penetrate this gigantic dust cloud from one side to the other.

But if the enemy was seeking only a hiding place, it was not going to be able to find shelter inside the gradually thickening dust before it was overtaken and brought to bay. Steadily, though with tantalizing slowness, Dirac's quarry was becoming more and more distinct in the yacht's telescopes, was coming almost within a reasonable range for using weapons.

Was the enemy trying to devise another ambush? Fanatically intense efforts at detection could discern no evidence of that. Perhaps the berserker's supply of auxiliary machines had been used up in the previous attempt, or perhaps it was hoarding them for a final confrontation.

One serpentine metal arm of Marcus the pilot made an inquiring gesture in the Premier's direction.

Dirac nodded. "We go."

If a new ambush had indeed been planned, it failed to appear. Perhaps it was avoided when Frank made one more daring gamble, undertaken with the Premier's grim blessing; one more jump through flightspace, with everyone else aboard snugged into their acceleration couches, praying or concentrating stoically according to personal preference.

This time no ambush materialized, and the gamble succeeded. When the yacht *Eidolon* emerged yet again into normal space, those aboard found themselves matching velocities almost perfectly with their fleeing foe, now only a few thousand kilometers distant. The pursuing humans very soon would be in a position where they might if they chose take a meaningful shot at the enemy or receive direct fire from its batteries.

That moment of possibility came and passed, and neither side opened fire.

Closing the range still more, the yacht would soon be near enough to assay some force-field grappling of the station the berserker doggedly dragged along. But any attempt to wrench the prize away by grappling seemed foreordained to failure, given the now-damaged condition of the yacht and the evidently tremendous power of the enemy.

But perhaps the berserker's power was not overwhelming after all, not anymore. Observers on the yacht, getting their first look at their foe from relatively short range, could see that the enemy's outer hull, at least, had sustained considerable damage. How much of that damage had been inflicted by the Imatran resistance, and how much before the enemy entered the Imatran system, was impossible to say. But since the berserker had carried out its raid successfully, it still had to be considered very formidable.

Twice in the space of a few seconds a subtle premonitory quiver of instrumental readings suggested that the enemy was about to fire at the yacht.

"Shields up!" The command as Dirac gave it seemed half a question, and in any case hopelessly belated—Kensing on hearing it wondered whether the old man was getting rattled.

But no matter. Frank, along with the autopilot to which his helmet now had him mentally melded, already had the defenses perfectly deployed. And in fact no enemy fire came.

Now Colonel Marcus, even as he laconically acknowledged Dirac's congratulations for his skill in getting his ship and shipmates into this situation alive, adjusted his angle of approach to bring the yacht directly behind the towed research station. In contrast to both berserker and yacht, the station's outer hull had so far revealed no sign of damage.

The enemy, which at least since the ambush had not been accelerating at all, was maintaining an almost straight course, jogging only slightly on occasion, a simple autopilot kind of maneuver to avoid high-density knots of nebular material. Frank had no difficulty at all in holding the yacht on station directly behind the double mass of the berserker and its captive. Now the actual variation in the yacht's distance from the station was minimal, no more than a few score meters.

With the *Eidolon* in this position, the bulk of the captive station hung directly between the adversaries, and prevented, or seemed to prevent, the berserker from bringing effectively to bear what must be its superior heavy weapons.

The Premier now ordered: "Get me in contact with them."

It was the political aide who objected: "Radio contact with the station? You're assuming—"

"Yes, I'm assuming there's someone still alive aboard that vessel. That's why we're here, remember? Now let's see if they're able to respond to an attempt at communication."

Several people probably thought that a ridiculous idea. But no one said so. "Acknowledge. We're transmitting. Hello, on the station? Anybody there?"

The only reply was a trickle of radio noise.

"No luck. Well, as for the berserker, the way it's acting, I think we have to assume the damned thing's dead. It must have taken some heavy shots a few days ago, and had some delayed reaction. If it wasn't dead, we probably would be by now."

Frank, with Dirac's concurrence, persisted in the tactic of staying as nearly as possible directly behind the towed station, so that its bulk continued to screen the yacht from the foe's presumably superior potential firepower.

The third radio attempt had now failed. Dirac nodded, calmly enough. Evidently he had already made up his mind as to the next step. "I'm going over there to see for myself. You're all volunteers on this mission, and I expect everyone who's not wounded to come with me. We've got enough small craft available. Nick, you take the helm here."

"Yes, sir."

"Frank, I want you to pilot our armed scoutship." There was just one such vessel.

"Right." Methodically Colonel Marcus got ready to turn over control of the yacht to Nicholas, whose driving would be augmented by the yacht's own computers.

Kensing, having extricated himself from his own acceleration couch, stood back to give Frank room while the boxed man skillfully maneuvered his personal containers out of the relatively cramped control room to go rolling with zestful celerity down a corridor, then down a ramp in the direction of the hangar deck where his specially fitted scoutship waited for him.

Kensing followed, suddenly feeling more afraid than he had ever felt before. It wasn't clear to him, and perhaps it didn't matter, whether the fear arose because he was soon going to be killed or because he was soon going to confront the truth about Annie.

One real scoutship, two couriers, two lightly armed launches, the latter pitifully small—not counting the three unsuitable lifeboats, there were five small craft aboard the *Eidolon* available for use in a boarding. The craft easily accommodated all of the remaining fit—and fleshly—crew members on the yacht, three or four to a vessel.

Dirac, who in the course of his career had been accused of many things but probably never of cowardice, was getting ready to drive the second-best small ship himself. This was a slightly modified courier, armed, but with much less combat capability than the military scout Frank was piloting.

When the arrangements to crew the small craft had been completed, the Premier quickly gave Nicholas Hawksmoor a few specific orders and left him in command of the yacht, supposedly the sole conscious tenant of the Premier's remaining fighting ship.

Nicholas Hawksmoor was impressed and somehow moved—and he also felt what he supposed must be a twinge of guilt—when the Premier went off regular intercom to confide privately to him that Nick was the one person he could totally trust not to run away.

Dirac confessed to Nick that he did not have such complete faith in any of his fleshly folk.

"Except for Marcus in this case," the Premier whispered. "And I want the colonel with us on the boarding."

Hawksmoor said, "That's understandable, sir. I think you've made a wise decision."

As soon as the five small craft were fully crewed, they began to emerge one at a time through the main hatch of the *Eidolon*'s hangar deck. Immediately upon emerging from the yacht, they deployed in a scattered formation nearby.

And from that rough formation, at a prearranged time, the tiny flotilla went darting simultaneously into action.

The little ships approached the silent research station quickly, on widely separated paths, all taking evasive action, though the enemy's weapons still remained quiet—

And then, in the blinking of an eye and a blinding flash of violence, the berserker was inert no longer.

The scarred hull of the monstrous mothership still remained silent and dark. But a swarm of small fighting machines erupted with weapons flaring from around the bulge of the enemy hull, speeding to intercept the approaching small Solarian vessels.

Nick, now isolated upon the yacht, his mind operating as always with the optelectronic analogue of nerves, reacted long milliseconds before any of the fleshly humans except Frank, whose mind was already securely melded with his scoutship's brain. The yacht's heaviest weapons, or at least the heaviest Hawksmoor dared to employ so near the station, lashed out at the swarm of counterattacking berserker machines, scattering, burning, crushing, wiping one after another of them out of existence.

In the moments immediately after Dirac had put full trust in him, Nick had briefly toyed with the idea of taking the battered yacht away when only he and his beloved Jenny were left aboard—but he had recognized that as a hopeless dream. Not because he, Nick, would be unable to betray a creator who had been foolish enough to have great faith in him; no, he had already managed to achieve betrayal. Rather, Nick had now become firmly convinced that his only chance of finding happiness with Jenny lay in helping his love regain her fleshly body. And only the bioresearch station, which was superbly equipped for just such experiments, offered any chance of that.

She was sleeping now, somewhere—as she would perceive it when she wakened—in the Abbey. Nick, as soon as he felt certain that this fight was imminent, had quietly and without asking her permission made sure that his beloved went to sleep. As soon as the combat was over, he would go back to her in the Abbey and knock gently on her bedroom door, and when she opened it for him, tell her of the victory. Had it been possible for Jenny to take any active role in the struggle against the berserker, things would of course have been different.

During the next minute, Hawksmoor's organic shipmates fought on grimly in their effort to board the station while he used the yacht's weapons conscientiously, blasting away with all of his considerable skill at the counterattacking enemy machines. He felt no temptation to turn the heavy weapons against Dirac's small ship—the berserker must be overcome before any lesser conflicts could be settled.

Besides, there was obviously a good chance that the berserker itself might eliminate Nick's rival, despite Nick's real efforts to protect him. Already one of the small Solarian ships was no longer visible at all, having been blasted by berserker weapons into fine debris. Another had been disabled and was drifting helplessly away. Hawksmoor's radio contact with the expeditionary force kept being disrupted, as was only to be expected, by battle noise.

At this point, long seconds into the space fight, three of the small human vessels, including the one Dirac was piloting, had survived the enemy counterattack.

Another of the surviving three was the scoutship, by far the most heavily armed and shielded of the attacking craft.

From the beginning of the action, Frank's heavily armed scoutship had drawn the heaviest enemy attention, a concentration of fire and ramming attempts by small kamikaze machines. It was only now, as Nick watched Frank fight his ship, that he realized how far the man in the boxes, an organic brain melded on the quantum level with state-of-the-art machinery, outclassed any purely nonorganic pilot; how he would indeed, almost certainly, outclass Nick himself.

Here came a pair of infernal berserker devices, hurling themselves in a direct attack upon the yacht!

In a moment Nick had vaporized them successfully.

But not before the *Eidolon* had been hit once more, and some further damage inflicted.

Meanwhile Frank, joyfully entering battle as if it were his natural habitat, had drawn much of the enemy force away from the other small human craft. His heavily armed scout became the enemy's chief target, being harried and followed by a swarm of enemy machines, and in a matter of seconds a virtual screen of them had cut him off from the yacht and from the two small, less well armed ships.

Frank, having assumed the job of flying interference for the actual boarding party, did not try to break through the screen. Instead, taking a gamble on being able to get away with the unexpected, he darted in the direction of the mammoth berserker itself. A sharp feint in this direction, and he ought to be able to swing back the other way.

Nick, observing these maneuvers with some surprise, was doing as much as he could with the yacht's weapons to help Frank, but Marcus was now entering a position where the yacht's weapons had an awkward time trying to reach the berserkers nearest him.

The difficulty was compounded by the fact that Nick was strongly constrained to avoid hitting the station.

Moving the yacht might make it possible to support Frank more effectively. But that might also bring the yacht—and Jenny's all-precious optelectronic life—within the line of fire of whatever heavy weapons the big berserker might be keeping in reserve. In microseconds Nick had decided against any such maneuver.

During the next few seconds, Colonel Marcus, his scoutship suddenly badly damaged, was being hounded farther away from the station by the pack of his pursuers, though their ranks were now thinned. The scoutship too had been shot up. It no longer mattered whether his aggressive move in the direction of the big berserker had been a feint or not. The remainder of his swarming foes kept after him, harrying his scout ever close to the great machine itself.

Nick was the only one besides Frank himself who had a chance to see what happened next. And even Nick, despite his speed of perception, was granted only a blurry look at the events.

Marcus, now finding himself isolated from his comrades in arms, chose, as his past record might have suggested, to adopt ever bolder tactics now that his situation was more desperate.

He drove right at the massive enemy.

Perhaps he had counted on being able to pull away at the last moment. What actually happened was that Frank's little scout, now appearing somewhat fouled in defensive force fields, closed with the berserker's hull and disappeared. Nick knew, though his angle of view and flaring interference kept him from actually recording it, that the colonel's ship must have landed, crashed, or been forced down somewhere upon the black, scarred immensity of the enemy hull—around the bulge of both hulls from Nick's place of observation on the yacht.

Nor had the scout's final fate been visible to any of the other surviving humans. The small handful still alive were at the moment totally absorbed in the problems of keeping themselves in that state, and getting aboard the station.

With the scoutship's disappearance, the enemy fire stopped.

A great many—perhaps all—of the small enemy machines that had come out to counterattack had been destroyed. Any that might have survived had ceased to oppose the boarding, had withdrawn out of the range of the yacht's still-formidable guns.

For a moment there was silence. Bright stars, dark nebula, looked on imperturbably from all directions.

Hastily checking the yacht's various systems for damage, Nick found the drive still functional. In a moment the temptation to cut and run away had risen again. Hawksmoor considered abandoning the Boss and all who had left the yacht with him, seizing the opportunity to get away cleanly with Jenny. Still arguing against any such rash decision was Nick's basic programming of obedience to Dirac and the equally fundamental commands that he serve and protect humanity—both still were very strong.

But again, he thought his final decision not to desert rested on the fact that the station still offered the only hope of reestablishing Jenny in the fleshly body she so fanatically demanded.

Despite considerable losses suffered by the human side, the boarding action now appeared to be succeeding in its main objective. Two small Solarian craft were attaching themselves to hatches over there, reestablishing a foothold on the station. But Nick observed that the victory gave every indication of turning out to be Pyrrhic. Only these two craft had survived this sharp clash.

Nick was presently able to reestablish radio contact with Dirac.

One of the Premier's first questions was "Where's the scoutship? How did Marcus come out?"

"He went down somewhere, it looked like, on the far side of the big berserker. I wouldn't count on him, sir, for any more help."

"Damn it. Any more bandits in sight?"

"Negative, sir. They went out of my sight along with the colonel."

"All right. Stand by, Nick. We're docked here now, and we're going in."

"The best of luck, sir." And at that moment, Nick was sure he meant it.

Frank Marcus was down, but not yet dead.

On finding his scoutship surrounded and harassed by a number of the foe, he had continued to fight aggressively. Triumphantly he had radioed word back—a signal that never got through—that he thought he had succeeded in breaking the back of the opposition by small machines. The number actively engaged against him had diminished to almost nothing. He had won for his shipmates the chance to land on the station virtually unopposed.

But now the scout with Frank inside was down, smashed down by grapples of overwhelming force upon the enemy's black, scarred hull. Still, Frank was not dead. The colonel came out of his wrecked ship fighting, having survived where no being entirely of flesh could have done so, his mobile boxes making him almost as agile and armored as a berserker.

It was time, and past time, for a retreat. But there was no way to retreat, and just staying where he was, until the berserker got around to looking for him, was pointless. He doubted very much that anyone was coming to his rescue.

That left him with the option of going forward. At least he wasn't finished fighting yet.

He hadn't gone far before he saw the chance, the possibility, of being able to do some more damage before the finish came. Ahead of him, as he clawed his way forward across the berserker's outer hull with his eight metallic limbs, Marcus now perceived a weakness, a place where his huge opponent's outer armor had been blown or ripped away in some fight thousands of years in the past.

It was just moments later, when he was in the act of actually entering the berserker, pushing ahead with his own boarding operation, that Frank suddenly understood, was perfectly convinced, that time and luck had run out at last. This was one daring effort that he was not going to survive. The realization did not interfere with his smooth flow of effort; if he had tried he couldn't have thought of any better way to die.

Naturally he had not come out of his little ship unarmed. Once inside the great berserker, near anything it thought important, he could still distract the enemy, make it pay a price. Show it that wiping out life from the universe was never going to be an easy job. Force the damned thing to divert part of its computing capacity and its material resources to finish him off. And maybe in the process he could give his fellow Solarians a chance to rob it of its prize, the bioresearch station it so badly wanted. Maybe Dirac and the rest would even be able to finish it off altogether.

Marcus indeed managed to get inside the hull. Then he had not far to go, in his one-man lunge for some outlying flange of the enemy's vitals, before he encountered heavy opposition.

Only Hawksmoor, alertly guarding his post aboard the *Eidolon*, received any of the last radio message Colonel Marcus sent. Only part of the message came through, and that in somewhat garbled form. And the last words that Nicholas, listening closely on the yacht, was able to hear from Frank were "Oh my God. Oh. My. God."

The two surviving small Solarian vessels had by now attached themselves to modest beachheads on the large hull of the biostation—itself small by comparison with the looming bulk of the berserker only a few hundred meters beyond it.

Dirac and those who were still alive and functioning with him—Kensing among them—were preparing, under the umbrella of Nick's potential firepower, to enter simultaneously two of the station's airlocks.

The boarders had to confront the possibility that the hatches might be booby-trapped or barricaded. Actually the station's outer skin appeared scorched or dented here and there, as if by near-miss explosions. But as far as could be ascertained from outside, the airlocks were intact. All indications were that the mating outer doors had functioned perfectly.

Now the Premier and his companions, wearing armor and carrying the best shoulder weapons available, climbed out of their acceleration couches and made their way one at a time through the small airlocks of their own craft and into the station's larger chambers, where there was room for several to stand together. Kensing moved among them, as eager and terrified as the rest—but his yearning to find Annie quenched his terror.

On entering the station's lock, they immediately discovered that the artificial gravity was still functioning at the normal level. Indications were that the internal atmosphere was normal also. But no one moved to open his or her helmet.

"Go ahead. We're going in."

Someone standing beside Kensing worked the manual controls set into a bulkhead. And now the station's inner door was cycling.

Kensing waited, weapon leveled, mind almost blank, his will holding the alphatrigger trembling on the edge of fire.

☀ EIGHT

The planetoid Imatra was ringed by the orbits of a score of artificial satellites, and several of these metal moons bristled with sophisticated astronomical equipment. Similar devices were revolving close to the larger members of the local planetary system. Now all of these instruments in orbit, as well as many on the ground, had been pressed into service, all focused in one direction. They provided anxious observers with some bizarre views, coming in from approximately ten light-days away.

The images received were at best spotty with distance, and incomplete as a result of interference from the Mavronari's outer fringe. Nor were the pictures nearly as detailed as the viewers could have wished. But under diligent interpretation they did indicate that the Premier and his pursing force had indeed—ten days earlier—managed to catch up with the fleeing enemy.

The additional fact that the encounter had been violent was suddenly revealed by the ominous spectra of weapon flashes. There were also the resulting briefly glowing clouds. Some kind of fierce though small-scale engagement was, or had been ten days ago, in progress.

Several of the worried observers in the Imatran system speculated that these flares and flashes limned an enemy attempt to ambush the pursuing yacht and its escorting ships. How successful the attempt had been, there was no way to be sure from this distance.

None of these observers from a distance detected anything, beyond the mere fact that Solarian ships had met the enemy, that could be construed as real encouragement to supporters of the Solarian cause. And some of the once-glowing clouds that were the aftermath of battle persisted, expanding enough to block any possible view of later events—assuming the chase had gone on to an even greater distance, beyond the site of the battle scene currently unfolding.

One of the few things that those who watched from Imatra were able to say with certainty was that there had been no detectable attempt at communication with their system by any of the Premier's ships, and no sign that any of those vessels had turned back.

More days passed with no new developments, no news. None of Dirac's ships came back in triumph, and if any had tried to turn back from a defeat, they had evidently been destroyed in the attempt. And if any had launched a robot communications courier, that too had been destroyed or had somehow gone astray. The people in the Imatran system lacked any means of confirming or elaborating on what they thought their telescopes had shown them.

Whether the Premier's whole squadron, including his yacht, had been wiped out or not was impossible to determine. One could only try to estimate the probabilities. There was not much to go on, really; just those final signals suggesting a space fight, if you knew where to look for them, and even those tenuous traces were fading day by day, hour by hour. Already it was impossible to record anything meaningful beyond the fact of those little glowing clouds, which one could assume to be the flame and smoke of distant battle. An ambiguous signal at best. And soon there would be nothing at all worth putting into memory.

"Well, we do have fairly good records of this whole unfortunate business. But the point is, are we sure we really want to be diligent about preserving them?"

"What do you mean?"

"I mean that as soon as all the directly interested worlds understand that not only Lady Genevieve is missing, but now Premier Dirac himself—"

"How can we be blamed for that? In all honesty, how can we be blamed in either case?"

"Well, I foresee we *are* probably going to be blamed by some people—unjustly, of course, but there it is—at least for the Lady Genevieve's being lost."

"Well, if we are to be blamed, let us at least not be accused of destroying records. That would only make it seem that we are covering up something, something truly . . . truly . . ."

And of course Sandro Kensing was gone too. But he had volunteered. The more the local authorities of the Imatran system contemplated their new situation, the more they concentrated on the problem of how best to protect themselves against possible damage from future investigations. Or even mere accusations or rumors.

The more they thought the matter over (now meeting, as they were, face-to-face, taking full advantage of the fine conference facilities on Imatra), the more it seemed to them that they were going to have to endure some kind of trouble along that line. Assuredly the Premier Dirac Sardou, the most powerful Solarian within a space of many light-years, was not going to be allowed to vanish unnoticed from Galactic politics and society.

Not that all the leading members of that society would be displeased by his absence. Inevitably, certain people were going to gain certain advantages if Dirac could reasonably be presumed, could legally be declared, dead. Others would just as surely lose thereby. Still others would benefit if the period of uncertainty could be prolonged. Any formal declaration of the Premier's demise would have to wait for at least seven standard years, but even now interested people were surely planning for that contingency.

A standard month after the Premier's departure with his squadron, the local authorities, despite their differences of opinion on other aspects of the situation, including the wording of the pending formal announcement, had no difficulty in agreeing that Dirac and his people and his ships were really hopelessly lost, and any attempt to speed a new force to their rescue would be foolish.

The Imatran leaders also carefully inspected the records of the actual attack, as well as those documenting the berserker's departure and the beginning of the Premier's pursuit. The local authorities discovered in these records nothing to cast doubt upon their own basic innocence regarding the recent tragic events. Therefore copies of the relevant recordings, in optical and other wavelengths, were freely produced for anyone who might be presumed to be strongly interested, and some copies were dispatched to other systems. Then the original records were routinely filed away.

❈   ❈   ❈

The inner door of the airlock slid open in front of the Premier and his handful of surviving volunteers, admitting them to the interior of the bioresearch station. They found themselves confronted by a normally lighted corridor, which appeared to contain nothing in the least out of the ordinary. Just down this corridor, a few meters to their right, the other boarding party was making an equally uneventful entrance.

Dirac addressed the station's optelectronic brain, ordering it to hold the inner doors of both airlocks open.

"Order acknowledged." The voice of the station's brain sounded slightly inhuman, which was perfectly normal for a Solarian-built robot device.

The doors obediently stayed open. So far. Jamming or welding them in that position would slow down a quick retreat, if such a maneuver became necessary.

The small party, reunited now and remaining together as they had planned, advanced a few meters down the corridor. And then a few meters more.

Dirac, undaunted by the disastrous losses suffered by his rescue mission thus far, was implacably determined to continue his search for his wife. There he stood now—where Kensing could get a good view of him—in the corridor just outside the main laboratory room, a middle-sized man in heavy but flexible armor, blinker (as opposed to alphatrigger) carbine carried in the crook of his right arm. Kensing got the impression that the Premier was perfectly well satisfied with the success of the rescue expedition up till now, heavy casualties and all.

A few meters ahead of the entering party, in perfect conformance with the computer model of the station they had all studied, the corridor branched. As far as it was possible to see along the curves, both branches stretched on, well lighted, filled with usable air at breathable pressure (or so Kensing's suit gauge continued to report), and utterly lifeless.

Standing beside the older man, Kensing could feel his own nerves still ringing with the violence of that last clash in space. *Well, here I am,* was what his mind kept telling itself, without being able to get much beyond that basic proposition. *Well, here I am, still alive.* Even Annie, it seemed, had been all but forgotten for the moment.

In a small voice scrambled and decoded again on the suit radios, someone murmured: "Would help if we could get Nick over here."

The Premier shook his head inside his helmet. His unmistakable radio voice responded: "Negative. At the moment I need Nick right where he is. Now we're going to look into the lab."

Kensing eased forward, holding his breath, his weapon cradled in his arms. The other people advanced behind him and beside him, brain waves close-coupled to the triggers of their carbines and projectors, ready and expecting from moment to moment to be plunged into yet another firefight.

No human's unaided reflexes, of course, could begin to compete against the speed and accuracy of machinery. Not even when the glance of an eye and an act of will, spark of a mind set on a hair trigger, were all it took to aim and fire. But technology made the contest less uneven. Shoulder arms and helmets were melded with the operator/wearer's human alpha waves in such wise that, if great care were not exercised, the whole armored suit could come perilously close to acting in berserker fashion. Weapons cradled in its arms or fastened to the helmet would blast at any visual silhouette that met certain programmed specifications, or simply at sudden noise or light or movement. The suits of armor in which the human fighters now stalked the biostation were also equipped with coded IFF, a hopefully accurate system of distinguishing friend from foe.

"Where are they?" Kensing couldn't be certain if the voice in his helmet was referring to the berserker's commensal machines or to its human victims.

Had Dirac and his party been facing a human enemy, the apparent withdrawal of the foe might easily have persuaded them that their enemy was frightened. But nothing could frighten a berserker. Whatever killing machines might have occupied this very corridor a day ago, an hour ago, five minutes ago, must be still lurking somewhere in these multitudinous compartments and spaces, awaiting the right moment, the savage signal, to spring out, as swiftly efficient as factory machinery, and kill.

Having failed to provoke any enemy response, Dirac ordered another cautious, methodical advance. His plan called for the territory that had been examined, apparently regained for human control, to be gradually extended. One corridor, one deck, after another.

Kensing had now warily eased his way just inside the doorway of the main laboratory room. Here were a thousand pieces of complex equipment of various sizes, shapes, and purposes, everything now standing still and silent. Annie had so often told him things about this chamber that even without studying the VR model in the yacht's ten-cube he would have had no trouble feeling almost at home inside it. This was where she worked. Her duty station, he felt sure, during the alert. So here was where berserker machines, assuming they had come aboard, had most likely caught up with her.

Keeping a tight grip on his nerve, Kensing eased his way in farther from the doorway. His weapon ready, he stood looking about.

The Solarian searchers were very few, and therefore even more tentative, more cautious than they might have been in greater numbers; the biostation was large and complex. To search every nook and cranny of the biostation for enemy machines, for booby traps and ambushes, would take a long time. Eventually, if things went well, Nick could be brought into action, and more ordinary robots used.

But Dirac and those with him could not wait; their primary goal was to discover whether there were human survivors.

Kensing was in midstep, tentatively advancing once again, when off to his right there burst a flash and crash of violence, an instant wave front of radiation and reflected heat dashing harmlessly against his armor. Before he could even turn his head in that direction, the skirmish was over, though in the following second of time another Solarian weapon or two—not Kensing's—echoed the first shots, letting go at a target already smashed, compounding the damage to unprotected laboratory gear and walls. The small berserker machine that had come leaping out of ambush from behind benign equipment had been felled by the first blasting volley, its six legs sliced from under it, the nozzles of its own weapons shriveled, its torso broken open to spill a waste of bloodless components across the deck. Nothing more now than a broken machine, fire leaping out of its insides to be rapidly drenched and quenched by a healing rain from built-in fountains in the lab's high overhead. The station's voice, intent on following the regulations, was insisting that all personnel evacuate the immediate area.

"There may be more—"

But moments passed and apparently there were no more. It was as if this single device, effectively trapped by the unexpected Solarian incursion, had come bounding out in order to be shot down by the alphatrigger weapons of people standing in the doorway.

Then one additional enemy machine was seen and shot at as it raced past in the corridor outside the lab, moving at the velocity of a speeding groundcar.

The Solarian fire missed its target this time, only damaging the inner hull just beyond the corridor's outer bulkhead.

Seconds of quiet stretched into a minute, into two. The knife edge of excitement dulled. An ominous new stillness descended upon the station, and this stillness was prolonged.

But peace was not completely quiet. Kensing, standing now near the middle of the big laboratory, made a soft little sound high in his throat. Annie, very much alive, looking rumpled but safe in a regular lab coat, had just come round a corner of machinery and was walking toward him.

In another moment, Acting Supervisor Zador, looking pale but very much intact, was clinging to Kensing in a miraculous reunion.

He had to resist an impulse to tear off his helmet and kiss her. All that kept him from doing so was the thought that in the next few minutes, before he could get her away and out of this damned place, she might yet need the most efficient protection he was able to provide.

"It's you, it's you!" Annie kept crying. She babbled on, words to the effect that seeing any free Solarian figure had been wonder enough when the people trapped on the station had already given themselves up for dead. But seeing *him* . . .

Kensing, in turn, demanded in a voice that barely functioned: "Did you think I wouldn't be coming after you?"

Other live Solarians were now appearing, as if by a miracle. A few paces behind Annie came a man she introduced as her colleague, Dan Hoveler. Then shortly a man she introduced as Scurlock, whose presence, unlike that of Hoveler, was totally unexpected by the rescuers. This development made Premier Dirac frown in concentration.

The survivors reported that, strange as it seemed, they had been largely unmolested by the machines when the station was overrun. On being surprised by the sudden sound of fighting, they had been free to take cover as best they could.

A minute later, Scurlock's unexpected appearance was followed by that of a dazed-looking woman named Carol.

There was no sign of Lady Genevieve. Dirac was already asking the survivors about her. "Have you seen my wife?"

Annie, Dan Hoveler, and Scurlock all looked at each other, while Carol stared distractedly at nothing. Then the three mentally alert survivors sadly but confidently assured Dirac that his beloved Lady Genevieve was simply not here at all, alive or dead. No one had seen her since the last courier departed, only minutes before the berserkers arrived.

Zador and Hoveler sadly reported that the Premier's unlucky bride must have joined the other visitors and most of the biolab's workers in boarding the ill-fated courier ship. That had been the last vessel to get away from the station before the berserker fell upon them.

Dirac was shaking his head. "I don't believe she did get on the courier. I believe that's been ruled out."

Now it was time for the Premier's colleagues to exchange glances with each other.

It came as a tragic shock to Hoveler and Zador to learn that the courier carrying their co-workers had been blown up days earlier, with all aboard presumably killed. They asked how much damage the attack had done in the Imatran system, and were somewhat relieved to learn that at least the overall destruction had been surprisingly small.

Sobering news had now somewhat muted their astonishment and delight that Dirac or anyone else had pursued and overtaken the berserker successfully.

"You've killed the berserker, then." It was Hoveler who was joyfully making this assumption. "But of course, you must have. You're sure it's dead?"

The Premier tilted his head back to gaze up toward overhead, the direction of the enemy's gigantic hull. "The big one? No, I'm afraid we can't be entirely sure. Certainly it's badly damaged. But it might have a trick or two to play yet."

The survivors, sobered, listened carefully, nodding. Now that this Galactic celebrity was here, Hoveler and Zador deferred to him, looked to him expectantly, joyfully for rescue, for leadership.

The station's brain, seemingly fully functional once more, blandly assured its questioners, when asked, that all of the berserker machines had now departed. At this point Dirac, leaving Kensing as an armed guard in the laboratory with Annie and the other survivors, took the rest of his people with him to pursue the search for Lady Genevieve on other decks.

The station intercom was still fully functional, and the search party used it to communicate with the lab, employing a quickly improvised code. During the first stages of their effort they encountered no resistance, no further signs of any current berserker presence. And no sign of the woman they were seeking.

Kensing, still thankfully marveling at his own miracle, looked back at Annie again. "So, the machines didn't even hurt you."

"No," she assured him, simply, solemnly. "They didn't really hurt any of us. I have no explanation for this. Except perhaps they wanted to learn something from us, just from watching our behavior."

Hoveler was nodding his puzzled agreement. "That's about the way it seemed to me."

Kensing said to Annie: "I won't demand explanations for a miracle. But I want to get you back aboard the yacht."

"I still have a job to do here." Her voice was intense.

"Then let me at least get you into some armor. All of you."

"All right."

But spare suits of armor were not readily at hand. And Kensing had to admit that perhaps it didn't matter after all. The discovery of living survivors and the absence of any further berserker activity were dulling the fine edge of alertness. It seemed to be true—whatever enemy devices had once occupied the station had now mysteriously withdrawn.

Scurlock had little to say, and Carol, now sitting slumped in a corner, said practically nothing. They both seemed much more deeply in shock than Annie or Dan.

After a few minutes had passed, Scurlock announced that he and Carol were withdrawing to their room, and added that she wasn't feeling well.

Looking after the beaten-looking couple as they left the lab with arms around each other, Dan Hoveler muttered: "They told us they were goodlife; we came near having a real fight a couple of times."

Kensing scowled. He hadn't expected to hear this. "Should we be—watching them?"

Hoveler shrugged. "I don't think they're armed, anything like that. As for claiming to be goodlife, it's probably just that the—pressure got to them."

"I can understand that."

Suddenly Annie was on the verge of tears. "I knew if we just held on . . ." And then she was weeping, with the intensity of relief.

Dirac and his people were soon back in the lab, with no substantial discoveries to report. The survivors' joy was further tempered when they understood how few their rescuers really were, and how seriously damaged was the ship in which they had arrived.

Kensing was emphatic: "We'd better get out of here as quickly as we can."

Nick was on the radio now, reporting in from the yacht, and his news was simply, seriously chilling: since the latest berserker attack, the yacht's drive was all but inoperative. Modest local maneuvers were still possible, but getting home on it was out of the question until—and unless—repairs could be effected. As soon as he could stand down from red alert, he'd get to work on the problem.

Somewhat to Kensing's surprise, Dirac delayed ordering a general evacuation to the yacht. Again and again the Premier demanded that the three coherent survivors tell him anything they could that might suggest the whereabouts of the Lady Genevieve.

In fact Kensing and others got the impression that Dirac was really paying little attention to the bad news concerning the yacht's drive. The prospect of being stranded here did not seem of much concern to him. He was still ferociously intent upon his search for his bride.

Despite the eyewitness testimony that she was not here, his attitude did not seem to be grief so much as suspicion and anger.

When someone boldly suggested that it was time to get back to the yacht, to repair its drive if nothing else, Dirac responded sharply that Nick and the maintenance robots could handle that as well as he could.

Annie and Hoveler, with growing concern, reiterated that there was no reason to expect to find his lady here. No one aboard the station had seen her since that last courier departed.

At last, hours after coming aboard the station, Premier Dirac, after trying to question the station's own brain and obtaining nothing helpful in regard to Lady Genevieve, seemed satisfied that this was the case.

But instead of giving way to grief or ordering a general retreat to the yacht, he seemed rather to withdraw mentally, hesitating as to what ought to be done next.

Nick called once more from the yacht to inform his boss that despite his own best efforts the yacht's drive still didn't work. Dirac's response was to send someone back to bring more arms and armor over to the station.

After the messenger's return, some of Dirac's own crew began making pointed suggestions as to what ought to be done next. People were saying that it was time—past time—to get out of here, board the rescuers' vessels and go back to the yacht. If the yacht still wasn't functional, it was time to concentrate on making her so.

And Dirac seemed to waver.

At that point Annie, now dressed in armor, as were Hoveler and Scurlock, faced him. "There's one problem with that plan," she announced.

"Yes, Dr. Zador?"

"Can your yacht carry everybody?"

The Premier's heavy brows contracted. "I don't understand. Assuming the drive can be repaired, there are only a handful of us here."

Anyuta Zador's voice rose slightly. "There are a great many more Solarians here than you seem to realize. Have you room aboard for a billion statglass tiles?"

For a long moment the Premier stared at her. Kensing, watching them, thought it was as if Annie had just offered the old man something he had been searching for. "You have a point there," Dirac conceded willingly.

People who had been suggesting a retreat now glared at Annie, but so far no one argued openly.

Evidently mention of the tiles reminded the Premier of something else. When he questioned the bioworkers again, they confirmed that the Lady Genevieve had indeed made her donation before the berserker attacked the station.

The Premier wanted to know: "Where is it now? The tile?"

Memories were uncertain on that point. Hoveler and Zador were honestly not sure whether the lab's robotic system had properly filed the First Protocolonist away or not. In any case the scrambling of the station's electronic wits, which Hoveler acknowledged having done, would keep anyone from immediately laying hands on any particular specimen.

Gathering his troops around him, Dirac issued a firm order to the effect that there would be no general evacuation of the station until the question of his protochild had been resolved.

Neither of the surviving bioworkers, having endured so much and done what they had done, all to defend the protocolonists, was ready to abandon them now. And everyone else now aboard the station, with the possible exception of Kensing, was accustomed to taking orders from Dirac.

Dirac, making sure that regular contact was maintained with Nick back on the *Eidolon* and having posted sentries at key locations on the station to watch for any berserker counterattack, took time out to watch a video showing his wife's arrival at the station a few days ago. He saw for himself the publicity opportunity that had turned into a panic as soon as the alert was called.

The color coding on the tile was barely discernible in some of the views. But with the retrieval system scrambled as it was, that was probably going to be of no help in finding it.

Hawksmoor had rather quickly made the decision to sabotage the yacht's drive and then to report it as malfunctioning, limited to low maneuvering power only. Of course he blamed the trouble on the recent enemy action. He'd done a thorough job of the disabling, but not so thorough that he would be unable to quickly put things back in their proper order if and when that became necessary—as he confidently expected that it would, sooner or later.

But probably not for a long time, Nick computed. Not until after he had managed to provide the Lady Genevieve with the living flesh her happiness demanded. And even after he had somehow arranged matters so he could use all the facilities of the biostation without hindrance, that was probably going to take years.

He didn't really want to make all these other fleshly people suffer, to disrupt their lives and in effect hold them prisoner. Especially not here, where they were almost within the grasp of a monster berserker that was probably still half alive. But what choice did he have?

Nick had to admit that the complexities of the whole situation were beginning to baffle him.

No, it wasn't fair, that the burden of others' lives should thus be placed upon him. He was supposed to be a pilot and an architect, not a philosopher. Not a political or spiritual or military leader. Not . . . not a lover and seducer.

He was able to cushion himself against this resentment and

uncertainty only by telling himself that his fretting over these insoluble problems offered strong evidence that whatever means his programmers had used in his creation, they had made him truly human.

☀ NINE

There was something about that last fragmentary message from Frank Marcus—chiefly the *tone*—which Nick found himself still pondering.

When he brought the message to the attention of Dirac and the others, the Premier listened once to the recording and then basically dismissed it.

"Humans often call upon God, some kind of god, in their last moments, Nick. Or so I'm told. Sad, tragic, like our other losses, but I wouldn't make too much of it. That's probably just the death Marcus would have chosen for himself. In fact, in a very real sense I'd say that he did choose it."

"Yes, sir." But Hawksmoor was unable to dismiss the matter as easily as his organic master did.

There were other pressing urgencies no one could dismiss. During the skirmish just past, the great berserker in crushing Frank's scoutship had demonstrated that it still possessed formidable short-range weapons, including the force-field grapples that had evidently pulled Frank in to his doom. The remaining small craft and the yacht itself would have to be kept at a safe distance from the berserker; of course no one could say with any confidence just what distance that might be.

Some of the debris from the space fight remained visible for almost an hour after the boarding, bits of junk metal and other substances swirling delicately in space, caught near the scene by some short-lived balance of incidental forces. But in an hour the last of this wreckage had gone, blown away in the vanishing faint wind of the ships' joint passage through never-quite-completely-empty space.

Every day, every hour as the hurtling cluster of objects drew closer to the depths of the Mavronari, the space through which they traveled, still vacuum by the standards of planetary atmosphere, was a little less empty than before.

Now space within several thousand kilometers in all directions indeed showed void of all small craft and machines, unpopulated by either friends or foes. Nicholas still stood guard faithfully, trying to decide whether he wanted the fleshly people to make themselves at home on the station or not, beginning to ponder what his own course of action was going to be in either case.

He could keep his post alertly enough now with half an eye, and far less than half a mind. He was free to spend more than half his time with Jenny. Joyfully, as soon as he had the chance, he awakened her with news of victory.

When Jenny came out of her bedroom again to talk to Nick, walking with him in the cool, dim vastness of the Abbey, she said: "So long as we remain nothing but clouds of light, hailstorms of electrons, all you and I can ever do is pretend to please each other, and pretend to be pleased. Maybe that would be enough for you. It could never be enough for me."

"Then, my lady, it cannot be enough for me either. No, Jenny, I want to be with you. I will be with you in one way or another, and I will make you happy."

The intensity in the lady's gaze made her eyes look enormous. "Then the two of us must have flesh. There is no other way."

"Then flesh we will have. I swear it. I will bring real human bodies into being for us."

"You have said that before. I doubt that you have such power."

"If I am allowed to use the resources on board the laboratory station, I do."

The Premier had chosen a woman of quick wit for his bride. "You mean the zygotes? The colonists?"

"One way would be to use those. There seem to be a billion potential bodies there to choose from."

The lady frowned. "But they are—"

"Are what? You mean there are moral objections, they are people? Hardly. More like genetic designs for organic vessels. Vessels we ought to be able to keep empty until we can fill them with ourselves. There must be some way."

Genevieve seemed unwilling to let herself believe that it was going to be possible. "Even if we could find a way to do that, it would take years. You mean to grow ourselves new bodies in the artificial wombs—I can't go back as an infant!"

"Nor would I choose to experience infancy." Nick shuddered inwardly. "Nor, I suppose, could adult minds be housed in brains so immature. But there *must* be a way to make that method work. As you are now, you could sleep for ten standard years, twenty years, while the body that would be yours was growing, developing somewhere. You could rest for a century, if there was any reason to prolong your slumber to that extent, and it would be no more to you than the blinking of an eye."

"And so could you."

"Yes, of course. Except that the Premier is not likely to let *me* rest without interruption for even an hour. And I must heed his orders if we are to survive. It's far from certain that the berserker is really dead." Nick paused, considering. "Fortunately, *he* seems in no rush about hurrying home. He hasn't given up on finding you; or finding a way to recover you in some sense."

"What do you mean?"

"He seems to be thinking about your child."

"Ah. So do I sometimes. But that child won't be me." The lady was silent for a little while, and then burst out: "Oh, Nick. If you can do this for me, put me back together, I will be yours forever." After a moment the lady added, "How will you do it? My—my husband, and the others mustn't—"

"Of course they mustn't find out. If I find a way to do this for you, you're not going back to him."

"I will go wherever you say, do whatever you want." New hope had been born in Genevieve's eyes. "And how will you gain access to the artificial wombs?"

"Access is no problem. There is nothing to keep me out of the circuitry over there. In general, the way things are on the station now, no one pays any attention to those devices, or would be aware of the fact if they were being used. Still, it would be better, of course, to use one or two of the machines that are physically isolated."

The Premier soon summoned Nick over to the station. Rather than transport the units in which he was physically stored, Hawksmoor chose to transmit himself by radio across the minor interval of intervening space, a mode of transportation he had sometimes used in the past.

Zador and Hoveler and Scurlock, all unaccustomed to the presence of recorded people or anthropomorphic programs, were startled when Nick showed up, as a kind of optelectronic ghost, in the station's circuitry and computers.

But the Premier was quick to reassure them. "That's Nick, he's on our side." A moment's pause; seeing that their recently frayed nerves needed more reassurance, Dirac added, "He's a mobile program, but it's all right."

Nick immediately went to work, at the Premier's direction, probing the immense complexity of circuits. Nowhere could he find any berserker booby traps or spot any but the most incidental residue of the berserker's presence. He did not forget the ten-cube and its stored programs.

He thoughtfully inspected the combat damage in the main laboratory, where an isolated berserker device had been gunned down, and in the nearby corridor, where a few shots had been wasted. It was very fortunate, he thought, that the onboard combat had been so limited. It wouldn't have taken a great deal of fighting to leave the station's fragile equipment entirely in ruins.

The onboard software was generally okay and did not appear to have been tampered with except for a certain serious confusion in the system that was supposed to keep track of the cargo of protocolonists. This was readily explained by Hoveler's actions immediately after the berserker occupation. Too bad, but it couldn't be helped now.

Nick pondered, wondering if there might be some way to turn the scrambling of the inventory system to advantage, for his own private purposes.

His and Jenny's.

Having completed the first phase of an intense inspection, Nick reported to Dirac and asked him, "What do I do next, boss?"

"She's here somewhere. You know, Nick?"

"*Sir?*"

Dirac raised eyes filled with an uncharacteristically dreamy expression. "The medics here on board took her genetic record, and they took our child. These things are a part of her, and they are here."

"Oh. Yes sir." The Boss had given Nick a bad moment there. But now Hawksmoor understood.

The scrambling of the inventory did not discourage Premier Dirac from pushing his search through the genetic records for his lost bride—or at least, as some of his crew muttered, for enough of her genes to do him some good dynastically.

"If the Lady Genevieve is dead, still, our child is not."

The days passed swiftly, and Dirac and his crew established something like a new routine. No new berserker presence was discovered on the station. But the enormous bulk of the enemy, its drive at least partly functional, still hung over everyone's head, dragging the research station, very slowly in terms of interstellar travel, toward some mysterious destination. Kensing, and doubtless others, had the feeling of living not far below the rim of a slumbering volcano.

Nick had now been placed in charge of a force of dull-witted serving robots, charged with a continued harrowing, a vigilant inspection and reinspection of the station, to guard against any surprise berserker counterattack.

And yet no additional berserker presence had been found, except for a couple of what appeared to be small spy devices. The existence of more was considered likely. Even with Nick on the job, there could be no absolute guarantee of security against them.

Nick, and one or two fleshly human workers, in consultation with Hoveler who had done the scrambling, were now trying to restore a normal inventory function to the station's brain. The outlook was not bright. Even were they apparently successful, the cargo might still be badly scrambled if the archivist robots had rearranged many of the tiles while the software was down. This seemed a distinct possibility.

Dirac insisted that this job of restoration be given the highest priority, though with a huge berserker of unknown capability only a few hundred meters distant, many of the Premier's shipmates would have preferred to concentrate their efforts on other matters, such as repairing the yacht's drive.

Nick, on snatching a few moments away from duty to spend them on his private affairs, felt shaken but triumphant when he considered events so far. He wondered at his own daring and success in secretly defying his powerful employer, in the matter of that employer's bride.

Not that this adventure with the lady had begun as an act of defiance. Far from it. Hawksmoor, reliving the chain of events in perfect memory, told himself that when he first drove his ship after the courier he had simply, very loyally, been trying to save her. A little later, when it had plainly been beyond his or the medirobot's powers to save her flesh from death, the next step had seemed to follow automatically.

Already at that point Hawksmoor had begun to dread the moment when the woman he had come to love would leave him to be restored to her husband. It had taken Nick somewhat longer to let himself be convinced that, since an electronic bride would do the Premier no good dynastically, she would never be going back to Dirac as any kind of political asset.

The glorious thing, of course, was that—Nick was sure of it!—she was now at least beginning to care for him. Not that she was ready to choose life with him, under the conditions of virtual reality, over having a real body once again. No, he was under no illusions as to that. Before she could choose life with him, he would have to provide her with a body. And he had yet to make sure that a means existed to accomplish that.

Most of the station's artificial wombs were on the same deck, actually in the same room. But five or six had been for some reason separated from the rest, scattered about in secluded spots. The possibility of Nick's being able to use one—he really needed two—of these without being discovered was something he would have to determine.

Nick said to Jenny: "I will find a way of growing flesh, since flesh you must have. I will grow bodies for us. Or," he added after a moment, "if something should prevent my doing that, I will take them, already grown."

That gave the lady pause, if only for a moment. "Take them from where? From whom?"

"Somehow. Somewhere. From people who would stop us if they knew what we are doing."

Now freely roaming about the station's circuits, Nick discovered the very treasures he needed to accomplish his goal. The station boasted a whole deck, actually somewhat more than one deck, packed with artificial wombs and their support equipment, perhaps a hundred or more of the glass-and-metal devices. All checked out functional, and all were sitting there just waiting to be used.

Technically, everything in that department seemed to be in perfect condition. Expert systems waited like genies in bottles to be called up, provided with the necessary genetic material, and given their orders to produce healthy human bodies. A full-scale effort along that line, of course, was supposed to take place only when the projected colonizing ship eventually reached its chosen destination.

Annie Zador, passing along information in all innocence, told Nick something about the most advanced prenatal expert system aboard, the one she and her co-workers had called Freya, after a Norse goddess of love and fertility.

And relating this point Nick, standing with his beloved companion near the high altar of the Abbey, lost his composure and attempted to embrace her fully. Whether he was really generating or only imagining the appropriate excitement was hard to say, but he was well on the way to undressing his companion before the lady, who at first had seemed joyously eager, suddenly pulled away, crying: "No! All wrong, all wrong!"

Then, when she had regained control of herself again: "Not this way, Nick. Not like this. One way or another, dear Nicholas, we must be flesh together."

Within the next hour, again having some respite from the duties assigned him by Dirac, Nick was again concentrating his consciousness in one of the comparatively remote areas of the biostation, earnestly studying the data banks and the equipment he would have to use to accomplish his and Jenny's secret project.

One of the many staggering problems he faced was to discover how the process by which a human mind was reduced or amplified to pure optics and electronics could be made to operate in reverse.

Hawksmoor very early interviewed the expert system called Freya by Annie Zador and her fellow fleshly bioworkers. Freya was distinct from the biolab's overall intelligence, and she—Nick definitely visualized her as a woman—had remained intact throughout Hoveler's efforts at disruption.

Nick's visualization of Freya was vague and variable. To him she was never actually anything more than an intellect expressed in a cool, compassionate voice.

Nick, having introduced himself to Freya, soon assumed—quite naturally, as part of his security function—the job of scanning Freya's programming. It really was part of his assigned job to make sure that, during the time when the station had been occupied territory, she had not become some kind of a berserker trick.

He verified that her programmed benevolence had not been poisoned. Then he talked with her some more and introduced his problem—without, of course stating it as his: "How fully developed would an organic brain need to be before I could download into it the patterns of myself?"

That was a stunner, even for Freya. It took her some time to frame an answer.

From the start of his investigation it had been obvious to Hawksmoor that the gray matter of a newborn infant, let alone that of a fetal brain, would never answer his purpose. Even were he capable of setting aside all his built-in moral objections to such a procedure, only a partial downloading could be accomplished under the restrictions of minimum space and complexity imposed by the infant brain.

The expert system too reacted with moral horror. Freya seemed on the verge of shutting herself down.

"The question is purely theoretical. No such operation is contemplated," Nick assured Freya firmly.

She in turn insisted that such an operation would not be technically possible, even under optimum conditions.

Hawksmoor continued his probing questions.

Freya upon reflection offered the opinion—purely theoretical, she insisted firmly—that there might be two ways in which an entity like Nick could obtain a carnal body for himself. One way would be to grow a body, from the stock of zygotes and/or other miscellaneous human genetic material available on the bioresearch station. To grow one selectively, taking care to preserve the developing brain as a tabula rasa, blank as regards any personality of its own, but capable of receiving his.

Of course, normally, bodies grown in the laboratory, just like those developed according to the ancient and organic course of nature, give every indication of being possessed by their own minds and spirits from the start.

The second possibility—and this, again, Freya was ready to admit only after persistent questioning, as a theoretical procedure, totally unacceptable in practice—would be to wipe clean an existing adult brain. This would involve inflicting an extensive pattern of carefully controlled microinjuries, to erase whatever personality pattern was currently present. Then the microstructure of the brain would be encouraged to heal, the healing brought about in such a way that the infusion of the new patterns was concomitant with it.

There would be some practical advantages to this ethically unacceptable scheme, the expert system admitted: instead of a minimum of fifteen or sixteen standard years, the host organ would be ready in a mere matter of months to receive the downloaded personality. But during that time the equipment would have to run steadily and undisturbed.

Nick went away to ponder in secret what he had learned.

Plainly it would be necessary to get free somehow of both the berserker and oppressive human authority before any such ambitious project could succeed.

Nick also considered attempting to run the experiment back on the yacht, where fleshly, inquisitive people now seldom visited. But it would be essential to move the necessary equipment from the station to the yacht—and again, he could not be sure of being able to work undisturbed for a long time. Moving Jenny and himself as required was easier.

Freya, when Nick talked to her again, insisted there was only one possible way to download the information content of an electronic man or woman into an organic brain, especially the only partially developed brain of an infant. It was at best a very tricky operation.

It would be something like the reverse of the process of recording, upon some optelectronic matrix, the personality pattern of a living brain. And even if some quicker method could be devised, it seemed inevitable that the incoming signals would scramble, destroy, whatever native pattern of personality the developing brain had already begun to form.

If a mature brain was used as the matrix, according to Freya, the native pattern would very likely triumph over the one being superimposed.

Or, given the two conflicting patterns, the resultant person might well be some hybrid of the two. Some memories, not all, would belong to the native personality.

The plan Nick finally decided on, one worked out in consultation with Freya (the latter requiring continual assurance that all this was merely theoretical), involved subjecting the maturing organic brain to alternating periods of deep though unfrozen sleep, in which the brain could grow organically, with periods of intense loading. First the rough outlines of the desired personality patterns would be impressed upon the developing matrix, and then later the details. Inevitably, Freya warned, certain errors would creep into the process; the resultant fleshly person would possess the memories of the electronic predecessor/ancestor, but could not be considered an exact copy.

"But then no fleshly human is, today, an exact copy of himself or herself of yesterday."

"I really hope the two of you are not working on an actual project. To deceive me in such a matter would be most unethical."

Nick, who had begun withdrawing along a path of circuits, turned back sharply. "The two of us?" He had not so much as ever hinted to Freya, he was sure of it, the actual existence of a program version of the Lady Genevieve.

"Yes." Freya was almost casual, as she usually was when anything but the sanctity of life was under discussion. "I have very recently given very much the same information to Premier Dirac. I assumed the two of you were having a discussion."

☀ TEN

Meanwhile, the handful of organic people living under Dirac's command found their initial relief at what had seemed a victory gradually turning into desperation.

But the Premier, supported by Brabant and Varvara Engadin, fiercely put down any open dissension before it could rise above the level of subdued muttering.

It's all right, Kensing tried to reassure himself. *At the moment we don't have a drive capable of getting us home—the small craft would be inadequate, starting from here within the nebula—and there's no use fretting about when to pull out until we have the capability. Meanwhile, someone has to be in charge, to keep up morale, to keep the people busy.* And who was better qualified as a leader than Dirac?

Besides, Kensing realized that even if the *Eidolon* was ready to go, Annie, and probably Hoveler as well, would still be determined not to abandon their billion protocolonists.

Eventually, Kensing hoped, it would be possible to somehow cut the station loose from the berserker's forcefields so that the restored yacht could eventually tow it home.

Meanwhile, things could have been worse. The berserker remained quiet, and all life-support systems on yacht and station were working. Things could have been much worse.

The Premier always had at least one organic person besides the automated systems standing sentry duty, watching the berserker for signs of activity. Meanwhile, under his firm command, his remaining handful of people were steadily consolidating their position aboard the research station.

The attempt to restore the cargo inventory system, in their ongoing effort to save the protocolonists, occupied most of Zador and Hoveler's time. The fact that Dirac put a high priority on saving the cargo enlisted the wholehearted support of the two surviving bioworkers.

Another project to which the Premier gave a high priority was that of establishing a relatively secure area from which any berserker spy devices had been absolutely excluded.

At the center of this domain Dirac had chosen a cabin for himself, and established his headquarters there.

Meanwhile, two other people aboard the station were under suspicion of being goodlife, despite the fact that since Dirac's boarding no one had heard them confess to that crime.

Dirac wanted to resolve that situation, to clear the air, as he put it. Quietly the Premier asked Scurlock to come and see him in his stateroom, and to bring Carol along.

Scurlock showed up alone, and entered the room to stand facing Dirac, who sat regarding him from a kind of rocking chair. A few of the cabins aboard had rather luxurious appointments.

When the Premier gestured to another chair, Scurlock took it uneasily. Then he reported that Carol had refused to come to the meeting. "She's not well, you know, Premier."

"Has Dr. Zador looked at her?" Dirac's voice indicated a fatherly concern. "Or have you taken her to a medirobot?"

"I've asked her to try one or the other, but she declines."

The Premier rocked a few times. "All right, let it go for now. I'll talk to you." He rocked a few more times, while Scurlock waited apprehensively. Then he said: "I can quite appreciate that the pair of you were in a very difficult situation when the berserker had you directly in its custody."

"Yes sir, it was difficult."

"I really think it would be unjust to blame you, either of you, for anything you may have said or done under those conditions."

"That's it, sir! That's very true. I'm only afraid that everyone isn't going to be so understanding." Scurlock's large, nervous hands had begun to wrestle with each other in his lap.

Dirac was soothing. "I think perhaps I can help you with the problems you face regarding other people's attitudes. That is, assuming that you and I can work together now. Understand that when—if—we eventually return to settled planets, you and Carol are going to need all the help that you can get. Accusations of goodlife activity are not taken lightly."

"Yes sir. I'm well aware of that."

Dirac spoke slowly. "At the moment we—all of us aboard the station—find ourselves in a situation not much different, I think, from that which you and Carol faced as actual prisoners of the machine. For us, too, some kind of accommodation with the machine, at least for the short term, is in order. Do you agree?"

"With the berserker, sir?"

"That's what I meant by the machine, yes."

"Oh, I do agree, Premier!"

"I'm not sure that the other people on board will be ready to understand this point as well as you and Carol will. So I'd like to keep this discussion just between us for the time being."

"I understand, Premier."

"Do you?" Dirac rocked and ruminated. "Of course the machine may now really be completely dead—except for its drive and autopilot. Or it may not. I would like to know the truth about its condition. That seems to me an essential first step."

Scurlock nodded.

"So I mean to send you on a scouting trip, Scurlock. I've chosen you because the machine knows you. It did not kill you or hurt you when it had the chance. Therefore I think you will do well as a scout, as my investigator."

Scurlock said nothing. He looked frightened, but not yet absolutely terrified.

Dirac nodded his apparent approval of this reaction. He continued: "If necessary, if the machine is not yet dead, then you will serve as my—ambassador."

Surlock let out a small sigh. Then he nodded.

The Premier continued. "There are certain things we—the people now in control of this station—want; first of all, that there be no further berserker attacks against us. Also there are certain things the machine—assuming it not yet dead—must want, according to its programming. We find ourselves now in a situation where total victory is not possible for either side. So, as I said before, an accommodation may be our only real choice."

And Scurlock nodded once again.

Nick, after a discussion with the Premier, nudged the *Eidolon* forward on its supposedly faltering drive, arranging for the yacht to hitch a ride by maneuvering into one edge of the berserker-generated towing field. Now the *Eidolon* too was being dragged along. Hawksmoor assured his organic companions that the yacht, even half crippled as it was, would be able to break free at a moment's notice. Meanwhile his efforts to repair the drive would be facilitated by being able to turn it completely off.

The violent berserker opposition to Dirac's boarding party had ceased so quickly that most of the Solarians still refused to believe that all the bad machines had been destroyed. Beyond that, Dirac himself had not yet publicly taken a position, but others were ready to argue on both sides of the question.

Brabant and Engadin were arguing.

The woman said: "Its machines have definitely retreated."

"Yes, but why? Ask yourself that. Berserkers don't just retreat. Or rather, they retreat only when they feel certain of gaining some advantage. It's obviously setting a trap for us."

Engadin disagreed strongly with the bodyguard: "I don't think they've retreated at all. What's happened, I believe, is that they've used up all their mobile hardware, or depleted it down to the last reserve. This giant thing on top of us is an ancient machine, judging by the look of its outer hull, and it's been through a lot of fights; I think the fact is that we've really blasted their last mobile unit."

Brabant looked doubtful. "That's a possibility, but we don't dare count on it."

"Anyway," Varvara Engadin insisted, "there are no active, mobile, berserker devices anywhere on the station. And just in time, I'd say." It was obvious to all that a little more onboard fighting might have left the station uninhabitable by breathing beings. "Rendering space installations uninhabitable is exactly what a berserker ought to try to do. I tell you, it's got nothing left to throw at us."

The big man shook his head gloomily. "I might be tempted to believe that. Except this berserker has been an exception right from the start. Seemingly utterly mad. A real oddball. It could easily have vaporized the station right where it was, in orbit around Imatra. Much less difficult than dragging a thing like this away."

"Which means what?"

"That question has a two-part answer, an easy part and a hard one. The easy part is, no, this berserker is not utterly mad. It had some coldly logical reason for not destroying this facility. Because it has, or had, some special use for it. Or for something or someone being carried aboard. And that might even explain why it's not fighting us now. It just doesn't want to risk having its prize shot up. It would rather bide its time and hope we fly away on the *Eidolon*."

The woman nodded slowly. "I have to admit you may be on to something there . . . and the hard part?"

"That is deciding what the special use could be."

"What else *could* it be but our billion protocolonists? So maybe, logically, the best thing we could do is shoot up the station's cargo ourselves."

The bioworkers were outraged when they heard this suggestion.

Once more, Dirac sided with them. "We can always shoot things up. But we do have a very valuable cargo here, and we are still exhausting every possibility to find the Lady Genevieve."

No one, except perhaps the Premier himself, actually believed that anymore. Several wondered why they were really lingering aboard, but no one dared insist upon an answer.

The bioworkers and Dirac as well had been relieved to discover that the period of active berserker occupation had involved no widespread destruction among the cargo of protopeople. Nor did any great volume of tiles seem to have been removed from their usual storage places—though given the immense number of stored units, and the severe confusion of the record-keeping system, it was impossible to be sure about that.

Certainly there was no evidence that the berserker had ever started to grow Solarians for some hypothetical corps of mamelukes, of goodlife slaves. None of the artificial wombs had been activated or moved from their original places of installation, though there was evidence suggesting one or more had been examined. As far as could be determined without detailed examination, none were damaged. None were currently in use.

Nick had to wait until this general inspection was over before he could hope to get his own secret project under way. Dirac was still conducting armed patrols, an armed and suited escort accompanying every fleshly technician's foray into the huge storerooms, in case something was still lurking.

Faced with the seemingly immense difficulties of providing bodies, Nick tried to persuade Jenny to abandon her demand for flesh. He kept promoting, subtly as he thought, virtual reality as a form of paradise, but Jenny, whenever she suspected him of doing this, continued to insist violently on regaining flesh.

She began to accuse Nick of having robbed her of her body; maybe his real goal all along had been to reduce her to his own fleshless, unreal condition, thinking to possess her that way. After all, she had only his word that her injuries had been so severe. Well, he could forget it, it wasn't going to work. No man was going to have her until she had been given her body back. The mere idea of electronic lovemaking, of attempting to program exquisite extrapolations on the sense of touch, was quite enough to make her sick.

Eventually the Premier, feeling increasingly confident about safety aboard, declared armed escorts now optional.

Early one morning—Dirac had set station time equal to ship's time aboard the *Eidolon*—Kensing, leaving the stateroom he now shared with Annie, asked her: "A zygote is basically a blueprint, correct? Basically very compactly stored information?"

"In the first place, a blueprint is neither human nor alive. I happen to believe that these are both."

"Even when frozen?"

"You wouldn't consider yourself dead, would you, lover, if you were riding unconscious in an SA chamber? Which brings us to the second place: you might as well argue that you or I or Nick or anyone is only a bundle of information."

"I didn't want to argue philosophy. What I was really getting at is this: could a billion zygotes have been stored much more compactly, and just as accurately, in digital form, as information records?"

Annie took deep thought over that one. "I don't know," she admitted at last. "You could fairly easily, I suppose, record anyone's genetic architecture, as it were. But not a protopersonality, as represented by the patterns of brain activity—in that sense a zygote has developed nothing to record. There is as yet no brain. Whereas even a three- or four-month fetus has quite a lot going on between the ears."

Scurlock was back. No one besides Dirac, and probably the reclusive Carol, even realized that he had been absent from the station for almost a full day.

He reported privately to Dirac, and he handed over to the Premier a small, mysterious, innocent-looking piece of hardware.

"You actually spoke to a functioning machine?"

"Sir, I did." The tall man was once more seated opposite the Premier in the latter's private quarters. He described how his physical journey had been accomplished according to plan. To make the secret journey possible, Dirac had taken an extra turn at sentry himself and had arranged for Hawksmoor to be distracted.

Dirac let out a long sigh. "Then I was right."

"Yes sir. You were right. The great machine is certainly not dead. Though I believe much weakened."

"And this?" Dirac was balancing the little piece of hardware in his hand. It looked like an anonymous spare part from somewhere inside one of a million complex Solarian devices.

"A secure communications device. So it informed me. Anything you say near it will be heard—over there. Now and then the machine may use it to talk to you. It said it would not talk to you very often, lest some speech come through at a moment when you might find it embarrassing."

"How considerate. So, it is listening to us now?"

"I assume so, Premier."

"And what else can you tell me? What were you able to observe?"

"Very little, Premier. I rode the space sled over there and looked around until I discovered what looked like a hatch. Then I waited, in accordance with your instructions. After several minutes the hatch opened and a small machine came out to investigate my presence."

"A small machine of the type you encountered here on the station, during the berserker occupation?"

"Yes, the same type, as far as I could tell."

"Go on."

"When I made an openhanded gesture to the small machine, it escorted me inside the hatch—it wasn't an airlock, of course. I didn't get any farther than just inside, and there was very little to see. Just metal walls. I didn't really learn anything about the machine's interior construction."

"I didn't really think you would be able to." Dirac tossed up the little piece of hardware and caught it in midair. "You have done well."

Jenny was delighted when Nick came to report that he was on the verge of starting their great secret project.

He had succeeded in copying Freya, without Freya's being aware of it, and in making the necessary alteration in the fundamental programming of Freya². Soon it should be possible to begin operations with a pair of the artificial wombs located in an area seldom visited by fleshly people.

Nothing ventured, nothing gained, Nick told himself and Jenny. If the secret work should be noticed, he could make some excuse, disguise the work as something other than what it was. But Nick thought it unlikely that anyone would even notice that the project was going on.

Jenny was growing enthusiastic. "But first, of course, we must select from the cargo the zygotes we want to use."

"Yes. We have a billion to choose from. If you don't want to go out there, I'll bring likely samples for your consideration."

"And after that, it is still going to take years."

"As I see it, we shall have years. I can control the yacht's drive indefinitely. And the Premier will not really be disappointed, I believe. I tell you, he is in no hurry at all to get started for home. The only thing that worries me . . ."

"Yes?"

"Never mind. An idle thought."

Nick didn't want to tell Jenny what he'd heard from Freya, that Dirac had apparently been contemplating a secret project of his own, something along the lines of Nick's.

He started to devise a simple program to let a robot sort through zygotes, a preliminary step in picking out the pair they'd use. One for Jenny's new body. And one for Nick's own body, the first and very likely the only fleshly form that he would ever have.

Nick's imagination kept coming back to the vital, difficult questions that could not be avoided. Might it be possible to push forward on two fronts at once, start trying to make both methods, growth and capture, work? Or would running two secret projects simply make discovery twice as likely?

The capture method would require him somehow to seize control of suitable adults and wipe their brains clear of pattern without killing any of the body's vital organs—to injure the brains delicately, precisely, without destroying the tissue's capacity to take and retain the patterns of thought once again.

Murder. Sheer murder of innocent bystanders. Despite his determination to be ruthless, he shrank from the thought. Not to mention the difficulties he and Jenny would face after technical success. Even if they could somehow avoid the Premier's wrath and that of other potential victims, what human society would give shelter to such murderers?

Of course it would be years quicker than growing zygotes. And the actual capture should pose no great difficulty. Nick, in his suit mode, could easily overpower any organic human not wearing armor, and few wore armor these days except on sentry duty.

The real difficulty was that very few adults were currently available; and none of the available bodies appeared to be ideal choices. On Nick's next visit to the yacht he entered the corridor housing the ship's medirobots and read the biological specifications on Fowler Aristov, the would-be colonist mentor who still reposed there in the deep freeze. Not Nick's ideal of a body for himself, but acceptable, he supposed, in an emergency.

But what about Jenny? She came first. He must find the right fleshly envelope for her, even if he failed to accomplish as much for himself. And among the organic females currently available, none, in Nick's opinion, came up to the standard of beauty that was required.

No, he had better stick to method one. Given sufficient time and care, human bodies could certainly be grown in the station's artificial wombs. There was an overabundance of zygotes aboard the station among which to rummage for desirable genetics. Despite the scrambled records, a suitable pair could certainly be located, given time for the slow mechanical search required.

That, of course, was only the beginning. Assuming that suitable bodies for himself and Jenny could be grown, the next step, loading their personalities into those immature brains, was surely going to present new difficulties. According to the plan he'd worked out with Freya[2], that phase would have to be accomplished concurrently with the process of organic growth. Organic brains and minds would have to be fabricated in successive levels of refinement, as a sculptor cuts away the stone in finer and finer increments.

And either method, stealing bodies or growing them, would eventually require that the information-storage masses in which the two disembodied people now resided—three skulls' volume each—be physically moved to the place where the organic vessels were being prepared.

Several members of Dirac's crew, now even Brabant and Engadin to some degree, were growing increasingly dissatisfied with his continued emphasis on somehow recouping his personal losses.

The political adviser scooped up a handful of tiles and let them go clattering to the deck, then watched moodily as a small machine came rushing to arrange the statglass rectangles in some kind of order. Varvara brooded: "First we spent our days searching for a woman who wasn't here when the berserkers came. Now we're looking for a tile, a single tile, that no one in God's universe could find!"

The bodyguard, grumbling in general agreement, compared the latter task to that of locating one star in the Galaxy, without a chart.

Dirac's adviser and mistress urged: "We've fought the berserker to a standstill. What we ought to be trying to do now, and I've already told him so, is get the whole station free of its grip. All right, sure, save the tiles if we can. The best way to do that is to go after the berserker now and make sure that it's dead."

"You mean go aboard it?"

"That's what I mean. Dangerous, sure. But if we wake up and think we'll realize that just staying here, devoting ourselves to meaningless tasks, is suicidal. If the berserker doesn't get us, the nebula is sooner or later going to close in and we'll be trapped."

"So? What do we do?"

"If repairing the yacht is really out of the question, then we must go aboard the berserker, make sure it's dead, and find some way to manipulate its drive. That's the only way we can start ourselves back in the right direction. That method saves the protolives as well; we can tow the station and its cargo out of the nebula again."

Everyone agreed on at least one point: If they maintained their present course, heading straight into the nebula, sooner or later they would inevitably get trapped in a shifting of the Mavronari's clouds, caught so that centuries instead of days of travel would be needed to restore them to their homes.

After long days of searching through cargo bins and various pieces of equipment, it still seemed impossible to determine whether or not the tile containing Lady Genevieve's donation had ever been turned over to the filing system. The problem of finding this protochild among nearly a billion others appeared to be practically impossible.

Barring success with the software, the only way to locate one tile among the billion might be to have people, or robots, physically examine all the stored tiles, one after another. "Is there only one machine on board designed to do such testing? Get through a million tiles a year, and we can finish the job in only ten centuries."

"Of course the chances are we'd find it in half that time."

Something like a hundred thousand tiles per standard month. That would mean three thousand a day. More than a hundred an hour.

Neither Zador or Hoveler could remember what had been done with that particular tile, in the panicky moments right after the alert was sounded, other than that it had been put down either on the arm of Hoveler's chair or on the edge of his console.

On several details the two bioworkers' memories were in conflict. Well, organic brains tended toward the unreliable in many ways.

Nevertheless Dirac continued to insist that a strong effort be made to find his family donation. The Premier had now publicly announced that he might be able to reclaim Jenny only by reconstituting her from her genes. Of course his wife's full genetic code would not be available from the zygote, but that would provide a start. And the full code might be here somewhere. Sometimes parents who donated a protochild to the colonizing project were asked to leave their own complete genetic records as well. Neither Hoveler nor Zador knew with certainty whether this had been done in the case of the Lady Genevieve. If it had, and the specimen could be found, then cloning should be possible. Zador and Hoveler themselves had performed such procedures in the past, for special medical reasons.

Dirac at about this time unveiled a surprise: a personal service system, really an elaborate bodyguard, which he called Loki. Nick was called upon to bring over from the station to the yacht, openly in this case, another container of three skulls' capacity. Yet another trustworthy personality, as the Premier explained to Nick, to relieve Nick of some of his duties and to provide protection if need be even against a berserker.

Days passed. Grumbling among the crew increased, but with Nick's and Loki's and Brabant's help, Dirac still remained firmly in control.

And even if Scurlock and Carol behaved strangely, and other people began to suspect that Dirac had opened negotiations with a berserker, he had long since established and would energetically maintain an iron control over the people with him.

"Nick, tell me—can a program experience true emotions?"

"I can indeed, sir."

"As I expected from you—a perfectly programmed response."

Dirac and Scurlock talked again, with the berserker's communication device locked away where they felt sure it would be able to hear nothing.

The Premier was saying: "All a berserker ever needs is life to kill, and a means of killing. One might argue that a protocolonist sealed inside a statglass tile is not really alive, but whether you call that entity a unit of life or of potential life is a fine philosophical point, probably not too interesting to a berserker."

"You mean, sir, that the zygotes will be valuable items with which to bargain for our own lives and freedom?"

Dirac, without actually saying anything, or even nodding, conveyed agreement.

The other man, pale-eyed, still very youthful in appearance, asked, "If it considers them alive, why didn't it kill them, destroy the tiles, when it had the chance?"

"For one thing, each tile is very tough, designed and built to protect its contents. They aren't that easy to destroy; you'd need individual attention to each one, or else very heavy weapons, to achieve mass destruction.

"But I think you're right, the berserker, as we've thought all along, must have had some reason beyond that. Some more ambitious scheme in mind—doubtless along the lines of growing and training a goodlife legion, as several have suggested. But our boarding evidently took it by surprise, and now it's lost that chance. Perhaps it was willing to open negotiations with us in an effort to win it back."

Kensing was having trouble standing the strain with no relief in sight. He approached Dirac with the urgent plea that everyone left alive suit up at once in armor, take up such weapons as they had available, and launch an expedition, a probing attack, against the berserker itself. The issue had to be resolved, and all the evidence suggested that the foe was almost if not entirely helpless.

Dirac was sharply critical of this proposal. "Don't be a fool! Don't you see it's doing its best to lure us into trying something of the kind?"

Kensing was ready to argue. "Or else it's preparing to launch some kind of an attack against us, fixing up what hardware it has left for a maximum effort. The more time we give it, the harder it's going to hit us when it's ready." He concluded with an anguished plea: "How else are we ever going to get home?"

The bioworkers had mixed feelings. They didn't want to provoke another berserker attack, but at the same time they fiercely resisted the idea of their billion charges being carried on helplessly into the Mavronari Nebula.

Dirac, helped in no small degree by his own reputation for ruthlessness, as well as his charisma, continued to squelch the plan put forward separately by Kensing and Engadin. He publicly opposed launching any kind of attack on the enemy just now, and provided reasons—the enemy was trying to lure them into something of the kind.

But Nick and a few others were becoming increasingly convinced that such a rash move would interfere with Dirac's own agenda, which required him not only to survive this disaster personally but to emerge from it with power intact.

Everything else, everyone else's plans and hopes, must wait while he continued his search for the all-important (to him) person he was determined not to lose. In truth, his real goal was power. His "beloved" had really never been anything more than a means to that.

Some of his more knowledgeable, cynical shipmates explained to others that for Dirac to go home without his politically necessary bride would be such a political disaster that doubtless he would prefer not to go home at all.

"What's that to us? Let him stay here if he wants to. We want to go home."

But even without using or directly threatening force, the Premier could always make most people see things his way.

☀ **ELEVEN**

Awakening to the sounds of water drilling and drumming on her high roof, the Lady Genevieve immediately remembered how, shortly before putting herself to sleep this last time, she had mentioned to Nick that when in her fleshly body she had liked listening to the rain.

Waking in this new mode of existence was always very unlike waking when she was in her body. Consciousness now came and went all in a piece, in an unmeasurable instant, like switching a light on or off, with none of either the luxury or the difficulty that had attended the process when she still inhabited her flesh. Coming out of deathlike sleep now, in semidarkness, she found herself occupying a very solid feeling though totally imaginary bed, somewhere in what ought to have been the Dean's Quarters. She was waking to the sound of earthly rain, British rain, London rain, drumming now for her unreal ears upon the distant imaginary slates of the imaginary Abbey's imaginary roof, cascading from the mouths of gargoyles onto the imaginary streets outside.

She wondered whether the real Abbey, somewhere very far from this spaceship, in which she was imprisoned, astronomically remote beyond light-years and light-years of busy space, carried any such creatures incorporated into its upper stonework, or whether these semi-reptilian monstrosities had been conceived and born only in some chaotic spasm of Nick's imagination. He had admitted to her wistfully that he lacked the historical resources to be sure his duplication was exact.

Effortlessly the lady willed herself to be no longer in her bed, but standing beside it—and there she was. Wet London was visible from one of her high windows when she rose on tiptoe to look out. It was gray morning, very gray, rain shining on the antique roofs of slate or shingle. The darkened sky was full of grating, grumbling thunder, and a realistic flare of lightning.

And the lady, in the bedroom privacy which Nicholas Hawksmoor had sworn and guaranteed for her, stripping off her white nightgown now, examined with fear and curiosity the white nakedness of the body image Nick had given her.

It wasn't the first time since coming to the Abbey that she had made a similar inspection. The first time she had seen her new self this way, she had been willing to agree: Yes, this is me. This at least looks like the flesh that I remember. But with each successive viewing her uncertainty had only increased.

The private portions of her body, those which had not been visible in any of the public videos on which the reconstruction had been based, now seemed to her to be the most changed from the flesh that she remembered. Or was she only imagining that this was so?

Willing her nightgown on again, the Lady Genevieve went out of her bedroom, along a passageway, into what ought to have been a public section of the Abbey. Then, finding her way through a small door and climbing a hundred steps and more without effort or breathlessness, she ascended a narrow stair within the north tower—the one without the clock.

Having counted a certain number of stairs, she stopped to open a small window, reached out and experimentally touched the rain upon the gray, slanting roof outside. The chill wet smoothness beneath her fingers still wasn't exactly right. Nothing was. Things changed here, now and then, but in their essentials they did not improve.

Descending from the tower again, she had hardly reentered her bedroom before there came a knock upon her door. Before responding she put on an imaged robe over the imaged nightdress in which she had climbed the tower. Taking her time, she shod her feet in slippers. Then she answered the door.

"Surprise, surprise," she said, hardly glancing at the figure that stood outside. "It's you."

Nick looked at her as if his thoughts were really elsewhere. "Who else were you expecting?" he inquired in honest momentary puzzlement.

She only gazed at him.

"Oh," he said at last, vaguely realizing that she was only registering a sarcastic complaint about her isolation. "Have you found things—to do? To think about?"

"No. How can I find anything here unless you give it to me?"

"I have said I'm willing to teach you how to exert control over this environment. You could experiment endlessly, make whatever changes you wanted. I should think it would be—fun."

"And I have said that I am not willing to endure this existence a moment longer than is absolutely necessary. What I want is to have my body back—or to be restored to another body that's at least as good."

"And I can only assure you, my darling, that I'm doing all I can." Nick was able to report some faintly encouraging news about the process of selecting zygotes, and the availability of artificial wombs.

By now they had strolled out into the church itself. "And I have brought you pictures, my dear."

Jenny was about to ask what else besides pictures he could possibly bring her as long as she was trapped here in unreality, but she forbore. Nick went on eagerly to explain. A robot searching the cargo under the direction of Freya[2] had already turned up a pair of zygotes whose genetic patterns closely matched the somatotypes Nick had ordered. He had created images showing what their new bodies would be like in early maturity, if grown from these zygotes.

"Well, when can I see them?"

"Here they are now."

Jenny looked over her shoulder to behold a handsome couple, entirely unclothed as for some nudist wedding ceremony, approaching side by side down the center of the nave. One of Nick, as he would look in his new fleshly mode, and one of her. His was very much like the virtual form that already stood beside her, looking anxiously for her approval. And hers ... she could see in it no more than a vague resemblance to what she thought she ought to look like.

The images, athletic and glowing with apparent health, but vacant-eyed and with no reaction to being observed, came within a few meters of the watching couple, then pirouetted and posed like holostage clothing models that someone had forgotten to provide with clothing.

"Well?"

"Close," said Jenny, not wanting to be too critical at this stage. "But I should be just a shade taller, don't you think? My breasts a little larger. And the chin, and the eyes—make her look back this way a moment—yes. The whole face, I think, is really not that much like mine. Like the way mine ought to be."

Nick nodded, unperturbed. "This is only a start, of course. The robot searched only a few million tiles to come up with these. It shouldn't take very long to turn up an even closer match—and what do you think of mine?"

"I think the resemblance is definitely closer there. It will certainly suit me if it suits you."

"Good. I'll use it, unless something even closer should turn up. Meanwhile we'll go forward with the search for yours. Meanwhile, what else can I do for you here, to make you as comfortable as possible?"

"Nick, I tell you I no longer know what comfort means. My only genuine feeling here, I can assure you, is one of helplessness."

That attitude, coming in place of the praise he felt that he had earned, horrified Hawksmoor. Or at least she got that sense of his reaction. "It pains me that it should be so, my lady!"

"Why should it pain *you*? I am absolutely in your power. Isn't that what you've really wanted all along?"

Horror doubled. "But I never wanted to have power over you!"

"You have deliberately robbed me of my freedom. Made me into a toy, a puppet."

"But I tell you I don't want such power! I took it and used it only when it was vitally essential, as if I were your doctor. Only when there was no choice if your life was to be saved.

"I'm sorry if you feel helpless here—again, I can only say that is the last thing I want. I repeat, I will teach you to control your own environment. Such teaching can be accomplished in a few moments. I will even give you the power to lock me out—"

"No, I don't want to lock you out!" The lady's panic was sudden and quite genuine; her unspoken fear was that this man upon whom she depended absolutely might grow angry and lock her in, instead. "Leaving me the privacy of my bedroom is quite enough for now. You saved me, you are the only one I can talk to. The only one who can possibly understand. The only one who can help."

"I have offered to provide other company for you."

She made a dismissive gesture. "Wraiths and phantoms—like these dummy images you have here now." The nude pair were still posing, angling their bodies, displaying themselves in a slow mindless dance. "Like that man in dark clothing who always appears off in some distant part of the church. The one you call the verger, whatever that is. No. I always turn away when I see him. None of this company you talk about are real or ever could be. Am I correct?"

"None of them are real," her companion admitted. "You and I are the only real people in this world."

"Then, please, spare me the phantoms and the wraiths."

"Very well, you will see them no more." And in an eye-blink the two body images were gone. "Until I've turned up another zygote for your consideration. Meanwhile, just remember that I am not a phantom."

"No, Nick." The lady's manner softened. "Oh no, I know you're not."

"I suppose that in the other world, the one you call real, there are many more people who love you than there are here. All I can promise you is that I love you more than any of those others do."

"Oh. Oh, Nick . . . I don't want to lock you out. I think . . ."

"What?"

"I think I want to lock you in."

"Jenny!"

She eluded his outstretched hand. "But I know that cannot be. Not while we are only ghosts. You must go out into that other world, and somehow you must do the one thing that I require of you. So are you going to do it? Nick?"

"I swear by . . . by the powers that programmed me, that I am going to find, or create for you, the body that you want. Meanwhile, if my Abbey displeases you, I tell you I would cheerfully grind all its gothic stones up into powder if that would make you happy."

The lady seemed to soften. "Destroy your Abbey? Oh, Nicholas, after all that you have done for me, it would be mean and horrible of me to do a thing like that, destroy something that you love. Even if it is only an image." She paused. "Please tell me, where are we now? Really, I mean?"

Nick felt deeply disheartened by the fact that Jenny could still use that last turn of phrase.

"Nicky, tell me?"

"Very well, the location of our physical storage units hasn't changed. We are still on the bioresearch station. In the sense you mean."

"Why were you so upset a moment ago? It must have been something I said."

"Because you said 'Where are we, really?' If my Abbey is not real, then neither am I—nor are you. You, I, and the Abbey—we are all made of the same stuff. Really."

"I see. Then you must provide us both with bodies, Nicholas. I know I am repeating myself monotonously. I know you are doing your best. My love."

Nick wanted to spend as much of his personal free time as he could with Jenny. Such satisfaction as these visits gave him could be gained in no more than a fraction of a second, as ship's time was kept aboard the station. But he worried that Dirac might have ways, ways Nick himself did not know about, of checking on him. To absent himself too frequently or too steadily from the company of Dirac and other people, and from his assigned duties, might arouse suspicions.

In the face of the ongoing berserker threat, duty still called with an urgent voice. Events in that mysterious outerworld of flesh and metal, only very indirectly controllable by anything inside a databank, still threatened her existence, and his own as well.

At odd intervals, Hawksmoor puzzled privately over the enigmatic tone of that message Frank Marcus had transmitted just before he died. He definitely missed Frank, despite Frank's expressed attitude toward talking programs.

Nick considered trying to share with Jenny his thoughts about the peculiarity of those last words. But then he decided she probably would not be interested.

Hawksmoor missed Frank, but his feelings about the Premier were undergoing a drastic transformation in the opposite direction ... as if betraying a man you had no logical reason to hate automatically made you his enthusiastic enemy. Nick had to admit that now he really would prefer his creator/employer to be dead.

The process of betrayal and rebellion, which had begun with minor disloyalties, a gradual process by which the old codes were degraded, was now moving along, he realized, to its natural conclusion.

Had the berserkers themselves, Nick wondered, at the moment when the prototypes broke free of their creators, experienced something like this ... epiphany?

In her fleshly existence the Lady Genevieve, compared with many other women, had very little experience of sexual behavior; the culture in which she had been born and raised prized virginity before marriage. Still, near virgin as she was, she obviously had infinitely more experience along this line than Nick.

And yet she had the feeling that, if and when they eventually tried to come together, things were going to seem the other way around. How puzzling ...

Intermittently the Lady Genevieve felt worrisome concern about her child—her protochild. This nagging feeling of loss had been with her, though dormant much of the time, from her first awakening in the Abbey.

"Suddenly those few cells inside their statglass and plastic nest are more real, more human, than I am. Or than I am ever likely to be again. Oh, God, but I must have my body back!"

" ... until death do you part."

Whether or not that line had been part of the aristocratic couple's wedding ceremony, Nick had absorbed it from somewhere, and tended to think about it in his moodier moments, when he pondered the significance of fleshly death, the invisible guest at all Solarian weddings, partner in all relationships.

Jenny had no patience with any of these solemn musings when he tried to discuss them with her. Her entire thought and will remained concentrated on regaining the state she considered real life.

But Hawksmoor was unable to dismiss any of the great human questions as easily as that. Was the transformation she had experienced, on the courier and in the medirobot, really death?

Had he, Nick, saved her life, or had he not? And did what had happened mean she was no longer Dirac's wife?

❈   ❈   ❈

Despite Nick's efforts to make her stay in the Abbey comfortable and to convince her of the advantages of optelectronic life in general, the lady's objections to her current mode of existence—and possibly to some of Nick's plans—were growing so vehement, her fear of remaining in this condition so great, that he feared for her psychological health. Not many hours after his first visit with the dancing images, Hawksmoor decided that it was better to shield her, to put her into a deep sleep for a time.

As usual, he did this to Jenny without warning. Recently she had told him she was now afraid to sleep, lest Nick somehow fail or betray her in a time when she effectively no longer existed, and flesh be denied her forever.

Hawksmoor retained, though he had not yet exercised, selective control over the lady's memories. He could see himself being tempted, if things weren't working out, to wipe out everything she had learned since becoming a computer program, and start over from that point.

If he was ever to do that, Jenny would once more find herself unexpectedly beginning a new life in the medieval cloister. The sunlit garth, the grass, the music. For her the experience would be completely fresh and new as she sat listening to the handsome minstrel sing. Maybe he would make the minstrel handsomer this time.

Trouble was, Nick realized, that it wouldn't be fresh and new for him—not unless he also chose to wipe out the relevant portions of his own memory. But that way would seem to be recursive madness.

Still, the thought of being able to start over again with Jenny was tempting. He could easily make himself more handsome this time.

What ultimately decided Nick against that approach was the certainty that no matter how carefully he might try, nothing could ever be exactly the same as before. Chaotic variation always threatened. Things could be better, but they could certainly be worse. Suppose that on the next iteration Jenny should go totally mad or reject him entirely?

Doggedly Nick battled other recurrent worries: Had Jenny's brain been directly damaged by her combat injuries, so that the recording of her personality had been a moment-to-moment race with death? Nick had had to hurry the process to have any chance at all of getting her.

Had the pattern-transfer been somehow faulty?

No plans for the future would mean anything if he and Jenny were unable to survive in the present. They—or he, at least, now that he had put her back to sleep—had to confront realistically the difficulties of their physical situation. Including the looming danger from the berserker that was not really dead. At least he had to assume that it was not.

Ahead, the full dead blackness of the Mavronari was working its way inexorably closer, its vast depth becoming incrementally more perceptible from one hour to the next. The stars ahead, their light very slightly blueshifted by the craft's velocity, were all beyond the nebula, and much dimmer than they ought to be. Within a cone of some sixty degrees, centered dead ahead, there was almost nothing to be seen but a black void. And minutely, gradually, with every passing hour, there was even less to see, as that void inexorably expanded. The berserker, blind and deaf—or, for whatever insane reason, giving a good imitation of that condition—along with its helpless prey and the scarcely less helpless yacht were all slowly plunging together, headfirst, into a limitless bag of soot.

Kensing took it upon himself to make certain observations, intended to determine whether the normal-space, subluminal velocity of the strange little cluster of spacecraft was still increasing, or whether perhaps relativistic effects were gradually becoming greater with regard to the ever-more-distant Imatran system and the rest of the universe.

The result of the observations was mildly encouraging. Actually the velocity of the several vessels relative to the nearest clouds of the surrounding nebula was diminishing. But only gradually; at such a rate of deceleration, coming to a complete stop relative to the Mavronari was going to take a number of years. Entrapment, sooner or later, seemed almost inevitable, though it might not happen for many centuries.

Even now, relatively little of the starry universe could be seen from either yacht or station, despite clear ports and free antennas. And things were going to get darker before they brightened.

Trying to consider all possible strategies, Nicholas considered what he might do in the worst-case scenario of a berserker attack on the station, ending in an enemy victory. As a last desperate try, under those circumstances, he might transmit both himself and Genevieve back toward Imatra. Subjectively, for them, the journey itself would be instantaneous, nothing at all—old Einstein would see to that. But it was obvious that after transmission over a distance of so many light-days, under less than optimum conditions, only poor, frazzled electronic skeletons of information would arrive, only a poor sketch of either Jenny or him would alight upon a world that in any case had no particular interest in helping them to reach their goals.

Useless! Only as an absolute last resort would he ever entertain the thought.

Besides, on Imatra or any other settled planet, neither he nor Jenny would ever be granted bodies. Her real home, the planet of her fleshly origins, was farther off among the stars, and she had evinced no particular desire to return there. And the concept of home, as applied to himself, was meaningless. He was wherever he happened to be, and that was all.

But he was now in some sense beginning to envision the possibility, in fact the necessity, of one day possessing a home somewhere.

Since meeting Jenny new ideas had begun to fill Nick's mind in profusion, multiplying explosively. Until now the coordinates of his physical location in the universe had been practically meaningless to Nicholas, but if and when he acquired a body, such matters would certainly have meaning for him.

And then there was, as always, the berserker.

Nick might, should he choose to be aggressive, beam himself directly toward the dark-hulled enemy. On arrival, assuming there were antennas that would let him in, he could try to negotiate a deal, one program to another. But Hawksmoor saw little likelihood of any benefit from such a step. He had no reason to think that his beamed self would be well received aboard the ominously silent berserker, or free to roam about at will. Whatever remained of the original power in charge there would not be friendly. Though Nick fully recognized the awesome danger of berserkers to humanity, he tended to think of them less as machines than as programs more or less like himself.

Most likely no version of himself would be allowed aboard the berserker at all. And if it was, it might well be caught there in some electronic trap, caught and safely confined for leisurely dissection by the foe. After a berserker had subjected Nick's alter ego to an exhaustive examination, it would have a much better idea of how to deal with his progenitor, stay-at-home Nick, homebody Hawksmoor, aboard the Premier's yacht.

An alternate plan would be to transmit some ineffective, weakened version of himself. But then if that entity was *not* trapped, was allowed to act at will when it arrived, it might well make some devastating blunder. Unless Nick were to dispatch Inferior Nick under the strictest orders to do nothing but facilitate the following transmission, in safety, of Nick Prime . . . and if he could depend upon that attenuated version of himself to follow orders . . .

Complications upon complications. It was all too much.

Would a berserker consider Jenny, a recorded human being, to be still alive, her death a good to be accomplished? And would its attitude be any different toward him?

Despite the great amounts of time and effort expended on the question, no Solarian knew exactly what standard berserkers used in judging between life and nonlife, in deciding which components of the universe were animated by vital force and therefore must be destroyed as abominations—and which were safely dead or inanimate, and therefore tolerable or even good.

Anyway, Nick doubted that a berserker would perceive Jenny—or him or any optelectronic person—as alive. Once he told her his opinion, and was glad that she seemed marginally relieved. But privately he thought the question was probably academic. Most likely a berserker would regard both Jenny and him as, if not alive, still dangerous oddities. Subjects to be experimented upon for the knowledge to be gained, and then to be snuffed out as treacherous devices, likely to behave with sympathy to the cause of life.

But, Nick realized, he could be wrong.

He had mentioned the subject once to Frank, in their discussions, and Frank had expressed doubt that the enemy used any of what Marcus had called "fancy psychology" to distinguish between the living and the satisfactorily dead. Berserkers probably applied some simple test or series of tests for anything organic. Some other possible interpretations of what it meant to be alive, used by humans themselves, would broaden the category to encompass even the berserkers, self-replicating machines with purposeful behavior.

Some indefinable oddity in Marcus's farewell message raised in Nick's mind the possibility that this berserker, which had already demonstrated a predilection for letting its victims live, had taken Frank as a (more or less) fleshly prisoner. If so, might it not have already learned from Frank of Nick's existence and his nature? Would the berserker then be able to foresee what course of action Nicholas Hawksmoor the artiman was most likely to attempt?

To Nick in his present situation, all pathways seemed to lead into shadowy danger, for the Lady and for himself. And at the moment not one of those pathways showed any real glimpse of sunlight at the end.

It was time to consult once more with Freya^2 and to check on the automated search that Nick had instituted for protocolonists whose genetic patterns met Jenny's and his own demanding specifications.

Freya^2, having been designed as a biddable co-conspirator, was quite ready to help Hawksmoor in his plan.

With the cargo inventory system still scrambled as it was, Nick felt once more compelled to awaken Jenny to discuss with her the great progress in and remaining hard facts of their situation, the continued difficulty, despite long effort, of implementing either of the two possible solutions to their problem of obtaining bodies.

Today the lady was moody, unwilling to hold such a discussion unless Hawksmoor forced her to do so. And he was reluctant to do that.

Finally, reluctantly, he once more put her, stealthily but forcibly, to sleep.

There were intervals—brief, so far—when Nick envied his companion her privilege of safe electronic sleep, oblivion on demand, whenever she felt like it. At least, thanks to him, she was as safe when sleeping as she was when awake.

As for himself, he sometimes tried to practice sleeping, lightly—for a time, trying to accustom himself to what a breathing life would be like. Then, worried, he would snap back to full tireless alertness.

☀ TWELVE

Hawksmoor now experienced moments when the most ordinary call of duty seemed a maddening distraction from his secret work for Jenny and himself. Even the enigmatic berserker, and the danger it represented to Jenny, to himself, and to his fleshly creators, shrank into the background.

But this attitude could never endure more than a moment, because his experiments, all his hopes for an eventual life of peace and freedom with Jenny, also depended upon the outcome of the various external struggles. If the berserker should win, the pair of them could hope for nothing better than enslavement and destruction.

In any case, Nick hastened whenever he could to rejoin his beloved within the Abbey's sanctuary. Usually he had to wake her when he arrived—because, seeing her bitterly unhappy, he had put her to sleep, without asking her consent, before his previous departure. Jenny never protested these intervals of enforced unconsciousness. And during her meetings with Nick she still steadfastly refused to be beguiled by the prospect of any kind of "dream world"—that was her word—he might concoct in an effort to distract her.

Hawksmoor dutifully restrained himself, both in movement and in observation, from ever crossing the threshold of Jenny's luxurious bedchamber. This was the lady's room, in which he held her privacy inviolate, where she went when she chose to sleep—or when he knocked her out.

During their talks he questioned her often about the world of the body, exactly where and how it differed from this virtual reality. Her catalogue of variation was voluminous.

And fascinating. In fact it was her world, her memories and descriptions of existence in the flesh, a life he had never experienced, that were seducing Hawksmoor. Day by day, hour by hour, under her influence Nick found himself changing, reveling in new thoughts and feelings. The world of organic humanity acquired in his daydreams a greater immediacy, a sharper reality than he would ever have believed possible.

Meanwhile his own mode of existence, the one whose merits he had tried to sell to Jenny, was coming to seem drab, inadequate. Is *this* life? he demanded of himself urgently, considering himself as a part of the world in which he dwelt—had always dwelt. He found himself in growing sympathy with her dissatisfaction. *Is this all it means to be alive?* The lightning speed and certainty of electronic thought, electronic movement, were not enough to compensate.

There were times now when even his beloved Abbey provoked in him this feeling of repugnance.

When that happened, he roamed abroad, into the farther reaches of the station's circuitry, seeking a way out.

Meanwhile his secret work continued. Still the search continued for the precisely correct zygotes, the genes that would give them, Jenny and himself, exactly the bodies that they craved, to please each other and themselves.

Drifting through the conductors and composites of many materials that wove the research facility into a kind of unity, turning on video eyes, looking at the statglass shells holding the invisible zygotes, Hawksmoor speculated about what quality of experience the protocolonists might know, lying as they were, helplessly inert, changeless, almost immune to time within their statglass tiles. He supposed a dozen or so paralyzed cells would be incapable of experiencing anything at all. But how was it possible to know that with certainty?

More than once he had invited Jenny to come exploring with him in the great world (by which he could only mean more wires, more circuits), to roam the universe of the station's electronics at his side.

Several times she had hesitated on the threshold, on the brink of losing the Abbey's comforting illusions, and flowing into and through a circuit. But she found it unendurable, and rejected any further suggestions along that line with revulsion and dread. "I'll go back to the real world as a human being when I go back at all!"

The implication that he was not human stung Nick badly; but

he told himself that Jenny should not be blamed for what she said when she was so upset.

Virtual reality, in her view, was bad enough. The mere thought of entering the even more alien cosmos of optelectronic circuits threatened her deepest perception of herself as human.

There were moments when, in spite of early setbacks and difficulties, he felt almost confident of success in either finding or creating bodies for them both. At other times, in growing horror, he was overcome by dread that his wooing of Jenny, though it might have begun promisingly, was doomed to failure.

Trying his clumsy best to express to this woman what he was feeling, Nicholas said to her: "Someday—it is my fondest wish that someday we will be happy, living together."

They were in the Abbey's grassy garth, where she had first glimpsed this world of his devising. It was one of the places that made her feel most human. "Oh Nick. Dear Nicholas. If only it could be so."

"But the first step is to guarantee that you will have your body back. I know. I'm doing what I can."

"I'm sure you are, Nick." She stared past him, into a world of memory that he had never made his own, where he could not really follow. "But sometimes . . . I despair."

Before replying he paused to make, unseen, an adjustment somewhere in the realm of control, a place where Jenny could not see—or rather, one where she had steadfastly refused to look. Still, his old hope would not die entirely, that she might learn to be happy with him here. If the body project came to nothing, ultimately.

Then Nick urged: "Give me your hand."

She did that willingly enough. Then she stared in surprise as the image of his extended fingers passed through that of hers.

"Did you feel that?" he asked. "Of course you did not. Nor did I. That was the best that I could do in imitating your world, when you first came to live with me."

Jenny's image shuddered. "Don't do that again! It's horrible. It makes me feel like a ghost."

"Very well. I just wanted to show you, remind you, how much progress we have made."

The lady said nothing.

Pausing briefly, Nick restored the adjustment he had made. Then he brought their hands together again. This time hers was unwilling, and he held her wrist with his free hand, exerting gentle force.

The contact came. "Better?"

"Yes, I suppose so." Considered visually, their virtually real fingers appeared to be pressing, pushing against each other solidly, no more capable of interpenetration than two dumb stones might be. Skin paled with the pressure.

"Push harder, if you like."

"Don't hurt me!"

Instantly Nick pulled back. "I can't hurt you, my love. Beyond the fact that I could never wish to do so, you no longer possess the capacity for physical pain; I took care at the start to make sure of that. But that absence may be one reason why it's been difficult to get the sense of touch adjusted within the range of high fidelity."

"Nick?" Suddenly the numbness of despair gave way once more to pleading.

"Yes?"

"Can't you make just a little bit of me real? Come up with enough blood and bone somewhere to make only my little finger, maybe, real and solid? Even if that meant having to put up with pain again?"

Nick, finding this attitude discouraging, fell silent for a time. After a pause he tried once more to explain: "The only real solid that has any chance of existing in this Abbey, the only physical substance that might be claimed to exist in this whole private world of ours, is the polyphase matter used to construct certain parts of VR chambers—any VR chambers. The facility that the Premier and his breathing shipmates would have to use, should they ever decide to walk through my Abbey. I suppose if you and I were in the program when they did that, we might meet them somewhere in it."

"You said there could be no real people here besides the two of us."

"I said I couldn't provide any, and I can't. Under certain conditions, the people you call real would have the power of entering my world, our world, this world. But that is something they have to do on their own initiative—do you see?"

"I think so. Then it is possible that I might meet another real person here—inside your Abbey."

"Yes, if we should run the Abbey program in the VR chamber—but I thought you didn't want to do that."

"I don't—I don't."

"Touch my hand again?"

Reluctantly she tried. This time the sensation seemed more realistic than ever before.

"Better, my love?"

"A little."

"I'm sure you can remember, from your earlier phase of life, the touch of other human fingers on your own. But I can only imagine what that must be like subjectively. Still, now that I have the station's medical information banks to draw on in addition to my other sources, I have been able to reprogram both of us to feel what

I imagine. And it means a great deal to me when you tell me that my programming is getting closer and closer to fleshly psychological reality."

The Lady Genevieve was silent.

He urged her: "You have known the touch of someone else's hand on yours. Tell me again whether the experience I have provided is the same."

Grudgingly she admitted: "In a way it is the same—or almost. I *think* it is almost the same. Or perhaps I think that only because you have—!" Genevieve broke off suddenly.

"Only because I have *what*?"

"Because you have somehow reprogrammed *me*, so that I now accept whatever my programmer tells me as the truth! If you say that this is how a human touch must feel, then that's it, as far as I'm concerned."

"I have not done anything like that." Nick made his voice convey outrage. Then he paused. Certainly he hadn't meant to do that. But—once he had started making subtle adjustments—could he be positive about what had happened?

For some time now it had been at least in the back of Nick's mind that, whatever delights the fleshly world might hold for them in years to come, the time ought to be ripe here and now in this world of his own to move on from simple touching, to make a start on the enormous project of trying to calculate and estimate and program all the delights of sexual love.

But now, with the lady still so uncertain and reluctant regarding the most elementary interactions, he saw that trying to go forward would be hopeless.

From time to time, hoping to learn more about the processes involved, Nick conducted certain tests on his secret companion. When he assured Jenny that these were necessary to learn more about how to accomplish her eventual downloading back to flesh, she gave her enthusiastic consent.

Part of the drill involved probing for the last event of the lady's fleshly life that her memory retained. And this—though she could not really recognize the experience for what it was—turned out to be the last thing that had happened before her physical organs perished. The process of being recorded, as her body had lain in the medirobot's couch, in the last awful minutes before brain death. Even at the time she had not understood what was really happening to her. Probably no suspicion of the truth had then entered her failing mind.

The last thing Genevieve could remember unambiguously was being rescued from the courier, carried from its shattered hull, by

Nick. She had thought at the time that she was being rescued in the conventional sense. The spacesuited, armored figure had come in and held her protectively in its arms. And in her relief she had kissed her rescuer.

She told Nick now that she still retained the disturbing memory of a strange, unsettling emptiness perceptible inside that figure's helmet. The recalled image came and went, as if the following knockout of short-term memory had all but wiped that view away.

Nick pondered whether the recording process, which had taken place in part after the main systems of her fleshly body had ceased to function, constituting as it did an electronic tracing of patterns, a draining, a pillaging of cells that had already begun to die in millions—whether that process in itself had tended to reinstate the short-term memory otherwise disabled.

Still he was unable to persuade Genevieve to venture out, even for a moment, from her VR sanctuary into the world of more prosaic circuitry. She spent all her time, with Nick, or alone, within the precincts of Westminster Abbey. The place was so huge she could not avoid the feeling that years of subjective time would be required to explore it with all the attention its details deserved. There were a vast number of things within and around the building complex that she wanted to think about and examine—even more things in which she would have been interested had not her own condition come to obsess her almost to the exclusion of other thoughts.

Retreating to her private room, she waited anxiously for Nick to come to her with a report. Sometimes she slept, knowing she would awaken when he came. She welcomed him each time he appeared to visit her; sometimes she was alerted by the distant sound of his boots on stone paving as he approached. And once, when she was awake and out of her room, his figure simply materialized, came instantly into being before her.

He'd played that last trick only once, for she'd immediately made him promise never to do such a startling and inhuman thing again.

During these usually peaceful visits, the couple spent more time in the grassy garth of the cloister than in any other single location. The lady yearned after the sun, but demurred when Nick suggested they might, they very easily could, go someplace else entirely, visit some mockery of a real-world location naturally much sunnier than London. Or he could just as easily brighten his artificial British daylight to tropical levels.

"No dear, don't do that. Will you never understand? I have the feeling that such reality as I still possess might fray out altogether if things keep changing around me as fast as you can change them."

Whenever she tired of the cloister's muted, confined beauty, or when some random program Nick had set in motion decreed unscheduled rain, graying the sky above the open garth and splashing their hands and faces with felt wetness, she welcomed the illusion of uncontrollable nature. At such times they moved indoors, pacing the gloomy depths of the Abbey itself, or taking refuge from rain and gloom in what Nick called the Jericho Parlour and the Jerusalem Chamber—old, incomprehensible names for parts of the living quarters whose timeless, insubstantial luxury now belied the ancient stonework of the walls.

Inside these living quarters, Nick, never giving up the fight for verisimilitude—as much to give himself a foretaste of fleshly life as to placate Jenny—had now arranged for imaged machines to serve them with imaged food and drink. The processes of eating and drinking, similar to what she could remember from her fleshly phase of life, relieved hunger and thirst—or effected changes that seemed to her analogous to satisfying real fleshly thirst and hunger—as she remembered those sensations.

Not that she was ever *really* hungry or thirsty here in the Abbey, or ever tired to the point of exhaustion—certainly she was never in pain. Nick in his concern had seen to it that her life was—endlessly comfortable. The sensual experiences she was allowed to have were all of them muted, different.

And gradually she understood that this existence must lack many things, subtle things, that were not as obvious as breathing or touching. It bothered Jenny that she could not remember exactly what those missing experiences were, of what else she was being deprived.

"Nick, I haven't told you everything that's missing here. A great many parts of real life are lacking."

Of course he was surprised—how stupid he could be sometimes!—and concerned. Dismayed and intrigued and challenged, all at once. "What things are they?" he demanded.

"That's just it! I don't know, yet I can feel the loss. If I knew what they were . . ." Jenny gestured, clenched her fists, gave up at last in exasperation.

Eventually words came to her in which to express at least one of the missing components of real life.

"Here in our world, as you call this existence, nothing can be depended on to last. Everything is exactly as changeable, as transient, as everything else. You, me, the rain, the stones, the sky—it's all the same."

"It seems to me," Nick retorted, "that it is out in what you call the real world that things are never permanent. Even our bodies, once we have them, will wear out and decay in time."

"But not for a long, long time, Nick. And as long as we have bodies, we'll be real."

Meanwhile her mind clung to the imaged stones of the Abbey, as at least suggesting endurance, a balanced struggle between permanence and change, a concept she found somewhat comforting.

Jenny once asked her sole companion whether he had ever known any other electronic people.

"No. Unless you count an expert system or two, like Freya, or the Boss's new bodyguard Loki—but that's really a very different thing."

"What is Loki like?"

"How can I tell you? A nature basically somewhat like mine—but very paranoid. Swift-moving, strong—in the ways an optelectronic man can be strong."

"Do you get along with him?"

"Not very well. I suppose no one could. Loki was not designed to get along with people."

One day Nick as a surprise, an attempted treat, suddenly furnished the Abbey with realistic sounds of running water besides the rain, a burbling stream somewhere, a sound that grew louder the closer Jenny approached the western entrance, those main doors which she had never opened. He pulled them open for her now, and London was gone; there was the little stream crossed by a mossy footbridge, beyond which a path went winding away into a virgin forest.

"No, Nick. No. Just close the door. I want no entertainments. All I want is—"

"Yes, I know, love. I know what you want, and I'm doing my best to get it for you."

Another day, high up in the north tower, he pointed out that the strong, silent tidal inflow of the Thames was visible if you knew where to look for it. And sure enough, looking over and around what Nick said were called the Houses of Parliament, which stood on the near bank, she saw the broad curving river as described. London's taller towers, far more modern, gray and monstrous, were half visible to virtual eyes behind the curtaining virtual rain, hanging in the virtual distance.

But none of that really helped at all. Genevieve's existence was made endurable only by the power she had been given to put herself to sleep whenever she wished, by simply willing the event. She availed herself of that refuge times beyond counting, often to find herself awake again, with little or no subjective sense of having rested, or of any duration whatsoever having passed. Her best hope to achieve the sensation of rest was to prolong the process of temporary extinction by simply entering her bedroom, an act that tended to bring on slowly increasing drowsiness.

Hawksmoor, alone with his thoughts while Jenny enjoyed one of her frequent periods of sleep—at least Nicholas hoped they were enjoyable—willed his own human image naked, and in that condition stood looking at himself in a virtual, multidimensional electronic mirror of his own devising. It was a mirror that could have existed in no ordinary space, and it showed the front and sides and top and back and bottom, all at once.

Nick's knowledge of human anatomy, and of the shapes and sizes and arrangements and textures of flesh that were ordinarily considered desirable, came not only from the databank references but from direct observation of human behavior, on this voyage and on others—including the behavior of a number of humans confident they were unobserved.

There had been a time, before the mobilization of the demonic Loki, when Nick's secret observations had extended even to the behavior of the Premier himself, especially on certain occasions when Varvara Engadin was sharing Dirac's room and bed.

But in Loki, Dirac possessed a handy means of keeping Nick at a distance when he didn't want him, as well as of summoning him when he did.

Nick told himself, almost convinced himself, that his knowledge of human love was already considerably more than merely theoretical. Ever since his creation—his own first memories were of being aboard the yacht, with control of most of a ship's circuitry at his electronic fingertips, his to do with as he pleased—he had been able to watch the most intimate biological activities of a succession of human shipmates, including people he knew as well as strangers. Obviously programs duplicating organic sexual excitement, love and pleasure, would have to be of enormous complexity—but Hawksmoor prided himself that programming acceptable variations of those things would not be beyond his powers.

But at the same time Nick felt—he considered it probably accurate to use the word "instinctively" to describe this feeling—that Jenny's yearning for a body was fundamentally right. Something, perhaps many things, had always been missing from his world, from the only universe of experience that he had ever known or, in his present form, could ever know. The events called joy and love and satisfaction had to be of greater potential than what he or any being could program into himself. To know such things in their full meaning there had to be a giving from outside. Jenny represented that—but what could Jenny, as miserable as she was now, give him?

"Until we have flesh of our own, we are doomed to be no more than ghosts." At some point she had spoken those words to him. And in the universe they shared what was once said could never be forgotten.

Eventually a standard year had passed since Dirac's daring boarding of the station and the loss of Frank Marcus, among others, in savage combat.

Still Nick had failed to convince Jenny to be satisfied with any of the zygote images he had presented for her approval. The project to grow bodies for Jenny and himself had been on hold for months.

☀ THIRTEEN

Loki, the Premier's optelectronic bodyguard, was wont to be irascible. He frequently reminded anyone, organic or not, who addressed him as if he were human that he was not a human being at all, but rather belonged to the category of events or objects more properly denoted personal systems.

But it seemed to Nick that Loki acted like a person in many ways.

Loki expressed no opinion, because he was not required to have one, on the humanity or lack thereof of Hawksmoor or any other entity save Loki himself—itself, if you please.

One important way in which the bodyguard-and-personal-servant system called Loki served the Premier was as a surefire means of summoning or dismissing his pilot, architect, and sometime bodyguard called Hawksmoor.

Fully self-aware or not, Loki was an effective, specialized AI being, capable of ordering Hawksmoor about when necessary.

When Nick thought about this situation, he supposed that he ought to have realized from the hour of his creation that Dirac would prudently have arranged some such way to maintain power over him. But actually the facts of Loki's existence and nature were a very recent and very disquieting discovery.

Fortunately for Nick's hopes of independence, for his secret projects, Loki was seldom fully mobilized, and when he was, he paid relatively little attention to Nick. But eventually Hawksmoor complained to his boss. Nick protested that Loki was harassing him. If Dirac wanted Nick to do the best possible job on all his multitude of assigned tasks, he would have to modify the system.

Dirac agreed to make some modifications, restricting Loki to a more purely defensive use.

Nick thanked the Boss and industriously returned to work.

Part of his self-assigned clandestine project was now to oversee a team of simple robots in the creation of a nursery. This was a small volume of space to be walled off from the rest of the station by new construction, a secret facility in which his and Jenny's new bodies, emerging fresh from the artificial wombs, could be safely brought to maturity, or near maturity, without being allowed to develop minds or personalities of their own. This nursery, as Nick called it in his own thoughts, would of course be located near the secretly operated wombs, in a part of the station where people rarely went.

Still Jenny hesitated, withholding her final approval from any of the zygotes Nick's searching robot managed to turn up. Millions more tiles had now been tested by the robot, but the surface of the cargo's possibilities had barely been scratched. Nick himself reviewed the most likely candidates before bringing the very cream of the crop to Jenny for her consideration. Then he set aside those she rejected—the rate was one hundred percent so far—keeping them on file for possible use if and when the lady should weary of her insistence on perfection.

Meanwhile, a slow parade of mindless images, of possible Jennys, were sent along by the searching robot to model for Hawksmoor alone. For a time the show of naked women amused and excited him, and added to his enjoyment by making the images behave in the manner of fleshly women he had secretly observed.

But presently this enjoyment wearied. And afterward Nick felt dirty, guilty. As if he had stood by, allowing the woman he loved to be defiled by someone else. Out of respect for his lady and for himself he turned the prancing parade into a slow, dutiful march. For of course the job of reviewing possible bodies still had to be done. He inspected succeeding candidates in the manner of one saddled with a weighty responsibility.

Nick's own yearnings to inhabit flesh were not entirely a result of his wish to be with Jenny. To some extent they certainly predated his rescue of the lady. But before he encountered her, such cravings might have been largely subconscious, and he might have thought them mere aberrations. In that epoch he had never questioned that he himself was perfectly at home, self-sufficient, in the current mode of his existence.

But now he could feel absolutely certain of almost nothing about himself.

"Or—I *think* I have feelings. I can see myself acting as if I do—how can I know myself any better than that?"

Yes, he thought that his own wish to have a body of his own had developed into a fixed idea, a compulsion, only when Genevieve, unequal to the task of trying to make do with images, swore that she had to have her body back—a beautiful, female, healthy, satisfactory body, of course—or go mad.

Nick was frightened to hear her say that. He feared madness, for himself as well as Jenny, and he felt it a distinct possibility, though he wasn't at all sure what it would mean for an electronic person to go mad.

In the back of Nick's mind another fear lurked, though he tried to convince himself that the worry was irrational: Would Genevieve, once reestablished in the flesh, be tempted to rejoin her husband? She said she now loved Nick and feared Dirac, but Dirac was, after all, the father of her child.

And yet another worry: What would happen if progress with the artificial wombs was made in such a way that Jenny was somehow to be granted her body before he, Nick, got his—what then?

She who had been Lady Genevieve was still haunted by recurrent fears over what might have become, and what was going to become, of her protochild. Hers and Dirac's.

Part of the feeling was resentment, a fear that the child would somehow become her rival, her replacement.

More and more now, Genevieve insisted to Nick that she was really terrified of Dirac. She would be happy never to see her tyrannical husband again.

Nick for the most part believed these protestations—because they made him so gloriously happy. Even in his moments of doubt he clung fervently to the hope that they were true.

Nicholas, ready to deal with the difficulties of obtaining two bodies rather than just one, ready to abandon the only world he knew to take on the mysterious burdens and glories of flesh—emphasized to Jenny his determination that, whatever else might happen, they should remain together.

What good would a body be to him if she had none?

But the corollary of that was, how could he bear to have her regain her flesh if she left him behind in the process?

"You really do want me to come with you when you go back to that world, don't you?"

"Of course, Nick."

"You have to understand that, one way or another, if I'm in that world, Dirac won't be. And vice versa. You must understand that. He'd never tolerate—what I have done. What you and I will be doing."

"Then we must make sure he's not around to bother us." She was quite calm and deadly about that.

Nick of course had never had genes before. Programmers who brought nonorganic people into existence did not approach their jobs by such a roundabout route. On first deciding to assume flesh, he had been ready to accept almost any presentable form. But now he had to face the fact that it was not only possible but necessary, with expert help and a lot of hard work, to choose what physical attributes he'd like to have, and then make up a suitable set, or find the closest possible approximation, from the existing Solarian supplies.

On assuming flesh he would of course be giving up a great deal of mental speed and sureness, and he could not help but regret in advance the losses he was going to suffer. Naturally there would be gains in other areas, compensations deriving from his new organic brain. But the compensations were subtler than the losses, harder for him in his current mode to define or even imagine.

Outweighing any such problems, of course, was the fact that in the fleshly mode he would have Jenny . . . *have* her, solid to solid, flesh to flesh. And this was a thing of awe, a profound mystery that he could not begin to fathom.

Nick needed to be reassured. He pleaded with his lady: "You'd want to be the one to show me how to live in a body? You must realize, the idea, the concept, of having real flesh is very strange to me. It'll take me a while, with my new organic brain, to learn to use muscles instead of thoughts. I'll forget where I am, I'll be terribly slow and clumsy. I'll fall down and bruise myself, and—and I don't know what."

He earned a laugh with that line. It was in fact the first real laugh that Nick had ever heard from her. But it was over in a moment.

Having been thus offered a kind of sympathy, Nick kept on. "I realize that kind of an existence is very natural for human beings, of course." *Just as being in the womb or in the cradle, is natural, but I don't want to do that.* "But still. I could wind up needing extensive medical therapy, surgery, just to keep my body alive. I could spend my first month or so of real life in a medirobot." In fact Freya[2] had warned him that such might be the case.

Jenny soothed him, offered comfort. "I'll show you how to live in your big clumsy body. I'll show you everything. And I'll take care of you if you need help. Oh, Nick . . . By the way, have you found a new model for yourself that you like better?"

Nick had, and now paraded the latest version of his potential self for her approval.

Genevieve frowned with interest at the walking, posing image. "That's rather a different look, Nick—"

"Don't you like it?" Suddenly he was anxious.

"Yes, I find it quite acceptable. And yet . . ."

"And yet what?"

"And yet, the face reminds me of something. Someone I've seen, somewhere before. But, I thought my memory was now completely digitized?"

"It is."

"If so, shouldn't that mean that I must either remember something or not remember it, not experience this—this—?"

It was also somewhat odd that she would find familiar the image of an unborn face. But chance, and quantum effects, could play strange tricks in any mind.

Nick was vaguely perturbed, but he tried to be soothing. "In most cases the process will work that way. For everything important, I hope. But—I don't wish to alarm you, but possibly there was some slight damage to your brain before I could start the recording. That could produce such an ambiguity. Also the recording process itself is rarely perfect. It's not surprising that there should be a few lacunae."

And Lady Genevieve continued to fret vaguely over her impression that she had seen this new face of Nick's somewhere before.

Nick, as he thought to himself and several times tried to explain to Jenny, suffered moral qualms at the thought of simply taking over some human's developed body—he at least doubted whether he was morally capable of doing that. His basic programming forbade him to kill humans or cause them harm—except possibly in a situation where anything he did would have some such effect.

Jenny appeared to be devoid of any such scruples. She proclaimed herself too desperate to afford them. There was a suggestion that she had been quite capable of hard and ruthless behavior in her fleshly past, when the situation seemed to call for it.

"Why do you think the Premier chose me for his bride? It wasn't entirely because of my family connections. Nor, I assure you, for my beauty—I had nothing spectacular in that department. No, he wanted a capable ally."

This revelation clashed violently with the ideal image of Genevieve that Nick had been developing. Resolutely he refused to give it thought.

Other seeming inconsistencies nagged at him. Nick was impressed and somewhat puzzled—alarmed and at the same time gratified—by his own progressively improving capability to disobey what had seemed the fundamentals of his programming.

He pondered the proposition: When complexity reaches a certain level, true life is born. And at a higher level yet, true freedom, true humanity?

And still Jenny hesitated over her choice of body.

So far, he thought bitterly, the great plan to achieve flesh, and carnal love, like almost everything else in the life of Nicholas Hawksmoor, remained entirely in his imagination, while the obstacles to its achievement unfortunately did not. The difficulties he faced were not susceptible of being solved by any rearrangement of symbols or reshuffling of information. He had observed that whenever the world of hardware and flesh came into contact with that of thought and pattern, the former tended to dominate.

But he was still fiercely determined to prevail. All the more important, then, that his calculations and patterns be as precise and as far-reaching as he could make them. He had to try to foresee everything.

Was it foolish to hope that the bodies could be grown under the noses of the fleshly humans who remained in control of the biostation, that the necessary years would be available to bring his and Jenny's new selves to maturity? Perhaps that was an unreasonable hope, but at least he would learn from the experience. And next time, next time, somehow, he would succeed.

And even suppose his plan succeeded, and at last he was somehow able, with the aid of the vast bioresearch computers, the artificial wombs, the available genetic samples, the help of Freya[2], to reconstruct the Lady Genevieve, and also embody himself in flesh.

The pair of them wouldn't be able to hide out indefinitely in bodies. Wasn't there bound to come a time, sooner or later, when he would be forced to explain, to attempt to justify, to the Premier or at least to other people what he had done? The time was bound to come. And when it came . . .

In his fancy Nicholas now brainstormed a series of elaborately mad scenarios, each one crazier than the last, he might be able to deceive and at the same time placate Dirac: On that day when the Premier's beloved showed up in the rosy flesh, somehow alive after all, quite recognizable though not precisely identical to her earlier self. And not a day older—probably younger, if anything.

For a time Hawksmoor toyed with the daring ploy of telling the truth, making a full confession. Was there any conceivable way to convince the Premier that Nick now wanted to have, really ought to be allowed to have, and one way or another was going to have, a body?

On the face of it, that scenario was the craziest of all. He was totally convinced that Dirac would never assent. For good old Nick to acquire bone and blood and muscle would forever abolish his unique usefulness.

And those difficulties, heroic as they might seem, would be only the start. Next would be the additional problem of explaining, how, why, the Lady Genevieve had been kept in hiding ever since her rescue. *Explain that to me, Nick.*

Hawksmoor, acutely conscious of these monumental impossibilities, wasted a good deal of time and thought trying to develop moderate, nonviolent solutions.

He even conjured up several explanations, each of which, while it was in the process of formation, he for some reason thought might work the miracle. For example: Suppose Jenny had never really been aboard the biostation at all. She had got someone else to impersonate her on that visit, while she herself, in a playful attempt to surprise her adored new husband, had stowed away aboard his yacht.

Toward the stern of the *Eidolon* were a couple of small state-rooms, guest cabins seldom used or even entered. It was a safe bet that the few people actually aboard had ignored these chambers throughout the crisis. Suppose, while hiding out in one of them, Lady Genevieve had accidentally drugged herself into a long sleep. Suppose Nick, again by sheer accident, had finally discovered her. No one but the lady herself, certainly not Nick, had known until just now that she was aboard.

Nonsense. He was fooling himself into thinking utter nonsense. It struck Hawksmoor that growing an acceptable pair of bodies might not be the hardest job he faced. Maybe developing some explanation that would leave him innocent of disobedience would, after all, be an even more gigantic task. Only a husband who was desperately willing to be convinced would swallow any of the stories Nick had managed to cook up so far; and that description did not begin to fit Dirac.

Of course he, Nicholas, could always try telling Old Master—that was a name he had begun of late to use, in his own thoughts, for the boss—the sober truth instead: That Jenny had indeed been present on the yacht since before they left Imatra, but only as an electronic ghost, a doppelgänger, symbolic life force drawn vampire fashion from dying flesh. Sucked out by Nick Hawksmoor, who had been acting without the knowledge or permission of his owner, who also happened to be the lady's lord and husband—and in whom (the lord and husband, that is) the lady was no longer interested.

Considering that plan, Hawksmoor thought it sounded like a fool-proof recipe for suicide. For his own virtually certain obliteration, as any other dangerously defective program would be wiped away. And the thought of being obliterated, erased, was now, for the first time in his life, profoundly unsettling. Because now for the first time he had something to live for.

For a little while after the boarding of the biostation, during the interval when communications between yacht and station had been cut off, Nick had felt a secret, guilty joy at the sudden thought that Dirac and all his fleshly companions might become victims of the berserker, lost forever to the fortunes of war.

One problem with that course of events, if it should really come to pass, was that it would leave him and Jenny confronting a giant berserker that was not really dead, probably contending with it for the biostation's facilities. Another problem was that, considering themselves as they did full members of the human race, they could hardly celebrate any kind of berserker victory.

Again and again Nick savored, vividly relived, his own thoughts, his own behavior at the time of the rescue. It was, in a way, as if his own life had begun only at that hour.

To project himself into the wrecked courier, he had taken over a semirobotic suit, a model designed to be either worn, or controlled at a distance, by a fleshly human.

And at the moment of rescue, she had seen him in what looked like human form—in appearance a spacesuited human—as he came aboard her blasted ship, carefully preserving the seals necessary to hold the inner chambers full of air. And in the moment when she saw him, she had jumped up from her acceleration couch, thinking she was saved—had kissed him, yes, right on the faceplate, not seeing or not caring in her joy about the emptiness inside.

Jenny kiss'd me when we met—

And then, in the next instant, one more blast . . .

The day came, at last, more than a year after that rescue, when he managed to prevail upon Jenny to make her final choice.

With that accomplished, Nick in suit mode took in hand the two tiles that had finally been chosen and went with them to Freya[2]. He was assailed by last-minute doubts that the expert system, despite his tinkering with her programming, was really going to help him. Any system complex enough to be useful at such a high level of intellectual endeavor must already have become, in some sense, a strong if monomaniacal intelligence; and Nick realized that he could never be absolutely sure that he had bound that other intelligence unbreakably to secrecy.

He also worried that someone, Loki or Dirac himself, might discover the existence of Freya^2 and question her. In Hawksmoor's experience, expert systems seldom volunteered information. But they naturally answered questions freely—that was their usual purpose—unless the project was labeled with a high security classification.

When he brought her the chosen pair of tiles, Freya^2 obeyed Nick's orders without question, almost without hesitation.

And now the pair of carefully cultivated Solarian fetuses were developing steadily, and in only a few months would be ready to come out of their artificial wombs. At that point, obviously, new arrangements would have to be made for their further development. Nick had several ideas on how he would go about that.

The two selected prenatal brains were taking shape under the stress of a pattern of carefully, precisely inflicted microinjuries, alternating with periods of healing in which the cells of the two brains were bathed, respectively, in a perfusion of Nick and Jenny personalities drawn from partial recordings. Theoretically no native patterns would be allowed the chance to start developing.

But this was obviously a difficult and delicate process, completely experimental. There were a great many ways in which things could go wrong.

PART TWO

☀ FOURTEEN

Following the disappearance of Dirac and his squadron, almost three hundred years passed in which the Imatran system remained essentially at peace, while new generations took control of politics and power. A strengthening of the system's military defenses was planned, with grim urgency, in the months immediately following the attack, and construction was energetically begun. But soon, for economic reasons, work on the projects slowed, then was several times interrupted. After almost three hundred years the defenses had been brought up only partially to their planned strength, with the remaining construction postponed indefinitely.

Meanwhile, within a month of Dirac's final departure, a series of very interesting rumors had begun to circulate: the vanished Premier was being accused of having somehow staged the whole show of attack and pursuit, though his accusers could put forward only the most nebulous reasons to explain why he might have done so.

Naturally the political situation was much changed by the Premier's disappearance. Years passed, then decades and centuries, and nothing was heard from him or from any of the other people who had gone in pursuit of the great berserker, or had been carried away by it.

There was certainly no shortage of rumors, though.

＊　＊　＊

And then, nearly three centuries after Dirac and his squadron had vanished, occasional rumor gave way to fact, violent, concrete, and bloody. Berserkers, a whole fleet of them this time, fell upon the planetoid Imatra in overwhelming force. This time their onslaught was no mysterious hit-and-run kidnapping. This time they did what was expected of berserkers, laboring in earnest to sterilize the planetoid.

Why, the modern dwellers on that unfortunate body asked themselves before they died in their deep shelters, why had the long-planned defenses never been completed? And, more fundamentally, why did people like themselves persist, anyway, in trying to live on this damned, doomed rock?

A great many of those who were unlucky enough to be caught in the latest attack had no time for such speculation. Others were not interested. At the moment, death had the last live man on the surface almost in its metallic grasp, and in another minute those grabbers, merciless as falling rocks, were going to close on his body and rend him limb from limb, armored suit and all, and he was certainly going to be dead.

Inescapable extinction had clothed itself in the form of a crippled steel insect, half again as tall as a man, and in this guise was chasing the survivor across the now suddenly devastated landscape of the planetoid, hounding him through the roaring swirls of mist, across the narrow bridges spanning the canals, stalking him with mechanical patience on four metal legs while two more legs hung broken. The broken legs had been shot almost completely off before the planetoid's defenses failed, and they dangled in the damned thing's way with every stride, slowing it down to the point where it could hardly catch an agile man who kept his nerve.

For an eternity in human terms, for perhaps a quarter of an hour by clocks less personal, ever since the last useless fortification had failed the people it was designed to defend, the man had been running away from death, splashing through the shallows of the scenic ponds and lakes, scrambling and falling and getting to his feet again. Waves of terror, each worse than the last, welled up inside the tight control he kept on his nerves, each wave in turn subjecting him to what felt like the last possible extremity of fear.

Exhausted muscles, almost out of chemical fuel except for that pumped in by fear, sent the wiry mass of his suited frame bounding almost out of control in the low natural gravity. His movements were hampered by the unfamiliar bulk of space armor as he struggled gasping across the uneven surface of the planetoid.

Though the space armor was slowing him down, during the last hour it had also more than once saved his life as improvised missiles, rocks crudely hurled by his pursuer, striking with a velocity worthy of bullets, had battered him and more than once knocked him off his feet, but so far had failed to kill or bring him down to stay.

Around the human survivor and his crippled pursuer, which came hobbling no more than fifty meters behind him now, the fog winds shrieked as the last of the planetoid's carefully created and tended atmosphere went boiling away from the surface under the repeated impact of major berserker weapons. The hulks of ruined buildings loomed out of the howling, rushing mist as the survivor ran toward them, and fell behind him as he bounded staggering past.

For long minutes now nothing but noise had come through on his radio. The last human voices exhorting the populace to be calm had long since been murdered. The exhausted rhythm of the running man's own breath was the loudest sound inside his helmet.

Only a single one of the deadly machines, and it among the smallest of them, had taken time from other tasks to pursue the man. He could not understand why the damned thing had chosen to zero on him as its next target, but it was obviously not going to be distracted. If it had not been damaged in the early fighting, two legs crippled, whatever projectile weapon it might possess evidently inactivated, he would have been dead long minutes past.

Relentlessly the insect shape came on, its framework skinny for its height, its color reminiscent of dried blood. Husbanding whatever powers it had left, methodically putting down one weakened leg after another, the machine advanced, evidently calculating that it could catch the fleeing life unit no matter what, and that it could not be stopped by anything one exhausted man in an armored suit could do. In any case a berserker was no more worried by the prospect of its own destruction than a table or a chair might be.

A bizarre twist in the long corkscrew path of destiny had given this man the chance of wearing space armor just when he most desperately needed it; but an accompanying trick of fate had denied him anything effective in the way of a personal weapon.

Running on foot, his reservoir of salvific luck surely almost exhausted now, the man tripped and fell, tumbled rolling downslope in the clumsy suit so that he ended lying with his face toward the sky. As he sprawled there, some curiously detached portion of his mind took notice of the fact that overhead the artificially blue vault of the Imatran atmosphere was fading swiftly, and the stars were becoming visible in the intervals between the weapon-flashes that still tormented nearby space and whatever might be left of the planetoid's upper atmosphere.

And still the fleeing human was not dead. Still his killer-to-be, tangled in its own broken legs, had not quite caught up. Struggling again to regain his feet, to gather breath enough to run again, he heard, above the shrieking of the wind outside, the loudness of his own gasping inside his helmet, the pounding of his own heart.

He tried once more, desperately, to call for help on radio.

No reply. Of course not. It seemed to him that in some sense this chase had been going on his whole life long.

For a moment, invincible hope surged up again, because he had momentarily lost sight of his pursuer. Trying to locate the damned machine again, struggling with an agony of hope, he looked around.

In the middle distance, no more than a few kilometers away across the planetoid's tightly curved surface, he could see, through a roaring, rushing curtain of mist, driven by the force of the escaping winds, certain recognizable human installations undergoing what must certainly be fatally destructive blows, a weapon-storm from space. Here and there structures stood out individually: marble columns, slabs of exotic materials still shimmeringly beautiful in texture and color, the divers temples of humanity tottering and falling.

A moment later, without warning, the berserker was upon him, no matter that he might have thought for a moment that he'd been granted some miraculous respite.

Only minutes ago this man had seen another human killed by this same berserker. Another man killed when the machine caught him, and with a motion quick and deft as that of any factory assembly robot, crushed in the fellow's helmet, and in the next instant twisted head and helmet completely off. And at the last instant, as his fellow human died, there had come to the ears of the survivor the shriek of a human voice on radio, and then the sound of breath and life and air departing.

But what had happened to others seemed irrelevant in the mind of the last man living on the Imatran surface. He himself had now been reduced to a state of mental and physical exhaustion in which it seemed to him that neither mind nor body could any longer move. He was no stranger to the earlier phases of this condition; but this time he knew in the foundation of his being something that he had never known before, that this time there was no way out. He could perceive distinctly, and with a curious detachment, just what final shape his termination had assumed. Skeletal and metallic, Death turned to him unhurriedly. Without hurry, but without delay—Death was wasting no time, though really there was all the time in the world for it to finish this job up properly.

... and there came a timeless, hideous moment, beyond anything that the survivor, who had thought he had already seen and known it all, would have been capable of imagining. When this moment arrived, the advancing machine was close enough for him to be able to look into at least some of its lenses as if they were eyes.

By this time the doomed man had struggled to his feet in what felt like a last effort and then fallen again, and struggled up once more, turning deliberately to confront Death, preferring that to feeling his doom grab him, strike him from behind.

And in that ultimate moment the man about to die was granted a good look into the lenses through which death gazed out at him . . .

. . . why should it move him so profoundly now, now when nothing in the world could matter, why should it make the least difference that those lenses were little mirrors?

. . . and what did it matter that he could see, if not his own face, at least his own helmet's faceplate, looking out at him expectantly?

A touching, even an exchange, of souls. As if he, in seeing the end of life so closely, had come to be Death, and meanwhile Death had come in behind his own eyes, and supplanted him . . .

. . . and then, just at that moment of triumph—as if the machine were concluding some inexplicable computation, reaching a decision that its goal had been achieved—just at that moment, the four metal legs still functioning stopped in their tracks. A moment later, without a pause, without a break, it had ceased to threaten its still-living victim and was backing away. In another moment the great steel insect had turned its back upon the last Solarian survivor and was running in the opposite direction, determined on an incredible retreat that looked even faster than its pursuit had been.

Still the man, whose lungs yet kept on breathing, could not move a voluntary muscle. He could only stare after the berserker. Blown dust and swirling fog obscured the metal shape, first thinly and then heavily. And then in another moment it was gone.

No, not completely. For long seconds the air mikes of the armored suit still brought him the vibration of the berserker's broken, dangling limbs, clashing against the members that still worked, a rhythmic sound that faded slowly, steadily, until it too had disappeared. The man who listened did not, could not, raise his eyes again or drag himself back to his feet.

With part of his mind he understood, vaguely but with a great inner conviction, that he had made some kind of pledge and that his offering must have been accepted. No words had been exchanged, but that made no real difference. The horror had departed from him because it was satisfied that now in some sense he belonged to it.

Only by the power of some satanic bargain was he still alive.

Somehow, in its terms and details, the bargain had still to be negotiated, given its final form. Sooner or later that must happen, and there was nothing to be done about it now. Right now the world of his survival was unreal. Still, when he let his eyelids close, he could see nothing but those reflective lenses, and those grippers raised and coming after him.

Some three standard hours later, the man who had survived was located, almost at the same spot, almost in the same position, by human searchers, who came looking for him armed and armored in their own swift-moving slave machines. Some of the joints of his armored suit had failed at last, so that he could no longer walk. His rescuers were led to where he huddled among the ruins by the slight vibration of his own still-trembling, still-living body.

✺ FIFTEEN

In the hours immediately following his seemingly miraculous escape, the survivor was examined and then given medical care in a field hospital hastily erected on one of the least damaged portions of the Imatran surface. In this facility he soon discovered a fact he considered to be of great significance—he was the only patient.

A number of people questioned this incredibly lucky man about his experiences, and he gave truthful answers, as best he could, to most of them. He skirted the truth by a wide margin when he was asked how he had come into possession of the space armor that had saved his life; otherwise he was generally truthful, except that he revealed nothing about what had gone on inside his head during those last horrible moments of confrontation with the machine that had come so close to killing him. He said nothing about reflections in lenses, or about any feeling he had of having come to an understanding with the enemy.

Lying in his hospital cot under a room-sized plastic dome, sometimes shifting his weight from side to side in obedience to the medirobot's brisk commands, he listened to the peculiar sounds attendant upon the efforts to restore the atmosphere outside, listened also for a certain recognizable tone of authority in the footsteps passing his room, and wondered if it would be of any practical value to steal and hide in some handy place, a scalpel someone had carelessly left upon a nearby table. He soon decided against that.

The survivor also reflected with awe upon the implications of the fact that out of several thousand humans populating the surface of Imatra when the attack began, he was the only one now still alive.

Stranger than that. Not just the only human survivor, which would have been bizarre enough. Not simply the only Earth-descended creature. Almost the only specimen of any biological species to outlast the onslaught. Scarcely a microbe, other than those in his body, clothing, and armor, had weathered the berserker aggression.

In the privacy of the man's own thoughts, the uniqueness of his position, and the questions that it raised, glowed with white-hot urgency. They were all really variants of the same problem: *What was the true nature of that last silent transaction that had taken place between himself and the machine?*

Something real must have happened between them, for it to have let him live.

What could a berserker have seen about him, known about him, detected in his voice, that had caused it to single him out for such special treatment?

And then there came a new thought, dancingly attractive, with—like all really attractive thoughts—a flavor of deep danger. Presently the man—who was startlingly handsome, and somewhat older than he looked—began to laugh. He kept the laughter almost entirely inside himself, in a way that he had long since mastered. No use encouraging his attendants to wonder just what he had found to laugh about. But the situation was really so amusing that he had to laugh. He wondered if the metal things that had so long and thoroughly terrorized humanity might have their own code of honor. For all he knew, it was conceivable that they did.

There was a certain long-established term in common use, a name with its translations and variants in every human society, for people who cooperated with berserkers. A name that had been originally bestowed upon such people by the machines themselves. The worst name that one could have, in most branches—maybe in any branch—of Solarian society.

Goodlife. That was the dirty word. What those who committed the vilest of crimes were called. One of the few crimes, the survivor thought, of which he himself had never been accused.

Not yet, anyway.

Abruptly he had ceased to laugh, and was shaking his head in private wonderment. What could the machine ever have learned about his past life, and by what means, that had given it cause to take him for an ally?

More immediately to the point, what concrete action did it expect of him?

He had never in all his life, before his arrival on Imatra, been within communicating distance of a berserker machine. Nor had he ever wanted to be. How could killing machines coming out of deep space to attack this system, where he had never been before, where he had never wanted to be—how could such machines have known anything, anything at all, about what he was like? Or that he would be here?

At whatever odds, under whatever conditions, he was the only survivor of their attack. Of only that one fact could he be certain.

A day after being admitted to the hospital, when he was on the verge of being released—he had suffered only inconsequential physical injuries—the survivor, somewhat to his own amazement, went into delayed shock.

The doctors said something about a natural psychic reaction. The patient didn't think it at all natural for him. Massive medical help was of course immediately available, and chemical therapy brought him out of the worst of the shock almost at once. But full healing in this case could not be achieved through chemistry, or at least the medics did not deem it wise to try. One of them wished aloud that he had the patient's medical history; but though that was available in a number of places, all those places were many days or even months away, upon the planets of other stars.

On the morning of the next standard day, having finally been given the doctors' permission to walk out of the hospital—even as machines were starting to disassemble the temporary building around him—the survivor trod the surface of a planetoid that was already enjoying a modest start on its way back to habitability; the complete journey was going to take a long time, judging by the way things looked. The diurnal cycle, disturbed when Imatra's period of rotation was thrown off by the violence of the attack, was slowly being returned to a period of twenty-four standard hours. Some tough ornamental plantings were still alive, still green, despite having endured some hours of virtual airlessness. Havot paused to gaze at them in admiration. A spacesuit was no longer required to walk about—atmospheric pressure, if not oxygen content, was well on the way back to normal. Humans working out of doors, who were the only people around except for the just-discharged patient, moved about protected by nothing more than respirators.

Unexpectedly, as if by some deep compulsion, he found himself heading back toward the place, the building, in which he had acquired his lifesaving suit of armor. Of course compulsive feelings could be dangerous, but this time he indulged them. As he drew near the site, his feet slowed to a stop. Silently he offered thanks to fate, to luck, the great faceless monsters who from somewhere ran the world, for at last coming back round to his side. Only a blasted shell of the edifice remained, on the edge of a disorienting ruin, stretching for kilometers, that had been one of the larger Imatran spaceports.

It would have been wiser, he supposed, to move away at once; but at the moment he was enjoying a feeling of invulnerability. He was still standing there, thoughtfully gazing at the ruins, when footsteps with a certain recognizable tone approached behind him. Only one pair of them.

He turned and found himself confronting a young woman dressed in executive style, who was of course wearing an inhalator like his own.

"Excuse me. Christopher Havot, is it not?" Her voice was soft, somehow inviting. "They told me your name at the hospital."

"That's right." The name he had given his rescuers was not one that he had ever used before, but he considered he had as much right to it as anyone else.

His questioner's moderate height was about the equal of his own. She (again like him) was strong-limbed and fair, and very cool and businesslike. She began fairly enough by introducing herself as Rebecca Thanarat, special agent of the Office of Humanity.

Havot looked innocently puzzled. "This is not my home world— far from it. I'm afraid I'm not entirely clear on what the Office of Humanity is. I suppose an 'office' would be some government bureau, or—?"

She nodded tolerantly. "Yes, the Imatran system is only one of four families of planets that fall under the jurisdiction of our OH office."

"I see." Havot had been right about the footsteps; he thought he could always tell when the law approached him, even though he was having some difficulty figuring out exactly what law, whose law, his interrogator was determined to enforce. Except he was certain that the Humanity Office could have no notion of who he really was. Not when they sent one casual young woman out to talk to him.

Obviously she was just feeling her way. She asked: "Then we do have the correct information, you are not an Imatran native?"

"No, I was just passing through. This was part of the spaceport, wasn't it?" He turned and gestured at the ruined plain before them. Actually he had no doubt of where he was. Only a few meters in front of where they were now standing had been the spaceport detention cell. As soon as the alert had sounded, one of his guards, who in other matters had not acted especially like an idiot, had begun to argue stoutly that the prisoner, whose life was totally dependent upon those who had him in their care, really ought to be unfettered, and be given the first chance at getting into an armored protective suit. It would be safe enough to give him armor, because certain of the suit's controls could be disabled first ...

After only a brief discussion they had given their prisoner the suit. Chris smiled remotely, fondly at the memory.

Meanwhile young Agent Thanarat was talking at him in her bright attractive voice, beginning a conversation. This is how we put the suspect at ease. More than likely she had been taught certain general rules, such as beginning most interrogations on a friendly note. But she seemed very young indeed, likely to have trouble keeping the friendliness from becoming genuine and spontaneous.

She was determined to accomplish her assigned job, no doubt about that. After a minute she led the talk rather awkwardly around to the question of why the berserkers had retreated so abruptly. What ideas did Havot have on that point?

Until this moment he had never really considered that larger aspect of the matter. He had assumed, without really thinking about it, that the enemy, having practically sterilized this little world, had moved on to bigger things, launching an attack on the more heavily populated sunward planets. Since he'd heard no weeping and wailing about horrendous casualty reports received from sunward, he assumed that the berserkers had been defeated there, or at least had been beaten off.

When he said as much, adopting a properly serious tone, his interlocutor gently informed him that nothing of the kind had happened.

"As soon as the berserkers broke off their attack on this planetoid, they very quickly withdrew from the entire system. The inner worlds were never menaced." When she said this, Agent Thanarat appeared to be watching carefully for his reaction.

Havot blinked. "Maybe they found out that a relief fleet was on its way."

"Possibly. But it still seems very strange. Or don't you think so? No one's ever frightened a berserker yet." Now Rebecca Thanarat was sounding tougher than she had seemed at first impression.

Havot turned his back on the ruins of the spaceport and started strolling, almost at random, putting his booted feet down among gray shards and dust that came drifting up feebly in the new air. Agent Thanarat came with him, walking with her hands clasped behind her back.

After a few paces Havot said: "But surely they have been known to retreat. If they'd known a superior force was coming to destroy them, they'd have backed away, wouldn't they? Withdraw to keep from being wiped out, so they could destroy more life another day?"

His companion nodded. "Sure, they retreat sometimes, for tactical reasons. But the human force approaching, the people who found you still alive, wasn't that much stronger than theirs. And even if they'd mistakenly computed that for once humanity had them outnumbered, that wouldn't throw machines into a panic—would it, now?"

"I hardly think it likely," agreed Havot, wondering at the tone of the question. The speaker had uttered it in the manner of one delivering the crushing conclusion to some serious debate.

His interlocutor nodded with evident satisfaction, as if she took Havot's answer as some kind of a concession. Then she went on: "The real question is, excuse me if I put it crudely, why couldn't they hang around another fraction of a minute to finish *you* off? If the version of your story that I've heard is the correct one, another few seconds would have done it."

"I hope you're not disappointed that I'm still here." He flashed a winning smile for just a second. Not too long; he had decided that Christopher Havot should be a basically shy young man.

"Not at all." The Humanity Office agent in turn favored him with a more personal look than any she had given him so far. Then—were her fair cheeks just a little flushed?—she lifted her blue eyes to stare into the sky. "We ought to have some verification shortly as to exactly what happened during the attack. A couple of ships are out there now looking for the relevant light."

"The relevant light? I don't understand."

Rebecca Thanarat made little jerky motions with her hands, illustrating the movement of craft in space. "A couple of ships have gone jumping out, antisunward in several directions, to overtake the sunlight that was reflected from this planetoid during the hours of the attack. It's a hazardous job, going c-plus this near a sun, and no one undertakes it except for the most serious reason. When the investigating ships have determined the exact distance, a couple of light-days out, they'll be able to sit there and watch the attack in progress. If all goes well, and they can fine-tune their distance exactly right, they'll be able to record the events just as they took place." The speaker, proud of her technical knowledge, was once more observing Havot closely.

Again the fortunate survivor nodded. He allowed himself to look impressed at this evidence of the investigators' skills. Yes, he had overheard people in the hospital discussing the same search process, calling it by some other name. Agent Thanarat seemed to assume it was of considerable importance.

❂   ❂   ❂

In the midst of this smiling discussion, something occurred to Havot that sent his inner alertness up a notch. During the attack his suit radio, meant to communicate with other suits and with local civil defense, had more than likely still been on when he surrendered to the berserker—someone might have picked up the signal of his voice, whatever words he'd said, out of the inferno of enemy-generated noise blanking out human communications in general. He couldn't really remember now if he'd said anything aloud or not. He might have.

—but surely those ships out there now, light-days away, would be unable to gather any radiant record of what one man, on the surface of the planetoid while the attack was going on, had said in the virtual privacy of his own helmet...

His interrogator, watching him keenly, persisted: "And still you say you have no idea why they fell back so precipitately?"

"Me? No. How could I have? Why do you ask me?" Havot, genuinely puzzled, was beginning to slide very naturally into the role of innocent victim of the bureaucrats. He had no problem sounding outraged. It was outrageous that these people of the Humanity Office, whatever that was exactly, might really have been able to find out something about his final confrontation with the berserker.

Already Havot had almost forgotten his physical injuries, which had never been more than trivial. His breathing was steady now and his pulse moderate and regular, but he had no doubt that he was in some sense still in shock.

Absorbed in his own newly restless thoughts, Havot moved on, leaving it up to the young woman whether she wanted to follow him and pursue the conversation or not.

She chose to stay with him. "Where are you going, Mr. Havot?" she inquired without apology.

"Walking. Am I required to account for my movements now?"

"No. Not at present. But have you any reason to object to a few questions?"

"Ask away. If I object, I won't leave you in doubt about it."

Agent Thanarat nodded. "Where are you from?"

He named a planet in a system many light-years distant, one with which he was somewhat familiar, far enough away that checking on him there was going to be a major undertaking.

"And what is your occupation?"

"I deal in educational materials."

Agent Thanarat seemed to accept that. If he'd needed any reassurance that they had not the faintest suspicion of his past, he had it now. So far no one had come close to guessing that he had been on Imatra only as a heavily guarded felon in the process of transportation.

Well, given the near totality of local destruction, the fortunate absence of all records and all witnesses came as no surprise.

He was going to have to be careful, though. Obviously these investigators were seriously wondering whether he might possibly be goodlife—or else for some reason they were trying to make him think they entertained such a suspicion. *What could their reason be?*

"Mr. Havot? What are your plans now?"

"If you mean am I planning to leave the system soon, I haven't decided. I'm still rather in shock."

Havot was wondering whether he should now separate from Agent Thanarat, or cultivate her acquaintance and see what happened, when a very different kind of person arrived, whose objective turned out to be the same as hers, finding Havot and asking him some questions. Different, because elderly and male, and yet fundamentally not all that different, because also the representative of authority.

The newcomer, a uniformed military officer of formidable appearance, described himself as being attached to the staff of Commodore Prinsep, who was fleet commander of the relief force that had entered the system an hour or so too late to do much but rescue Havot from the field of desolation.

"The commodore would definitely like to see you, young fellow."

Havot glanced at Thanarat. She remained silent, but looked vaguely perturbed at the prospect of having her suspect—if Havot indeed fit in that category—taken away from her.

"Why not?" was Havot's response to the man. "I'm not busy with anything else at the moment." He smiled at Becky Thanarat; he much preferred to deal with two authorities rather than one, as such a situation always created some possibility of playing one off against the other. Still, he reacted rather coolly to the newcomer, and started grumbling, like your ordinary, innocent taxpaying citizen, about the unspecified suspicion to which he had just been subjected.

And got some confirmation of his own suspicions, as soon as he and the officer from Prinsep's staff were alone together in a groundcar, heading for a different part of the demolished spaceport. "Your real problem, Mr. Havot, may be that there were no other survivors."

"How's that?"

"I mean, there's no one else around, in this case, for agent Thanarat and her superiors to suspect of goodlife activity."

"Goodlife!" Havot felt sure that his look of stunned alarm was indistinguishable from the real thing. "You mean they really suspect *me*? That's ridiculous. We were just talking."

The officer pulled at his well-worn mustache. "I'm afraid certain people, people of the type who tend to become agents of the

Human Office, may have a tendency to see goodlife, berserker lovers, everywhere."

"But me? They can't be serious. Say, I hope that Commodore, uh—"

"Commodore Prinsep."

"Prinsep, yes. I hope *he* doesn't have any thought that I—"

"Oh, I don't think so, Mr. Havot." The officer was reassuring. "Just a sort of routine debriefing about the attack, I expect. You're about the only one who was on the scene that *we* have left to talk to."

In another moment the groundcar was slowing to a stop at the edge of a cleared-off, decontaminated corner of the spaceport once more open for business, and already busy enough to give a false impression of thriving commerce. In the square kilometer of land ahead, several ships—warships, Havot supposed—had landed and were now squatting on the ground like deformed metallic spheres or footballs. Their dimensions ranged from small to what Havot, no expert on ordnance, considered enormous. The surface details of some of the larger hulls were blurry with screens of force.

He and the officer got out of the car, and together started walking toward one of the smaller ships.

Currently, and Havot took comfort from the fact, there did not appear to be a crumb of evidence to support any charge of goodlife activity against him—beyond the mere fact of his survival, insofar as anyone might count *that* evidence.

Nor did he see, really, how any such evidence could exist. The truth was that the machine chasing him had been crippled. It had earnestly tried for some time to kill him, and its failure had not been for want of trying. Anyway, the damned machines were known to kill goodlife as readily as they slaughtered anyone else, once they computed that the usefulness of any individual in that category had come to an end.

Inwardly Havot's feelings were intensely mixed when he considered that name, that swear word, being seriously applied to himself. Like everyone else he knew, he had always considered goodlife to be slimy creatures—not, of course, that he had ever actually seen such a person, to his knowledge, or even given them any serious thought. And now, all of a sudden, he himself . . . well, it certainly was not the first time he had moved on into a new category.

As to that final moment before the crippled berserker turned away—well, something had happened, hadn't it? Some kind of transaction had taken place between him and the machine. Or so it had seemed to Havot at the time. So he remembered it now.

He and the killing machine had reached an understanding of some kind—? Or had they?

At the moment Havot couldn't decide in his own mind whether he ought to be taking this memory, this impression, seriously.

During that last confrontation, no words had been spoken on either side, no deal spelled out. Bah. How could he know now exactly what had been going through his own mind then, let alone what the machine's purpose might have been?

There was no use fooling himself, though. He brought the memory back as clearly as possible. He had to admit that the machine must have meant *something* by its odd behavior in letting him survive. Somehow it had expected Havot living to be worth more to the berserker cause than Havot dead. Because otherwise no berserker would have turned its back and let him go. Not when another five seconds of effort would have finished him off.

"I shouldn't worry." His escort, evidently misinterpreting Havot's grim expression, was offering reassurance. "The old man's not that hard to deal with, as a rule."

Boarding the space shuttle with his escort, Havot sighed. All his private, inward signs were bad, indicating that the Fates were probably about to treat him to some new kind of trouble. Whereas the old familiar kinds would have been quite sufficient.

There were indications that Commodore Prinsep might really be impatient for this interview. The small shuttle craft, carrying Havot and the officer from the fleet commander's staff, was being granted top-priority clearance into and through the fleet's formation space. Entering space in the steadily moving shuttle, Havot could see the surface of the water-spotted planetoid curved out below, already showing the results of the first stage of rehabilitation.

From casual remarks dropped by some of his fellow passengers, Havot soon learned that the reconstruction work had been suspended for the time being, at the fleet commander's order. Almost all energies were to be directed toward the coming pursuit of the enemy—as soon as everyone could be sure that the enemy was not about to double back and attack the system again.

And now, close above the rapidly rising shuttle, the fleet that hung in orbit seemed to be spreading out. Its fifteen or twenty ships made a hard-to-judge formation of dim points and crescents, picked out by the light of the distant Imatran sun.

Though unified under the command of one person—a high-ranking political (Havot gathered) officer of easygoing nature named Ivan Prinsep—the fleet was composed of ships and people from several planets and societies—all of them Solarian, of course.

Havot also overheard talk to the effect that Commodore Prinsep's task force, which had almost caught up with the marauding berserkers here, had been chasing the same machines, or some of them, for a long time, probably for months.

Unlike Dirac's berserker in the days of yore, these modern machines had approached Imatra from a direction almost directly opposite from that of the Mavronari Nebula. The task force, reaching the scene just in time to salvage Havot in his broken suit from the abandoned battlefield, had arrived from the same general direction as the berserkers, but several hours too late to confront them.

Havot was already mulling over the idea of trying to get taken along with the fleet as some kind of witness or consultant, or simply as a stranded civilian in need of help. That would certainly be preferable to waiting around on blasted Imatra or on one of the system's inner planets until Rebecca Thanarat and her suspicious colleagues had had time to check out his background.

Fortunately for Havot's cause, Fleet Commander Prinsep, rather than order a hot pursuit, had delayed in the Imatran system, waiting for reinforcements. While he waited, he had been managing at least to look busy by meeting with various authorities from the inward planets.

"Flagship's coming up, dead ahead."

Looking out of the shuttle through a cleared port, Havot beheld what must be a battle craft, or ship of the line, called the *Symmetry*. As they drew near he could read the name, clearly marked upon a hull that dwarfed those landed ships he had so recently judged enormous.

Moments later, the shuttle was being whisked efficiently in through a battle hatch to a landing on the flight deck amidships of the commodore's flagship.

Quickly Havot was ushered into a kind of bridge or command center, a cavernous place replete with armor and displays, everything he would have imagined the nerve center of a battleship to be.

Despite his escort's reassurances, he had been expecting a grim, no-nonsense warrior. Thus he was startled when he first set eyes on the commodore, a pudgy, vaguely middle-aged figure in a rumpled uniform.

Havot blinked. A few of the other chairs in the dim, dramatic room were occupied by organic humans, faces impassive, going on about their business. At the moment, the leader of the punitive task force was giving his full attention to a holostage beside his command chair, conducting a dialogue, discoursing learnedly in a petulant voice with some expert system regarding what sounded like a complicated arrangement of food and drink. Havot learned of things called Brussels sprouts and baked Alaska. Something called guacamole. Green chili-chicken soup.

The newcomer, realizing that he had not exactly entered the den of a tiger thirsting for combat, felt cheered by the discovery. So much, thought Havot, for any serious concerns he might have had about the dangers of combat if he accompanied the fleet on its departure.

The commodore's business with the menu had evidently been concluded. Now he turned his vaguely feminine and somewhat watery gaze on Havot, invited him to sit down, and questioned him about his experience with the berserker.

Havot, perching on the edge of another power chair nearby, told essentially the same story as before.

Prinsep, gazing at him sadly, prodded his own fat cheek with a forefinger, as if checking tenderly on the state of a sore tooth. But what the commodore said was: "The Humanity Office is interested in you, young man."

"I've discovered that, Commodore." Havot wondered just how ingratiating and pleasant he wanted to appear. Well, he certainly wasn't going to overdo it.

But his pudgy questioner, for the moment at least, was again distracted from any interest in his job—or in handsome young men. What must be today's dinner menu, complete with graphic illustrations, was taking now shape upon the nearby 'stage, and this drew the commodore's attention for a while.

But presently he was regarding his visitor again. "Hmf. For the time being, I believe you had better eat and sleep aboard this ship. I'll put you on as a civilian consultant; I want to talk to you at greater length about your experiences on the surface. Some of my people will want to conduct a proper debriefing."

Havot made a small show of hesitation, but inwardly felt ready to jump at the suggestion, not caring whether or not it really amounted to an order. Instinct told him that right now the Humanity Office were the people he had to worry about, and Prinsep seemed to offer the best chance of staying out of their clutches. Havot was still unclear on the precise nature of the HO. As a full-fledged organization devoted purely to anti-goodlife activity, it had no counterpart in the regions of the Solarian-settled Galaxy with which Havot was generally familiar. But on principle he loathed any governmental body that questioned and arrested people.

Somewhat to Havot's surprise, he had no sooner left the control room than he encountered Becky Thanarat again. Looking thoroughly at home here on the *Symmetry*, she greeted him in a friendly manner, told him she had come up to the flagship in an HO shuttle, and in general conducted herself as if she had a right to be aboard.

Privately, Havot felt a wary contempt for the cool and seemingly confident young agent. He thought he could detect some basic insecurity in her, and had already begun to imagine with pleasure how he would attempt her seduction if the opportunity should ever arise.

And he was ready to deal with more questions about berserkers, if the need arose. His calm denial, in his own mind, that he had ever trafficked with them did not even feel like lying. That confrontation with the killer machine had been quite real, but it had been a separate and distinct reality from this one—Havot was no stranger to this kind of dichotomy. It greatly facilitated effective lying—he had never yet met the lie detector that could catch him out.

Superintendent Gazin of the Imatran HO office, accompanied by Lieutenant Ariari, evidently one of his more senior agents, presently came to reinforce Becky Thanarat aboard the flagship.

Superintendent Gazin was a dark, bitter, and ascetic-looking man, and Ariari his paler-looking shadow. Both men gave Havot the impression of nursing a fanatical hatred not only of berserkers and goodlife, but of the world in general. That was not Havot's way; he rarely thought of himself as hating anyone.

It was soon plain that the superintendent and his trusted aide had come up to the flagship solely to see Havot, whom they now quickly summoned to a meeting.

The meeting took place in quarters assigned to the Office of Humanity representatives. The results, thought Havot, were inconclusive. He was not exactly threatened, but it was obvious that the OH was preparing, or trying to prepare, some kind of case against him.

Becky Thanarat seemed drawn to Havot by something other than sheer duty. Waiting for him in the semi-public corridor at the conclusion of the formal meeting, she informed him of word, or at least rumor, which had reached her, to the effect that legal minds at high levels were even now wrangling over a proposed declaration of martial law on the planetoid of Imatra. This would give prosecutors locally considerable power beyond what they were ordinarily permitted to exercise.

"Just wanted to warn you," she concluded.

"Thanks. Though I don't suppose there's much I can do about it. By the way, aren't you worried that your boss will see you socializing on jolly terms with me?"

"Not a bit. He's directed me to do just that."

"Oh. I see. To win my confidence?"

"And having done so, be witness to some damning admissions from your own lips."

"I take it you're not recording this?"

"Not yet, but I'm about to start. Ready? . . . there." He couldn't see that Becky had made any overt physical movement to turn anything on. Some alphatriggered device, no doubt.

Ultimately, Havot felt sure it would be up to the commodore to decide whether martial law should be declared, because Prinsep was camped here with the weapons and the power to do just about anything he liked.

The fleet commander did take action of a sort. Calling before him the people chiefly concerned, Prinsep, looking vaguely distressed in the presence of Havot and the OH people, considered the question of martial law.

"I don't understand this request." His voice, as usual, was petulant. "What smattering of legal knowledge I possess whispers to me that the purpose of martial law is the control of an otherwise unmanageable population."

One of his own aides nodded briskly. "That is correct, Commodore."

"Then I really fail to understand." He stared with watery eyes at the OH people. "What population are you trying to control, anyway? I get the idea, don't you know, that they're all dead hereabouts." The statement concluded with a final little shudder of repugnance.

At that point Humanity Office Superintendent Gazin, no doubt confident of his target, decided to try a lightly veiled threat. "There is only one proper way to approach the situation, Fleet Commander. Or perhaps for some reason you don't approve of the Humanitarian point of view in general?"

Prinsep only blinked at him and looked distressed. "Dear me. But whatever personal feelings I might have in the matter must surely be put aside. No, as a matter of military necessity, Superintendent, our only living witness to the attack must be kept available to the military, for ah, continued debriefing."

This was all, as far as Havot could see, political sparring. In fact the commodore and his advisers hadn't bothered Havot very much with questions so far. And however much Havot might have been willing to help, the fact was that he honestly could give them very little about berserkers. He thought of trying to fabricate some interesting tidbits, just to confirm the commodore's conviction of his usefulness, but decided that would be too risky.

Still Havot, despite his earlier forebodings, was convinced that things were now going well for him. Fortune still smiled, the furious Fates were held at bay, and he was content for the time being to wait in his newly assigned cabin, small but adequate, aboard the flagship *Symmetry*. In a day or two this impressive weapon was going to carry him safely out of the chaos of the Imatran system, whisk him away before any word of his true identity and legal status could arrive in-system and reach the anxious hands of Superintendent Gazin and his HO cohorts.

Havot had one worry: delay. He doubted very much that the gourmandizing commodore was going to break his neck hurrying after the fleeing berserker fleet. With fine wines and exotic foods to be enjoyed, why risk bringing about a real confrontation with that murderous collection of machines?

Now, having got through what he could hope would be his last unpleasant confrontation with the superintendent, Havot spent most of his time inspecting one shipboard display or another, or chatting with any crew members who happened to be free. He also took note of the fact that additional Solarian fighting ships kept appearing in-system at irregular intervals of hours or minutes, and attaching themselves to the fleet.

The continuing buildup of force was impressive. Arguably ominous. But Havot was not personally very much afraid of combat; and he still doubted seriously that Prinsep was the type of leader to make serious use of the strength he was being given.

He enjoyed arguing this, and other matters, with Becky Thanarat. And of course he took it for granted that she was recording him, even, or especially, when she assured him she was not.

As for Commodore Prinsep: all right, the man was jealous of his own prerogatives, and able to stand up for his own authority; but to go out and fight berserkers was a different matter. He'd go out and look for them, all right, but doubtless be careful not to come too close.

So much the better for Havot, who wasn't particularly anxious to ride into battle against berserkers. Not after his experience with one on the Imatran surface.

And yet, in the background, the ominous drum roll of preparation continued, hour after hour. Havot could not avoid being interested, drawn to the swift lethal combat scouts, some near spheres, some jagged silhouettes like frozen lightning, which darted past the *Symmetry* to descend to the Imatran surface, or nuzzled at their mother ships in low orbit.

A member of the flagship's crew informed Havot that some of these scouts, having just survived the perils of in-system jumping to intercept the relevant light, were bringing back the eagerly anticipated recordings of the berserker attack he alone had been lucky enough to survive.

Word drifted out of the fleet commander's quarters that Prinsep was now inspecting these video records of the recent raid. The OH people had also been given access to them, but evidently had been able to learn nothing offering new fuel for their suspicions.

To the suspect's vast relief, he soon learned—from Agent Thanarat, who was showing signs of becoming rather more than sympathetic—that the superintendent had been given permission to search the archives of the fleet, but had found there no evidence connecting Havot with crimes of any kind.

But Becky also confirmed, matter-of-factly, something Havot had already assumed: more than a day ago the superintendent had dispatched Havot's fingerprints and other identifying characteristics to one of the sunward planets. Communications were still upset because of the recent attack, but a response might be forthcoming at any time.

"Why in all the hells has he decided to pick on me?" Havot flared for just a moment—then he worried that the woman might have seen the predator's claws come out.

But it seemed that Becky hadn't noticed anything special in his reaction. She said: "I don't know. It might be just political; he's trying to boost the power of the Office any way he can." They walked on a little farther. "I don't know," she repeated. "When I signed up with them, I didn't think it would be like this."

"No?"

"No. I thought—I believed in what they always claim their objectives are, promoting the values of humanity, and . . ."

She fell abruptly silent, and her feet slowed to a stop. Havot was stopping, frozen too.

Emerging from around the next bend of corridor into their field of view, there walked upon a dozen stubby legs a barrel-shaped non-Solarian creature like nothing either of them had ever seen before. No more than a meter tall, but massive as a large man, dressed in something green and flowing . . .

"A Carmpan," Havot breathed. Then in the next moment he had rallied somewhat. Neither Havot nor Becky, like the vast majority of their fellow Solarians, had ever seen such a creature before except on holostages, where they, or rather skillfully imaged imitations, tended to show up frequently in fantastic space-adventure stories.

The creature—the Carmpan human—had evidently heard him. He—or she—paused and turned to the two young Solarians.

"I am called Fourth Adventurer." The words came tumbling, chopped but quite distinct, from a definitely non-Solarian mouth. "I am male, if this is of concern in how you think of me."

The Solarians in turn introduced themselves. Talking freely to both of them, but seeming especially interested in Havot, Fourth Adventurer explained that he had been for some years an accredited diplomat to several high Solarian powers, and for some months now a usually reclusive passenger on the *Symmetry*.

Fourth Adventurer soon invited both Havot and Thanarat to attend, as his guests, the commodore's next planning session.

Havot, at least, was intrigued. "I'd love to. If the commodore doesn't mind." And indeed it soon appeared that Prinsep had no objection to the young people's attendance, if the Carmpan diplomat wanted them there.

Once in the meeting, the Carmpan settled into his specially shaped chair, saying very little but seeming to listen attentively to everything.

There was only one rational reason, some Solarian proclaimed in a kind of opening statement, for berserkers to withdraw as precipitately as this particular set had done, from a target where their attack had been successful but had not yet been pushed to its deadly conclusion.

Someone else interrupted: "I don't see how they could even be sure they'd done as thorough a job as they really had. If they were playing by their own usual rules, they'd have stayed around at least a little longer to make sure that everything was dead."

"The only possible explanation is that their early withdrawal somehow gave them the opportunity of eventually being able to harvest still more lives—preferably human lives—here or somewhere else. Or they were convinced it would have that effect."

"And as we all know, their preferred target of all targets is human life—Solarian human in particular."

No one, least of all the listening Carmpan, disputed that point. Berserkers understood very well that only one species of life in the Galaxy—or at least in this part of it—seriously contested the dominance of the killing machines, really gave them a hard time in carrying out their mission. Therefore, in the berserkers' reversed scale of values, the elimination of one Earth-descended human life was worth the destruction of a vast number of animals or plants.

But then some other person in the discussion put forward a second possible reason for the enemy's withdrawal—though this possibility was really a variation of the first. Suppose the berserkers had captured some person or thing on the Imatran surface or had gained some information there—had somehow attained a prize that was to them of overwhelming value. So overwhelming, indeed, that their own advantage demanded that they carry this prize away with them at all costs, and without a moment's delay.

"Even if doing so meant leaving behind some human life unharvested."

"Even so."

Everyone turned involuntarily to look. It must, Havot realized, have been the first time the Carmpan had spoken in council.

⊛ SIXTEEN

This was the first time Havot had ever been aboard a warship, and he was somewhat surprised at how few people made up the crew of even a ship of the line, as leviathans like *Symmetry* were called. Onboard society was rather restricted, but it was interesting.

Havot's amusement grew from hour to hour, though he kept it well concealed. He was enjoying the situation. He liked to watch Commodore Prinsep, plump fingers fluttering, agonizing, in consultation with his robot chef, over his choices for tonight's dinner and tomorrow's lunch. He sat or stood about his office looking timid and seeming to waver, his mind on other things—and actually he did not yield a centimeter on anything of substance.

So Havot, confident that he still enjoyed the commodore's protection, was privately more amused than worried by the various maneuvers on the part of his potential persecutors. It appeared to him that he had little to worry about as long as he remained under the protective custody of the fleet commander. His current situation allowed him to lounge about in comfort in the wardroom, the library, or the gymnasium of the warship, or in the small private cabin he had been assigned. This cabin was fairly large, he gathered, by military standards, being about three paces square, big enough for bunk and table, chair and plumbing and holostage. It had probably been intended to house midlevel dignitaries who were visiting aboard or being transported.

The Carmpan, Fourth Adventurer, was housed in a similar room just down the corridor. And Havot, rather enjoying his constrained but comfortable stay aboard the flagship, and accustomed to feeling like an alien himself, felt some kinship with this other alien, who appeared to be doing very much the same thing.

Havot soon discovered that none of the Solarians aboard seemed to know the Carmpan's reason for having joined this expedition, though of course there was a lot of speculation. Fourth Adventurer was evidently too eminent a diplomat for anyone to risk offending, too important to be prevented from doing anything that he was seriously determined to accomplish. A great rarity indeed, a Carmpan traveling on a Solarian vessel far from any of the homeworlds of that race so everlastingly enigmatic to Earth folk.

Rumors of long standing had it that this race could do strange things with mental contact, telepathic achievement all but completely beyond Solarian capability. In Havot's mind that added a risk of discovery, a touch of danger. Fascinated, he found himself staring at the non-Solarian whenever the opportunity arose. If the Carmpan had any objection to this intense inspection, he said nothing.

Fourth Adventurer looked, to Solarian eyes, pretty much indistinguishable from the other Carmpan, real or image-faked, who appeared from time to time on holostage. Some Solarians described their race's slow and squarish bodies as machine-like, in contrast with their visionary minds.

A small handful of Carmpan individuals were famous in Solarian annals as Prophets of Probability, and Havot took the next good opportunity to ask Fourth Adventurer the truth about that title—or office, or activity. The young man admitted he did not know how it should be described.

"I prefer to speak on other topics," said Fourth Adventurer; and that was that.

Becky too was curious about their exotic fellow passenger. She reminded Havot of the famous historical scene shortly preceding the legendary battle of the Stone Place, where in all the dramatic re-creations a Prophet appeared, festooned with ganglions of wire and fiber stretching to make a hundred connections with Carmpan animals and equipment around him ...

"Show business," Havot commented scornfully. But he didn't know if he was right.

... and then Fourth Adventurer, at a moment when Becky happened to be absent, looked Havot over even as the Solarian impassively studied the blocky, slablike Carmpan body. At length the non-Solarian diplomat assured Havot that he, the young Solarian, must have been spared death at the hands of the berserkers for some good if still mysterious reason. It sounded to Havot as if the non-Solarian were talking about something like God's plan, even if the Carmpan did not use those exact words.

Havot was somewhat disappointed; he wasn't sure what he had expected from this exotic being, but something more. In his experience, anyone who professed a belief in a God was very likely to be cracked or, more likely, actively out to defraud his listeners.

But Havot did draw a pleasant, unexpected comfort from the fact that at least one influential person seemed to believe strongly in his, Havot's, fundamental innocence. One had to keep on meeting new people if one expected to enjoy that attitude; as soon as people got to know one, they tended to lose faith.

The HO Superintendent, still confidently on board, had demanded and received from Commodore Prinsep—who would not think of refusing any reasonable request by duly constituted authority—access to the recently obtained military recordings of the latest berserker attack. The same records, seized on eagerly by the intelligence analysts aboard, were broken into sections by computer, recombined, examined over and over again.

Certain facts could be solidly established by the recordings. Among these were the precise direction of the berserkers' hurried departure, and the strength of the force that had carried out the most recent attack. This fleet had included ten large spacegoing machines, each equipped with a small army of boarding devices, landers, and other infernal gadgets.

One or two of the berserker motherships and a large number of landers had been destroyed by the ground defenses, which had been greatly, if not sufficiently, improved since the last attack three centuries ago. No single berserker, not even one the size of Dirac's, which had dwarfed the more modern units, would have succeeded in this year's raid. But still this year's enemy fleet had been too strong.

The strategists and would-be strategists on board the *Symmetry* scratched their chins and rubbed their eyes and pondered: what was the significance of the direction of the enemy fleet's departure?

"There's just nothing out that way but the Mavronari . . . of course it's possible they deliberately headed out-system in the wrong direction, trying to mislead us as to their ultimate destination."

"That's hardly consistent with their being in such a rush that they couldn't spare five seconds to clean up one more human life."

By means of diligent and clever computer enhancement, tricks performed by the warship's expert graphics systems, the video record from deep space could be made to show with surprising clarity certain details of the planetoid's surface during the attack. Details as fine as a rough image of the individual machine, only a little larger than a man, that had been chasing Havot.

Some of the enhancements of the action on the surface even displayed a barely discernible dot, which all analysts agreed was probably the armor-suited Havot himself.

Superintendent Gazin and Ariari, his senior agent, also spent some time watching this part of the show over and over, displaying keen interest and suspicion. But the OH representatives must have been disappointed; they saw nothing to suggest overt goodlife activity on Havot's part.

The only thing even ambiguously suspicious in the recorded images was the apparent hesitancy of the killing machine that had confronted Havot. And even that could be explained by the fact that it was crippled.

Havot, on expressing a modest curiosity, was invited by the commodore to take a look at the recording.

The young man managed to get the seat next to Agent Thanarat at the next showing, and made some further impression on her.

To the suspect's relief it proved impossible to derive from the little dancing images any evidence about most of the things he had actually been doing to get himself away from one of the enemy.

Of course to the senior Humanity agent, and to the superintendent of the Office, the enhanced pictures of Havot on the Imatran surface looked pretty damned suspicious. Or so they claimed.

"We're trying to get a line on this man, and eventually we will—but right now communications throughout the system are pretty much in turmoil, as you might expect."

Havot felt comfortably confident that no local record of his presence at the spaceport, as a convicted murderer undergoing transportation, had survived the raid. Of course sooner or later, if he stayed around, his fingerprints or other ID were going to doom him.

Meanwhile Commodore Prinsep and his staff were continuing their own study of the maddeningly enigmatic images of the attack, a study in which Havot's individual conduct or fate played only a small part.

During the last phase of the onslaught, a number of small berserker auxiliaries could be seen at various points on the Imatran surface. All the machines still fully functional were lashing about them with death rays and other weapons, laboring methodically at their endless task of sterilizing the universe.

Someone, muttering in surprise, stopped the show, freezing the recorded berserkers temporarily in their tracks. "Back up, and let's take a look at that again." The recording was run back a few seconds and then restarted. It was no mistake, no glitch in the recording. All the berserkers of the landing party simultaneously dropped what they were doing—the machine that had been menacing Havot turned away in step with all the rest. And all of them went darting for their respective landing craft, the vehicles that had brought them to the surface.

Plainly all the berserkers on the surface had begun to retreat at precisely the same time, within a fraction of a second.

"This could have been the miracle that saved our friend Havot—yes, I would say that's very likely. Just look at the timing here."

Prinsep, his attention called to the timing of the berserker retreat, was very much impressed.

"Their motherships must have transmitted a recall signal, virtually simultaneously, to all their machines on the ground."

"Obviously. But the speed of the response by the landing devices suggests something more than an ordinary recall signal. I mean, this was something with a real *priority*. It stopped them all in their tracks!"

"We haven't been able to catch up with any such transmission, but you're right. It must have been a command of the highest priority, overriding everything else, ordering all the landers in effect to drop whatever they were doing and come home to mother at once."

"As if their mothers were suddenly fearful of a trap?"

"No, I don't think so. Let's not get into using the word 'fear' when we assign motives to berserkers. Their own survival in itself means absolutely nothing to them. The only real value they esteem is death. And observe that for whatever reason their motherships did not abandon their landing machines. They waited for every last one of them before heading out of the system."

"Right. I was about to comment that the damned pigs got every one of their fighting machines back on board, even those which had been seriously damaged, before they left."

"And that tells us—?"

"It tells me that the berserkers expected to need all of their fighting strength whenever they got to wherever they were going next."

"Perhaps they pulled out because word had just reached them, of some new target—?"

There was a muttering around the table, and a shuffling of imaged documents. "What target could possibly rate such a high priority that it would cause them to abandon this attack?"

"Possibly it wasn't another target at all, in that sense. Possibly the enemy hurried away to defend one of their own bases, some real nerve center, against some kind of threat?"

"I don't get it. Here's a fleet fully engaged in an attack. How could they have suddenly discovered a new target while all their attention was focused on this one? Or how could they have learned that one of their own bases needed help? They didn't receive any incoming message couriers while the fight was going on."

"Are you sure?"

"None that we could detect."

"We've been looking pretty closely at these recordings, and they are pretty good; I think we're about ready to rule out any additional radio signals of key importance—where would one come from? And we have to assume that we'd be able to detect the arrival of even a small courier."

"All right; but if we grant that, we seem to be forced to the conclusion that something the berserkers learned *here*, on Imatra, while the fighting was still in progress, forced them into a very abrupt and drastic change of plans."

"It does look that way. Something . . . but where on the planetoid did they learn anything? And what was it they learned?"

No one could come up with an answer.

Meanwhile the methodical electronic sieving of in-system space for useful signals continued. Gradually it became possible to rule out any chance that the berserkers, while in the midst of their attack, had received a communication from others of their kind elsewhere. In theory, radio and laser signals could not be entirely eliminated, but such means of communication were hopelessly slow over interstellar distances, though eminently useful near at hand. In any case there did not seem to have been any particularly interesting signals creeping through nearby space while the attack was going on.

"Then what are we left with?"

"All we can find out just reinforces the conclusion that the enemy, in the course of their raiding and ravaging the surface, discovered something *on the planetoid*. Something or some piece of information that they considered overwhelmingly important. So vital to their cause that responding to it in an appropriate way took precedence over everything else. Everything!"

"A thing, or a piece of information. Such as what?"

"Possibly something this man Havot passed to one of them. We really don't know who he is."

"Bah. I can't credit that. Why should a man spend an hour or more running away from a berserker if he intended passing it information? But then if it wasn't something they somehow gained from Havot, what was it? I haven't the faintest idea. Let's run that last sequence again."

In the course of the next playback, one berserker lander in particular caught someone's attention. This device, several kilometers from Havot's position, appeared to have gone underground, the only instance of one of the marauders doing so.

"What's there? In that place where it went down?"

Someone pulled up a diagram on holostage. "This map just says 'archive.'"

"See if we can find out something to clarify that."

The common information utility on Imatra was readily available, but it had been left in strands and fragments by the attack. At the moment it was not much good for answering even the simplest questions.

"We'll keep trying. Meanwhile let's take another look at this recording."

Commodore Prinsep ordered an increased enhancement of the sequence of events from three minutes before to three minutes after the sudden berserker decision to withdraw. The job at this level of difficulty took several minutes for the computer to accomplish.

When the computer's organic masters looked at the latest, most intensely enhanced version, they saw the berserker landing device reemerge from underground to stand perfectly still for a moment facing its mothership at a distance of more than a kilometer—almost out of line-of-sight, around the sharp curvature of the small planetoid. The emergence of the unit from the archive came just a hair-trigger interval before the recall command was transmitted—time perhaps for a human being to shout a warning or draw a gun. Too swift a response to be accepted as purely coincidental, too slow to be merely routine. The berserker command computers had devoted a couple of seconds—for them a vast gulf of time—to calculation before making their decision to withdraw as rapidly as possible.

Still, the devastated Imatran information banks could not be induced to say anything more informative about the underground archive buried at that point on the planetoid's surface.

"Could just be a coincidence after all, this one unit coming up out of the ground just there, and then the recall being sent a few seconds later."

"I tend not to believe in coincidences." Prinsep's voice was for once not tentative. "I want to go down there as soon as possible, travel physically to the place where it says 'archive,' and take a first-hand look."

Within a couple of hours a group comprising most of the strategic planners, including key members of the commodore's staff, had shuttled down to the Imatran surface. There they were soon crowded into a single much smaller vehicle, and headed for the location of the mysterious underground facility.

The Carmpan had stayed aboard the flagship, but Havot had come down with the group—no one tried to stop him. And Becky Thanarat, of course, to keep an eye on him for the Humanity Office.

Not much of any construction on the surface of Imatra had been left standing. But neither had all of the housing, all the conference centers and other public buildings, been totally obliterated. Here and there a few units even appeared intact. The remnant still standing included some relatively old, quaint-looking structures. Havot had heard that these had been designed to imitate certain buildings back on Earth, though most people who saw this fairly common style had no idea where it had originated. The majority of those who lived on or visited Imatra, like most Solarians across the settled Galaxy, had never been to Earth—unless colonists had come here directly from the original homeworld.

Arriving at the spot in an antigrav flyer, the investigators, all wearing respirators, stood regarding the charred and shattered aperture, of a size to accommodate an ordinary stairway, which evidently led down to some kind of subterranean installation.

None of the people present had been familiar with Imatra in its normal configuration; several had never set foot on it before. Nothing they were looking at now gave them any clue as to why the small berserker might have come to this place, or what it might have unearthed.

"Just what was stored down there, anyway?"

"One way to find out."

Fortunately several people had had the forethought to bring flashlights. The stone stairs themselves, and what could be seen of a door standing partially open at their foot, appeared to be essentially undamaged.

"Let's go down."

But one of the investigators dallied, standing at the head of the stair. Said she, frowning: "Something doesn't feel right about this."

Whoever had started down the stairs now paused and turned. "What do you mean?"

"Look, I'm a killer machine, standing right here, as the recording shows. I've come from that way." A thumb over a shoulder indicated a direction. "Over there"—pointing in a different direction—"on ground level, readily accessible, I can see a house, looking undamaged. Over that way's another one. So, do I take a shot at either building? Or do I rush over and check 'em out, see if there's anyone hiding inside? No. Instead I choose to blast open the door to this underground vault."

"Maybe the machine saw someone in the act of taking shelter down here. Or it somehow detected signs of life from underground. Heard breathing, or . . ."

There seemed little point in continued speculation, when the truth might be readily available. In silence the little company started to file down the stairs. Then someone had a thought. "I'm not absolutely sure that our machines have checked this out yet, though they've covered most of the surface. Better watch out for booby traps."

On that suggestion the company retreated, promptly enough, back up the stairs, and a robot was summoned. None had been brought along, because all of the useful, versatile robots were extremely busy just now. But this group of investigators had high priority when they chose to assert it. Within a couple of minutes one of the busy machines now engaged in rehabilitating/decontaminating the nearby surface had been temporarily commandeered.

It was a man-sized crawler with many useful limbs, and like other advanced robots built by the children of Earth, it possessed intelligence of a sort. But it also resembled its fellows in being anything but anthropomorphic in physical or intellectual design.

Docilely the eight-limbed device received its orders, acknowledged them in its pleasing mechanical voice, and nimbly descended the stair.

The doors at the bottom no longer offered any obstacle to entry. They appeared to have been blasted or broken by the berserker.

The people waiting on the surface tuned in their wrist-video units and watched the pictures sent back by the investigating robot. Inside the first door below had been a stronger set, now also demolished.

Beyond the shattered doors the remote video showed extensive ruin occupying a space the size of a small house. At first glance there was nothing particularly interesting about more piles of rubble. The underground vault showed no immediate sign of human or even animal casualties.

Within a minute or two the robot, having stomped and vibrated its way backward and forward through the debris, pronounced the area free of booby traps.

"Can we believe that?"

"It would really be an oddity if the enemy had planted any such devices here. We haven't found any elsewhere on the planetoid's surface."

"Is that unusual?"

"I'd say so. If this had been an ordinary raid with landers, setting traps would have been their last step before withdrawing."

"Nothing ordinary about this operation. Everything seems to confirm the idea that once the damned machines decided to pull out, they were unwilling to delay their departure by a single second. Shall we go down?"

Moments later the humans were gathered at the foot of the stairs, inside the broken doors, gazing directly at devastation in the brightness of the robot's lights. From here it was easy to see that this was, or had been, an archive designed to hold physical samples—of something. It was a common way of insuring that electronic data would not be lost—keep copies disconnected, physically separated, from all electronic systems, preventing electronic accidents or vandalism.

People who had brought their own lights flashed them around. The room had been arranged in narrow aisles between rows of tall cabinets. Enough of some of the cabinets had survived to show that each had many drawers, many if not all of the drawers subdivided into small compartments. Gingerly at first, then more freely, people picked up samples.

"These are recordings. Mostly civic records of various kinds. Videos of meetings, celebrations . . . This was not meant to be a bombproof vault. There seems to have been no great effort made toward preserving these against accident or attack."

The drawers and cabinets held little boxes, for the most part made of ordinary plastic or metal or composite materials. At the request of one human investigator, the helpful robot plugged one of the records into its own thorax and played it. The robot's upper surface became a simple holostage. The video with sound displayed people sitting around a table, what had to be a local Imatran council meeting of some kind. They were discussing the esthetics of a new spaceport.

"Hardly news to shake the empire of death to its foundations. Can we be sure the berserker didn't just come down here chasing someone?" He scraped a booted foot across the singed and littered floor. "A human body might have been completely—destroyed."

The robot, given new and more precise instructions, began at once to take samples from the new air, and from several of the scorched surfaces within the vault. Even before gathering its last sample, it assured its masters that analysis was proceeding without delay.

While they were waiting for the results, someone said: "At least there doesn't seem to have been anything as big as a cat or dog in here when the berserker roasted the place."

Within a minute the robot interrupted the humans' conversation to assure them in its soft droning voice that it was highly unlikely any organic mass the size of a human body had recently been burned or fragmented in this room.

The commodore sniffed disdainfully. "'Fragmented'—yes, an evocative suggestion."

"Well? I think, sir, we can eliminate simple killing as that berserker's purpose in coming down here.

"But the course it followed over the surface, from its mothership to the entrance to this archive, suggests that it was making a beeline for this place."

Somebody commented on the diversity of information storage systems represented in the surviving drawers and cabinets. "Not everything here is standardized, far from it, though one can observe a long-term tendency in that direction. Some of these, perhaps most of them, seem to go back centuries."

"Presumably berserkers conduct intelligence operations just as we do. Any organization would want to learn about the way its enemies, in this case Solarian humans, store data."

"About all the damned machines could have gleaned by rummaging around down here is a history of the ways their enemies saved information a few hundred years ago—sorry, I just can't see them being overwhelmingly interested. Not so fascinated that they'd break off a successful attack in progress, just to communicate the secret techniques of the Imatran archive a little more quickly to some hypothetical distant confederates of theirs."

"All right. Then if it wasn't Imatra's antique storage methods they found so fascinating, it must have been something else. How about the *information* in one or more of these old files? Is that what set them roaring off at top speed, squeaking 'Eureka!' in a berserker voice?"

"Is there any way we can find out just what, if anything, the machine actually removed from this room?"

The discussion went on. Havot found himself being ignored for the time being; he had been all the help that he was going to be. He might be able to walk away unnoticed, hide himself and disappear. But what would he do then?

Meanwhile, he was having no more luck than anyone else in figuring out why the berserkers should have been rooting around down in this cellar. He was trying to picture the machine that had almost killed him, reacting to something in its orders, in its programming, so that instead of seeking breathing victims it had come down here . . . but come down here to do what? Anyway, this machine had been a different one altogether.

The degree of destruction inside the vault augured serious difficulty in determining what materials might be missing.

Everyone in the group pondered this problem for a while. Havot, entering into the spirit of things—asked: "What chance is there that all the files here were kept in duplicate somewhere else?"

Someone responded: "The Imatran society enjoys a reputation as good record keepers. I'd say it's worth looking into."

Information from someone who had dealt with the late local authorities confirmed that the general policy was to create duplicates.

Prinsep nodded. "Good. Let's find them if they exist. Meanwhile I want some people and machines down here, working to restore this junk to its original condition, or at least identifying it as accurately as possible. Whatever items appear to be completely missing, we'll hypothesize that perhaps the berserker took them, and see where that gets us."

Within an hour it had been determined that a duplicate archive did exist on one of the Imatran system's sunward planets. It would be possible to get any record—or a VR simulation of it—beamed to the planetoid in a few hours by radio, which was still the fastest dependable communication this close to a sun.

The commodore and his people were soon back on the flagship, while a hastily assembled team in the devastated archive began the task of reconstruction.

Within a few hours the first stage of their job had been completed.

According to the reconstruction, there was at least an eighty percent probability that the records taken by the berserker lander were those dealing with the famous raid of nearly three hundred years before.

"That's the one where some oddball berserker, historians call it Dirac's berserker now, grabbed the bioresearch station right out of orbit and carried it off."

"I don't remember that story, I grew up a long way from here. It carried off a what? A bioresearch station, you say?"

"Yes, a sizable spacegoing lab—actually it seems to have been kind of a pilot plant for a huge colonization project that never really got going. And then, if I remember correctly, within a matter of days after the attack, Premier Dirac, whose bride happened to get carried away with the station, was here in-system, putting together a small squadron of ships, making brave speeches and rushing off to get her back."

"How romantic."

"I guess. His whole squadron disappeared with all hands—that was the expedition where Colonel Marcus was lost."

"Colonel who?"

"You're not up on the history of the Berserker Wars, are you? Never mind, I'll show you later."

Duplicate Imatran records of the old raid, urgently requested, would soon be on their way from one of the sunward worlds by tight-beam transmission and should be available on the flagship in a few hours. Meanwhile, now that the investigators had some idea of what they were looking for, they could call up routine news reports from the days immediately following that attack; some were available in the flagship's general information banks.

Easily discernible in these records was the course taken by Dirac's berserker in its flight. The cylindrical research station, being towed behind the enemy by forcefields, was briefly but clearly visible.

"Now here we are a few days later. And there go Dirac's three ships, following exactly the same course."

"Yep. So what good does this information do us?"

"I don't know. My first reaction is, that as berserker attacks go, that one seems to have been truly unique. A very different kind of oddity from ours. The raid three centuries ago inflicted very little surface damage on Imatra."

Prinsep, working and giving orders in his unhurried, dogged way, kept everyone moving productively. Several times he repeated: "I want to know more about that bioresearch station."

The official history was fairly easy to come by.

At dinner that evening in the *Symmetry*'s wardroom, the discussion turned briefly to the general subject of colonization, on which opinions had not changed all that enormously in three hundred years.

"How long have we—Solarian humans—been trying to colonize the Galaxy, anyway?"

"I don't know—a thousand years?"

Some problems had not changed that much, either. There still remained in Solarian societies the question of what to do with inconvenient zygotes and fetuses. It was true that Solarian planets now in general seemed to produce fewer of these problem items than in Premier Dirac's day.

Continued discussion of the subject elicited from someone a mention of von Neumann probes.

"What were they?"

"It's an ancient scheme, a theory, going way back, to when all the Earth-descended folk in the Galaxy were actually still on Earth.

"The theory outlines techniques by which a civilization of quite modest technology, starting on one planet, would supposedly be able to explore the entire Galaxy in a quite reasonable time—even without the benefit of superluminal drive. To make it work properly, though, you have to be able to design some very smart and capable machines. And to overcome some serious problems in the engineering and construction. But the real problem appears, of course, when you send out your unmanned probes. At that point you have to really turn them loose—say goodbye and let them go, to roam the Galaxy unsupervised. You must be willing to let them represent you, your whole species, in whatever encounters they may have. These devices have to be self-repairing and self-replicating, like berserkers; able to improve their own design, like berserkers again. And with industrial capabilities, for mining and smelting ore and so on, that can easily be employed as formidable weapons."

More than one among the listeners shuddered faintly.

"Just send them out unsupervised?"

"That was the idea."

"Have Solarians ever actually built anything like that?"

"I'd have to look it up."

"Try. It shouldn't take long."

And it did not. The ship's general archive soon provided answers: Few people in recent centuries had thought it a good idea to send out von Neumann probes, either in slowship or c-plus form. Not in a galaxy known to be infested by true berserkers. Not when such devices necessarily contained in some form the Galactic coordinates at which the people who sent them could be found.

The archive even obligingly produced an example or two of worlds, branches of Solarian civilization, which in the very early years of the berserker encounter had implemented such a plan and had lived just long enough to regret it.

☀ SEVENTEEN

Havot got a kick out of waiting for the Humanity Office people to revise their initial opinion of the commodore. Havot was ready to admit that he himself had been fooled at first. Almost everyone, on first meeting Ivan Prinsep, must get the impression that he was a decadent creampuff, who had been given command of this expedition as an exercise in politics—that much at least, Havot had heard, was true—who intended to conduct it as an exercise in fancy dining and other indulgence, meanwhile looking for some way to abandon the pursuit well before it became really dangerous. It hadn't taken Havot himself long to become convinced that this first impression was mistaken; but he thought that Superintendent Gazin and his troops still had an awakening coming.

All components of the combat fleet that had descended to the planetoid's surface were now lifting off again under pressure of the commodore's relentless though unstressed orders. The desired information about the buried archive was on its way from one of the sunward worlds, and otherwise essential readiness had been achieved. The rising craft rendezvoused in low orbit with their fellows, and the entire fleet—eighteen ships, according to the last count Havot had heard—set out together.

Despite the efforts at rehabilitation Havot had witnessed on the planetoid's surface, the task force was leaving behind it a deserted, practically uninhabitable body. The planetoid's gravitational augmenters had been demolished. Its remaining atmosphere was once more racked by horrendous winds, so in a matter of days probably only a dead surface would remain. This time, in contrast with the situation of three hundred years ago, all of the local leadership, the people with the greatest interest in revitalizing and rebuilding, had been wiped out. This time the military left only robots behind on Imatra, certain machines of little value in combat, but capable of working industriously with a minimum of human supervision to restore that planetoid's hard-won habitability.

Officially, the restoration work had now been temporarily, perhaps indefinitely, postponed. In fact it might really have been completely abandoned. Two raids in three centuries, and we give up—in this case, anyway.

The duplicate archive material, transmitted in a tight beam from an inner planet in virtual reality format, arrived on the *Symmetry* before the task force had made much headway getting out of the system.

Other urgent information, this concerning Havot personally, came in at about the same time, specially coded for the Humanity Office. Agent Thanarat signed a receipt for the message and took it away for private decoding.

A few minutes later, she sought out Havot privately, and demanded: "I want you to explain something to me."

From the change in her look, her manner, he suspected what had happened.

But he was innocently cheerful. "Gladly, if I can."

"There's a—" Becky started, temporarily lost the power of speech, and had to start again. Her voice was taut, withholding judgment. "Read this. I'd like to hear what you have to say about it." And she thrust toward him a solid, secret, nonelectronic piece of paper, the kind of form often employed for very confidential messages and records.

Meanwhile, people who had been waiting for the data from the duplicate Imatran archive now hurried to the flagship's VR chamber. Others were already in that spacious room, doing some preliminary studies.

The two senior Humanity investigators were on hand, waiting for the information as anxiously as anyone. The OH Superintendent, in making his decision to accompany the expedition, remained smugly confident that Prinsep was going to turn back, or proceed to some other safe system, before he actually caught up with any berserkers.

Meanwhile, some of the people milling about on the lower level of the ten-cube were arguing ancient history.

The old suspicion, going back nearly as far as the event itself, would not die, however illogical it might be: that Premier Dirac, feeling his base of power slipping, had somehow arranged the whole disastrous attack and kidnapping himself. Proponents of this theory claimed that the Premier had lived in hiding for a long time afterward, even that he was still alive somewhere, on some remote world. The corollary, of course, was that the supposed berserker he had been chasing had really been nothing of the kind, but rather a ship under the control of Dirac's human allies. Or else, an even more sinister accusation, Dirac had made some kind of goodlife bargain with the real thing.

Those who gave credence to these theories were not swayed by the fact that no one had ever been able to generate a shred of evidence to support any of them. The most persistent suspicion, a common element in all the theories, was that in one way or another the berserker of three centuries ago had not been genuine. Some people, none of whom were considered tough-minded experts in the subject, still argued for that.

On the other hand, if Dirac's berserker was accepted as genuine, then anyone who had arranged a deal with that machine undoubtedly qualified as goodlife. Any evidence that Dirac had tried to arrange such a deal might cast doubt on the legitimacy of all claims made by his modern heirs.

Havot meanwhile was now alone with Becky Thanarat in her small cabin—a mere cubicle, smaller than his own—and for the past few minutes he had been making an all-out effort to explain away the damning information which had just arrived.

"You do believe me, don't you? Becky? Love?" The young man had no difficulty in sounding genuinely stricken.

At the moment she was once more having trouble speaking.

"I *mean* . . ." Havot did the best he could to generate a tone of amused contempt. "Murder, rape, knifings and torture . . . how many victims am I supposed to have destroyed? What did they say, again?" He reached politely for the paper; she handed it over. He waved it in distress. "Some really improbable total. You see, they rather overplayed their hand. Much more convincing if they'd simply said I was wanted for accidental manslaughter somewhere."

"Explain it to me again." She was sitting on her bunk, her hands white-knuckled clutching at the mattress, while he stood in the middle of the little private space. He almost had her; she was wavering. No, he really did have her, she was wavering so hard. She was begging to be convinced. "How there could be a mistake like this. You say these enemies of yours are—"

"It's a local police department." He named a real planet, very distant naturally. "Very corrupt. How I became their enemy is a long story, and it shows just how rotten and ugly the world can be. I'm sure they'll be able to explain this message convincingly, when they're eventually called to account for it, by saying it's all some horrible computer error. That they innocently confused me with some real psychopath somewhere. Meanwhile they can hope I'll be shackled, mistreated, or even killed . . . are there any other copies of this aboard, love?"

Becky slowly shook her head. Hope, her lover's vindication, was winning the struggle in her mind. In another minute or two she might be able to start to smile.

"Think. Sure there aren't? This would cause me no end of trouble if your boss got hold of it."

"I'm sure." Already a very attenuated, virtual-reality smile was struggling to be born. "We don't want spare copies of any of our confidential communications floating around."

"Good." And he crumpled the paper softly in his fist.

Meanwhile, at the flagship's ten-cube, a planning meeting was informally in session, being presided over by the commodore himself.

"I say we must concern ourselves with ancient history. What we must endeavor to determine now, my people, is just what today's berserkers find so compelling about this record." Prinsep tapped a pudgy finger on the case. "As we have seen, it delineates their own—or their predecessors'—attack upon the Imatran system three hundred years ago. Can we deduce why our current enemies should be so interested in history?"

"It may help, sir, if we take a closer look."

"By all means."

People who wanted to experience to the full the chamber's powers and effects were required on entering to put on helmets equipped with sensory and control feedbacks. Some were starting to do that now, getting ready to scrutinize the new information as intensely as possible when it came in. A thousand cubic meters of interior space made the flagship's VR chamber as large as a small house—few spaceships of only moderate size indulged in the luxury of having one. Such a generous volume allowed a party of a dozen or more to participate simultaneously in reasonable comfort—and this time there were almost that many.

Once inside, taking advantage of force supports and a few rubbery, polyphase matter projections from the walls—and of the partial nullification of artificial gravity inside the chamber's walls—those experienced in this game showed others how they could leap and climb and "swim" about in almost perfect freedom and safety.

A display on one wall listed the titles of some of the software available. Posted almost invisibly was even a game list, including items called JUNGLE VINES, MASTS AND RIGGING, and CITY GIRDERS.

No time for games today. Someone already had a model of the Milky Way Galaxy up and running.

The idea had been to avoid wasting time, to keep from looking as if one were wasting time—and also to take a look at the Mavronari, in hopes of coming up with some clue as to why one berserker attack force after another had attacked the same planetoid and then fled into the same shelter, taking precisely the same direction.

The first scene evoked in GALACTIC MODEL showed an overview of the whole Galaxy. The central, lens-shaped disk was some thirty kiloparsecs, or about one hundred thousand light-years, in diameter. The component spiral arms of this great wheel were surrounded by a much vaguer and dimmer englobement of individual stars, star clusters, clouds of gas and dust, and an assortment of other objects considerably less routine.

The brightest region in the display represented what was generally known to the Solarian military as CORESEC. This was the Galactic core, a star-crowded, roughly spherical volume perhaps a thousand light-years in diameter, holding at its unattainable center some of the unfathomable mysteries of creation.

There at the Galaxy's very heart lay, among other things, that great enigma which for the last several centuries Solarian humanity had called the Taj, a name devised as a military code word but soon generally adopted as expressing the exotic and magnificent.

Only a few Earth-descended beings had ever reached even the outer strata of the Taj, and fewer still had ever managed to return. Notable among the very few had been the legendary Colonel Frank Marcus, missing for the last three hundred years upon another quest. Nor had any of that harrowed and honored handful been able to bring much information away with them from the Galactic heart—and what little news they had gathered there did not encourage further attempts at exploration.

In fact only about five percent of the Galaxy's volume had ever been explored by Solarian ships, and much of that exploration had been nominal, a mere cataloguing of stars of beacon brightness, a mapping of the more substantial and readily visible nebulae and of the flow of subspace currents in the quasi-mathematical understrata of reality, that still-almost-unknown realm where c-plus travel could be brought within the range of possibility.

The approximate center of Solarian territory lay at Sol System, three-quarters of the way out from CORESEC to the Rim, along the great spiral curve of what was still called the Orion-Cygnus arm (after a pair of constellations in old Earth's night sky). From one point on the roughly outlined sphere of ED dominion, a narrow tendril of exploration went snaking in, a symbol of Earth-descended boldness, to touch and barely penetrate the Core. The snaking indirectness was due to the unusually difficult physics of travel in that part of the Galaxy.

Within the small part of the Milky Way's volume through which the ships of Earth had traveled, intelligent life forms were breathtakingly rare. Certainly many more sterile planets had been discovered than those bearing even elementary forms of life. And there were far more of the latter than there were of those on which organic intelligence had actually bloomed. Among contemporary intelligent races, the Solarians were almost uniquely aggressive; not until berserkers entered Earth-descended territory had the killing machines ceased to enjoy their hunting almost unopposed.

The Carmpan were the unearthly, extraterrestrial, variant of humanity with whom the expanding Solarians had had most contact—and there had been precious little of that. Against berserkers the Carmpan Prophets of Probability had on occasion given great though indirect assistance.

The other organic thinkers known currently to inhabit the Galaxy were even less well known and understood among Solarians than were the Carmpan. Even more retiring and shadowy than the Carmpan, they appeared utterly repelled by the idea of face-to-face confrontation with their violent Solarian cousins on neutral ground, let alone by the possibility of opening their homeworlds to such visitors.

Not that these others were really hostile to the strange folk from Sol, under whose shield of protective violence their several races still survived. Nor were they unwilling to express their gratitude.

Only the distant Builders and their ancient opponents, both their races all but completely invisible behind the barricades of time, seemed to have been similar in mind and behavior to the offspring of Earth. Of the Builders' organic foes, not even a name now survived—but evidently they too had been combative. There was one word of their language left, a name, *qwib-qwib,* denoting a kind of machine they had evidently built to hunt out and destroy berserkers. That had proved dangerous hunting—it was uncertain whether in all the Galaxy a single *qwib-qwib* yet survived. And of the Builders themselves, their own all-too-effective weapons, the berserkers, had left nothing but a few obscure records—video and voice recordings. Those videos had recorded slender, fine-boned beings, topologically like Solarian humans with the sole visible exception of the eye, which in the Builder species was a single organ, stretching clear across the upper face, with a bright bulging pupil that slid rapidly back and forth.

One statement about the Galaxy was certainly possible to make with confidence—that among its hundred billion stars and planetary systems, a vast number of surprises, happy and otherwise, still awaited the determined explorer.

Everyone gathered in the ten-cube room today had used similar devices before, though the design was not completely standardized, and some initial confusion arose. Each VR helmet presented its wearer with a visual keyboard, floating in apparent space at the lower left or lower right—the wearer's choice—of the visual field. The controls were accessible through directed vision and practiced will—no hands necessary. Some users found it easier to manage by means of eyeblinks.

One of the basic controls managed the scale of the display; the effect produced was as if the wearer's body were shrinking or swelling to accommodate the wish to explore or observe, at one level or another of physical size.

The vast majority of the stars appearing in the display were only statistical approximations, artifacts of the VR computer. But information on several million real stars and systems had also been fed in from the standard astrogation models.

The computer at the moment was using no color or other distinguishing shading to represent berserker territory. In fact, as the slow tide of the long conflict ebbed and flowed, it would have been impossible to delimit that wasteland with anything like up-to-date accuracy. Nor could anyone say with any substantial probability where the damned machines had originated, though the captured records, sketchy as they were, offered a tersely convincing explanation of how they had come into being.

In this particular display, a somewhat outdated version of their domain of devastation could be marked out, demarcated by tagging the suns of all the worlds known to have been attacked in the era of Solarian civilization. A smaller domain, largely enclosed within the first, represented that of the planets known to have been sterilized of life.

One of the investigators had now keyed in these presentations, evoking a strategic situation inevitably some years out of date. No one in the group now gathered expected to find in this database much in the way of berserker bases, factories, or strongholds.

If some person of ordinary height, employing the witchcraft of virtual reality within this chamber, swelled in a moment by a factor of a billion in physical height and width, he or she was still somewhat less than two billion meters (two million kilometers) tall. The observer was now in effect much bigger than the biggest planet, yet in his eyes the scale of the surrounding display, as far as its more distant reaches were concerned, seemed hardly to have changed.

His body length had now become comparable to the diameter of Sol, a roughly average star. But if the explorer's objective in using the chamber had been to bring the Galaxy down to a size through which he might hope to climb or swim in a few minutes' effort, he had really made little headway. The division (in effect) of all the distances involved by a factor of a thousand million still left the expanded human facing mind-cracking immensity.

"Unless you want to swim in one place all day, you'll have to grow a lot more than that."

Math conquers all—if only numbers are to be evaluated. Eventually, having evoked more multiples, the hopeful swimmer attained a scale on which the Galaxy looked no bigger than a tall building. This did not occur until the would-be observer had magnified his own height to something like a thousand light-years. On this scale any solar system had long since disappeared into the microscopic—or would have done so had the computer not been careful to create beacons.

Now, moving about within the VR chamber, temporarily free of the restraints of gravity, one got the impression that the whole Galaxy had indeed been made to fit inside. On this scale the three main spiral arms were readily distinguishable, with Sol—thanks to the computer—findable as a tiny blinking beacon well out in the Orion-Cygnus curve.

Someone made the necessary adjustments to bring the display's version of the Mavronari Nebula into focus at a handy size. The investigators looked and felt their way around and through the image without coming to any helpful insights.

Someone remarked that most astronomers and astrogators would ordinarily regard the Mavronari as tremendously dull. There were a hundred other nebulas much like it in known space, and they were of interest only as obstacles to astrogation, save to a few cosmologists. Anyway, whoever had created and updated the display had evidently possessed few details on the subject.

The small black box that one of the fleet commander's staff was now loading into the VR mechanism contained information exactly duplicating that in the box which the berserkers had recently stolen from the Imatran archive, or which—in a scenario considered less likely—that machine had quickly read in the archive and then utterly destroyed.

The computers controlling the display inside the ten-meter cube granted each observer a central viewpoint this time, choosing as a first scene a defense controller's bunker slightly below the Imatran surface. Then the scenario was run in other modes—at first look none of them very helpful.

Realtime rolled by as the study continued. Disappointment soon set in once more.

"Run it again?" asked a software specialist.

"Yes. No. Yes, in a minute. But first—" Commodore Prinsep rubbed tired eyes. "Well, people, all I can actually see when I look at this record is what appears to be a very peculiar berserker attack. Unique in its own way. The most recent onslaught upon Imatra was also thoroughly untypical, but the two were unlike in at least one intriguing characteristic—I mean that the attacker of three centuries ago retreated after having shed relatively little blood."

There was a murmur of agreement.

The speaker went on: "Have any of the rest of you yet discerned any additional nontrivial contrasts, or similarities, between the two engagements?"

"Not I."

"Nor I. Not yet." There was a chorus of similar answers around the circle.

The commodore pushed at the point relentlessly. "So no one yet has any idea what our contemporary berserkers might have found in this record to cause them to break off their own attack so abruptly?"

No one did. But one adviser offered: "Viewing the recording certainly brings home the essential strangeness of that raid of three hundred years ago. One sees excerpts, and reads the accounts, of course, but somehow one doesn't grasp the full peculiarity of the event that way. As you say, sir, it was a mugging, a mass kidnapping, rather than a wholesale murder."

"Yes. While, as we all know, wholesale murder is a berserker's sole aim in life."

No one smiled.

"In a way, such a great peculiarity worries me more than simple slaughter. Because it indicates that there's something very important that we don't understand.

"Dirac's contemporaries were worried by it too, and so were a number of people in the years immediately following that raid. They were bothered by the oddity, even those who didn't believe it was all a great plot by the Premier. People theorized that the berserker had taken a whole planetary population of protocolonist tiles in order to raise a vast colony of goodlife humans somewhere, goodlife to be its servants, its fanatical warriors.

"A lot of people in the years immediately following Dirac's disappearance spent a lot of time looking at copies of this very record. Gradually, of course, interest declined. If I'd wanted a copy recently I don't suppose I'd have known where to look for it, except on Imatra."

"Speaking of looking for things—" This was Ensign Dinant, an astrogator.

Prinsep blinked at him. "Yes?"

"I was wondering: Just where is it now after three hundred standard years? Where is Dirac's berserker? The machine that wanted to steal a billion protopeople—or whatever the exact number really was—and for all we know, succeeded. It shows up fairly clearly in this display. But I wonder where it's got to?

"It's easy to see, on this record, which way that berserker went, and easy to see that Dirac and his people took the same course, going directly after it. But whatever trail that machine or those ships might have left has faded long ago. After three centuries, Dirac's berserker could be in a lot of different places. It could be well along in the task of nurturing that goodlife colony—if you subscribe to that theory."

The commodore nodded. "After three hundred years I should think it could. I also think that we should be seeing some results. And it needs no profound insight to observe that Dirac himself could be in a lot of places—if he's still alive."

The pudgy Prinsep rapped sharply on his table. "Let me remind you, my friends, my dear counselors: the primary question that we face is still: 'Why should today's berserkers be so interested in what happened to either the machines or the badlife Solarians of yesteryear?'"

"I say they can't," Dinant argued stubbornly. "Therefore it's got to be something else on this recording, something we haven't noticed so far, that hit them so hard, struck an electronic nerve."

Perhaps, another adviser suggested tentatively, the vital clue had something to do with the glimpses the recording afforded of Premier Dirac's yacht.

But why should anything at all about that vessel be of any importance now?

No one could guess. But Commodore Prinsep remained determined to find out. Speaking softly, but making the orders unequivocal, he ordered a team comprising both humans and robots to begin at once a grimly thorough, minutely detailed, expert analysis of the recording.

Meanwhile his task force went plowing steadily ahead.

☸ EIGHTEEN

Havot overheard Superintendent Gazin commenting that the majority of Prinsep's personal staff were expert computer systems—and sneering that a majority of *them* seemed to be devoted exclusively to food preparation. Havot was developing a somewhat different idea;

he could observe for himself that the organic component of the commodore's staff, a handful of people who had known the commodore and worked with him for some time, was fiercely loyal. At first Havot had taken this attitude for mere politics on their part. Now he was not so sure.

And Havot wondered if perhaps the Humanity Office superintendent and his senior agent, were beginning to worry about the fleet's catching up with some active berserkers after all.

Talking to Fourth Adventurer, Havot learned something more surprising: the Carmpan professed to see in Commodore Prinsep a tendency to mysticism.

"Mysticism, Fourth Adventurer?"

"Indeed, Christopher Havot." The Carmpan stood looking up at him from its one-meter height, out of a face that by Solarian standards was scarcely a face at all. The non-Solarian gestured with several limbs. "And I make the same statement with reference to you yourself."

"Me?" Havot stood there, for once astonished, feeling the foolish grin hanging on his face like a mask. "A mystic? No." At the same time he felt a surprisingly powerful urge to tell Fourth Adventurer of his experience with the berserker on the Imatran surface. But he held back from making any revelations.

Actually the commodore was very far from Havot's idea of what a mystic ought to be—almost as far as he was himself. Prinsep, between his businesslike planning sessions, spent most of his time dealing with nothing more abstract than nibbling grapes, or making out his menu for dinner.

Perhaps Fourth Adventurer had only been trying to be complimentary. Or he simply had the wrong word, the wrong Solarian concept. The difficulty in matching mental constructs must work both ways.

The commodore, Havot discovered, did spend a fair amount of time with the only non-Solarian human on his ship. It seemed unlikely that they were fellow gourmets—the Carmpan could be seen consuming Solarian food from time to time, but only after running it through his personal processing device, from which everything emerged as a kind of neutral-looking paste.

By this time the fleet was well launched on its pursuit of the berserker enemies, whose formation was intermittently in sight ahead. Astern, Imatra's sun dimmed fast with increasing distance. No more messages from Imatra were likely to catch up—Havot could relax a little.

At the moment, of course, the key to his fate was Becky. Let her let slip a word to Prinsep, or worse, her own boss, about the information that had come in, and her new lover was certain to see one of the brig's isolation cells or perhaps deep freeze in an SA chamber until someone decided to let him out.

And he was well aware that the senior representatives of the Humanitarian Office were still watching him, biding their time, looking for a chance to place him under arrest. They didn't bother trying to keep him under continuous surveillance; he wasn't going to run away.

Concerning Agent Rebecca Thanarat, Havot was considering several courses of action, all of which had certain drawbacks. For the moment he had to be sure, at all costs, that she was in love with him, content with their relationship. Havot smoothly stepped up the pace of his campaign of seduction, keeping in mind that getting her into bed was infinitely less important than winning her total devotion. Frequently, he had observed, the two did not go very closely together.

Havot tended to believe Rebecca's assurance that no other copy existed of the incriminating message. But naturally he could not be absolutely sure. He had disposed of the first paper copy very carefully.

Like many of the other women who had fallen in love with Havot at one point or another, Becky wanted to know all about his background. He repeated to her with some elaboration his earlier lie that he had worked as a dealer in educational materials. The story had now expanded to make him a former teacher.

She wasn't that interested in pursuing details of Havot's fictitious teaching career. "You were going to tell me how you got into trouble with that awful police department."

"Well . . . it had to do with an abused child." By now Havot had had the time necessary to prepare a prizewinning narrative. He knew Becky well enough to know how her sympathies could be most easily aroused and enlisted.

Aboard the several ships of the pursuing task force—now preparing for the first c-plus jump out of the system—the commodore and his chief advisers, including the subordinate ship captains, were gathered in electronic conference, the optelectronic brains of the ships themselves exchanging speech in the form of scrambled signals.

The leaders summoned into conference by the commodore were military people, except for the Carmpan—who this time courteously declined the honor—and the Humanity Superintendent.

The planners continued to struggle with the problem of the enemy's motivation in their sudden withdrawal and flight.

❀   ❀   ❀

The electronic spoor of the mysterious lone raider of three centuries ago had long since dissipated. But on the old records the course of Dirac's berserker was easily discernible, and telescopic observations confirmed the fact that today's powerful but swiftly fleeing force of death machines were indeed staying very close to their predecessor's vanished track.

Havot was not usually invited to sit in on Prinsep's strategic planning sessions. But much of what was said in these discussions soon became common knowledge aboard ship, as did the observed behavior of the contemporary enemy.

To anyone who studied the problem, it began to seem that the modern berserkers' discovery of their predecessor's escape route must indeed have been the event that triggered their own abrupt flight from the Imatran surface, virtually in midraid.

One of Prinsep's advisers was thinking aloud. "The conclusion seems irresistible that the enemy just pulled out the instant they identified the path taken by their predecessor, Dirac's berserker, on its way out of the system—in fact the evidence strongly suggests that this year's berserkers *came to Imatra primarily to gain that information.* The record they took from the underground archive contains nothing else that could conceivably be of interest to them."

"No! No no no!" The commodore was shaking his head emphatically. "Quite unacceptable! We can't be satisfied with the conclusion that they must be pursuing one of their own machines."

"And who can say dogmatically what our enemies will find interesting and what they will not? The record they went to such pains to steal contains an astronomical number of bits of information."

Prinsep made a dismissive gesture. "So does a picture of a blank wall. A great deal of what technically must be called information is really meaningless. What else in that recording, besides their colleague's route, could have any importance for berserkers?"

Prinsep paused for emphasis: "When a berserker computes that saving a few seconds is more important than terminating one more Solarian human life—you may take it that from that berserker's point of view, something very unusual, very important, is going on."

Meanwhile, the OH superintendent who had privately doubted Prinsep's determination sat silent and thoughtful, looking less knowing and more grave. The retreating berserkers continued to follow very closely the route followed by the chase of three hundred years ago. Therefore, so did the hunting pack of Solarian humans and machines.

❀   ❀   ❀

The contemporary chase wore on, hour after hour, day after day, with the Solarian fleet now seeming to gain a little ground and now again to lose a little. All of the human pilots were military people trained in formation flight, and worked smoothly with their associated computers. Commodore Prinsep was pushing the chase hard, but not hard enough to have cost him any ships.

The first c-plus jump essayed by the fleet's astrogators was far from a new experience for Havot, who in his comparatively short lifetime had seen a great many of the Galaxy's thousands of Solarian-settled worlds. Many more than most people ever got to see.

But travel outside and beyond the limitations of normal space was a totally new experience for agent Thanarat.

The first jump lasted for a subjective ship's time of some ten seconds, long enough for Becky, with Havot romantically at her side, to be initiated into the sensation of looking out through a cleared port into the eye-watering, nerve-grating irrelevance of flightspace—a scene often described as dim lights behind a series of distorting lenses.

Their cabins were both too far inboard to boast an actual cleared port. And to call up such a port on holostage was not the way, Havot assured her, to experience the full effect. There was something in the quality of the light, the images brought inboard through clear statglass, that any ordinary holosystem struggled inadequately to reproduce.

At the conclusion of each collective jump, on the fleet's reemergence into normal space, the people and computers on the flagship's bridge rapidly counted the ships composing the fleet, after which the human decision makers relaxed momentarily. But with the next breath drawn, people and machines began the calculations for the next jump, a process occupying a few seconds at the minimum.

In the short intervals between jumps, other crew members and their machines scanned space in every direction, testing the enemy's electronic spoor for freshness and exact position, and restored the desired tightness to their own ships' formation. Then a last round of intership communications, concluded in milliseconds. Then, at a signal, *jump* again in unison.

Each time one of the fleet's vessels reemerged in normal space, its sensors were already looking ahead, probing for signs of recent traffic, trying to catch some clue, some disturbance in the radiation patterns of normal space, indicating what general physical conditions would be encountered in that direction. So far they found no sign that the most recent band of marauders had deviated from the escape route used by their forerunner of three centuries ago.

Until now, the human hunters and their faithful slave machines had been able to see nothing directly of that antique chase. Nor had there seemed any point in wasting time and equipment trying to detect images of the fabled, vanished *Eidolon* or of the deadly object the old Premier had been hunting; the light that had once borne those images would be hundreds of light-years distant now, even if it had not long ago dispersed into a faintness far beyond the capability of any receiver to capture and restore to intelligibility.

No one in Prinsep's fleet was looking for the old trail now; the more recent attackers required the hunters' full attention. Today's berserkers were certainly leaving a fresh, distinct wake of their own. The suggestion was that to them, sheer speed had now become all-important. As if, against the blind urgency of their mysterious quest, the pursuing Solarian fleet hardly weighed in their calculations at all, any more than had the human left alive back on Imatra. The killing machines would outrun their hunters if they could, but otherwise seemed determined to ignore them as long as possible.

Commodore Prinsep thought, and several times speculated in the presence of one or more of his subordinates, that these tactics were possibly meant to set his fleet up for an ambush. He tried to estimate the chances of this, looking much grimmer than was his wont. But he still refused to slow the pace of his pursuit.

The *Symmetry*'s battle computer, and the expert systems Prinsep had grafted to it, did their best to calculate the odds in favor of berserker trickery. Prinsep did not make the calculations public. After all, the decision was up to him.

And then the odds were altered slightly by sheer accident. Two large berserkers, several light-hours ahead of the pursuing fleet, could be observed jump-crashing in their terrible haste, tearing themselves apart on specks and spikes of gravity jutting into spacetime from bits of nearby matter; the remaining members of their pack were compelled to slow down, or face destruction by laws of physics as remorseless as themselves.

Everyone aboard the flagship except the fleet commander himself kept expecting Prinsep to order a slowdown, or some change of tactics. But he did not.

The fleet gained.

Becky Thanarat came back to the cabin she now shared with Havot, and reported (to the amusement and delight of her new lover) that the Humanity Office superintendent and his senior agent, neither of whom had ever seen a real berserker in their lives, were beginning to look a little pale.

Presently the pursuing fleet reduced its speed at the fleet commander's orders. But only minimally.

Pursued and pursuers went tearing on in the same direction,

plunging boldly in among the ever-so-slowly thickening fringes of dark nebula.

Meanwhile Becky was suddenly called on the carpet by her superiors for her apparent failure to pass a decoded message along to them. Ship's communications had presented evidence, strong if not indisputable, that some radio communication coded for the HO had been received aboard the *Symmetry* several days earlier, just as the fleet was reaching the limit of good reception from the Imatran system.

Word reached Havot indirectly that Becky was unable to come up with any acceptable explanation.

Gazin evidently suspected, but could not prove, the truth, and ordered Agent Thanarat thrown in the brig.

Commodore Prinsep, who had to give his approval before any such drastic action could be taken, called in Havot as part of his own effort to get to the bottom of the situation.

"What do you know about this, Havot? We are on the verge of entering combat, and I cannot tolerate these distractions."

The youth was properly, tremulously outraged. "Superintendent Gazin has declared himself my enemy—why, I don't know. I supposed he has finally discovered that Agent Thanarat and I are now lovers, and that this is some plot on his part to get at me through her—I know nothing about any supposedly missing message."

Prinsep sighed and studied the young man who stood before him. Ultimately all decisions here in space, in wartime conditions, were up to the fleet commander.

Then Prinsep said unexpectedly: "Our Carmpan passenger has advised me to rely upon you, Havot. Know any reason why Fourth Adventurer should have said that?"

"No sir, I don't." Havot for once could think of nothing clever to say.

"Well, then, I am going to allow the young woman her freedom. For the time being, at least. I suppose I shall have to answer to the Humanity people for it when we get home." It was obvious that the commodore detested the HO and all the thought-control business that it stood for.

Havot showed a relieved smile. "I don't think you'll regret it, Commodore."

"See to it that I don't, Mr. Havot. Please see to it that I don't."

❋ NINETEEN

To the Solarians in the pursuing fleet, Dirac's berserker, along with the Premier and his people who had vanished in its pursuit, had never been more than dim historical shadows. But now, throughout the fleet, people were once again beginning to speculate on the possibility that Premier Dirac might turn out to be still alive, after all.

The discovery of a living Dirac would certainly have some contemporary political effect. But just what that effect might be was not so easy to say.

Havot mused: "If Dirac or any of his people were still breathing, they'd be old, old folks by this time."

But as Prinsep several times remarked to colleagues, not absolutely, impossibly too old. He had been studying the history. Many individuals did live longer than three hundred years; and Dirac had been fairly young, his bride even younger, hardly more than a girl, at the time of their disappearance. Also it seemed only natural that people trapped in a bioresearch station where SA chambers were readily available might very well make use of them.

Provided, of course, that berserkers' prisoners still had any mastery over their own fate. There was really no reason to expect that any human being taken, anytime, anywhere, by the unliving enemy, would long survive.

Havot once overheard the senior Humanity Office agent, who tended to lean politically to the side of the Premier's old enemies, envisioning a scenario in which Dirac had become goodlife, or had been goodlife all along, and was now, or had been, helping the berserker raise a goodlife force of millions of Solarians, all slaves and servants of the death machines.

Still, leaving aside political suspicions and accusations, the questions would not go away: Why should the modern berserkers set such overwhelming importance upon their discovery of the route by which their predecessor had withdrawn? And why should they, ever since making that discovery, have been slavishly following that same route at a near-suicidal speed?

And still, no one had answers.

Were the modern machines consumed with an urge to overtake their own mysterious forerunner? Or did they crave, for some unimaginable reason, to catch up with Dirac's yacht, which had preceded them on the same trail? Surprisingly, the best and latest computer calculations carried out aboard the flagship showed that such a feat of astrogation lay well within the bounds of possibility—assuming either Dirac's ship or the berserker he was chasing had gone plowing along on the same course, more or less straight ahead, ever deeper into the Mavronari's fringes. But why should either human or berserker have done that?

Three centuries of incremental improvements in interstellar drives and control systems, as well as in the techniques of getting through difficult nebulae, assured the modern pursuers that at least they ought to be able to make better time than had their enigmatic predecessor, Premier Dirac.

Some recently constructed berserkers were also known to have incorporated certain improvements over those of Dirac's time. And the machines which had carried out the latest attack on Imatra, or some of them at least, had given evidence of belonging to the improved class. So neither pursuit nor combat was likely to be any easier for the modern fleet than it had been for Dirac's people.

No member of the modern human task force was willing to express a belief that any of the participants in that earlier chase were still out there ahead of this one, gamely plowing on into the dark nebula. The odds were just overwhelmingly against it.

No, when you looked at the situation realistically, that contest must have been settled, long ago, one way or another. It was almost certain that the Premier together with his fleshly friends and enemies were centuries dead, their ships and the missing bioresearch station destroyed in combat or in desperate flight. And as for the giant berserker that had come to bear his name, if it had not sustained terminal injuries in one fire-fight or another, it might have changed course and broken free somehow of the Mavronari. Or else it had somehow stalled itself, and perhaps its captured prey, inside that endless blackness.

But in any case the modern fleet, under a commander showing an unexpected but seemingly natural combination of boldness and tenacity, appeared to have a good chance of overtaking the contemporary berserker force.

Despite the predicted imminence of battle, morale in all the ships seemed high—or would have, had it not been for the situation involving Havot and the Humanity Office representatives.

The fleet's captains and the other officers who were taking part in the ongoing planning sessions, kept coming back to the same point: to determine why the modern berserkers were following the cold trail of the old chase, it might be very helpful to learn what that ancient enemy's goal had been.

Ensign Dinant mused: "I suppose today's bandits, independently of any discovery they've turned up on Imatra, *might* retain some history of which target one of their number went after three hundred years ago, and even what tactics it employed then. On the other hand, I can easily believe that our modern death cultivators preserve no record of anything like that, because I *don't* see any reason why they should give a damn."

After a moody silence, Lieutenant Tongres, a pilot, cleared her throat. "Look at it this way. As far as we can tell, the only important thing these old Imatran records reveal is the exact line of retreat taken by Dirac's berserker. As far as we know that machine did succeed in getting away, and maybe it even worked a successful ambush on the Premier when he came after it. And if a tactic succeeds once, you use it again."

"Bah! There appears to be no astrogational advantage to this particular pathway—nothing that would make an ambush easier or more effective than if the flight had followed a route a million kilometers to one side or another. For our modern berserkers to head for cover again in the nearest dark nebula would be repeating a tactic. But for them to follow the *exact same trail* as their predecessor is . . . something else. Something more than tactics. I don't know what. A reenactment. But why? why? why?" The Ensign beat a fist upon a table.

Tongres shook her head. "As I see it, it's not really that our modern enemies want to follow the exact same trail. The point is, they want to arrive at the exact same place."

"Oh? And what place might that be?"

"How about a hidden entrance to a clear pathway inside the Mavronari, a quick passage to its interior? A direct route all the way through it and out the other side?"

"The interior, so far as we know, is very little more than a bag of dust. All right, a direct route through would have some value. But not much."

"Maybe—maybe they're carrying important news to berserker headquarters. And the grand berserker headquarters is located on some world inside the Mavronari."

Dinant was unconvinced. "So now we have a whole fleet of berserkers devoting their time and energy to a mission that a single machine could readily accomplish. Bah. Anyway, aren't you arguing in a circle? I trust that the important news they're carrying to their own headquarters is something other than the coordinates of that headquarters' location."

The lieutenant bristled, but before she could retort another crew member interrupted:

"How important to these bandits of ours could *any* news be, extracted from a three-hundred-year-old recording they just happened to dig up on the surface of Imatra?"

"Ah, perhaps you weren't here for the early showing, the matinee. It doesn't appear that they 'just happened' to dig this information up. The landing machine that did the digging up headed straight for the archive as soon as it touched down, for all the world as if it had been dispatched upon that particular mission. As if they knew somehow that the record they wanted would be there."

"How would any berserker know that?" Dinant wanted to know.

"A very good question." Tongres looked thoughtful. "Someone would have to tell them, I suppose."

This real hint of goodlife activity was met by an interval of silence. Neither Havot nor either of the OH men was present at the moment.

The moment passed.

The third crewmember inquired, "And so the prize our enemies were hoping for, and gleaned from the buried record, was nothing more or less than the direction of the earlier berserker's flight?"

"What else?" Tongres shrugged. "We've all seen the show a hundred times now. Just what else could the big secret possibly have been?"

Dinant was struck with a sudden thought. "Wait. What if . . ."

"Yes?"

"Suppose, after all, for the sake of argument, that Dirac was goodlife. All right, I know, there's nothing in his public record to suggest that. But if no other explanation makes sense, we ought at least to consider the possibility. Say he was at least goodlife enough to make a deal with the damned machines, in hopes of furthering his own career. So he arranges somehow to give the machines a whole bioresearch station, containing some millions of protopeople for them to kill, or to—use."

"All right, granted for the sake of argument. Though there's no evidence he did anything at all to help them. Anyway, what were they supposed to give him in return?"

The ensign paused. "I don't know. Maybe the plan was that they'd get rid of some of his political enemies. Only the deal went sour, from the goodlife's point of view, and the berserker ate him alive, along with a few other people on his ships and on the research station."

"And bolted down about a billion protopeople for dessert. Well, it doesn't sound convincing to me, but again, for the sake of argument, suppose it's true. How does any of it explain the behavior of these machines we're chasing?"

Dinant had no answer.

Tongres sighed.

At last the third member of the conversation spoke again. "But I wonder . . . the damned berserkers have operated, continue to operate, over a truly enormous stretch of space and time. As far as I know, no one's ever demonstrated they even have a central headquarters or command center, any more than Solarian humanity does."

"Interesting thought, though. To consider that the berserkers might have one. Even more interesting to think that we, here, now, might be hurrying as fast as we can along the road that leads to it."

Over a number of centuries, beginning well before the first berserker raid on Imatra, the interior of the Mavronari had been partially, desultorily explored. The nebula was known to be almost if not entirely lifeless, but also not totally devoid of the possibilities of life. At certain widely scattered locations within the vast sprawl of silent darkness, the light-pressure of isolated suns was sufficient to keep shadowing dust and thin gas at bay, establishing adequate orbital space for modest families of planets.

One or two of these systems of worlds, which according to the flagship's data banks had never been inhabited (and were all but completely uninhabitable), were known to lie in the general direction of the recurrent berserker flights from Imatra. These isolated systems within the Mavronari had proven to be reachable by narrow, roundabout channels of relatively clear space winding through the occluding interstellar dust. The enemy did not appear to be trying to reach any of these channels. And the fleet commander, with access to prodigious amounts of military information on berserker sightings and activity, could find nothing in his information banks to indicate that the Mavronari had ever been suspected of harboring berserker installations.

Of course other solar systems, known to the berserkers but never discovered by humanity, might well exist inside the sprawling nebula. And worlds unusable by life might still offer space for dock facilities and shipyards, and minerals for production, to the unliving foe.

The Solarians who were now engaged in planning the pursuit felt themselves being forced to the conclusion, for lack of any better, that the enemy were probably indeed on their way to one of those worlds, and had chosen to get there by plowing in the back way, the slow way. But again, *why?* Certainly any ship or machine, constrained by dust to travel only in normal space, fighting the nebula every meter of the way, would need more than three hundred years to reach any of those bodies from the modern berserkers' current position.

Prinsep now rechecked the astrogational possibilities. The result was available to anyone in the fleet who expressed an interest: In three hundred years there had not been time for either Dirac's berserker or Dirac's yacht to complete the long dark tunneling and emerge at any of those known isolated systems.

"Maybe time enough to tunnel their way to some system we don't know about? I don't think so, but I can't say it's impossible."

"Do you suppose that one of the berserkers we're chasing now could be Dirac's?"

That question earned the one who asked it a strange look. "Not if Dirac's berserker stayed on the course it was last seen to be following. If it kept to that course, it's still in there somewhere, plowing through the dust."

"Maybe there is some secret passage we don't know about. Some high-speed lane through the Mavronari that we can't see from here, a route humans have never discovered."

One of the captains ran up on her holostage some model images, such profiles of the modern machines as could be compiled from intelligence reports and telescopic sightings.

"None of these correspond with the image of Dirac's berserker on the old record. You're suggesting that the thing may have been chasing itself around in a three-hundred-year circle, recruiting a force of helpers as it goes?"

"No, not exactly. Not if you put it that way. I mean that possibly such a machine hangs out in the Mavronari, comes out at intervals to make another hit-and-run attack on Imatra—or some other target—and then ducks back inside."

The other thought it over. Shook her head. "Historically, there haven't been many attacks anywhere in the vicinity of the Mavronari. Not a single other attack on Imatra besides the two that we're concerned about. And why make a raid only every three hundred years? Doesn't even sound like a berserker."

"Well, what does it sound like, then?" This was the commodore speaking, cutting through debate with authority. "If anyone here is still clinging to some notion that these objects we're chasing may not be real berserkers, I advise you to forget that theory right now. We've picked up more than enough of their debris, intercepted more than enough of their combat communications, to clinch the fact beyond any doubt... and so did Dirac make sure of his opponent, as the records show, before he started out on his last chase. The things we're fighting here, and the one he was fighting, are the genuine bad machines. Absolutely!"

Someone else put in: "Remember, berserkers do sometimes randomize their tactics, doing things that seem stupid just for the sake of remaining unpredictable."

Prinsep shook his head. "Sometimes they do. But three hundred years of deliberate stupidity? Of inefficiency, of downright waste of time and effort and firepower, just to give us something to fret about? If that's true I give up. No I don't. Never mind. I'm tired, I'm going to grab some sack time." His chef's usual signal, a muted dinner gong, chimed upon the nearby holostage, but for once the commodore waved the menu away without comment.

The fleet managed to gain some ground on the fleeing foe during the next couple of c-plus jumps. But after that, gaining more became bleakly difficult; the commodore considered accepting an increased risk of collisions with stray matter, but decided against it. Even so, the chase was becoming more and more dangerous, almost prohibitively so, as the hunters followed their quarry ever more deeply into the outlying regions of the dark nebula.

Over the next four or five standard days, it seemed that some ground was being lost. The trail left in subspace by their berserker prey grew intermittently colder and more difficult to follow.

The fleet commander gritted his teeth, weighed his chances—some said he spent time alone in his cabin, saying his prayers to whatever form of deity he favored (no one was quite sure what that might be)—and ordered a slight additional acceleration.

And a moment after issuing that command turned, with a put-upon sigh, his attention to the possibilities for lunch.

Meanwhile, Havot and Becky had been reunited. She had supposedly been relieved of all her HO duties, but that punishment—if such it was—was the limit of what her superiors were able to inflict upon her at the moment. She was now living blissfully with Havot in a reprieve of uncertain duration, and of course she was no longer recording what he said and did.

At least, Havot thought, that was what he was supposed to take for granted.

All his life he had been blessed—that was how he regarded the condition—with an incredibly suspicious mind. Which of course was one of the main reasons why he was still alive.

Anyway, spy devices could be very small and hard to spot, and he continued to assume that whatever happened between him and Becky would be overheard, and very likely watched, any place they might go on the ship.

So he was impeccably tender with her, very innocent and loving.

❂   ❂   ❂

Meanwhile Havot had to grapple with inner demons of some subtlety. As the chase progressed, and it became more and more evident that the commodore was in deadly, inflexible earnest, Havot found the prospect of once more confronting a berserker, or perhaps a whole fleet of them, somewhat disturbing.

In private moments and in dreams he tried to clarify in his inner thoughts his impression, his fading memory, of what exactly had happened between him and the crippled killing machine, back there on the Imatran surface. Had he really—when death seemed certain, the prospect of being able to draw another breath a fantasy—had he really, in that moment, committed himself in some way to serve the berserker cause?

His present situation did not distress him. He was experiencing the usual mixture of enchantment and mesmerizing fear that any perilous enterprise could give him—the sense of being, at least for a short time, fully alive. It was a kick that nothing but serious danger could deliver.

When Havot heard how the berserkers had taken the record from the subterranean archive, he began to think that the action of the berserker machine in sparing him had really not been based on anything he had or had not done. But the trouble with being eternally suspicious was that you could never be quite sure.

There was another question, a related one, that tended to keep the fugitive awake when he lay sleepless, alone, or with his newly released lover, in his bunk: Would the berserkers, when he met them again, be somehow able to recognize him as one of their own? Had the substance of his confrontation with one battered machine somehow been communicated to the others?

Maybe the real question was: Did he, Havot, really want to fight on the berserkers' side or not?

Given the unexpected ferocity with which Commodore Prinsep was pursuing the berserkers, Havot thought it distinctly possible that he was soon going to find out.

Lying now in the small berth with Becky, his body pressed against hers in the constricted space, Havot looked fondly at his sleeping lover, stroked her blond hair, and smiled to himself.

He allowed himself to whisper, sweetly, inaudibly, one word: "Badlife!"

☀ TWENTY

The first jolting impact of a berserker weapon against the flagship's force-shielded hull jarred Havot out of the sack, and a moment later Rebecca's naked body landed directly on top of him.

Yet once more, for perhaps the hundredth time since the task force had left Imatra—Havot had long ago lost count—the flagship had ended a jump with sudden reemergence into normal space.

But this reentry was different. In the next instant after the *Symmetry* appeared in normal space the first hammer blow from the enemy struck home. A second or two later the ship's alarms belatedly set up their deadly, muted clamor.

Ruthlessly pushing aside the half-wakened Becky, Havot ignored her confused cries. Even before his mind was fully conscious, his own body was struggling to get into the suit of space armor that for some days had been resting underneath his bunk.

Becky of course had armor too, but hers waited some distance down the corridor in her cabin, so more than Becky's modesty and reputation were going to be at risk while she ran, half-nude and struggling to pull on clothing, the necessary meters to get at it. Havot could picture others in the corridor perhaps looking at her strangely, even in the midst of their own travail.

Havot accepted her parting kiss without allowing himself to be distracted from the task of getting his own armor on. He did not particularly want her to put hers on, but he could not very well try to stop her or advise her against it.

None of the crew members or passengers aboard the vessels of the task force—with the possible exception of those actually on watch at the time—had been granted any warning at all before their world exploded.

Gambling to overtake the fleeing foe, the fleet commander had accepted a certain risk of ambush. Therefore the berserker counter-attack could not be counted as a total surprise, but still its specific timing and its strength were unexpected.

A theory advanced earlier by one of the astrogators, but never supported by solid evidence, held that the enemy had fled in this precise direction because the distribution of various types of matter in the space along this trail offered unequaled possibilities for ambush. Regardless of whether the astrogator's theory was right or wrong, the practical outcome was almost completely disastrous from the human point of view. The commodore's continued gamble for speed had finally been lost.

The ten or fifteen lesser vessels of the task force, emerging from flightspace within milliseconds of the flagship, and all within a few hundred kilometers of each other, were also attacked at once. Some of them were instantly destroyed.

The small civilian contingent aboard the *Symmetry*—Havot, the three HO people, and the Carmpan—had been warned, coached, and rehearsed days ago, soon after the fleet's departure from Imatra, about their duties once a red alert had sounded. They were to put on armor, get to their acceleration couches as rapidly as possible, and stay in them for the duration of the emergency.

Havot, alone in his cabin, was just completing the process of putting on his suit when he was knocked off his feet by the second direct hit on the flagship. Grimly he struggled erect; his hands were shaking now. The weight and smell and look of the bulky outfit, very much like the one that had saved his life on the Imatran surface, strongly evoked the terrifying chase and then the confrontation by the berserker.

Even as he fastened the last connector on the suit, he ran out into the corridor, keeping an eye open for Becky or either of her senior associates while he headed for his acceleration couch. Not that he expected yet to be able to do anything about them, but perhaps in the heat of battle a window of opportunity would arise. Certainly not here and now. The restricted space of the corridor seemed filled by a jostling crowd of bulky suits and helmets, most of them bright with identification markings of one kind or another.

Bumping his way along toward his assigned battle station, amid the unfamiliar noises and pressures of the confined environment, Havot found his imagination gripped, inflamed, by the idea that he could feel the death machines in space ahead of him, and on all sides, as they came hurtling past the *Symmetry* at unimaginable velocities. He could sense their lifeless bodies, smell them, just outside the hull—

With an effort he brought his mind back to current reality. Here was the room just off the bridge where all the passengers were to occupy their assigned acceleration couches until the all clear was sounded. Superintendent Gazin and Senior Agent Ariari were in the room already. Their armored suits bore some insignia of the HO office. Havot wondered if that would make them special targets for the berserkers, but decided, to his own private amusement, that this was unlikely.

Meanwhile the ship repeatedly lurched and sounded—hull ringing and groaning like great gongs—under the continued impact of enemy weapons. Blended in now were the space-twitching detonations of her own guns firing back.

Here came Becky, in her suit and apparently unhurt, staggering her way across the unsteady deck to the acceleration couch beside Havot's. Inside her faceplate he could see her relief to find him still unhurt and already well protected.

The commodore's amplified voice could be heard, still calm, still in control:

"Stand by to repel boarders. I repeat—"

Boarders! Something that tended to happen frequently in the space adventure stories and surprisingly often in real life as well.

Modern defenses were capable of turning sheer kinetic energy back upon itself. Fighting ships and machines, each muffled in a protective envelope of defensive force, were often more susceptible to the slow approach of a grappling and boarding device than to the screaming velocity of missiles.

Already the ship's brain, taking over momentarily from the commodore, was reporting in its dispassionate voice that several small enemy attack units had rammed themselves in through the flagship's force-field protection.

Havot reached out an armored hand to touch that of Becky in the couch beside his. Beyond her, the other two Humanity Office agents seemed to be lying there inertly.

Then the chief of the Humanity Office, as if sensing that Havot was looking at him, turned his head and glared back, doubtless trying to express his suspicion that Havot would try to take the berserkers' side now that battle had been joined.

By contrast, Lieutenant Ariari looked too pale and terrified inside his helmet to be worrying about the suspected goodlife or anyone else. He looked in fact like a man about to soil his underwear—if such a thing was possible in a properly fitted suit of space combat armor, with its built-in miniaturized plumbing.

In the small room there was one acceleration couch still unoccupied, this one of drastically different shape. The Carmpan had evidently elected to remain in his cabin. Definitely against the commodore's orders, but it seemed unlikely that anyone was going to try to enforce obedience in the case of Fourth Adventurer.

And now an arming robot, having evidently concluded its tasks in the control room next door, came rolling into the passengers' compartment.

No doubt Gazin and Ariari, if anyone had asked them, would have strongly objected to either Havot or the now-disgraced Agent Thanarat being issued weapons. But apparently no one had yet sought their opinion. Certainly the robot from the weapons shop was not about to do so.

Instead it proceeded as it had been programmed, rolling along the short row of acceleration couches, using its metal arms to issue each passenger his or her choice of alphatrigger or blink-triggered shoulder weapon. Gazin and Ariari selected theirs mechanically and the robot moved along. Havot could see even before it reached him that it bore racked on its flanks rows of what he took to be grenades, hanging there like ripe tempting fruit, waiting for any eager Solarian hand to pluck. Havot was no military ordnance expert, but these looked to him like the type called drillbombs. Just the thing to use when you got within arm's length of a berserker machine—or someone you didn't like, whether or not he was wearing an armored suit.

Accepting an alphatrigger carbine with his left hand, Havot used his right to quickly harvest three grenades, one after another, from the handy rack. Three, he thought, would probably be plenty.

The drillbombs fitted snugly, as if the space had been designed for them, into a belt pouch attached to Havot's armor. He held the carbine cradled in his arm. It was basically an energy projector, whose beam cracked and shivered hard armor, but could be safely turned against soft flesh. The beam induced intense vibrations in whatever it struck; in a substance as soft as flesh, the vibrations damped out quickly and harmlessly. In hard material the result was quite different.

Hard surfaces could be protected by treatment with a spray of the proper chemical composition. The robot as it issued weapons was also treating all the surfaces of friendly armor with chemical protection. The formula was varied from one day, or one engagement, to the next, to prevent the enemy's being able to duplicate it.

The aiming and firing of the blink-triggered weapons were controlled by the user's eyes. Sights tracked a reflection of the operator's pupils and aimed along the line of vision; the weapon was triggered by a hard blink. Sometimes the thing fired unintentionally—when the system was armed and ready, you tended to avoid looking straight at anyone or anything you wanted to protect.

Alphatriggering was an alternative and even faster system, one considered somewhat more reliable, though it took a little longer to learn to use. Such weapons were also aimed visually, but fired by the controllable alphawave signal of the operator's organic brain.

❋   ❋   ❋

Apart from a few staggering shocks, the flagship's artificial gravity had so far maintained itself through the violence of combat, cushioning and protecting the tender flesh and bone of crew and passengers against the g forces created by enemy weapons and by the warship's own maneuvers. Only once so far had the *Symmetry's* gravity faltered badly enough to pile people up in corners, allowing a surge in local g forces intense enough to inflict serious casualties despite the fact that all aboard were now in armor. And that failure had been on another deck, far from the control room.

Havot was pleasurably calculating his chances of getting rid of either or both of the senior HO officers as soon as he could do so without exposing himself to retribution. His main objective, though, was still to make sure that Becky was permanently silenced. She was the only one aboard, as far as he knew, who possessed damning knowledge of the coded message.

Once the presence of berserker units aboard could be confirmed, almost anything that happened could be blamed on them. If he could catch her out of her armor, a knife would do as well as any more spectacular high-tech weapon—as long as there was no prospect of the wound's being examined after she was dead.

Knives could wait. Right now Havot would bide his time, watching for the proper opportunity with the calm he was usually able to enjoy on desperate occasions—more than one enemy had described his serene composure as inhuman.

He was pleased when, after a further exchange of heavy-weapons fire, an actual berserker boarding was confirmed by a ship's announcement. At least three devices were thought to have penetrated the inner hull.

Someone was whimpering on intercom—Havot supposed it might be Ariari. Most of the regular crew, at least most who were still alive, seemed to be carrying on with their duties, almost calmly, to judge by their voices tersely exchanging jargon.

And then a different report. A terrified human voice, breathing raggedly as if the speaker would soon be dead, came on intercom to say one of the things was moving down a corridor in the direction of the control room.

Smoothly, unthinkingly as if he were letting his body take over, Havot hit the release on his couch. He stood up, the powered joints of his heavy suit bringing him easily to his feet, carbine in the crook of his arm swinging into firing position. The backpack holding the compact hydrogen power lamp—enough kick there to stop a runaway ground train—slipped neatly into its proper position on his back as he got up.

Regulations sternly forbade passengers to leave their couches for any reason during combat, and naturally such a rule had force enough to keep Becky and the two HO men, sticklers all for law and order, in their chairs a little longer.

But after only a moment Becky slid out of her couch too, determined to be with her lover.

First Gazin and then Ariari did the same, as if they were somehow compelled to follow anything that looked like leadership.

Havot gestured savagely for them to keep back. Hoping they were going to stay out of his way, nursing his carbine into just the position where he wanted it, Havot moved as quietly as his armored bulk would let him to a position from which he ought to be able to ambush anything or anyone appearing in the doorway.

Subvocalizing a command to his suit's small built-in brain, he turned up the sensitivity on his helmet's airmikes. Now he could hear the berserker coming, slowly. Something was out there in the hallway now, moving closer, walking, humping, sliding upon damaged, subtly grating parts. Lurching forward, then waiting, pausing as if to watch and listen. From where it was, it ought to be able to see right past Havot's ambush, into the control room itself.

Havot had no doubt that this machine approaching now was going to kill him if he did not kill it. Any half-baked bargain that he might or might not have made back on the Imatra surface had long ago gone up in smoke, in wisps of unreality. If the berserkers were truly hoping to enlist him for goodlife, they were going to have to come right out and say so, offer him a better and more clear-cut deal than they had done before.

Out in the corridor, the killer machine once more centimetered forward, this time stopping no more than four meters from where Havot crouched, close enough for him to glimpse one flange of its forward surface, to see how badly it was damaged, spots slagged and glowing at a temperature that at this distance would have scorched unprotected human skin—and then, with all the speed it could still muster, the machine rushed the apparently unguarded control-room door.

Havot's alphatrigger beam, striking from one side, swifter than any conscious human thought, sliced out to destroy. At point-blank range a blade of light and force skinned berserker armor back like fruit peel, evoking an internal blast and spray, dropping the monster in its tracks, no more than halfway through the doorway.

The other passengers were thrown into panic, and two of them at least were firing their shoulder weapons now, slicing already demolished berserker hardware into smaller bits. Beams glanced back harmlessly from armored suits, from treated bulkheads and the deck.

Now Havot saw his chance. Dodging back into the midst of the sliding and bumping confusion of armored bodies, the billowing smoke and fumes from the demolished foe, he picked out Becky's suited form, stepped close, and slapped one of his three drillbomb grenades hard against her armored back.

The suited figure convulsed, its faceplate glowed like a searchlight for an instant; the grenade's force, focused into a molten, armor-piercing jet, evoking secondary interior explosions, was certain death to any human being in the suit.

Turning, wondering if he had the time to try for one of the HO men, Havot was stunned to see Becky's anxious countenance gazing out at him from the helmet of another suit.

And there was Gazin, also still alive. Havot realized that he had wasted a chance, killed the wrong person, wiped out no one more dangerous than a bureaucratic coward. Only Ariari was in that suit down on the deck, well cooked by now inside his armor bubbling with fumes and heat. Here, curse her, was Becky Thanarat still alive and on her feet, tearfully glad to see that Havot himself had survived uninjured this almost hand-to-gripper fight with a berserker.

Terse exchanges of conversation assured Havot that the other two were blaming the man's death on the berserker. And now things had calmed down a little; it would be necessary to wait before he tried to use another grenade on Becky.

Aroused by fear and the proximity of death, Havot was now gripped by an almost physical yearning for a knife. Almost certainly there would be a good selection of edged weapons from which to choose, available among Prinsep's elaborate table cutlery.

Checking the charge on his shoulder weapon, Havot left the room and started down the corridor. Someone called after him on scrambler radio, and he tersely put them off, saying he was only scouting.

Down one deck, he went prowling through the deserted galley, excited by a profusion of knives arrayed in high racks, left lying carelessly on wooden cutting boards among the meat and fruit. Choosing hastily, he picked the biggest weapon that would fit into one of his suit pouches and stowed it there for later use.

Of course the knife was not going to be of much use as long as Agent Thanarat continued to wear armor, and she wasn't likely to take her armor off until the combat concluded—if she was still living then. Havot considered other ways, such as possibly pushing Agent Thanarat into some berserker's grasp. And even her death would not completely set Havot's mind at ease. He still suspected that some of the incriminating message might be around, perhaps still waiting to be decoded. He'd have to search Becky's dead body, if at all possible, and then her quarters.

The latest estimate from what still survived of Damage Control was that two or three or four small berserker boarding machines had actually entered the flagship. It was now thought that all but one of these had been destroyed, but only after bitter fighting that had left much of the vessel's interior in a shambles.

No one knew at the moment where the single surviving berserker boarder was.

Meanwhile, heavy-weapons fire was still being exchanged with large berserker units. By now the *Symmetry's* drive had been somewhat weakened, and the outer and inner hulls both damaged.

Havot, after picking up his knife, made his way back to the control room. On the way the only humans he saw were dead, and he encountered no more berserkers. When he arrived he discovered that Fourth Adventurer had finally emerged from his cabin to join the other passengers, wearing his own Carmpan version of space armor.

Havot, in what he imagined was something like proper military style, reported to Prinsep that he had disposed of one berserker—said nothing about the objectionable human—and that he was present and available for duty.

Prinsep, his hands totally full with other matters, only looked at him and nodded.

That was all right. Havot again went out and down the corridor a little distance, to look for at least one more metal killer. This was fun, more fun than he had expected.

Meanwhile Prinsep, still in the fleet commander's chair, his human staff badly decimated around him, was attempting on intercom to raise crew members in other parts of the ship. The results were discouraging. It sounded like only a few wounded survived anywhere in the ship.

Then something made him look up, to discover where the last berserker boarder was. Much more nimble than its predecessor, it had just come popping out of God knew where to appear at the very entrance of the control room. One of its grippers, blurring sideways at machine-speed, knocked Havot's armored body smashing into a bulkhead before the man could get his carbine into firing position. In the next eyeblink the berserker had selected a target and fired its own weapon, killing Becky Thanarat, who had her carbine almost raised.

The next shot, fully capable of piercing Solarian body armor, was snapped off a fraction of a second later at Prinsep, a conspicuous target in his central chair. It missed the commodore only by centimeters, and no doubt would have killed him had not Fourth Adventurer, unequipped with formal weapons, propelled his suited body at that moment right into the berserker's legs. Gripper arms beat at the Carmpan like the blades of a propeller, snagged and tore his suit, mangled his flesh.

Havot was not dead. Firing while still flat on his back, slashing away coolly with his alphatrigger weapon, he cut the berserker's legs from under it, and a moment later detonated something vital deep inside its torso.

A stunned, ear-ringing silence fell.

Slowly, his back against the bulkhead, weapon ready, Havot centimetered his way back to his feet. His armor had saved him. He had been momentarily stunned, but was not really hurt.

Dead people were lying everywhere. Becky was among them, Havot saw; at the moment he hardly cared. He picked his way around and over fallen bodies, smashed machinery, back into the control room, where Prinsep still presided, though one support of his acceleration couch, that nearest his left ear, had been neatly shot away. He and the surviving human pilot, and even the surviving HO superintendent were now all looking at Havot with something like awe.

Minutes passed, while outside the flagship's battered, straining metal, heavy weapons thundered, the tides of battle still ebbed and flowed.

The embattled commodore, still presiding over his half-ruined control room from his chair near the flagship's center of mass, grimly continued to receive damage reports, news of disaster from almost every deck.

Commodore Prinsep, the once-bright armor encasing his pudgy body now battle-stained and scorched, the outer surface splashed with Carmpan as well as Solarian blood, seemed to be gradually slumping lower in the webs of his acceleration chair.

At the moment his face bore an expression of wistful calm that might almost have been despair. Yet minute after minute he continued to make decisions, to answer questions softly, logically, purposefully. Something in his very attitude of inertness, his immobility, inspired confidence.

More minutes passed, and casualty reports kept coming in, while inside the fleet's few surviving hulls, machines and people fought desperately to control battle damage, to determine the positions of surviving friends and foes, to recharge weapons and maintain shields at the highest strength attainable.

Communication among the ships in the task force had now become intermittent at best. Contact was cut off altogether for many seconds at a stretch, with nearby space a howling hell of every kind of radiation. But the coders and transmitters had been designed to cope with hell, and there were moments when cohesive packets of information did come through. Some of the human vessels were being vaporized while others were claiming kills against the enemy.

The flagship's brain, delivering with unshakable calm its best evaluation of the fight, concluded that the enemy must have sent half or more of his force dropping back to spring this ambush.

Although to some of those who lived through it, the battle seemed to go on forever, actually, by the usual standards of combat between forces of this size, it was mercifully short. In a very brief time, no more than a quarter of a standard hour, several berserkers had been destroyed. On the debit side, every vessel in the ambushed fleet was badly shot up, and half of them were gone.

Now there were suggestions that berserker reinforcements were arriving.

In any case the signals from other friendly vessels were fading, one by one, and they did not come back. Their images disappeared from the tactical stage.

Prinsep expressed a hope that some at least of the other Solarian ships were getting away; with all the noise in space, it was impossible to distinguish intact departures from obliteration.

Havot, almost at ease, one arm round a stanchion in case the artificial gravity should stutter again, was cheerful, in his element at last.

"What do we do now, chief?" he inquired. Again, Prinsep only looked at him.

No matter. Havot looked back serenely.

To extricate his vessel from the ambush, the fleet commander closed his eyes and ordered his surviving organic and optelectronic pilots to jump his ship ahead.

Before normal space dropped away, several of the survivors aboard the flagship caught a last glimpse of several ravening berserkers, barely detectable by the humans' instruments as they came darting with abandon after their escaping prey, only to encounter pulverizing collisions with almost insubstantial dust, vaporizing themselves or being sufficiently disabled to be thrown permanently out of the fight.

❖   ❖   ❖

Somehow or other the *Symmetry*, though limping and with a number of its compartments hissing air, survived its desperate bid to break free, carrying to relative safety Havot and a handful of other survivors, half of them wounded, along with a number of dead.

With a last effort, straining the damaged drive very nearly to its limit, the computers guiding the damaged ship sought out the most open channel and maneuvered the scarred hull into it.

Not only did the flagship survive, but it temporarily retained enough speed, power, and mobility to break away from the several surviving ambushers.

The dead Carmpan, and a number of Solarian dead, still lay in the corners of the control room and the adjoining chamber.

The human pilot, Lieutenant Tongres, said: "I took what I could get, Commodore—and now astrogation's got us back on the same old trail again."

The commodore for once looked haggard, but his voice was still steady. "Any more bandits ahead?"

"Don't see any yet. But I can't see much of anything for all the dust, so there might well be. I don't believe that was their whole force we just engaged."

"Thank all the gods of space we avoided a few of them at least."

Someone in a remote area of the ship was still on intercom, with repeated desperate pleas for help.

And so Ivan Prinsep bestirred himself—heaved himself out of his acceleration couch for the first time since the battle had started—and went to check on the wounded elsewhere in his ship. The organic pilot was busy. A couple of other people lay in their couches free of serious physical injury but totally exhausted.

Havot, so far virtually unscratched, almost jauntily volunteered to come with the commodore as bodyguard, in case any enemy boarding devices were still lurking in the corners.

Prinsep nodded his acceptance.

☀ TWENTY-ONE

The flagship's surviving human pilot, Lieutenant Tongres, was discussing the situation with Ensign Dinant, the only other person still functional in the control room, even as they worked on the flagship's damaged instrumentation.

Soon a startling fact was confirmed: beginning approximately at the present location of the flagship, an open channel cut through the enclosing nebular material, offering relatively smooth passage. This crude tunnel of comparatively clear space led on in the general direction the enemy had originally been following.

The lieutenant marveled. "Look at it. Almost like it was dredged clear somehow."

"Almost." Dinant's admission was reluctant; the actual accomplishment of such a feat on the scale now visible would have been far beyond any known technology, and similar natural features were not unheard of. "Wouldn't be surprised if Dirac's berserker once came right down this channel, with the old man himself driving his yacht right after it."

"Wouldn't be surprised." Tongres went on intercom. "Commodore, you there? We're really hurting. Drive, shields, everything."

Around the still-breathing pair of officers the control room's surviving holostages were sizzling, erupting like white holes in strange and improbable virtual images. The display system, like all the flagship's systems now, was obviously damaged. Power was being conserved wherever possible.

Presently Prinsep's voice came back, redundantly transmitted on audio intercom and scrambled suit radio: "Do what you can. I'll be back with you in a minute. We're going to have a problem with the wounded. We don't seem to have an intact medirobot left aboard."

Prinsep, escorted by a serene Havot, soon reappeared in the control room. They had not tried to move the seriously wounded yet.

Turning to the commodore, the pilot asked: "I think she's got about one more jump left in her legs, sir. Do we try it, or do we just hang here?"

With a sigh the commodore let himself down in his blasted chair. "We try it. We look around first, and catch our breath, and see if anything else is left of our task force. And if after that we find ourselves still alone, we jump again. Because there's nothing here."

Havot had seated himself nearby—there were a number of empty couches now available—and was attending with interest.

Ensign Dinant asked: "Which way do we aim? And how far?"

"We aim dead ahead, straight down that channel you're showing me." Prinsep's helmet nodded awkwardly to indicate direction. "Let the autopilot decide the range. Because we know what we have behind us here—berserkers—and we can see what we have on all sides. There's nothing for us in the deep dust."

It was true that at the moment cleared ports showed the flagship hanging, seemingly motionless, in a wilderness of dust and plasma. In several directions rolled disturbances that a fanciful observer might have been taken for Earthly thunderstorms magnified to planetary sizes but condemned to eerie silence, dark clouds sparkling and flashing with electrical discharges.

In every direction, except straight forward and astern, spread the subtle tentacles of the Mavronari, deep dust leaving ominously few stars in view, black arms outstretched as if about to bestow the last embrace that any of the intruding humans were ever going to feel. From this point even the Core could barely be distinguished with the naked eye, and that only if you knew where to look. Only straight astern, in the direction of Imatra, could anything like a normal Galactic complement of stars be seen. Straight ahead lay the night.

"Where's the rest of our fleet?"

"With any luck, we'll be able to rendezvous with them, somewhere up ahead."

Gradually Havot, not forgetting to watch the doorways while he listened to the crew talk jargon, got a better grasp on what was happening. The commodore hadn't just cut and run out of the space fight; in ordering that last escape jump, he'd had some reason to hope that his other ships or several of them—or at least one—might also have managed to escape the ambush by jumping on ahead. It appeared to be certain that at least a couple of other vessels had made the attempt to do so. Now the flagship was coming into a position from which he might expect to contact those ships again.

Now Prinsep and what was left of his crew were repeatedly trying to do so, but so far with no success.

After a conference with Dinant, his surviving astrogator, the commodore decided that his only remaining hope of reassembling his fleet, or what might be left of it, was to rendezvous with any other vessels somewhere ahead.

"The rest of our people are up there, ahead, if they are anywhere. If they are not there, they are almost certainly all dead."

"So we jump again."

"We do."

"Yes sir."

Once more flightspace closed in, then fell away. All those who still lived and breathed—except the badly wounded who had not been moved—were still gathered in the control room of the *Symmetry*, and they sent up a tentative collective sigh of relief.

They had just survived the last c-plus jump that the battered warship was likely ever to achieve. The drive had taken them out of normal space and brought them back again more or less intact.

But where had reentry dropped them? Into what looked like a

murky tunnel, a half-clogged remnant, extension, of the intra-nebular channel from which they had just jumped.

The ship's computers were quick to offer the calculation that the last jump had covered millions of kilometers. More important, the flagship was no longer alone. In the control room, even an inexperienced reader of displays and instruments like Havot could tell that.

An approximately ship-sized object—in fact several of them— lay nearly dead ahead, within much less than interplanetary distances.

The flagship's remaining weapons had already locked themselves automatically upon the largest target, which, Havot now realized, was vastly larger than the *Symmetry*. Again, he felt peculiar, conflicting feelings as he studied that monstrous shape.

But for the moment Solarian hardware and systems were holding their peace. And so far no enemy fire sprouted.

Under tighter optical focusing this target was quickly resolved into a double object. The larger component, amply big enough in itself to qualify as a large berserker, dwarfed the smaller one, and was only very slightly more distant than the smaller. And behind the smaller object of the pair, no more than a couple of kilometers from it and also in line with the approaching flagship, hung a third image, target or vessel, by a slight margin the smallest of the three.

Within moments, this last blip had been tentatively identified from the old records as Premier Dirac's armed yacht. The *Eidolon* was now holding its position relative to what gave every appearance of being Dirac's berserker, actually still linked to the space station it had kidnapped three centuries ago.

None of the handful of survivors gathered in the control room had time or energy to spend on great excitement. What resources they had left were now concentrated in an effort to assure their own continued survival.

To which the appearance of yet another berserker was decidedly relevant. Someone asked in a dead calm voice: "Are those vessels dead?"

"We'll soon see. At the moment none of them, including the berserker, are radiating anything more than you'd expect from so much scrap metal. But stay locked on with whatever arms we still have."

"Acknowledge." Pause. "We're still closing on them, sir."

"Well, keep closing. Prepare to match velocities." The commodore felt no need to spell out the reasons for this decision—if it could be ranked as a decision. They hardly had any choice. A quick inventory, balancing damage already sustained against resources available, had already disclosed to the ship's surviving officers and their computer aides such a degree of irreparable ruin that much calculation would have to be undertaken, much energy expended, just to preserve from moment to moment the lives of those aboard.

"The last thing we need right now is another fight." That, from Superintendent Gazin, was too obvious to need saying, or to deserve comment after it was said.

But Prinsep made the effort anyway. "I'm no longer looking for a fight. I'm looking for a way to stay alive. I'm assuming that's Dirac's berserker we're locked onto, and if it's not already shooting at us, I think we may risk the assumption that it's dead.

"If that object just this side of the berserker is really the missing bioresearch station, we might just possibly be able to board it and find some of the help we need. I don't see any other course of action that offers us even a ghost of a chance."

Within an hour the battered flagship had closed to no more than a few hundred kilometers from the small parade of objects dominated by the huge, dark, silent, but very ominous mass occupying the lead position.

Everyone kept watching that leading unit, expecting weapon flashes or some sharp maneuver, alert for a display of violence that, for whatever reason, did not come. All that happened was that the images of the three objects became ever more clearly visible.

"It is a berserker," Prinsep announced laconically at last. "A damned big one."

"Yes sir. It sure is—or was," Lieutenant Tongres added hopefully. "I suppose we can safely assume, given the presence of the other objects nearby, that it's Dirac's."

"Yes."

Havot, watching and listening with the others, had a hard time making any connection between the enigmatic, half-ruined mass ahead and the murderous machine that had once cornered him back on the Imatran surface.

"Hold battle stations," the commodore ordered. But still, despite urgings from his crew to get in the first blow, he refused to pull the trigger and order aggressive action.

Commodore Prinsep allowed the closure with the three tandem units to continue, while his two crew members still fit for duty, along with such shipboard robots as were still functioning, took turns applying themselves to damage control, caring for the wounded, and attempting emergency repairs of life support and weapons systems.

An ongoing monitoring of the situation confirmed that repairs to the drive and power systems were impossible, and the other palliative measures taken to keep equipment functioning were going to prove futile in a matter of hours at the most.

"Fleet Commander Prinsep." It was his dying ship itself which thus so formally addressed him.

"That is my name," he replied softly. "But I no longer have a fleet."

"Strongly suggest that you issue orders to abandon ship."

"I acknowledge the suggestion."

Still, the commodore delayed giving that command. Now a mechanical voice from the deck where the wounded lay began calling urgently for help, until one of the people in the control room, who had no more help to give, overrode the system's programming and shut it up.

At this point the commodore tried to obtain from his instruments a better optical image of the station. In his quietly controlled near desperation, Prinsep continued to pursue the chance—at first mentally rejected by Havot and others as fantastically improbable—that he might be able to find some functional help for his wounded aboard the captive biostation—if the giant berserker was really as dead as it appeared.

"A facility like that, for biological research, certainly ought to have medirobots on board, oughtn't it?" He sounded almost wistful.

Tongres said: "Sir, I suppose it would have mounted some such devices, three hundred years ago. What it must have on board right now is berserkers, if anything."

Prinsep shrugged fatalistically. "If things turn out like that, maybe we can at least take a few more of them with us. One thing I can assure you—all of you—if we simply sit here on this ship, we're all going to die in a few hours. A day or two at best."

"Are we to abandon ship, sir?"

"Let's not rush it. But I want to get the wounded into a lifeboat. And I'd rather not be seen abandoning ship if the enemy is indeed observing us."

A pair of undamaged lifeboats remained aboard the flagship, offering survival perhaps for many days, but hopelessly inadequate to the task of getting home.

There was now every reason to expect the warship to self-destruct uncontrollably within a matter of hours, perhaps a standard day at the most. With this in mind the commodore, having got his wounded packed into one of the lifeboats, did not bother trying to program the *Symmetry* to blow itself up. The near hulk would be of no value to the berserker enemy if they should take it over. Prinsep contented himself with making sure that key encryption systems and a few other secrets were destroyed.

As the minutes passed, with closure continuing at a steadily slowing rate, the nature of the most distant object became more and more unmistakably, ominously clear. The nearer vessels were far too small to obscure much of it. That most distant shape of the three was defining itself with deadly finality—if any confirmation were still needed—as a berserker of truly awesome size. One huge enough to have given Prinsep's original fleet all it could handle in the way of battle—if its murderous brain and its arsenal of weaponry still worked. For this berserker too had been through hellish combat.

What appeared to be functional weapons were to be seen projecting from its hull—and indeed, the giant, half-ruined enemy had been for some time in range, and was certainly in position, though not absolutely the best position, to fire on the new arrival approaching from astern. But, for whatever reason, the berserker's weapons still remained silent as minute after minute of the battered flagship's approach wore on.

Dinant had an announcement. "Sir, I can detect some kind of heavy forcefield, connecting the berserker and the station."

"A field like that could be a relic. Am I not correct? I mean it might persist locally, surrounding the objects to which it had been attached, for an indefinite time after the machine that created it was effectively dead?"

"Possibly, sir. The berserker's drive is obviously still functioning also. Putting out very steady, low power. At the moment only course-correcting, not accelerating. The towing field could be driven from the drive, or it could be on some low-intelligence automatic function. We can still hope that its real brain is dead."

Both the trailing yacht at the end of the small parade, and the berserker in the lead, showed signs of substantial damage, while the station, at least at this distance, did not. Some of the damage to the supposed berserker could now be observed to be fresh, judging by the heat radiation from the scars, and some definite outgassing of various elements and compounds.

Was there a thin cloud of fine, very recent debris drifting in nearby space, dispersing at a rate that proved it could not be very old? Yes, something of the kind could be confirmed.

"Where the hell did that come from?"

It created some excitement. The commodore, on observing this evidence of recent combat, said: "We must assume that our ships, or some of them, did get through this far after all, and did engage the enemy."

"Then where are our other ships now?"

"If they're not here, they evidently didn't survive the fight."

"Unless they simply gave it up as too tough a job, pulled out and headed for home?"

In either case the missing Solarian vessels were not going to be of any help to Havot and his shipmates.

❄   ❄   ❄

The people on board the slowly approaching warship were now also getting a clearer look at the kidnapped bioresearch station. The identification could now be absolutely confirmed by matching the appearance of this object against images on the duplicate old recording the approaching humans had brought out here with them from Imatra. After three hundred years the outer hull of this structure at least appeared essentially undamaged, though there was some scarring such as might have been caused by heavy explosions in nearby space.

Presently the approaching Solarians, whose autopilot had now reduced their rate of closure to only a few kilometers per minute, were able to get a better look at the antique forcefield bonds that held the berserker and the bioresearch station together. The opinion that this was a relic field received some support from further observations.

Meanwhile the continued gentle deceleration—almost at the limit of what the flagship's failing drive could have managed in any case—steadily slowed the rate of closure. The *Symmetry* was going to come to rest relative to the yacht when the two were no more than a few kilometers apart—perhaps less than one kilometer.

The little triad of antique objects, and now the warship that had joined them, were moving quite slowly relative to the surrounding nebula.

Dirac's yacht, now the nearest to the new arrivals, had been identified beyond any possibility of doubt. The *Eidolon* drifted steadily at the outer limit of the field uniting its two companions and maintained the same inert silence. Perhaps, someone mused, it was only by accident that the yacht had become attached to them and was being gently towed along.

"Evidently Premier Dirac did succeed in catching up," someone commented.

"Much good it did him, from the way things look."

Under the careful supervision of her surviving human pilot, the flagship had now succeeded in smoothly matching velocities with Dirac's once-proud vessel.

And Ensign Dinant, the remaining astrogator, now came up with a plausible explanation for the flagship's emergence from flightspace so close to the three antique machines. The explanation had to do with the channel in the nebula, which locally provided minimum resistance and maximum speed. The distribution of matter and force in nearby space and flightspace was such that any vessel traveling nearby would tend to drift into this channel; it was a path, a condition, that would not have changed substantially over the last three hundred years.

So far, as they had done ever since the flagship had come into observational range, yacht, berserker, and research station continued to maintain virtual radio silence, none of them emitting anything like a deliberate signal at any frequency.

At last Commodore Prinsep let out a sigh of something approximating relief. "You can see as well as I can, my people, that this berserker appears to be dead. But as we know, some very active bandits were close on our heels when we risked that last jump. If it's so damned easy for everything that comes this way to wind up on the same path, we might find them joining us at any moment. I fear we must assume they're going to try."

"I wouldn't be at all surprised, sir, if the berserkers we got away from do show up. If we did in fact leave any of them still functional." Ensign Dinant, a combat veteran when this voyage began, paused. "God, Commodore, but that was a fight."

"Yes, young man, indeed it was. But as we all know, those of our opponents who survived were not in the least discouraged by it. They will be doing their best to grope and crawl their way in our direction. So we must continue to bear in readiness whatever loaded arms we have."

"Sir?" This was Tongres. "Our ships aren't the only ones missing. We can't forget that there was another component to their force too. I don't think they used their full strength to ambush us."

"No, I don't suppose they did. Given the fanaticism of their pursuit of these three objects, some of them must have stayed with that. But that component of their force must somehow have overshot, or else have been thrown off the trail. Because they're not here now, which is one small piece of luck for us."

It was Superintendent Gazin who amended: "At least they're not here yet." He had not spoken for a long time, and everyone turned to look at him.

Havot had a contribution too. "We keep coming back to the same question. We can't avoid it. If only we knew what the big damned attraction is out this way, the berserkers' object in starting this whole rat race . . ."

The commodore shook his head. "We can only guess at that. But the immediate goal of *our* berserkers seems pretty well confirmed now. I think they must have been simply trying to catch up with this parade, the antique component of this rat race, as you put it." He nodded in the direction of the three enigmatic spacecraft so neatly miniaturized upon the one holostage now functioning, their short file graded in size from front to rear.

"And when they do catch up?"

"Then possibly, if we are still on the scene, we will learn

something. Perhaps at least the mystery of their behavior will be solved."

Returning to the familiar argument served at least to give the surviving Solarians something to talk about, a minimal relief from contemplating their own desperate situation.

Ensign Dinant argued, "I still say that whatever the goal of the berserkers we've been chasing, it couldn't have been simply to catch up with the Premier and his yacht. Berserkers absolutely would not have abandoned a successful attack, in a heavily populated system, just to come to grips with this man who for three hundred years has been effectively if not actually dead—a man who no longer has any fleets, no power of any kind."

Tongres was ready to debate. "All right. Then tell me what they are hunting, if not Dirac and his yacht?"

"I admit that the alternatives seem little if any more reasonable. Possibility Two seems to be that our modern berserkers are trying to overtake a bioresearch station full of prenatal specimens of Solarian humanity—specimens which have been effectively frozen as long as or longer than Dirac's been gone.

"And Possibility Three—ah, that's the real winner. It says that a whole berserker fleet is fanatically chasing one of their own machines—don't ask me why. And there you have all the apparent choices. I don't like any of them. But, damn it, there just isn't anything else out here."

Anxiously the small group of human survivors, aided by such of their faithful slave-machines as were still in operation, scanned observable space in every direction, at every moment fearing and expecting to discover fresh berserker hosts. But no enemy materialized.

The sensors and the analyzing systems on the warship were, like everything else, degraded by battle damage; but there definitely was fresh hot debris in nearby space in clouds already very thin and still rapidly dispersing, indications of recent fighting. And some of the damage on the huge berserker, whose details became plainer the longer they were studied, could now be confirmed as intriguingly recent, inflicted perhaps within the past few hours: still flaring, still glowing, traces of the great machine's inner chemistry still outgassing.

Commodore Prinsep, his face a study in despair, nevertheless continued to be relentlessly decisive in his low-key way. "We're going to check out the yacht first. I intend to lead a live boarding party over there. If we survive that excursion, but fail to obtain the help we need, we'll try pulling up right behind the bioresearch station and checking it out."

"Boarding!"

"Yes, Lieutenant, boarding. Do you have a better suggestion?"

There was none.

With a gesture Prinsep indicated displays showing the most recent damage control reports. "I'm afraid we really have no choice, given the condition of our drive and our life support. If we can find functioning medirobots on either the yacht or the station, and put them to work, our wounded may have some chance. Not to mention the fact that if the yacht's drive is still working—and for all we know that's possible—it might be capable of taking us all home."

Those words brought a general murmur of enthusiasm.

The commodore went on: "If we can't obtain help from one of these vessels, none of us are going to keep on breathing very much longer."

Prinsep had no indecision as to who should go with him to the yacht—he wanted Havot at his side. Havot nodded agreeably at the prospect.

Prinsep added: "Our task may be easier in one respect. I think we must assume that the biostation is, or has been at some time, occupied by berserkers. I do not believe the same assumption need necessarily be made about the yacht."

There followed a technical discussion, which Havot did not really understand and largely ignored, of the nature of the force-field connections obviously binding all three of the antique objects together—how strong those fields might be at various locations, and whether they represented any danger to small craft or suited humans entering them.

The consensus of opinion now was that the yacht had probably been accidentally enmeshed; it appeared to be much more weakly connected than the other two bodies.

The commodore calmly began such simple personal preparations as were necessary to go aboard the yacht. Havot watched him for a moment and then began to get ready too.

They were to attempt the boarding in one of the small and unarmed lifeboats.

Two possible sources of hope, faint but real, lay before them. The yacht and the biolab. Two out of the three antique objects. As for the third . . .

Commodore Prinsep thought to himself that no one was going to board a berserker willingly, not even a berserker as dead-looking as this one. Not while there was any other way to go.

Then he thought of an exception. Maybe Havot would.

☀ TWENTY-TWO

Havot was on a high, far removed from any care about what might be going to happen two hours from now, or three.

It was going to be damned interesting to see what happened next. On top of everything else, it gave him a kick to realize that by shooting down two berserkers he had now achieved heroic status in the eyes of his shipmates. Even Superintendent Gazin seemed to be impressed. Doubtless there were any number of planets where he'd be nominated for great honors—provided all the identities he'd had before that of Christopher Havot could be wiped away, and provided he and any of his shipmates did manage to survive.

At least any charge of goodlife activity would now look utterly ridiculous. And as for Havot's inner demons—whatever mesmerized pledge he might once have been coerced into making to the bad machines, he didn't belong in that category now.

The commodore, though, was not entirely taken in. Havot thought he could tell by the way the man sometimes looked at him.

To hell with it. He, Havot, was not going to hurt Commodore Prinsep; being around him was too much fun.

And Havot understood, too, whenever he stopped to really think about it, that if he should survive and return to what people called civilization, someone might propose him for a medal, but they'd bring it to him in a cell. He could not actually expect any kind of pardon. No human society tolerated the kind of things he'd done. But what the hell. He hadn't lost anything by getting free back at the spaceport, and at the moment he was content to ride the wave, to see what the universe put up to amuse him in the next hour or so.

Meanwhile, Christopher Havot was enjoying the way his shipmates looked at him. Sheer survival had now become the sole concern of all the flagship's remaining survivors, and under these conditions he was a good man to have around.

For the time being, at least. He understood quite well how swiftly attitudes could change.

After a short pause for rest and reorganization, he followed Prinsep to the flight deck—which was badly shot up, like every other part of the flagship—and into one of the two still-functional lifeboats.

The two men in the lifeboat, and the people they'd left on the flagship, all kept casting nervous looks in the direction of the huge berserker—or the seeming hulk that had once been a berserker. That mountainous, half-mangled mass of metal still gave no sign of life. If it was tracking the little lifeboat now beginning to move toward the yacht, they could not tell.

The name of the vessel they were approaching, *Eidolon,* was clearly visible as Prinsep and Havot in their tiny craft drew near. Dirac's antique yacht was not all that much smaller than the battered flagship, but both were dwarfed by the berserker.

In the middle of their passage in the lifeboat there came a strange silent moment in which the two men exchanged glances in a way that seemed to indicate some mutual understanding. Havot could see fear in Prinsep's eyes, but since the battle had begun he himself had experienced no fear at all. It was usually this way for Havot when he got into something genuinely exciting. He was eager to do this thing for its own sake, to go forward, to go and see whatever there was to see aboard the seemingly lifeless yacht. Active danger lured him on, as always. And there was also the reluctance to die passively. If there was any way out of this situation, it would be found only by going forward.

On impulse he said: "I'm glad you picked me to come along, Commodore."

Prinsep nodded slowly. "I rather thought you might enjoy it. And you're good with weapons. Better than any of the rest of us."

Havot tried to look modest.

"Sorry about Becky. I know the two of you were close."

Havot felt uncomfortable.

The commodore checked to make sure that for the moment they were securely alone, maintaining radio silence with regard to the outside world. Then he added quietly: "No, I'm not worried that you're going to murder me, Havot."

"What?"

"Not yet, at least. First, I can see you've decided to sign on with me, as it were, and second, the chances are that both of us are soon going to be dead anyway. But right now we make a great team, you and I. And I don't care what you did before you got on my ship, and I don't want to know."

"Murder, Commodore?" But even as he said the words, he knew they sounded false; he wasn't capable just now of uttering them with the proper shocked surprise. He supposed his heart just wasn't in the effort of trying to fool Commodore Prinsep, who kept looking at him steadily.

Getting the little lifeboat next to the yacht and selecting one of the yacht's airlocks presented no particular problem. The yacht routinely accepted docking.

Moments later, Havot and Prinsep, both with weapons ready, were standing inside the yacht's airlock, and its outer door had closed behind them, shutting them in, and now the inner door was opening. *Here ought to be the trap, or the first trap. When the door opens, a berserker will be crouched there, ready to kill—*

But the inner door slid out of their way routinely, very quietly, and there was nothing. Only the prosaic corridor extending to right and left, adequately lighted, properly atmosphered according to the visitors' suit gauges, oriented by normal shipboard gravity.

A few minutes later, having made a good start on exploring the yacht, Prinsep and Havot had found nothing to indicate that it was not really deserted, peacefully abandoned, as forsaken as might be expected in the case of a ship last heard from three hundred years ago.

At least the vessel on first inspection gave evidence of having been completely lifeless for a long time, though the *Eidolon*'s life-support systems were still functional.

That was puzzling, in a way, as Prinsep murmured to his companion. The yacht's own brain might have been expected to shut down life support when it became apparent after some substantial length of time that nobody was using it. But that evidently hadn't happened. Which suggested that someone—or something—might have told the yacht's brain not to do that.

Ship's Systems responded promptly to routine checkout commands when Prinsep tried them. It told the newcomers: "Drive inoperable," but could give no explanation.

Prinsep sighed.

The ship responded promptly to his next questions, about the location and availability of medirobots, showing how to reach them from the explorers' present location.

As they moved about the yacht, both Havot and Prinsep noticed certain old signs of combat damage.

The hangar deck was as deserted as the rest of the ship, empty of all small vessels.

Soon the two explorers found their way to the yacht's control room, without provoking any berserker counterattack, or, indeed, discovering any signs of berserkers' presence. At this point Prinsep, risking the division of his modest search party, dispatched Havot to seek out the medirobots, to confirm by direct inspection that such units were available on board.

Meanwhile the commodore himself stayed in the control room, and started checking out its systems. He totally ignored the possibility of booby traps—things were too desperate to worry about that—and concentrated on trying to start up the drive and weapons systems.

Havot gave brief consideration to the idea of quietly disobeying the commodore's order, lurking around the control room instead, protecting Prinsep, waiting to see if a berserker indeed appeared as soon as the two of them had separated. It would be fun to ambush another of the deadly machines. But just waiting for a berserker seemed too passive a course. Still, he took his time about making his way through the large, unfamiliar vessel. He moved alertly but not hesitantly, feeling intensely alive. He would play this game at his own pace, in his own way.

As if his indifference were paying off, the directions given by the ship's brain proved correct. Be ready for tricks and you didn't get them. Havot easily found his way to a narrow corridor housing the medirobot berths. There were five of the devices, like fancy coffins, each clearly marked with the Galactic emergency symbols.

Havot observed with mild surprise that one medirobot was currently occupied. Stepping close, he saw that it was doing duty as an SA device. He gazed briefly at the indistinct image of a frozen face, Solarian and male, directly visible behind statglass. Then he called up and read the legend, a plethora of detail regarding one Fowler Aristov, a youthful man who three hundred years ago had evidently volunteered to spend his life nurturing innocent young colonists as part of some grandiose pioneering scheme hatched by the Sardou Foundation. Whatever that had been.

"Knock, knock, Fowler Aristov. Time to get up. You haven't paid your rent," said Havot, taking care not to transmit his words anywhere. Even as he spoke, his gauntleted fingers were locating, arming, and activating the EMERGENCY REVIVAL control. Muted lights within and around the occupied coffin immediately indicated that things were happening. Time for Fowler Aristov to rise and shine; the commodore wanted to put someone else in this nice comfortable bed; and Havot, for the time being at least, was backing the commodore all the way.

It occurred to him to wonder whether after three hundred years these medirobots were still fully functional. He'd warm them up, get them ready for the commodore's people. Hitching his weapon into a different—but still handy—position, Havot went down the row, calling upon each unit for a checkout. Indicators showed that the special berths were all in good shape, the currently vacant ones ready to receive patients. Presumably the one currently occupied would be available in a matter of minutes. It was common practice to make such units interchangeably useable for suspended animation—in therapeutic use, hopeless cases were generally shunted by the robot into the SA mode, pending the availability of superior medical help or at least an organic decision maker.

Warily trying out the yacht's intercom, Havot communicated with Prinsep in the control room. The commodore sounded faintly surprised to hear from him—and very tired. He wasn't having any luck in getting the yacht's drive up and running.

Havot soon made his way uneventfully back to the control room, where the commodore, a study in exhaustion slumped in a command chair, looked up at him.

"Damn. Whatever's wrong with this drive, it's going to take some work, if there's any chance at all to get it going—but you say at least the medirobots are operational?"

"Yes."

"How many of them?"

"Five."

"Too bad there's not eight. But at least we can get our five worst cases into care as quickly as possible. Let's call up Tongres and Dinant, and get them started ferrying people over here."

Sandy Kensing was slowly coming up out of deep SA sleep. It was different from the arousal from ordinary sleep, vaguely like recovering from a long illness—only faster—and vaguely like being drugged. Over the last four or five subjective years of Kensing's life the sensation had come to be familiar to him, and he recognized it at once.

The gossamer threads of some glorious dream had just begun to weave themselves together, as part of the sensation of being drugged, when they were brutally torn apart. The dream had had to do with Annie and him. In it they were, for once, both out of the deep freeze at the same time, and Dirac was going to let them go, somehow send them home . . .

But already the dream was gone. Kensing was on the biostation, where he had been for too many years, for what seemed like eternity. Where he was always going to be.

Still on the biostation, in his usual SA unit. And a big man, graying, powerfully built, was bending over Kensing's coffin. "Time to get up, kid," he urged in his rasping voice.

"What?" Kensing still lay there in his glassy box, half dazed. "Give me a few minutes."

"No. Wake up now." The big man was relentless. "You're the defense-systems expert, and I want to talk to you before I go waking the boss. He's very touchy about being got up. But we've got information that someone's moving around on the yacht."

The temporary disorientation attendant upon revival from SA sleep was passing quickly. Sandy Kensing was sitting up in his glassy coffin, remembering.

"How many years this time?" he demanded of Dirac's body-guard, Brabant. At the moment, with mind and eyes a little foggy still, asking was still easier than looking at the indicators for himself.

The graying man didn't look any older than Kensing remembered him. But Brabant himself had doubtless spent most of the interval asleep. He answered: "How many years have you been out? Shade under five. Not very long."

Kensing nodded. That would make the total length of this damned voyage—if this ordeal could be called a voyage—still only a little over three centuries. He himself had not spent more than four or five years out of those three centuries awake and active, metabolizing and aging. But subjectively he thought that he could feel every second of them, and more.

"What's up?" His coffin lid had now retracted itself all the way, and Sandy Kensing moved his legs and started to get up. "I want a shower."

"Shower later." Brabant moved back a couple of steps to give him room. "Right now I need a consultation. Someone's visiting the yacht. Someone, or something."

Naked, Kensing climbed out of his coffin, reaching to accept the clothing offered by an attendant service robot. Automatically his eyes sought the other medirobots nearby, in which several of his shipmates lay temporarily entombed. Not Dirac, of course. The Premier, damn him, took his rest imperiously apart.

In *that* one, there, lay Annie. The readouts on that unit all looked normal—and that was as close as he was going to be allowed to get to Annie now.

On the way to the flight deck, where they would board a shuttle for the short trip to the yacht, Kensing asked: "Who's on the yacht?"

Brabant looked at him morosely. "That's what we're going to find out. If anyone's really there. Nick got me up, with some half-assed story about intruders, and the first thing I did was come to get you. I'm having a little trouble communicating with Nick."

"Oh?"

"He's probably over there on the yacht now. But I want to see for myself what's going on, and I want you to back me up."

Meanwhile, Commodore Prinsep was temporarily abandoning the yacht's control room, shifting his efforts to other areas of the ship. He was determined to wake up its drive and weapons systems, if at all possible.

It would be a hideous disappointment after discovering this ship, seemingly miraculously intact, to be denied its use as a means of escape.

As for the yacht's weapons, the indications were that firepower still remained; but Prinsep was not about to risk arousing the berserker with a live test.

Superintendent Gazin of the Humanity Office had slipped without protest into the role of ordinary spaceman, at least for the time being. He and the two active survivors of Prinsep's crew, Lieutenant Tongres and Ensign Dinant, were taking turns watching the berserker, making as sure as possible that the enigmatic mass at the head of the small procession was still completely quiet.

Seen from this close—berserker and yacht were less than a kilometer apart—that mass was big enough to stop a Solarian's thought processes altogether, if he allowed himself to think of it as a berserker. Its hull, rugose with damage, bulged out on all sides past the considerable bulk of the captive bioresearch station.

The lifeboat carrying the badly wounded people from the *Symmetry* had now docked successfully with the yacht, and Prinsep led his troops in their effort to stretcher the five worst cases in through airlock and corridors and lodge them in the yacht's five medirobots. He was pleased to find that Havot had the quintet of devices all checked out, warmed up, and ready.

Havot acknowledged the commodore's commendation with a dreamy smile. "What next, sir?"

"Next, you and I go to check out the research station. Dinant, you and the superintendent hang around here and keep an eye on our people. Tongres, go to the control room and take a look at the drive on this bird. Possibly I missed something."

No one questioned the implicit decision to abandon the flagship. The risks of returning to that vessel were steadily mounting, as the *Symmetry* telemetered indications that a killing explosion threatened at any moment.

Despite their growing weariness, Havot and the commodore soon reembarked in their lifeboat and headed for the research station. As they approached within a few meters of the station's outer hull, their instruments allowed them to observe closely the binding web of forcefields connecting the station with the giant berserker. But the towing field was discontinuous, leaving large areas of the station's hull readily accessible. The two explorers had no trouble in locating a suitable airlock and docking their lifeboat.

Brabant and Sandy Kensing, approaching the yacht, observed the flagship—obviously Solarian military, and looking very seriously damaged—just beyond it. And there was some movement of lifeboats between the two large ships.

"Not a false alarm, then. We've really got visitors." Kensing paused, knowing a feeling of mingled awe and hope. He looked at the body-guard. "You didn't wake the Premier yet?"

"No." Brabant hesitated marginally. "I don't know if Nick has or not. Or if Loki would let him. Anyway, I got my orders not to wake him unless it's something I can't deal with—but in this case I better."

Kensing said nothing. It would be fine with him if Dirac was allowed to sleep on through all eternity.

Brabant, opening a tight communication beam to the station, roused Loki, and debated briefly with his optelectronic counterpart. Brabant's temper had been aroused before he felt satisfied that the guardian program was really going to initiate the hour-long process of waking Premier Dirac from his self-scheduled slumber.

"Now," said Brabant to Kensing, "you and I are going to see what's really going on. So we can let the boss know as soon as possible." He eased forward on the little shuttle's drive.

As far as they could tell, none of the small handful of people plying between the mysterious, damaged warship and the yacht had yet sighted Brabant and Kensing's small craft. "Must be intent on their work, whatever it is they're doing."

Soon Kensing and Brabant had docked against the *Eidolon*, on the far side from the hatches where the boats from the strange ship had attached themselves.

Once inside the yacht, Brabant paused near the airlock to open one of the ship's lockers and take out a holstered sidearm that he attached to his belt. "You'd better wait here, Kensing. I want to take a look at these people, see what they're up to." The bodyguard hesitated marginally, then gestured at the arms locker. "Maybe you'd better put on a gun too, just in case."

So, Sandy thought, *you're going to trust me with a weapon?* But of course the answer was yes. Brabant, and Scurlock, and Dirac himself, would know that Kensing could be trusted—as long as Annie lay in suspended animation, effectively the Premier's hostage.

Kensing helped himself to one of the handguns in the locker, and then with a silent wave saw Brabant off on his reconnoitering mission.

A few seconds later, Kensing followed. Entranced by the prospect of seeing new Solarian faces for the first time in three hundred years, he was not going to wait.

He hadn't gone far before he tensed and stopped. Someone in space armor—not Brabant, he hadn't been wearing armor—was walking down a side passage toward him.

Then Kensing relaxed, recognizing the insignia, twin antique towers of masonry painted on the armored torso. It was only Nicholas Hawksmoor, in suit-form.

Even after all these years, looking in through the blank faceplate, seeing only the empty helmet, gave Kensing an unsettled feeling. He said: "Nick, I hear there are strange people on this ship."

"Yes," said the airspeakers of Nick's suit. His voice, as always, sounded very human. The suit came to a stop near Kensing. Its speakers said nothing more.

"You've changed, Nick," Kensing remarked impulsively.

"Yes, I have, haven't I? But people always change, don't they?"

"Yes, of course."

"But you meant something more. How have I changed, specifically?"

"Oh. I suppose all I meant was—well, thinking back to before you were reprogrammed—then you were—different."

"That seems a tautology, Sandy."

"Yes." Kensing considered that it probably wouldn't be wise to encourage Nick to ponder his own history. At least it could be dangerous.

But now the subject had been raised, Nick was not disposed to let it drop. "How have I changed? I'm really interested."

"Oh . . . I think you were more independent several years ago."

"Was that why I was reprogrammed? I was too independent? You know, I'm certain large chunks of my memory were taken out."

"You'll have to ask our master about that. No one's ever told me the details. But obviously you were reprogrammed about four years ago—in my subjective time, that is. Just about the time the Premier announced that Lady Genevieve had been found and was rejoining us."

"I wonder if there was a connection?" Hawksmoor sounded innocently puzzled.

Kensing said nothing.

"I'll ask the Premier sometime," Nick decided. "He's not awake right now."

"He soon will be. I think Brabant has argued Loki into getting the old man out of his box."

Nick seemed to have mixed feelings about that, because his suit turned this way, turned that way, shook its empty helmet. "He doesn't want to be awakened, ever, unless something we can't handle should come up."

"That's what Brabant said . . . so, who are these people coming aboard the yacht? Their own ship looks all shot up."

"I noticed that, of course. But I don't know who they are. All the organic humans I know are in their assigned places—except one."

"Oh? Who's that?"

Hawksmoor sounded uncharacteristically uncertain. "I had thought his name was Fowler Aristov, but now I'm not sure of his identity. I'm not sure of what to do."

"Where is he now?"

Nick's suit raised an arm and pointed down the corridor.

Kensing started that way, turned back. "Coming?"

"Not now. You go and look. See what you think. I'll join you later."

Moments after that, Kensing was near the place where the medirobots were installed, when he heard someone call his name.

"Sandy?" The word was spoken in a soft, incredulous whisper. The voice, coming from somewhere behind Kensing's left shoulder, startled him so that he spun round.

A white-faced figure, wearing common shipboard-issue shirt and trousers and sandals like Kensing's own, was advancing toward him out of a softly lit side passage. The form was that of a young man, backlit by ambient illumination so that Kensing could not at first get a good look at the face. But the more he did see of the young man's face as he approached, the crazier it seemed. Because this looked like—like—

But it couldn't be—

"Sandy?" And now the voice, a sound from the dim past, was thoroughly recognizable. "Sandy, is Dad here? What's going on?—I know this is his yacht. I woke up here an hour ago, lying in a medirobot—"

Kensing took a step closer to the tottering figure. Softly, incredulously, he whispered: "*Mike?* Michael Sardou?"

Going aboard the bioresearch station with Commodore Prinsep, prowling and exploring, Havot happened to be the one to make the first historic contact with one of the long-term residents.

Advancing cautiously through one of the biostation's corridors, a passage astonishingly almost choked by a mass of semicultivated greenery, he encountered a woman who was proceeding cautiously toward him. The look on her face suggested that she was expecting to encounter something out of the ordinary.

Her small body was glad in casual shipboard garb. She was youthful in appearance, with coppery-brown curls framing pretty, vaguely Indonesian features.

On catching sight of Havot, an armored figure pushing his way through vines and stalks, the young woman stopped, staring at him in pure, open wonder. "Who are you?" she demanded. "And bearing weapons? Why? What—?"

"Only a poor shipwrecked mariner, ma'am." He gave a little helmet nod by way of bow. "And who are you?" Although Havot, who in his spare time on the voyage had studied the history of Dirac and his times, felt fairly certain that he had already identified this woman from her pictures.

She confirmed his recognition in a kind of automatic whisper, as if she were still shocked by his very presence. "I am the Lady Genevieve, wife of the Supreme Premier, Dirac Sardou."

It was only a few seconds later when Commodore Prinsep, advancing cautiously in stable artificial gravity, through air as good—if somewhat oddly scented due to the prolific greenery—as that he'd ever breathed on any other ship, rounded a corner and, to his considerable surprise, encountered Havot speaking with Lady Genevieve.

Shortly thereafter the threesome were joined by Dirac, a living, reasonably healthy, and unmistakably recognizable Premier.

Clad in a self-designed uniform of sparkling elegance, but blinking and rubbing his eyes as if he'd just been wakened, the Premier spoke imperiously to the newcomers, in his eloquent actor's bass. "You won't need your weapons, gentlemen, I assure you."

Prinsep allowed the muzzle of his carbine, which was already low, to droop still farther; but Havot still held his in a position from which it could be leveled in a fraction of a second.

And Havot, now finding himself confronted by creatures of flesh and blood rather than metal, moved one hand casually on his weapon's stock, unobtrusively detuning the OUTPUT control to razor-beam setting, for greater effectiveness against a softer target.

The imperious man, having verbally dismissed the weapons, now ignored them. As if he found the newcomers' silence offensive, he snapped at them: "Probably you can recognize me as Dirac Sardou? Or am I overestimating my historical durability after this length of time? In any case, you have the advantage of me."

The commodore, in a voice dominated by fatigue, introduced himself. "And this is Mr. Havot."

Conversation proceeded slowly. Dirac explained that he had been asleep when the newcomers unexpectedly arrived. "Rather a deep sleep, gentlemen. One needs perhaps an hour for full recovery, before one can function as one would like. But come, I am forgetting my hospitality. It's been rather a long time since we've had visitors."

Other denizens of the station now began to appear. As Prinsep and Havot later realized, these were only people Dirac now wanted awake, including Varvara Engadin and a man called Scurlock. Scurlock mentioned his companion Carol, who evidently slept on, as did Drs. Hoveler and Zador. Men named Brabant and Kensing were absent somewhere at the moment.

None of the long-term inhabitants who appeared looked anywhere near three hundred years old, and Prinsep commented on the fact.

The Premier explained tersely. "We have a great many SA units available, and we've been taking advantage of them, relying a great deal on our nonorganic people to stand watch."

Prinsep was not interested in nonorganics at the moment. He said: "I hope you have at least three ready to be used."

"Sir?"

"The SA units you mentioned. I have wounded who need them badly. We went aboard the yacht first—found five medirobots there and filled them up. But three more of my crew still need help as soon as we can get it for them."

Dirac's countenance had suddenly assumed a strange expression. "One of those units on the yacht was occupied," he pronounced in a changed voice.

Frowning at the solemnity of this objection, seeing that it must be taken seriously, Prinsep turned to his companion. "Havot?"

The young man nodded casually. "True, one of the machines had a tenant. A would-be colonist, as his label described him. I turned him out to make room for our wounded."

Dirac stared at Havot for several seconds, as if he were deeply interested; perhaps almost as much in Havot as in what these intruders might have done on the yacht. Then he asked: "Where is he now? The one you turned out?"

Havot shrugged.

For a moment, Havot thought, something quietly murderous looked out at him from the cave of Dirac's eyes—as if perhaps it had been three centuries since anyone had treated any of the Premier's demanding questions quite so casually. Well, well.

Prinsep hastily stepped in, offering to communicate with the people he had left on the yacht. He would ask them to look out for "—what's his name?"

The Premier looked at him thoughtfully. "Fowler Aristov. Thank you for your concern, but I believe some of my own people are on that vessel now. You may summon yours to join us here." It sounded like a command. "Now, if you will excuse me, I think I had better go over to the *Eidolon* myself."

"Certainly, Premier Dirac. But before you go, let me repeat that three more of my people coming from the yacht will need intensive care."

Dirac, already stalking away, snapped over his shoulder orders for his associates to take care of whatever number of blasted wounded might arrive, and to see that Dr. Zador was awakened. Then he was gone.

✴   ✴   ✴

The tall, disheveled man named Scurlock, under the beaming supervision of the Lady Genevieve, hastened to assure the new arrivals that the station offered more than enough medirobots to care for all of Prinsep's wounded.

The commodore rejoiced to hear it. But he suggested rather firmly that the injured he had already installed in units on the yacht be allowed to remain there. "Moving them again would certainly be traumatic. Unless there is some compelling reason—?"

Lady Genevieve was soothing. "I expect Premier Dirac will have no objection."

Scurlock also assured the newcomers that live medical help in the person of Dr. Zador would be available in about an hour. The process of her awakening, he said, had already been begun.

The necessity of dealing with recently wounded people naturally led to the discussion of berserkers, and this to description of the brisk fight the newcomers had just been through.

With sudden apprehension, Scurlock asked: "I take it, Commodore, you have not engaged in any hostilities with the machine? I mean the one we're attached to?"

Prinsep blinked. "No. You sound concerned. So this giant berserker may still be active?"

"I should think we have very little to worry about in that regard. But with berserkers one can never be sure, can one?"

"I suppose not. No, a few hours ago we found ourselves pitted against a different enemy. A more modern force." And Prinsep briefly outlined recent events, beginning with the latest raid on Imatra.

Dinant and Tongres, and the three severely wounded crew people still in their care, soon joined the group on the station. They had lost track of Superintendent Gazin, they said, somewhere on the yacht, and hadn't wanted to delay their passage to search for him.

Havot, though now weighed down by a leaden weariness, retained the curiosity to ask: "Lady Genevieve, we'll all be interested in hearing how you personally managed to survive."

"Survive, young man?"

"Your first encounter with the berserker, back in the Imatran system. Historians are almost unanimously agreed that you died then." And he favored the lady with his most winning and seductive smile.

Seated in one of the spare cabins on the yacht, Mike Sardou was telling his old friend Sandy Kensing how he had very recently awakened, to his own intense astonishment, in the glassy coffin of an operational SA device here on his father's yacht. He didn't know how he'd come to be there or who had given the order to revive him. He didn't know how long he'd been there, until Sandy broke the news.

Michael related now how, as his mind had cleared fully, he'd prudently kept out of sight of Prinsep's people, while watching them bring their seriously wounded aboard and start putting them into the medirobots.

Here was evidence that some kind of battle was going on, or had recently been concluded. Mike couldn't recognize any of the people, or even the space armor they were wearing.

Nor could he guess what connection they had with his own predicament. But Mike strongly suspected that his father—or some faction among his father's supporters—had put him in the coffin, under a false identity, in an effort to get rid of him. Alternatively, he might for all he knew have been kidnapped by some of the Premier's enemies.

Kensing asked: "Does the name 'Fowler Aristov' mean anything to you?"

"That's the name that was on my SA unit. Beyond that, no, I never—" Mike broke off. Someone was coming down the corridor.

In a moment Nicholas Hawksmoor, still in suit-form, had appeared in the half-open doorway.

Kensing quickly performed the necessary introduction. Hawksmoor with his encyclopedic memory had already recognized the Premier's son, the image of whose face showed up in a thousand records of one kind or another.

But all the records to which Nick had access also agreed that young Mike had gone off on some kind of a long trip, only vaguely specified, three hundred years ago. His confirmed presence aboard the *Eidolon* was contradictory and astounding.

At first Nick was suspicious of the contradiction in his records. "You're Mike Sardou?"

"Yes." Warily.

The wariness existed on both sides. "What're you doing here? Your father told me, told everyone, that you had gone off traveling."

"If my father really said that, then obviously my father lied."

Nick didn't answer.

Mike went on: "Damned if I know what I'm doing here; I mean, I'm not surprised to find myself here on the yacht, because the last thing I can recall is going to bed in my stateroom . . . where are we, by the way? Where in space?"

It took the others a couple of minutes to bring him up to date on events, after which there was a pause while Mike tried to digest the information. Then Nick demanded: "Can you think of any reason why you should have been put to sleep, under the name of Fowler Aristov, three hundred years ago?"

Mike looked at them, his first stunned incomprehension swiftly turning into rage. "Yes, I can think of a reason—of a man who thought he had reasons, and who would have stopped at nothing—my father. Oh, damn him. Damn him!"

Nick's helmet nodded. "I can believe that, yes. You've been ... reprogrammed, in a way. As I have. By the same man. Our father. I acknowledge him as my creator too, you see ..."

Nick paused, lifting, turning his empty helmet to reposition the airmikes, in an eerie semblance of a human tilting his head to listen. In a moment the others heard the footsteps too.

Brabant arrived, to stand in the doorway looking at them all in indecisive anger.

Mike recognized him immediately. "Brabant, what is this?"

"Kid, I think you just got a little too big for your britches, is what it is. The old man doesn't put up with any back talk. You should've known that."

"So he did this to me." There was a seething, quiet rage behind the words, reminding all the others of the Old Man himself.

Brabant looked around at the others, then back at Mike. "If you hadn't been his son, he would've wiped you out, instead of saving you here. But he doesn't put up with any crap, from you or anyone else."

Nick said: "Our father puts up with nothing from anyone. He always gets what he wants."

Brabant's expression altered profoundly. "So, you've figured it out."

There was silence for a moment.

The bodyguard, sensing a crisis but uncertain of its exact nature, went on: "What the hell, kid? It could be worse. Part of you's had fun for three hundred years, being an architect and a pilot on the old man's staff. And the other part's had a nice long peaceful nap. Maybe the old man will let you reintegrate sometime."

Brabant's voice trailed off as it came home to him the way the other three were looking at him.

"We hadn't figured it out," said Kensing slowly. "Not quite. But we have now. Dirac recorded him. Recorded his own son, and then reprogrammed him, to make him what he wanted—a useful, obedient architect and pilot."

"All of you," said a new, unfamiliar voice. "Stay where you are."

All four turned to see a stranger in an armored suit, aiming at them a weapon usually effective only against hard surfaces. Superintendent Gazin, suspicious, as always, of goodlife.

❋ ❋ ❋

On the station variegated greenery, grown from odd stocks of potential colonial materials, much of it deliberately mutated, had over the centuries overgrown rooms and corridors, almost a whole deck, not originally intended as gardens. Vines twisted around doors, groped blindly for controls, tested the seals of hatches. Already, as a result of neglect, the growth was hiding some things, keeping others from working properly.

Dirac's lady and his aide Scurlock were smoothly cooperative in the effort to care for Prinsep's wounded, and quite properly concerned. Soon the Lady Genevieve, with the air of a gracious monarch, assigned the commodore and his surviving shipmates a corridor of cabins on the station.

There were a good many cabins and staterooms waiting to be used. Overcrowding had not been a problem, even if, as some remarks by the old inhabitants suggested, the Lady Genevieve had not been the only person born—or reborn—here in the last three hundred years.

As soon as the commodore's bleary eyes had seen to it that all of his wounded were receiving the best treatment available, and that the handful of his people who were suffering from nothing worse than exhaustion were as well off as seemed possible under the circumstances, he considered giving in to his own need for rest. But for the time being he still struggled to stay awake.

Privately Prinsep now at least half suspected all of these long-term survivors, or at least Dirac, of having become some exotic kind of goodlife. But he didn't want to voice his suspicions until he could talk them over with his own trusted people—the remnant he had left.

With this in mind the commodore, struggling yet a little longer to keep awake, warned Dirac's contemporaries that there was a good possibility of continued danger from the pack of bandits he and his people had just been fighting.

The commodore worriedly renewed his inquiry: "I take it your berserker here hasn't made any aggressive moves toward you lately?"

"It has not," Scurlock reassured him. "I think we may assume our ancient foe poses no immediate threat. We've had no trouble with it for a long time. But if you were planning—some aggressive move toward it—I'd advise caution."

"Aggressive moves on our part were a possibility as long as we had our flagship. But now ... unfortunately, as you can see, we are here in the character of refugees rather than rescuers. At the moment we find ourselves needing help rather than offering protection. Of course, we do bring certain weapons and equipment that you may have been lacking. If there is anything that we can do ..."

"There's no hurry, after three centuries—can it really have been that long? We must begin by offering what we can in the way of hospitality."

Sounding urbane and eminently reasonable, Scurlock, after checking with Lady Genevieve, commanded the still-working service robots to bring refreshment for everyone.

Gradually the story of the past three centuries aboard began to be told by the long-term residents—or enough interesting fragments to make it possible to start trying to guess the pattern of the whole.

And now Prinsep, though almost asleep on his feet and about to retire to his room, inquired with anxious delicacy about food; he was visibly relieved to hear that that area of life support was still in excellent condition.

Prinsep, divesting himself of armor in his newly assigned cabin, on the verge of letting himself give way to exhaustion, in turn warned the best available approximation of a trusted aide—Havot had to play the role—that they would have to watch out for Dirac.

They were talking through the coded communication still available in their helmets.

"You want me to watch out for him?" Havot nodded. "I was about to suggest the same thing myself."

"I see signs that he's a dangerous man, Havot—is that really your name, by the way?" Then the commodore shook his head. He shed the last bit of his armor and in his underwear reeled toward his bed, speaking uncoded words in air. "Sorry, I'm getting punchy. No matter. Yes, I want you to do the watching-out."

"You still trust me, then."

"Oh yes. Actually there are some matters, Christopher—is *that* really your name?—in which I trust you profoundly."

Havot thought it over. "You know, Commodore . . . ?"

But the commodore was sound asleep.

☀ TWENTY-THREE

Kensing watched, poised for action, as the stranger advanced one hesitant step and then another. The weapon in the newcomer's armored hands swung unsteadily to aim at first one and then another of the four men who confronted him. Blink-trigger carbine, alpha, or simply manual firing? It could make a very important difference.

"I am Superintendent Gazin of the Humanity Office," he proclaimed, in a voice that seemed to be struggling to establish authority. "Investigating goodlife activity."

Brabant's voice was infinitely more confident, though his own weapon still rested in its holster. "I'd take it kindly if you didn't point that thing at me."

Immediately the barrel of the superintendent's weapon swung back to aim at him. "Drop your own gun first!" he commanded. Then Gazin glanced at Nick, who was standing in suit-form near Brabant. In the next instant the superintendent seemed to freeze, as he became aware of the empty helmet and, presumably, of some of its implications.

Exactly what triggered the eruption of violence Kensing could not have said. He threw himself down, rolling on the deck, trying to get his own unarmored body out of the way as Gazin's weapon flared, beam searing ineffectually at Nick's armor. Beside Kensing, Mike Sardou was also trying to save himself.

The man from the Humanity Office—whatever that might be—had fired at Nick, and Brabant had shot back. Brabant's heavy sidearm proved the most effective weapon, force packets puncturing Gazin's suit and driving the man staggering against the bulkhead behind him. Gazin's weapon fell from his arms and he crumpled to the deck on top of it.

Nick, his armor scorched and glowing but still intact, had already decided on his next move, and now performed it with nerveless optelectronic speed. He spun toward Brabant, both metal gauntlets of the hollow suit lashing out.

The bodyguard went down at once and soundlessly. Brabant, his head smashed, twitched on the deck and died without another word.

Kensing, climbing slowly to his feet, found his own sidearm in his hand. Slowly he reholstered it.

Mike—the two examples of him—stood beside Kensing, his organic form close to Sandy Kensing's right side. The hollow suit, inhabited only by patterns of information, was just at his left.

"Two men dead," said Kensing, gazing with gradually developing shock at the still forms on the deck, Brabant and the stranger. "What do we do now?"

"Easy," said Mike, raising his eyes to look past Kensing into the empty helmet of the other version of himself.

The airspeakers on Nick's armor had the answer ready: "We go after the old man."

Mike nodded. "He'll be coming over here, all right. To see what's happened."

"And I know just where we can take him," the speakers said. "I know just how."

"Nick?"

No answer.

Dirac was standing now in the cavernous space of the *Eidolon*'s flight deck, right beside the open hatch of the little shuttle from which he had just disembarked.

He tried again, raising his voice—only modestly, he didn't want to advertise his presence on the yacht to any of Prinsep's people who might still be around.

"Nick?"

Still no reply. The sheltering spaces of the *Eidolon* around him were all silent. A certain quality in the ship's silence, he thought, momentarily letting himself be fanciful, suggested that his once-proud yacht had been waiting for him. Well, he would investigate, and by the time Loki had transmitted himself over from the station, he, the Premier, might have uncovered some answers. Loki had orders to remain on the station until Scurlock felt sure of being able to manage these well-armed intruders.

As for himself, fully armored and armed as he was, the Premier felt confident of being able to deal with any emergency that was at all likely to come up, at least until Loki should arrive.

Proceeding cautiously to the deck where the medirobots were located, Dirac found all five units occupied, just as the ineffective-looking commodore had announced. None of the devices were in SA mode, and each of them contained a semiconscious stranger, man or woman.

There was no one else around. The members of Prinsep's crew who were still active had by now probably joined their commanding officer on the station. But where were Nick and Kensing and Brabant?

And—on a deep level the most disturbing question—what had happened to Mike?

When Dirac tried asking the ship directly, its bland, imperturbable voice informed him that the people he was trying to locate could be found in the ten-cube.

"Why in the devil—" But there was no use trying to debate these matters with the ship. He would go and see for himself.

At the threshold of the VR chamber, the Premier discovered that the facility was indeed in use. Most of the interior was glowing with a huge and elaborate presentation.

Letting the entrance door close behind him, Dirac frowned at what he saw. Nick—or someone else?—had called up and was displaying a certain design project the Premier had meant to keep secret for some time yet. The display was not truly interactive, a simple holograph that required no special helmet for viewing. It was the model of a projected colony, the heart of a new plan he had been perfecting in secret. It showed how the colony he now intended to found would very likely look when construction was well along.

The solar system and the world on which this plan would eventually take form were yet to be determined, of course, still unknown even to Dirac himself. The site would depend to a great extent upon where his—partner—wanted to take them.

At the center of the model as it was now being presented arose a palatial residence . . .

And voices were discussing it. He couldn't see the speakers—he supposed they were behind some portion of the glowing image—but he could hear them plainly.

"—and whose house is that going to be?"

"Can't you guess?"

Two voices, those of Nick and Mike. They were quite different. Both sounds were intensely, equally familiar to Dirac, though he had not heard one of them for centuries.

Mike was saying: "The great mansion must belong to the man who even now—in his own warped mind—is becoming less and less a man, and more and more a god. The one who's going to rule it all."

And Nick: "Except that he isn't going to have the chance."

"To sit in this house and rule this colony."

"Oh yes, definitely, this is a colonial plan. The outer defenses. Right here in the middle, the palace for god to occupy. And a lot of other housing round it."

"But—I wonder what this is over here? Some kind of temple? Church? Monument?"

Dirac judged that it was time for him to break in. "That is another kind of house," he proclaimed in a loud voice. "For the machine. I think it will be pleased to have that kind of a facility."

"Hear that? he calls it a machine," Mike's voice commented, its owner still invisible to the Premier. "What he means is the berserker."

Dirac saw no reason to put up with any argument. "The machine with which we have been coexisting for three hundred years. Whatever we call it, it's basically only another machine. As such, it can be managed, used, if the problem is approached with sufficient intelligence, and the proper attitude."

Even before he had finished speaking, a vast rippling, a sea change, passed over the holographic representation before him.

The glowing images re-formed themselves, dimmed and cooled their colors, became old stone washed in the mellow illumination of stained glass transmitting sunlight.

Dirac found himself standing in the Abbey near the foot of the few steps leading up to the sanctuary, looking east, in the direction of the high altar just beyond.

What he was seeing was a true VR display, and it ought not to have been so clearly visible, accessible, through a helmet faceplate built to withstand harsh reality and not for playing games and dealing symbols. The fact that he could see the imaged Abbey with such clarity must mean that someone—it had to be Nick, of course—was directly manipulating the light of the image as it approached the Premier's eyes.

Was this an attempt to induce him to take his helmet off, thus exposing himself to physical attack?

The image frayed and flickered at one side. Now Dirac could see Brabant, walking in his armored suit, coming toward him through layers of illusion, raising one arm in an urgent gesture, beckoning the Premier to come closer.

Dirac, suspecting something was wrong, did not move. Fighting down a momentary impulse to panic, the Premier realized that he had at least temporarily no control over what was happening around him.

Urgently he attempted to summon Loki by means of his suit radio. But he feared that the signal was not getting through; Loki had been temporarily baffled, cut off from contact with his master.

Now another human figure loomed, this one towering above the Premier as it confronted him. It was the magnified image of his son. Dirac could not be sure if this was real at all, but he brought up his weapon. Mike's clothing kept varying, in some quirk of the disturbed Abbey programming, from medieval robes to imaged armor to modern shipboard dress and back again. His hands looked empty, but Dirac knew better than to assume they really were.

The huge mouth of Mike's image moved, and a voice came forth. "Do you recognize me?" it demanded.

"I—" For some reason the Premier found it difficult to speak.

The young man, his expression distorted and unreadable, was staring directly at him. "I'm here, in the flesh, just as you are. Father. *Do you recognize me?*"

"All right. I know you. Mike."

"You don't know me."

"How about me?" This voice came from a different direction, and Dirac spun around. An armored suit, its helmet empty, was standing in the south transept, down near Poets' Corner. Nick's voice pressed at him. "Who am I? *Father,* can you tell me who I am?"

"Nick, someone's been fooling with your programming." He wanted to sound calm and eminently reasonable. "You shouldn't be acting like this." *(Loki, where are you? Come to my help at once!)*

The empty suit advanced a step. "Fooling with my programming? My programming! Someone's been doing worse than that."

Now letting his anger show, the Premier demanded: "Is this your poor idea of a joke, Nick? What does this mean?"

And now Brabant's image loomed once more, shambling toward him from the north transept, beckoning and clad in armor.

"Brabant—?"

Then the bodyguard's armor became modern, and the Premier realized with a hideous shock that Brabant's face inside the walking suit was dead.

With his gun he shot down the walking corpse.

Return fire blasted at Dirac. His armor, the best made anywhere, pounded at his body, burned him, but it saved his life. He caught brief glimpses of Kensing and of Mike, both armed with heavy pistols though unarmored. They were shooting from positions concealed in the VR's room distorting displays.

Dirac cut loose with more rounds of his own, setting his weapon on full automatic. Meanwhile he went groping his way backward through the virtual reality of the Abbey, around stone columns, past stone skeletons on tombs, trying to find the exit. No wonder they had lured him in here to be assassinated; here in the ten-cube Nick had some hope of being able to control the flow of events. Or thought he did.

Nick's voice came at him, inexorably. "This is my territory, Father. Only my dreams can be real in here, not yours. And Loki will not be able to get in here to help you."

Dirac fired again. And again. Plenty of force packets left. He couldn't tell what he had hit. But get off enough rounds, and the machinery maintaining the VR world was bound to be damaged into failure.

The complex battle circuits in his helmet had now wakened, tuning in to alpha waves and feeding back. As lower levels of his consciousness inevitably became engaged, symbolic images emerged to confuse and trouble him.

And then a fragmentary message came through on Dirac's suit radio, just a few words and it broke off again, but it was enough to provide a surge of hope. Loki was aware of his peril, was coming to his aid, was raging just outside the barriers put up by Nick, an immaterial juggernaut, a tidal wave of information assaulting an optelectronic drawbridge, battering and roaring to get in.

Here inside the VR pit, the fight was very material and real.

Dirac, still heavily protected by his armor in spite of everything, still only battered and bruised, not seriously hurt, battled for his life. At moments of great fear or horror he closed his eyes to avoid the images, but that was little or no help. The terrible images still offered information, if he could interpret them coolly.

Before him he saw dueling knights, and one of them was himself— thoughts of conflict, of weapons, evoked images of medieval swords and armor.

Now the combatants were dueling gargoyles, as the stone creatures crawled down from their waterspout niches, marking the edges and the channels of the Abbey's leaded roof.

A hideous throng of demonic enemies swarmed about him.

Knight against monster, bright sword against white fangs, then points and edges all blood red. But he no longer knew which combatant he was, or which he chose to be.

And then at some point the portcullis failed, the gates gave way, and Loki came roaring in—inevitably, because Dirac had taken great care in his creation to make sure that Loki should be stronger than Hawksmoor.

From that point on, the tide turned swiftly, and cold reality was winning. Solid flesh and blood, and metal, would inevitably have their way with dreams and images.

Swathes of deceptive image were peeling and falling away now, exposing to Dirac's eager, realistic gaze the dull black walls of the ten-cube chamber.

Moments later, most of the images were gone, and Dirac could see out of his helmet clearly and realistically again. At this point, when a last burst from his weapon seemed to slice open the imaged stone of one of the Abbey's royal tombs—Henry Seventh, master of his own transcendent chapel—he discovered the body of Superintendent Gazin lying there in state.

The fight was over now. Mike had fallen, and so had Kensing. Only the latter was still alive. Loki, bursting in physically at last, animating his own team of armored suits, had simply been too strong.

In the ringing silence after the battle, looking down coldly at the fleshly body of his dead son, Dirac thought: what a terrible mistake. I should have—I should have—

But he didn't know, he couldn't tell himself, just what his mistake had been. Having a son in the first place? He didn't know. He couldn't say just what it was he should have done.

Nick had held out longer than the organic men against Loki's overwhelming power, but Loki after all had been designed and built to be able to manage Nick. Now Hawksmoor, still in his suit, was being confined, bottled up like a genie, like so much hydrogen power plasma.

The suit Nick inhabited was now effectively paralyzed, able to maintain its balance only by leaning against one of the VR chamber's polyphase matter walls. Meanwhile Nick was being granted an experience very few humans ever had, that of looking on his own dead body.

Nick, the loser, had a few last words to say before he was turned off. Perhaps it was involuntary, because Loki was already rifling his programming—Dirac did not particularly want to listen, but he could tell that Hawksmoor's voice seemed to be reciting, almost singing, ancient poetry. Something about a kiss, and a chair.

Dirac shook his head sadly. "Well, here we go again. Goodbye, Nick—only until you can be reprogrammed, mind. We've been through this before, but I'm not ready to give up on you. Not by a long shot."

Loki invisibly clamped down.

Nick's suit, now truly empty, crumpled softly to the padded deck.

Dirac and his guard Loki were left standing as victors upon the field of half-shattered images.

Slowly, wearily, Dirac loosened his helmet and pulled it off. The sight of the distorted, gun-riddled chamber round him was no help. Ten meters, three stories high, the same distance wide and deep. Now he could confirm the dull black reality of the ten-cube room, dusty and littered with the mixed debris of battle damage.

For a few moments all was silence. Then a small force of prosaic robots, summoned by Loki, were coming in to clean things up.

The dead bodies of Mike Sardou and Superintendent Gazin and Brabant the bodyguard were left to be disposed of by the service robots.

Wearily Dirac gave the machines their orders. "Yes, just get rid of all three of them somehow. I don't care how."

Kensing was the only survivor on the losing side. Loki, still in solid suit-form, with tatters of medieval armor-image clinging to his shape as long as he remained inside the ten-cube, and Dirac himself, dragged the half-conscious Sandy Kensing away. Loki had methodically, neatly, bound the captive's hands and feet.

"Don't kill him. Don't hurt him seriously. He'll have value, as an intact life unit, being given away."

Commodore Prinsep, on waking with a start from the sleep he had so desperately needed, found himself sprawled in his underwear on the bunk in his comfortable new quarters aboard the station. Havot, still in his armor and with his carbine at his side, was sleeping on the floor directly in front of the room's only entrance.

Sitting up, the commodore made it his first duty to cast a wary, jaundiced eye at Havot's carbine, reassuring himself about the relative safety of the setting. Then he began to dress.

The slight sound of movement aroused Havot. The two men talked briefly.

Then Prinsep set about communicating with Tongres and Dinant, who were lodging in the rooms on either side of his. He made sure that his remaining crew members were safe for the moment, and that their most urgent needs had been met.

Where was Superintendent Gazin? None of Prinsep's people had yet seen him aboard the station. Not that any of them felt vitally concerned.

In a few minutes Dr. Zador, alerted by the station's brain to the fact that the newcomers were now awake, came calling with news. Premier Dirac had returned from the yacht only a couple of hours ago, in a glum, uncommunicative mood. Now the Premier was sleeping in his quarters—ordinary sleep, not suspended animation—having left orders not to be disturbed except for the most serious emergency.

Deciding there was no use fretting over Gazin for the time being, Prinsep sat down to enjoy a vitally needed breakfast with Annie Zador and with Havot, who had at last shed his armor. Both men had showered and ordered up new clothing.

Poached eggs and ship-grown asparagus came to Prinsep's order, with commendable speed. He was relieved to find that robot service was as good here as on most ships. Nothing to complain about, though of course not up to the commodore's preferred gourmet standards.

In the course of their morning meal Prinsep resumed his historical probing in conversation with Dr. Zador. One of the commodore's main objectives was to find out all he could about Dirac's berserker. But he was also concerned about the obvious peculiarities marking this society. It gave a first impression of having evolved into a kind of benevolent-seeming dictatorship.

"The kind of thing that historically is often not really benevolent at all."

Dr. Zador several times expressed concern over what might have happened to Kensing. She feared that the Premier might have ordered him put back to sleep, this time before she had even had a chance to talk to him. She said that Scurlock and the optelectronic Loki obeyed Dirac slavishly and would have seen to it.

Havot was eating pancakes with a good appetite, and listening with interest. But he offered no comment.

Prinsep made no bones about his objections. "A bit high-handed, isn't it? Ordering people to spend years in unconsciousness, without regard for what they might want?"

Annie Zador said with quiet bitterness: "The Premier keeps reminding us that he is in command of this ship, and that we are all subject to discipline. No one disputed that at first. What we have now is a situation that's—crept up on us somehow."

The commodore let that pass for the moment. He told Dr. Zador that he would like her, as soon as possible, to check on his seriously wounded people occupying medirobots both here on the station and on the yacht.

Zador agreed. She was eager to go over to the yacht, because she was beginning to be worried about Sandy. Dirac on his return had refused to say anything about Kensing at all.

Before Prinsep and his two companions had quite finished their meal, a woman the commodore had not seen before appeared, to stand in the doorway of his room looking at him balefully. Zador informed him tersely that this was Carol, Scurlock's consort.

To Prinsep, this latest caller at first glance appeared mentally unstable. Her behavior during her visit did nothing to counteract this impression.

"So," she began, having subjected Prinsep and Havot to a prolonged scrutiny. "Does the machine know that new people, you people, have come aboard here? But of course it does."

"The machine?" the commodore inquired politely.

"Don't play innocent with me!" she flared at him. "I mean what the badlife call the big berserker. Very big. Do you know, I have seen the shadows of a hundred berserkers, crossing the face of the full moon?"

Havot chuckled artlessly; he found this entertaining. Prinsep frowned at him, then turned to ask the glaring woman: "The full moon? What planet's moon is that?"

"Don't play innocent with me. I have seen them. I have watched! I know!" Havot's louder laughter bothered Carol and she snarled something and moved on, stopping several times in her passage down the corridor to look back.

Dr. Zador, who was now casting uncertain looks at Havot, informed the men that Carol was periodically tranquilized. But she was still demented, a crabbed and crazy elder, still youthful in appearance because she was usually brought out of deep sleep only when Scurlock wanted her.

Prinsep asked: "Have I met everyone now? All of your contemporaries?"

"You haven't met Dr. Hoveler. A good man, you must talk to him. But he will still be in the freezer, I expect."

"Then we must see about getting him out. Nor have I seen much of the Lady Genevieve. Now hers must be a curious story."

Annie Zador told them as much of it as she knew. Not much about how the lady had been recorded, something of how she had been restored to flesh. And other people, other bodies at least, had been born on the station during the past three hundred years. When the advanced machinery was properly employed, a human body could be grown to physical maturity in only three or four years.

Prinsep listened carefully. "I shouldn't think this—this voyage, this exile, whatever it is, was precisely the situation where one would expect reproduction to be high on the list of desirable activities."

Havot yawned and stretched—deep moralistic talk was boring. Presently he rose, murmured some polite excuse, and drifted away. The young man was wearing fresh garments ordered from the robots this morning, a fashionable outfit topped by a flowing robe. It suddenly occurred to the commodore to wonder whether the flowing robe concealed weapons. Considering the nature of the authority that now ruled here, he didn't know whether to hope that it did, or that it did not.

Today he meant to bear his own weapon as if it were just part of a uniform.

◈ TWENTY-FOUR

Kensing regained consciousness slowly, with the feeling that the universe was roaring and collapsing around him, a titanic VR display being suddenly reprogrammed by some indifferent god.

He was lying on his back in an acceleration couch, and his immediate surroundings made it plain that he was now aboard some very small space vessel. In fact it had to be one of the little shuttles commonly used to travel from station to yacht and back again. From where Kensing was lying he couldn't really see out, but he could tell from subtle hints of sound that the small craft was in motion.

When he tried to move, he realized with a chill that his ankles were tied together, his wrists firmly bound behind him.

His last clear memory was of the fight in the yacht's ten-cube. But he could not recall just what had knocked him out. His body felt battered and bruised, but he seemed to have suffered no very serious injury, apart from having been stunned.

The shuttle seemed to be making one of its usual brief unhurried passages. Turning his head, Kensing could see that Scurlock, not wearing armor, was at the controls. No one else appeared to be on board.

Whoever had bound Kensing's arms and legs—probably Loki, he supposed—had done a well-nigh perfect job, doing no injury but leaving not the least room for trying to work free.

"We're going back to the station," he murmured aloud, with the fog of unconsciousness still not quite cleared from his mind.

Scurlock turned his head to give his passenger—his captive—a look that was hard to read. "Not exactly."

Kensing made an effort to consider that, but was forced to abandon it. "Where are the others?" he asked at last.

"The Premier is seeing to the cleanup. Brabant is dead, as I'm sure you must remember."

"Mike?"

"I don't know of anyone by that name. You also killed a volunteer mentor called Fowler Aristov."

Kensing took a few deep breaths. "Scurlock," he said. "You don't really believe that, do you? That that was his name, or that I killed him?"

Scurlock turned his gaze forward again. "The Premier and Loki have explained to me what happened on the yacht."

The shuttle suddenly dipped and sighed in flight, then grated on something hard. It didn't sound like any ordinary docking. Kensing was suddenly shocked into full consciousness.

"It doesn't matter what you think," said Scurlock, getting out of his own couch and coming to undo the fastenings on Kensing's. He sounded as if he were talking to himself.

"Wait a minute. What're you doing now? What's going on?"

Scurlock chose not to answer Kensing directly. "You're getting off here," he remarked.

Still it took Kensing another moment or two to realize that they must actually have docked with some other object than the station. The berserker? If so, then at some time during the last three centuries an actual airlock must have been put into its hull, matching the specifications of Solarian hardware.

The shuttle's little airlock was opening now, into a larger, alien chamber—and in that somewhat greater space stood a machine, a typical berserker boarding device, waiting for what was evidently a prearranged meeting of some kind.

Scurlock was strong; he lifted Kensing's helpless body from the couch quite easily against the shuttle's standard gravity.

Only now did Kensing understand how Dirac must be bargaining, arranging to stay on good terms with his unliving partner. Only now did he finally let out a yell. As Scurlock dragged him into the airlock, the berserker machine stepped forward and reached out, ready to take Kensing in its grippers and carry him down into the black lightless guts of the great metal killer.

An hour or so after that, Havot and his companion of the moment were jarred out of dozing sleep, rocked by some remote shock that set the whole massive station quivering around them.

"What was that?" the Lady Genevieve demanded in a hoarse whisper. Here in this remote cabin the two of them had felt quite safe from observation; Nick was still in the shop, so to speak, being reprogrammed, and Loki as a rule concerned himself only with people who approached Dirac.

Havot said what he thought the noise had been: the blast of the commodore's flagship finally exploding, the impact of wavefronts of radiation and fine material debris slamming, in indistinguishably rapid succession, against the station's protective outer hull.

"That must be it!" And Genevieve, relieved, sank back in bed beside him.

He hadn't needed a great deal of time, nor much exertion of his seductive powers, to maneuver himself into this position with the Lady Genevieve. He was soon going to try to get Varvara Engadin off in some remote stateroom or secluded leafy bower, and see what fun it was possible to have with her.

Havot's current companion, like so many women, found his handsome youth quite fascinating. He knew he could project an image of almost childish innocence. Somewhat irreverent, but basically a decent fellow—a dealer in educational materials.

He'd told the Lady Genevieve: "Your husband is a very fortunate man indeed—of course I'm sure he deserves his good fortune."

The lady didn't know quite how to take such a compliment. Probably, living with Dirac, she had not heard much flattery of any kind over the last century or two.

Now she snuggled up to him as if seeking protection, reassurance. Apropos of nothing, seemingly, she inquired: "Christopher? What is it that frightens you?"

"Not very many things, I suppose." He paused, thinking. "There was a time when berserkers really did."

"But they don't now?"

He lay with hands clasped behind his head, studying her. Then he responded to her last question with one of his own. "What really frightens you? The Premier?"

Jenny began now to tell Havot, in a rush, of her experiences with Nick, of the horrors of discarnate life as she remembered them. The body Havot was now gazing at, stroking, with such obvious appreciation, was actually the fourth she'd had since her return to flesh. Dirac was interested in keeping her freshly young, and also in the experiments themselves.

The truth was that Jenny, ever since Nick had plucked her from the courier's wreckage, whether in a body or not, had become obsessed with her own image. She felt compelled to refine her appearance to match some dazzling ideal of her own, but at the same time she wanted to remain unchanged, recognizable to anyone who had known her in her first incarnation.

Several times she had discussed with Havot her difficulties in finding the exactly perfect body. She craved reassurance from him regarding her appearance.

Havot was intrigued by the idea of people being able to replace their bodies practically at will. But it was not something he wanted to try personally. He felt well satisfied with the way he looked, the way his natural body functioned.

Havot was always interested in finding out what truly frightened people. Sometimes it was something really surprising. Now he probed at Genevieve, trying, gently at first, to discover the best way to provoke her. He said: "Sooner or later you won't be able to turn up such close genetic matches for your original appearance—even if you do have a billion samples to search through for a match."

"I'll worry about that when it happens. We won't come close to running out of close matches for a long time yet."

Immediately after breakfast, Prinsep had convened a planning session with Lieutenant Tongres and Ensign Dinant.

The commodore said: "The questions of overriding importance are, as I see them, first: Has this damned berserker really been finished off, or hasn't it? Second, if it's not really dead, can it be killed? And—this is a rather more breathtaking question, if possible—can its drive be taken over, in one way or another, to help a group of stranded Solarians get home?"

The more Prinsep looked at the situation, the more certain he became of one thing: for whatever reason, Premier Dirac had evidently placed himself squarely in the path of any such enterprise, as if determined to prevent it.

Over the next few hours, while Dirac's aides were still maintaining that the great man was resting and not to be disturbed, Prinsep

found that the station's other long-term residents either would not
or could not help him much. Carol uttered vaguely disturbing nonsense, when she said anything at all. Scurlock was openly antagonistic
to the newcomers' intrusion, and neither the Lady Genevieve nor
Varvara Engadin was inclined to be useful.

Compounding Prinsep's other worries, Superintendent Gazin was
still missing, as were Sandy Kensing and the man called Brabant,
the latter evidently Dirac's bodyguard.

Scurlock, who came to keep Prinsep company for a time, dropped
a few hints that all three absent people might have fallen foul of
the berserker in some way.

"Then it is still active? There might be berserker devices on the
yacht?"

Scurlock replied mildly: "When you've had a chance to accustom
yourselves to our situation—which has now become your situation
as well—you'll understand that we are neither goodlife, nor exactly
prisoners."

"Perhaps you will explain to us, then, just what our situation is?"

Scurlock looked up past Prinsep's shoulder, and his face changed
with relief. "Here comes the Premier. He can explain these things
better than I can."

Dirac, elegantly dressed and looking somber, was approaching from the direction of his private quarters. He appeared to
be ready to carry on with the explanations. "Your people in the
medirobots, Commodore, are healing peacefully, or at least resting undisturbed."

"Where's Sandy?" Annie Zador, just arriving on the scene, urgently
wanted to know. She appeared to have been waiting for Dirac so
as to question him.

The Premier turned his gloomy gaze upon her. "I don't know any
good way to break the bad news to you, Dr. Zador."

Annie stared at him a moment, then brought both hands up to
her cheeks and screamed.

Dirac, grim and unbending, went on: "There was a fight on the
yacht. Your Superintendent Gazin"—he shot a glance at Prinsep—
"evidently killed the unfortunate Fowler Aristov and then shot it out
with Brabant and Kensing. All four men are dead. And the events
left Nicholas Hawksmoor in a state of shock that necessitates his
being reprogrammed." He looked back at Annie, his gaze at last
softening into a kind of sympathy.

Meanwhile Tongres and Dinant had opened a conversation with
Varvara Engadin and were hearing a larger version of the truth
from her. Four years ago, rebellious Nick had done something that

enraged Dirac tremendously. His offense had had something to do with the Lady Genevieve.

On that occasion, Nick had been caught by Loki and Dirac, overpowered and reprogrammed, forcibly regressed to his state before the berserker had attacked the station. Something vaguely similar seemed to have happened again.

An hour after Dirac's announcement of the deaths, Dr. Daniel Hoveler was awakened, partly at Prinsep's request and partly in response to the pleas of the violently grieving Annie.

Both Zador and Hoveler, when Prinsep talked to them alone, were inclined to doubt Dirac's version of the deaths of Kensing and the others.

Commodore Prinsep wanted to learn for himself what other resources and assets, concealed by Dirac or perhaps unknown to him, might be available. And he was concerned about the poisonous, mysterious mental atmosphere of the place as it had evolved under Dirac's dictatorship. Therefore he requested a general meeting of everyone on board the station and currently awake.

Dirac agreed, with seeming willingness.

When everyone had gathered, the commodore demanded: "What really keeps us from making a concerted effort to take over the berserker's drive and using it to get home?"

In response the Premier argued that between the forcefield obstacles, and other passive defenses the berserker was sure to have in place, reaching either its brain or its drive was quite impossible, and any effort along that line must be suicidal.

Another argument, this one put forward by Scurlock, was that the dead grip of the berserker's forcefields on the station was just too powerful to be overcome by the technology available to the station's inhabitants. It would be physically impossible for them to get to the berserker and to penetrate its hull, if they tried.

"How can you know until you do try?"

None of the long-termers had an answer satisfactory to Prinsep and his aggressive crew members.

Prinsep said: "Well, we've brought with us a few items, at least, in the way of technological reinforcement. And in the absence of any convincing arguments to the contrary, we intend to try them. If the yacht can't move, our only way out of this situation may be to board the berserker and turn it around—or at least turn it off!"

Prinsep turned back to Dirac. "In your opinion, Premier, is the berserker towing this vessel dead or not? Or how would you describe its condition?"

The other was, as usual, icily ready for a confrontation. "This berserker has been for some centuries basically inert."

"For some centuries, you say. Could you be a little more specific about the time?"

Dirac said: "It has been inert almost from the start."

"You're telling me that this berserker's condition, its behavior, hasn't changed substantially in three hundred years? And still you haven't been able to do anything against it?"

"It may be easy for you, Commodore, to accuse—"

"You haven't even *tried*?"

"I say, it may be easy, for one who has not shared our struggle for survival over the last three centuries, to criticize the path which we have followed. I'm sure that technically the berserker is not entirely defunct."

"Because its drive is active."

"Partly that, yes."

"And because some kind of astrogation system is evidently functional. An autopilot, enough instrumentation to keep the machine on a steady course. And the towing forcefields, obviously. Anything else?"

"Beyond that we enter the realm of speculation. We wouldn't want to trust a berserker, though, would we?"

"Let me put it this way. It long ago stopped trying to kill people, as far as you know?"

Dirac, a model of tolerant restraint, shook his head. "I fear it may be only—exercising a great deal of patience."

"I don't understand. What about the three men who seem to have perished on the yacht? Did they really all die simply as a result of a fight among themselves?"

"None of them were members of your crew. I don't consider that what they were doing is necessarily any of your business."

"Members of my crew are in medirobots aboard that vessel. And I—"

"Your crew members are as safe as any of the rest of us. Commodore, you are an impetuous man. We have reached a point where I think I had better state bluntly a fact I had planned to withhold until you had a better appreciation of our situation here. The fact is that we have been in communication with this berserker from time to time."

"Ah. What kind of communication?"

"It has been necessary for us to reach a truce with it. An accommodation." The Premier announced the fact calmly, with no hesitation or indication of guilt. Guilt and Dirac Sardou were strangers; they had never met.

"What sort of accommodation?"

"An implied one." The Premier gave the impression of being still very much in control. "You do not begin to understand our situation, sir."

Lieutenant Tongres burst out: "It is now our situation too!"

Dirac looked at her imperturbably. "Agreed. But you still do not seem to understand it."

The commodore raised a hand, putting a stop to the accusations, at least for the time being. He asked, reasonably: "I very much want to understand our situation, as you call it. In fact I'd damn well better know what's going on. We all had. I insist on knowing: Just what do you mean by having reached a truce?"

"It will take time for you to understand. Do not attempt to bully me, Commodore Prinsep. I am not subject to your authority on this vessel. Actually you are subject to mine." And Dirac turned his back, majestically, and walked away.

Scurlock intervened, almost apologetically, when some of Prinsep's people would have gone after the Premier: "All he's trying to say is that it comes down to this. We don't try to kill it; it doesn't try to kill us."

Commodore Prinsep, putting aside his dark suspicions concerning Dirac's sanity and intentions, also tried to avert or at least postpone a showdown. He feared an all-out fight among the humans now present on the station.

Still, the more Prinsep considered the situation, the worse it seemed. The appearance of the long-term survivors at their first meeting had been deceptive. Everyone on board when the people from the *Symmetry* arrived had appeared at least tolerably well fed and clothed. The station life-support systems were still functioning smoothly and unobtrusively, at least as well as those aboard the yacht; here too the hydrogen power lamps still put out power—as they could be expected to do for many generations. Maintenance machines still worked. Medirobots obviously had retained the ability to care effectively for even serious illnesses and injuries.

The fields created by the station's own artificial gravity system still held their proper configuration inside the hull. Recycling machines could be programmed to regularly produce new fabrics—if anyone cared—and were quite capable of coming up with new designs—if anyone was interested. Some machines aboard might have been originally installed for testing with a view to eventual use by future colonists.

Prinsep also continued to be concerned about his wounded, trying to keep an eye out for their welfare even after they were all safely lodged in medirobots. He saw to it that these units were inspected regularly by one of his own people, or by Dr. Zador.

❀   ❀   ❀

Hoveler and Zador questioned Prinsep closely about what might have happened to the remainder of his fleet. The medical workers now longed for—even as others aboard feared—the arrival at any hour of more people, real victorious Solarian rescuers in a powerful ship. The Premier was at the same time wary of this happening. For Dirac saw his own new dreams of power endangered by the arrival of possible intruders. Centuries ago he had written off any real possibility of rescue. In his planning he had ceased to allow for any such turn of events.

Prinsep decided it would be wise to give the impression that he believed the arrival of a fresh ship was a real possibility, even though his belief was quite different. Simply considering the possibility would tend to undermine Dirac's control.

The latest version of Nicholas Hawksmoor, just restored to duty after his reprogramming, pondered the situation of great complexity in which he found himself.

Other people on board, the ones who had evidently known two earlier versions of himself, were now calling him Nick[3]. To Nick himself those earlier versions usually seemed utterly remote, even though he shared certain memories with them.

One of the few things he could be sure of, in this entrancing and perilous world he was now being allowed to reenter, was that the Lady Genevieve was very beautiful. Another thing, which Nick discovered almost immediately upon returning to his duties, was that this intriguing and appealing woman was now having an affair with Christopher Havot—whom Nick immediately began to hate.

One more discovery was that the Lady Genevieve was very wary around Nick, as if she were afraid of him. He had no idea why this should be so. He could not believe that any earlier version of himself could ever have caused her any harm.

Tentatively he approached her, establishing his presence on holo-stage, in her room, at a time when she was alone and he could feel reasonably certain they were not going to be interrupted.

He said: "Mistress, I think you know me."

She looked sharply at the unexpected intruder. "I know you are called Nick. Nicholas Hawksmoor. What do you want?"

"Only to reassure you. I have the impression that you fear me, and I don't know why. I want to promise you in the strongest terms that you have nothing to fear from me. Doing you any harm, even alarming you, would be the last thing in the world—"

"Thank you, Nick, thank you. Was there anything else? If not, please let me alone."

"Yes, my lady. But if you would answer one question for me first?"

"What is it?" Reluctantly.

"I do not sleep, as I suppose you know. Yet there have been times—I suppose it has something to do with being reprogrammed—times when it has seemed to me that I have dreamed. Dreamed that I was in a body, and you were in a body too, and with me. I don't know if you can tell me anything about these dreams of mine—if that is what they are—but I felt I had to say something to you about them."

The lady was staring at him in an entirely new way. "How very strange," she breathed.

"My lady?"

"No, Nick, we have never been in bodies together. You have never had a body at all."

"I know that."

"But you do appear in certain of my dreams. Just as you say I have appeared in yours. Gods of all space, how I wish I could be rid of them!"

Moments later, Hawksmoor withdrew, relieved that the lady did not seem to hate him, but otherwise no wiser than before.

He found the thought of being subject to endless cycles of reprogramming somehow depressing, though it did seem to confer a kind of immortality.

Nick, as far as he could remember, had never made a backup copy of himself, nor did he want to do so.

But he was afraid that Dirac might well have copies of him.

Havot told Prinsep and others the story of Nick's rescue and recording of Dirac's bride, and her subsequent restoration to the flesh, as he, Havot, had heard it from the lady herself.

For Dirac, the confirmation of his bride's death, like any other obstacle he had ever encountered, had evidently been only a temporary setback. In fact it was not really Genevieve herself he needed—though he had chosen his bride from several candidates because of her valuable qualities—but rather the power, the alliance, she represented. He refused to allow himself to be deprived of those advantages.

Actually, before the Premier learned that a recording of the Lady Genevieve's personality existed, he had already begun to calculate how closely an organically grown approximation would have to resemble his original bride to be acceptable politically.

One thing was certain: by the time the battered flagship had arrived with its small band of refugee survivors, Dirac had been operating the artificial wombs intermittently for centuries. His first determined effort had been to duplicate his beloved—or to recover their child, as a first step in bringing back its mother. And fairly soon he had discovered that Nick[1], with the help of Freya[2], was conducting a very similar operation.

After the treachery of Nick[1] had come to light, and that unfortunate version of Hawksmoor had been reprogrammed into Nick[2], Dirac had continued his own experiments, but now with different aims in mind.

Zador and Hoveler agreed with Prinsep and his people in their doubts about Dirac's version of what had happened to Sandy Kensing and the other men who had disappeared on the yacht.

"Why such a delayed announcement of their deaths? Why the cleanup before anyone was notified?"

Dirac on being confronted with these questions responded that he was not required to account to anyone for his decisions. But he denied that there was any real mystery.

In general the Premier seemed rather surprisingly indifferent to reports of what had been happening back in civilization, even on the worlds he had once ruled. He seemed to choose to disbelieve whatever news he didn't like. When he talked at all about the people he had formerly governed, he spoke as one assuming those folk—or their descendants—would still be eager to have him back, if they were given the choice.

Dirac spoke calmly of how much he missed his homeworld and his people. But he did not seem to have any real wish to rejoin them.

Prinsep thought he was gradually coming to understand the situation. Ever since the station had been isolated, centuries ago, Dirac had become increasingly the prisoner of his own mania for power. The tricks with the artificial wombs were a significant part of the story, but no more than a part. He had also read the labels on thousands of tiles, hatching one zygote after another, in an effort to recover, reconstitute, his lost beloved. Putting himself away in a guarded vault for years, sometimes decades, between hatchings of his latest experiments, thus preserving his relative youth, and avoiding long subjective waits to see how the latest specimen had turned out.

Dirac would trust no human, and only one artifact, to stand guard over him while he slept his long sleeps.

Only Loki, the specialist.

And Prinsep felt sure there must be times when the Premier worried about Loki.

☀ TWENTY-FIVE

Nick[3] had been summoned to see the boss, and now he was waiting for Loki to let him in.

Hawksmoor had not come to the Premier's private quarters in suit-form—in fact he had been ordered not to do so. Rather he tarried in electronic suspension, poised in certain delay circuits, anticipating the command that would allow him to appear upon the Premier's holostage. Meanwhile he tried, with no success, to hold some conversation with Loki. Nick now perceived Loki as he usually did, only an ominous presence, rather like a heavy static charge on the verge of outbreak. Loki communicated orders or questions and listened to the replies, but that was all.

Word from the boss came at last, and Nick, admitted to the inner sanctum, hovered optelectronically on a holostage close beside the master's ordinary bed.

Not far from the ordinary bed there was another. The Premier'd had his own private medirobot installed in this stateroom fairly early on in the voyage. The device sat there like an elaborate food freezer or a glassy coffin, overlooking the much more ordinary bed. Digits of information glowed in muted light from several panels on its sides. A bier surrounded, in Nick's enhanced perception, by a ring of fire—a visual manifestation of the electronic being called Loki.

Nick[3], in the long moment before Dirac spoke to him, found himself wondering exactly what Dirac's face must look like during those long stretches of time when it was frozen hard and solid. In a way Hawksmoor thought that his master's countenance might look quite natural that way.

Loki had already informed Nick that a woman was with Dirac, and Nick had speculated—uselessly, as far as provoking any reaction from Loki—as to who today's visitor might be. Hawksmoor doubted very much that the Premier's private caller was Dr. Zador, who loathed Dirac more with every passing year. And the Premier had as yet made no effort to get the female newcomer, Lieutenant Tongres, into his room and bed—he was intrigued by her, though. Nick felt sure of that.

Today's visitor turned out to be the Lady Genevieve, her attitude and her expression quite unhappy. And Hawksmoor felt sure, as soon as he got a look at the couple, that they had been arguing. It did not seem that the lady was here today for any purpose of romantic dalliance; both of the organic people were on their feet and fully dressed.

The Lady Genevieve barely nodded in response to Hawksmoor's formal greeting. The Premier too was ready to go straight to business. "Nick, I have a question for you. An important question."

"I'll do my best, sir."

"I'm counting on that. I believe I can still safely count on that, although your predecessors both lied to me egregiously. You—Nick[3], I mean—you haven't been in existence long enough to be corrupted yet. Have you, Hawksmoor? D'you still want to keep that name, by the way?"

"Yes sir, I'll keep it. Unless there's another name that you'd prefer I use."

"Let the name stand for now. Well, Nick? Here's my question: Has my lovely wife here been granting her favors to any other man?"

Nick was fully, terribly, aware of the lady's pleading eyes, though he took care that the eyes of his own image should not be observed to turn toward her at this moment. He answered with restrained shock. "Sir, I have never seen a molecule of evidence to support any such—such—"

"Oh, spare us, Hawksmoor, your imitation of a righteous pillar of the community. I swear, you're blushing. I don't know how you manage to acquire these routines. In fact there is much I don't know how you manage to acquire."

"Sir, to the best of my knowledge the Lady Genevieve is completely innocent."

"Have you ever seen my wife alone with the man called Christopher Havot?"

There had been a few totally innocent encounters, in corridors or other public places, as there would have been between any two organic folk aboard the station. Briskly and precisely Nick recounted the ones he had happened to witness, omitting any meetings that were not completely innocent.

Dirac questioned him on details. It was futile, of course, for a man relying on a merely, purely organic brain to try to catch out an optelectronic intelligence in omissions or contradictions concerning details. Nick, when he chose to do so, could weave a seamless cloak of deception regarding such matters, and do it all in a moment.

Presently Dirac seemed to realize this fact. He charged Nick with the responsibility of spying on Havot in the future, and soon after that dismissed him.

Nick's immediate reward from the lady, the last thing he saw as he vanished from the holostage, was a look of desperate gratitude.

As he resumed his regular chores, Nick pondered his new assignment. He was quite willing to create trouble for Havot, but not at the price of causing the lady any embarrassment.

Perhaps, he thought, his wisest course would be to warn Havot to stay away from her. Hoping to accomplish this indirectly, Nick sought out Commodore Prinsep.

Prinsep appeared to take little notice of Nick's indirect attempts to pass along a warning. The commodore had other things in mind. He tried to question Nick about the yacht's defective drive and other matters.

Nick thought he could be somewhat helpful in the matter of the drive. He remembered perfectly that three hundred years ago the yacht's drive had been damaged in the fighting when Dirac's little squadron of ships had caught up with the berserker and its captured station.

"Are you sure, Nick?"

"I have an excellent memory, Commodore," Hawksmoor ironically reminded the organic man. But then Nick paused, vaguely wondering. The memory of how that damage had occurred was quite cool and unemotional, like something learned from a history tape.

"What's wrong, Nick?"

Nick tried to explain.

"Like something you learned from a tape, hey? Or, maybe, like something that never really happened, that was only programmed in?"

"What do you mean?"

"I don't know much about your programming, Nick. But I do know that the yacht's drive shows no physical evidence of damage. Take a look for yourself next time you're over there."

Nick went over to the *Eidolon*, and looked at the undamaged hardware, wondering. He no longer knew which fleshly people deserved his loyalty—if any of them did. But he was determined to do everything he could for Jenny.

Brooding about the yacht's drive, and about why he had been programmed with erroneous information, led Hawksmoor into fantasizing about finding a quick and easy way of restoring the machinery to full function, and then taking off in that vessel—with only himself and the Lady Genevieve aboard.

Nick[3] in general disapproved of fantasies. He supposed he was subject to them only as a result of some stubborn defect in his programming. Experimenting with your will only in the privacy of your own mind was like fanning the air, shadowboxing. It accomplished nothing and proved nothing.

Nick had already spent—wasted, as he saw the matter now—a great deal of time wondering how he had been able to manage the seemingly profound betrayals that, as the facts and his memory assured him, he had already accomplished.

By now Nick[3] had deduced that the long process of his betrayal of the Premier must have started when he—or rather his predecessor Nick[1]—had flown to the damaged courier to try to help the Lady Genevieve. Up to that point he had still been running firmly, or so he seemed to remember now, on the tracks of his programmed loyalty. His only objective in boarding the doomed vessel had been to save his employer's lady any way he could.

But no, any betrayal that had really happened must have started later. Because in fact his saving the lady, and his recording her mind and personality, had in the end been a benefit to Dirac. Suppose he had not interfered. Now Jenny would be really dead, just as her husband had long believed she was. How would the Premier have gained by that? He'd have lost her permanently. And the stretch of time she'd spent in optelectronic mode hadn't caused Dirac any suffering—at least not until he had found out about it.

Prinsep, following his talk with Nick, picked up Lieutenant Tongres and Ensign Dinant and went with Dr. Hoveler into a region of the laboratory they had not seen before, to inspect the site of the experiments and bioengineering projects Dirac had been and evidently still was conducting.

Hoveler had been involved only intermittently in that work, and only reluctantly admitted his participation, because he had serious reservations about the morality of using the zygotes to grow new bodies in which to house old personalities. He served as a good if sometimes reluctant guide.

Dirac, as Hoveler explained, had always felt himself perfectly justified in trying to recover his lost bride by whatever means were necessary. And other experiments had grown out of that.

Hoveler introduced the new arrivals to Freya[2], and explained to them how and why she had been created by Nick[1].

Freya appeared to her visitors on a holostage in the lab, using an image Nick had once suggested to her, that of the head of a handsome woman, her age indeterminate, long silvery-blond hair in motion as if some breeze were blowing through the optelectronic world in which Freya dwelt.

After a brief exchange of pleasantries, Prinsep got down to business.

"Freya, can you tell me what is commonly done with dead organic bodies, here on the station or on the yacht?"

The imaged woman seemed serenely immune to surprise. "Ordinarily, Commodore, there are no dead bodies of any organic species. Such food products as meat and eggs are synthesized directly by the life-support machinery."

"I am thinking of the Solarian human species in particular. There must be experimental failures here in the laboratory. And lately there have also been dead adult human males."

"I store all such material for future use in genetic work. So far, the storage space available is more than adequate."

"Ah. And may we see what specimens you now have in storage? I am thinking particularly of adult humans."

"You may." It was Freya's business to answer questions.

She directed the visitors to another alcove of the laboratory complex, where presently they stood gazing through glass at three human corpses. Freya said the service robots, instructed only to get rid of them, had brought them to her as organic debris. Hoveler instantly recognized Brabant's body, and Prinsep and his shipmates identified Superintendent Gazin's, which was marked with obvious gunshot wounds.

The commodore stared blankly at the third body. "But who's this fellow?"

"It's certainly not Sandy Kensing," replied Hoveler, scowling. "I was expecting to see Kensing. But this definitely is someone else."

Freya told them: "Nick has identified this body as that of Fowler Aristov."

"Ah." Prinsep nodded. "The would-be colonial mentor Havot evicted from the medirobot on the yacht."

The body of Sandy Kensing remained notably missing. Freya knew nothing of what might have happened to him, alive or dead.

Nick, having noticed what the newcomers were doing, and growing curious, presently joined the group. His image, standing beside Freya's on the 'stage, confirmed the identity of Aristov. Before Nick's latest reprogramming, he'd seen that face in one of the yacht's medirobots—a memory, as clear and calm as that of the yacht's damaged drive, assured him of the fact.

Nick dropped out again at that point, but the tour proceeded. Soon Prinsep and his two aides, in the company of Nick[3] as well as Freya[2], were observing a developing female Solarian fetus, through the glass sides of an artificial womb.

"Another body for Lady Genevieve?"

Hoveler unhappily admitted that he didn't know the purpose of this particular project, or even how many bioengineering projects might currently be running.

Freya said firmly that she had been constrained not to discuss such matters in any depth, unless the Premier was present.

A few minutes later, when the tour was over, Prinsep sought out Dirac, who seemed willing and even anxious to talk to him. The commodore discussed what he had seen in the lab. But he left out all mention of the three adult corpses.

Dirac appeared eager to know what the commodore thought about the growth, the manipulation, of new human bodies.

Actually the Premier felt a great urge to explain, to someone whose opinion he respected, the advantages of his gradually developed plan to cooperate with the berserker. Prinsep was undoubtedly the best candidate currently available.

Dirac began by asking: "You disapprove of my efforts in bioengineering?"

"I have some doubts about what I've seen so far."

"Commodore Prinsep, I would like to satisfy your doubts. The fact is, that since our isolation here, I have become intensely interested in truly fundamental questions."

"Such as?"

"Such as: What is humanity? For a long time there has been no simple answer to that question. But now there are fresh ideas."

"And you look forward to exploring them."

"Shouldn't we all? *Think,* my friend, of what kind of society could be built with the variety of human components now available! The word *society* seems inadequate to describe the transcendent possibilities. And we here, on this vessel, as an isolated offshoot of humanity, we are free to remake ourselves anew."

"And what part does the berserker play in this brave new world you plan to forge?"

"Death, Commodore Prinsep, is an inevitable part of any world. Death and life are perpetually bound in coexistence. Either would be quite meaningless without the other, don't you agree?"

"Perhaps." Prinsep frowned. He had never been much for the abstract pleasures of philosophy. "Do you mean that when it becomes necessary for some of the human components of your new world to die—"

"I mean that their deaths will not be random, or entirely meaningless. In the form of the machine, death becomes quantified, organized, manageable and meaningful at last."

The commodore stared at the Premier. Dirac's face wore an expression of achievement, of satisfaction, as if what he was saying did indeed make sense to him.

"And who," the commodore demanded, "is to quantify and organize, as you put it? To decide which human life units are to die so meaningfully, and when, and for what purpose?"

"Who decides? The minds with the clearest, deepest vision!"

Prinsep did not try to hide his anger. "Reaching a truce with a crippled berserker, more or less by default, is perhaps forgivable. But this—no, what you seem to be suggesting is intolerable!"

Dirac drew himself up. He reminded his accuser that for the great mass of a billion protopeople aboard, the only possible future lay on some new world where some kind of independent colony might eventually be established. They were not wanted elsewhere; that was why they were here now.

He challenged Prinsep to name any Solarian world, whatever its type or degree of civilization, that would extend a cheerful welcome to a billion strangers, that would take in that number of people who, no matter how much they might eventually contribute, would first have to be nurtured through all the difficulties of immaturity.

Prinsep shook his head, condemning. "You would give them life only to serve you. To be coins in some damned bargain you think that you can make with death."

"I say it is only my bargaining with death, as you put it, Commodore, that has kept us all from being exterminated."

Prinsep demanded: "Then you have definite evidence that the berserker retains a capability for aggressive action?"

Dirac nodded slowly. "It is possible that it does. More than possible."

"You seem to know a lot about it."

Slowly the Premier was becoming enraged. "At least you should admit that I know more on this subject than you. You've been here in our little world a matter of days, my friend. I have been dealing with this problem, keeping my people alive, for three centuries."

Prinsep, on leaving Dirac, went wandering the decks and corridors of the station alone, trying gloomily to decide whether his only course was bloody conflict to overthrow the Premier's rule. Such a conflict might well kill every Solarian on board, and only succeed in doing the berserker's work.

The commodore's feet carried him into Freya's territory, and presently he once more stood looking down at the three dead men she was preserving.

He mused aloud: "Too bad their minds could not have been recorded. I suppose there was no hope of that by the time they reached you."

"None," agreed Freya[2]. Her image had sprouted in welcome on a nearby 'stage. "The mind, the personality, ceases to be detectable with organic death. It is still possible for some hours afterward—longer with good preservation—to obtain a distinctive individual pattern from

the brain cells, a pattern which would appear also in the recorded
personality. But as yet we can do no more than that."

"Interesting," was Prinsep's comment. "So, for example, if the Lady
Genevieve's original body were still available—"

"Yes, it could be shown to be hers. Even as this body here is readily
identifiable as the organic basis for Nicholas Hawksmoor's matrix."
And she indicated the still, dead form of Fowler Aristov.

Prinsep's head turned slowly, wonderingly. He stared at the calm
image of Freya, her long hair tossed gently by an invisible wind.
"Tell me that again?" he asked slowly.

Nick³ soon heard the story of his own origins, from Prinsep.
The story as Freya told it included the fact of Dirac's parenthood,
which she had been able to deduce from the Premier's genetic pattern kept on file.

When Nick knew the truth, his thoughts churned with murderous rage—as had those of his immediate predecessor on hearing the
same revelation. He wanted to strike for revenge, this time beginning
directly against Loki. But Loki's physical storage was inaccessible to
him, almost certainly in Dirac's private stateroom.

It would only be possible to get in there when Dirac was elsewhere, and Loki with him, concentrating his attention as always on
protecting Dirac.

Meanwhile, the Premier wanted to consult once more with the
berserker, before making a final choice on what his own next
move should be. Now, less worried than before about the secret
contacts being discovered, he had taken steps to establish a video
link—he wanted to present the graphic of his proposed colonial
design.

He had wondered, with deep curiosity, what image if any a
berserker would present upon a holostage to represent itself in a
dialogue with Solarians. The answer turned out to be that there
was only noisy emptiness. No real video signal at all was coming through.

Dirac was ready to concede that his plan for a new colony, a
new mode of human life, might well require additional centuries
to perfect. Probably it had been a mistake to talk about the plan
to Prinsep. He had known from the day the commodore and his
people arrived that there would be virtually no hope of getting them
to cooperate in the scheme. No. They would have to be dealt with
in some other way.

He paced now in the narrow cleared space of his private quarters,
occasionally turning his head to glance at the image of noisy fog,
as if he half expected the noise to coalesce into something more

meaningful. The little communicator Scurlock had brought the Premier so long ago now lay forgotten on a table. Scurlock and Varvara Engadin stood by listening anxiously.

Dirac was saying to the berserker's chaotic image: "It has been obvious from the beginning of our—I might say partnership—that you are being forced to operate under severe physical limitations. That massive damage of one kind or another prevents you from fulfilling the basic commands of your programming directly."

Only a droning near silence came through the audio channel.

Dirac paced some more. "For three hundred years now you have been in possession of a billion potential Solarian lives—and you are still unable to put them to your original purpose. To an organic intelligence, this would be very frustrating indeed. You must experience some analogous . . . feeling."

At last the voice of the machine responded. It was clear enough, but it seemed to come from a great distance, and it spoke as always in unpleasantly ugly tones, as if even the minimal amount of stress thus created might be of value in wearing away the endless resistance of Solarian humanity.

It said: "I assume these statements indicate that you have some further accommodation to propose?"

Dirac nodded. "I have. A long-term plan indeed. A great bargain between life and death, the organic and the inorganic. A number of details will have to be worked out. But I have a holographic display to show you—and I will soon send you another Solarian life unit. Perhaps several of them."

The holostage in Havot's cabin lit up, showing the signal which meant that someone was trying to call in. He had been lying in his bunk—alone—and thinking, and now he rolled halfway over, raising himself on one elbow. "Display," he said.

The head and shoulders of the Lady Genevieve appeared. Breathlessly Jenny's image demanded: "Chris? I must see you at once."

He was surprised. "Won't that be rather dangerous for you, given your husband's suddenly suspicious attitude? I don't know . . ."

"He's out of the way for the moment. Come as soon as you can. To the place you called our leafy bower. Will you come?"

Havot sighed. He smiled. "All right, within the hour."

"Please hurry!" The stage went dark.

Frowning thoughtfully, Havot was halfway through the process of getting dressed when his 'stage lit up again. "Display!" he ordered the device.

This time the imaged head was that of Nicholas Hawksmoor, who wasted no time in preliminaries. "Havot, I know you've just been summoned to a meeting. But you'd best not go. I don't care much what happens to you, but I want to save the Lady Genevieve from any further trouble."

The movements of Havot's arms, pulling on his clothing, slowed to a stop. "Ah. Aha. What sort of trouble exactly?"

"That wasn't really her, you know. The image on your holostage just now."

"What?" Though now that the suggestion had been made, Havot realized that something about the image had been just a little— *odd*.

Hawksmoor nodded. "It was Loki. He can do tricks with recorded images and voices. Not quite as well as I can do them, but still well enough to serve the purpose."

"And I suppose if I respond to the summons, I'll die?"

Nick seemed to hesitate momentarily. "Perhaps you won't die instantly. But something will happen that you won't like. Loki is already waiting in suit-form near the rendezvous. And a small shuttle is standing by, with Scurlock at the controls."

Havot sighed. "Thanks for the warning."

"I don't give it for your sake."

"I see. Thanks anyway." He paused. "Nick? One good turn deserves another. We ought to be able to work out something where I do one for you."

The image of Nick³ looked at Havot steadily for what seemed to Havot a long time. Then Hawksmoor said: "At the moment I am inclined to give an alliance favorable consideration."

☀ TWENTY-SIX

Nick needed only moments to locate the Lady Genevieve. He knew that currently she was nowhere near the leafy bower, nor was she in her quarters, where, unknown to her, her enemies and Nick's were ready to monitor any incoming calls. Instead, Jenny had gone wandering through the laboratory deck, and now at Freya's recommendation she was visiting the station's ten-cube.

Jenny was suddenly aware of a need to come to grips with, attain an understanding of, her own past life.

Three centuries ago, as Dirac's bride, she had come aboard this station intending a brief visit for a special purpose. Having handed over her offspring, boy or girl—actually she could not remember ever asking the sex—to the blandly tender organic doctors and machines, the Premier's young bride had then fled the station and proceeded to get herself killed—or so almost everyone had been convinced.

Her donation of three hundred years ago, the zygote sought so assiduously by the Premier when he first came aboard, had never been located. Evidently that tile had been truly lost among the enormous mass of other genetic material, as a result of Hoveler's successful scrambling of the records.

Certainly, she thought now, as she watched the development of the elaborate display that she had ordered up at Freya's suggestion, her husband was right about one thing: for the billion protopeople aboard the biostation the future existed, if it existed anywhere at all, only on some new world, where a Solarian colony could eventually be established.

Jenny's fanatical determination to cling to her restored flesh had never wavered. But she had come to feel only hate and fear for her husband. And he was jealous of her, not because he cared for her particularly as a woman, but as he would have resented any other encroachment upon his exclusive rights to anything.

Recently Dirac, gripped by jealousy, had threatened his wife with something worse than an extended deep freeze: a re-recording, followed by a reprogramming such as he had more than once inflicted upon Nick.

Centuries ago, when this Solarian bioresearch station had functioned normally, its VR chamber, like similar devices in many other scientific establishments throughout the Solarian portion of the Galaxy, had been one of the most favored research tools aboard.

Inside such a facility, researchers could easily blow up a microscopic zygote—or even a single cell or a single molecule—to room size or to the imaged size of Westminster Abbey, accommodated within a comparatively modest thousand cubic meters of real room, and could go climbing around among the imaged components sculpted by the chamber's software out of polyphase matter. Working through such modeling, researchers could obtain exactly the view they wanted of their subject; and then, with the proper tools connected, they could alter individual molecules, or even atoms, as desired.

Under normal conditions, one of the most important uses of the chamber on the biostation had been the imaging of individual specimens, in preparation for various efforts at genetic engineering.

Freya of course did not need this kind of help in grasping physical relationships and patterns. Nor did Nick. But for organic humans such graphics could be a great aid to visualization.

Today, somewhat to Nick's surprise, he found the lady standing among gigantic representations of complex molecules, getting what was evidently her first serious look at the image of human origins, the architecture of genetics.

She looked at Nick through the eyes of the VR helmet and greeted him abstractedly. He delayed delivering the warning that had brought him here long enough to conduct a very brief tutorial session, explaining what some of the exotic shapes in the graphic represented.

Lady Genevieve appeared to be impressed with all the looping, spiraling intricacies. "So, this is what we are."

"This is how we start, my lady. Or, rather, what we look like only a very little way out of the starting gate. Or while we're still in the gate, if you prefer to look at the matter that way."

"Nick, you say 'we.' But none of this really applies to you."

"Jenny, there is something I have just learned about myself. Something I want you to know."

And even as Nick explained to the lady his recent discoveries about himself, he was simultaneously carrying out two other operations, jobs that would not, could not wait.

First, acting in discrete microsecond intervals, slices of time abstracted from his talk with Jenny, he was skillfully deceiving Loki as to Havot's whereabouts.

Actually Havot, clad now in full armor and carrying his carbine, was stalking Loki near the leafy bower, approaching from a direction in which Loki was not expecting to see him. As the young man advanced, he remained in almost continuous communication with Nick. And Nick, by employing various service machines he had at his disposal, was able to provide slight noises, carefully timed distractions meant to conceal the slight sound of Havot's quiet movements from Loki's perception.

Presently Havot came to a stop, standing very quietly in front of a door that impeded further progress. Silently he lifted his carbine in both arms.

Nick silently and partially slid open the door in front of Havot.

Not ten meters down the corridor which was now revealed, Havot could now see Loki. Dirac's optelectronic bodyguard was waiting in suit-form, his inorganic attention focused away from Havot. Somewhat farther in the same direction, just round the next corner, Nick was using a service robot to fabricate the sound of cautious human footsteps, thus creating a phantom Havot, a pseudovictim, who was walking steadily if somewhat suspiciously straight into the planned ambush.

And where was Dirac himself? For a moment Nick was frightened, thinking he had lost track of the Premier. But no, there he was, in a small room just out of sight of the spot where Loki waited. The old man, in accordance with his usual behavior nowadays, was curious and jealous and worried about what his wife was doing. But for the moment at least the Premier was ignoring her. Intent on getting word from Loki and Scurlock, he was standing by to make sure that the intended abduction of Havot went off without a hitch.

And Nick, even while talking with Jenny and guiding Havot, was concurrently conducting yet a third enterprise. At this moment he came bursting, in suit-form, into Dirac's private quarters, his violent entry triggering alarms that for the moment rang unheeded. There was also the detonation at knee level of some kind of booby trap. The explosion was only partially successful against Nick's armored suit, which lost one leg just at the knee.

But that was not enough to stop him. Even damaged, Nick's armored shape crawled on to discover Loki's physical storage, three skulls' volume of metal concealed behind a bulkhead panel. In a moment Nick was rooting out his enemy with fire.

And on another deck, at the last possible moment, the avatar of Loki waiting to ambush Havot became aware of the threat behind him. Loki's suit-form blurred into evasive action at superhuman speed. But the bodyguard program had been waiting to take Havot alive, not to kill him. Therefore Loki had to draw a weapon before he could shoot back, and the fraction of a second's delay proved fatal.

For once the optelectronic reactions could not be fast enough. Havot's alphatriggered carbine stuttered and flared, spitting armor-piercing packets of force. Enough of the missiles hit home to blast another set of Loki's hardware into ruin.

And now events outside of the ten-cube abruptly demanded Hawksmoor's undivided attention. When he suddenly abandoned the Lady Genevieve, just as the distant sound of alarms and fighting reached her ears, the lady was terrified.

The unexpected sounds of fighting also interrupted a conference Prinsep had been having with Lieutenant Tongres, Ensign Dinant, and Drs. Zador and Hoveler.

Before the fighting started, the commodore had been telling his allies that there seemed no way to avoid launching a direct assault on the berserker, but how soon they could mount any such operation depended to a great extent on Dirac.

Some of those present thought that before undertaking such a desperate course of action it would first be necessary to depose Dirac as de facto ruler.

❀   ❀   ❀

When Dirac to his horror saw the pieces of Loki's armored suit scattered along a corridor seared and pocked with fragments of debris, and when the Premier's bodyguard ominously failed to respond to an emergency call for help, he quickly realized that he had been deprived at least temporarily of his most powerful and loyal defender.

Catching a brief glimpse of Havot in the distance, he fired a few shots in his direction, with no effect. Then the Premier, his mind almost paralyzed in terror and rage, hurried to the waiting shuttle which Scurlock was holding ready at an airlock near the site of the failed ambush.

Prinsep and his allies were astounded to learn facts that were soon confirmed by Nick. First, Loki had effectively been destroyed in a two-pronged attack. Second, Dirac, accompanied by Scurlock and Varvara Engadin, had fled the station in a small shuttle. The shuttle had not gone to the yacht, where Nick would soon have had the fugitives at his mercy. Instead it had gone to the berserker.

Evidently the Premier had been ready to risk the danger of seeking sanctuary with a berserker, confident that he could talk it into helping him, still holding out his offer of collaboration in the disposal of a billion protolives.

Christopher Havot, having survived without a scratch the shots taken at him by Dirac, as well as the firefight with Loki, was smiling and enjoying himself, quite ready to go along with whatever plan the commodore might think up next.

When he looked at the situation objectively, however, Havot had to admit that the Premier still seemed more likely than Prinsep to come out on top in this complicated struggle. Utter ruthlessness counted for a lot, as Havot understood full well. And the last thing Havot really wanted was to be returned to mainstream of Solarian civilization, where he would sooner or later inevitably face punishment for his crimes.

But Havot did not want to be part of any group controlled by Dirac. And anyway, what did such future considerations matter against the joys of the moment? This was fun!

Hawksmoor, still retaining his built-in but rather vague compulsion to protect Solarian humanity in general, felt a great wariness regarding the likelihood of continued bloody conflict among the Solarian factions. Definitely inappropriate, especially with a berserker waiting to pick up the pieces.

Nick thought about all that. But mostly he thought about his father, and what Dirac might be doing now and planning to do next.

Nick said to the commodore: "If he's gone to the berserker—well, we're going to have to go after him."

☀ TWENTY-SEVEN

Prinsep, having convened a meeting of his little force of friends and allies, looked earnestly round the circle of their faces. There were Havot, Drs. Hoveler and Zador, Lieutenant Tongres, and Ensign Dinant. Lady Genevieve and Carol, the only two other organic people on the station, had declined to attend the meeting and were in their respective quarters at the moment. Nick Hawksmoor had said that he would be on call when he was wanted.

The group had completed as best they could an inventory of both problems and resources. It was now time to discuss their chances of somehow surviving their present predicament and eventually getting home.

Prinsep began by admitting that he did not claim military authority over most of those present, adding that in a matter as grave as the decision they now faced, all had a right to be heard from.

Seeing encouragement on the faces around him, he went on. He maintained that, with Dirac now absent, there was no longer any reason to delay an armed invasion of the dead or dying berserker. Unless they confronted the monster directly, there appeared to be no hope of ever escaping from its grip.

It was true, the commodore admitted, that pushing the plan of direct confrontation to its ultimate conclusion appeared almost suicidally dangerous. Eventually it would involve cannibalizing drive units, or components, from the berserker, modifying them, sometimes drastically, with the help of service robots, and installing them in the yacht as a means of restoring that vessel's drive. Such a technical feat would present heroic difficulties, but it was not necessarily utterly impossible.

An alternate plan, which all agreed would be of equal or even greater difficulty, would be to completely (or adequately) pacify the berserker itself, take over control of it and establish habitable living quarters there, then drive it into the vicinity of some trade route. There they would abandon it for fear of being blasted by human warships, commit themselves to the deep in one of the existing small craft, improvise a beacon, and hope to be picked up.

Taking his turn to speak, Ensign Dinant protested that, while he was still ready to obey orders, an invasion of the berserker would be disastrous. "For a handful of us, armed as we are, to attack a berserker of this size directly won't be *almost* suicidal. It'll be the real thing. I say the damned monster must have some powers in reserve. Even if it lacks mobility, it will have booby-trapped everything. There'll be traps and tricks everywhere inside its own machinery."

Lieutenant Tongres held a different opinion. "Of course the berserker would do that if it could. But really, the thing must be dead, or very nearly so. And we can send a robot ahead. If Nick's willing to try transmitting himself, he can try getting in through the berserker's antenna systems. It must have a great variety of those. If that doesn't work he can do his tricks inhabiting the suit."

A number of armored suits in a variety of designs were still available, including those worn aboard by the newcomers, as well as suits that had been standard equipment on the station. And there was no lack of hand and shoulder weapons powerful enough to be effective against berserkers—against the enemy's man-sized units, anyway.

When Prinsep summoned him, Nick appeared promptly on holostage, ready to present technical information. The current physical separation between the captive station and its enigmatic captor was only about a hundred meters; this distance had varied over the range of a few hundred meters during the course of the long voyage.

The forcefields with which the alien marauder had attached itself to its prey three hundred years ago were still as strong as ever, as far as Hawksmoor or anyone else on the station could tell.

Tongres and Dinant, who both had engineering training, agreed that those fields must require continuous and substantial power to maintain the great machine's firm grip on its prize catch—to that extent at least the berserker could not be dead.

The balloting on the question of direct attack was tied after six folk had voted, with Prinsep, Havot, and Tongres in favor, Dinant and the two medical workers opposed.

Prinsep looked to the holostage. "Nick?"

The optelectronic man had been silent during the voting, as if unsure whether the others wanted to include him. Now he answered instantly: "I still say we must go."

When it came to a discussion of tactics, Hawksmoor decided against testing the hospitality of the berserker's antenna farm. Rather he would traverse the gap between vessels in suit-form, carrying a duplicate of his physical storage in his own belly as he moved.

He informed the Lady Genevieve that he was leaving his own

prime physical storage units on the station, in a place where she would be able to activate them if she needed help.

After a final hour spent in preparations, the party of armed investigators—Ensign Dinant, true to his word, made no further protest—assembled on the flight deck, boarded a shuttle, and in moments had departed from the station through one of its hatches on the side away from the berserker. This route was chosen in the hope that the enemy might not notice, for a time at least, what they were up to.

The party was equipped with several small relay communication units, through which they hoped to be able to maintain contact with the people remaining on the station. Drs. Zador and Hoveler had promised to do what they could from the station to support the effort.

Both bioengineer Hoveler and physician Zador still regarded their billion helpless wards as a myriad of still-sleeping brothers and sisters. Hoveler regretted his work with Dirac in a series of ever more radical experiments. Both bioworkers retained a strong feeling of kinship with the vast horde of protolives, and some of their shipmates more or less shared these feelings.

On departing the station, Lieutenant Tongres took the shuttle out in a wide slow loop, then approached the berserker's hull from a different direction.

Through the shuttle's cleared ports, surrounding space pressed in on every side, the tendrils of the Mavronari engaged in their slow inevitable drift to close in berserker and Solarian ships alike. The peril was probably not immediate, but was inexorably increasing. The last hope of any swift escape would probably be destroyed within a few years. Such a change might be brought on more quickly by the disturbances resulting from their own and the berserkers' intrusion into the nebula. Here the bow wave of a ship or a large berserker machine could produce something analogous to projected sonic shocks against steep mountainsides piled with snow.

And now the planetoid-sized mass of the berserker grew ahead of them, a lifeless landscape of sprouting weapons and old destruction, some surrealist artist's curse of war. Clutching at the faintest hope of concealment from the dreadful machine which held them captive, Tongres took the little shuttle close along one bowed strand of the towing forcefields. Even inside the shuttle, inside their armor, the invaders felt themselves being pulled or pressed, first one way then another, as if something analogous to tidal force was trying to turn them around inside their suits.

But worse was the fear, now grown much more intense. Was the berserker only allowing them to crawl into a trap before it exerted its last reserves of weakened power and finished them off?

❉　　❉　　❉

Actually the passage, even conducted at a drifting slowness, was very short. Soon they were free of the towing fields and Tongres was bringing their little craft with feathery gentleness into contact with the enemy's scarred hull.

As silently and stealthily as possible the Solarians disembarked. Naturally there was no welcoming airlock to be found, no artificial gravity. According to plan, with Prinsep in the lead, Havot and suited Hawksmoor close behind him, they began to make their way in an irregular file along the scarred and blackened outer surface, suits clinging with light magnetism to the metal beneath them, seeking the best place to try an entry.

Ensign Dinant had the feeling that a great cold was soaking into him from the ancient fabric, even through the insulation of his suit. He was keenly aware that he and his companions were climbing over, making their way around and through, metalwork that might be almost as old as *Homo sapiens.*

Prinsep moved steadily ahead, as if he knew what he was looking for, even where he was going. No use expecting a berserker to mark its hatches plainly for the convenience of live visitors, and indeed none were marked. But certainly any vessel, any machine of this size would need hatches of some kind. And there were obviously other, unplanned openings in the ravaged outer hull, the damage of a dozen or perhaps a hundred battles down through the millennia.

Then the commodore, maintaining radio silence, was gesturing for a halt, and pointing. They had reached the rim of a deep crater, where the berserker's outer hull had once been holed by some weapon of infernal violence, metal thick as a house left slagged and torn and folded back upon itself. Far down within the underlying cavity, the intruders' suit lights picked out the damaged complexities that had to represent a second layer of defense.

Nick, alone, went down a little way to look. Then he paused, shook his empty helmet at his companions, and came back. He could see no viable passage leading on in that direction.

Exercising relentless patience, Prinsep next led his band of adventurers climbing, drifting, and crawling, maneuvering among minor craters and patches of slagged metal, following a zigzag course fully a quarter of the distance around the berserker's bulk. Twice they stopped to position small communication relay units. Periodically their armor pinged and rang, buffeted almost palpably by shrieking gusts of nebular dust particles.

Dinant had begun to think they were not going to be able to get in, and he was beginning to experience a strange feeling, half let down, half elation, at the prospect.

But within a few minutes the commodore had located a more promising path. Here, where one damage crater had impinged upon an earlier one, overlapping, disrupting what appeared to have been an earlier effort at repair, destruction had left an opening of adequate size for human passage, through a crack that appeared to penetrate the full thickness of the ancient, ravaged hull.

With the commodore still in the lead, the party moved in.

Moments later they found themselves in another surrealist region, airless and lightless of course, surrounded by shapes and constructions of no immediately discoverable purpose. Now Prinsep decided to allow limited, coded, radio communication.

Proceeding with suit lights extinguished, faceplates tuned for broad-spectrum vision, including the infrared, they soon determined that they were now standing on an inner hull, which was connected to the outer by gigantic pillars and struts.

The inner hull stretched away to right and left, forward and rear, so big that standing on it was almost like standing on the surface of a planetoid. Here too signs of damage were everywhere, though not as ruinous as on the outer hull above. Still, whole segments of this inner shield were missing, some gaps looking as if material had been cut out neatly, perhaps cannibalized for repairs elsewhere. This machine badly needed a repair dock, or a complete rebuilding while it rested in secure orbit somewhere.

The intrusive Solarians steadily made their way inward, though experiencing some setbacks, encountering some blind alleys in these uncharted passageways.

"Look here."

A sizable hatchway had appeared in the inner hull, evidently giving on some passage meant to be used by maintenance machines. The door was standing open, and Prinsep used a weapon to weld it in that position before once more leading the way inward.

Now the intruders had truly reached their enemy's interior. Real hope began to dawn that they would be able to force a passage all the way to the berserker's unliving heart.

But it soon became obvious that the great machine around them was not truly dead. There were occasional vibrations, distant heavy movement, once even a dim flare of light revealing twisted alien shapes of unknown purpose.

The brief flash startled them all. "What in all the hells was that?" asked Havot.

The commodore grunted. "I don't know. Maybe it's welding something somewhere, trying to do repairs."

They moved on.

Some of the intruders knew moments when they were near to

panic. Now once more their goal began to seem discouragingly remote, perhaps impossible to reach.

But Prinsep methodically persisted. He drew encouragement from, and called the attention of his followers to, the absence so far of active opposition.

Progress continued, though with painful slowness. Twice, then three times, it was necessary to enlarge tiny openings to human size to allow passage. Nick took the lead during these operations, cutting and then even blasting their way through bulkheads and too-small hatches, creating a crude tunnel.

Then suddenly Prinsep called a halt. Reading his suit gauges carefully, he called the attention of his companions to something very strange.

"There's been a recent minor outgassing of oxygen somewhere in this vicinity. I'm picking up traces of helium and nitrogen too, as if from a breathable atmosphere."

"Dirac?—Dirac and his people, maybe. The damned thing might have made some space to keep its goodlife in."

"That's reasonable. It probably once had Carol and Scurlock aboard."

"See if we can follow the traces."

The scent was picked up again, lost, then found, somewhat stronger. The evidence now seemed solid that some kind of life-support system was, or very recently had been, in operation here.

"This is Builders' metal," Dinant muttered presently, after scraping off a minute sample of an exposed structural member, and analyzing it on the spot with an engineer's gadget he took from his belt.

Lieutenant Tongres was ready to argue. "Were you still in doubt of what this thing is? It's a berserker, all right. But it's a very old berserker, much, much older than our station. Older than *Homo sapiens* would be a safe estimate. And in fact, though there's still some hardware movement, it's now practically dead."

"All right, old, I grant you. Worn out—it could well be. Unable to be properly aggressive—quite possible. But how can you be so confident it's dead?"

"Look where we are! Look at what it's allowing us to do! How long has the whole station been riding tied to its tail? Its drive is still at least partly functional, but nothing else can be. Certainly its brain has to be moribund. If it wasn't dead, it would have long ago accelerated until it destroyed itself and the station with it."

There came a new flare of light, much brighter than before, from somewhere above, in the direction of the outer surface.

Pressing on, the explorers soon reached a passage where the traces of atmospheric oxygen were very strong on sensitive detectors, and another meter sensed the field of artificial gravity nearby. Then, without warning, came another scare. Machines that looked like service and maintenance robots could be seen moving at a distance of less than fifty meters. Obviously the great berserker was not totally dead.

At this point the first message came through, from Dr. Zador back on the station. An ominous sign, because the people there had agreed not to initiate communication except in an emergency. This message was a string of mostly garbled sounds indicating that at least the chain of little relay devices were functioning, but barely. In content, this signal was not reassuring.

" . . . there's fighting going on, in space . . ."

A few more words came through intermittently. The burden of Zador's message seemed to be that the explosions of combat were brightening the darkness of the Mavronari. Judging by what she and Hoveler could see, looking out of their cleared ports, some kind of onrushing attack force had englobed the three closely positioned objects, station, yacht, and the scarred berserker hull. But the attackers were facing fierce opposition from some source.

At one point Annie's words suggested that small units of some kind might be landing directly on the station.

Prinsep's frame was locked in rigid concentration. "Say again? Can't read you, Zador. Say again?"

" . . . fighting . . . one more . . ."

And, for the moment, that was all.

When contact with the station was so ominously broken off, Nick hastily informed Prinsep that he was abandoning the expedition to rush back to the station, to defend his beloved Jenny at all costs.

The commodore was suddenly a powerful leader. "But you are there already. You left a version of yourself aboard the station, didn't you? For just this contingency? So you stay here. Going back would only create confusion. Dirac is here, and the berserker. We're going to have to beat them here, if we're going to do your Jenny any good at all."

☀ TWENTY-EIGHT

Dan Hoveler, feeling as he usually did hopelessly awkward in an armored suit, had grabbed up a weapon and left the laboratory deck, waving Annie Zador what he thought was going to be his last goodbye. Hoveler was hurrying as fast as he could to defend the precious cargo bays. Only moments ago the station's brain, working on full alert, had reported the intrusive presence aboard of what appeared to be a pair of berserker boarding devices, entering the station separately on opposite sides.

Annie Zador, also armed and armored, was sticking to her regular battle station near the middle of the laboratory deck.

As Hoveler passed between decks, the station rocked and sang around him. Fighting still flared, even more viciously than before, in nearby space, apparently surrounding the station on every side. The people aboard had been unable to tell, so far, what forces were arrayed against each other there—certainly none of the contenders had made any effort to communicate with them.

Hoveler, even while running in his clumsy armor, continued to receive regular reports from the ship's brain which helped him keep track of the intruders. He was faintly surprised to find that neither boarding device appeared to be intent on destroying a billion Solarian zygotes, as he had somehow presumed they would be. Perhaps such an assumption was irrational, given the berserker's long peculiar history. But for whatever reason, both invaders were now converging on the deck where the great majority of the station's artificial wombs were housed.

A number of the helpless unborn—exactly how many, only Freya knew, and presumably Dirac—were there too, in Freya's semi-secret laboratory.

Dan Hoveler ran as hard as he could, doing his best to head off the mechanical killers, though he hardly expected to survive the encounter.

Moments later he dashed around a corner, only to be abruptly engulfed by a murderous crossfire from weapons much heavier than the one he carried. One of Hoveler's armored feet slid on a patch of newly molten metal, and he went down, skidding across the passageway flat on his back, the accidental fall undoubtedly saving his life. The whole corridor around him was erupting in flame and detonation.

Force-packets reflecting from the bulkheads beat like great hammers at his body. He needed a timeless moment to realize that the crisscrossing gunfire passing centimeters above his helmet was not aimed at him.

There to his right, no more than about ten meters away, the well-known and long-dreaded shape of a berserker boarder crouched on its cluster of metallic legs, twin weapons flashing from ports built into its shoulders. Hoveler had the dreamlike feeling that he could count the flashes in slow motion.

And there, back at his left, coming into view as his own body completed a sliding roll, stood what looked like the very twin of the first machine, the two of them shooting it out *against* each other.

The intensity of destruction could not endure. The machine on Hoveler's left started to go down, legs shot from under it. The metal torso was caught by three more blasts in the second before it hit the deck, transformed into a great spewing, driven splash of molten wreckage.

The roar of battle filling the enclosed space broke off abruptly. Near silence reigned, a quiet warped by the groaning of the corridor's tortured metal.

Hoveler, dazed by the battering he had received despite his suit, regained his knees and then his feet. As if he were observing the scene from a great distance, he noted that the passageway around him was ruined, shattered, wavering with heat from the bombardment. Without his armor he would have been roasted, cindered, in a second. Overhead, the long pipes of Damage Control, somehow surviving, began projecting damping fields; later there would be cooling sprays of liquid.

But one of the berserkers had survived the duel.

Unsteady on his feet, aware of his fatal organic clumsiness, knowing himself completely outclassed as a warrior, Hoveler began to raise his weapon.

His gunbarrel quivered with the unsteadiness of his grip. Just down the corridor, the victorious piece of hardware was not aiming at him, but waving metallic tentacles. And now speech came from it—its speakers were producing very unberserkerlike words, in the tones of a very human voice indeed.

It said: "Don't shoot, don't shoot! Colonel Frank Marcus here."

The Lady Genevieve, tremulous when she heard that her husband had fled the station, terror-stricken when the fighting started, had sought counsel and protection by hastily evoking the station's version of Nick[3].

Immediately after Nick joined her, she had retreated with him, at his urging, to the sheltering cool stonework of Westminster Abbey.

Standing in the ten-cube—unlike the yacht's, the station's facility was still intact—the lady pulled on the VR helmet and started walking down the long nave. This was the scene of her recurring nightmares of being bodiless again, and yet at Nick's urging she found the strength to face it.

"Will I be safe here from the machines?" She could hardly recognize the tones of her own voice.

Nick, now appearing to her in his familiar minstrel garb, was walking at her side. "I don't know about being safe. But when your husband—my father—comes looking for you, we will both of us be as ready as we can be to meet him."

Nick guided her steadily onward, as if he had some well-defined goal in mind, through the cavernous spaces of imaged stone. Oddly, Genevieve's first terror at finding herself again in these long-dreaded surroundings soon abated. This was the first time she'd seen the Abbey through organic eyes; and the differences, though subtle, gave her an important feeling of being in control.

Premier Dirac was congratulating himself on having neatly out-flanked his enemies.

When, to his surprise, they had dared to follow him to the ber-serker, he had been able to observe their approach. Then he had dared to double back and return alone to the station, the base his persecutors had abandoned. That was where his only real chances lay for his future, for his power—if the battle flaring now in space around them, evidently some new Solarian attack, was going to leave him any chance at all.

Landing his shuttle again on the station's flight deck, oblivious for the moment to any other conflict taking place on board, Dirac was welcomed by Varvara Engadin and Carol, the latter looking even more than ordinarily demented and distraught.

"Where's Scurlock?" Carol demanded, looking with wild eyes past the Premier into the little empty shuttle.

"He decided to stay back there on the berserker. I don't need him. Where's my wife?"

"She's gone into the ten-cube," Varvara informed him, and paused. Then she added bitterly: "I thought perhaps you had come back for me."

Dirac at the moment had no interest in what Varvara thought, or said. He snapped: "I'm going after her. You'd better wait here." And he stalked on in his armor, toward the ten-cube.

Scurlock had indeed elected to remain with his old protector, the berserker. He was in his heart glad to be rid of the Premier, and he had no wish at all to go back out into those other, dangerous places. The machine had fitted out a snug little anteroom, just inboard from a small private airlock, a room as big as he needed, and comfortable with properly humidified air, easy gravity, and a few items of furniture. There was even a little holostage, offering a means of looking out into space. But Scurlock wasn't really interested in those.

The little anteroom had another door, in the inboard bulkhead, obviously leading to regions deeper inside the machine. But that door hadn't opened yet. Maybe it never would.

When the shuttle docked again at the airlock, Carol got out of it alone and came into the little room.

Scurlock smiled a twisted smile to see her, and that she was alone. She smiled back, and even seemed to relax a little. It was almost like the old days, the two of them all alone with the great berserker. He had the feeling that the machine was once more going to take care of them.

He had come to realize that it was only when other people came around that trouble started.

Dirac found, as he had expected, that the ten-cube was firmly in Nick's control. This time the Premier did not have Loki at his side, but he refused to let that lack deter him. He pushed on.

He had gone quite a distance inside the Abbey, as far as St. Michael's chapel in the north transept, when he was brought to a halt by a startling sight. This was the tomb of Lady Elizabeth Nightingale, mounting on its top eighteenth-century statues that despite their nature had somehow escaped Dirac's notice until now, here among a thousand other antique images. Skeletal Death had been carved bursting out of a tomb, drawing back a spear with which to skewer the cringing Lady Elizabeth. Meanwhile a stone man, presumably her husband, stretched out an arm to try to block the blow.

"Father," said a soft voice behind him, and Dirac spun around to discover that Nick[3], the optelectronic thing that had once been his son, was there, clutching a weapon that the VR circuits molded visually into a barbed lance very like the stone one wielded by Death.

"So, you'll never learn!" the Premier snarled, and raised his own weapon and fired point-blank.

Commodore Prinsep did not want to admit the fact, even to himself, but he feared that the tenuous link of communication between his party and their friends back in the station might now have been broken. No more messages were coming through.

Quite likely the break had not been accidental. The Solarian expeditionary force had just caught a glimpse, at a range of forty meters or so, of a mobile machine very much resembling a berserker boarding device. Havot had snapped off a shot at it, but with no visible effect.

If the enemy's plan had been to trap the small band of human challengers, it seemed that the trap might well be closing now.

However that might be, the commodore had no intention of trying to turn back. Instead he continued to concentrate to the best of his ability upon the original objective: to go after the berserker's central brain and at all costs to *neutralize* it.

That was the only way to win. But Prinsep could admit in the privacy of his own thoughts that it was really a bleak and almost hopeless prospect; anyone who knew anything about berserkers understood that it would be difficult if not impossible to disable or destroy the brain without setting off some final monstrous destructor charge.

At that point, as Dinant now bitterly remarked, all their seeming success so far would mean very little.

The version of Nick[3] who was still accompanying Prinsep's people in suit-mode pressed forward in a fierce search for his hated father.

Now that he was here on the berserker, one unanswered question that had lain for centuries in the back of Nick's mind was once more nagging him insistently: exactly what had happened to Frank Marcus all those many years ago?

Almost three hundred years had passed since the arrival of Frank Marcus's intriguing and enigmatic last message, in the brief interval when he, optelectronic Nick, had been the only conscious entity aboard the yacht. But the memory of Nick[3] still preserved without detectable degradation every word, every tone and shading in that voice. It had been an odd but very human voice, produced by mechanical speakers that were driven ultimately by the neurons of an organic Solarian brain.

Of course, as Nick was well aware, eventually an epoch must arrive, thousands or tens of thousands of years in the future, when even his memory would fade.

And he reflected that such a span of life would be part of what he would give up if—when—he finally succeeded in his renewed ambition of equipping himself with a fleshly body.

But the last message from Frank Marcus had never ceased to puzzle him. Thousands of times he had played back those words and their tones, out of one bank or another of his own memory, doing his best to calculate the right interpretation.

It had sounded like a very important message, coming from a man who, everyone agreed, would much rather have died than work out any accommodation with a berserker. From a man who worshiped life as much as the berserkers hated it. From one who cherished and guarded—some would say beyond all reason—the last few handfuls of the living flesh with which he had been born, and who moved his fleshly remnant around in armored boxes. From Colonel Marcus himself.

Nick had never doubted that the important-sounding communication had really come from Frank. Berserkers, without exception, were as notoriously poor at imitating the voices of human beings as they were at mimicking human appearance. Whatever the real reasons for this deficiency, it conveyed the impression that the killers detested life so violently that they refused even to assume its likeness. Or else they were too contemptuous of human resistance to make such an effort at deception. The voices used by the bad machines, whenever they deemed it necessary or convenient to employ human language, were no better than a parody of speech. In some cases this parody was said to have been molded clumsily from real voices, the recorded syllables of tortured prisoners.

Though his acquaintance with the colonel had been brief, Nick, if asked, would have described Frank Marcus as probably the least suicidal person he had ever met. Frank's move directly against the foe hadn't been simply a gallant sacrifice. If the odds were hopelessly against Colonel Marcus—a situation he had encountered often enough—well, that was what they were. Whatever the odds, he went on sincerely trying to defeat his enemy, to keep himself alive and win.

Nick had enormous respect for Frank, despite the emanations of contempt he had sensed radiating in the other direction. No, contempt wasn't quite the right word for the colonel's attitude. Frank had been constitutionally incapable of feeling contempt for a computer program, any more than he would have wasted energy disdaining a map or a pair of pliers. All these items were useful tools, deserving of respect and proper use.

The explorers continued to advance, sometimes in a group, sometimes strung out along a corridor or two parallel corridors, but being careful not to lose contact with one another.

To everyone's intense surprise, they once caught a glimpse of what looked for all the world like green plants, vegetation actually growing behind glass somewhere inside this—this *thing*.

That seemed an extremely unlikely amenity for any goodlife quarters, no matter how willing Death might be in some cases to pamper its fleshly worshipers.

Havot, greatly intrigued by the incredible sight, wanted to turn aside and check on it.

But Prinsep insisted they stick to the goal for which they had begun this perilous exploration. He sharply warned the more easily distracted that anything alluring, enigmatic, or interesting visible down a side passage might be part of an elaborate and deliberate trap.

Dinant seconded that. "It's had plenty of time to get ready for us. To make its plans and charge whatever weapons it has left."

Lieutenant Tongres said: "And I say it is dead, or as near as makes no difference. We're right here in its guts, and it hasn't been able to kill us yet."

They moved on.

☀ ☀ ✸

After a time, the voice of one of their number, murmuring on suit radio, could be heard uttering a prayerful hope for help.

The embattled survivors could feel reasonably sure that the reinforcements the commodore had called for, before leaving Imatra, would sooner or later be probing space in this general direction, looking for them. But "sooner or later" and "general direction" were cold comfort. There was no guarantee, far from it, that the search would succeed, even if it was pushed hard—and every reason to fear that it would not even be pushed. Realistically, the chance of any relief expedition, from Imatra or elsewhere, actually reaching them in the near future, was vanishingly small.

Back on the station, the alien boarding machine that claimed to be Colonel Marcus had insisted on accompanying Hoveler, peacefully and companionably, back to the lab deck. It had been a long time, the colonel's voice said from the alien hardware as they walked, a long time since he had been able to talk to anyone. Actually he didn't sound all that much dismayed about the fact.

Annie Zador came to meet them at the door to the main lab. Her skin, despite its strong component of African heritage, paled at the sight of Hoveler's companion.

Hoveler could only stutter ineffectually in an effort to explain. But the machine at his side seemed eager to converse. Its male Solarian voice rasped out: "This is not a berserker you're looking at, people. This is me, Frank Marcus, badlife in a box. I can explain—more or less. I got put in this new box because it gives me a definite advantage in my current job."

The machine proceeded to explain. It seemed that in any battle against the common unliving foe, one important component of the value of Colonel Frank Marcus (ret.) or any other comparably equipped Solarian human, lay in the fact that this person in his box or boxes, into which no normal human adult body could fit, was able to imitate a small berserker machine in such a way that he might fool a real berserker—especially one not being particularly attentive.

Annie Zador said dazedly: "Of course the presumption among us has always been that Marcus was killed."

Hoveler nodded agreement. "I didn't suppose there was ever any question about his being killed, even if at first the berserker didn't recognize his little pile of hardware as human. It would certainly recognize it as something dangerous."

The machine scoffed. It laughed a human laugh. "*I'd* be recognized, all right. Knowing me, I'd probably find some way to advertise the fact. 'Here I am, what're you going to do about it?'"

Then the colonel's voice, issuing from what still looked like berserker hardware, told both bioworkers that his current job had brought him aboard the station to stand guard over the valuable cargo.

Zador and Hoveler, their minds reeling, agreed that the cargo of a billion protolives was very valuable.

The colonel—neither of his hearers any longer disputed his identity—said: "Right. No argument. But that's not exactly the cargo my present employer is worried about."

The station rocked with a nearby explosion. Hoveler demanded: "What's all this fighting in space around us? Who's attacking?"

"Berserkers, who else?" And with that the colonel left them, to take up his guard duties where he could best protect the deck of artificial wombs.

But just as he went out the door, he turned back a kind of metallic eyestalk and added: "If one of you, or both of you, want to come along, I'll tell you where I've been for the past three hundred years."

For some time after his recent awakening by the great machine, Frank, despite the startling things he'd glimpsed just before his capture, had clung fiercely to his first belief that he was the captive of a berserker, any other suggestion was nothing but sheer berserker trickery.

The machine, ignoring this attitude for the time being, told Frank in good Solarian speech that it had recalled him to duty because he was the finest tool available with which to fight real berserkers. No one else could do that quite as well.

And very quickly he had been forced to abandon his belief, because the machine could show him too much evidence, evidence that he must at last accept. Puzzling objects, of which Frank had caught only tantalizing glimpses before he had been overcome and captured and put to sleep, were now offered for his free inspection.

At last he had admitted: "All right then, you're not a berserker—or at least you're the damndest berserker I've ever . . . you know, the standard behavior pattern is very simple. Berserker see life, berserker kill. Just like that."

At that point Frank had stopped, and sighed, and capitulated; the sigh was a realistic sound, a good imitation of real organic lungs, an effect practiced for so long that Frank now used it unconsciously. "But you don't operate that way. You never have. You've killed, but you don't live for killing. All right, I give up. You look exactly like a berserker, but you're not a berserker. You can't be. But then just what in all the hells *are* you?"

It told him, and then it showed him. It had the evidence to prove these statements too.

Frank thought about it. "The artificial wombs," he said. "That's it, isn't it? They're what you've wanted all along."

☀ TWENTY-NINE

Dirac, heavily armed and armored, was stalking the latest optelectronic version of his son through the ten-cube's virtual version of Westminster Abbey.

And vice versa.

Devoutly the Premier wished that he could turn off at least some of these damned images. But at the moment the full complement of illusions was still firmly in Nick's control, and Nick had the interactive quotient high.

He, Dirac, would have to prevail once more by managing reality.

Dirac told himself, not for the first time, that virtual people, programs, had their drawbacks just like those of flesh and blood. One of the problems with the former, from his point of view, was that beings like Nick could not really be made to suffer.

Light falling through graphic images of stained glass painted the virtual stones of the original, antique Hawksmoor's towers in muted pastels, and left deep shadows around and behind the roots of tombs and monuments and columns. Dirac as he advanced became aware, by means of subtle clues of sight and sound, of another presence in the Abbey besides his own and Nick's. But one glimpse of this additional form in passing, wreathed in the virtual image of an angelic statue, indicated that it was only Jenny. The Premier decided that she, definitely a nonviolent woman, could be safely disregarded for the moment.

His stalking had carried him a considerable way in the virtual dimensions of the ten-cube, some distance east of the high altar and well into the royal chapels, before a more suspicious movement caught his eye, an unwonted stirring in the detailed mirage. The Premier pounced quickly, moving to grapple with his armored hands the lid of a great stone sarcophagus. The polyphase matter of the ten-cube's deck and walls instantly reshaped itself to accommodate the signals from his own visual cortex, feedback forming a firm stone ledge for him to grab.

With a surge of violence Premier Dirac wrenched open the last resting place of the half sisters Elizabeth the First and Mary. But in this time and place it was neither of the ancient queens who lay inside. The form of a much more modern woman leaped up screaming.

Dirac shouted retribution at his wife, and drove her off, a screaming wraith among the monuments and tombs.

He prowled on, himself a solid ghost among the thousand imaged graves and statues.

Without warning gunfire chattered near him, missiles glancing from the Premier's superb armor. The salvo bruised him, spun him round and sent him staggering, but that was all. It'd need a better angle, at shorter range, to bring him down.

Dirac gritted his teeth, delaying his return fire till he should have a clear target. He was wary of shooting this facility to pieces as he had the ten-cube on the yacht. He meant to do a lot of planning yet in this one, designing his new colony.

Once more Nick[3], still successfully keeping himself concealed, was shouting threats and imprecations.

His father shouted condemnation back and then moved promptly in pursuit.

"I am damned," Dirac was muttering now to himself, "damned if I am going to be killed, or beaten, by any recorded person—or, to state the thing conservatively, with legalistic prudence—by any computer program that behaves as if it believes itself to be a recorded person."

And Dirac stalked on, gloriously aware of his own fleshly mortality. He was now entering the huge, magnificent chapel of Henry the Seventh, fan vaulting as delicate as forest leaves above his head. He had always disdained having any backup recording of himself. The Premier enjoyed being flesh, and intended to retain his body.

More than once over the years Dirac had considered having himself recorded, as insurance against accidents or assassinations. There had been moments when the idea seemed tempting, but he had always rejected it. Because such a procedure could not fail to create a real potential rival.

The Premier had even imagined how it would be to undergo the experience, the splitting of his very self in *half*: he would put on the helmet and then later take it off, and nothing would have changed. At the same time, and just as validly, he would put the same helmet on, and then gradually become aware that he had said goodbye to his flesh forever. No. A deeply unsatisfactory invasion of the center of his being.

He had come out of Henry's great chapel now, letting his instincts move him back toward the center, spiritual if not quite geometrical, of the whole Abbey. Just ahead of him Edward the Confessor's chapel waited, cavernous and complex, a temple within a temple, centered on the shrine of green porphyry. There in the real Abbey's early centuries, or so the stories said, miracles abounded.

The Premier entered.

Abruptly the empty helmet of Nick's suit, transformed by illusion into a medieval casque, loomed up before his father. In the same instant Dirac's carbine, alphatriggered, shot it clean off the armored suit, which crashed and fell into a corner of illusion.

Dirac kicked at it jubilantly. "Reprogramming again for you, young man! What is it about you that you can never learn? What is it—"

Dirac was never able to complete the thought. For that was the moment when Varvara Engadin, who had followed her former lover broodingly into the Abbey, came up close behind Dirac and shot him in the back.

And now the Premier was down, and knew that he was dying. This time his superb armor had saved him from instantaneous death, but that was all.

Dimly he was aware that Freya had come from somewhere and was bending over him, long hair blowing in an invisible wind. Dirac couldn't grasp the details of what she was saying, but it seemed that, after all, he was going to be recorded.

Commodore Prinsep's mind was whirling as he and his small band of followers advanced. It was maddening, it was impossible, that there should be such an altogether inordinate amount of breathing space on board any berserker. They had now been moving for long minutes inside that space, having entered it by means of the most startling discovery yet, an actual working airlock. The controls and markings of that lock were formed according to no Solarian system that the explorers had ever heard of, yet the functioning had been smooth and accurate.

"This thing is a bloody *ship*. It's got to be." The words were delivered in a harsh, fierce whisper by Nick, who understood that they bore incalculable implications.

The other intruders, being careful to keep their suits and helmets sealed, stared at the empty helmet that had just spoken.

One of them objected: "But it can't be a ship!"

"Well, what *is* it then?"

"The damned machines didn't build a whole ship just to accommodate goodlife! They couldn't, they wouldn't."

"Maybe . . ."

"Never! Not a battlewagon like this one."

Still the intruders had encountered no real opposition. Weapons ready, they continued to advance cautiously through one of the incredible, incongruous air-filled corridors that wound its way through the belly of the beast.

Here and there on the bulkheads, which in certain corridors had been worn smooth by the agelong passage of serving machines, were engraved signs obviously intended to be read by living eyes. These notices, mostly located near apertures or controls, were in the recognizable script or printing of the Builders. A few of the signs still glowed, while time and wear at last had entirely sapped the energy from others.

Following certain lines and conduits that appeared to be concerned with information input and control, making their way through twisted corridors and voluminous ducts, avoiding any moving machinery they saw, the survivors advanced, still seeking the berserker's brain in order to destroy it.

But what the armed intruders came upon instead was something very different,

"Come look at this."

"*Damn it, keep radio silence—*"

"No. No more radio silence. I tell you that doesn't matter anymore. Come look."

Those who had been summoned went to look. And found themselves entering a steel-vaulted chamber whose deck space was well nigh filled with screens and chairs and stages.

The stages and the screens were acrawl with information in alien and unreadable symbols.

At the center of the vaulted space, a dais supported three chairs or couches of peculiar shape, somewhat bigger and more elaborate than those in the lower levels of the room. The three central chairs were all closely surrounded by the most intricate machinery, and two of them had been swiveled to face away from the people who were now entering.

This chamber could be nothing but a bridge, a control room, whatever you might call it. The suggestion was overwhelming that this was an insulated, defended place from which the huge machine could be commanded.

The invaders gazed at one another in wonder. No Solarian had ever seen or heard of a berserker mounting any facility at all like this.

Besides the peculiar chairs or acceleration couches—a dozen of them in all, including those in the farther reaches of the room—there were visual displays, some utterly unearthly, some tantalizingly almost familiar.

Was it still within the range of possibility that this, all this, was only some virtual reality, berserker subterfuge, illusion? The hardware in the room felt every bit as solid as it looked. No virtual reality, no polyphase matter, here.

The Solarians, advancing slowly, were momentarily lost, distracted, in sheer wonder. Such substantial, comprehensive controls could never have been built for goodlife.

From somewhere outside the vast machine, dimly apprehended here, came the whine and scream and smash and vibration of heavy combat.

The controls and furniture in this chamber had been designed to accommodate creatures about the size and strength and dexterity of ED humans, but whose bodies must have differed from the Solarian standard in several important ways. The lighting, for one thing, designed for different vision. For another, the intended occupants of this room had obviously been somewhat taller and a great deal thinner than Solarians. The shape and positioning of the controls also implied considerable differences.

"No." Dinant was denying, rejecting, what he saw.

Havot muttered, "A mockup, then. The damned thing has constructed a real-world simulation of some human ship."

"Not a Solarian ship," said Prinsep. "And I think not a simulation."

"This room is full of air, good breathable air." Lieutenant Tongres at least seemed on the verge of opening her helmet, declaring her acceptance of the miracle.

Havot was bewildered. "Some Carmpan vessel, then?"

That suggestion moved the commodore to something like amusement. "When did the Carmpan ever build a ship like this, or want one? No, not Carmpan either."

And then all of the intruders fell silent.

Because the central chair on the dais, which had presented its high back to the intruders, was swiveling around. And that high seat was occupied.

Filled by a figure instantly recognizable, because it came out of ancient video recordings with which all the visitors were familiar. But this was not video. The intruders were standing in the presence of a live Builder, perhaps clothed—it was hard to tell—though not visibly armored in any way. He (or just as likely, she) was sitting there regarding the intruders with a single eye centered just below the forehead, an eye whose bright pupil slid back and forth with a quivering speed that somehow suggested an insect. The being on the dais appeared, by Solarian standards, inhumanly thin.

Skin and flesh moved in the lower portion of the face, the face of a living body whose ancestors had never known the light of Sol. From between folds of loose saffron skin, a voice emerged, a muted torrent of clicks and whines. The sound was being amplified, translated for the visitors' airmikes by an artificial speaker somewhere.

It was a Builder who confronted them. Beyond all argument, a living Builder. A fabled relic, incredibly alive, rising from his (or her) control chair, staring at the intruders with his/her liquidly mobile central eye of gray or blue.

"I am the acting captain of this vessel," the being on the dais told them, "and I welcome you aboard my ship."

☀ THIRTY

The Builder who now stood towering over the gaping little audience of intruders was a slender, fine-boned being, taller than all but a very few Solarian men but topologically like a Solarian except for the single eye that stretched across the upper face, with a bright bulging pupil that slid to and fro with the rapidity of thought.

After a stunned pause, Commodore Prinsep responded to the short speech of welcome, but the commodore was never able afterward to remember exactly what he had said. The thin orange-and-yellow figure looming above him on the dais listened as a machine swiftly translated Prinsep's words into bursts of whistles and clicks.

From the first moment, the ship's captain was a convincing presence. Neither Prinsep nor any of his companions had any doubt of the nature of the being now confronting them. All of them had seen, times beyond counting, images of the Builder race, pictures extracted from a precious handful of alien video records that were older than Solarian humanity. Copies of those videos reposed in every general encyclopedia, in every comprehensive data storage bank. Images of Builders were as widely recognizable as those of Solarians from the first century of photography.

In most of the ancient Builder graphics, no matter how elegantly enhanced, the berserkers' creators showed as hardly more than stick drawings of orange glowing substance. Now for the first time in history it was plain to Solarian eyes that that orange color and brightness were the result of some kind of clothing, the exposed skin being a dullish yellow where it showed on the face, the four-fingered hands, and across part of the chest.

Before the commodore and his boarding party had fully absorbed one shock, another fell. A new flurry of excitement passed among them when one of their own species suddenly appeared on the dais within arm's length of the captain. A biologically youthful man with sandy hair, dressed in modern ship's issue clothing, arose from another of the central chairs, the tall back of which had concealed him.

Among the people who had come in with Prinsep, only Nick immediately recognized Sandy Kensing. Nick quickly informed the others of his identity.

Kensing distractedly greeted the new arrivals. From the moment he rose from his chair, he had been looking anxiously among them for Annie Zador. Now he was relieved to hear that Dr. Zador had been well when last reported. It came as no surprise to Kensing to learn that she and Dr. Hoveler had elected to remain back on the station.

"But we had given you up for dead," Prinsep reminded Kensing sharply.

The youth looked haggard. "I know that—I was about ready to give up myself, until Colonel Marcus welcomed me aboard here. Now he's gone back to the station to try to help out."

"What? Who's gone where?"

"I'll explain as best I can about the colonel's survival and my own. But first I'd better tell you we've got immediate problems—real berserkers are attacking, and this vessel—the one we're on—is their prime target. And it always has been. To berserkers, this particular ship has a higher priority for destruction than any Solarian ship. Much higher than a mere billion Solarian protolives."

Then Kensing, taking pity on the hopeless silence of bewilderment before him, drew a deep breath and slowed down a little. "I can quite appreciate your confusion, shipmates. I've been in the deep freeze, and I'm only a few hours ahead of you in the process of learning about—this."

His expansive gesture included the self-proclaimed captain beside him, as well as the ship around them all. "But you're better off than I was. When I came on board, Dirac and Scurlock thought they were giving me to a berserker. And I believed them, until . . ."

The speaker drew another breath. "Let me start over, by introducing the captain more thoroughly. Her name—his name—I'm not yet sure which—will translate at least approximately as 'Carpenter.'"

The captain, still listening to simultaneous machine translation, bowed, a strange, stiff gesture.

Tersely Kensing went on to inform his compatriots that Captain Carpenter was very likely the last mature Builder surviving in the universe. Originally part of the ship's reserve crew, he/she had also been thawed out, at the orders of this ship's optelectronic brain, only a few hours ago—but in the captain's case, after a longsleep of some fifty thousand standard years.

Acting Captain Carpenter was one of an elite corps of individuals, fanatically dedicated to the preservation of the Builders' race, who had boarded this ship when it set out on its desperate voyage—part of a last effort to escape the destruction being visited on the Builders' civilization by their own creation, the berserkers.

Prinsep, who had been attending carefully, supposed that under the circumstances he could accept that. Actually he supposed that he had very little choice. "All right," the commodore demanded, "then what is this damned thing, anyway? Where are we?"

Kensing gazed at the older man uncertainly. "The best translation I can give you, Commodore, for the function of this vessel seems to be 'seedship.'"

Captain Carpenter, following the conversation with the aid of his own machines, quickly confirmed the fact. The vessel they were on was only one—almost certainly, the last surviving—of a great many similar craft that had been launched by Carpenter's desperate race in its last days, and represented their last-ditch attempt to establish a beachhead in the future for their posterity. It was a frenzied gamble they had undertaken only when they realized that their war against their own creations, the berserkers, was certain to be lost.

The great majority of seedships had been destroyed by the implacable berserkers soon after they were built. Also obliterated at that time had been all of the Builders' other ships and other spacegoing installations.

Every one of the Builders' planets, fruit of a long, aggressive campaign to expand their empire, had been sterilized.

But this one seedship, and most likely this one alone—its individual name seemed to translate as something like *Phoenix*—had escaped destruction. Though it had been heavily damaged, its original live crew wiped out, it was still carrying deep in its metal guts more than a billion encapsulated zygotes—almost certainly the only examples of Builder genetics still extant anywhere in the universe.

But all of the artificial wombs it had originally carried, as well as the capacity to construct more, had been destroyed by berserker boarding devices and other weapons.

Relentlessly pursued almost from the moment of its launching, this vessel fifty thousand years ago had narrowly escaped destruction by plunging into a deep nebula—that which Solarians now called the Mavronari—a cloud of gas and dust hanging broad and high and dense enough in Galactic space to baffle any effective pursuit. Inside this nebula, travel at c-plus velocities was impossible.

Ensign Dinant was still inclined to be skeptical. "It looks just like a berserker. All our experts have identified it as one."

Kensing nodded soberly. "Of course it does, of course they have. Not only did it come out of one of the same original Builder shipyards, but it was deliberately designed and built to look like a berserker—enough to fool, if possible, the killing machines themselves."

Except for the basically benign programming of this vessel's computers, the match had been very close indeed. Certainly close enough to fool Solarians. But of course the objective of fooling the unliving enemy had ultimately failed of attainment.

Evidently sensing that some doubts still lingered. Captain Carpenter was willing to offer proof. A simultaneous translation of his speech came through: "We must be quick. But I will show you all this vessel's cargo. Please follow me."

Even a freight consisting of some billions of encapsulated zygotes, a cargo having the same magnitude of volume as that of the Solarian research station, did not occupy a high proportion of the space available. Not on a battlewagon the size of this one.

And now, as Kensing, accompanied by Captain Carpenter conducted Prinsep and his companions on a tour of this vessel's cargo holds, their last lingering doubts were satisfied.

Prinsep picked up a sample to inspect it closely. Each Builder zygote was protected inside a small circular plate, not much different in size, though substantially dissimilar in texture and composition, from the Solarian tiles with which all the Earth-descended people present were well familiar.

Tongres even did some half-abstracted calculations: A billion tiles or disks would seem to need a volume of about 90 meters x 90 meters x 50 meters.

Prinsep wondered, keeping the question to himself for now, whether Builders knew sexual attraction and love in the Solarian sense. And decided in his own mind that probably they did.

Even this vessel, immense enough to tuck away such a bulk of cargo, was still only in the middle range of size for a berserker mothership. In this vast interior, the secret cargo might remain indefinitely unexamined and unremarked by a handful of tired, frightened boarders who were necessarily intent on other matters, in particular their own survival.

And still, around them, the fight against the latest attacking waves of real berserkers was going on. From time to time, Captain Carpenter in a few terse phrases reminded his visitors of the fact. The full combat resources of the *Phoenix*, hoarded for millennia against the need for this final stand, an arsenal including extra defensive shields, and weapons that could have annihilated the planetoid Imatra a hundred times over, were being mobilized and thrown into action now.

"What can we do to help?" asked Prinsep.

An immediate expression of gratitude came from Captain Carpenter together with the answer: not much at the moment. But if and when the berserkers could again be beaten off, perhaps a great deal.

Not only were their own human lives at stake, Carpenter explained, but also the survival of a viable drive aboard the seedship. And, aboard the bioresearch station, the survival of a fleet of artificial wombs which would be usable by either species.

That statement momentarily staggered the commodore and those with him. "Usable by either species?"

"Right!" said Kensing, adding: "And that, you see, is the key to the whole mystery of this ship's behavior."

For one race's artificial wombs to be used on the other's zygotes would certainly require heavy modification in both hardware and software. But both races shared the same fundamental chemistry of life. Tools and energy and comprehensive libraries of information were available. It had been determined centuries ago that with time and effort and ingenuity, the Solarian wombs could be modified to handle satisfactorily the protoindividuals of the other race.

Briefly interrupting Kensing's explanation, Captain Carpenter clicked and whistled for his new allies a kind of apology for the way his ship had treated certain Solarians over the course of the past three hundred years.

When the live crew of the *Phoenix* had been wiped out early in the agelong voyage, leaving the seedship's computers to do their best absent the conscious control of any living Builder, the elaborate software entities inhabiting those machines labored under the certainty that ultimate success or failure rode on the decisions they were now forced to make. At times the strain had proven too much for the command computers, leading to decisions that were contradictory and counterproductive.

Approximately fifty thousand standard ED years (as confirmed rather precisely by the seedship's master clocks) after plunging into the sheltering nebula, this particular ship had at last emerged again. In the course of its tortuous passage through that protective but also dangerous darkness, it had found one or two sites where a colony might be established. But without the hardware to grow organic beings, or the necessary software to construct and operate it, the sites were useless.

Therefore, a very little more than three hundred years ago, on emerging from the dark nebula into more or less clear, normal space, the bright, wary, dangerous shipboard computers, charged with the preservation of their cargo, and the eventual establishment of colonies at any and all costs, had begun to cast about for the means of making a colony once more possible.

And the computers commanding the *Phoenix* encountered something

Fred Saberhagen

new. The signals of Solarian civilization, sent into space both deliberately and accidentally for centuries in this part of the Galaxy, were
detectable at several points along the radiation spectrum commonly
used for communications.

For a Solarian standard year or two after its emergence from the
most heavily constricting clouds, the ship had hung back in the
fringes of the Mavronari. For all its computers knew, the Galaxy
into which it had reemerged, some fifty thousand years older than
the one it had escaped, might well be completely dominated by
berserkers; indeed the shipboard computers felt compelled to assign
a pessimistically high probability to that situation.

During the dark millennia of steady groping through obscurity the
onboard computers had done such research as they could manage
on the problem of surviving the berserkers and ultimately defeating
them. The odds were not good. Further delay in the establishment
of a colony was undesirable.

But reckless haste, their basic programming impressed upon them,
might produce results that were disastrously worse.

With mechanical patience, using such tools as remained after the
long-accumulated damage of battle, time, and travel, the seedship's
computers investigated the new world before them. They again evaluated the option of reviving one of the precious few organic Builders
of the reserve crew, but continued to judge that the optimum time
for that step had not yet arrived.

The computers representing the last hope of the Builders began,
cautiously, an active search along the Coreward fringe of the Mavronari, still seeking favorable places for the establishment of a live
colony, but concentrating upon the lack of nurturing hardware and
software.

The course followed by the seedship in its seeking, along the
ever-more-attenuated outer fringe of the Mavronari brought a
fortuitous discovery that altered and delayed all of the computers'
other plans.

Traces of very fresh activity on the part of the newly dominant
intelligent race suddenly appeared in the electromagnetic spectrum.
These were rapidly decaying signals, undoubtedly artificial, echoing
in multiple reflections from one interstellar cloud to another, no
more than a few years old but already faint almost beyond the most
sophisticated detection.

The seedship computers expanded their field antennas as best they
could. They watched and listened, recording all artificial signals with
an omnivorous greed for information.

Presently scout machines were programmed and dispatched,
clever, heavily armed devices superficially indistinguishable from
berserker scouts. These moved swiftly, in wary silence, homing on

the signals just discovered and listening with particular attention for more.

Presently more such transmissions were detected, recorded and analyzed, and bearings taken. One of the seedship's scouts returned with new information.

Presently the small scouting machines drifted forward again, as warily as possible, in the direction of the signals' source. They listened again, and then advanced and listened once more, to younger and ever younger samples of the alien communications spectrum. Thus cautious exploration proceeded in small increments.

Eventually direct contact was effected. Abruptly a small Solarian ship—an utterly new phenomenon to the seedship computers—was detected within visual range.

The electronic strategists were wary about approaching the Solarians openly, because they knew that, to humans of any race who knew anything about berserkers, their vessel was virtually certain to be identified as an old, battered berserker.

Surreptitious observation had not continued long before certain evidence came to the attention of the seedship computers, evidence tending to confirm that the small vessel was under the control of living beings, not berserkers. Warily, and experiencing something analogous to gratitude and joy, the computers accepted this fact as evidence that even now, some fifty thousand years after their victory over their creators, the berserkers had been unable to expunge intelligent life completely from the Galaxy.

But caution was still essential. For one thing, the seedship knew that it looked like a berserker. Perhaps its controlling software entities were capable of appreciating irony. To be attacked and destroyed as a berserker, after fifty thousand years of strained survival...

Provoking either attack or panicked flight on the part of the alien was undesirable.

There was another goal: whatever effort might be necessary, it was very important to learn at least one Solarian language, or preferably several. In the absence of any wealth of recorded information, there seemed no alternative to either taking an unacceptably long time about the job, or else learning from live beings.

To somehow establish contact with such beings without alerting their whole race to the presence of a formidable stranger seemed essential—on the other hand, to be caught taking prisoners was predictably almost certain to create hostility among the very beings the ship hoped ultimately to enlist as allies.

Therefore the ship planned very carefully the acquisition of its language tutors—though in the end it had little real choice as to who they were going to be.

❖   ❖   ❖

It appeared feasible to capture the small ship, and that was easily accomplished.

Upon investigation it became clear that the little craft had been part of a small, private operation in space, with only a couple of people on board. Fortunately for the seedship's purposes, it was small enough to be taken undamaged and without a fight.

Unfortunately the universe held other deadly dangers besides the killing machines. The Builders' own history demonstrated amply that one intelligent race could be perfectly capable of waging war upon another. Were this not a fact, the berserkers would never have been created. Therefore great diplomacy was called for; the seedship's brain would have to predict (and much depended upon the accuracy of the prediction) just what the attitude of these unknown beings was going to be toward a billion Builder zygotes.

Ensign Dinant was the last to doubt. "But—when it attacked Imatra—it killed defenders, it seized the station violently and carried it off."

The commodore responded soberly. "Of course, the Builders and their machinery would have been willing to wipe out all Solarian life—if such a thing were possible—if they saw that as the only way to capture our biostation or its equivalent. The only way to save their own race. Hell, we'd do the same to them, right?"

The Builder who had ordered the first Imatran raid, Carpenter's predecessor as captain, might have planned to tell his pair of kidnapped Solarians the truth. But he, having gone out in a small combat scout to oversee the operation, had unluckily been killed in the first fighting. And after his sudden death his machines, once more forced to grapple with unwelcome responsibility, had failed to carry out that plan.

At the conclusion of the violent combat that had accompanied the seedship's seizing and carrying off the station, the stored body of only one adult Builder remained in viable condition—and the computers soon decided that before they risked playing that final card, rousing their sole remaining master, they had better gather as much information as possible about the newly discovered Solarian race.

Early in their occupation of the station, the machines examined several of the Solarian artificial wombs, the priceless replacements for Builder devices destroyed beyond recovery. The captured machinery appeared to be adaptable—and so, as far as could be determined, were Freya and her counterparts. But no real trial had been attempted. The tricky complexities of alien biology were difficult even for big computers; and their situation would have to be even more desperate than it was before they would have dared experiment on Builder zygotes without prolonged and intensive computer modeling.

And the computers had been willing to accept almost any risk rather than allow the Solarians to realize just what the real prize was—these invaluable artificial wombs, and the expert systems that made them functional.

The one disaster the computers had never dared to risk was the destruction of these priceless nurturing devices, so miraculously obtained. At the threat of open fighting aboard the Solarian bio-station, the seedship it had withdrawn its combat machines, leaving the belligerent Solarians to their own devices while keeping open some channels of communication and observation.

The seedship had installed sensors, recorders, on the Solarian station's womb-deck, and some of these devices had survived the Solarians' suspicious search. The Builders' master computers wanted constant reassurance that the Solarians left in control of the station were doing nothing that would put the artificial wombs and associated systems at risk.

Hundreds of years had passed since the seedship computers had seized and made off with their Solarian treasure. In that interval they had succeeded in getting it almost out of sight of berserkers and Solarians alike. The planners could afford to be patient. It was necessary only to outlast the few Solarians still on the station—those violent, weapon-carrying beings living in such perilously close proximity to the artificial wombs. For a time the all-important goal grew more and more likely of attainment.

Then suddenly, without warning, upsetting all calculations, more Solarians had come threading their way out of the nebula in a badly damaged warship, bringing with them confirmation of an approaching berserker presence in nearby space. Now mobilization was necessary, preparations must be made to fight off these potential attackers.

The whole situation, long fraught with possibilities for disaster beyond calculation, suddenly became vastly more complicated and dangerous.

The damaged seedship computers, working sometimes on the verge of breakdown, continued to do the best they could.

In its first contact with Solarians, the seedship had deliberately passed itself off as a berserker. First, because it would have been difficult to convince suspicious humans that it was anything else. Later, it preferred not to reveal to the handful of organic aliens what an advantage they had in controlling all the artificial wombs.

If the Solarian aliens were willing to accept their captor as a berserker and still to maintain communication with it, then the seedship would humor them. To try to argue them into the truth seemed to carry the risk of unguessable complications. And it was possible to make the hopeful computation that in a few years, a few decades, a few centuries at the most, they would all be conveniently dead.

And thus, more or less gradually, the deal between Dirac Sardou and the alien machine had evolved.

Through discussions between Dirac and his unliving counterpart, their plan for establishing a cooperative colony had evolved—each partner in the scheme planning to double-cross the other as soon as possible.

Up to the time when the commodore's band of refugees arrived at the bioresearch station, the seedship brain had been uncertain about the value of the treacherous, brutal Premier as any kind of long-term ally. Of course the Builders' machine had had little choice; the man had firmly established himself as leader of the small surviving group of humans. And alliance was at least a possibility, with any known entity other than a berserker.

In fact the seedship's archives held records of certain Builder individuals who had equaled or surpassed Dirac in the capacity for violence and personal ambition. There was no reason to assume that Dirac was more closely typical of human leaders than those Builders had been of their own race.

In any case, the ship had trouble coming up with a better plan for using these aliens, or learning more about them.

But now other and perhaps more satisfactory human partners had become available, in the form of the fleet commander and his associates. The Builder ended by telling them that he would bring out the reserve fighting machines the ship had been hiding, and depose Dirac.

Hawksmoor had listened to the story with a sympathy for those beleaguered Builder programs.

In Nick's opinion, any advanced computer or advanced program ordinarily felt intrinsically more comfortable dealing with another computer or another program than with a fleshly person. The Builders' creation was surely no exception to this rule.

Nick could sympathize with his program counterparts aboard the seedship, though now from the vantage point of what he considered to be his own dual nature, he judged them rather colorless.

Another question that occurred to Nick was this: Had the Builders ever experienced any ethical, moral, or social problems with the idea of making electronic recordings of themselves? Well, he wasn't going to raise the point just now; there seemed to be plenty of other problems that would have to be considered first.

❂   ❂   ❂

Captain Carpenter resumed the story. The seedship's plans for retreating to some hidden sanctuary, and building its colony with the help of Solarian equipment, had to be put on hold as soon as it received convincing evidence—from listening to Solarian communications, or from its own observations—that the bad machines might be about to appear.

At that point, feeling some computer analogue of desperation, the seedship computers had awakened Frank Marcus.

An array of other Solarian people were also being kept frozen in the seedship's archives—those who had been sent to it by Dirac in the belief that he was placating a great berserker.

At the moment Frank was taken prisoner, he had already been half convinced that the machine he was fighting was no berserker.

The seedship's brain continually reconsidered the possibility of reviving the sole remaining qualified Builder, and when (s)he was checked out healthy, relieving *itself* of command.

But the last time the seedship controller had revived a Builder, shortly before the first raid on Imatra, he/she promptly got himself killed by the Solarian humans; and now it had only one mature Builder left. No margin remained to accommodate another error.

If the seedship was ever to make an open and serious partnership with Solarians, it would not want to be perceived as guilty of slaughtering the young that they were making at least some effort to preserve.

For centuries now the seedship had been trying to protect its own most vital secrets from the Solarians, even while struggling to learn theirs. But ultimately it would rather reveal its true nature to these intruders than kill them off. They were not necessarily its mortal enemies, but berserkers were.

The seedship had now spent three hundred years studying the alien species who called themselves Solarians. But for any machines to study any of the Galactic varieties of humanity was extremely difficult, and the seedship was extremely reluctant to reach any firm conclusions without still more study, now that additional subjects were at last available.

The seedship knew it must to make a deal with the quarrelsome Solarians—or with one faction among them, if they were divided in deadly earnest.

But now, with real berserkers coming to the attack, time for hesitation had run out.

As had the time for explanations.

"Battle stations, everyone. We must at all costs defend the bridge," said Captain Carpenter.

One of the seedship's service machines was already bringing Kensing battle armor, tailored to his Solarian shape and size. Prinsep and Havot, Nick and Tongres and Dinant, readied their arms.

Reports from the Builders' auxiliary machines were now coming in rapidly, and Carpenter ordered immediate translation of all messages. The news was grim: more berserker machines had landed on the *Phoenix* and were even now fighting their way inboard.

Carpenter remained in command on the bridge, while on the captain's orders Prinsep swiftly deployed his people to guard the passageway through which they'd entered. Their armored forms took shelter as best they could in niches and corners, and behind hastily mobilized service robots.

In moments the enemy was upon them, in the form of bizarre shapes darting forward at inhuman speed. In a hail of fire and force, fighting side by side with the Builders' defensive robots, they tried to protect the bridge and other vital installations against the boarding machines.

Kensing, his senses ringing with the violence of battle, saw Nick in suit-form on his right fighting until a swiftly advancing berserker caught him and crushed the suit to scrap. On Kensing's left, Havot and at least one other Solarian went down, to be dragged off by friendly service machines, whether bound for medirobots, or simply for disposal as dead flesh, Kensing could not tell.

And then, quite suddenly, the shooting stopped again. Prinsep was saying in his helmet radio that an all clear had been sounded, and Sandy Kensing realized that he himself was still alive.

Still, for long moments, he had trouble breathing. Until word came that contact with the station had been restored ... and yes, Annie was still there. She was still alive, and for the moment safe.

☀ THIRTY-ONE

Something like twenty-four standard hours had gone by since the last shot quelling the failed berserker boarding attempt. The enemy had not been heard from again during that time, but it was entirely possible that more of the killing machines would materialize out of the nebular dust at any moment, coming on in another kamikaze charge.

Certainly the Galaxy still harbored vast numbers of berserkers, and they would still be making every effort to locate the *Phoenix*.

From the point of view of the enemies of life, an alliance between warlike Builders, with their intimate knowledge of how berserkers were originally built and programmed, and the bellicose Solarians, who had already taught themselves to fight berserkers to a standstill, would be about the worst possible scenario.

Sandy Kensing and Annie Zador, both of them still in armored suits and ready to grab up weapons at a moment's notice, were walking together through the Builders' gigantic vessel, exploring some of its more interesting byways. They and their shipmates visiting aboard moved in artificial gravity that Captain Carpenter had ordered especially tailored for Solarian comfort.

At the moment, Zador and Kensing were watching some of Captain Carpenter's service robots bringing out from the engine room of the *Phoenix* the small physical storage units containing an expert engineering system.

Fortunately the Builders' ship was able to spare an analytical expert system, which in theory ought to be capable of bypassing if not undoing Nick's old scrambling of the drive controls upon the *Eidolon*. In return, Carpenter had been granted a working share of the biostation's hardware and expertise, including several versions of Freya and forty Solarian artificial wombs, which would soon be on their way over from the station to the Builders' craft.

Annie, breaking a short silence, asked her companion bluntly: "Are you coming with us?"

Sandy Kensing did not answer impulsively. Instead he gave himself another long moment to think about it. This was literally a once-in-a-lifetime decision.

If all went well, the yacht, with its stardrive restored to marginal function (better than marginal was possible, but not to be counted on) would be ready in another day for the attempt by some of the surviving Solarians to return to their own worlds.

"If our jury-rigging doesn't blow up on us halfway there," Prinsep had warned them. "And if we don't run into more berserkers."

The trip home would be a dangerous gamble, but some people were ready to risk it.

Declining to take that risk would mean accepting another at least as great.

Drs. Zador and Hoveler, still dedicated to the welfare of the entities they thought of as their billion children, had elected not to try to have the biostation towed back to civilization by the yacht, a clumsy arrangement certain to increase greatly the perils of that voyage for all concerned. Nor did they want to overload the yacht by somehow packing aboard it a billion zygotes—miniature life units, in the berserker term—thus returning the protopeople to a place where they weren't wanted anyway.

Instead, Drs. Zador and Hoveler had elected to go on, joining the fortunes of their children with those of Captain Carpenter and his. If a real future existed for these Solarians anywhere, it was not at home.

Annie did not want to leave Sandy Kensing, far from it. But it seemed that her conception of duty left her no choice.

The seedship, its own mission rendered viable by Solarian technology, would of course continue towing the station on into the Mavronari, still seeking a good site for a Builder colony.

Prinsep was determined to bring Scurlock and Carol back to civilization with him, under forcible confinement, though it was doubtful whether any indictment for goodlife activity could be made to stand against them. Havot, currently in a medirobot with critical injuries, was also going back.

The Premier, too, was returning to the worlds he had once ruled, though he—or at least his optelectronic version, which was all that now survived—had not been consulted in the matter. Prinsep had left it up to the Lady Genevieve, as next of kin, to decide what ought to be done with her husband's recorded personality; none of the Solarians currently in a position to make decisions were in the mood to give Dirac Sardou, or any program by that name, the right to decide anything.

Anyway the Premier in his newly discarnate mode could simply be left turned off for the time being. There were still more immediate problems to worry about.

One version of Nicholas Hawksmoor, kept in reserve on the station by Premier Dirac, had survived all the shooting. By common consent this version, an equivalent of Nick[2], had been turned on, brought up to date on the situation, and allowed to make his own decision.

This avatar of Hawksmoor had needed only a fraction of a second to renounce all future possibility of contact with the Lady Genevieve, and to go on, accompanying the seedship in its effort to find a new world deep in the Mavronari.

And Sandy Kensing was going to have to decide his own future quickly, before the *Eidolon*'s drive was fixed. The yacht's departure could not be postponed, for with every passing hour the nebula around grew thicker, the journey home more difficult. Captain Carpenter was refusing to consider any course adjustments that would delay his vessel and keep it in this region, where at any moment more berserkers might arrive to finish its destruction.

Kensing turned to stare into the Builder analogue of a holostage nearby. At the moment the device displayed a graphic of the three small vessels moving in deep space, ahead of them the blankness of the Mavronari, like an unknowable future.

"I don't know what I'll do if you're not with us, Sandy," Annie said suddenly, as if his prolonged silence was suddenly too much for her.

"Hey, Annie. Relax, relax!" Kensing reached for his woman, took her armored hands in his. "A future with you in it, and a billion screaming kids—"

"More like two billion," she said, "counting Builders."

"Two billion, then. Hey, I wouldn't miss that for anything."